*As the great thoat and his rider hurtled past,
Carthoris swung his long-sword in a mighty cut.*

THREE MARTIAN NOVELS

Thuvia, Maid of Mars
The Chessmen of Mars
The Master Mind of Mars

BY

EDGAR RICE BURROUGHS.

DOVER PUBLICATIONS
NEW YORK

This new Dover edition, first published in 1962, is an unabridged and unaltered republication of the following works by Edgar Rice Burroughs:

Thuvia, Maid of Mars, first published in 1920.

The Chessmen of Mars, first published in 1922.

The Master Mind of Mars, first published in 1928.

Illustrations for this edition are by J. Allen St. John and have been selected from among those in earlier editions.

Standard Book Number: 486-20039-6
Library of Congress Catalog Card Number: 62-3086

Manufactured in the United States of America
Dover Publications, Inc.
180 Varick Street
New York, N.Y. 10014

CONTENTS

For but an instant the searchlight halted upon Thuvia of Ptarth.

Thuvia, Maid of Mars

By

EDGAR RICE BURROUGHS

*With a savage cry of triumph, Thar Ban disap-
peared down the black canyon of the Avenue of
Quays.*

CONTENTS

Between them and the city raged a terrific battle.

CHAPTER I

CARTHORIS AND THUVIA

UPON A MASSIVE bench of polished ersite beneath the gorgeous blooms of a giant pimalia a woman sat. Her shapely, sandaled foot tapped impatiently upon the jewel-strewn walk that wound beneath the stately sorapus trees across the scarlet sward of the royal gardens of Thuvan Dihn, Jeddak of Ptarth, as a dark-haired, red-skinned warrior bent low toward her, whispering heated words close to her ear.

"Ah, Thuvia of Ptarth," he cried, "you are cold even before the fiery blasts of my consuming love! No harder than your heart, nor colder is the hard, cold ersite of this thrice happy bench which supports your divine and fadeless form! Tell me, O Thuvia of Ptarth, that I may still hope —that though you do not love me now, yet someday, some day, my princess, I—"

The girl sprang to her feet with an exclamation of surprise and displeasure. Her queenly head was poised haughtily upon her smooth red shoulders. Her dark eyes looked angrily into those of the man.

"You forget yourself, and the customs of Barsoom, Astok," she said. "I have given you no right thus to address the daughter of Thuvan Dihn, nor have you won such a right."

The man reached suddenly forth and grasped her by the arm.

"You shall be my princess!" he cried. "By the breast of Issus, thou shalt, nor shall any other come between Astok, Prince of Dusar, and his heart's desire. Tell me that there is another, and I shall cut out his foul heart and fling it to the wild calots of the dead sea-bottoms!"

At touch of the man's hand upon her flesh the girl went pallid beneath her coppery skin, for the persons of the royal women of the courts of Mars are held but little less than sacred. The act of Astok, Prince of Dusar, was profanation. There was no terror in the eyes of Thuvia of Ptarth —only horror for the thing the man had done and for its possible consequences.

"Release me." Her voice was level—frigid.

The man muttered incoherently and drew her roughly toward him.

"Release me!" she repeated sharply, "or I call the guard, and the Prince of Dusar knows what that will mean."

Quickly he threw his right arm about her shoulders and strove to draw her face to his lips. With a little cry she struck him full in the mouth with the massive bracelets that circled her free arm.

"Caiot!" she exclaimed, and then: "The guard! The guard! Hasten in protection of the Princess of Ptarth!"

In answer to her call a dozen guardsmen came racing across the scarlet sward, their gleaming long-swords naked in the sun, the metal of their accouterments clanking against that of their leathern harness, and in their throats hoarse shouts of rage at the sight which met their eyes.

But before they had passed half across the royal garden to where Astok of Dusar still held the struggling girl in his grasp, another figure sprang from a cluster of dense foliage that half hid a golden fountain close at hand. A tall, straight youth he was, with black hair and keen gray eyes; broad of shoulder and narrow of hip; a clean-limbed fighting man. His skin was but faintly tinged with the copper color that marks the red men of Mars from the other races of the dying planet—he was like them, and yet there was a subtle difference greater even than that which lay in his lighter skin and his gray eyes.

There was a difference, too, in his movements. He came on in great leaps that carried him so swiftly over the ground that the speed of the guardsmen was as nothing by comparison.

Astok still clutched Thuvia's wrist as the young warrior confronted him. The newcomer wasted no time and he spoke but a single word.

"Calot!" he snapped, and then his clenched fist landed beneath the other's chin, lifting him high into the air and depositing him in a crumpled heap within the center of the pimalia bush beside the ersite bench.

Her champion turned toward the girl. "Kaor, Thuvia of Ptarth!" he cried. "It seems that fate timed my visit well."

"Kaor, Carthoris of Helium!" the princess returned the young man's greeting, "and what less could one expect of the son of such a sire?"

He bowed his acknowledgment of the compliment to his father, John Carter, Warlord of Mars. And then the guardsmen, panting from their charge, came up just as the Prince of Dusar, bleeding at the mouth, and with drawn sword, crawled from the entanglement of the pimalia.

Astok would have leaped to mortal combat with the son of Dejah Thoris, but the guardsmen pressed about him, preventing, though it was clearly evident that naught would have better pleased Carthoris of Helium.

"But say the word, Thuvia of Ptarth," he begged, "and naught will give me greater pleasure than meting to this fellow the punishment he has earned."

"It cannot be, Carthoris," she replied. "Even though he has forfeited all claim upon my consideration, yet he is the guest of the jeddak, my father, and to him alone may he account for the unpardonable act he has committed."

"As you say, Thuvia," replied the Heliumite. "But afterward he shall account to Carthoris, Prince of Helium, for this affront to the daughter of my father's friend." As he spoke, though, there burned in his eyes a fire that proclaimed a nearer, dearer cause for his championship of this glorious daughter of Barsoom.

The maid's cheek darkened beneath the satin of her transparent skin, and the eyes of Astok, Prince of Dusar, darkened, too, as he read that which passed unspoken between the two in the royal gardens of the jeddak.

"And thou to me," he snapped at Carthoris, answering the young man's challenge.

The guard still surrounded Astok. It was a difficult position for the young officer who commanded it. His prisoner was the son of a mighty jeddak; he was the guest of Thuvan Dihn—until but now an honored guest upon whom every royal dignity had been showered. To arrest him forcibly could mean naught else than war, and yet he had done that which in the eyes of the Ptarth warrior merited death.

The young man hesitated. He looked toward his princess. She, too, guessed all that hung upon the action of the coming moment. For many years Dusar and Ptarth had been at peace with each other. Their great merchant ships plied back and forth between the larger cities of the two nations.

Even now, far above the gold-shot scarlet dome of the jeddak's palace, she could see the huge bulk of a giant freighter taking its majestic way through the thin Barsoomian air toward the west and Dusar.

By a word she might plunge these two mighty nations into a bloody conflict that would drain them of their bravest blood and their incalculable riches, leaving them all helpless against the inroads of their envious and less powerful neighbors, and at last a prey to the savage green hordes of the dead sea-bottoms.

No sense of fear influenced her decision, for fear is seldom known to the children of Mars. It was rather a sense of the responsibility that she, the daughter of their jeddak, felt for the welfare of her father's people.

"I called you, Padwar," she said to the lieutenant of the guard, "to protect the person of your princess, and to keep the peace that must not be violated within the royal gardens of the jeddak. That is all. You will escort me to the palace, and the Prince of Helium will accompany me."

Without another glance in the direction of Astok she turned, and taking Carthoris' proffered hand, moved slowly toward the massive marble pile that housed the ruler of Ptarth and his glittering court. On either side marched a file of guardsmen. Thus Thuvia of Ptarth found a way out of a dilemma, escaping the necessity of placing her father's royal guest under forcible restraint, and at the same time separating the two princes, who otherwise would have been at each other's throat the moment she and the guard had departed.

Beside the pimalia stood Astok, his dark eyes narrowed to mere slits of hate beneath his lowering brows as he watched the retreating forms of the woman who had aroused the fiercest passions of his nature and the man whom he now believed to be the one who stood between his love and its consummation.

As they disappeared within the structure Astok shrugged his shoulders and with a murmured oath crossed the gardens toward another wing of the building where he and his retinue were housed.

That night he took formal leave of Thuvan Dihn, and though no mention was made of the happening within the garden, it was plain to see through the cold mask of the jed-

dak's courtesy that only the customs of royal hospitality restrained him from voicing the contempt he felt for the Prince
of Dusar.

Carthoris was not present at the leave-taking, nor was
Thuvia. The ceremony was as stiff and formal as court etiquette could make it, and when the last of the Dusarians
clambered over the rail of the battleship that had brought
them upon this fateful visit to the court of Ptarth, and the
mighty engine of destruction had risen slowly from the ways
of the landing stage, a note of relief was apparent in the voice
of Thuvan Dihn as he turned to one of his officers with a
word of comment upon a subject foreign to that which had
been uppermost in the minds of all for hours.

But, after all, was it so foreign?

"Inform Prince Sovan," he directed, "that it is our wish
that the fleet which departed for Kaol this morning be recalled to cruise to the west of Ptarth."

As the warship, bearing Astok back to the court of his
father, turned toward the west, Thuvia of Ptarth, sitting
upon the same bench where the Prince of Dusar had affronted her, watched the twinkling lights of the craft growing smaller in the distance. Beside her, in the brilliant light of
the nearer moon, sat Carthoris. His eyes were not upon the
dim bulk of the battleship, but on the profile of the girl's
upturned face.

"Thuvia," he whispered.

The girl turned her eyes toward his. His hand stole out to
find hers, but she drew it gently away.

"Thuvia of Ptarth, I love you!" cried the young warrior.
"Tell me that it does not offend."

She shook her head sadly. "The love of Carthoris of Helium," she said simply, "could be naught but an honor to any
woman; but you must not speak, my friend, of bestowing
upon me that which I may not reciprocate."

The young man got slowly to his feet. His eyes were wide in
astonishment. It never had occurred to the Prince of Helium
that Thuvia of Ptarth might love another.

"But at Kadabra!" he exclaimed. "And later here at your
father's court, what did you do, Thuvia of Ptarth, that might
have warned me that you could not return my love?"

"And what did I do, Carthoris of Helium," she returned,

"that might lead you to believe that I *did* return it?"

He paused in thought, and then shook his head. "Nothing, Thuvia, that is true; yet I could have sworn you loved me. Indeed, you well knew how near to worship has been my love for you."

"And how might I know it, Carthoris?" she asked innocently. "Did you ever tell me as much? Ever before have words of love for me fallen from your lips?"

"But you *must* have known it!" he exclaimed. "I am like my father—witless in matters of the heart, and of a poor way with women; yet the jewels that strew these royal garden paths—the trees, the flowers, the sward—all must have read the love that has filled my heart since first my eyes were made new by imaging your perfect face and form; so how could you alone have been blind to it?"

"Do the maids of Helium pay court to their men?" asked Thuvia.

"You are playing with me!" exclaimed Carthoris, not, however, without appeal in his voice. "Say that you are but playing, and that after all you love me, Thuvia!"

"I cannot tell you that, Carthoris, for I am promised to another."

Her tone was level, but was there not within it the hint of an infinite depth of sadness? Who may say?

"Promised to another?" Carthoris scarcely breathed the words. His face went almost white, and then his head came up as befitted him in whose veins flowed the blood of the overlord of a world.

"Carthoris of Helium wishes you every happiness with the man of your choice," he said. "With—" and then he hesitated, waiting for her to fill in the name.

"Kulan Tith, Jeddak of Kaol," she replied. "My father's friend and Ptarth's most puissant ally."

The young man looked at her intently for a moment before he spoke again.

"You love him, Thuvia of Ptarth?" he asked earnestly.

"I am promised to him," she replied simply.

He did not press her. "He is of Barsoom's noblest blood and mightiest fighters," mused Carthoris. "My father's friend and mine—would that it might have been another!" he muttered almost savagely. What the girl thought was hidden by

the mask of her expression, which was tinged only by a little
shadow of sadness that might have been for Carthoris, herself, or for them both.

Carthoris of Helium did not ask, though he noted it, for
his loyalty to Kulan Tith was the loyalty of the blood of
John Carter of Virginia for a friend, greater than which could
be no loyalty.

He raised a jewel-encrusted bit of the girl's magnificent
trappings to his lips.

"To the honor and happiness of Kulan Tith and the
priceless jewel that has been bestowed upon him," he said,
and though his voice was husky there was the true ring of sincerity in it. "I told you that I loved you, Thuvia, before I
knew that you were promised to another. I may not tell you
it again, but I am glad that you know it, for there is no dishonor in it either to you or to Kulan Tith or to myself. My
love is such that it may embrace as well Kulan Tith—if you
love him." There was almost a question in the statement.

"I am promised to him," she replied.

Carthoris backed slowly away. He laid one hand upon his
heart, the other upon the pommel of his long-sword.

"These are yours—always," he said. A moment later he had
entered the palace, and was gone from the girl's sight.

Had he returned at once he would have found her prone
upon the ersite bench, her face buried in her arms. Was she
weeping? There was none to see.

Carthoris of Helium had come all unannounced to the
court of his father's friend that day. He had come alone in a
small flier, sure of the same welcome that always awaited him
at Ptarth. As there had been no formality in his coming
there was no need of formality in his going.

To Thuvan Dihn he explained that he had been but testing an invention of his own with which his flier was equipped
—a clever improvement of the ordinary Martian air compass, which when set for a certain destination, will remain
constantly fixed thereon, making it only necessary to keep a
vessel's prow always in the direction of the compass needle
to reach any given point upon Barsoom by the shortest route.

Carthoris' improvement upon this consisted of an auxiliary
device which steered the craft mechanically in the direction
of the compass, and upon arrival directly over the point for

which the compass was set, brought the craft to a standstill
and lowered it, also automatically, to the ground.

"You readily discern the advantages of this invention," he
was saying to Thuvan Dihn, who had accompanied him to
the landing stage upon the palace roof to inspect the compass
and bid his young friend farewell.

A dozen officers of the court with several body servants
were grouped behind the jeddak and his guest, eager listen-
ers to the conversation—so eager on the part of one of the
servants that he was twice rebuked by a noble for his for-
wardness in pushing himself ahead of his betters to view the
intricate mechanism of the wonderful "controlling destination compass," as the thing was called.

"For example," continued Carthoris, "I have an all-night
trip before me, as tonight. I set the pointer here upon the
right-hand dial, which represents the eastern hemisphere of
Barsoom, so that the point rests upon the exact latitude and
longitude of Helium. Then I start the engine, roll up in my
sleeping silks and furs, and with lights burning, race through
the air toward Helium, confident that at the appointed hour
I shall drop gently toward the landing stage upon my own
palace, whether I am still asleep or no."

"Provided," suggested Thuvan Dihn, "you do not chance
to collide with some other night wanderer in the meanwhile."

Carthoris smiled. "No danger of that," he replied. "See
here," and he indicated a device at the right of the destination
compass. "This is my 'obstruction evader,' as I call it. This
visible device is the switch which throws the mechanism on or
off. The instrument itself is below deck, geared both to the
steering apparatus and the control levers.

"It is quite simple, being nothing more than a radium gen-
erator diffusing radio-activity in all directions to a distance
of a hundred yards or so from the flier. Should this enveloping force be interrupted in any direction a delicate instrument
immediately apprehends the irregularity, at the same time
imparting an impulse to a magnetic device which in turn actuates the steering mechanism, diverting the bow of the flier
away from the obstacle until the craft's radio-activity sphere
is no longer in contact with the obstruction, then she falls once
more into her normal course. Should the disturbance approach from the rear, as in the case of a faster-moving craft

overhauling me, the mechanism actuates the speed control as well as the steering gear, and the flier shoots ahead and either up or down, as the oncoming vessel is upon a lower or higher plane than herself.

"In aggravated cases, that is when the obstructions are many, or of such a nature as to deflect the bow more than forty-five degrees in any direction, or when the craft has reached its destination and dropped to within a hundred yards of the ground, the mechanism brings her to a full stop, at the same time sounding a loud alarm which will instantly awaken the pilot. You see I have anticipated almost every contingency."

Thuvan Dihn smiled his appreciation of the marvelous device. The forward servant pushed almost to the flier's side. His eyes were narrowed to slits.

"All but one," he said.

The nobles looked at him in astonishment, and one of them grasped the fellow none too gently by the shoulder to push him back to his proper place. Carthoris raised his hand.

"Wait," he urged. "Let us hear what the man has to say—no creation of mortal mind is perfect. Perchance he has detected a weakness that it will be well to know at once. Come, my good fellow, and what may be the one contingency I have overlooked?"

As he spoke Carthoris observed the servant closely for the first time. He saw a man of giant stature and handsome, as are all those of the race of Martian red men; but the fellow's lips were thin and cruel, and across one cheek was the faint, white-line of a sword-cut from the right temple to the corner of the mouth.

"Come," urged the Prince of Helium. "Speak!"

The man hesitated. It was evident that he regretted the temerity that had made him the center of interested observation. But at last, seeing no alternative, he spoke.

"It might be tampered with," he said, "by an enemy."

Carthoris drew a small key from his leathern pocket-pouch.

"Look at this," he said, handing it to the man. "If you know aught of locks, you will know that the mechanism which this unlooses is beyond the cunning of a picker of locks. It guards the vitals of the instrument from crafty tampering. Without it an enemy must half wreck the device to reach its heart, leaving his handiwork apparent to the most casual observer."

The servant took the key, glanced at it shrewdly, and then as he made to return it to Carthoris dropped it upon the marble flagging. Turning to look for it he planted the sole of his sandal full upon the glittering object. For an instant he bore all his weight upon the foot that covered the key, then he stepped back and with an exclamation as of pleasure that he had found it, stooped, recovered it, and returned it to the Heliumite. Then he dropped back to his station behind the nobles and was forgotten.

A moment later Carthoris had made his adieux to Thuvan Dihn and his nobles, and with lights twinkling had risen into the star-shot void of the Martian night.

CHAPTER II

SLAVERY

AS THE RULER of Ptarth, followed by his courtiers, descended from the landing stage above the palace, the servants dropped into their places in the rear of their royal or noble masters, and behind the others one lingered to the last. Then quickly stooping he snatched the sandal from his right foot, slipping it into his pocket-pouch.

When the party had come to the lower levels, and the jeddak had dispersed them by a sign, none noticed that the forward fellow who had drawn so much attention to himself before the Prince of Helium departed, was no longer among the other servants.

To whose retinue he had been attached none had thought to inquire, for the followers of a Martian noble are many, coming and going at the whim of their master, so that a new face is scarcely ever questioned, as the fact that a man has passed within the palace walls is considered proof positive that his loyalty to the jeddak is beyond question, so rigid is the examination of each who seeks service with the nobles of the court.

A good rule that, and only relaxed by courtesy in favor of

the retinue of visiting royalty from a friendly foreign power.

It was late in the morning of the next day that a giant serving man in the harness of the house of a great Ptarth noble passed out into the city from the palace gates. Along one broad avenue and then another he strode briskly until he had passed beyond the district of the nobles and had come to the place of shops. Here he sought a pretentious building that rose spirelike toward the heavens, its outer walls elaborately wrought with delicate carvings and intricate mosaics.

It was the Palace of Peace in which were housed the representatives of the foreign powers, or rather in which were located their embassies; for the ministers themselves dwelt in gorgeous palaces within the district occupied by the nobles.

Here the man sought the embassy of Dusar. A clerk arose questioningly as he entered, and at his request to have a word with the minister asked his credentials. The visitor slipped a plain metal armlet from above his elbow, and pointing to an inscription upon its inner surface, whispered a word or two to the clerk.

The latter's eyes went wide, and his attitude turned at once to one of deference. He bowed the stranger to a seat, and hastened to an inner room with the armlet in his hand. A moment later he reappeared and conducted the caller into the presence of the minister.

For a long time the two were closeted together, and when at last the giant serving man emerged from the inner office his expression was cast in a smile of sinister satisfaction. From the Palace of Peace he hurried directly to the palace of the Dusarian minister.

That night two swift fliers left the same palace top. One sped its rapid course toward Helium; the other—

Thuvia of Ptarth strolled in the gardens of her father's palace, as was her nightly custom before retiring. Her silks and furs were drawn about her, for the air of Mars is chill after the sun has taken his quick plunge beneath the planet's western verge.

The girl's thoughts wandered from her impending nuptials, that would make her empress of Kaol, to the person of the trim young Heliumite who had laid his heart at her feet the preceding day.

Whether it was pity or regret that saddened her expression

as she gazed toward the southern heavens where she had watched the lights of his flier disappear the previous night, it would be difficult to say.

So, too, is it impossible to conjecture just what her emotions may have been as she discerned the lights of a flier speeding rapidly out of the distance from that very direction, as though impelled toward her garden by the very intensity of the princess' thoughts.

She saw it circle lower above the palace until she was positive that it but hovered in preparation for a landing.

Presently the powerful rays of its searchlight shot downward from the bow. They fell upon the landing stage for a brief instant, revealing the figures of the Ptarthian guard, picking into brilliant points of fire the gems upon their gorgeous harnesses.

Then the blazing eye swept onward across the burnished domes and graceful minarets, down into court and park and garden to pause at last upon the ersite bench and the girl standing there beside it, her face upturned full toward the flier.

For but an instant the searchlight halted upon Thuvia of Ptarth, then it was extinguished as suddenly as it had come to life. The flier passed on above her to disappear beyond a grove of lofty skeel trees that grew within the palace grounds.

The girl stood for some time as it had left her, except that her head was bent and her eyes downcast in thought.

Who but Carthoris could it have been? She tried to feel anger that he should have returned thus, spying upon her; but she found it difficult to be angry with the young prince of Helium.

What mad caprice could have induced him so to transgress the etiquette of nations? For lesser things great powers had gone to war.

The princess in her was shocked and angered—but what of the girl!

And the guard—what of them? Evidently they, too, had been so much surprised by the unprecedented action of the stranger that they had not even challenged; but that they had no thought to let the thing go unnoticed was quickly evidenced by the skirring of motors upon the landing stage and the quick shooting airward of a long-lined patrol boat.

Thuvia watched it dart swiftly eastward. So, too, did

other eyes watch.

Within the dense shadows of the skeel grove, in a wide avenue beneath o'erspreading foliage, a flier hung a dozen feet above the g.ound. From its deck keen eyes watched the far-fanning searchlight of the patrol boat. No light shone from the enshadowed craft. Upon its deck was the silence of the tomb. Its crew of a half dozen red warriors watched the lights of the patrol boat diminishing in the distance.

"The intellects of our ancestors are with us tonight," said one in a low tone.

"No plan ever carried better," returned another. "They did precisely as the prince foretold."

He who had first spoken turned toward the man who squatted before the control board.

"Now!" he whispered. There was no other order given. Every man upon the craft had evidently been well schooled in each detail of that night's work. Silently the dark hull crept beneath the cathedral arches of the dark and silent grove.

Thuvia of Ptarth, gazing toward the east, saw the blacker blot against the blackness of the trees as the craft topped the buttressed garden wall. She saw the dim bulk incline gently downward toward the scarlet sward of the garden.

She knew that men came not thus with honorable intent. Yet she did not cry aloud to alarm the nearby guardsmen, nor did she flee to the safety of the palace.

Why?

I can see her shrug her shapely shoulders in reply as she voices the age-old, universal answer of the woman: Because!

Scarce had the flier touched the ground when four men leaped from its deck. They ran forward toward the girl.

Still she made no sign of alarm, standing as though hypnotized. Or could it have been as one who awaited a welcome visitor?

Not until they were quite close to her did she move. Then the nearer moon, rising above the surrounding foliage, touched their faces, lighting all with the brilliancy of her silver rays.

Thuvia of Ptarth saw only strangers—warriors in the harness of Dusar. Now she took fright, but too late!

Before she could voice but a single cry, rough hands

seized her. A heavy silken scarf was wound about her head. She was lifted in strong arms and borne to the deck of the flier. There was the sudden whirl of propellers, the rushing of air against her body, and, from far beneath the shouting and the challenge from the guard.

Racing toward the south another flier sped toward Helium. In its cabin a tall red man bent over the soft sole of an upturned sandal. With delicate instruments he measured the faint imprint of a small object which appeared there. Upon a pad beside him was the outline of a key, and here he noted the results of his measurements.

A smile played upon his lips as he completed his task and turned to one who waited at the opposite side of the table.

"The man is a genius," he remarked, admiration in his voice.

"Only a genius could have evolved such a lock as this is designed to spring. Here, take the sketch, Larok, and give all thine own genius full and unfettered freedom in reproducing it in metal."

The warrior-artificer bowed. "Man builds naught," he said, "that man may not destroy." Then he left the cabin with the sketch.

As dawn broke upon the lofty towers which mark the twin cities of Helium—the scarlet tower of one and the yellow tower of its sister—a flier floated lazily out of the north.

Upon its bow was emblazoned the insignia of a lesser noble of a far city of the empire of Helium. Its leisurely approach and the evident confidence with which it moved across the city aroused no suspicion in the minds of the sleepy guard. Their round of duty nearly done, they had little thought beyond the coming of those who were to relieve them.

Peace reigned throughout Helium. Stagnant, emasculating peace. Helium had no enemies. There was naught to fear.

Without haste the nearest air patrol swung sluggishly about and approached the stranger. At easy speaking distance the officer upon her deck hailed the incoming craft.

The cheery "Kaor!" and the plausible explanation that the owner had come from distant parts for a few days of pleasure in gay Helium sufficed. The air-patrol boat sheered off, passing again upon its way. The stranger continued toward a public landing stage, where she dropped into the ways and came to rest.

At about the same time a warrior entered her cabin.

"It is done, Vas Kor," he said, handing a small metal key to the tall noble who had just risen from his sleeping silks and furs.

"Good!" exclaimed the latter. "You must have worked upon it all during the night, Larok."

The warrior nodded.

"Now fetch me the Heliumetic metal you wrought some days since," commanded Vas Kor.

This done, the warrior assisted his master to replace the handsome jeweled metal of his harness with the plainer ornaments of an ordinary fighting man of Helium, and with the insignia of the same house that appeared upon the bow of the flier.

Vas Kor breakfasted on board. Then he emerged upon the aerial dock, entered an elevator, and was borne quickly to the street below, where he was soon engulfed by the early morning throng of workers hastening to their daily duties.

Among them his warrior trappings were no more remarkable than is a pair of trousers upon Broadway. All Martian men are warriors, save those physically unable to bear arms. The tradesman and his clerk clank with their martial trappings as they pursue their vocations. The schoolboy, coming out into the world, as he does, almost adult from the snowy shell that has encompassed his development for five long years, knows so little of life without a sword at his hip that he would feel the same discomfiture at going abroad unarmed that an Earth boy would experience in walking the streets knickerbockerless.

Vas Kor's destination lay in Greater Helium, which lies some seventy-five miles across the level plain from Lesser Helium. He had landed at the latter city because the air patrol is less suspicious and alert than that above the larger metropolis, where lies the palace of the jeddak.

As he moved with the throng in the parklike canyon of the thoroughfare the life of an awakening Martian city was in evidence about him. Houses, raised high upon their slender metal columns for the night, were dropping gently toward the ground. Among the flowers upon the scarlet sward which lies about the buildings children were already playing, and comely women laughing and chatting with their neighbors as they culled gorgeous blossoms and graceful ferns for the vases within doors.

The pleasant "kaor" of the Barsoomian greeting fell continually upon the ears of the stranger as friends and neighbors took up the duties of a new day.

The district in which he had landed was residential—a district of merchants of the more prosperous sort. Everywhere were evidences of luxury and wealth. Slaves appeared upon every house top with gorgeous silks and costly furs, laying them in the sun for airing. Jewel-encrusted women lolled even thus early upon the carven balconies before their sleeping apartments. Later in the day they would repair to the roofs when the slaves had arranged couches and pitched silken canopies to shade them from the sun.

Strains of inspiring music broke agreeably from open windows, for the Martians have solved the problem of attuning the nerves pleasantly to the sudden transition from sleep to waking that proves so difficult a thing for most Earth folk.

Above him raced the long, light passenger fliers, plying, each in its proper plane, between the numerous landing stages for internal passenger traffic. Landing stages that tower high into the heavens are for the great international passenger liners. Freighters have other landing stages at various lower levels, to within a couple of hundred feet of the ground; nor dare any flier rise or drop from one plane to another except in certain restricted districts where horizontal traffic is forbidden.

Along the close-cropped sward which paves the avenue ground fliers were moving in continuous lines in opposite directions. For the greater part they skimmed along the surface of the sward, soaring gracefully into the air at times to pass over a slower-going driver ahead, or at intersections, where the north and south traffic has the right of way and that going east and west must rise above it.

From private hangers upon many a roof top, fliers were darting into the line of traffic. Gay farewells and parting admonitions mingled with the whirring of motors and the subdued noises of the city.

Yet with all the swift movement and the countless thousands rushing hither and thither, the predominant suggestion was that of luxurious ease and soft noiselessness.

Martians dislike harsh, discordant clamor. The only loud noises they can abide are the martial sounds of war, the clash of arms, the collision of two mighty dreadnaughts of the air. To them there is no sweeter music than this.

At the intersection of two broad avenues Vas Kor descended from the street level to one of the great pneumatic stations of the city. Here he paid before a little wicket the fare to his destination with a couple of the dull, oval coins of Helium.

Beyond the gatekeeper he came to a slowly moving line of what to Earthly eyes would have appeared to be conical-nosed, eight-foot projectiles for some giant gun. In slow procession the things moved in single file along a grooved track. A half dozen attendants assisted passengers to enter, or directed these carriers to their proper destination.

Vas Kor approached one that was empty. Upon its nose was a dial and a pointer. He set the pointer for a certain station in Greater Helium, raised the arched lid of the thing, stepped in and lay down upon the upholstered bottom. An attendant closed the lid, which locked with a little click, and the carrier continued its slow way.

Presently it switched itself automatically to another track, to enter, a moment later, one of a series of dark-mouthed tubes.

The instant that its entire length was within the black aperture it sprang forward with the speed of a rifle ball. There was an instant of whizzing—a soft, though sudden, stop, and slowly the carrier emerged upon another platform, another attendant raised the lid and Vas Kor stepped out at the station beneath the center of Greater Helium, seventy-five miles from the point at which he had embarked.

Here he sought the street level, stepping immediately into a waiting ground flier. He spoke no word to the slave sitting in the driver's seat. It was evident that he had been expected, and that the fellow had received his instructions before his coming.

Scarcely had Vas Kor taken his seat when the flier went quickly into the fast-moving procession, turning presently from the broad and crowded avenue into a less congested

street. After a time it left the thronged district behind to enter
a section of small shops, where it stopped before the entrance
to one which bore the sign of a dealer in foreign silks.

Vas Kor entered the low-ceilinged room. A man at the
far end motioned him toward an inner apartment, giving
no further sign of recognition until he had passed in after
the caller and closed the door.

Then he faced his visitor, saluting deferentially.

"Most noble—" he commenced, but Vas Kor silenced him
with a gesture.

"No formalities," he said. "We must forget that I am aught
other than your slave. If all has been as carefully carried out
as it has been planned, we have no time to waste. Instead
we should be upon our way to the slave market. Are you
ready?"

The merchant nodded, and, turning to a great chest, produced the unemblazoned trappings of a slave. These Vas Kor
immediately donned. Then the two passed from the shop
through a rear door, traversed a winding alley to an avenue
beyond, where they entered a swift flier which awaited
them.

Five minutes later the merchant was leading his slave to the
public market, where a great concourse of people filled the
large open space in the center of which stood the slave block.

The crowds were enormous today, for Carthoris, Prince
of Helium, was to be the principal bidder.

One by one the masters mounted the rostrum beside the
slave block upon which stood their chattels. Briefly and clearly
each recounted the virtues of his particular offering.

When all were done, the major-domo of the Prince of
Helium recalled to the block such as had favorably impressed
him. For such he made a fair offer.

There was little haggling as to price, and none at all when
Vas Kor was placed upon the block. His merchant-master accepted the first offer that was made for him, and thus a Dusarian noble entered the household of Carthoris.

CHAPTER III
TREACHERY

THE DAY FOLLOWING the coming of Vas Kor to the palace of the Prince of Helium great excitement reigned throughout the twin cities, reaching its climax in the palace of Carthoris. Word had come of the abduction of Thuvia of Ptarth from her father's court, and with it the veiled hint that the Prince of Helium might be suspected of considerable knowledge of the act and the whereabouts of the princess.

In the council chamber of John Carter, Warlord of Mars, was Tardos Mors, Jeddak of Helium; Mors Kajak, his son, Jed of Lesser Helium; Carthoris, and a score of the great nobles of the empire.

"There must be no war between Ptarth and Helium, my son," said John Carter. "That you are innocent of the charge that has been placed against you by insinuation, we well know; but Thuvan Dihn must know it well, too.

"There is but one who may convince him, and that one be you. You must hasten at once to the court of Ptarth, and by your presence there as well as by your words assure him that his suspicions are groundless. Bear with you the authority of the Warlord of Barsoom, and of the Jeddak of Helium to offer every resource of the allied powers to assist Thuvan Dihn to recover his daughter and punish her abductors, whomsoever they may be.

"Go! I know that I do not need to urge upon you the necessity for haste."

Carthoris left the council chamber, and hastened to his palace.

Here slaves were busy in a moment setting things to right for the departure of their master. Several worked about the swift flier that would bear the Prince of Helium rapidly toward Ptarth.

At last all was done. But two armed slaves remained on guard. The setting sun hung low above the horizon. In a moment darkness would envelop all.

One of the guardsmen, a giant of a fellow across whose right cheek there ran a thin scar from temple to mouth, approached his companion. His gaze was directed beyond and above his comrade. When he had come quite close he spoke.

"What strange craft is that?" he asked.

The other turned about quickly to gaze heavenward. Scarce was his back turned toward the giant than the short-sword of the latter was plunged beneath his left shoulder blade, straight through his heart.

Voiceless, the soldier sank in his tracks—stone dead. Quickly the murderer dragged the corpse into the black shadows within the hangar. Then he returned to the flier.

Drawing a cunningly wrought key from his pocket-pouch, he removed the cover of the righthand dial of the controlling destination compass. For a moment he studied the construction of the mechanism beneath. Then he returned the dial to its place, set the pointer, and removed it again to note the resultant change in the position of the parts affected by the act.

A smile crossed his lips. With a pair of cutters he snipped off the projection which extended through the dial from the external pointer—now the latter might be moved to any point upon the dial without affecting the mechanism below. The eastern hemisphere dial was useless.

Now he turned his attention to the western dial. This he set upon a certain point. Afterward he removed the cover of this dial also, and with keen tool cut the steel finger from the under side of the pointer.

As quickly as possible he replaced the second dial cover, and resumed his place on guard. To all intents and purposes the compass was as efficient as before; but, as a matter of fact, the moving of the pointers upon the dials resulted now in no corresponding shift of the mechanism beneath—and the device was set, immovably, upon a destination of the slave's own choosing.

Presently came Carthoris, accompanied by but a handful of his gentlemen. He cast but a casual glance upon the single slave who stood guard. The fellow's thin, cruel lips, and the sword cut that ran from temple to mouth aroused the suggestion of an unpleasant memory within him. He wondered where Saran Tal had found the man—then the matter faded from his thoughts, and in another moment the Prince of Helium was laughing and chatting with his companions, though below the surface his heart was cold with dread, for what contingencies confronted Thuvia of Ptarth he could not even guess.

First to his mind, naturally, had sprung the thought that Astok of Dusar had stolen the fair Ptarthian; but almost simultaneously with the report of the abduction had come news of the great fêtes at Dusar in honor of the return of the jeddak's son to the court of his father.

It could not have been he, thought Carthoris, for on the very night that Thuvia was taken Astok had been in Dusar, and yet—

He entered the flier, exchanging casual remarks with his companions as he unlocked the mechanism of the compass and set the pointer upon the capital city of Ptarth.

With a word of farewell he touched the button which controlled the repulsive rays, and as the flier rose lightly into the air, the engine purred in answer to the touch of his finger upon a second button, the propellers whirred as his hand drew back the speed lever, and Carthoris, Prince of Helium, was off into the gorgeous Martian night beneath the hurtling moons and the million stars.

Scarce had the flier found its speed ere the man, wrapping his sleeping silks and furs about him, stretched at full length upon the narrow deck to sleep.

But sleep did not come at once at his bidding.

Instead, his thoughts ran riot in his brain, driving sleep away. He recalled the words of Thuvia of Ptarth, words that had half assured him that she loved him; for when he had asked her if she loved Kulan Tith, she had answered only that she was promised to him.

Now he saw that her reply was open to more than a single construction. It might, of course, mean that she did not love Kulan Tith; and so, by inference, be taken to mean that she loved another.

But what assurance was there that the other was Carthoris of Helium?

The more he thought upon it the more positive he became that not only was there no assurance in her words that she loved him, but none either in any act of hers. No, the fact was, she did not love him. She loved another. She had not been abducted—she had fled willingly with her lover.

With such pleasant thoughts filling him alternately with

despair and rage, Carthoris at last dropped into a deep sleep of utter mental exhaustion.

The breaking of the sudden dawn found him still asleep. His flier was rushing swiftly above a barren, ochre plain—the world-old bottom of a long-dead Martian sea.

In the distance rose low hills. Toward these the craft was headed. As it approached them, a great promontory might have been seen from its deck, stretching out into what had once been a mighty ocean, and circling back once more to enclose the forgotten harbor of a forgotten city, which still stretched back from its deserted quays, an imposing pile of wondrous architecture of a long-dead past.

The countless dismal windows, vacant and forlorn, stared, sightless, from their marble walls; the whole sad city taking on the semblance of scattered mounds of dead men's sun-bleached skulls—the casements having the appearance of eyeless sockets, the portals, grinning jaws.

Closer came the flier, but now its speed was diminishing—yet this was not Ptarth.

Above the central plaza it stopped, slowly settling Marsward. Within a hundred yards of the ground it came to rest, floating gently in the light air, and at the same instant an alarm sounded at the sleeper's ear.

Carthoris sprang to his feet. Below him he looked to see the teeming metropolis of Ptarth. Beside him, already, there should have been an air patrol.

He gazed about in bewildered astonishment. There indeed was a great city, but it was not Ptarth. No multitudes surged through its broad avenues. No signs of life broke the dead monotony of its deserted roof tops. No gorgeous silks, no priceless furs lent life and color to the cold marble and the gleaming ersite.

No patrol boat lay ready with its familiar challenge. Silent and empty lay the great city—empty and silent the surrounding air.

What had happened?

Carthoris examined the dial of his compass. The pointer was set upon Ptarth. Could the creature of his genius have thus betrayed him? He would not believe it.

Quickly he unlocked the cover, turning it back upon its hinge. A single glance showed him the truth, or at least a

part of it—the steel projection that communicated the movement of the pointer upon the dial to the heart of the mechanism beneath had been severed.

Who could have done the thing—and why?

Carthoris could not hazard even a faint guess. But the
thing now was to learn in what portion of the world he was,
and then take up his interrupted journey once more.

If it had been the purpose of some enemy to delay him, he
had succeeded well, thought Carthoris, as he unlocked the
cover of the second dial, the first having shown that its
pointer had not been set at all.

Beneath the second dial he found the steel pin severed as in
the other, but the controlling mechanism had first been set
for a point upon the western hemisphere.

He had just time to judge his location roughly at some
place southwest of Helium, and at a considerable distance
from the twin cities, when he was startled by a woman's
scream beneath him.

Leaning over the side of the flier, he saw what appeared
to be a red woman being dragged across the plaza by a huge,
green warrior—one of those fierce, cruel denizens of the dead-
sea bottoms and deserted cities of dying Mars.

Carthoris waited to see no more. Reaching for the control
board, he sent his craft racing plummet-like toward the
ground.

The green man was hurrying his captive toward a huge
thoat that browsed upon the ochre vegetation of the once
scarlet-gorgeous plaza. At the same instant a dozen red warriors leaped from the entrance of a nearby ersite palace,
pursuing the abductor with naked swords and shouts of rageful warning.

Once the woman turned her face upward toward the falling flier, and in the single swift glance, Carthoris saw that it
was Thuvia of Ptarth!

CHAPTER IV

A GREEN MAN'S CAPTIVE

WHEN THE LIGHT of day broke upon the little craft to whose deck the Princess of Ptarth had been snatched from her father's garden, Thuvia saw that the night had wrought a change in her abductors.

No longer did their trappings gleam with the metal of Dusar, but instead there was emblazoned there the insignia of the Prince of Helium.

The girl felt renewed hope, for she could not believe that in the heart of Carthoris could lie intent to harm her.

She spoke to the warrior squatting before the control board.

"Last night you wore the trappings of a Dusarian," she said. "Now your metal is that of Helium. What means it?"

The man looked at her with a grin.

"The Prince of Helium is no fool," he said.

Just then an officer emerged from the tiny cabin. He reprimanded the warrior for conversing with the prisoner, nor would he himself reply to any of her inquiries.

No harm was offered her during the journey, and so they came at last to their destination with the girl no wiser as to her abductors or their purpose than at first.

Here the flier settled slowly into the plaza of one of those mute monuments of Mars' dead and forgotten past—the deserted cities that fringe the sad ochre sea-bottoms where once rolled the mighty floods upon whose bosoms moved the maritime commerce of the peoples that are gone forever.

Thuvia of Ptarth was no stranger to such places. During her wanderings in search of the River Iss, that time she had set out upon what, for countless ages, had been the last, long pilgrimage of Martians, toward the Valley Dor, where lies the Lost Sea of Korus, she had encountered several of these sad reminders of the greatness and the glory of ancient Barsoom.

And again, during her flight from the temples of the Holy Therns with Tars Tarkas, Jeddak of Thark, she had seen them with their weird and ghostly inmates, the great white apes of Barsoom.

She knew, too, that many of them were used now by the

nomadic tribes of green men, but that among them all was no city that the red men did not shun, for without exception they stood amidst vast, waterless tracts, unsuited for the continued sustenance of the dominant race of Martians.

Why, then, should they be bringing her to such a place? There was but a single answer. Such was the nature of their work that they must needs seek the seclusion that a dead city afforded. The girl trembled at thought of her plight.

For two days her captors kept her within a huge palace that even in decay reflected the splendor of the age which its youth had known.

Just before dawn on the third day she had been aroused by the voices of two of her abductors.

"He should be here by dawn," one was saying. "Have her in readiness upon the plaza—else he will never land. The moment he finds that he is in a strange country he will turn about—methinks the prince's plan is weak in this one spot."

"There was no other way," replied the other. "It is wondrous work to get them both here at all, and even if we do not succeed in luring him to the ground, we shall have accomplished much."

Just then the speaker caught the eyes of Thuvia upon him, revealed by the quick-moving patch of light cast by Thuria in her mad race through the heavens.

With a quick sign to the other, he ceased speaking, and advancing toward the girl, motioned her to rise. Then he led her out into the night toward the center of the great plaza.

"Stand here," he commanded, "until we come for you. We shall be watching, and should you attempt to escape it will go ill with you—much worse than death. Such are the prince's orders."

Then he turned and retraced his steps toward the palace, leaving her alone in the midst of the unseen terrors of the haunted city, for in truth these places are haunted in the belief of many Martians who still cling to an ancient superstition which teaches that the spirits of Holy Therns who die before their allotted one thousand years, pass, on occasions, into the bodies of the great white apes.

To Thuvia, however, the real danger of attack by one of these ferocious, manlike beasts was quite sufficient. She no

longer believed in the weird soul transmigration that the
therns had taught her before she was rescued from their
clutches by John Carter; but she well knew the horrid fate
that awaited her should one of the terrible beasts chance to
spy her during its nocturnal prowlings.

What was that?

Surely she could not be mistaken. Something had moved,
stealthily, in the shadow of one of the great monoliths that
line the avenue where it entered the plaza opposite her!

Thar Ban, jed among the hordes of Torquas, rode swiftly
across the ochre vegetation of the dead sea-bottom toward
the ruins of ancient Aaanthor.

He had ridden far that night, and fast, for he had but
come from the despoiling of the incubator of a neighboring
green horde with which the hordes of Torquas were per-
petually warring.

His giant thoat was far from jaded, yet it would be well,
thought Thar Ban, to permit him to graze upon the ochre
moss which grows to greater height within the protected
courtyards of deserted cities, where the soil is richer than
on the sea-bottoms, and the plants partly shaded from the
sun during the cloudless Martian day.

Within the tiny stems of this dry-seeming plant is sufficient
moisture for the needs of the huge bodies of the mighty
thoats, which can exist for months without water, and for
days without even the slight moisture which the ochre moss
contains.

As Thar Ban rode noiselessly up the broad avenue which
leads from the quays of Aaanthor to the great central plaza,
he and his mount might have been mistaken for specters
from a world of dreams, so grotesque the man and beast, so
soundless the great thoat's padded, nailless feet upon the
moss-grown flagging of the ancient pavement.

The man was a splendid specimen of his race. Fully fifteen feet towered his great height from sole to pate. The
moonlight glistened against his glossy green hide, sparkling
the jewels of his heavy harness and the ornaments that
weighted his four muscular arms, while the upcurving tusks
that protruded from his lower jaw gleamed white and
terrible.

At the side of his thoat were slung his long radium rifle and his great, forty-foot, metal-shod spear, while from his own harness depended his long-sword and his short-sword, as well as his lesser weapons.

His protruding eyes and antennae-like ears were turning constantly hither and thither, for Thar Ban was yet in the country of the enemy, and, too, there was always the menace of the great white apes, which, John Carter was wont to say, are the only creatures that can arouse in the breasts of these fierce denizens of the dead sea-bottoms even the remotest semblance of fear.

As the rider neared the plaza, he reined suddenly in. His slender, tubular ears pointed rigidly forward. An unwonted sound had reached them. Voices! And where there were voices, outside of Torquas, there, too, were enemies. All the world of wide Barsoom contained naught but enemies for the fierce Torquasians.

Thar Ban dismounted. Keeping in the shadows of the great monoliths that line the Avenue of Quays of sleeping Aaanthor, he approached the plaza. Directly behind him, as a hound at heel, came the slate-gray thoat, his white belly shadowed by his barrel, his vivid yellow feet merging into the yellow of the moss beneath them.

In the center of the plaza Thar Ban saw the figure of a red woman. A red warrior was conversing with her. Now the man turned and retraced his steps toward the palace at the opposite side of the plaza.

Thar Ban watched until he had disappeared within the yawning portal. Here was a captive worth having! Seldom did a female of their hereditary enemies fall to the lot of a green man. Thar Ban licked his thin lips.

Thuvia of Ptarth watched the shadow behind the monolith at the opening to the avenue opposite her. She hoped that it might be but the figment of an overwrought imagination.

But no! Now, clearly and distinctly, she saw it move. It came from behind the screening shelter of the ersite shaft.

The sudden light of the rising sun fell upon it. The girl trembled. The *thing* was a huge green warrior!

Swiftly he sprang toward her. She screamed and tried to flee; but she had scarce turned toward the palace when a giant hand fell upon her arm, she was whirled about, and half dragged, half carried toward a huge thoat that was slowly grazing out of the avenue's mouth onto the ochre moss of the plaza.

At the same instant she turned her face upward toward the whirring sound of something above her, and there she saw a swift flier dropping toward her, the head and shoulders of a man leaning far over the side; but the man's features were deeply shadowed, so that she did not recognize them.

Now from behind her came the shouts of her red abductors. They were racing madly after him who dared to steal what they already had stolen.

As Thar Ban reached the side of his mount he snatched his long radium rifle from its boot, and, wheeling, poured three shots into the oncoming red men.

Such is the uncanny marksmanship of these Martian savages that three red warriors dropped in their tracks as three projectiles exploded in their vitals.

The others halted, nor did they dare return the fire for fear of wounding the girl.

Then Thar Ban vaulted to the back of this thoat, Thuvia of Ptarth still in his arms, and with a savage cry of triumph disappeared down the black canyon of the Avenue of Quays between the sullen palaces of forgotten Aaanthor.

Carthoris' flier had not touched the ground before he had sprung from its deck to race after the swift thoat, whose eight long legs were sending it down the avenue at the rate of an express train; but the men of Dusar who still remained alive had no mind to permit so valuable a capture to escape them.

They had lost the girl. That would be a difficult thing to explain to Astok; but some leniency might be expected could they carry the Prince of Helium to their master instead.

So the three who remained set upon Carthoris with their long-swords, crying to him to surrender; but they might as successfully have cried aloud to Thuria to cease her mad hurtling through the Barsoomian sky, for Carthoris of Helium was a true son of the Warlord of Mars and his incomparable Dejah Thoris.

Carthoris' long-sword had been already in his hand as

he leaped from the deck of the flier, so the instant that he realized the menace of the three red warriors, he wheeled to face them, meeting their onslaught as only John Carter himself might have done.

So swift his sword, so mighty and agile his half-earthly muscles, that one of his opponents was down, crimsoning the ochre moss with his lifeblood, when he had scarce made a single pass at Carthoris.

Now the two remaining Dusarians rushed simultaneously upon the Heliumite. Three long-swords clashed and sparkled in the moonlight, until the great white apes, roused from their slumbers, crept to the lowering windows of the dead city to view the bloody scene beneath them.

Thrice was Carthoris touched, so that the red blood ran down his face, blinding him and dyeing his broad chest. With his free hand he wiped the gore from his eyes, and with the fighting smile of his father touching his lips, leaped upon his antagonists with renewed fury.

A single cut of his heavy sword severed the head of one of them, and then the other, backing away clear of that point of death, turned and fled toward the palace at his back.

Carthoris made no step to pursue. He had other concern than the meting of even well-deserved punishment to strange men who masqueraded in the metal of his own house, for he had seen that these men were tricked out in the insignia that marked his personal followers.

Turning quickly toward his flier, he was soon rising from the plaza in pursuit of Thar Ban.

The red warrior whom he had put to flight turned in the entrance to the palace, and, seeing Carthoris' intent, snatched a rifle from those that he and his fellows had left leaning against the wall as they had rushed out with drawn swords to prevent the theft of their prisoner.

Few red men are good shots, for the sword is their chosen weapon; so now as the Dusarian drew bead upon the rising flier and touched the button upon his rifle's stock, it was more to chance than proficiency that he owed the partial success of his aim.

The projectile grazed the flier's side, the opaque coating breaking sufficiently to permit daylight to strike in upon the powder vial within the bullet's nose. There was a sharp explosion. Carthoris felt his craft reel drunkenly beneath him, and the engine stopped.

The momentum the air boat had gained carried her on over the city toward the sea-bottom beyond.

The red warrior in the plaza fired several more shots, none of which scored. Then a lofty minaret shut the drifting quarry from his view.

In the distance before him Carthoris could see the green warrior bearing Thuvia of Ptarth away upon his mighty thoat. The direction of his flight was toward the northwest of Aaanthor, where lay a vast mountainous country little known to red men.

The Heliumite now gave his attention to his injured craft. A close examination revealed the fact that one of the buoyancy tanks had been punctured, but the engine itself was uninjured.

A splinter from the projectile had damaged one of the control levers beyond the possibility of repair outside a machine shop; but after considerable tinkering, Carthoris was able to propel his wounded flier at low speed, a rate which could not approach the rapid gait of the thoat, whose eight long, powerful legs carried it over the ochre vegetation of the dead sea-bottom at terrific speed.

The Prince of Helium chafed and fretted at the slowness of his pursuit, yet he was thankful that the damage was no worse, for now he could at least move more rapidly than on foot.

But even this meager satisfaction was soon to be denied him, for presently the flier commenced to sag toward the port and by the bow. The damage to the buoyancy tanks had evidently been more grievous than he had at first believed.

All the balance of that long day Carthoris crawled erratically through the still air, the bow of the flier sinking lower and lower, and the list to port becoming more and more alarming, until at last, near dark, he was floating almost bow-down, his harness buckled to a heavy deck ring to keep him from being precipitated to the ground below.

His forward movement was now confined to a slow drifting with the gentle breeze that blew out of the southeast, and when this died down with the setting of the sun, he let the flier sink gently to the mossy carpet beneath.

Far before him loomed the mountains toward which the green man had been fleeing when last he had seen him, and with dogged resolution the son of John Carter, endowed with the indomitable will of his mighty sire, took up the pursuit on foot.

All that night he forged ahead until, with the dawning of a new day, he entered the low foothills that guard the approach to the fastness of the mountains of Torquas.

Rugged, granitic walls towered before him. Nowhere could he discern an opening through the formidable barrier; yet somewhere into this inhospitable world of stone the green warrior had borne the woman of the red man's heart's desire.

Across the yielding moss of the sea-bottom there had been no spoor to follow, for the soft pads of the thoat but pressed down in his swift passage the resilient vegetation, which sprang up again behind his fleeing feet, leaving no sign.

But here in the hills, where loose rock occasionally strewed the way; where black loam and wild flowers partially replaced the somber monotony of the waste places of the lowlands, Carthoris hoped to find some sign that would lead him in the right direction.

Yet, search as he would, the baffling mystery of the trail seemed likely to remain forever unsolved.

It was drawing toward the day's close once more when the keen eyes of the Heliumite discerned the tawny yellow of a sleek hide moving among the boulders several hundred yards to his left.

Crouching quickly behind a large rock, Carthoris watched the thing before him. It was a huge banth, one of those savage Barsoomian lions that roam the desolate hills of the dying planet.

The creature's nose was close to the ground. It was evident that he was following the spoor of meat by scent.

As Carthoris watched him, a great hope leaped into the man's heart. Here, possibly, might lie the solution to the mystery he had been endeavoring to solve. This hungry carnivore, keen always for the flesh of man, might even now be trailing the two whom Carthoris sought!

Cautiously the youth crept out upon the trail of the man-eater. Along the foot of the perpendicular cliff the creature moved, sniffing at the invisible spoor, and now and then emitting the low moan of the hunting banth.

Carthoris had followed the creature for but a few minutes when it disappeared as suddenly and mysteriously as though dissolved into thin air.

The man leaped to his feet. Not again was he to be cheated as the man had cheated him. He sprang forward at a reckless pace to the spot at which he last had seen the great, skulking brute.

Before him loomed the sheer cliff, its face unbroken by any aperture into which the huge banth might have wormed its great carcass. Beside him was a small, flat boulder, not larger than the deck of a ten-man flier, nor standing to a greater height than twice his own stature.

Perhaps the banth was in hiding behind this? The brute might have discovered the man upon his trail, and even now be lying in wait for his easy prey.

Cautiously, with drawn long-sword, Carthoris crept around the corner of the rock. There was no banth there, but something which surprised him infinitely more than would the presence of twenty banths.

Before him yawned the mouth of a dark cave leading downward into the ground. Through this the banth must have disappeared. Was it his lair? Within its dark and forbidding interior might there not lurk not one but many of the fearsome creatures?

Carthoris did not know, nor, with the thought that had been spurring him onward upon the trail of the creature uppermost in his mind, did he much care; for into this gloomy cavern he was sure the banth had trailed the green man and his captive, and into it he, too, would follow, content to give his life in the service of the woman he loved.

Not an instant did he hesitate, nor yet did he advance rashly; but with ready sword and cautious steps, for the way was dark, he stole on. As he advanced, the obscurity became impenetrable blackness.

CHAPTER V

THE FAIR RACE

DOWNWARD ALONG a smooth, broad floor led the strange tunnel, for such Carthoris was now convinced was the nature of the shaft he at first had thought but a cave.

Before him he could hear the occasional low moans of the banth, and presently from behind came a similar uncanny note. Another banth had entered the passageway on *his* trail!

His position was anything but pleasant. His eyes could not penetrate the darkness even to the distinguishing of his hand before his face, while the banths, he knew, could see quite well, though absence of light were utter.

No other sounds came to his ears than the dismal, blood-thirsty moanings of the beast ahead and the beast behind.

The tunnel had led straight, from where he had entered it beneath the side of the rock furtherest from the unscalable cliffs, toward the mighty barrier that had baffled him so long.

Now it was running almost level, and presently he noted a gradual ascent.

The beast behind him was gaining upon him, crowding him perilously close upon the heels of the beast in front. Presently he should have to do battle with one, or both. More firmly he gripped his weapon.

Now he could hear the breathing of the banth at his heels. Not for much longer could he delay the encounter.

Long since he had become assured that the tunnel led beneath the cliffs to the opposite side of the barrier, and he had hoped that he might reach the moonlit open before being compelled to grapple with either of the monsters.

The sun had been setting as he entered the tunnel, and the way had been sufficiently long to assure him that darkness now reigned upon the world without.

He glanced behind him. Blazing out of the darkness, seemingly not ten paces behind, glared two flaming points of fire. As the savage eyes met his, the beast emitted a frightful roar and then he charged.

To face that savage mountain of onrushing ferocity, to stand unshaken before the hideous fangs that he knew were bared in slavering bloodthirstiness, though he could not see

them, required nerves of steel; but of such were the nerves
of Carthoris of Helium.

He had the brute's eyes to guide his point, and, as true as
the sword hand of his mighty sire, his guided the keen
point to one of those blazing orbs, even as he leaped lightly
to one side.

With a hideous scream of pain and rage, the wounded
banth hurtled, clawing, past him. Then it turned to charge
once more; but this time Carthoris saw but a single gleaming
point of fiery hate directed upon him.

Again the needle point met its flashing target. Again the
horrid cry of the stricken beast reverberated through the rocky
tunnel, shocking in its torture-laden shrillness, deafening in
its terrific volume.

But now, as it turned to charge again, the man had no
guide whereby to direct his point. He heard the scraping of
the padded feet upon the rocky floor. He knew the thing was
charging down upon him once again, but he could see nothing.

Yet, if he could not see his antagonist, neither could his
antagonist now see him.

Leaping, as he thought, to the exact center of the tunnel,
he held his sword point ready on a line with the beast's chest.
It was all that he could do, hoping that chance might send
the point into the savage heart as he went down beneath the
great body.

So quickly was the thing over that Carthoris could scarce
believe his senses as the mighty body rushed madly past him.
Either he had not placed himself in the center of the tunnel,
or else the blinded banth had erred in its calculations.

However, the huge body missed him by a foot, and the
creature continued on down the tunnel as though in pursuit
of the prey that had eluded him.

Carthoris, too, followed the same direction, nor was it long
before his heart was gladdened by the sight of the moonlit
exit from the long, dark passage.

Before him lay a deep hollow, entirely surrounded by gigantic cliffs. The surface of the valley was dotted with enormous trees, a strange sight so far from a Martian waterway.
The ground itself was clothed in brilliant scarlet sward,
picked out with innumerable patches of gorgeous wild flowers.

Beneath the glorious effulgence of the two moons the scene was one of indescribably loveliness, tinged with the weirdness of strange enchantment.

For only an instant, however, did his gaze rest upon the natural beauties outspread before him. Almost immediately they were riveted upon the figure of a great banth standing across the carcass of a new-killed thoat.

The huge beast, his tawny mane bristling around his hideous head, kept his eyes fixed upon another banth that charged erratically hither and thither, with shrill screams of pain, and horrid roars of hate and rage.

Carthoris quickly guessed that the second brute was the one he had blinded during the fight in the tunnel, but it was the dead thoat that centered his interest more than either of the savage carnivora.

The harness was still upon the body of the huge Martian mount, and Carthoris could not doubt but that this was the very animal upon which the green warrior had borne away Thuvia of Ptarth.

But where were the rider and his prisoner? The Prince of Helium shuddered as he thought upon the probability of the fate that had overtaken them.

Human flesh is the food most craved by the fierce Barsoomian lion, whose great carcass and giant thews require enormous quantities of meat to sustain them.

Two human bodies would have but whetted the creature's appetite, and that he had killed and eaten the green man and the red girl seemed only too likely to Carthoris. He had left the carcass of the mighty thoat to be devoured after having consumed the more toothsome portion of his banquet.

Now the sightless banth, in its savage, aimless charging and counter-charging, had passed beyond the kill of its fellow, and there the light breeze that was blowing wafted the scent of new blood to its nostrils.

No longer were its movements erratic. With outstretched tail and foaming jaws it charged straight as an arrow, for the body of the thoat and the mighty creature of destruction that stood with forepaws upon the slate-gray side, waiting to defend its meat.

When the charging banth was twenty paces from the dead thoat the killer gave vent to its hideous challenge, and with a mighty spring leaped forward to meet it.

The battle that ensued awed even the warlike Barsoomian. The mad rending, the hideous and deafening roaring, the implacable savagery of the blood-stained beasts held him in the paralysis of fascination, and when it was over and the two creatures, their heads and shoulders torn to ribbons, lay with their dead jaws still buried in each other's bodies, Carthoris tore himself from the spell only by an effort of the will.

Hurrying to the side of the dead thoat he searched for traces of the girl he feared had shared the thoat's fate, but nowhere could he discover anything to confirm his fears.

With slightly lightened heart he started out to explore the valley, but scarce a dozen steps had he taken when the glistening of a jeweled bauble lying on the sward caught his eye.

As he picked it up his first glance showed him that it was a woman's hair ornament, and emblazoned upon it was the insignia of the royal house of Ptarth.

But, sinister discovery, blood, still wet, splotched the magnificent jewels of the setting.

Carthoris half choked as the dire possibilities which the thing suggested presented themselves to his imagination. Yet he could not, would not believe it.

It was impossible that that radiant creature could have met so hideous an end. It was incredible that the glorious Thuvia should ever cease to be.

Upon his already jewel-encrusted harness, to the strap that crossed his great chest beneath which beat his loyal heart, Carthoris, Prince of Helium, fastened the gleaming thing that Thuvia of Ptarth had worn, and wearing, had made holy to the Heliumite.

Then he proceeded upon his way into the heart of the unknown valley.

For the most part the giant trees shut off his view to any but the most limited distances. Occasionally he caught glimpses of the towering hills that bounded the valley upon every side, and though they stood out clear beneath the light of the two moons, he knew that they were far off, and that the extent of the valley was immense.

For half the night he continued his search, until presently he was brought to a sudden halt by the distant sound of squealing thoats.

Guided by the noise of these habitually angry beasts, he stole forward through the trees until at last he came upon a level, treeless plain, in the center of which a mighty city reared its burnished domes and vividly colored towers.

About the walled city the red man saw a huge encampment of the green warriors of the dead sea-bottoms, and as he let his eyes rove carefully over the city he realized that here was no deserted metropolis of a dead past.

But what city could it be? His studies had taught him that in this little-explored portion of Barsoom the fierce tribe of Torquasian green men ruled supreme, and that as yet no red man had succeeded in piercing to the heart of their domain to return again to the world of civilization.

The men of Torquas had perfected huge guns with which their uncanny marksmanship had permitted them to repulse the few determined efforts that nearby red nations had made to explore their country by means of battle fleets of airships.

That he was within the boundary of Torquas, Carthoris was sure, but that there existed there such a wondrous city he never had dreamed, nor had the chronicles of the past even hinted at such a possibility, for the Torquasians were known to live, as did the other green men of Mars, within the deserted cities that dotted the dying planet, nor ever had any green horde built so much as a single edifice, other than the low-walled incubators where their young are hatched by the sun's heat.

The encircling camp of green warriors lay about five hundred yards from the city's walls. Between it and the city was no semblance of breastwork or other protection against rifle or cannon fire; yet distinctly now in the light of the rising sun Carthoris could see many figures moving along the summit of the high wall, and upon the roof tops beyond.

That they were beings like himself he was sure, though they were at too great a distance from him for him to be positive that they were red men.

Almost immediately after sunrise the green warriors commenced firing upon the little figures upon the wall. To Carthoris' surprise the fire was not returned, but presently the last of the city's inhabitants had sought shelter from the weird marksmanship of the green men, and no further sign of life was visible beyond the wall.

Then Carthoris, keeping within the shelter of the trees that fringed the plain, began circling the rear of the besiegers' line, hoping against hope that somewhere he would obtain sight of Thuvia of Ptarth, for even now he could not believe that she was dead.

That he was not discovered was a miracle, for mounted warriors were constantly riding back and forth from the camp into the forest; but the long day wore on and still he continued his seemingly fruitless quest, until, near sunset, he came opposite a mighty gate in the city's western wall.

Here seemed to be the principal force of the attacking horde. Here a great platform had been erected whereon Carthoris could see squatting a huge green warrior, surrounded by others of his kind.

This, then, must be the notorious Hortan Gur, Jeddak of Torquas, the fierce old ogre of the southwestern hemisphere, as only for a jeddak are platforms raised in temporary camps or upon the march by the green hordes of Barsoom.

As the Heliumite watched he saw another green warrior push his way forward toward the rostrum. Beside him he dragged a captive, and as the surrounding warriors parted to let the two pass, Carthoris caught a fleeting glimpse of the prisoner.

His heart leaped in rejoicing. Thuvia of Ptarth still lived!

It was with difficulty that Carthoris restrained the impulse to rush forward to the side of the Ptarthian princess; but in the end his better judgment prevailed, for in the face of such odds he knew that he should have been but throwing away, uselessly, any future opportunity he might have to succor her.

He saw her dragged to the foot of the rostrum. He saw Hortan Gur address her. He could not hear the creature's words, nor Thuvia's reply; but it must have angered the green monster, for Carthoris saw him leap toward the prisoner, striking her a cruel blow across the face with his metalbanded arm.

Then the son of John Carter, Jeddak of Jeddaks, Warlord of Barsoom, went mad. The old, blood-red haze through which his sire had glared at countless foes, floated before his eyes.

His half-Earthly muscles, responding quickly to his will,

sent him in enormous leaps and bounds toward the green monster that had struck the woman he loved.

The Torquasians were not looking in the direction of the forest. All eyes had been upon the figures of the girl and their jeddak, and loud was the hideous laughter that rang out in appreciation of the wit of the green emperor's reply to his prisoner's appeal for liberty.

Carthoris had covered about half the distance between the forest and the green warriors, when a new factor succeeded in still further directing the attention of the latter from him.

Upon a high tower within the beleaguered city a man appeared. From his upturned mouth there issued a series of frightful shrieks; uncanny shrieks that swept, shrill and terrifying, across the city's walls, over the heads of the besiegers, and out across the forest to the uttermost confines of the valley.

Once, twice, thrice the fearsome sound smote upon the ears of the listening green men, and then far, far off across the broad woods came sharp and clear from the distance an answering shriek.

It was but the first. From every point rose similar savage cries, until the world seemed to tremble to their reverberations.

The green warriors looked nervously this way and that. They knew not fear, as Earth men may know it; but in the face of the unusual their wonted self-assurance deserted them.

And then the great gate in the city wall opposite the platform of Hortan Gur swung suddenly wide. From it issued as strange a sight as Carthoris ever had witnessed, though at the moment he had time to cast but a single fleeting glance at the tall bowmen emerging through the portal behind their long, oval shields; to note their flowing auburn hair; and to realize that the growling things at their side were fierce Barsoomian lions.

Then he was in the midst of the astonished Torquasians. With drawn long-sword he was among them, and to Thuvia of Ptarth, whose startled eyes were the first to fall upon him, it seemed that she was looking upon John Carter himself, so strangely similar to the fighting of the father was that of the son.

Even to the famous fighting smile of the Virginian was the resemblance true. And the sword arm! Ah, the subtleness of it, and the speed!

All about was turmoil and confusion. Green warriors were leaping to the backs of their restive, squealing thoats. Calots were growling out their savage gutturals, whining to be at the throats of the oncoming foemen.

Thar Ban and another by the side of the rostrum had been the first to note the coming of Carthoris, and it was with them he battled for possession of the red girl, while the others hastened to meet the host advancing from the beleaguered city.

Carthoris sought both to defend Thuvia of Ptarth and reach the side of the hideous Hortan Gur that he might avenge the blow the creature had struck the girl.

He succeeded in reaching the rostrum, over the dead bodies of two warriors who had turned to join Thar Ban and his companion in repulsing this adventurous red man, just as Hortan Gur was about to leap from it to the back of his thoat.

The attention of the green warriors turned principally upon the bowmen advancing upon them from the city, and upon the savage banths that paced beside them—cruel beasts of war, infinitely more terrible than their own savage calots.

As Carthoris leaped to the rostrum he drew Thuvia up beside him, and then he turned upon the departing jeddak with an angry challenge and a sword thrust.

As the Heliumite's point pricked his green hide, Hortan Gur turned upon his adversary with a snarl, but at the same instant two of his chieftains called to him to hasten, for the charge of the fair-skinned inhabitants of the city was developing into a more serious matter than the Torquasians had anticipated.

Instead of remaining to battle with the red man, Hortan Gur promised him his attention after he had disposed of the presumptuous citizens of the walled city, and, leaping astride his thoat, galloped madly off to meet the rapidly advancing bowmen.

The other warriors quickly followed their jeddak, leaving Thuvia and Carthoris alone upon the platform.

Between them and the city raged a terrific battle. The fair-skinned warriors, armed only with their long bows and a kind of short-handled war-ax, were almost helpless beneath the savage mounted green men at close quarters; but at a distance their sharp arrows did fully as much execution as the radium projectiles of the green men.

But if the warriors themselves were outclassed, not so their savage companions, the fierce banths. Scarce had the two lines come together when hundreds of these appalling creatures had leaped among the Torquasians, dragging warriors from their thoats—dragging down the huge thoats themselves, and bringing consternation to all before them.

The numbers of the citizenry, too, was to their advantage, for it seemed that scarce a warrior fell but his place was taken by a score more, in such a constant stream did they pour from the city's great gate.

And so it came, what with the ferocity of the banths and the numbers of the bowmen, that at last the Torquasians fell back, until presently the platform upon which stood Carthoris and Thuvia lay directly in the center of the fight.

That neither was struck by a bullet or an arrow seemed a miracle to both; but at last the tide had rolled completely past them, so that they were alone between the fighters and the city, except for the dying and the dead, and a score or so of growling banths, less well trained than their fellows, who prowled among the corpses seeking meat.

To Carthoris the strangest part of the battle had been the terrific toll taken by the bowmen with their relatively puny weapons. Nowhere that he could see was there a single wounded green man, but the corpses of their dead lay thick upon the field of battle.

Death seemed to follow instantly the slightest pinprick of a bowman's arrow, nor apparently did one ever miss its goal. There could be but one explanation: the missiles were poison-tipped.

Presently the sounds of conflict died in the distant forest. Quiet reigned, broken only by the growling of the devouring banths. Carthoris turned toward Thuvia of Ptarth. As yet neither had spoken.

"Where are we, Thuvia?" he asked.

The girl looked at him questioningly. His very presence had seemed to proclaim a guilty knowledge of her abduction. How else might he have known the destination of the flier that brought her!

"Who should know better than the Prince of Helium?" she asked in return. "Did he not come hither of his own free will?"

"From Aaanthor I came voluntarily upon the trail of the green man who had stolen you, Thuvia," he replied; "but from the time I left Helium until I awoke above Aaanthor I thought myself bound for Ptarth.

"It had been intimated that I had guilty knowledge of your abduction," he explained simply, "and I was hastening to the jeddak, your father, to convince him of the falsity of the charge, and to give my service to your recovery. Before I left Helium someone tampered with my compass, so that it bore me to Aaanthor instead of to Ptarth. That is all. You believe me?"

"But the warriors who stole me from the garden!" she exclaimed. "After we arrived at Aaanthor they wore the metal of the Prince of Helium. When they took me they were trapped in Dusarian harness. There seemed but a single explanation. Whoever dared the outrage wished to put the onus upon another, should he be detected in the act; but once safely away from Ptarth he felt safe in having his minions return to their own harness."

"You believe that I did this thing, Thuvia?" he asked.

"Ah, Carthoris," she replied sadly, "I did not wish to believe it; but when everything pointed to you—even then I would not believe it."

"I did not do it, Thuvia," he said. "But let me be entirely honest with you. As much as I love your father, as much as I respect Kulan Tith, to whom you are betrothed, as well as I know the frightful consequences that must have followed such an act of mine, hurling into war, as it would, three of the greatest nations of Barsoom—yet, notwithstanding all this, I should not have hesitated to take you thus, Thuvia of Ptarth, had you even hinted that it would not have displeased *you*.

"But you did nothing of the kind, and so I am here, not in my own service, but in yours, and in the service of the man to whom you are promised, to save you for him, if it lies within the power of man to do so," he concluded, almost bitterly.

Thuvia of Ptarth looked into his face for several moments.

Her breast was rising and falling as though to some resistless emotion. She half took a step toward him. Her lips parted as though to speak—swiftly and impetuously.

And then she conquered whatever had moved her.

"The future acts of the Prince of Helium," she said coldly, "must constitute the proof of his past honesty of purpose."

Carthoris was hurt by the girl's tone, as much as by the doubt as to his integrity which her words implied.

He had half hoped that she might hint that his love would be acceptable—certainly there was due him at least a little gratitude for his recent acts in her behalf; but the best he received was cold skepticism.

The Prince of Helium shrugged his broad shoulders. The girl noted it, and the little smile that touched his lips, so that it became her turn to be hurt.

Of course she had not meant to hurt him. He might have known that after what he had said she could not do anything to encourage him! But he need not have made his indifference quite so palpable. The men of Helium were noted for their gallantry—not for boorishness. Possibly it was the Earth blood that flowed in his veins.

How could she know that the shrug was but Carthoris' way of attempting, by physical effort, to cast blighting sorrow from his heart, or that the smile upon his lips was the fighting smile of his father with which the son gave outward evidence of the determination he had reached to submerge his own great love in his efforts to save Thuvia of Ptarth for another, because he believed that she loved this other!

He reverted to his original question.

"Where are we?" he asked. "I do not know."

"Nor I," replied the girl. "Those who stole me from Ptarth spoke among themselves of Aaanthor, so that I thought it possible that the ancient city to which they took me was that famous ruin; but where we may be now I have no idea."

"When the bowmen return we shall doubtless learn all that there is to know," said Carthoris. "Let us hope that they prove friendly. What race may they be? Only in the most ancient of our legends and in the mural paintings of the deserted cities of the dead sea-bottoms are depicted such a race of auburn-haired, fair-skinned people. Can it be that we have stumbled upon a surviving city of the past which all Barsoom believes buried beneath the ages?"

Thuvia was looking toward the forest into which the green men and the pursuing bowmen had disappeared. From a great distance came the hideous cries of banths, and an occasional shot.

"It is strange that they do not return," said the girl.

"One would expect to see the wounded limping or being carried back to the city," replied Carthoris, with a puzzled frown. "But how about the wounded nearer the city? Have they carried them within?"

Both turned their eyes toward the field between them and the walled city, where the fighting had been most furious.

There were the banths, still growling about their hideous feast.

Carthoris looked at Thuvia in astonishment. Then he pointed toward the field.

"Where are they?" he whispered. *"What has become of their dead and wounded?"*

CHAPTER VI

THE JEDDAK OF LOTHAR

THE GIRL LOOKED her incredulity.

"They lay in piles," she murmured. "There were thousands of them but a minute ago."

"And now," continued Carthoris, "there remain but the banths and the carcasses of the green men."

"They must have sent forth and carried the dead bowmen away while we were talking," said the girl.

"It is impossible!" replied Carthoris. "Thousands of dead lay there upon the field but a moment since. It would have required many hours to have removed them. The thing is uncanny."

"I had hoped," said Thuvia, "that we might find an asylum with these fair-skinned people. Notwithstanding their valor upon the field of battle, they did not strike me as a ferocious or warlike people. I had been about to suggest that we seek

entrance to the city, but now I scarce know if I care to venture among people whose dead vanish into thin air."

"Let us chance it," replied Carthoris. "We can be no worse
off within their walls than without. Here we may fall prey to
the banths or the no less fierce Torquasians. There, at least,
we shall find beings molded after our own images.

"All that causes me to hesitate," he added, "is the danger of
taking you past so many banths. A single sword would scarce
prevail were even a couple of them to charge simultaneously."

"Do not fear on that score," replied the girl, smiling. "The
banths will not harm us."

As she spoke she descended from the platform, and with
Carthoris at her side stepped fearlessly out upon the bloody
field in the direction of the walled city of mystery.

They had advanced but a short distance when a banth,
looking up from its gory feast, descried them. With an angry
roar the beast walked quickly in their direction, and at the
sound of its voice a score of others followed its example.

Carthoris drew his long-sword. The girl stole a quick
glance at his face. She saw the smile upon his lips, and it was
as wine to sick nerves; for even upon warlike Barsoom where
all men are brave, woman reacts quickly to quiet indifference
to danger—to dare-deviltry that is without bombast.

"You may return your sword," she said. "I told you that
the banths would not harm us. Look!" and as she spoke she
stepped quickly toward the nearest animal.

Carthoris would have leaped after her to protect her, but
with a gesture she motioned him back. He heard her calling
to the banths in a low, singsong voice that was half purr.

Instantly the great heads went up and all the wicked eyes
were riveted upon the figure of the girl. Then, stealthily,
they commenced moving toward her. She had stopped now
and was standing waiting them.

One, closer to her than the others, hesitated. She spoke to
him imperiously, as a master might speak to a refractory
hound.

The great carnivore let its head droop, and with tail between its legs came slinking to the girl's feet, and after it
came the others until she was entirely surrounded by the
savage man-eaters.

Turning she led them to where Carthoris stood. They growled a little as they neared the man, but a few sharp words of command put them in their places.

"How do you do it?" exclaimed Carthoris.

"Your father once asked me that same question in the galleries of the Golden Cliffs within the Otz Mountains, beneath the temples of the therns. I could not answer him, nor can I answer you. I do not know whence comes my power over them, but ever since the day that Sator Throg threw me among them in the banth pit of the Holy Therns, and the great creatures fawned upon instead of devouring me, I ever have had the same strange power over them. They come at my call and do my bidding, even as the faithful Woola does the bidding of your mighty sire."

With a word the girl dispersed the fierce pack. Roaring, they returned to their interrupted feast, while Carthoris and Thuvia passed among them toward the walled city.

As they advanced the man looked with wonder upon the dead bodies of those of the green men that had not been devoured or mauled by the banths.

He called the girl's attention to them. No arrows protruded from the great carcasses. Nowhere upon any of them was the sign of mortal wound, nor even slightest scratch or abrasion.

Before the bowmen's dead had disappeared the corpses of the Torquasians had bristled with the deadly arrows of their foes. Where had the slender messengers of death departed? What unseen hand had plucked them from the bodies of the slain?

Despite himself Carthoris could scarce repress a shudder of apprehension as he glanced toward the silent city before them. No longer was sign of life visible upon wall or roof top. All was quiet—brooding, ominous quiet.

Yet he was sure that eyes watched them from somewhere behind that blank wall.

He glanced at Thuvia. She was advancing with wide eyes fixed upon the city gate. He looked in the direction of her gaze, but saw nothing.

His gaze upon her seemed to arouse her as from a lethargy. She glanced up at him, a quick, brave smile touching her lips, and then, as though the act was involuntary, she came close to his side and placed one of her hands in his.

He guessed that something within her that was beyond her conscious control was appealing to him for protection. He threw an arm about her and thus they crossed the field. She did not draw away from him, so engrossed was she in the mystery of the strange city before them.

They stopped before the gate. It was a mighty thing. From its construction Carthoris could but dimly speculate upon its unthinkable antiquity.

It was circular, closing a circular aperture, and the Heliumite knew from his study of ancient Barsoomian architecture that it rolled to one side, like a huge wheel, into an aperture in the wall.

Even such world-old cities as ancient Aaanthor were as yet undreamed of when the races lived that built such gates as these.

As he stood speculating upon the identity of this forgotten city, a voice spoke from above. There, leaning over the high wall, was a man.

His hair was auburn, his skin fair—fairer even than that of John Carter, the Virginian. His forehead was high, his eyes large and intelligent.

The language that he used was intelligible to the two below, yet there was a marked difference between it and their Barsoomian tongue.

"Who are you?" he asked. "And what do you here before the gate of Lothar?"

"We are friends," replied Carthoris. "This be the princess, Thuvia of Ptarth, who was captured by the Torquasian horde. I am Carthoris of Helium, Prince of the house of Tardos Mors, Jeddak of Helium, and son of John Carter, Warlord of Mars, and of his wife, Dejah Thoris."

" 'Ptarth'?" repeated the man. " 'Helium'?" He shook his head. "I never have heard of these places, nor did I know that there dwelt upon Barsoom a race of thy strange color. Where may these cities lie? From our loftiest tower we have never seen another city than Lothar."

Carthoris pointed toward the northeast.

"In that direction lie Helium and Ptarth," he said. "Helium is over eight thousand haads from Lothar, while Ptarth lies nine thousand five hundred haads northeast of Helium."[1]

Still the man shook his head.

"I know of nothing beyond the Lotharian hills," he said. "Naught may live there beside the hideous green hordes of Torquas. They have conquered all Barsoom except this single valley and the city of Lothar. Here we have defied them for countless ages, though periodically they renew their attempts to destroy us. From whence you come I cannot guess unless you be descended from the slaves the Torquasians captured in early times when they reduced the outer world to their vassalage; but we had heard that they destroyed all other races but their own."

Carthoris tried to explain that the Torquasians ruled but a relatively tiny part of the surface of Barsoom, and even this only because their domain held nothing to attract the red race; but the Lotharian could not seem to conceive of anything beyond the valley of Lothar other than a trackless waste peopled by the ferocious green hordes of Torquas.

After considerable parleying he consented to admit them to the city, and a moment later the wheel-like gate rolled back within its niche, and Thuvia and Carthoris entered the city of Lothar.

All about them were evidences of fabulous wealth. The façades of the buildings fronting upon the avenue within the wall were richly carven, and about the windows and doors were ofttimes set foot-wide borders of precious stones, intricate mosaics, or tablets of beaten gold bearing bas-reliefs depicting what may have been bits of the history of this forgotten people.

---

[1] On Barsoom the *ad* is the basis of linear measurement. It is the equivalent of an Earthly foot, measuring about 11.694 Earth inches. As has been my custom in the past, I have generally translated Barsoomian symbols of time, distance, etc., into their Earthly equivalents, as being more easily understood by Earth readers. For those of a more studious turn of mind it may be interesting to know the Martian table of linear measurement, and so I give it here:

     10 safads = 1 ad.
     200 ads   = 1 haad.
     100 haads = 1 karad.
     360 karads = 1 circumference of Mars at equator.

A haad, or Barsoomian mile, contains about 2,339 Earth feet. A karad is one degree. A sofad about 1.17 Earth inches.

He with whom they had conversed across the wall was in the avenue to receive them. About him were a hundred or more men of the same race. All were clothed in flowing robes and all were beardless.

Their attitude was more of fearful suspicion than antagonism. They followed the newcomers with their eyes; but spoke no word to them.

Carthoris could not but notice the fact that though the city had been but a short time before surrounded by a horde of bloodthirsty demons yet none of the citizens appeared to be armed, nor was there sign of soldiery about.

He wondered if all the fighting men had sallied forth in one supreme effort to rout the foe, leaving the city all unguarded. He asked their host.

The man smiled.

"No creature other than a score or so of our sacred banths has left Lothar today," he replied.

"But the soldiers—the bowmen!" exclaimed Carthoris. "We saw thousands emerge from this very gate, overwhelming the hordes of Torquas and putting them to rout with their deadly arrows and their fierce banths."

Still the man smiled his knowing smile.

"Look!" he cried, and pointed down a broad avenue before him.

Carthoris and Thuvia followed the direction indicated, and there, marching bravely in the sunlight, they saw advancing toward them a great army of bowmen.

"Ah!" exclaimed Thuvia. "They have returned through another gate, or perchance these be the troops that remained to defend the city?"

Again the fellow smiled his uncanny smile

"There are no soldiers in Lothar," he said. "Look!"

Both Carthoris and Thuvia had turned toward him while he spoke, and now as they turned back again toward the advancing regiments their eyes went wide in astonishment, for the broad avenue before them was as deserted as the tomb.

"And those who marched out upon the hordes today?" whispered Carthoris. "They, too, were unreal?"

The man nodded.

"But their arrows slew the green warriors," insisted Thuvia.

"Let us go before Tario," replied the Lotharian. "He will tell you that which he deems it best you know. I might tell you too much."

"Who is Tario?" asked Carthoris.

"Jeddak of Lothar," replied the guide, leading them up the broad avenue down which they had but a moment since seen the phantom army marching.

For half an hour they walked along lovely avenues between the most gorgeous buildings that the two had ever seen. Few people were in evidence. Carthoris could not but note the deserted appearance of the mighty city.

At last they came to the royal palace. Carthoris saw it from a distance, and guessing the nature of the magnificent pile wondered that even here there should be so little sign of activity and life.

Not even a single guard was visible before the great entrance gate, nor in the gardens beyond, into which he could see, was there sign of the myriad life that pulses within the precincts of the royal estates of the red jeddaks.

"Here," said their guide, "is the palace of Tario."

As he spoke Carthoris again let his gaze rest upon the wondrous palace. With a startled exclamation he rubbed his eyes and looked again. No! He could not be mistaken. Before the massive gate stood a score of sentries. Within, the avenue leading to the main building was lined on either side by ranks of bowmen. The gardens were dotted with officers and soldiers moving quickly to and fro, as though bent upon the duties of the minute.

What manner of people were these who could conjure an army out of thin air? He glanced toward Thuvia. She, too, evidently had witnessed the transformation as her brow was drawn in perplexing thought.

With a little shudder she pressed more closely toward him.

"What do you make of it?" she whispered. "It is most uncanny."

"I cannot account for it," replied Carthoris, "unless we have gone mad."

Carthoris turned quickly toward the Lotharian. The fellow was smiling broadly.

"I thought that you just said that there were no soldiers in Lothar," said the Heliumite, with a gesture toward the guardsmen. "What are these?"

"Ask Tario," replied the other. "We shall soon be before him."

Nor was it long before they entered a lofty chamber at one end of which a man reclined upon a luxurious, regal couch that stood upon a high dais.

As the trip approached, the man turned dreamy eyes sleepily upon them. Twenty feet from the dais their conductor halted, and, whispering to Thuvia and Carthoris to follow his example, threw himself headlong to the floor. Then rising to hands and knees, he commenced crawling toward the foot of the throne, swinging his head to and fro and wiggling his body as you have seen a hound do when approaching its master.

Thuvia glanced quickly toward Carthoris. He was standing erect, with high-held head and arms folded across his broad chest. A haughty smile curved his lips.

The man upon the dais was eying him intently, and Carthoris of Helium was looking straight into the other's face.

"Who be these, Jav?" asked the man of him who crawled upon his belly along the floor.

"O Tario, most glorious Jeddak," replied Jav, "these be strangers who came with the hordes of Torquas to our gates, saying that they were prisoners of the green men. They tell strange tales of cities far beyond Lothar."

"Arise, Jav," commanded Tario, "and ask these two why they show not to Tario the respect that is his due."

Jav arose and faced the strangers. At sight of their erect positions his face went livid. He leaped toward them.

"Creatures!" he screamed. "Down! Down upon your bellies before the last of the jeddaks of Barsoom!"

CHAPTER VII

THE PHANTOM BOWMAN

AS JAV LEAPED toward him Carthoris laid his hand upon the hilt of his long-sword. The Lotharian halted. The great apartment was empty save for the four at the dais, yet as Jav stepped back from the menace of the Heliumite's threatening attitude the latter found himself surrounded by a score of bowmen.

From whence had they sprung? Both Carthoris and Thuvia looked their astonishment.

Now the former's sword leaped from its scabbard, and at the same instant the bowmen drew back their slim shafts.

Tario had half raised himself upon one elbow. For the first time he saw the full figure of Thuvia, who had been concealed behind the person of Carthoris.

"Enough!" cried the jeddak, raising a protesting hand, but at that very instant the sword of the Heliumite cut viciously at its nearest antagonist.

As the keen edge reached its goal Carthoris let the point fall to the floor, as with wide eyes he stepped backward in consternation, throwing the back of his left hand across his brow. His steel had cut but empty air—his antagonist had vanished—there were no bowmen in the room!

"It is evident that these are strangers," said Tario to Jav. "Let us first determine that they knowingly affronted us before we take measures for punishment."

Then he turned to Carthoris, but ever his gaze wandered to the perfect lines of Thuvia's glorious figure, which the harness of a Barsoomian princess accentuated rather than concealed.

"Who are you," he asked, "who knows not the etiquette of the court of the last of the mighty jeddaks?"

"I am Carthoris, Prince of Helium," replied the Heliumite. "And this is Thuvia, Princess of Ptarth. In the courts of our fathers men do not prostrate themselves before royalty. Not since the First Born tore their immortal goddess limb from limb have men crawled upon their bellies to any throne upon Barsoom. Now think you that the daughter of one mighty jeddak and the son of another would so humiliate themselves?"

Tario looked at Carthoris for a long time. At last he spoke.

"There is no other jeddak upon Barsoom than Tario," he said. "There is no other race than that of Lothar, unless the hordes of Torquas may be dignified by such an appellation. Lotharians are white; your skins are red. There are no women left upon Barsoom. Your companion is a woman."

He half rose from the couch, leaning far forward and pointing a long accusing finger at Carthoris.

"You are a lie!" he shrieked. "You are both lies, and you dare to come before Tario, last and mightiest of the jeddaks of Barsoom, and assert your reality. Someone shall pay well for this, Jav, and unless I mistake it is yourself who has dared thus flippantly to trifle with the good nature of your jeddak.

"Remove the man. Leave the woman. We shall see if both be lies. And later, Jav, you shall suffer for your temerity. There be few of us left, but—Komal must be fed. Go!"

Carthoris could see that Jav trembled as he prostrated himself once more before his ruler, and then, rising, turned toward the Prince of Helium.

"Come!" he said.

"And leave the Princess of Ptarth here alone?" cried Carthoris.

Jav brushed closely past him, whispering:

"Follow me—he cannot harm her, except to kill; and that he can do whether you remain or not. We had best go now—trust me."

Carthoris did not understand, but something in the urgency of the other's tone assured him, and so he turned away, but not without a glance toward Thuvia in which he attempted to make her understand that it was in her own interest that he left her.

For answer she turned her back full upon him, but not without first throwing him such a look of utter contempt that brought the scarlet to his cheek.

Then he hesitated, but Jav seized him by the wrist.

"Come!" he whispered. "Or he will have the bowmen upon you, and this time there will be no escape. Did you not see how futile is your steel against thin air!"

Carthoris turned unwillingly to follow. As the two left the room he turned to his companion.

"If I may not kill thin air," he asked, "how, then, shall I fear that thin air may kill me?"

"You saw the Torquasians fall before the bowmen?" asked Jav.

Carthoris nodded.

"So would you fall before them, and without one single

chance for self-defense or revenge."

As they talked Jav led Carthoris to a small room in one of the numerous towers of the palace. Here were couches, and Jav bid the Heliumite be seated.

For several minutes the Lotharian eyed his prisoner, for such Carthoris now realized himself to be.

"I am half convinced that you are real," he said at last.

Carthoris laughed.

"Of course I am real," he said. "What caused you to doubt it? Can you not see me, feel me?"

"So may I see and feel the bowmen," replied Jav, "and yet we all know that they, at least, are not real."

Carthoris showed by the expression of his face his puzzlement at each new reference to the mysterious bowmen—the vanishing soldiery of Lothar.

"What then may they be?" he asked.

"You really do not know?" asked Jav.

Carthoris shook his head negatively.

"I can almost believe that you have told us the truth and that you are really from another part of Barsoom, or from another world. But tell me, in your own country have you no bowmen to strike terror to the hearts of the green hordesmen as they slay in company with the fierce banths of war?"

"We have soldiers," replied Carthoris. "We of the red race are all soldiers, but we have no bowmen to defend us, such as yours. We defend ourselves."

"You go out and get killed by your enemies!" cried Jav incredulously.

"Certainly," replied Carthoris. "How do the Lotharians?"

"You have seen," replied the other. "We send out our deathless archers—deathless because they are lifeless, existing only in the imaginations of our enemies. It is really our giant minds that defend us, sending out legions of imaginary warriors to materialize before the mind's eye of the foe.

"They see them—they see their bows drawn back—they see their slender arrows speed with unerring precision toward their hearts. And they die—killed by the power of suggestion."

"But the archers that are slain?" exclaimed Carthoris. "You call them deathless, and yet I saw their dead bodies piled high upon the battlefield. How may that be?"

"It is but to lend reality to the scene," replied Jav. "We picture many of our own defenders killed that the Torquasians may not guess that there are really no flesh and blood creatures opposing them.

"Once that truth became implanted in their minds, it is the theory of many of us, no longer would they fall prey to the suggestion of the deadly arrows, for greater would be the suggestion of the truth, and the more powerful suggestion would prevail—it is law."

"And the banths?" questioned Carthoris. "They, too, were but creatures of suggestion?"

"Some of them were real," replied Jav. "Those that accompanied the archers in pursuit of the Torquasians were unreal. Like the archers, they never returned, but, having served their purpose, vanished with the bowmen when the rout of the enemy was assured.

"Those that remained about the field were real. Those we loosed as scavengers to devour the bodies of the dead of Torquas. This thing is demanded by the realists among us. I am a realist. Tario is an etherealist.

"The etherealists maintain that there is no such thing as matter—that all is mind. They say that none of us exists, except in the imagination of his fellows, other than as an intangible, invisible mentality.

"According to Tario, it is but necessary that we all unite in imagining that there are no dead Torquasians beneath our walls, and there will be none, nor any need for the fierce scavenging banths."

"You, then, do not hold Tario's beliefs?" asked Carthoris.

"In part only," replied the Lotharian. "I believe, in fact I know, that there are some truly ethereal creatures. Tario is one, I am convinced. He has no existence except in the imaginations of his people.

"Of course, it is the contention of all us realists that all etherealists are but figments of the imagination. They contend that no food is necessary, nor do they eat; but anyone of the most rudimentary intelligence must realize that food is a necessity to creatures having actual existence."

"Yes," agreed Carthoris, "not having eaten today I can readily agree with you."

"Ah, pardon me," exclaimed Jav. "Pray be seated and

satisfy your hunger," and with a wave of his hand he indicated a bountifully laden table that had not been there an instant before he spoke. Of that Carthoris was positive, for he had searched the room diligently with his eyes several times.

"It is well," continued Jav, "that you did not fall into the hands of an etherealist. Then, indeed, would you have gone hungry."

"But," exclaimed Carthoris, "this is not real food—it was not here an instant since, and real food does not materialize out of thin air."

Jav looked hurt.

"There is no real food or water in Lothar," he said; "nor has there been for countless ages. Upon such as you now see before you have we existed since the dawn of history. Upon such, then, may you exist."

"But I thought you were a realist," exclaimed Carthoris.

"Indeed," cried Jav, "what more realistic than this bounteous feast? It is just here that we differ most from the etherealists. They claim that it is unnecessary to imagine food; but we have found that for the maintenance of life we must thrice daily sit down to hearty meals.

"The food that one eats is supposed to undergo certain chemical changes during the process of digestion and assimilation, the result, of course, being the rebuilding of wasted tissue.

"Now we all know that mind is all, though we may differ in the interpretation of its various manifestations. Tario maintains that there is no such thing as substance, all being created from the substanceless matter of the brain.

"We realists, however, know better. We know that mind has the power to maintain substance even though it may not be able to create substance—the latter is still an open question. And so we know that in order to maintain our physical bodies we must cause all our organs properly to function.

"This we accomplish by materializing food-thoughts, and by partaking of the food thus created. We chew, we swallow, we digest. All our organs function precisely as if we had partaken of material food. And what is the result? What must be the result? The chemical changes take place through both direct and indirect suggestion, and we live and thrive."

Carthoris eyed the food before him. It seemed real enough. He lifted a morsel to his lips. There was substance indeed. And flavor as well. Yes, even his palate was deceived.

Jav watched him, smiling, as he ate.

"Is it not entirely satisfying?" he asked.

"I must admit that it is," replied Carthoris. "But tell me, how does Tario live, and the other etherealists who maintain that food is unnecessary?"

Jav scratched his head.

"That is a question we often discuss," he replied. "It is the strongest evidence we have of the nonexistence of the etherealists; but who may know other than Komal?"

"Who is Komal?" asked Carthoris. "I heard your jeddak speak of him."

Jav bent low toward the ear of the Heliumite, looking fearfully about before he spoke.

"Komal is the essence," he whispered. "Even the etherealists admit that mind itself must have substance in order to transmit to imaginings the appearance of substance. For if there really was no such thing as substance it could not be suggested—what never has been cannot be imagined. Do you follow me?"

"I am groping," replied Carthoris dryly.

"So the essence must be substance," continued Jav. "Komal is the essence of the All, as it were. He is maintained by substance. He eats. He eats the real. To be explicit, he eats the realists. That is Tario's work.

"He says that inasmuch as we maintain that we alone are real we should, to be consistent, admit that we alone are proper food for Komal. Sometimes, as today, we find other food for him. He is very fond of Torquasians."

"And Komal is a man?" asked Carthoris.

"He is All, I told you," replied Jav. "I know not how to explain him in words that you will understand. He is the beginning and the end. All life emanates from Komal, since the substance which feeds the brain with imaginings radiates from the body of Komal.

"Should Komal cease to eat, all life upon Barsoom would cease to be. He cannot die, but he might cease to eat, and, thus, to radiate."

"And he feeds upon the men and women of your belief?"

cried Carthoris.

"Women!" exclaimed Jav. "There are no women in Lothar. The last of the Lotharian females perished ages since, upon that cruel and terrible journey across the muddy plains that fringed the half-dried seas, when the green hordes scourged us across the world to this our last hiding place—our impregnable fortress of Lothar.

"Scarce twenty thousand men of all the countless millions of our race lived to reach Lothar. Among us were no women and no children. All these had perished by the way.

"As time went on, we, too, were dying and the race fast approaching extinction, when the Great Truth was revealed to us, that mind is all. Many more died before we perfected our powers, but at last we were able to defy death when we fully understood that death was merely a state of mind.

"Then came the creation of mind-people, or rather the materialization of imaginings. We first put these to practical use when the Torquasians discovered our retreat, and fortunate for us it was that it required ages of search upon their part before they found the single tiny entrance to the valley of Lothar.

"That day we threw our first bowmen against them. The intention was purely to frighten them away by the vast numbers of bowmen which we could muster upon our walls. All Lothar bristled with the bows and arrows of our ethereal host.

"But the Torquasians did not frighten. They are lower than the beasts—they know no fear. They rushed upon our walls, and standing one upon the shoulders of others they built human approaches to the wall tops, and were on the very point of surging in upon us and overwhelming us.

"Not an arrow had been discharged by our bowmen—we did but cause them to run to and fro along the wall top, screaming taunts and threats at the enemy.

"Presently I thought to attempt the thing—*the great thing*. I centered all my mighty intellect upon the bowmen of my own creation—each of us produces and directs as many bowmen as his mentality and imagination is capable of conjuring up.

"I caused them to fit arrows to their bows for the first time. I made them take aim at the hearts of the green men. I made

the green men see all this, and then I made them see the arrows fly, and I made them think that the points pierced
their hearts.

"It was all that was necessary. By hundreds they toppled
from our walls, and when my fellows saw what I had done
they were quick to follow my example, so that presently the
hordes of Torquas had retreated beyond the range of our
arrows.

"We might have killed them at any distance, but one rule
of war we have maintained from the first—the rule of realism.
We do nothing, or rather we cause our bowmen to do nothing within sight of the enemy that is beyond the understanding of the foe. Otherwise they might guess the truth, and that
would be the end of us.

"But after the Torquasians had retreated beyond bow-shot,
they turned upon us with their terrible rifles, and by constant
popping at us made life miserable within our walls.

"So then I bethought the scheme to hurl our bowmen
through the gates upon them. You have seen this day how
well it works. For ages they have come down upon us at intervals, but always with the same results."

"And all this is due to your intellect, Jav?" asked Carthoris.
"I should think that you would be high in the councils of
your people."

"I am," replied Jav, proudly. "I am next to Tario."

"But why then your cringing manner of approaching the
throne?"

"Tario demands it. He is jealous of me. He only awaits the
slightest excuse to feed me to Komal. He fears that I may
some day usurp his power."

Carthoris suddenly sprang from the table.

"Jav!" he exclaimed. "I am a beast! Here I have been eating
my fill, while the Princess of Ptarth may perchance be still
without food. Let us return and find some means of furnishing her with nourishment."

The Lotharian shook his head.

"Tario would not permit it," he said. "He will, doubtless,
make an etherealist of her."

"But I must go to her," insisted Carthoris. "You say that
there are no women in Lothar. Then she must be among men
and if this be so I intend to be near where I may defend her

if the need arises."

"Tario will have his way," insisted Jav. "He sent you away and you may not return until he sends for you."

"Then I shall go without waiting to be sent for."

"Do not forget the bowmen," cautioned Jav.

"I do not forget them," replied Carthoris, but he did not tell Jav that he remembered something else that the Lo - tharian had let drop—something that was but a conjecture, possibly, and yet one well worth pinning a forlorn hope to, should necessity arise.

Carthoris started to leave the room. Jav stepped before him, barring his way.

"I have learned to like you, red man," he said; "but do not forget that Tario is still my jeddak, and that Tario has commanded that you remain here."

Carthoris was about to reply, when there came faintly to the ears of both a woman's cry for help.

With a sweep of his arm the Prince of Helium brushed the Lotharian aside, and with drawn sword sprang into the corridor without.

CHAPTER VIII

THE HALL OF DOOM

AS THUVIA OF PTARTH saw Carthoris depart from the presence of Tario, leaving her alone with the man, a sudden qualm of terror seized her.

There was an air of mystery pervading the stately chamber. Its furnishings and appointments bespoke wealth and culture, and carried the suggestion that the room was often the scene of royal functions which filled it to its capacity.

And yet nowhere about her, in antechamber or corridor, was there sign of any other being than herself and the recumbent figure of Tario, the jeddak, who watched her through half-closed eyes from the gorgeous trappings of his regal couch.

For a time after the departure of Jav and Carthoris the man

eyed her intently. Then he spoke.

"Come nearer," he said, and, as she approached: "Whose creature are you? Who has dared materialize his imaginings of woman? It is contrary to the customs and the royal edicts of Lothar. Tell me, woman, from whose brain have you sprung? Jav's? No, do not deny it. I know that it could be no other than that envious realist. He seeks to tempt me. He would see me fall beneath the spell of your charms, and then he, your master, would direct my destiny and—my end. I see it all! I see it all!"

The blood of indignation and anger had been rising to Thuvia's face. Her chin was up, a haughty curve upon her perfect lips.

"I know naught," she cried, "of what you are prating! I am Thuvia, Princess of Ptarth. I am no man's 'creature.' Never before today did I lay eyes upon him you call Jav, nor upon your ridiculous city, of which even the greatest nations of Barsoom have never dreamed.

"My charms are not for you, nor such as you. They are not for sale or barter, even though the price were a real throne. And as for using them to win your worse than futile power—" She ended her sentence with a shrug of her shapely shoulders, and a little scornful laugh.

When she had finished Tario was sitting upon the edge of his couch, his feet upon the floor. He was leaning forward with eyes no longer half closed, but wide with a startled expression in them.

He did not seem to note the *lèse majesté* of her words and manner. There was evidently something more startling and compelling about her speech than that.

Slowly he came to his feet.

"By the fangs of Komal!" he muttered. "But you are *real*! A *real* woman! No dream! No vain and foolish figment of the mind!"

He took a step toward her, with hands outstretched.

"Come!" he whispered. "Come, woman! For countless ages have I dreamed that some day you would come. And now that you are here I can scarce believe the testimony of my eyes. Even now, knowing that you are real, I still half dread that you may be a lie."

Thuvia shrank back. She thought the man mad. Her hand

stole to the jeweled hilt of her dagger. The man saw the move, and stopped. A cunning expression entered his eyes. Then they became at once dreamy and penetrating as they fairly bored into the girl's brain.

Thuvia suddenly felt a change coming over her. What the cause of it she did not guess; but somehow the man before her began to assume a new relationship within her heart.

No longer was he a strange and mysterious enemy, but an old and trusted friend. Her hand slipped from the dagger's hilt. Tario came closer. He spoke gentle, friendly words, and she answered him in a voice that seemed hers and yet another's.

He was beside her now. His hand was upon her shoulder. His eyes were down-bent toward hers. She looked up into his face. His gaze seemed to bore straight through her to some hidden spring of sentiment within her.

Her lips parted in sudden awe and wonder at the strange revealment of her inner self that was being laid bare before her consciousness. She had known Tario forever. He was more than a friend to her. She moved a little closer to him. In one swift flood of light she knew the truth. She loved Tario, Jeddak of Lothar! She had always loved him.

The man, seeing the success of his strategy, could not restrain a faint smile of satisfaction. Whether there was something in the expression of his face, or whether from Carthoris of Helium in a far chamber of the palace came a more powerful suggestion, who may say? But something there was that suddenly dispelled the strange, hypnotic influence of the man.

As though a mask had been torn from her eyes, Thuvia suddenly saw Tario as she had formerly seen him, and, accustomed as she was to the strange manifestations of highly developed mentality which are common upon Barsoom, she quickly guessed enough of the truth to know that she was in grave danger.

Quickly she took a step backward, tearing herself from his grasp. But the momentary contact had aroused within Tario all the long-buried passions of his loveless existence.

With a muffled cry he sprang upon her, throwing his arms about her and attempting to drag her lips to his.

"Woman!" he cried. "Lovely woman! Tario would make

you queen of Lothar. Listen to me! Listen to the love of
the last of the jeddaks of Barsoom."

Thuvia struggled to free herself from his embrace.

"Stop, creature!" she cried. "Stop! I do not love you. Stop,
or I shall scream for help!"

Tario laughed in her face.

" 'Scream for help,' " he mimicked. "And who within the
halls of Lothar is there who might come in answer to your
call? Who would dare enter the presence of Tario, unsum-
moned?"

"There is one," she replied, "who would come, and, coming, dare to cut you down upon your own throne, if he
thought that you had offered affront to Thuvia of Ptarth!"

"Who, Jav?" asked Tario.

"Not Jav, nor any other soft-skinned Lotharian," she replied; "but a real man, a real warrior—Carthoris of Helium!"

Again the man laughed at her.

"You forget the bowmen," he reminded her. "What could
your red warrior accomplish against my fearless legions?"

Again he caught her roughly to him, dragging her towards
his couch.

"If you will not be my queen," he said, "you shall be my
slave."

"Neither!" cried the girl.

As she spoke the single word there was a quick move of her
right hand, Tario, releasing her, staggered back, both hands
pressed to his side. At the same instant the room filled with
bowmen, and then the jeddak of Lothar sank senseless to the
marble floor.

At the instant that he lost consciousness the bowmen
were about to release their arrows into Thuvia's heart. Involuntarily she gave a single cry for help, though she knew that
not even Carthoris of Helium could save her now.

Then she closed her eyes and waited for the end. No slender shafts pierced her tender side. She raised her lids to see
what stayed the hand of her executioners.

The room was empty save for herself and the still form of
the jeddak of Lothar lying at her feet, a little pool of crimson
staining the white marble of the floor beside him. Tario was
unconscious.

Thuvia was amazed. Where were the bowmen? Why had

they not loosed their shafts? What could it all mean?

An instant before the room had been mysteriously filled with armed men, evidently called to protect their jeddak; yet now, with the evidence of her deed plain before them, they had vanished as mysteriously as they had come, leaving her alone with the body of their ruler, into whose side she had slipped her long, keen blade.

The girl glanced apprehensively about, first for signs of the return of the bowmen, and then for some means of escape.

The walls behind the dais was pierced by two small door-ways, hidden by heavy hangings. Thuvia was running quickly toward one of these when she heard the clank of a warrior's metal at the end of the apartment behind her.

Ah, if she had but an instant more of time she could have reached that screening arras and, perchance, have found some avenue of escape behind it; but now it was too late—she had been discovered!

With a feeling that was akin to apathy she turned to meet her fate, and there, before her, running swiftly across the broad chamber to her side, was Carthoris, his naked long-sword gleaming in his hand.

For days she had doubted the intentions of the Heliumite. She had thought him a party to her abduction. Since Fate had thrown them together she had scarce favored him with more than the most perfunctory replies to his remarks, unless at such times as the weird and uncanny happenings at Lothar had surprised her out of her reserve.

She knew that Carthoris of Helium would fight for her; but whether to save her for himself or another she was in doubt.

He knew that she was promised to Kulan Tith, Jeddak of Kaol, but if he had been instrumental in her abduction, his motives could not be prompted by loyalty to his friend, or regard for her honor.

And yet, as she saw him coming across the marble floor of the audience chamber of Tario of Lothar, his fine eyes filled with apprehension for her safety, his splendid figure personifying all that is finest in the fighting men of martial Mars, she could not believe that any faintest trace of perfidy lurked beneath so glorious an exterior.

Never, she thought, in all her life had the sight of any man been so welcome to her. It was with difficulty that she refrained from rushing forward to meet him.

She knew that he loved her; but, in time, she recalled that she was promised to Kulan Tith. Not even might she trust herself to show too great gratitude to the Heliumite, lest he misunderstand.

Carthoris was by her side now. His quick glance had taken in the scene within the room—the still figure of the jeddak sprawled upon the floor—the girl hastening toward a shrouded exit.

"Did he harm you, Thuvia?" he asked.

She held up her crimsoned blade that he might see it.

"No," she said, "he did not harm me."

A grim smile lighted Carthoris' face.

"Praised be our first ancestor!" he murmured. "And now let us see if we may not make good our escape from this accursed city before the Lotharians discover that their jeddak is no more."

With the firm authority that sat so well upon him in whose veins flowed the blood of John Carter of Virginia and Dejah Thoris of Helium, he grasped her hand and, turning back across the hall, strode toward the great doorway through which Jav had brought them into the presence of the jeddak earlier in the day.

They had almost reached the threshold when a figure sprang into the apartment through another entrance. It was Jav. He, too, took in the scene within at a glance.

Carthoris turned to face him, his sword ready in his hand, and his great body shielding the slender figure of the girl.

"Come, Jav of Lothar!" he cried. "Let us face the issue at once, for only one of us may leave this chamber alive with Thuvia of Ptarth." Then, seeing that the man wore no sword, he exclaimed: "Bring on your bowmen, then, or come with us as my prisoner until we have safely passed the outer portals of thy ghostly city."

"You have killed Tario!" exclaimed Jav, ignoring the other's challenge. "You have killed Tario! I see his blood upon the floor—real blood—real death. Tario was, after all, as real as I. Yet he was an etherealist. He would not materialize his sustenance. Can it be that they are right? Well, we, too, are right. And all these ages we have been quarreling—each saying that the other was wrong!

"However, he is dead now. Of that I am glad. Now shall Jav come into his own. Now shall Jav be jeddak of Lothar!"

As he finished, Tario opened his eyes and then quickly sat up.

"Traitor! Assassin!" he screamed, and then: "Kadar! Kadar!" which is the Barsoomian for guard.

Jav went sickly white. He fell upon his belly, wriggling toward Tario.

"Oh, my Jeddak, my Jeddak!" he whimpered. "Jav had no hand in this. Jav, your faithful Jav, but just this instant entered the apartment to find you lying prone upon the floor and these two strangers about to leave. How it happened I know not. Believe me, most glorious Jeddak!"

"Cease, knave!" cried Tario. "I heard your words: 'However, he is dead now. Of that I am glad. Now shall Jav come into his own. Now shall Jav be jeddak of Lothar.'

"At last, traitor, I have found you out. Your own words have condemned you as surely as the acts of these red creatures have sealed their fates—unless—" He paused. "Unless the woman—"

But he got no further. Carthoris guessed what he would have said, and before the words could be uttered he had sprung forward and struck the man across the mouth with his open palm.

Tario frothed in rage and mortification.

"And should you again affront the Princess of Ptarth," warned the Heliumite, "I shall forget that you wear no sword —not forever may I control my itching sword hand."

Tario shrank back toward the little doorways behind the dais. He was trying to speak, but so hideously were the muscles of his face working that he could utter no word for several minutes. At last he managed to articulate intelligibly.

"Die!" he shrieked. "Die!" and then he turned toward the exit at his back.

Jav leaped forward, screaming in terror.

"Have pity, Tario! Have pity! Remember the long ages that I have served you faithfully. Remember all that I have done for Lothar. Do not condemn me now to the death hideous. Save me! Save me!"

But Tario only laughed a mocking laugh and continued to back toward the hangings that hid the little doorway.

Jav turned toward Carthoris.

"Stop him!" he screamed. "Stop him! If you love life, let him not leave this room," and as he spoke he leaped in pur- suit of his jeddak.

Carthoris followed Jav's example, but the "last of the jed- daks of Barsoom" was too quick for them. By the time they reached the arras behind which he had disappeared, they found a heavy stone door blocking their further progress.

Jav sank to the floor in a spasm of terror.

"Come, man!" cried Carthoris. "We are not dead yet. Let us hasten to the avenues and make an attempt to leave the city. We are still alive, and while we live we may yet endeavor to direct our own destinies. Of what avail, to sink spineless to the floor? Come, be a man!"

Jav but shook his head.

"Did you not hear him call the guards?" he moaned. "Ah, if we could have but intercepted him! Then there might have been hope; but, alas, he was too quick for us."

"Well, well," exclaimed Carthoris impatiently. "What if he did call the guards? There will be time enough to worry about that after they come—at present I see no indication that they have any idea of over-exerting themselves to obey their jeddak's summons."

Jav shook his head mournfully in utter dejection.

"You do not understand," he said. "The guards have al- ready come—and gone. They have done their work and we are lost. Look to the various exits."

Carthoris and Thuvia turned their eyes in the direction of the several doorways which pierced the walls of the great chamber. Each was tightly closed by huge stone doors.

"Well?" asked Carthoris.

"We are to die the death," whispered Jav faintly.

Further than that he would not say. He just sat upon the edge of the jeddak's couch and waited.

Carthoris moved to Thuvia's side, and, standing there with naked sword, he let his brave eyes roam ceaselessly about the great chamber, that no foe might spring upon them unseen.

For what seemed hours no sound broke the silence of their living tomb. No sign gave their executioners of the time or manner of their death. The suspense was terrible. Even

Carthoris of Helium began to feel the terrific strain upon his nerves. If he could but know how and whence the hand of death was to strike, he could meet it unafraid, but to suffer longer the hideous tension of this blighting ignorance of the plans of their assassins was telling upon him grievously.

Thuvia of Ptarth drew quite close to him. She felt safer with the feel of his arm against hers, and with the contact of her the man took a new grip upon himself. With his old-time smile he turned toward her.

"It would seem that they are trying to frighten us to death," he said, laughing; "and, shame be upon me that I should confess it, I think they were close to accomplishing their designs upon me."

She was about to make some reply when a fearful shriek broke from the lips of the Lotharian.

"The end is coming!" he cried. "The end is coming! The floor! The floor! Oh, Komal, be merciful!"

Thuvia and Carthoris did not need to look at the floor to be aware of the strange movement that was taking place.

Slowly the marble flagging was sinking in all directions toward the center. At first the movement, being gradual, was scarce noticeable; but presently the angle of the floor became such that one might stand easily only by bending one knee considerably.

Jav was shrieking still, and clawing at the royal couch that had already commenced to slide toward the center of the room, where both Thuvia and Carthoris suddenly noted a small orifice which grew in diameter as the floor assumed more closely a funnel-like contour.

Now it became more and more difficult to cling to the dizzy inclination of the smooth and polished marble. Carthoris tried to support Thuvia, but himself commenced to slide and slip toward the ever-enlarging aperture.

Better to cling to the smooth stone he kicked off his sandals of zitidar hide and with his bare feet braced himself against the sickening tilt, at the same time throwing his arms supportingly about the girl.

In her terror her own hands clasped about the man's neck. Her cheek was close to his. Death, unseen and of unknown form, seemed close upon them, and because unseen and unknowable infinitely more terrifying.

The man turned dreamy eyes sleepily upon them.

*The jeddak of Lothar sank senseless to the marble
floor.*

"Courage, my princess," he whispered cheeringly.

She looked up into his face to see smiling lips above hers and brave eyes, untouched by terror, drinking deeply of her own.

Then the floor sagged and tilted more swiftly. There was a sudden slipping rush as they were precipitated toward the aperture.

Jav's screams rose weird and horrible in their ears, and then the three found themselves piled upon the royal couch of Tario, which had stuck within the aperture at the base of the marble funnel.

For a moment they breathed more freely, but presently they discovered that the aperture was continuing to enlarge. The couch slipped downward. Jav shrieked again. There was a sickening sensation as they felt all let go beneath them, as they fell through darkness to an unknown death.

CHAPTER IX

THE BATTLE OF THE PLAIN

THE DISTANCE FROM the bottom of the funnel to the floor of the chamber beneath it could not have been great, for all three of the victims of Tario's wrath alighted unscathed.

Carthoris, still clasping Thuvia tightly to his breast, came to the ground catlike, upon his feet, breaking the shock for the girl. Scarce had his feet touched the rough stone flagging of this new chamber than his sword flashed out ready for instant use. But though the room was lighted, there was no sign of enemy about.

Carthoris looked toward Jav. The man was pasty white with fear.

"What is to be our fate?" asked the Heliumite. "Tell me, man! Shake off your terror long enough to tell me, so I may be prepared to sell my life and that of the Princess of Ptarth as dearly as possible."

"Komal!" whispered Jav. "We are to be devoured by Komal!"

"Your deity?" asked Carthoris.

The Lotharian nodded his head. Then he pointed toward a low doorway at one end of the chamber.

"From thence will he come upon us. Lay aside your puny sword, fool. It will but enrage him the more and make our sufferings the worse."

Carthoris smiled, gripping his long-sword the more firmly.

Presently Jav gave a horrified moan, at the same time pointing toward the door.

"He has come," he whimpered.

Carthoris and Thuvia looked in the direction the Lotharian had indicated, expecting to see some strange and fearful creature in human form; but to their astonishment they saw the broad head and great-maned shoulders of a huge banth, the largest that either ever had seen.

Slowly and with dignity the mighty beast advanced into the room. Jav had fallen to the floor, and was wriggling his body in the same servile manner that he had adopted toward Tario. He spoke to the fierce beast as he would have spoken to a human being, pleading with it for mercy.

Carthoris stepped between Thuvia and the banth, his sword ready to contest the beast's victory over them. Thuvia turned toward Jav.

"Is this Komal, your god?" she asked.

Jav nodded affirmatively. The girl smiled, and then, brushing past Carthoris, she stepped swiftly toward the growling carnivore.

In low, firm tones she spoke to it as she had spoken to the banths of the Golden Cliffs and the scavengers before the walls of Lothar.

The beast ceased its growling. With lowered head and catlike purr, it came slinking to the girl's feet. Thuvia turned toward Carthoris.

"It is but a banth," she said. "We have nothing to fear from it."

Carthoris smiled.

"I did not fear it," he replied, "for I, too, believed it to be only a banth, and I have my long-sword."

Jav sat up and gazed at the spectacle before him—the slender girl weaving her fingers in the tawny mane of the huge creature that he had thought divine, while Komal rubbed his hideous snout against her side.

"So this is your god!" laughed Thuvia.

Jav looked bewildered. He scarce knew whether he dared chance offending Komal or not, for so strong is the power of superstition that even though we know that we have been reverencing a sham, yet still we hesitate to admit the validity of our new-found convictions.

"Yes," he said, "this is Komal. For ages the enemies of Tario have been hurled to this pit to fill his maw, for Komal must be fed."

"Is there any way out of this chamber to the avenues of the city?" asked Carthoris.

Jav shrugged.

"I do not know," he replied. "Never have I been here before, nor ever have I cared to be."

"Come," suggested Thuvia, "let us explore. There must be a way out."

Together the three approached the doorway through which Komal had entered the apartment that was to have witnessed their deaths. Beyond was a low-roofed lair, with a small door at the far end.

This, to their delight, opened to the lifting of an ordinary latch, letting them into a circular arena, surrounded by tiers of seats.

"Here is where Komal is fed in public," explained Jav. "Had Tario dared it would have been here that our fates had been sealed; but he feared too much thy keen blade, red man, and so he hurled us all downward to the pit. I did not know how closely connected were the two chambers. Now we may easily reach the avenues and the city gates. Only the bowmen may dispute the right of way, and, knowing their secret, I doubt that they have power to harm us."

Another door led to a flight of steps that rose from the arena level upward through the seats to an exit at the back of the hall. Beyond this was a straight, broad corridor, running directly through the palace to the gardens at the side.

No one appeared to question them as they advanced, mighty Komal pacing by the girl's side.

"Where are the people of the palace—the jeddak's retinue?" asked Carthoris. "Even in the city streets as we came through I scarce saw sign of a human being, yet all about are evidences of a mighty population."

Jav sighed.

"Poor Lothar," he said. "It is indeed a city of ghosts. There are scarce a thousand of us left, who once were numbered in the millions. Our great city is peopled by the creatures of our own imaginings. For our own needs we do not take the trouble to materialize these peoples of our brain, yet they are apparent to us.

"Even now I see great throngs lining the avenue, hastening to and fro in the round of their duties. I see women and children laughing on the balconies—these we are forbidden to materialize; but yet I see them—they are here. . . . . But why not?" he mused. "No longer need I fear Tario—he has done his worst, and failed. Why not indeed?

"Stay, friends," he continued. "Would you see Lothar in all her glory?"

Carthoris and Thuvia nodded their assent, more out of courtesy than because they fully grasped the import of his mutterings.

Jav gazed at them penetratingly for an instant, then, with a wave of his hand, cried: "Look!"

The sight that met them was awe-inspiring. Where before there had been naught but deserted pavements and scarlet swards, yawning windows and tenantless doors, now swarmed a countless multitude of happy, laughing people.

"It is the past," said Jav in a low voice. "They do not see us —they but live the old dead past of ancient Lothar—the dead and crumbled Lothar of antiquity, which stood upon the shore of Throxus, mightiest of the five oceans.

"See those fine, upstanding men swinging along the broad avenue? See the young girls and the women smile upon them? See the men greet them with love and respect? Those be seafarers coming up from their ships which lie at the quays at the city's edge.

"Brave men, they—ah, but the glory of Lothar has faded! See their weapons. They alone bore arms, for they crossed the five seas to strange places where dangers were. With their passing passed the martial spirit of the Lotharians, leaving, as the ages rolled by, a race of spineless cowards.

"We hated war, and so we trained not our youth in warlike ways. Thus followed our undoing, for when the seas dried and the green hordes encroached upon us we could do naught but flee. But we remembered the seafaring bowmen of the days of our glory—it is the memory of these which we hurl upon our enemies."

As Jav ceased speaking, the picture faded, and once more the three took up their way toward the distant gates, along deserted avenues, uncanny in their sepulchral silence.

Twice they sighted Lotharians of flesh and blood. At sight of them and the huge banth which they must have recognized as Komal, the citizens turned and fled.

"They will carry word of our flight to Tario," cried Jav, and soon he will send his bowmen after us. Let us hope that our theory is correct, and that their shafts are powerless against minds cognizant of their unreality. Otherwise we are doomed.

"Explain, red man, to the woman the truths that I have explained to you, that she may meet the arrows with a stronger counter-suggestion of immunity."

Carthoris did as Jav bid him; but they came to the great gates without sign of pursuit developing. Here Jav set in motion the mechanism that rolled the huge, wheel-like gate aside, and a moment later the three, accompanied by the banth, stepped into the plain before Lothar.

Scarce had they covered a hundred yards when the sound of many men shouting arose behind them. As they turned they saw a company of bowmen debouching upon the plain from the gate through which they had but just passed.

Upon the wall above the gate were a number of Lotharians, among whom Jav recognized Tario. The jeddak stood glaring at them, evidently concentrating all the forces of his trained mind upon them. That he was making a supreme effort to render his imaginary creatures deadly was apparent.

Jav turned white, and commenced to tremble. At the crucial moment he appeared to lose the courage of his conviction. The great banth turned back toward the advancing bowmen and growled. Carthoris placed himself between Thuvia and the enemy and, facing them, awaited the outcome of their charge.

Suddenly an inspiration came to Carthoris.

"Hurl your own bowmen against Tario's!" he cried to Jav. "Let us see a materialized battle between two mentalities."

The suggestion seemed to hearten the Lotharian, and in another moment the three stood behind solid ranks of huge bowmen who hurled taunts and menaces at the advancing company emerging from the walled city.

Jav was a new man the moment his battalions stood between him and Tario. One could almost have sworn the man believed these creatures of his strange hypnotic power to be real flesh and blood.

With hoarse battle cries they charged the bowmen of Tario. Barbed shafts flew thick and fast. Men fell, and the ground was red with gore.

Carthoris and Thuvia had difficulty in reconciling the reality of it all with their knowledge of the truth. They saw utan after utan march from the gate in perfect step to reinforce the outnumbered company which Tario had first sent forth to arrest them.

They saw Jav's forces grow correspondingly until all about them rolled a sea of fighting, cursing warriors, and the dead lay in heaps about the field.

Jav and Tario seemed to have forgotten all else beside the struggling bowmen that surged to and fro, filling the broad field between the forest and the city.

The wood loomed close behind Thuvia and Carthoris. The latter cast a glance toward Jav.

"Come!" he whispered to the girl. "Let them fight out their empty battle—neither, evidently, has power to harm the other. They are like two controversialists hurling words at one another. While they are engaged we may as well be devoting our energies to an attempt to find the passage through the cliffs to the plain beyond."

As he spoke, Jav, turning from the battle for an instant, caught his words. He saw the girl move to accompany the Heliumite. A cunning look leaped to the Lotharian's eyes.

The thing that lay beyond that look had been deep in his heart since first he had laid eyes upon Thuvia of Ptarth. He had not recognized it, however, until now that she seemed to pass out of his existence.

He centered his mind upon the Heliumite and the girl for an instant.

Carthoris saw Thuvia of Ptarth step forward with outstretched hand. He was surprised at this sudden softening toward him, and it was with a full heart that he let his fingers close upon hers, as together they turned away from forgotten Lothar, into the woods, and bent their steps toward the distant mountains.

As the Lotharian had turned toward them, Thuvia had been surprised to hear Carthoris suddenly voice a new plan.

"Remain here with Jav," she had heard him say, "while I go to search for the passage through the cliffs."

She had dropped back in surprise and disappointment, for she knew that there was no reason why she should not have accompanied him. Certainly she should have been safer with him than left here alone with the strange Lotharian she could not understand.

And Jav watched the two and smiled his cunning smile.

When Carthoris had disappeared within the wood, Thuvia seated herself apathetically upon the scarlet sward to watch the seemingly interminable struggles of the bowmen.

The long afternoon dragged its weary way toward darkness and still the imaginary legions charged and retreated. The sun was about to set when Tario commenced to withdraw his troops slowly toward the city.

His plan for cessation of hostilities through the night evidently met with Jav's entire approval, for he caused his forces to form themselves in orderly utans and march just within the edge of the wood, where they were soon busily engaged in preparing their evening meal, and spreading down their sleeping silks and furs for the night.

Thuvia could scarce repress a smile as she noted the scrupulous care with which Jav's imaginary men attended to each tiny detail of deportment as truly as if they had been real flesh and blood warriors.

Sentries were posted between the camp and the city. Officers clanked hither and thither issuing commands and seeing to it that they were properly carried out.

Thuvia turned toward Jav.

"Why is it," she asked, "that you observe such careful nicety in the regulation of your creatures when Tario knows quite as well as you that they are but figments of your brain? Why not permit them simply to dissolve into thin air until you again require their futile service?"

"You do not understand them," replied Jav. "While they

exist they are real. I do but call them into being now, and in a way direct their general actions. But thereafter, until I dissolve them, they are as actual as you or I. Their officers command them, under my guidance. I am the general—that is all. And the psychological effect upon the enemy is far greater than were I to treat them merely as substanceless vagaries.

"Then, too," continued the Lotharian, "there is always the hope, which with us is little short of belief, that some day these materializations will merge into the real—that they will remain, some of them, after we have dissolved their fellows, and that thus we shall have discovered a means for perpetuating our dying race.

"Some there are who claim already to have accomplished the thing. It is generally supposed that the etherealists have quite a few among their number who are permanent materializations. It is even said that such is Tario, but that cannot be, for he existed before we had discovered the full possibilities of suggestion.

"There are others among us who insist that none of us is real. That we could not have existed all these ages without material food and water had we ourselves been material. Although I am a realist, I rather incline toward this belief myself.

"It seems well and sensibly based upon the belief that our ancient forebears developed before their extinction such wondrous mentalities that some of the stronger minds among them lived after the death of their bodies—that we are but the deathless minds of individuals long dead.

"It would appear possible, and yet in so far as I am concerned I have all the attributes of corporeal existence. I eat, I sleep—" He paused, casting a meaning look upon the girl—"I love!"

Thuvia could not mistake the palpable meaning of his words and expression. She turned away with a little shrug of disgust that was not lost upon the Lotharian.

He came close to her and seized her arm.

"Why not Jav?" he cried. "Who more honorable than the second of the world's most ancient race? Your Heliumite? He has gone. He has deserted you to your fate to save himself. Come, be Jav's!"

Thuvia of Ptarth rose to her full height, her lifted shoulder turned toward the man, her haughty chin upraised, a scornful twist to her lips.

"You lie!" she said quietly. "The Heliumite knows less of disloyalty than he knows of fear, and of fear he is as ignorant as the unhatched young."

"Then where is he?" taunted the Lotharian. "I tell you he has fled the valley. He has left you to your fate. But Jav will see that it is a pleasant one. Tomorrow we shall return into Lothar at the head of my victorious army, and I shall be jeddak and you shall be my consort. Come!" And he attemped to crush her to his breast.

The girl struggled to free herself, striking at the man with her metal armlets. Yet still he drew her toward him, until both were suddenly startled by a hideous growl that rumbled from the dark wood close behind them.

CHAPTER X

KAR KOMAK, THE BOWMAN

AS CARTHORIS MOVED through the forest toward the distant cliffs with Thuvia's hand still tight pressed in his, he wondered a little at the girl's continued silence, yet the contact of her cool palm against his was so pleasant that he feared to break the spell of her new-found reliance in him by speaking.

Onward through the dim wood they passed until the shadows of the quick coming Martian night commenced to close down upon them. Then it was that Carthoris turned to speak to the girl at his side.

They must plan together for the future. It was his idea to pass through the cliffs at once if they could locate the passage, and he was quite positive that they were now close to it; but he wanted her assent to the proposition.

As his eyes rested upon her, he was struck by her strangely ethereal appearance. She seemed suddenly to have dissolved into the tenuous substance of a dream, and as he continued to gaze upon her, she faded slowly from his sight.

For an instant he was dumfounded, and then the whole truth flashed suddenly upon him. Jav had caused him to believe that Thuvia was accompanying him through the wood while, as a matter of fact, he had detained the girl for himself!

Carthoris was horrified. He cursed himself for his stupidity, and yet he knew that the fiendish power which the Lotharian had invoked to confuse him might have deceived any.

Scarce had he realized the truth than he had started to retrace his steps toward Lothar, but now he moved at a trot, the Earthly thews that he had inherited from his father carrying him swiftly over the soft carpet of fallen leaves and rank grass.

Thuria's brilliant light flooded the plain before the walled city of Lothar as Carthoris broke from the wood opposite the great gate that had given the fugitives egress from the city earlier in the day.

At first he saw no indication that there was another than himself anywhere about. The plain was deserted. No myriad bowmen camped now beneath the overhanging verdure of the giant trees. No gory heaps of tortured dead defaced the beauty of the scarlet sward. All was silence. All was peace.

The Heliumite, scarce pausing at the forest's verge, pushed on across the plain toward the city, when presently he descried a huddled form in the grass at his feet.

It was the body of a man, lying prone. Carthoris turned the figure over upon its back. It was Jav, but torn and mangled almost beyond recognition.

The prince bent low to note if any spark of life remained, and as he did so the lids raised and dull, suffering eyes looked up into his.

"The Princess of Ptarth!" cried Carthoris. "Where is she? Answer me, man, or I complete the work that another has so well begun."

"Komal," muttered Jav. "He sprang upon me . . . . and would have devoured me but for the girl. Then they went away together into the wood—the girl and the great banth . . . . her fingers twined in his tawny mane."

"Which way went they?" asked Carthoris.

"There," replied Jav faintly, "toward the passage through the cliffs."

The Prince of Helium waited to hear no more, but springing to his feet, raced back again into the forest.

It was dawn when he reached the mouth of the dark tunnel that would lead him to the other world beyond this valley of ghostly memories and strange hypnotic influences and menaces.

Within the long, dark passages he met with no accident or obstacle, coming at last into the light of day beyond the mountains, and no great distance from the southern verge of the domains of the Torquasians, not more than one hundred and fifty haad at the most.

From the boundary of Torquas to the city of Aaanthor is a distance of some two hundred haads, so that the Heliumite had before him a journey of more than one hundred and fifty Earth miles between him and Aaanthor.

He could at best but hazard a chance guess that toward Aaanthor Thuvia would take her flight. There lay the nearest water, and there might be expected some day a rescuing party from her father's empire; for Carthoris knew Thuvan Dihn well enough to know that he would leave no stone unturned until he had tracked down the truth as to his daughter's abduction, and learned all that there might be to learn of her whereabouts.

He realized, of course, that the trick which had laid suspicion upon him would greatly delay the discovery of the truth, but little did he guess to what vast proportions had the results of the villainy of Astok of Dusar already grown.

Even as he emerged from the mouth of the passage to look across the foothills in the direction of Aaanthor, a Ptarth battle fleet was winging its majestic way slowly toward the twin cities of Helium, while from far distant Kaol raced another mighty armada to join forces with its ally.

He did not know that in the face of the circumstantial evidence against him even his own people had commenced to entertain suspicions that he might have stolen the Ptarthian princess.

He did not know of the lengths to which the Dusarians had gone to disrupt the friendship and alliance which existed between the three great powers of the eastern hemisphere—Helium, Ptarth, and Kaol.

How Dusarian emissaries had found employment in important posts in the foreign offices of the three great nations, and how, through these men, messages from one jeddak to another were altered and garbled until the patience and pride of the three rulers and former friends could no longer endure the humiliations and insults contained in these falsified papers—not any of this he knew.

Nor did he know how even to the last John Carter, Warlord of Mars, had refused to permit the jeddak of Helium to declare war against either Ptarth or Kaol, because of his implicit belief in his son, and that eventually all would be satisfactorily explained.

And now two great fleets were moving upon Helium, while the Dusarian spies at the court of Tardos Mors saw to it that the twin cities remained in ignorance of their danger.

War had been declared by Thuvan Dihn, but the messenger who had been dispatched with the proclamation had been a Dusarian who had seen to it that no word of warning reached the twin cities of the approach of a hostile fleet.

For several days diplomatic relations had been severed between Helium and her two most powerful neighbors, and with the departure of the ministers had come a total cessation of wireless communication between the disputants, as is usual upon Barsoom.

But of all this Carthoris was ignorant. All that interested him at present was the finding of Thuvia of Ptarth. Her trail beside that of the huge banth had been well marked to the tunnel, and was once more visible leading southward into the deep foothills.

As he followed rapidly downward toward the dead seabottom, where he knew he must lose the spoor in the resilient ochre vegetation, he was suddenly surprised to see a naked man approaching him from the northeast.

As the fellow drew closer, Carthoris halted to await his coming. He knew that the man was unarmed, and that he was apparently a Lotharian, for his skin was white and his hair auburn.

He approached the Heliumite without sign of fear, and when quite close called out the cheery Barsoomian "kaor" of greeting.

"Who are you?" asked Carthoris.

"I am Kar Komak, odwar of the bowmen," replied the other. "A strange thing has happened to me. For ages Tario has been bringing me into existence as he needed the services of the army of his mind. Of all the bowmen it has been Kar Komak who has been oftenest materialized.

"For a long time Tario has been concentrating his mind upon my permanent materialization. It has been an obsession with him that some day this thing could be accomplished and the future of Lothar assured. He asserted that matter was nonexistent except in the imagination of man—that all was mental, and so he believed that by persisting in his suggestion he could eventually make of me a permanent suggestion in the minds of all creatures.

"Yesterday he succeeded, but at such a time! It must have come all unknown to him, as it came to me without my knowledge, as, with my horde of yelling bowmen, I pursued the fleeing Torquasians back to their ochre plains.

"As darkness settled and the time came for us to fade once more into thin air, I suddenly found myself alone upon the edge of the great plain which lies yonder at the foot of the low hills.

"My men were gone back to the nothingness from which they had sprung, but I remained—naked and unarmed—a lone creature in this vast wilderness.

"At first I could not understand, but at last came a realization of what had occurred. Tario's long suggestions had at last prevailed, and Kar Komak had become a reality in the world of men; but my harness and my weapons had faded away with my fellows, leaving me naked and unarmed in a hostile country far from Lothar."

"You wish to return to Lothar?" asked Carthoris.

"No!" replied Kar Komak quickly. "I have no love for Tario. Being a creature of his mind, I know him too well. He is cruel and tyrannical—a master I have no desire to serve. Now that he has succeeded in accomplishing my permanent materialization, he will be unbearable, and he will go on until he has filled Lothar with his creatures. I wonder if he has succeeded as well with the maid of Lothar."

"I thought there were no women there," said Carthoris.

"In a hidden apartment in the palace of Tario," replied Kar Komak, "the jeddak has maintained the suggestion of a beautiful girl, hoping that some day she would become permanent. I have seen her there. She is wonderful! But for her

sake I hope that Tario succeeds not so well with her as he has
with me.

"Now, red man, I have told you of myself—what of you?"

Carthoris liked the face and the manner of the bowman.
There had been no sign of doubt or fear in his expression as
he approached the heavily armed Heliumite, and he had
spoken directly and to the point.

So the Prince of Helium told the bowman of Lothar who
he was and what adventure had brought him to this far
country.

"Good!" exclaimed the other, when he had done. "Kar
Komak will accompany you. Together we shall find the Princess of Ptarth, and with you Kar Komak will return to the
world of men—such a world as he knew in the long-gone past
when the ships of mighty Lothar plowed angry Throxus, and
the roaring surf beat against the mighty barrier of these
parched and dreary hills."

"What mean you?" asked Carthoris. "Had you really a
former actual existence?"

"Most assuredly," replied Kar Komak. "In my day I commanded the fleets of Lothar—mightiest of all the fleets that
sailed the five salt seas.

"Wherever men lived upon Barsoom there was the name of
Kar Komak known and respected. Peaceful were the land
races in those distant days—only the seafarers were warriors;
but now has the glory of the past faded, nor did I think until
I met you that there remained upon Barsoom a single person
of our own mold who lived and loved and fought as did the
ancient seafarers of my time.

"Ah, but it will seem good to see men once again—real
men! Never had I much respect for the landsmen of my day.
They remained in their walled cities wasting their time in
play, depending for their protection entirely upon the sea
race. And the poor creatures who remain, the Tarios and Javs
of Lothar, are even worse than their ancient forebears."

Carthoris was a trifle skeptical as to the wisdom of permitting the stranger to attach himself to him. There was always the chance that he was but the essence of some hypnotic
treachery which Tario or Jav was attempting to exert upon
the Heliumite; and yet, so sincere had been the manner
and the words of the bowman, so much the fighting man did

he seem, that Carthoris could not find it in his heart to doubt him.

The outcome of the matter was that he gave the naked od-war leave to accompany him, and together they set out upon the spoor of Thuvia and Komal.

Down to the ochre sea-bottom the trail led. There it disappeared, as Carthoris had known that it would; but where it entered the plain its direction had been toward Aaanthor, and so toward Aaanthor the two turned their faces.

It was a long and tedious journey, fraught with many dangers. The bowman could not travel at the pace set by Carthoris, whose muscles carried him with great rapidity over the face of the small planet, the force of gravity of which exerts so much less retarding power than that of the Earth. Fifty miles a day is a fair average for a Barsoomian, but the son of John Carter might easily have covered a hundred or more miles had he cared to desert his new-found comrade.

All the way they were in constant danger of discovery by roving bands of Torquasians, and especially was this true before they reached the boundary of Torquas.

Good fortune was with them, however, and although they sighted two detachments of the savage green men, they were not themselves seen.

And so they came, upon the morning of the third day, within sight of the glistening domes of distant Aaanthor. Throughout the journey Carthoris had ever strained his eyes ahead in search of Thuvia and the great banth; but not till now had he seen aught to give him hope.

This morning, far ahead, halfway betweeen themselves and Aaanthor, the men saw two tiny figures moving toward the city. For a moment they watched them intently. Then Carthoris, convinced, leaped forward at a rapid run, Kar Komak following as swiftly as he could.

The Heliumite shouted to attract the girl's attention, and presently he was rewarded by seeing her turn and stand looking toward him. At her side the great banth stood with uppricked ears, watching the approaching man.

Not yet could Thuvia of Ptarth have recognized Carthoris, though that it was he she must have been convinced, for she waited there for him without sign of fear.

Presently he saw her point toward the northwest, beyond

him. Without slackening his pace, he turned his eyes in the direction she indicated.

Racing silently over the thick vegetation, not half a mile behind, came a score of fierce green warriors, charging him upon their mighty thoats.

To their right was Kar Komak, naked and unarmed, yet running valiantly toward Carthoris and shouting warning as though he, too, had but just discovered the silent, menacing company that moved so swiftly forward with couched spears and ready long-swords.

Carthoris shouted to the Lotharian, warning him back, for he knew that he could but uselessly sacrifice his life by placing himself, all unarmed, in the path of the cruel and relentless savages.

But Kar Komak never hesitated. With shouts of encouragement to his new friend, he hurried onward toward the Prince of Helium. The red man's heart leaped in response to this exhibition of courage and self-sacrifice. He regretted now that he had not thought to give Kar Komak one of his swords; but it was too late to attempt it, for should he wait for the Lotharian to overtake him or return to meet him, the Torquasians would reach Thuvia of Ptarth before he could do so.

Even as it was, it would be nip and tuck as to who came first to her side.

Again he turned his face in her direction, and now, from Aaanthor way, he saw a new force hastening toward them— two medium-sized war craft—and even at the distance they still were from him he discerned the device of Dusar upon their bows.

Now, indeed, seemed little hope for Thuvia of Ptarth. With savage warriors of the hordes of Torquas charging toward her from one direction, and no less implacable enemies, in the form of the creatures of Astok, Prince of Dusar, bearing down upon her from another, while only a banth, a red warrior, and an unarmed bowman were near to defend her, her plight was quite hopeless and her cause already lost ere ever it was contested.

As Thuvia saw Carthoris approaching, she felt again that unaccountable sensation of entire relief from responsibility and fear that she had experienced upon a former occasion. Nor could she account for it while her mind still tried to convince her heart that the Prince of Helium had been instrumental in her abduction from her father's court. She only knew that she was glad when he was by her side, and that with him there all things seemed possible—even such impossible things as escape from her present predicament.

Now had he stopped, panting, before her. A brave smile of encouragement lit his face.

"Courage, my princess," he whispered.

To the girl's memory flashed the occasion upon which he had used those same words—in the throneroom of Tario of Lothar as they had commenced to slip down the sinking marble floor toward an unknown fate.

Then she had not chidden him for the use of that familiar salutation, nor did she chide him now, though she was promised to another. She wondered at herself—flushing at her own turpitude; for upon Barsoom it is a shameful thing for a woman to listen to those two words from another than her husband or her betrothed.

Carthoris saw her flush of mortification, and in an instant regretted his words. There was but a moment before the green warriors would be upon them.

"Forgive me!" said the man in a low voice. "Let my great love be my excuse—that, and the belief that I have but a moment more of life," and with the words he turned to meet the foremost of the green warriors.

The fellow was charging with couched spear, but Carthoris leaped to one side, and as the great thoat and its rider hurtled harmlessly past him he swung his long-sword in a mighty cut that clove the green carcass in twain.

At the same moment Kar Komak leaped with bare hands clawing at the leg of another of the huge riders; the balance of the horde raced in to close quarters, dismounting the better to wield their favorite long-swords; the Dusarian fliers touched the soft carpet of the ochre-clad sea-bottom, disgorging fifty fighting men from their bowels; and into the swirling sea of cutting, slashing swords sprang Komal, the great banth.

CHAPTER XI

GREEN MEN AND WHITE APES

A TORQUASIAN SWORD smote a glancing blow across the forehead of Carthoris. He had a fleeting vision of soft arms about his neck, and warm lips close to his before he lost consciousness.

How long he lay there senseless he could not guess; but when he opened his eyes again he was alone, except for the bodies of the dead green men and Dusarians, and the carcass of a great banth that lay half across his own.

Thuvia was gone, nor was the body of Kar Komak among the dead.

Weak from loss of blood, Carthoris made his way slowly toward Aaanthor, reaching its outskirts at dark.

He wanted water more than any other thing, and so he kept on up a broad avenue toward the great central plaza, where he knew the precious fluid was to be found in a half-ruined building opposite the great palace of the ancient jeddak, who once had ruled this mighty city.

Disheartened and discouraged by the strange sequence of events that seemed foreordained to thwart his every attempt to serve the Princess of Ptarth, he paid little or no attention to his surroundings, moving through the deserted city as though no great white apes lurked in the black shadows of the mystery-haunted piles that flanked the broad avenues and the great plaza.

But if Carthoris was careless of his surroundings, not so other eyes that watched his entrance into the plaza, and followed his slow footsteps toward the marble pile that housed the tiny, half-choked spring whose water one might gain only by scratching a deep hole in the red sand that covered it.

And as the Heliumite entered the small building a dozen mighty, grotesque figures emerged from the doorway of the palace to speed noiselessly across the plaza toward him.

For half an hour Carthoris remained in the building, digging for water and gaining the few much-needed drops which were the fruits of his labor. Then he rose and slowly left the structure. Scarce had he stepped beyond the threshold than twelve Torquasian warriors leaped upon him.

No time then to draw long-sword; but swift from his harness flew his long, slim dagger, and as he went down beneath them more than a single green heart ceased beating at the bite of that keen point.

Then they overpowered him and took his weapons away; but only nine of the twelve warriors who had crossed the plaza returned with their prize.

They dragged their prisoner roughly to the palace pits, where in utter darkness they chained him with rusty links to the solid masonry of the wall.

"Tomorrow Thar Ban will speak with you," they said. "Now he sleeps. But great will be his pleasure when he learns who has wandered amongst us—and great will be the pleasure of Hortan Gur when Thar Ban drags before him the mad fool who dared prick the great jeddak with his sword."

Then they left him to the silence and the darkness.

For what seemed hours Carthoris squatted upon the stone floor of his prison, his back against the wall in which was sunk the heavy eye-bolt that secured the chain which held him.

Then, from out the mysterious blackness before him, there came to his ears the sound of naked feet moving stealthily upon stone—approaching nearer and nearer to where he lay, unarmed and defenseless.

Minutes passed—minutes that seemed hours—during which time periods of sepulchral silence would be followed by a repetition of the uncanny scraping of naked feet slinking warily upon him.

At last he heard a sudden rush of unshod soles across the empty blackness, and at a little distance a scuffling sound, heavy breathing, and once what he thought the muttered imprecation of a man battling against great odds. Then the clanging of a chain, and a noise as of the snapping back against stone of broken link.

Again came silence. But for a moment only. Now he heard once more the soft feet approaching him. He thought that he discerned wicked eyes gleaming fearfully at him through the darkness. He knew that he could hear the heavy breathing of powerful lungs.

Then came the rush of many feet toward him, and the *things* were upon him.

Hands terminating in manlike fingers clutched at his throat and arms and legs. Hairy bodies strained and struggled against his own smooth hide as he battled in grim silence against these horrid foemen in the darkness of the pits of ancient Aaanthor.

Thewed like some giant god was Carthoris of Helium, yet in the clutches of these unseen creatures of the pit's Stygian night he was helpless as a frail woman.

Yet he battled on, striking futile blows against great, hispid breasts he could not see; feeling thick, squat throats beneath his fingers; the drool of saliva upon his cheek, and hot, foul breath in his nostrils.

Fangs, too, mighty fangs, he knew were close, and why they did not sink into his flesh he could not guess.

At last he became aware of the mighty surging of a number of his antagonists back and forth upon the great chain that held him, and presently came the same sound that he had heard at a little distance from him a short time before he had been attacked—his chain had parted and the broken end snapped back against the stone wall.

Now he was seized upon either side and dragged at a rapid pace through the dark corridors—toward what fate he could not even guess.

At first he had thought his foes might be of the tribe of Torquas, but their hairy bodies belied that belief. Now he was at last quite sure of their identity, though why they had not killed and devoured him at once he could not imagine.

After half an hour or more of rapid racing through the underground passages that are a distinguishing feature of all Barsoomian cities, modern as well as ancient, his captors suddenly emerged into the moonlight of a courtyard, far from the central plaza.

Immediately Carthoris saw that he was in the power of a tribe of the great white apes of Barsoom. All that had caused him doubt before as to the identity of his attackers was the hairiness of their breasts, for the white apes are entirely hairless except for a great shock bristling from their heads.

Now he saw the cause of that which had deceived him— across the chest of each of them were strips of hairy hide, usually of banth, in imitation of the harness of the green warriors who so often camped at their deserted city.

GREEN MEN AND WHITE APES   93

Carthoris had read of the existence of tribes of apes that seemed to be progressing slowly toward higher standards of intelligence. Into the hands of such, he realized, he had fallen; but—what were their intentions toward him?

As he glanced about the courtyard, he saw fully fifty of the hideous beasts, squatting on their haunches, and at a little distance from him another human being, closely guarded.

As his eyes met those of his fellow-captive a smile lit the other's face, and: "Kaor, red man!" burst from his lips. It was Kar Komak, the bowman.

"Kaor!" cried Carthoris, in response. "How came you here, and what befell the princess?"

"Red men like yourself descended in mighty ships that sailed the air, even as the great ships of my distant day sailed the five seas," replied Kar Komak. "They fought with the green men of Torquas. They slew Komal, god of Lothar. I thought they were your friends, and I was glad when finally those of them who survived the battle carried the red girl to one of the ships and sailed away with her into the safety of the high air.

"Then the green men seized me, and carried me to a great, empty city, where they chained me to a wall in a black pit. Afterward came these and dragged me hither. And what of you, red man?"

Carthoris related all that had befallen him, and as the two men talked the great apes squatted about them watching them intently.

"What are we to do now?" asked the bowman.

"Our case looks rather hopeless," replied Carthoris ruefully. "These creatures are born man-eaters. Why they have not already devoured us I cannot imagine—there!" he whispered. "See? The end is coming."

Kar Komak looked in the direction Carthoris indicated to see a huge ape advancing with a mighty bludgeon.

"It is thus they like best to kill their prey," said Carthoris.

"Must we die without a struggle?" asked Kar Komak.

"Not I," replied Carthoris, "though I know how futile our best defense must be against these mighty brutes! Oh, for a long-sword!"

"Or a good bow," added Kar Komak, "and a utan of bowmen."

At the words Carthoris half sprang to his feet, only to be dragged roughly down by his guard.

"Kar Komak!" he cried. "Why cannot you do what Tario and Jav did? They had no bowmen other than those of their own creation. You must know the secret of their power. Call forth your own utan, Kar Komak!"

The Lotharian looked at Carthoris in wide-eyed astonishment as the full purport of the suggestion bore in upon his understanding.

"Why not?" he murmured.

The savage ape bearing the mighty bludgeon was slinking toward Carthoris. The Heliumite's fingers were working as he kept his eyes upon his executioner. Kar Komak bent his gaze penetratingly upon the apes. The effort of his mind was evidenced in the great beads of sweat upon his contracted brows.

The creature that was to slay the red man was almost within arm's reach of his prey when Carthoris heard a hoarse shout from the opposite side of the courtyard. In common with the squatting apes and the demon with the club he turned in the direction of the sound to see a company of sturdy bowmen rushing from the doorway of a nearby building.

With screams of rage the apes leaped to their feet to meet the charge. A volley of arrows met them halfway, sending a dozen rolling lifeless to the ground. Then the apes closed with their adversaries. All their attention was occupied by the attackers—even the guard had deserted the prisoners to join in the battle.

"Come!" whispered Kar Komak. "Now may we escape while their attention is diverted from us by my bowmen."

"And leave those brave fellows leaderless?" cried Carthoris, whose loyal nature revolted at the merest suggestion of such a thing.

Kar Komak laughed.

"You forget," he said, "that they are but thin air—figments of my brain. They will vanish, unscathed, when we have no further need for them. Praised be your first ancestor, red man, that you thought of this chance in time! It would never have occurred to me to imagine that I might wield the same power that brought me into existence."

"You are right," said Carthoris. "Still, I hate to leave them, though there is naught else to do," and so the two turned from the courtyard, and making their way into one of the broad avenues, crept stealthily in the shadows of the building toward the great central plaza upon which were the buildings occupied by the green warriors when they visited the deserted city.

When they had come to the plaza's edge Carthoris halted.

"Wait here," he whispered. "I go to fetch thoats, since on foot we may never hope to escape the clutches of these green fiends."

To reach the courtyard where the thoats were kept it was necessary for Carthoris to pass through one of the buildings which surrounded the square. Which were occupied and which not he could not even guess, so he was compelled to take considerable chances to gain the enclosure in which he could hear the restless beasts squealing and quarreling among themselves.

Chance carried him through a dark doorway into a large chamber in which lay a score or more green warriors wrapped in their sleeping silks and furs. Scarce had Carthoris passed through the short hallway that connected the door of the building and the great room beyond it than he became aware of the presence of something or someone in the hallway through which he had but just passed.

He heard a man yawn, and then, behind him, he saw the figure of a sentry rise from where the fellow had been dozing, and stretching himself resume his wakeful watchfulness.

Carthoris realized that he must have passed within a foot of the warrior, doubtless rousing him from his slumber. To retreat now would be impossible. Yet to cross through that roomful of sleeping warriors seemed almost equally beyond the pale of possibility. The crucial moment had come.

Carthoris shrugged his broad shoulders and chose the lesser evil. Warily he entered the room. At his right, against the wall, leaned several swords and rifles and spears—extra weapons which the warriors had stacked here ready to their hands should there be a night alarm calling them suddenly from slumber. Beside each sleeper lay his weapon—these were never far from their owners from childhood to death.

The sight of the swords made the young man's palm itch.

He stepped quickly to them, selecting two short-swords—one for Kar Komak, the other for himself; also some trappings for his naked comrade.

Then he started directly across the center of the apartment among the sleeping Torquasians.

Not a man of them moved until Carthoris had completed more than half of the short though dangerous journey. Then a fellow directly in his path turned restlessly upon his sleeping silks and furs.

The Heliumite paused above him, one of the short-swords in readiness should the warrior awaken. For what seemed an eternity to the young prince the green man continued to move uneasily upon his couch, then, as though actuated by springs, he leaped to his feet and faced the red man.

Instantly Carthoris struck, but not before a savage grunt escaped the other's lips. In an instant the room was in turmoil. Warriors leaped to their feet, grasping their weapons as they rose, and shouting to one another for an explanation of the disturbance.

To Carthoris all within the room was plainly visible in the dim light reflected from without, for the further moon stood directly at zenith; but to the eyes of the newly awakened green men objects as yet had not taken on familiar forms—they but saw vaguely the figures of warriors moving about their apartment.

Now one stumbled against the corpse of him whom Carthoris had slain. The fellow stooped and his hand came in contact with the cleft skull. He saw about him the giant figures of other green men, and so he jumped to the only conclusion that was open to him.

"The Thurds!" he cried. "The Thurds are upon us! Rise, warriors of Torquas, and drive home your swords within the hearts of Torquas' ancient enemies!"

Instantly the green men began to fall upon one another with naked swords. Their savage lust of battle was aroused. To fight, to kill, to die with cold steel buried in their vitals! Ah, that to them was Nirvana.

Carthoris was quick to guess their error and take advantage of it. He knew that in the pleasure of killing they might fight on long after they had discovered their mistake, unless their attention was distracted by sight of the real cause of the altercation, and so he lost no time in continuing across the room to the doorway upon the opposite side, which opened into the inner court, where the savage thoats were squealing and fighting among themselves.

Once here he had no easy task before him. To catch and mount one of these habitually rageful and intractable beasts was no child's play under the best of conditions; but now, when silence and time were such important considerations, it might well have seemed quite hopeless to a less resourceful and optimistic man than the son of the great warlord.

From his father he had learned much concerning the traits of these mighty beasts, and from Tars Tarkas, also, when he had visited that great green jeddak among his horde at Thark. So now he centered upon the work in hand all that he had ever learned about them from others and from his own experience, for he, too, had ridden and handled them many times.

The temper of the thoats of Torquas appeared even shorter than their vicious cousins among the Tharks and Warhoons, and for a time it seemed unlikely that he should escape a savage charge on the part of a couple of old bulls that circled, squealing, about him; but at last he managed to get close enough to one of them to touch the beast. With the feel of his hand upon the sleek hide the creature quieted, and in answer to the telepathic command of the red man sank to its knees docile as a lamb.

In a moment Carthoris was upon its back, guiding it toward the great gate that leads from the courtyard through a large building at one end into an avenue beyond.

The other bull, still squealing and enraged, followed after his fellow. There was no bridle upon either, for these strange creatures are controlled entirely by suggestion—when they are controlled at all.

Even in the hands of the giant green men bridle reins would be hopelessly futile against the mad savagery and mastodonic strength of the thoat, and so they are guided by that strange telepathic power with which the men of Mars have learned to communicate in a crude way with the lower orders of their planet.

With difficulty Carthoris urged the two beasts to the gate, where, leaning down, he raised the latch. Then the thoat that he was riding placed his great shoulder to the skeel-wood planking, pushed through, and a moment later the man and the two beasts were swinging silently down the avenue to the edge of the plaza, where Kar Komak hid.

Here Carthoris found considerable difficulty in subduing the second thoat, and as Kar Komak had never before ridden one of the beasts, it seemed a most hopeless job; but at last the bowman managed to scramble to the sleek back, and again the two beasts fled softly down the moss-grown avenues toward the open sea-bottom beyond the city.

All that night and the following day and the second night they rode toward the northeast. No indication of pursuit developed, and at dawn of the second day Carthoris saw in the distance the waving ribbon of great trees that marked one of the long Barsoomian waterways.

Immediately they abandoned their thoats and approached the cultivated district on foot. Carthoris also discarded the metal from his harness, or such of it as might serve to identify him as a Heliumite, or of royal blood, for he did not know to what nation belonged this waterway, and upon Mars it is always well to assume every man and nation your enemy until you have learned the contrary.

It was mid-forenoon when the two at last entered one of the roads that cut through the cultivated districts at regular intervals, joining the arid wastes on either side with the great white, central highway that follows through the center from end to end of the far-reaching, threadlike farm lands.

The high wall surrounding the fields served as a protection against surprise by raiding green hordes, as well as keeping the savage banths and other carnivora from the domestic animals and the human beings upon the farms.

Carthoris stopped before the first gate he came to, pounding for admission. The young man who answered his summons greeted the two hospitably, though he looked with considerable wonder upon the white skin and auburn hair of the bowman.

After he had listened for a moment to a partial narration of their escape from the Torquasians, he invited them within, took them to his house and bade the servants there prepare food for them.

As they waited in the low-ceiled, pleasant living room of the farmhouse until the meal should be ready, Carthoris drew his host into conversation that he might learn his nationality, and thus the nation under whose dominion lay the waterway where circumstance had placed him.

"I am Hal Vas," said the young man, "son of Vas Kor of Dusar, a noble in the retinue of Astok, Prince of Dusar. At present I am Dwar of the Road for this district."

Carthoris was very glad that he had not disclosed his identity, for though he had no idea of anything that had transpired since he had left Helium, or that Astok was at the bottom of all his misfortunes, he well knew that the Dusarian had no love for him, and that he could hope for no assistance within the dominions of Dusar.

"And who are you?" asked Hal Vas. "By your appearance I take you for a fighting man, but I see no insignia upon your harness. Can it be that you are a panthan?"

Now, these wandering soldiers of fortune are common upon Barsoom, where most men love to fight. They sell their services wherever war exists, and in the occasional brief intervals when there is no organized warfare between the red nations, they join one of the numerous expeditions that are constantly being dispatched against the green men in protection of the waterways that traverse the wilder portions of the globe.

When their service is over they discard the metal of the nation they have been serving until they shall have found a new master. In the intervals they wear no insignia, their war-worn harness and grim weapons being sufficient to attest their calling.

The suggestion was a happy one, and Carthoris embraced the chance it afforded to account satisfactorily for himself. There was, however, a single drawback. In times of war such panthans as happened to be within the domain of a belligerent nation were compelled to don the insignia of that nation and fight with her warriors.

As far as Carthoris knew Dusar was not at war with any other nation, but there was never any telling when one red nation would be flying at the throat of a neighbor, even though the great and powerful alliance at the head of which was his father, John Carter, had managed to maintain a long peace upon the greater portion of Barsoom.

A pleasant smile lighted Hal Vas' face as Carthoris admitted his vocation.

"It is well," exclaimed the young man, "that you chanced to come hither, for here you will find the means of obtaining service in short order. My father, Vas Kor, is even now with me, having come hither to recruit a force for the new war against Helium."

CHAPTER XII

TO SAVE DUSAR

THUVIA OF PTARTH, battling for more than life against the lust of Jav, cast a quick glance over her shoulder toward the forest from which had rumbled the fierce growl. Jav looked, too.

What they saw filled each with apprehension. It was Komal, the banth-god, rushing wide-jawed upon them!

Which had he chosen for his prey? Or was it to be both?

They had not long to wait, for though the Lotharian attempted to hold the girl between himself and the terrible fangs, the great beast found him at last.

Then, shrieking, he attempted to fly toward Lothar, after pushing Thuvia bodily into the face of the man-eater. But his flight was of short duration. In a moment Komal was upon him, rending his throat and chest with demoniacal fury.

The girl reached their side a moment later, but it was with difficulty that she tore the mad beast from its prey. Still growling and casting hungry glances back upon Jav, the banth at last permitted itself to be led away into the wood.

With her giant protector by her side Thuvia set forth to find the passage through the cliffs that she might attempt the seemingly impossible feat of reaching far-distant Ptarth across the more than seventeen thousand haads of savage Barsoom.

She could not believe that Carthoris had deliberately deserted her, and so she kept a constant watch for him; but as she bore too far to the north in her search for the tunnel she

passed the Heliumite as he was returning to Lothar in search
of her.

Thuvia of Ptarth was having difficulty in determining the
exact status of the Prince of Helium in her heart. She could
not admit even to herself that she loved him, and yet she had
permitted him to apply to her that term of endearment and
possession to which a Barsoomian maid should turn deaf ears
when voiced by other lips than those of her husband or
fiancé—"my princess."

Kulan Tith, Jeddak of Kaol, to whom she was affianced,
commanded her respect and admiration. Had it been that she
had surrendered to her father's wishes because of pique that
the handsome Heliumite had not taken advantage of his visits
to her father's court to push the suit for her hand that she
had been quite sure he had contemplated since that distant
day the two had sat together upon the carved seat within the
gorgeous Garden of the Jeddaks that graced the inner courtyard of the palace of Salensus Oll at Kadabra?

Did she love Kulan Tith? Bravely she tried to believe that
she did; but all the while her eyes wandered through the
coming darkness for the figure of a clean-limbed fighting
man—black-haired and gray-eyed. Black was the hair of Kulan Tith; but his eyes were brown.

It was almost dark when she found the entrance to the
tunnel. Safely she passed through to the hills beyond, and
here, under the bright light of Mars' two moons, she halted
to plan her future action.

Should she wait here in the hope that Carthoris would
return in search of her? Or should she continue her way
northeast toward Ptarth? Where, first, would Carthoris
have gone after leaving the valley of Lothar?

Her parched throat and dry tongue gave her the answer—
toward Aaanthor and water. Well, she, too, would go first to
Aaanthor, where she might find more than the water she
needed.

With Komal by her side she felt little fear, for he would
protect her from all other savage beasts. Even the great white
apes would flee the mighty banth in terror. Men only need
she fear, but she must take this and many other chances before
she could hope to reach her father's court again.

When at last Carthoris found her, only to be struck down

by the long-sword of a green man, Thuvia prayed that the
same fate might overtake her.

The sight of the red warriors leaping from their fliers had,
for a moment, filled her with renewed hope—hope that Carthoris of Helium might be only stunned and that they would
rescue him; but when she saw the Dusarian metal upon
their harness, and that they sought only to escape with her
alone from the charging Torquasians, she gave up.

Komal, too, was dead—dead across the body of the Heliumite. She was, indeed, alone now. There was none to protect
her.

The Dusarian warriors dragged her to the deck of a flier.
All about them the green warriors surged in an attempt to
wrest her from the red.

At last those who had not died in the conflict gained the
decks of the two craft. The engines throbbed and purred—
the propellers whirred. Quickly the swift boats shot heavenward.

Thuvia of Ptarth glanced about her. A man stood near,
smiling down into her face. With a gasp of recognition she
looked full into his eyes, and then with a little moan of terror
and understanding she buried her face in her hands and sank
to the polished skeel-wood deck. It was Astok, Prince of
Dusar, who bent above her.

Swift were the fliers of Astok of Dusar, and great the need
for reaching his father's court as quickly as possible, for the
fleets of war of Helium and Ptarth and Kaol were scattered
far and wide above Barsoom. Nor would it go well with
Astok of Dusar should any one of them discover Thuvia of
Ptarth a prisoner upon his own vessel.

Aaanthor lies in fifty south latitude, and forty east of Horz,
the deserted seat of ancient Barsoomian culture and learning,
while Dusar lies fifteen degrees north of the equator and
twenty degrees east from Horz.

Great though the distance is, the fliers covered it without
a stop. Long before they had reached their destination Thuvia of Ptarth had learned several things that cleared up the
doubts that had assailed her mind for many days. Scarce had
they risen above Aaanthor than she recognized one of the crew
as a member of the crew of that other flier that had borne
her from her father's gardens to Aaanthor. The presence of

Astok upon the craft settled the whole question. She had been stolen by emissaries of the Dusarian prince—Carthoris of Helium had had nothing to do with it.

Nor did Astok deny the charge when she accused him. He only smiled and pleaded his love for her.

"I would sooner mate with a white ape!" she cried, when he would have urged his suit.

Astok glowered sullenly upon her.

"You shall mate with me, Thuvia of Ptarth," he growled, "or, by your first ancestor, you shall have your preference—and mate with a white ape."

The girl made no reply, nor could he draw her into conversation during the balance of the journey.

As a matter of fact Astok was a trifle awed by the proportions of the conflict which his abduction of the Ptarthian princess had induced, nor was he over comfortable with the weight of responsibility which the possession of such a prisoner entailed.

His one thought was to get her to Dusar, and there let his father assume the responsibility. In the meantime he would be as careful as possible to do nothing to affront her, lest they all might be captured and he have to account for his treatment of the girl to one of the great jeddaks whose interest centered in her.

And so at last they came to Dusar, where Astok hid his prisoner in a secret room high in the east tower of his own palace. He had sworn his men to silence in the matter of the identity of the girl, for until he had seen his father, Nutus, Jeddak of Dusar, he dared not let anyone know whom he had brought with him from the south.

But when he appeared in the great audience chamber before the cruel-lipped man who was his sire, he found his courage oozing, and he dared not speak of the princess hid within his palace. It occurred to him to test his father's sentiments upon the subject, and so he told a tale of capturing one who claimed to know the whereabouts of Thuvia of Ptarth.

"And if you command it, Sire," he said, "I will go and capture her—fetching her here to Dusar."

Nutus frowned and shook his head.

"You have done enough already to set Ptarth and Kaol

and Helium all three upon us at once should they learn your part in the theft of the Ptarth princess. That you succeeded in shifting the guilt upon the Prince of Helium was fortunate, and a masterly move of strategy; but were the girl to know the truth and ever return to her father's court, all Dusar would have to pay the penalty, and to have her here a prisoner amongst us would be an admission of guilt from the consequences of which naught could save us. It would cost me my throne, Astok, and that I have no mind to lose.

"If we had her here—" the elder man suddenly commenced to muse, repeating the phrase again and again. "If we had her here, Astok," he exclaimed fiercely. "Ah, if we but had her here and none knew that she was here! Can you not guess, man? The guilt of Dusar might be forever buried with her bones," he concluded in a low, savage whisper.

Astok, Prince of Dusar, shuddered.

Weak he was; yes, and wicked, too; but the suggestion that his father's words implied turned him cold with horror.

Cruel to their enemies are the men of Mars; but the word "enemies" is commonly interpreted to mean men only. Assassination runs riot in the great Barsoomian cities; yet to murder a woman is a crime so unthinkable that even the most hardened of the paid assassins would shrink from you in horror should you even dare to suggest such a thing to him.

Nutus was apparently oblivious to his son's all-too-patent terror at his suggestion. Presently he continued:

"You say that you know where the girl lies hid, since she was stolen from your people at Aaanthor. Should she be found by any one of the three powers her unsupported story would be sufficient to turn them all against us.

"There is but one way, Astok," cried the older man. "You must return at once to her hiding place and fetch her hither in all secrecy. And, look you here! Return not to Dusar without her, upon pain of death!"

Astok, Prince of Dusar, well knew his royal father's temper. He knew that in the tyrant's heart there pulsed no single throb of love for any creature.

Astok's mother had been a slave woman. Nutus had never loved her. He had never loved another. In youth he had tried to find a bride at the courts of several of his powerful neighbors, but their women would have none of him.

After a dozen daughters of his own nobility had sought self-destruction rather than wed him he had given up. And then it had been that he had legally wed one of his slaves that he might have a son to stand among the jeds when Nutus died and a new jeddak was chosen.

Slowly Astok withdrew from the presence of his father. With white face and shaking limbs he made his way to his own palace. As he crossed the courtyard his glance chanced to wander to the great east tower looming high against the azure of the sky.

At sight of it beads of sweat broke out upon his brow.

Issus! No other hand than his could be trusted to do the horrid thing. With his own fingers he must crush the life from that perfect throat, or plunge the silent blade into the red, red heart.

Her heart! The heart that he had hoped would brim with love for him!

But had it done so? He recalled the haughty contempt with which his protestations of love had been received. He went cold and then hot at the memory of it. His compunctions cooled as the self-satisfaction of a near revenge crowded out the finer instincts that had for a moment asserted themselves— the good that he had inherited from the slave woman was once again submerged in the bad blood that had come down to him from his royal sire; as, in the end, it always was.

A cold smile supplanted the terror that had dilated his eyes. He turned his steps toward the tower. He would see her before he set out upon the journey that was to blind his father to the fact that the girl was already in Dusar.

Quietly he passed in through the secret way, ascending a spiral runway to the apartment in which the Princess of Ptarth was immured.

As he entered the room he saw the girl leaning upon the sill of the east casement, gazing out across the roof tops of Dusar toward distant Ptarth. He hated Ptarth. The thought of it filled him with rage. Why not finish her now and have it done with?

At the sound of his step she turned quickly toward him. Ah, how beautiful she was! His sudden determination faded beneath the glorious light of her wondrous beauty. He would wait until he had returned from his little journey of decep-

tion—maybe there might be some other way then. Some
other hand to strike the blow—with that face, with those eyes
before him, he could never do it. Of that he was positive. He
had always gloried in the cruelty of his nature, but, Issus! he
was not that cruel. No, another must be found—one whom he
could trust.

He was still looking at her as she stood there before him
meeting his gaze steadily and unafraid. He felt the hot passion of his love mounting higher and higher.

Why not sue once more? If she would relent, all might yet
be well. Even if his father could not be persuaded they
could fly to Ptarth, laying all the blame of the knavery and
intrigue that had thrown four great nations into war,
upon the shoulders of Nutus. And who was there that would
doubt the justice of the charge?

"Thuvia," he said, "I come once again, for the last time, to
lay my heart at your feet. Ptarth·and Kaol and Dusar are
battling with Helium because of you. Wed me, Thuvia, and
all may yet be as it should be."

The girl shook her head.

"Wait!" he commanded, before she could speak. "Know the
truth before you speak words that may seal not only your
own fate but that of the thousands of warriors who battle
because of you.

"Refuse to wed me willingly, and Dusar would be laid waste
should ever the truth be known to Ptarth and Kaol and
Helium. They would raze our cities, leaving not one stone upon another. They would scatter our peoples across the face of
Barsoom from the frozen north to the frozen south, hunting
them down and slaying them, until this great nation remained only as a hated memory in the minds of men.

"But while they are exterminating the Dusarians countless
thousands of their own warriors must perish—and all because of the stubbornness of a single woman who would not
wed the prince who loves her.

"Refuse, Thuvia of Ptarth, and there remains but a single
alternative—no man must ever know your fate. Only a handful of loyal servitors besides my royal father and myself know
that you were stolen from the gardens of Thuvan Dihn by
Astok, Prince of Dusar, or that today you be imprisoned in
my palace.

"Refuse, Thuvia of Ptarth, and you must die to save Dusar—there is no other way. Nutus, the jeddak, has so decreed.
I have spoken."

For a long moment the girl let her level gaze rest full upon
the face of Astok of Dusar. Then she spoke, and though the
words were few, the unimpassioned tone carried unfathomable depths of cold contempt.

"Better all that you have threatened," she said, "than you."

Then she turned her back upon him and went to stand once
more before the east window, gazing with sad eyes toward
distant Ptarth.

Astok wheeled and left the room, returning after a short
interval of time with food and drink.

"Here," he said, "is sustenance until I return again. The
next to enter this apartment will be your executioner. Com-
mend yourself to your ancestors, Thuvia of Ptarth, for within
a few days you shall be with them."

Then he was gone.

Half an hour later he was interviewing an officer high in
the navy of Dusar.

"Whither went Vas Kor?" he asked. "He is not at his palace."

"South, to the great waterway that skirts Torquas," replied the other. "His son, Hal Vas, is Dwar of the Road
there, and thither has Vas Kor gone to enlist recruits among
the workers on the farms."

"Good," said Astok, and a half-hour more found him rising
above Dusar in his swiftest flier.

CHAPTER XIII

TURJUN, THE PANTHAN

THE FACE OF CARTHORIS of Helium gave no token of
the emotions that convulsed him inwardly as he heard from
the lips of Hal Vas that Helium was at war with Dusar, and
that fate had thrown him into the service of the enemy.

That he might utilize this opportunity to the good of Hel-

ium scarce sufficed to outweigh the chagrin he felt that he
was not fighting in the open at the head of his own loyal
troops.

To escape the Dusarians might prove an easy matter; and
then again it might not. Should they suspect his loyalty (and
the loyalty of an impressed panthan was always open to suspicion), he might not find an opportunity to elude their
vigilance until after the termination of the war, which might
occur within days, or, again, only after long and weary years
of bloodshed.

He recalled that history recorded wars in which actual
military operations had been carried on without cessation for
five or six hundred years, and even now there were nations
upon Barsoom with which Helium had made no peace
within the history of man.

The outlook was not cheering. He could not guess that
within a few hours he would be blessing the fate that had
thrown him into the service of Dusar.

"Ah!" exclaimed Hal Vas. "Here is my father now. Kaor!
Vas Kor. Here is one you will be glad to meet—a doughty
panthan—" He hesitated.

"Turjun," interjected Carthoris, seizing upon the first appellation that occurred to him.

As he spoke his eyes crossed quickly to the tall warrior who
was entering the room. Where before had he seen that giant
figure, that taciturn countenance, and the livid sword cut
from temple to mouth?

"Vas Kor," repeated Carthoris mentally. "Vas Kor!" Where
had he seen the man before?

And then the noble spoke, and like a flash it all came back
to Carthoris—the forward servant upon the landing stage at
Ptarth that time that he had been explaining the intricacies
of his new compass to Thuvan Dihn; the lone slave that had
guarded his own hangar that night he had left upon his ill-
fated journey for Ptarth—the journey that had brought him
so mysteriously to far Aaanthor.

"Vas Kor," he repeated aloud, "blessed be your ancestors
for this meeting," nor did the Dusarian guess the wealth of
meaning that lay beneath that hackneyed phrase with which
a Barsoomian ackowledges an introduction.

"And blessed be yours, Turjun," replied Vas Kor.

Now came the introduction of Kar Komak to Vas Kor, and as Carthoris went through the little ceremony there came to him the only explanation he might make to account for the white skin and auburn hair of the bowman; for he feared that the truth might not be believed and thus suspicion be cast upon them both from the beginning.

"Kar Komak," he explained, "is, as you can see, a thern. He has wandered far from his icebound southern temples in search of adventure. I came upon him in the pits of Aaanthor; but though I have known him so short a time, I can vouch for his bravery and loyalty."

Since the destruction of the fabric of their false religion by John Carter, the majority of the therns had gladly accepted the new order of things, so that it was now no longer uncommon to see them mingling with the multitudes of red men in any of the great cities of the outer world, so Vas Kor neither felt nor expressed any great astonishment and no alarm.

All during the interview Carthoris watched, catlike, for some indication that Vas Kor recognized in the battered panthan the erstwhile gorgeous Prince of Helium; but the sleepless nights, the long days of marching and fighting, the wounds and the dried blood had evidently sufficed to obliterate the last remnant of his likeness to his former self; and then Vas Kor had seen him but twice in all his life. Little wonder that he did not know him.

During the evening Vas Kor announced that on the morrow they should depart north toward Dusar, picking up recruits at various stations along the way.

In a great field behind the house a flier lay—a fair-sized cruiser-transport that would accommodate many men, yet swift and well armed also. Here Carthoris slept, and Kar Komak, too, with the other recruits, under guard of the regular Dusarian warriors that manned the craft.

Toward midnight Vas Kor returned to the vessel from his son's house, repairing at once to his cabin. Carthoris, with one of the Dusarians, was on watch. It was with difficulty that the Heliumite repressed a cold smile as the noble passed within a foot of him—within a foot of the long, slim, Heliumitic blade that swung in his harness.

How easy it would have been! How easy to avenge the cowardly trick that had been played upon him—to avenge

Helium and Ptarth and Thuvia!

But his hand moved not toward the dagger's hilt, for first Vas Kor must serve a better purpose—he might know where Thuvia of Ptarth lay hidden now, if it had truly been Dusarians that had spirited her away during the fight before Aaanthor.

And then, too, there was the instigator of the entire foul plot. He must pay the penalty; and who better than Vas Kor could lead the Prince of Helium to Astok of Dusar?

Faintly out of the night there came to Carthoris's ears the purring of a distant motor. He scanned the heavens.

Yes, there it was far in the north, dimly outlined against the dark void of space that stretched illimitably beyond it, the faint suggestion of a flier passing, unlighted, through the black Barsoomian night.

Carthoris, knowing not whether the craft might be friend or foe of Dusar, gave no sign that he had seen, but turned his eyes in another direction, leaving the matter to the Dusarian who stood watch with him.

Presently the fellow discovered the oncoming craft, and sounded the low alarm which brought the balance of the watch and an officer from their sleeping silks and furs upon the deck nearby.

The cruiser-transport lay without lights, and resting as she was upon the ground, must have been entirely invisible to the oncoming flier, which all presently recognized as a small craft.

It soon became evident that the stranger intended making a landing, for she was now spiraling slowly above them, dropping lower and lower in each graceful curve.

"It is the *Thuria*," whispered one of the Dusarian warriors. "I would know her in the blackness of the pits among ten thousand other craft."

Right you are!" exclaimed Vas Kor, who had come on deck. And then he hailed:

"Kaor, *Thuria!*"

"Kaor!" came presently from above after a brief silence. Then: "What ship?"

"Cruiser-transport *Kalksus*, Vas Kor of Dusar."

"Good!" came from above. "Is there safe landing alongside?"

"Yes, close in to starboard. Wait, we will show our lights," and a moment later the smaller craft settled close beside the *Kalksus*, and the lights of the latter were immediately extinguished once more.

Several figures could be seen slipping over the side of the *Thuria* and advancing toward the *Kalksus*. Ever suspicious, the Dusarians stood ready to receive the visitors as friends or foes as closer inspection might prove them.

Carthoris stood quite near the rail, ready to take sides with the newcomers should chance have it that they were Heliumites playing a bold stroke of strategy upon this lone Dusarian ship. He had led like parties himself, and knew that such a contingency was quite possible.

But the face of the first man to cross the rail undeceived him with a shock that was not at all unpleasurable—it was the face of Astok, Prince of Dusar.

Scarce noticing the others upon the deck of the *Kalksus*, Astok strode forward to accept Vas Kor's greeting, then he summoned the noble below. The warriors and officers returned to their sleeping silks and furs, and once more the deck was deserted except for the Dusarian warrior and Turjun, the panthan, who stood guard.

The latter walked quietly to and fro. The former leaned across the rail, wishing for the hour that would bring him relief. He did not see his companion approach the lights of the cabin of Vas Kor. He did not see him stoop with ear close pressed to a tiny ventilator.

"May the white apes take us all," cried Astok ruefully, "if we are not in as ugly a snarl as you have ever seen! Nutus thinks that we have her in hiding far away from Dusar. He has bidden me bring her there."

He paused. No man should have heard from his lips the thing he was trying to tell. It should have been forever the secret of Nutus and Astok, for upon it rested the safety of a throne. With that knowledge any man could wrest from the Jeddak of Dusar whatever he listed.

But Astok was afraid, and he wanted from this older man the suggestion of an alternative. He went on.

"I am to kill her," he whispered, looking fearfully around. "Nutus merely wishes to see the body that he may know his commands have been executed. I am now supposed to be

gone to the spot where we have her hidden that I may fetch
her in secrecy to Dusar. None is to know that she has ever
been in the keeping of a Dusarian. I do not need to tell you
what would befall Dusar should Ptarth and Helium and
Kaol ever learn the truth."

The jaws of the listener at the ventilator clicked together
with a vicious snap. Before he had but guessed at the identity
of the subject of this conversation. Now he knew. And they
were to kill her! His muscular fingers clenched until the nails
bit into the palms.

"And you wish me to go with you while you fetch her to
Dusar," Vas Kor was saying. "Where is she?"

Astok bent close and whispered into the other's ear. The
suggestion of a smile crossed the cruel features of Vas Kor. He
realized the power that lay within his grasp. He should be a
jed at least.

"And how may I help you, my Prince?" asked the older
man suavely.

"I cannot kill her," said Astok. "Issus! I cannot do it! When
she turns those eyes upon me my heart becomes water."

Vas Kor's eyes narrowed.

"And you wish—" He paused, the interrogation unfinished,
yet complete.

Astok nodded.

"*You* do not love her," he said.

"But I love my life—though I am only a lesser noble," he
concluded meaningly.

"You shall be a greater noble—a noble of the first rank!"
exclaimed Astok.

"I would be a jed," said Vas Kor bluntly.

Astok hesitated.

"A jed must die before there can be another jed," he
pleaded.

"Jeds have died before," snapped Vas Kor. "It would doubtless be not difficult for you to find a jed you do not love, Astok—there are many who do not love you."

Already Vas Kor was commencing to presume upon his
power over the young prince. Astok was quick to note and
appreciate the subtle change in his lieutenant. A cunning
scheme entered his weak and wicked brain.

"As you say, Vas Kor!" he exclaimed. "You shall be a jed

when the thing is done," and then, to himself: "Nor will it
then be difficult for me to find a jed I do not love."

"When shall we return to Dusar?" asked the noble.

"At once," replied Astok. "Let us get under way now—there
is naught to keep you here?"

"I had intended sailing on the morrow, picking up such
recruits as the various Dwars of the Roads might have collected for me, as we returned to Dusar."

"Let the recruits wait," said Astok. "Or, better still, come
you to Dusar upon the *Thuria,* leaving the *Kalksus* to follow
and pick up the recruits."

"Yes," acquiesced Vas Kor; "that is the better plan. Come;
I am ready," and he rose to accompany Astok to the latter's
flier.

The listener at the ventilator came to his feet slowly, like
an old man. His face was drawn and pinched and very white
beneath the light copper of his skin. She was to die! And he
helpless to avert the tragedy. He did not even know where
she was imprisoned.

The two men were ascending from the cabin to the deck.
Turjun, the panthan, crept close to the companionway, his
sinuous fingers closing tightly upon the hilt of his dagger.
Could he despatch them both before he was overpowered? He
smiled. He could slay an entire utan of her enemies in his
present state of mind.

They were almost abreast of him now. Astok was speaking.

"Bring a couple of your men along, Vas Kor," he said. "We
are short-handed upon the *Thuria,* so quickly did we depart."

The panthan's fingers dropped from the dagger's hilt. His
quick mind had grasped here a chance for succoring Thuvia
of Ptarth. He might be chosen as one to accompany the assassins, and once he had learned where the captive lay he could
despatch Astok and Vas Kor as well as now. To kill them before he knew where Thuvia was hid was simply to leave her
to death at the hands of others; for sooner or later Nutus
would learn her whereabouts, and Nutus, Jeddak of Dusar,
could not afford to let her live.

Turjun put himself in the path of Vas Kor that he might
not be overlooked. The noble aroused the men sleeping upon the deck, but always before him the strange panthan
whom he had recruited that same day found means for keep-

ing himself to the fore.

Vas Kor turned to his lieutenant, giving instruction for the bringing of the *Kalksus* to Dusar, and the gathering up of the recruits; then he signed to two stalwart warriors who stood close behind the padwar.

"You two accompany us to the *Thuria*," he said, "and put yourselves at the disposal of her dwar."

It was dark upon the deck of the *Kalksus*, so Vas Kor had not a good look at the faces of the two he chose; but that was of no moment, for they were but common warriors to assist with the ordinary duties upon a flier, and to fight if need be.

One of the two was Kar Komak, the bowman. The other was not Carthoris.

The Heliumite was mad with disappointment. He snatched his dagger from his harness; but already Astok had left the deck of the *Kalksus*, and he knew that before he could overtake him, should he despatch Vas Kor, he would be killed by the Dusarian warriors, who now were thick upon the deck. With either one of the two alive Thuvia was in as great danger as though both lived—it must be both!

As Vas Kor descended to the ground Carthoris boldly followed him, nor did any attempt to halt him, thinking, doubtless, that he was one of the party.

After him came Kar Komak and the Dusarian warrior who had been detailed to duty upon the *Thuria*. Carthoris walked close to the left side of the latter. Now they came to the dense shadow under the side of the *Thuria*. It was very dark there, so that they had to grope to find the rope ladder.

Kar Komak preceded the Dusarian. The latter reached upward for the swinging rounds, and as he did so steel fingers closed upon his windpipe and a steel blade pierced the very center of his heart.

Turjun, the panthan, was the last to clamber over the rail of the *Thuria*, drawing the rope ladder in after him.

A moment later the flier was rising rapidly, headed for the north.

At the rail Kar Komak turned to speak to the warrior who had been detailed to accompany him. His eyes went wide as they rested upon the face of the young man whom he had met beside the granite cliffs that guard mysterious Lothar. How had he come in place of the Dusarian?

A quick sign, and Kar Komak turned once more to find the *Thuria*'s dwar that he might report himself for duty. Behind him followed the panthan.

Carthoris blessed the chance that had caused Vas Kor to choose the bowman of all others, for had it been another Dusarian there would have been questions to answer as to the whereabouts of the warrior who lay so quietly in the field beyond the residence of Hal Vas, Dwar of the Southern Road; and Carthoris had no answer to that question other than his sword point, which alone was scarce adequate to convince the entire crew of the *Thuria*.

The journey to Dusar seemed interminable to the impatient Carthoris, though as a matter of fact it was quickly accomplished. Some time before they reached their destination they met and spoke with another Dusarian war flier. From it they learned that a great battle was soon to be fought southeast of Dusar.

The combined navies of Dusar, Ptarth, and Kaol had been intercepted in their advance toward Helium by the mighty Heliumitic navy—the most formidable upon Barsoom, not alone in numbers and armament, but in the training and courage of its officers and warriors, and the zitidaric proportions of many of its monster battleships.

Not for many a day had there been the promise of such a battle. Four jeddaks were in direct command of their own fleets—Kulan Tith of Kaol, Thuvan Dihn of Ptarth, and Nutus of Dusar upon one side; while upon the other was Tardos Mors, Jeddak of Helium. With the latter was John Carter, Warlord of Mars.

From the far north another force was moving south across the barrier cliffs—the new navy of Talu, Jeddak of Okar, coming in response to the call from the warlord. Upon the decks of the sullen ships of war black-bearded yellow men looked over eagerly toward the south. Gorgeous were they in their splendid cloaks of orluk and apt. Fierce, formidable fighters from the hothouse cities of the frozen north.

And from the distant south, from the Sea of Omean and the cliffs of gold, from the temples of the therns and the gardens of Issus, other thousands sailed into the north at the call of the great man they all had learned to respect, and, respecting, love. Pacing the flagship of this mighty fleet, second only to the navy of Helium, was the ebon Xodar, Jeddak of the First Born, his heart beating strong in anticipation of the coming moment when he should hurl his savage crews and the weight of his mighty ships upon the enemies of the warlord.

But would these allies reach the theater of war in time to be of avail to Helium? Or, would Helium need them?

Carthoris, with the other members of the crew of the *Thuria*, heard the gossip and the rumors. None knew of the two fleets, the one from the south and the other from the north, that were coming to support the ships of Helium, and all of Dusar were convinced that nothing now could save the ancient power of Helium from being wiped forever from the upper air of Barsoom.

Carthoris, too, loyal son of Helium that he was, felt that even his beloved navy might not be able to cope successfully with the combined forces of three great powers.

Now the *Thuria* touched the landing stage above the palace of Astok. Hurriedly the prince and Vas Kor disembarked and entered the drop that would carry them to the lower levels of the palace.

Close beside it was another drop that was utilized by common warriors. Carthoris touched Kar Komak upon the arm.

"Come!" he whispered. "You are my only friend among a nation of enemies. Will you stand by me?"

"To the death," replied Kar Komak.

The two approached the drop. A slave operated it.

"Where are your passes?" he asked.

Carthoris fumbled in his pocket pouch as though in search of them, at the same time entering the cage. Kar Komak followed him, closing the door. The slave did not start the cage downward. Every second counted. They must reach the lower level as soon as possible after Astok and Vas Kor if they would know whither the two went.

Carthoris turned suddenly upon the slave, hurling him to the opposite side of the cage.

"Bind and gag him, Kar Komak!" he cried.

Then he grasped the control lever, and as the cage shot downward at sickening speed, the bowman grappled with the slave. Carthoris could not leave the control to assist his companion, for should they touch the lowest level at the speed at which they were going, all would be dashed to instant death.

Below him he could now see the top of Astok's cage in the parallel shaft, and he reduced the speed of his to that of the other. The slave commenced to scream.

"Silence him!" cried Carthoris.

A moment later a limp form crumpled to the floor of the cage.

"He is silenced," said Kar Komak.

Carthoris brought the cage to a sudden stop at one of the higher levels of the palace. Opening the door, he grasped the still form of the slave and pushed it out upon the floor. Then he banged the gate and resumed the downward drop.

Once more he sighted the top of the cage that held Astok and Vas Kor. An instant later it had stopped, and as he brought his car to a halt, he saw the two men disappear through one of the exits of the corridor beyond.

CHAPTER XIV

KULAN TITH'S SACRIFICE

THE MORNING OF THE second day of her incarceration in the east tower of the palace of Astok, Prince of Dusar, found Thuvia of Ptarth waiting in dull apathy the coming of the assassin.

She had exhausted every possibility of escape, going over and over again the door and the windows, the floor and the walls.

The solid ersite slabs she could not even scratch; the tough Barsoomian glass of the windows would have shattered to nothing less than a heavy sledge in the hands of a strong man. The door and the lock were impregnable. There was no escape. And they had stripped her of her weapons so that she could not even anticipate the hour of her doom, thus robbing them of the satisfaction of witnessing her last moments.

When would they come? Would Astok do the deed with his own hands? She doubted that he had the courage for it. At heart he was a coward—she had known it since first she had heard him brag as, a visitor at the court of her father, he had sought to impress her with his valor.

She could not help but compare him with another. And with whom would an affianced bride compare an unsuccessful suitor? With her betrothed? And did Thuvia of Ptarth now measure Astok of Dusar by the standards of Kulan Tith, Jeddak of Kaol?

She was about to die; her thoughts were her own to do with as she pleased; yet furthest from them was Kulan Tith. Instead the figure of the tall and comely Heliumite filled her mind, crowding therefrom all other images.

She dreamed of his noble face, the quiet dignity of his bearing, the smile that lit his eyes as he conversed with his friends, and the smile that touched his lips as he fought with his enemies—the fighting smile of his Virginian sire.

And Thuvia of Ptarth, true daughter of Barsoom, found her breath quickening and heart leaping to the memory of this other smile—the smile that she would never see again. With a little half sob the girl sank to the pile of silks and furs that were tumbled in confusion beneath the east window, burying her face in her arms.

In the corridor outside her prison-room two men had paused in heated argument.

"I tell you again, Astok," one was saying, "that I shall not do this thing unless you be present in the room."

There was little of the respect due royalty in the tone of the speaker's voice. The other, noting it, flushed.

"Do not impose too far upon my friendship for you, Vas Kor," he snapped. "There is a limit to my patience."

"There is no question of royal prerogative here," returned Vas Kor. "You ask me to become an assassin in your stead, and against your jeddak's strict injunctions. You are in no position, Astok, to dictate to me; but rather should you be glad to accede to my reasonable request that you be present, thus sharing the guilt with me. Why should I bear it all?"

The younger man scowled, but he advanced toward the locked door, and as it swung in upon its hinges, he entered the room beyond at the side of Vas Kor.

Across the chamber the girl, hearing them enter, rose to her feet and faced them. Under the soft copper of her skin she blanched just a trifle; but her eyes were brave and level, and the haughty tilt of her firm little chin was eloquent of loathing and contempt.

"You still prefer death?" asked Astok.

"To *you*, yes," replied the girl coldly.

The Prince of Dusar turned to Vas Kor and nodded. The noble drew his short-sword and crossed the room toward Thuvia.

"Kneel!" he commanded.

"I prefer to die standing," she replied.

"As you will," said Vas Kor, feeling the point of his blade with his left thumb. "In the name of Nutus, Jeddak of Dusar!" he cried, and ran quickly toward her.

"In the name of Carthoris, Prince of Helium!" came in low tones from the doorway.

Vas Kor turned to see the panthan he had recruited at his son's house leaping across the floor toward him. The fellow brushed past Astok with an: "After him, you—calot!"

Vas Kor wheeled to meet the charging man.

"What means this treason?" he cried.

Astok, with bared sword, leaped to Vas Kor's assistance. The panthan's sword clashed against that of the noble, and in the first encounter Vas Kor knew that he faced a master swordsman in his antagonist.

Before he half realized the stranger's purpose he found the man between himself and Thuvia of Ptarth, at bay facing the two swords of the Dusarians. But he fought not like a man at bay. Ever was he the aggressor, and though always he kept his flashing blade between the girl and her enemies, yet he managed to force them hither and thither about the room, calling to the girl to follow close behind him.

Until it was too late neither Vas Kor nor Astok dreamed of that which lay in the panthan's mind; but at last as the fellow stood with his back toward the door both understood —they were penned in their own prison, and now the intruder could slay them at his will, for Thuvia of Ptarth was bolting the door at the man's direction, first taking the key from the opposite side, where Astok had left it when they had entered.

Astok, as was his way, finding that the enemy did not fall immediately before their swords, was leaving the brunt of the fighting to Vas Kor, and now as his eyes appraised the panthan carefully they presently went wider and wider, for slowly he had come to recognize the features of the Prince of Helium.

The Heliumite was pressing close upon Vas Kor. The noble was bleeding from a dozen wounds. Astok saw that he could not for long withstand the cunning craft of that terrible sword hand.

"Courage, Vas Kor!" he whispered in the other's ear. "I have a plan. Hold him but a moment longer and all will be well," but the balance of the sentence, "with Astok, Prince of Dusar," he did not voice aloud.

Vas Kor, dreaming no treachery, nodded his head, and for a moment succeeded in holding Carthoris at bay. Then the Heliumite and the girl saw the Dusarian prince run swiftly to the opposite side of the chamber, touch something in the wall that sent a great panel swinging inward, and disappear into the black vault beyond.

It was done so quickly that by no possibility could they have intercepted him. Carthoris, fearful lest Vas Kor might similarly elude him, or Astok return immediately with reinforcements, sprang viciously in upon his antagonist, and a moment later the headless body of the Dusarian noble rolled upon the ersite floor.

"Come!" cried Carthoris. "There is no time to be lost. Astok will be back in a moment with enough warriors to overpower me."

But Astok had no such plan in mind, for such a move would have meant the spreading of the fact among the palace gossips that the Ptarthian princess was a prisoner in the east tower. Quickly would the word have come to his father, and no amount of falsifying could have explained away the facts that the jeddak's investigation would have brought to light.

Instead Astok was racing madly through a long corridor to reach the door of the tower-room before Carthoris and Thuvia left the apartment. He had seen the girl remove the key and place it in her pocket-pouch, and he knew that a dagger point driven into the keyhole from the opposite side would imprison them in the secret chamber till eight dead worlds circled a cold, dead sun.

As fast as he could run Astok entered the main corridor that led to the tower chamber. Would he reach the door in time? What if the Heliumite should have already emerged and he should run upon him in the passageway? Astok felt a cold chill run up his spine. He had no stomach to face that uncanny blade.

He was almost at the door. Around the next turn of the corridor it stood. No, they had not left the apartment. Evidently Vas Kor was still holding the Heliumite!

Astok could scarce repress a grin at the clever manner in which he had outwitted the noble and disposed of him at the same time. And then he rounded the turn and came face to face with an auburn-haired, white giant.

The fellow did not wait to ask the reason for his coming; instead he leaped upon him with a long-sword, so that Astok had to parry a dozen vicious cuts before he could disengage himself and flee back down the runway.

A moment later Carthoris and Thuvia entered the corridor from the secret chamber.

"Well, Kar Komak?" asked the Heliumite.

"It is fortunate that you left me here, red man," said the bowman. "I but just now intercepted one who seemed over-anxious to reach this door—it was he whom they call Astok, Prince of Dusar."

Carthoris smiled.

"Where is he now?" he asked.

"He escaped my blade, and ran down this corridor," replied Kar Komak.

"We must lose no time then!" exclaimed Carthoris. "He will have the guard upon us yet!"

Together the three hastened along the winding passages through which Carthoris and Kar Komak had tracked the Dusarians by the marks of the latter's sandals in the thin dust that overspread the floors of these seldom-used passageways.

They had come to the chamber at the entrances to the lifts before they met with opposition. Here they found a handful of guardsmen, and an officer, who, seeing that they were strangers, questioned their presence in the palace of Astok.

Once more Carthoris and Kar Komak had recourse to their blades, and before they had won their way to one of the lifts the noise of the conflict must have aroused the entire palace, for they heard men shouting, and as they passed the many levels on their quick passage to the landing stage they saw armed men running hither and thither in search of the cause of the commotion.

Beside the stage lay the *Thuria*, with three warriors on guard. Again the Heliumite and the Lotharian fought shoulder to shoulder, but the battle was soon over, for the Prince of Helium alone would have been a match for any three that Dusar could produce.

Scarce had the *Thuria* risen from the ways ere a hundred or more fighting men leaped to view upon the landing stage. At their head was Astok of Dusar, and as he saw the two he had thought so safely in his power slipping from his grasp, he danced with rage and chagrin, shaking his fists and hurling abuse and vile insults at them.

With her bow inclined upward at a dizzy angle, the *Thuria* shot meteor-like into the sky. From a dozen points swift patrol boats darted after her, for the scene upon the landing stage above the palace of the Prince of Dusar had not gone unnoticed.

A dozen times shots grazed the *Thuria's* side, and as Carthoris could not leave the control levers, Thuvia of Ptarth turned the muzzles of the craft's rapid-fire guns upon the enemy as she clung to the steep and slippery surface of the deck.

It was a noble race and a noble fight. One against a score now, for other Dusarian craft had joined in the pursuit; but Astok, Prince of Dusar, had built well when he built the *Thuria*. None in the navy of his sire possessed a swifter flier; no other craft so well armored or so well armed.

One by one the pursuers were distanced, and as the last of them fell out of range behind, Carthoris dropped the *Thuria* nose to a horizontal plane, as with lever drawn to the last notch, she tore through the thin air of dying Mars toward the east and Ptarth.

Thirteen and a half thousand haads away lay Ptarth—a stiff thirty-hour journey for the swiftest of fliers, and between Dusar and Ptarth might lie half the navy of Dusar, for in this direction was the reported seat of the great naval battle that even now might be in progress.

Could Carthoris have known precisely where the great fleet of the contending red nations lay, he would have hastened to them without delay, for in the return of Thuvia to her sire lay the greatest hope of peace.

Half the distance they covered without sighting a single war-ship, and then Kar Komak called Carthoris' attention to a distant craft that rested upon the ochre vegetation of the great dead sea-bottom, above which the *Thuria* was speeding.

About the vessel many figures could be seen swarming. With the aid of powerful glasses, the Heliumite saw that they were green warriors, and that they were repeatedly charg-ing down upon the crew of the stranded airship. The nation-ality of the latter he could not make out at so great a distance.

It was not necessary to change the course of the *Thuria* to permit of passing directly above the scene of battle, but Carthoris dropped his craft a few hundred feet that he might have a better and closer view.

If the ship was of a friendly power, he could do no less than stop and direct his guns upon her enemies, though with the precious freight he carried he scarcely felt justified in landing, for he could offer but two swords in reinforcement—scarce enough to warrant jeopardizing the safety of the Princess of Ptarth.

As they came close above the stricken ship, they could see that it would be but a question of minutes before the green horde would swarm across the armored bulwarks to glut the ferocity of their bloodlust upon the defenders.

"It would be futile to descend," said Carthoris to Thuvia. "The craft may even be of Dusar—she shows no insignia. All that we may do is fire upon the hordesmen," and as he spoke he stepped to one of the guns and deflected its muzzle toward the green warriors at the ship's side.

At the first shot from the *Thuria* those upon the vessel below evidently discovered her for the first time. Immediately a device fluttered from the bow of the warship on the ground. Thuvia of Ptarth caught her breath quickly, glancing at Car-thoris.

The device was that of Kulan Tith, Jeddak of Kaol—the man to whom the Princess of Ptarth was betrothed!

How easy for the Heliumite to pass on, leaving his rival to the fate that could not for long be averted! No man could accuse him of cowardice or treachery, for Kulan Tith was in arms against Helium, and, further, upon the *Thuria* were not enough swords to delay even temporarily the outcome that already was a foregone conclusion in the minds of the watchers.

What would Carthoris, Prince of Helium, son of the illustrious war-lord, do?

Scarce had the device broken to the faint breeze ere the bow of the *Thuria* dropped at a sharp angle toward the ground.

"Can you navigate her?" asked Carthoris of Thuvia.

The girl nodded.

"I am going to try to take the survivors aboard," he continued. "It will need both Kar Komak and myself to man the guns while the Kaolians take to the boarding tackle. Keep her bow depressed against the rifle fire. She can bear it better in her forward armor, and at the same time the propellers will be protected."

He hurried to the cabin as Thuvia took the control. A moment later the boarding tackle dropped from the keel of the *Thuria*, and from a dozen points along either side stout, knotted leathern lines trailed downward. At the same time a signal broke from her bow:

"Prepare to board us."

A shout arose from the deck of the Kaolian warship. Carthoris, who by this time had returned from the cabin, smiled sadly. He was about to snatch from the jaws of death the man who stood between himself and the woman he loved.

"Take the port bow gun, Kar Komak," he called to the bowman, and himself stepped to the gun upon the starboard bow.

They could now feel the sharp shock of the explosions of the green warriors' projectiles against the armored sides of the staunch *Thuria*.

It was a forlorn hope at best. At any moment the repulsive ray tanks might be pierced. The men upon the Kaolian ship were battling with renewed hope. In the bow stood Kulan Tith, a brave figure fighting beside his brave warriors, beating back the ferocious green men.

The *Thuria* came low above the other craft. The Kaolians were forming under their officers in readiness to board, and then a sudden fierce fusillade from the rifles of the green warriors vomited their hail of death and destruction into the side of the brave flier.

Like a wounded bird she dived suddenly Mars-ward, careening drunkenly. Thuvia turned the bow upward in an effort to avert the imminent tragedy, but she succeeded only in lessening the shock of the flier's impact as she struck the ground beside the Kaolian ship.

When the green men saw only two warriors and a woman upon the deck of the *Thuria*, a savage shout of triumph arose from their ranks, while an answering groan broke from the lips of the Kaolians.

The former now turned their attention upon the new arrival, for they saw her defenders could soon be overcome and that from her deck they could command the deck of the better-manned ship.

As they charged a shout of warning came from Kulan Tith, upon the bridge of his own ship, and with it an appreciation of the valor of the act that had put the smaller vessel in these sore straits.

"Who is it," he cried, "that offers his life in the service of Kulan Tith? Never was wrought a nobler deed of self-sacrifice upon Barsoom!"

The green horde was scrambling over the *Thuria's* side as there broke from the bow the device of Carthoris, Prince of Helium, in reply to the query of the jeddak of Kaol. None upon the smaller flier had opportunity to note the effect of this announcement upon the Kaolians, for their attention was claimed solely now by that which was transpiring upon their own deck.

Kar Komak stood behind the gun he had been operating, staring with wide eyes at the onrushing hideous green warriors. Carthoris, seeing him thus, felt a pang of regret that, after all, this man that he had thought so valorous should prove, in the hour of need, as spineless as Jav or Tario.

"Kar Komak—man!" he shouted. "Grip yourself! Remember the days of the glory of the seafarers of Lothar. Fight! Fight, man! Fight as never man fought before. All that remains to us is to die fighting."

Kar Komak turned toward the Heliumite, a grim smile upon his lips.

"Why should we fight," he asked, "against such fearful odds? There is another way—a better way. Look!" He pointed toward the companionway that led below deck.

The green men, a handful of them, had already reached the *Thuria's* deck, as Carthoris glanced in the direction the Lotharian had indicated. The sight that met his eyes set his heart to thumping in joy and relief—Thuvia of Ptarth might yet be saved! For from below there poured a stream of giant bowmen, grim and terrible. Not the bowmen of Tario or Jav, but the bowmen of an odwar of bowmen—savage fighting men eager for the fray.

The green warriors paused in momentary surprise and consternation, but only for a moment. Then with horrid warcries they leaped forward to meet these strange, new foemen.

A volley of arrows stopped them in their tracks. In a moment the only green warriors upon the deck of the *Thuria* were dead warriors, and the bowmen of Kar Komak were leaping over the vessel's sides to charge the hordesmen upon the ground.

Utan after utan tumbled from the bowels of the *Thuria* to launch themselves upon the unfortunate green men. Kulan Tith and his Kaolians stood wide-eyed and speechless with amazement as they saw thousands of these strange, fierce warriors emerge from the companionway of the small craft that could not comfortably have accommodated more than fifty.

At last the green men could withstand the onslaught of overwhelming numbers no longer. Slowly, at first, they fell back across the ochre plain. The bowmen pursued them. Kar Komak, standing upon the deck of the *Thuria*, trembled with excitement.

At the top of his lungs he voiced the savage warcry of his forgotten day. He roared encouragement and commands at his battling utans, and then, as they charged further and further from the *Thuria*, he could no longer withstand the lure of battle.

Leaping over the ship's side to the ground, he joined the last of his bowmen as they raced off over the dead sea-bottom in pursuit of the fleeing green horde.

Beyond a low promontory of what once had been an island the green men were disappearing toward the west. Close upon their heels raced the fleet bowmen of a bygone day, and forging steadily ahead among them Carthoris and Thuvia could see the mighty figure of Kar Komak, brandishing aloft the Torquasian short-sword with which he was armed, as he urged

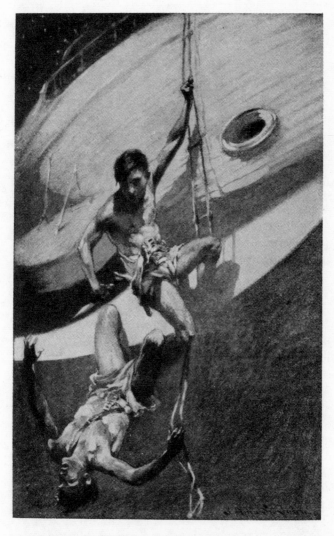

A steel blade pierced the very center of his heart.

"Stay, my chieftain. Stay — I love you!"

his creatures after the retreating enemy.

As the last of them disappeared behind the promontory, Carthoris turned toward Thuvia of Ptarth.

"They have taught me a lesson, these vanishing bowmen of Lothar," he said. "When they have served their purpose they remain not to embarrass their masters by their presence. Kulan Tith and his warriors are here to protect you. My acts have constituted the proof of my honesty of purpose. Good-by," and he knelt at her feet, raising a bit of her harness to his lips.

The girl reached out a hand and laid it upon the thick black hair of the head bent before her. Softly she asked:

"Where are you going, Carthoris?"

"With Kar Komak, the bowman," he replied. "There will be fighting and forgetfulness."

The girl put her hands before her eyes, as though to shut out some mighty temptation from her sight.

"May my ancestors have mercy upon me," she cried, "if I say the thing I have no right to say; but I cannot see you cast your life away, Carthoris, Prince of Helium! Stay, my chieftain. Stay—I love you!"

A cough behind them brought both about, and there they saw standing, not two paces from them, Kulan Tith, Jeddak of Kaol.

For a long moment none spoke. Then Kulan Tith cleared his throat.

"I could not help hearing all that passed," he said. "I am no fool, to be blind to the love that lies between you. Nor am I blind to the lofty honor that has caused you, Carthoris, to risk your life and hers to save mine, though you thought that that very act would rob you of the chance to keep her for your own.

"Nor can I fail to appreciate the virtue that has kept your lips sealed against words of love for this Heliumite, Thuvia, for I know that I have but just heard the first declaration of your passion for him. I do not condemn you. Rather should I have condemned you had you entered a loveless marriage with me.

"Take back your liberty, Thuvia of Ptarth," he cried, "and bestow it where your heart already lies enchained, and when the golden collars are clasped about your necks you will see

that Kulan Tith's is the first sword to be raised in declaration of eternal friendship for the new Princess of Helium
and her royal mate!"

The Chessmen of Mars

By

EDGAR RICE BURROUGHS

To the girl's horror, the headless body moved.

CONTENTS

A giant Martian rat was gnawing upon his arm!

Prelude

JOHN CARTER COMES TO EARTH

SHEA HAD JUST beaten me at chess, as usual, and, also as usual, I had gleaned what questionable satisfaction I might by twitting him with this indication of failing mentality by calling his attention for the nth time to that theory, propounded by certain scientists, which is based upon the assertion that phenomenal chess players are always found to be from the ranks of children under twelve, adults over seventy-two or the mentally defective—a theory that is lightly ignored upon those rare occasions that I win. Shea had gone to bed and I should have followed suit, for we are always in the saddle here before sunrise; but instead I sat there before the chess table in the library, idly blowing smoke at the dishonored head of my defeated king.

While thus profitably employed I heard the east door of the living-room open and someone enter. I thought it was Shea returning to speak with me on some matter of tomorrow's work; but when I raised my eyes to the doorway that connects the two rooms I saw framed there the figure of a bronzed giant, his otherwise naked body trapped with jewel-encrusted harness from which there hung at one side an ornate short-sword and at the other a pistol of strange pattern. The black hair, the steel-gray eyes, brave and smiling, the noble features—I recognized them at once, and leaping to my feet I advanced with outstretched hand.

"John Carter!" I cried. "You?"

"None other, my son," he replied, taking my hand in one of his and placing the other upon my shoulder.

"And what are you doing here?" I asked. "It has been long years since you revisited Earth, and never before in the trappings of Mars. Lord! but it is good to see you—and not a day older in appearance than when you trotted me on your knee in my babyhood. How do you explain it, John Carter, Warlord of Mars, or do you try to explain it?"

"Why attempt to explain the inexplicable?" he replied. "As I have told you before, I am a very old man. I do not

133

know how old I am. I recall no childhood; but recollect only
having been always as you see me now and as you saw me first
when you were five years old. You, yourself, have aged,
though not as much as most men in a corresponding number of years, which may be accounted for by the fact that the
same blood runs in our veins: but I have not aged at all. I
have discussed the question with a noted Martian scientist, a friend of mine; but his theories are still only theories.
However, I am content with the fact—I never age, and I love
life and the vigor of youth.

"And now as to your natural question as to what brings me
to Earth again and in this, to earthly eyes, strange habiliment.
We may thank Kar Komak, the bowman of Lothar. It was he
who gave me the idea upon which I have been experimenting
until at last I have achieved success. As you know I have long
possessed the power to cross the void in spirit, but never before have I been able to impart to inanimate things a similar
power. Now, however, you see me for the first time precisely
as my Martian fellows see me—you see the very short-sword
that has tasted the blood of many a savage foeman; the harness with the devices of Helium and the insignia of my rank;
the pistol that was presented to me by Tars Tarkas, Jeddak of
Thark.

"Aside from seeing you, which is my principal reason for
being here, and satisfying myself that I can transport inanimate things if I so desire, I have no purpose. Earth is not for me.
My every interest is upon Barsoom—my wife, my children,
my work; all are there. I will spend a quiet evening with you
and then back to the world I love even better than I love life."

As he spoke he dropped into the chair upon the opposite side
of the chess table.

"You spoke of children," I said. "Have you more than Carthoris?"

"A daughter," he replied, "only a little younger than Carthoris, and, barring one, the fairest thing that ever breathed the
thin air of dying Mars. Only Dejah Thoris, her mother, could
be more beautiful than Tara of Helium."

For a moment he fingered the chessmen idly. "We have a
game on Mars similar to chess," he said, "very similar. And
there is a race there that plays it grimly with men and naked
swords. We call the game *jetan*. It is played on a board like

yours, except that there are a hundred squares and we use twenty pieces on each side. I never see it played without thinking of Tara of Helium and what befell her among the chessmen of Barsoom. Would you like to hear her story?"

I said that I would and so he told it to me, and now I shall try to re-tell it for you as nearly in the words of The Warlord of Mars as I can recall them, but in the third person. If there be inconsistencies and errors, let the blame fall not upon John Carter, but rather upon my faulty memory, where it belongs. It is a strange tale and utterly Barsoomian.

Gahan of Gathol smote the man from his mount.

CHAPTER I

TARA IN A TANTRUM

TARA OF HELIUM rose from the pile of silks and soft furs upon which she had been reclining, stretched her lithe body languidly, and crossed toward the center of the room, where, above a large table a bronze disc depended from the low ceiling. Her carriage was that of health and physical perfection—the effortless harmony of faultless coordination. A scarf of silken gossamer crossing over one shoulder was wrapped about her body; her black hair was piled high upon her head. With a wooden stick she tapped upon the bronze disc, lightly, and presently the summons was answered by a slave girl, who entered, smiling, to be greeted similarly by her mistress.

"Are my father's guests arriving?" asked the princess.

"Yes, Tara of Helium, they come," replied the slave. "I have seen Kantos Kan, Overlord of the Navy, and Prince Soran of Ptarth, and Djor Kantos, son of Kantos Kan," she shot a roguish glance at her mistress as she mentioned Djor Kantos' name, "and—oh, there were others, many have come."

"The bath, then, Uthia," said her mistress. "And why, Uthia," she added, "do you look thus and smile when you mention the name of Djor Kantos?"

The slave girl laughed gaily. "It is so plain to all that he worships you," she replied.

"It is not plain to me," said Tara of Helium. "He is the friend of my brother, Carthoris, and so he is here much; but not to see me. It is his friendship for Carthoris that brings him thus often to the palace of my father."

"But Carthoris is hunting in the north with Talu, Jeddak of Okar," Uthia reminded her.

"My bath, Uthia!" cried Tara of Helium. "That tongue of yours will bring you to some misadventure yet."

"The bath is ready, Tara of Helium," the girl responded, her eyes still twinkling with merriment, for she well knew that in the heart of her mistress was no anger that could dis-

137

place the love of the princess for her slave. Preceding the
daughter of The Warlord she opened the door of an adjoining room where lay the bath—a gleaming pool of scented water in a marble basin. Golden stanchions supported a chain of
gold encircling it and leading down into the water on either
side of marble steps. A glass dome let in the sunlight, which
flooded the interior, glancing from the polished white of
marble walls and the procession of bathers and fishes, which,
in conventional design, were inlaid with gold in a broad band
that circled the room.

Tara of Helium removed the scarf from about her and
handed it to the slave. Slowly she descended the steps to the
water, the temperature of which she tested with a symmetrical
foot, undeformed by tight shoes and high heels—a lovely foot,
as God intended that feet should be and seldom are. Finding
the water to her liking, the girl swam leisurely to and fro
about the pool. With the silken ease of the seal she swam,
now at the surface now below, her smooth muscles rolling
softly beneath her clear skin—a wordless song of health and
happiness and grace. Presently she emerged and gave herself into the hands of the slave girl, who rubbed the body of
her mistress with a sweet smelling semi-liquid substance
contained in a golden urn, until the glowing skin was covered
with a foamy lather, then a quick plunge into the pool, a dry-
ing with soft towels, and the bath was over. Typical of the
life of the princess was the simple elegance of her bath—no
retinue of useless slaves, no pomp, no idle waste of precious
moments. In another half hour her hair was dried and built
into the strange, but becoming, coiffure of her station; her
leathern trappings, encrusted with gold and jewels, had been
adjusted to her figure and she was ready to mingle with the
guests that had been bidden to the midday function at the
palace of The Warlord.

As she left her apartments to make her way to the gardens
where the guests were congregating, two warriors, the insignia of the House of the Prince of Helium upon their harness, followed a few paces behind her, grim reminders that
the assassin's blade may never be ignored upon Barsoom,
where, in a measure, it counterbalances the great natural
span of human life, which is estimated at not less than a
thousand years.

As they neared the entrance to the garden another woman, similarly guarded, approached them from another quarter of the great palace. As she neared them Tara of Helium turned toward her with a smile and a happy greeting, while her guards knelt with bowed heads in willing and voluntary adoration of the beloved of Helium. Thus always, solely at the command of their own hearts, did the warriors of Helium greet Dejah Thoris, whose deathless beauty had more than once brought them to bloody warfare with other nations of Barsoom. So great was the love of the people of Helium for the mate of John Carter it amounted practically to worship, as though she were indeed the goddess that she looked.

The mother and daughter exchanged the gentle, Barsoomian, "kaor" of greeting and kissed. Then together they entered the gardens where the guests were. A huge warrior drew his short-sword and struck his metal shield with the flat of it, the brazen sound ringing out above the laughter and the speech.

"The Princess comes!" he cried. "Dejah Thoris! The Princess comes! Tara of Helium!" Thus always is royalty announced. The guests arose; the two women inclined their heads; the guards fell back upon either side of the entrance-way; a number of nobles advanced to pay their respects; the laughing and the talking were resumed and Dejah Thoris and her daughter moved simply and naturally among their guests, no suggestion of differing rank apparent in the bearing of any who were there, though there was more than a single Jeddak and many common warriors whose only title lay in brave deeds, or noble patriotism. Thus it is upon Mars where men are judged upon their own merits rather than upon those of their grandsires, even though pride of lineage be great.

Tara of Helium let her slow gaze wander among the throng of guests until presently it halted upon one she sought. Was the faint shadow of a frown that crossed her brow an indication of displeasure at the sight that met her eyes, or did the brilliant rays of the noonday sun distress her? Who may say! She had been reared to believe that one day she should wed Djor Kantos, son of her father's best friend. It had been the dearest wish of Kantos Kan and The Warlord that this should be, and Tara of Helium had accepted it as a mat-

ter of all but accomplished fact. Djor Kantos had seemed to
accept the matter in the same way. They had spoken of it
casually as something that would, as a matter of course, take
place in the indefinite future, as, for instance, his promotion
in the navy, in which he was now a padwar; or the set functions of the court of her grandfather, Tardos Mors, Jeddak of
Helium; or Death. They had never spoken of love and that
had puzzled Tara of Helium upon the rare occasions she
gave it thought, for she knew that people who were to wed
were usually much occupied with the matter of love and she
had all of a woman's curiosity—she wondered what love was
like. She was very fond of Djor Kantos and she knew that he
was very fond of her. They liked to be together, for they
liked the same things and the same people and the same
books and their dancing was a joy, not only to themselves but
to those who watched them. She could not imagine wanting
to marry anyone other than Djor Kantos.

So perhaps it was only the sun that made her brows contract just the tiniest bit at the same instant that she discovered Djor Kantos sitting in earnest conversation with Olvia Marthis, daughter of the Jed of Hastor. It was Djor Kantos' duty immediately to pay his respects to Dejah Thoris and
Tara of Helium; but he did not do so and presently the
daughter of The Warlord frowned indeed. She looked long
?t Olvia Marthis, and though she had seen her many times
before and knew her well, she looked at her today through
new eyes that saw, apparently for the first time, that the girl
from Hastor was noticeably beautiful even among those
other beautiful women of Helium. Tara of Helium was disturbed. She attempted to analyze her emotions; but found
it difficult. Olvia Marthis was her friend—she was very fond of
her and she felt no anger toward her. Was she angry with
Djor Kantos? No, she finally decided that she was not. It was
merely surprise, then, that she felt—surprise that Djor Kantos
could be more interested in another than in herself. She was
about to cross the garden and join them when she heard her
father's voice directly behind her.

"Tara of Helium!" he called, and she turned to see him
approaching with a strange warrior whose harness and metal
bore devices with which she was unfamiliar. Even among the
gorgeous trappings of the men of Helium and the visitors

from distant empires those of the stranger were remarkable for their barbaric splendor. The leather of his harness was completely hidden beneath ornaments of platinum thickly set with brilliant diamonds, as were the scabbards of his swords and the ornate holster that held his long, Martian pistol. Moving through the sunlit garden at the side of the great Warlord, the scintillant rays of his countless gems enveloping him as in an aureole of light imparted to his noble figure a suggestion of godliness.

"Tara of Helium, I bring you Gahan, Jed of Gathol," said John Carter, after the simple Barsoomian custom of presentation.

"Kaor! Gahan, Jed of Gathol," returned Tara of Helium.

"My sword is at your feet, Tara of Helium," said the young chieftain.

The Warlord left them and the two seated themselves upon an ersite bench beneath a spreading sorapus tree.

"Far Gathol," mused the girl. "Ever in my mind has it been connected with mystery and romance and the half-forgotten lore of the ancients. I cannot think of Gathol as existing today, possibly because I have never before seen a Gatholian."

"And perhaps too because of the great distance that separates Helium and Gathol, as well as the comparative insignificance of my little free city, which might easily be lost in one corner of mighty Helium," added Gahan. "But what we lack in power we make up in pride," he continued, laughing. "We believe ours the oldest inhabited city upon Barsoom. It is one of the few that has retained its freedom, and this despite the fact that its ancient diamond mines are the richest known and, unlike practically all the other fields, are today apparently as inexhaustible as ever."

"Tell me of Gathol," urged the girl. "The very thought fills me with interest," nor was it likely that the handsome face of the young jed detracted anything from the glamour of far Gathol.

Nor did Gahan seem displeased with the excuse for further monopolizing the society of his fair companion. His eyes seemed chained to her exquisite features, from which they moved no further than to a rounded breast, part hid beneath its jeweled covering, a naked shoulder or the symmetry of a perfect arm, resplendent in bracelets of barbaric magnificence.

"Your ancient history has doubtless told you that Gathol was built upon an island in Throxeus, mightiest of the five oceans of old Barsoom. As the ocean receded Gathol crept down the sides of the mountain, the summit of which was the island upon which she had been built, until today she covers the slopes from summit to base, while the bowels of the great hill are honeycombed with the galleries of her mines. Entirely surrounding us is a great salt marsh, which protects us from invasion by land, while the rugged and oft-times vertical topography of our mountain renders the landing of hostile airships a precarious undertaking.

"That, and your brave warriors?" suggested the girl.

Gahan smiled. "We do not speak of that except to enemies," he said, "and then with tongues of steel rather than of flesh."

"But what practice in the art of war has a people which nature has thus protected from attack?" asked Tara of Helium, who had liked the young jed's answer to her previous question, but yet in whose mind persisted a vague conviction of the possible effeminacy of her companion, induced, doubtless, by the magnificence of his trappings and weapons which carried a suggestion of splendid show rather than grim utility.

"Our natural barriers, while they have doubtless saved us from defeat on countless occasions, have not by any means rendered us immune from attack," he explained, "for so great is the wealth of Gathol's diamond treasury that there yet may be found those who will risk almost certain defeat in an effort to loot our unconquered city; so thus we find occasional practice in the exercise of arms; but there is more to Gathol than the mountain city. My country extends from Polodona (Equator) north ten karads and from the tenth karad west of Horz to the twentieth west, including thus a million square haads, the greater proportion of which is fine grazing land where run our great herds of thoats and zitidars.

"Surrounded as we are by predatory enemies our herdsmen must indeed be warriors or we should have no herds, and you may be assured they get plenty of fighting. Then there is our constant need of workers in the mines. The Gatholians

consider themselves a race of warriors and as such prefer not
to labor in the mines. The law is, however, that each male
Gatholian shall give an hour a day in labor to the government. That is practically the only tax that is levied upon
them. They prefer however, to furnish a substitute to perform this labor, and as our own people will not hire out for
labor in the mines it has been necessary to obtain slaves,
and I do not need to tell you that slaves are not won without
fighting. We sell these slaves in the public market, the pro-
ceeds going, half and half, to the government and the warriors who bring them in. The purchasers are credited with
the amount of labor performed by their particular slaves.
At the end of a year a good slave will have performed the
labor tax of his master for six years, and if slaves are plentiful
he is freed and permitted to return to his own people."

"You fight in platinum and diamonds?" asked Tara, indicating his gorgeous trappings with a quizzical smile.

Gahan laughed. "We are a vain people," he admitted,
good-naturedly, "and it is possible that we place too much
value on personal appearances. We vie with one another in
the splendor of our accoutrements when trapped for the
observance of the lighter duties of life, though when we take
the field our leather is the plainest I ever have seen worn by
fighting men of Barsoom. We pride ourselves, too, upon our
physical beauty, and especially upon the beauty of our women.
May I dare to say, Tara of Helium, that I am hoping for the
day when you will visit Gathol that my people may see one
who is really beautiful?"

"The women of Helium are taught to frown with displeasure upon the tongue of the flatterer," rejoined the girl,
but Gahan, Jed of Gathol, observed that she smiled as she
said it.

A bugle sounded, clear and sweet, above the laughter and
the talk. "The Dance of Barsoom!" exclaimed the young
warrior. "I claim you for it, Tara of Helium."

The girl glanced in the direction of the bench where she
had last seen Djor Kantos. He was not in sight. She inclined
her head in assent to the claim of the Gatholian. Slaves were
passing among the guests, distributing small musical instruments of a single string. Upon each instrument were
characters which indicated the pitch and length of its tone.

The instruments were of skeel, the string of gut, and were shaped to fit the left forearm of the dancer, to which it was strapped. There was also a ring wound with gut which was worn between the first and second joints of the index finger of the right hand and which, when passed over the string of the instrument, elicited the single note required of the dancer.

The guests had risen and were slowly making their way toward the expanse of scarlet sward at the south end of the gardens where the dance was to be held, when Djor Kantos came hurriedly toward Tara of Helium. "I claim—" he exclaimed as he neared her; but she interrupted him with a gesture.

"You are too late, Djor Kantos," she cried in mock anger. "No laggard may claim Tara of Helium; but haste now lest thou lose also Olvia Marthis, whom I have never seen wait long to be claimed for this or any other dance."

"I have already lost her," admitted Djor Kantos ruefully.

"And you mean to say that you came for Tara of Helium only after having lost Olvia Marthis?" demanded the girl, still simulating displeasure.

"Oh, Tara of Helium, you know better than that," insisted the young man. "Was it not natural that I should assume that you would expect me, who alone has claimed you for the Dance of Barsoom for at least twelve times past?"

"And sit and play with my thumbs until you saw fit to come for me?" she questioned. "Ah, no, Djor Kantos; Tara of Helium is for no laggard," and she threw him a sweet smile and passed on toward the assembling dancers with Gahan, Jed of far Gathol.

The Dance of Barsoom bears a relation similar to the more formal dancing functions of Mars that The Grand March does to ours, though it is infinitely more intricate and more beautiful. Before a Martian youth of either sex may attend an important social function where there is dancing, he must have become proficient in at least three dances—The Dance of Barsoom, his national dance, and the dance of his city. In these three dances the dancers furnish their own music, which never varies; nor do the steps or figures vary, having been handed down from time immemorial. All Barsoomian dances are stately and beautiful, but The Dance of Barsoom is a

wondrous epic of motion and harmony—there is no grotesque posturing, no vulgar or suggestive movements. It has
been described as the interpretation of the highest ideals of a
world that aspired to grace and beauty and chastity in
woman, and strength and dignity and loyalty in man.

Today, John Carter, Warlord of Mars, with Dejah Thoris,
his mate, led in the dancing, and if there was another couple
that vied with them in possession of the silent admiration of
the guests it was the resplendent Jed of Gathol and his beautiful partner. In the ever-changing figures of the dance the
man found himself now with the girl's hand in his and again
with an arm about the lithe body that the jeweled harness
but inadequately covered, and the girl, though she had
danced a thousand dances in the past, realized for the first
time the personal contact of a man's arm against her naked
flesh. It troubled her that she should notice it, and she looked
up questioningly and almost with displeasure at the man
as though it was his fault. Their eyes met and she saw
in his that which she had never seen in the eyes of Djor
Kantos. It was at the very end of the dance and they both
stopped suddenly with the music and stood there looking
straight into each other's eyes. It was Gahan of Gathol who
spoke first.

"Tara of Helium, I love you!" he said.

The girl drew herself to her full height. "The Jed of
Gathol forgets himself," she exclaimed haughtily.

"The Jed of Gathol would forget everything but you, Tara
of Helium," he replied. Fiercely he pressed the soft hand that
he still retained from the last position of the dance. "I love
you, Tara of Helium," he repeated. "Why should your ears
refuse to hear what your eyes but just now did not refuse to
see—and answer?"

"What meanest thou?" she cried. "Are the men of Gathol
such boors, then?"

"They are neither boors nor fools," he replied, quietly.
"They know when they love a woman—and when she loves
them."

Tara of Helium stamped her little foot in anger. "Go!" she
said, "before it is necessary to acquaint my father with the
dishonor of his guest."

She turned and walked away. "Wait!" cried the man. "Just

another word."

"Of apology?" she asked.

"Of prophecy," he said.

"I do not care to hear it," replied Tara of Helium, and left him standing there. She was strangely unstrung and shortly thereafter returned to her own quarter of the palace, where she stood for a long time by a window looking out beyond the scarlet tower of Greater Helium toward the northwest.

Presently she turned angrily away. "I hate him!" she exclaimed aloud.

"Whom?" inquired the privileged Uthia.

Tara of Helium stamped her foot. "That ill-mannered boor, the Jed of Gathol," she replied.

Uthia raised her slim brows.

At the stamping of the little foot, a great beast rose from the corner of the room and crossed to Tara of Helium where it stood looking up into her face. She placed her hand upon the ugly head. "Dear old Woola," she said; "no love could be deeper than yours, yet it never offends. Would that men might pattern themselves after you!"

CHAPTER II

AT THE GALE'S MERCY

TARA OF HELIUM did not return to her father's guests, but awaited in her own apartments the word from Djor Kantos which she knew must come, begging her to return to the gardens. She would then refuse, haughtily. But no appeal came from Djor Kantos. At first Tara of Helium was angry, then she was hurt, and always she was puzzled. She could not understand. Occasionally she thought of the Jed of Gathol and then she would stamp her foot, for she was very angry indeed with Gahan. The presumption of the man! He had insinuated that he read love for him in her eyes. Never had she been so insulted and humiliated. Never had she so thoroughly hated a man. Suddenly she turned toward Uthia.

"My flying leather!" she commanded.

"But the guests!" exclaimed the slave girl, "Your father, The Warlord, will expect you to return."

"He will be disappointed," snapped Tara of Helium.

The slave hesitated. "He does not approve of your flying alone," she reminded her mistress.

The young princess sprang to her feet and seized the unhappy slave by the shoulders, shaking her. "You are becoming unbearable, Uthia," she cried. "Soon there will be no alternative than to send you to the public slave-market. Then possibly you will find a master to your liking."

Tears came to the soft eyes of the slave girl. "It is because I love you, my princess," she said softly. Instantly Tara of Helium melted. She took the slave in her arms and kissed her.

"I have the disposition of a thoat, Uthia," she said. "Forgive me! I love you and there is nothing that I would not do for you and nothing would I do to harm you. Again, as I have so often in the past, I offer you your freedom."

"I do not wish my freedom if it will separate me from you, Tara of Helium," replied Uthia. "I am happy here with you —I think that I should die without you."

Again the girls kissed. "And you will not fly alone, then?" questioned the slave.

Tara of Helium laughed and pinched her companion. "You persistent little pest," she cried. "Of course I shall fly—does not Tara of Helium always do that which pleases her?"

Uthia shook her head sorrowfully. "Alas! she does," she admitted. "Iron is the Warlord of Barsoom to the influences of all but two. In the hands of Dejah Thoris and Tara of Helium he is as potters' clay."

"Then run and fetch my flying leather like the sweet slave you are," directed the mistress.

Far out across the ochre sea-bottoms beyond the twin cities of Helium raced the swift flier of Tara of Helium. Thrilling to the speed and the buoyancy and the obedience of the little craft the girl drove toward the northwest. Why she should choose that direction she did not pause to consider. Perhaps because in that direction lay the least known areas of Barsoom, and, *ergo*, Romance, Mystery, and Adventure. In that direction also lay far Gathol; but to that fact she gave no conscious thought.

She did, however, think occasionally of the jed of that distant kingdom, but the reaction to these thoughts was scarcely pleasurable. They still brought a flush of shame to her cheeks and a surge of angry blood to her heart. She was very angry with the Jed of Gathol, and though she should never see him again she was quite sure that hate of him would remain fresh in her memory forever. Mostly her thoughts revolved about another—Djor Kantos. And when she thought of him she thought also of Olvia Marthis of Hastor. Tara of Helium thought that she was jealous of the fair Olvia and it made her very angry to think that. She was angry with Djor Kantos and herself, but she was not angry at all with Olvia Marthis, whom she loved, and so of course she was not jealous really. The trouble was, that Tara of Helium had failed for once to have her own way. Djor Kantos had not come running like a willing slave when she had expected him, and, ah, here was the nub of the whole thing! Gahan, Jed of Gathol, a stranger, had been a witness to her humiliation. He had seen her unclaimed at the beginning of a great function and he had had to come to her rescue to save her, as he doubtless thought, from the inglorious fate of a wallflower. At the recurring thought, Tara of Helium could feel her whole body burning with scarlet shame and then she went suddenly white and cold with rage; whereupon she turned her flier about so abruptly that she was all but torn from her lashings upon the flat, narrow deck. She reached home just before dark. The guests had departed. Quiet had descended upon the palace. An hour later she joined her father and mother at the evening meal.

"You deserted us, Tara of Helium," said John Carter. "It is not what the guests of John Carter should expect."

"They did not come to see me," replied Tara of Helium. "I did not ask them."

"They were no less your guests," replied her father.

The girl rose, and came and stood beside him and put her arms about his neck.

"My proper old Virginian," she cried, rumpling his shock of black hair.

"In Virginia you would be turned over your father's knee and spanked," said the man smiling.

She crept into his lap and kissed him. "You do not love me any more," she announced. "No one loves me," but she could not compose her features into a pout because bubbling laughter insisted upon breaking through.

"The trouble is there are too many who love you," he said. "And now there is another."

"Indeed!" she cried. "What do you mean?"

"Gahan of Gathol has asked permission to woo you."

The girl sat up very straight and tilted her chin in the air. "I would not wed with a walking diamond-mine," she said. "I will not have him."

"I told him as much," replied her father, "and that you were as good as betrothed to another. He was very courteous about it; but at the same time he gave me to understand that he was accustomed to getting what he wanted and that he wanted you very much. I suppose it will mean another war. Your mother's beauty kept Helium at war for many years, and—well, Tara of Helium, if I were a young man I should doubtless be willing to set all Barsoom afire to win you, as I still would to keep your divine mother," and he smiled across the sorapus table and its golden service at the undimmed beauty of Mars' most beautiful woman.

"Our little girl should not yet be troubled with such matters," said Dejah Thoris. "Remember, John Carter, that you are not dealing with an Earth child whose span of life would be more than half completed before a daughter of Barsoom reached actual maturity."

"But do not the daughters of Barsoom sometimes marry as early as twenty?" he insisted.

"Yes, but they may still be desirable in the eyes of men after forty generations of Earth folk have returned to dust—there is no hurry, at least, upon Barsoom. We do not fade and decay here as you tell me those of your planet do, though you, yourself, belie your own words. When the time seems proper Tara of Helium shall wed with Djor Kantos, and until then let us give the matter no further thought."

"No," said the girl, "the subject irks me, and I shall not marry Djor Kantos, or another—I do not intend to wed."

Her father and mother looked at her and smiled. "When Gahan of Gathol returns he may carry you off," said the former.

"He has gone?" asked the girl.

"His flier departs for Gathol in the morning," John Carter replied.

"I have seen the last of him then," remarked Tara of Helium with a sigh of relief.

"He says not," returned John Carter.

The girl dismissed the subject with a shrug and the conversation passed to other topics. A letter had arrived from Thuvia of Ptarth, who was visiting at her father's court while Carthoris, her mate, hunted in Okar. Word had been received that the Tharks and Warhoons were again at war, or rather that there had been an engagement, for war was their habitual state. In the memory of man there had been no peace between these two savage green hordes—and only a single temporary truce. Two new battleships had been launched at Hastor. A little band of holy therns was attempting to revive the ancient and discredited religion of Issus, who they claimed still lived in spirit and had communicated with them. There were rumors of war from Dusar. A scientist claimed to have discovered human life on the further moon. A madman had attempted to destroy the atmosphere plant. Seven people had been assassinated in Greater Helium during the last ten zodes (the equivalent of an Earth day).

Following the meal Dejah Thoris and The Warlord played at jetan, the Barsoomian game of chess, which is played upon a board of a hundred alternate black and orange squares. One player has twenty black pieces, the other, twenty orange pieces. A brief description of the game may interest those Earth readers who care for chess, and will not be lost upon those who pursue this narrative to its conclusion, since before they are done they will find that a knowledge of jetan will add to the interest and the thrills that are in store for them.

The men are placed upon the board as in chess upon the first two rows next the players. In order from left to right on the line of squares nearest the players, the jetan pieces are Warrior, Padwar, Dwar, Flier, Chief, Princess, Flier, Dwar, Padwar, Warrior. In the next line all are Panthans except the end pieces, which are called Thoats, and represent mounted warriors.

The Panthans, which are represented as warriors with one feather, may move one space in any direction except backward; the Thoats, mounted warriors with three feathers, may move one straight and one diagonal, and may jump intervening pieces; Warriors, foot soldiers with two feathers, straight in any direction, or diagonally, two spaces; Padwars, lieutenants wearing two feathers, two diagonal in any direction, or combination; Dwars, captains wearing three feathers, three spaces straight in any direction, or combination; Fliers, represented by a propellor with three blades, three spaces in any direction, or combination, diagonally, and may jump intervening pieces; the Chief, indicated by a diadem with ten jewels, three spaces in any direction, straight, or diagonal; Princess, diadem with a single jewel, same as Chief, and can jump intervening pieces.

The game is won when a player places any of his pieces on the same square with his opponent's Princess, or when a Chief takes a Chief. It is drawn when a Chief is taken by any opposing piece other than the opposing Chief; or when both sides have been reduced to three pieces, or less, of equal value, and the game is not terminated in the following ten moves, five apiece. This is but a general outline of the game, briefly stated.

It was this game that Dejah Thoris and John Carter were playing when Tara of Helium bid them good night, retiring to her own quarters and her sleeping silks and furs. "Until morning, my beloved," she called back to them as she passed from the apartment, nor little did she guess, nor her parents, that this might indeed be the last time that they would ever set eyes upon her.

The morning broke dull and gray. Ominous clouds billowed restlessly and low. Beneath them torn fragments scudded toward the northwest. From her window Tara of Helium looked out upon this unusual scene. Dense clouds seldom overcast the Barsoomian sky. At this hour of the day it was her custom to ride one of those small thoats that are the saddle animals of the red Martians, but the sight of the billowing clouds lured her to a new adventure. Uthia still slept and the girl did not disturb her. Instead, she dressed quietly and went to the hangar upon the roof of the palace directly above her quarters where her own swift flier was housed. She had never driven through the clouds. It was an adventure that always she had longed to experience. The

wind was strong and it was with difficulty that she maneu-
vered the craft from the hangar without accident, but once
away it raced swiftly out above the twin cities. The buffeting
winds caught and tossed it, and the girl laughed aloud in
sheer joy of the resultant thrills. She handled the little ship
like a veteran, though few veterans would have faced the
menace of such a storm in so light a craft. Swiftly she rose
toward the clouds, racing with the scudding streamers of the
storm-swept fragments, and a moment later she was swal-
lowed by the dense masses billowing above. Here was a new
world, a world of chaos unpeopled except for herself; but it
was a cold, damp, lonely world and she found it depressing
after the novelty of it had been dissipated, by an overpower-
ing sense of the magnitude of the forces surging about her.
Suddenly she felt very lonely and very cold and very little.
Hurriedly, therefore, she rose until presently her craft broke
through into the glorious sunlight that transformed the upper surface of the somber element into rolling masses of
burnished silver. Here it was still cold, but without the
dampness of the clouds, and in the eye of the brilliant sun her
spirits rose with the mounting needle of her altimeter. Gazing
at the clouds, now far beneath, the girl experienced the sensation of hanging stationary in mid-heaven; but the whirring
of her propellor, the wind beating upon her, the high figures
that rose and fell beneath the glass of her speedometer, these
told her that her speed was terrific. It was then that she determined to turn back.

The first attempt she made above the clouds, but it was
unsuccessful. To her surprise she discovered that she could
not even turn against the high wind, which rocked and buffeted the frail craft. Then she dropped swiftly to the dark
and wind-swept zone between the hurtling clouds and the
gloomy surface of the shadowed ground. Here she tried
again to force the nose of the flier back toward Helium, but
the tempest seized the frail thing and hurled it remorselessly
about, rolling it over and over and tossing it as it were a cork
in a cataract. At last the girl succeeded in righting the flier,
perilously close to the ground. Never before had she been so
close to death, yet she was not terrified. Her coolness had
saved her, that and the strength of the deck lashings that held
her. Traveling with the storm she was safe, but where was it

bearing her? She pictured the apprehension of her father and mother when she failed to appear at the morning meal. They would find her flier missing and they would guess that somewhere in the path of the storm it lay a wrecked and tangled mass upon her dead body, and then brave men would go out in search of her, risking their lives; and that lives would be lost in the search, she knew, for she realized now that never in her lifetime had such a tempest raged upon Barsoom.

She must turn back! She must reach Helium before her mad lust for thrills had cost the sacrifice of a single courageous life! She determined that greater safety and likelihood of success lay above the clouds, and once again she rose through the chilling, wind-tossed vapor. Her speed again was terrific, for the wind seemed to have increased rather than to have lessened. She sought gradually to check the swift flight of her craft, but though she finally succeeded in reversing her motor the wind but carried her on as it would. Then it was that Tara of Helium lost her temper. Had her world not always bowed in acquiescence to her every wish? What were these elements that they dared 'to thwart her? She would demonstrate to them that the daughter of The Warlord was not to be denied! They would learn that Tara of Helium might not be ruled even by the forces of nature!

And so she drove her motor forward again and then with her firm, white teeth set in grim determination she drove the steering lever far down to port with the intention of forcing the nose of her craft straight into the teeth of the wind, and the wind seized the frail thing and toppled it over upon its back, and twisted and turned it and hurled it over and over; the propeller raced for an instant in an air pocket and then the tempest seized it again and twisted it from its shaft, leaving the girl helpless upon an unmanageable atom that rose and fell, and rolled and tumbled—the sport of the elements she had defied. Tara of Helium's first sensation was one of surprise—that she had failed to have her own way. Then she commenced to feel concern—not for her own safety but for the anxiety of her parents and the dangers that the inevitable searchers must face. She reproached herself for the thoughtless selfishness that had jeopardized the peace and safety of others. She realized her own grave danger, too; but she was still unterrified, as befitted the daughter of Dejah

Thoris and John Carter. She knew that her buoyancy tanks might keep her afloat indefinitely, but she had neither food nor water, and she was being borne toward the least-known area of Barsoom. Perhaps it would be better to land immediately and await the coming of the searchers, rather than to allow herself to be carried still further from Helium, thus greatly reducing the chances of early discovery; but when she dropped toward the ground she discovered that the violence of the wind rendered an attempt to land tantamount to destruction and she rose again, rapidly.

Carried along a few hundred feet above the ground she was better able to appreciate the Titanic proportions of the storm than when she had flown in the comparative serenity of the zone above the clouds, for now she could distinctly see the effect of the wind upon the surface of Barsoom. The air was filled with dust and flying bits of vegetation and when the storm carried her across an irrigated area of farm land she saw great trees and stone walls and buildings lifted high in air and scattered broadcast over the devastated country; and then she was carried swiftly on to other sights that forced in upon her consciousness a rapidly growing conviction that after all Tara of Helium was a very small and insignificant and helpless person. It was quite a shock to her self-pride while it lasted, and toward evening she was ready to believe that it was going to last forever. There had been no abatement in the ferocity of the tempest, nor was there indication of any. She could only guess at the distance she had been carried for she could not believe in the correctness of the high figures that had been piled upon the record of her odometer. They seemed unbelievable and yet, had she known it, they were quite true—in twelve hours she had flown and been carried by the storm full seven thousand haads. Just before dark she was carried over one of the deserted cities of ancient Mars. It was Torquas, but she did not know it. Had she, she might readily have been forgiven for abandoning the last vestige of hope, for to the people of Helium Torquas seems as remote as do the South Sea Islands to us. And still the tempest, its fury unabated, bore her on.

All that night she hurtled through the dark beneath the clouds, or rose to race through the moonlit void beneath the glory of Barsoom's two satellites. She was cold and hungry and altogether miserable, but her brave little spirit refused to admit that her plight was hopeless even though reason proclaimed the truth. Her reply to reason, sometimes spoken aloud in sudden defiance, recalled the Spartan stubbornness of her sire in the face of certain annihilation: "I still live!"

That morning there had been an early visitor at the palace of The Warlord. It was Gahan, Jed of Gathol. He had arrived shortly after the absence of Tara of Helium had been noted, and in the excitement he had remained unannounced until John Carter had happened upon him in the great reception corridor of the palace as The Warlord was hurrying out to arrange for the dispatch of ships in search of his daughter.

Gahan read the concern upon the face of The Warlord. "Forgive me if I intrude, John Carter," he said. "I but came to ask the indulgence of another day since it would be foolhardy to attempt to navigate a ship in such a storm."

"Remain, Gahan, a welcome guest until you choose to leave us," replied The Warlord; "but you must forgive any seeming inattention upon the part of Helium until my daughter is restored to us."

"Your daughter! Restored! What do you mean?" exclaimed the Gatholian. "I do not understand."

"She is gone, together with her light flier. That is all we know. We can only assume that she decided to fly before the morning meal and was caught in the clutches of the tempest. You will pardon me, Gahan, if I leave you abruptly—I am arranging to send ships in search of her;" but Gahan, Jed of Gathol, was already speeding in the direction of the palace gate. There he leaped upon a waiting thoat and followed by two warriors in the metal of Gathol, he dashed through the avenues of Helium toward the palace that had been set aside for his entertainment.

CHAPTER III

THE HEADLESS HUMANS

ABOVE THE ROOF of the palace that housed the Jed of Gathol and his entourage, the cruiser *Vanator* tore at her stout moorings. The groaning tackle bespoke the mad fury of the gale, while the worried faces of those members of the crew whose duties demanded their presence on the straining craft gave corroborative evidence of the gravity of the situation. Only stout lashings prevented these men from being swept from the deck, while those upon the roof below were constantly compelled to cling to rails and stanchions to save themselves from being carried away by each new burst of meteoric fury. Upon the prow of the *Vanator* was painted the device of Gathol, but no pennants were displayed in the upper works since the storm had carried away several in rapid succession, just as it seemed to the watching men that it must carry away the ship itself. They could not believe that any tackle could withstand for long this Titanic force. To each of the twelve lashings clung a brawny warrior with drawn short-sword. Had but a single mooring given to the power of the tempest eleven short-swords would have cut the others; since, partially moored, the ship was doomed, while free in the tempest it stood at least some slight chance for life.

"By the blood of Issus, I believe they will hold!" screamed one warrior to another.

"And they do not hold may the spirits of our ancestors reward the brave warriors upon the *Vanator*," replied another of those upon the roof of the palace, "for it will not be long from the moment her cables part before her crew dons the leather of the dead; but yet, Tanus, I believe they will hold. Give thanks at least that we did not sail before the tempest fell, since now each of us has a chance to live."

"Yes," replied Tanus, "I should hate to be abroad today upon the stoutest ship that sails the Barsoomian sky."

It was then that Gahan the Jed appeared upon the roof. With him were the balance of his own party and a dozen warriors of Helium. The young chief turned to his followers.

"I sail at once upon the *Vanator*," he said, "in search of Tara

156

of Helium who is thought to have been carried away upon
a one-man flier by the storm. I do not need to explain to you
the slender chances the *Vanator* has to withstand the fury of
the tempest, nor will I order you to your deaths. Let those
who wish remain behind without dishonor. The others will
follow me," and he leaped for the rope ladder that lashed
wildly in the gale.

The first man to follow him was Tanus and when the last
reached the deck of the cruiser there remained upon the palace roof only the twelve warriors of Helium, who, with naked
swords, had taken the posts of the Gatholians at the moorings.

Not a single warrior who had remained aboard the *Vanator*
would leave her now.

"I expected no less," said Gahan, as with the help of those
already on the deck he and the others found secure lashings.
The commander of the *Vanator* shook his head. He loved
his trim craft, the pride of her class in the little navy of Gathol.
It was of her he thought—not of himself. He saw her lying
torn and twisted upon the ochre vegetation of some distant
sea-bottom, to be presently overrun and looted by some savage, green horde. He looked at Gahan.

"Are you ready, San Tothis?" asked the jed.

"All is ready."

"Then cut away!"

Word was passed across the deck and over the side to
the Heliumetic warriors below that at the third gun they
were to cut away. Twelve keen swords must strike simultaneously and with equal power, and each must sever completely
and instantly three strands of heavy cable that no loose end
fouling a block bring immediate disaster upon the *Vanator*.

Boom! The voice of the signal gun rolled down through the
screaming wind to the twelve warriors upon the roof. *Boom!*
Twelve swords were raised above twelve brawny shoulders.
Boom! Twelve keen edges severed twelve complaining moorings clean and as one.

The *Vanator*, her propellors whirling, shot forward with
the storm. The tempest struck her in the stern as with a
mailed fist and stood the great ship upon her nose, and then
it caught her and spun her as a child's top spins; and upon
the palace roof the twelve men looked on in silent helplessness
and prayed for the souls of the brave warriors who were go-

ing to their death. And others saw, from Helium's lofty landing stages and from a thousand hangars upon a thousand
roofs; but only for an instant did the preparations stop that
would send other brave men into the frightful maelstrom
of that apparently hopeless search, for such is the courage of
the warriors of Barsoom.

But the *Vanator* did not fall to the ground, within sight of
the city at least, though as long as the watchers could see her
never for an instant did she rest upon an even keel. Sometime
she lay upon one side or the other, or again she hurtled along
keel up, or rolled over and over, or stood upon her nose or her
tail at the caprice of the great force that carried her along.
And the watchers saw that this great ship was merely being
blown away with the other bits of débris great and small that
filled the sky. Never in the memory of man or the annals of
recorded history had such a storm raged across the face of
Barsoom.

And in another instant was the *Vanator* forgotten as the
lofty, scarlet tower that had marked Lesser Helium for ages
crashed to ground, carrying death and demolition upon
the city beneath. Panic reigned. A fire broke out in the ruins.
The city's every force seemed crippled, and it was then that
The Warlord ordered the men that were about to set forth
in search of Tara of Helium to devote their energies to the
salvation of the city, for he too had witnessed the start of the
Vanator and realized the futility of wasting men who were
needed sorely if Lesser Helium was to be saved from utter destruction.

Shortly after noon of the second day the storm commenced
to abate, and before the sun went down, the little craft upon
which Tara of Helium had hovered between life and death
these many hours drifted slowly before a gentle breeze above
a landscape of rolling hills that once had been lofty mountains upon a Martian continent. The girl was exhausted from
loss of sleep, from lack of food and drink, and from the nervous reaction consequent to the terrifying experiences through
which she had passed. In the near distance, just topping an
intervening hill, she caught a momentary glimpse of what appeared to be a dome-capped tower. Quickly she dropped the
flier until the hill shut it off from the view of the possible
occupants of the structure she had seen. The tower meant to

her the habitation of man, suggesting the presence of water and perhaps, of food. If the tower was the deserted relic of a bygone age she would scarcely find food there, but there was still a chance that there might be water. If it was inhabited, then must her approach be cautious, for only enemies might be expected to abide in so far distant a land. Tara of Helium knew that she must be far from the twin cities of her grandfather's empire, but had she guessed within even a thousand haads of the reality, she had been stunned by realization of the utter hopelessness of her state.

Keeping the craft low, for the buoyancy tanks were still intact, the girl skimmed the ground until the gently-moving wind had carried her to the side of the last hill that intervened between her and the structure she had thought a man-built tower. Here she brought the flier to the ground among some stunted trees, and dragging it beneath one where it might be somewhat hidden from craft passing above, she made it fast and set forth to reconnoiter. Like most women of her class she was armed only with a single slender blade, so that in such an emergency as now confronted her she must depend almost solely upon her cleverness in remaining undiscovered by enemies. With utmost caution she crept warily toward the crest of the hill, taking advantage of every natural screen that the landscape afforded to conceal her approach from possible observers ahead, while momentarily she cast quick glances rearward lest she be taken by surprise from that quarter.

She came at last to the summit, where, from the concealment of a low bush, she could see what lay beyond. Beneath her spread a beautiful valley surrounded by low hills. Dotting it were numerous circular towers, dome-capped, and surrounding each tower was a stone wall enclosing several acres of ground. The valley appeared to be in a high state of cultivation. Upon the opposite side of the hill and just beneath her was a tower and enclosure. It was the roof of the former that had first attracted her attention. In all respects it seemed identical in construction with those further out in the valley—a high, plastered wall of massive construction surrounding a similarly constructed tower, upon whose gray surface was painted in vivid colors a strange device. The towers were about forty ads in diameter, approximately forty earth-feet, and sixty in height to the base of the dome. To an Earth man they would have immediately suggested the silos in which dairy farmers store ensilage for their herds, but closer scrutiny, revealing an occasional embrasured opening together with the strange construction of the domes, would have altered such a conclusion. Tara of Helium saw that the domes seemed to be faced with innumerable prisms of glass, those that were exposed to the declining sun scintillating so gorgeously as to remind her suddenly of the magnificent trappings of Gahan of Gathol. As she thought of the man she shook her head angrily, and moved cautiously forward a foot or two that she might get a less obstructed view of the nearer tower and its enclosure.

As Tara of Helium looked down into the enclosure surrounding the nearest tower, her brows contracted momentarily in frowning surprise, and then her eyes went wide in an expression of incredulity tinged with horror, for what she saw was a score or two of human bodies—naked and headless. For a long moment she watched, breathless; unable to believe the evidence of her own eyes—that these grewsome things moved and had life! She saw them crawling about on hands and knees over and across one another, searching about with their fingers. And she saw some of them at troughs, for which the others seemed to be searching, and those at the troughs were taking something from these receptacles and apparently putting it in a hole where their necks should have been. They were not far beneath her—she could see them distinctly and she saw that there were the bodies of both men and women, and that they were beautifully proportioned, and that their skin was similar to hers, but of a slightly lighter red. At first she had thought that she was looking upon a shambles and that the bodies, but recently decapitated, were moving under the impulse of muscular reaction; but presently she realized that this was their normal condition. The horror of them fascinated her, so that she could scarce take her eyes from them. It was evident from their groping hands that they were eyeless, and their sluggish movements suggested a rudimentary nervous system and a correspondingly minute brain. The girl wondered how they subsisted for she could not, even by the wildest stretch of imagination, picture these imperfect creatures as intelligent tillers of the soil. Yet that the soil of the valley was tilled was evident and that these things had food was equally so. But who tilled the soil? Who kept and fed these unhappy things, and for what purpose? It was an enigma beyond her powers of deduction.

The sight of food aroused again a consciousness of her own gnawing hunger and the thirst that parched her throat. She could see both food and water within the enclosure; but would she dare enter even should she find means of ingress? She doubted it, since the very thought of possible contact with these grewsome creatures sent a shudder through her frame.

Then her eyes wandered again out across the valley until presently they picked out what appeared to be a tiny stream winding its way through the center of the farm lands—a strange sight upon Barsoom. Ah, if it were but water! Then she might hope with a real hope, for the fields would give her sustenance which she could gain by night, while by day she hid among the surrounding hills, and sometime, yes, sometime she knew, the searchers would come, for John Carter, Warlord of Barsoom, would never cease to search for his daughter until every square haad of the planet had been combed again and again. She knew him and she knew the warriors of Helium and so she knew that could she but manage to escape harm until they came, they would indeed come at last.

She would have to wait until dark before she dare venture into the valley, and in the meantime she thought it well to search out a place of safety nearby where she might be reasonably safe from savage beasts. It was possible that the district was free from carnivora, but one might never be sure in a strange land. As she was about to withdraw behind the brow of the hill her attention was again attracted to the enclosure below. Two figures had emerged from the tower. Their beautiful bodies seemed identical with those of the headless creatures among which they moved, but the newcomers were not headless. Upon their shoulders were heads that seemed human, yet which the girl intuitively sensed were not human. They were just a trifle too far away for her to see them distinctly in the waning light of the dying day, but she knew that they were too large, they were out of proportion to the perfectly proportioned bodies, and they were oblate in form. She could see that the men wore some manner of harness to which were slung the customary long-sword and short-sword of the Barsoomian warrior, and that about their short necks were massive leather collars cut to fit closely over the shoulders and snugly to the lower part of the head. Their features were scarce discernible, but there was a suggestion of grotesqueness about them that carried to her a feeling of revulsion.

The two carried a long rope to which were fastened, at intervals of about two sofads, what she later guessed were light manacles, for she saw the warriors passing among the poor creatures in the enclosure and about the right wrist of each they fastened one of the manacles. When all had been thus fastened to the rope one of the warriors commenced to pull and tug at the loose end as though attempting to drag the headless company toward the tower, while the other went among them with a long, light whip with which he flicked them upon the naked skin. Slowly, dully, the creatures rose to their feet and between the tugging of the warrior in front and the lashing of him behind the hopeless band was finally herded within the tower. Tara of Helium shuddered as she turned away. What manner of creatures were these?

Suddenly it was night. The Barsoomian day had ended, and then the brief period of twilight that renders the transition from daylight to darkness almost as abrupt as the switching off of an electric light, and Tara of Helium had found no sanctuary. But perhaps there were no beasts to fear, or rather to avoid—Tara of Helium liked not the word fear. She would have been glad, however, had there been a cabin, even a very tiny cabin, upon her small flier; but there was no cabin. The interior of the hull was completely taken up by the buoyancy tanks. Ah, she had it! How stupid of her not to have thought of it before! She could moor the craft to the tree beneath which it rested and let it rise the length of the rope. Lashed to the deck rings she would then be safe from any roaming beast of prey that chanced along. In the morning she could drop to ground again before the craft was discovered.

As Tara of Helium crept over the brow of the hill down toward the valley, her presence was hidden by the darkness of the night from the sight of any chance observer who might be loitering by a window in the nearby tower. Cluros, the farther moon, was just rising above the horizon to commence his leisurely journey through the heavens. Eight zodes later he would set—a trifle over nineteen and a half Earth hours—and during that time Thuria, his vivacious mate, would have circled the planet twice and be more than half way around on her third trip. She had but just set. It would be more than three and a half hours before she shot above the opposite horizon to hurtle, swift and low, across the face of the dying planet. During this temporary absence of the mad moon Tara of Helium hoped to find both food and water, and gain again the safety of her flier's deck.

She groped her way through the darkness, giving the tower and its enclosure as wide a berth as possible. Sometimes she stumbled, for in the long shadows cast by the rising Cluros objects were grotesquely distorted, though the light from the moon was still not sufficient to be of much assistance to her. Nor, as a matter of fact, did she want light. She could find the stream in the dark, by the simple expedient of going down hill until she walked into it and she had seen that bearing trees and many crops grew throughout the valley, so that she would pass food in plenty ere she reached the stream. If the moon showed her the way more clearly and thus saved her from an occasional fall, he would, too, show her more clearly to the strange denizens of the towers, and that, of course, must not be. Could she have waited until the following night conditions would have been better, since Cluros would not appear in the heavens at all and so, during Thuria's absence, utter darkness would reign; but the pangs of thirst and the gnawing of hunger could be endured no longer with food and drink both in sight, and so she had decided to risk discovery rather than suffer longer.

Safely past the nearest tower, she moved as rapidly as she felt consistent with safety, choosing her way wherever possible so that she might take advantage of the shadows of the trees that grew at intervals and at the same time discover those which bore fruit. In this latter she met with almost immediate success, for the very third tree beneath which she halted was heavy with ripe fruit. Never, thought Tara of Helium, had aught so delicious impinged upon her palate, and yet it was naught else than the almost tasteless usa, which is considered to be palatable only after having been cooked and highly spiced. It grows easily with little irrigation and the trees bear abundantly. The fruit, which ranks high in food value, is one of the staple foods of the less well-to-do, and because of its cheapness and nutritive value forms one of the principal rations of both armies and navies upon Barsoom, a use which has won for it a Martian *sobriquet* which, freely translated into English, would be, The Fighting Potato. The girl was wise enough to eat but sparingly, but she filled her pocket-pouch with the fruit before she continued upon her way.

Two towers she passed before she came at last to the stream, and here again she was temperate, drinking but little and that very slowly, contenting herself with rinsing her mouth frequently and bathing her face, her hands, and her feet; and even though the night was cold, as Martian nights are, the sensation of refreshment more than compensated for the physical discomfort of the low temperature. Replacing her sandals she sought among the growing truck near the stream for whatever edible berries or tubers might be planted there, and found a couple of varieties that could be eaten raw. With these she replaced some of the usa in her pocket-pouch, not only to insure a variety but because she found them more palatable. Occasionally she returned to the stream to drink, but each time moderately. Always were her eyes and ears alert for the first signs of danger, but she had neither seen nor heard aught to disturb her. And presently the time approached when she felt she must return to her flier lest she be caught in the revealing light of low swinging Thuria. She dreaded leaving the water for she knew that she must become very thirsty before she could hope to come again to the stream. If she only had some little receptacle in which to carry water, even a small amount would tide her over until the following night; but she had nothing and so she must content herself as best she could with the juices of the fruit and tubers she had gathered.

After a last drink at the stream, the longest and deepest she had allowed herself, she rose to retrace her steps toward the hills; but even as she did so she became suddenly tense with apprehension. What was that? She could have sworn that she saw something move in the shadows beneath a tree not far away. For a long minute the girl did not move—she scarce breathed. Her eyes remained fixed upon the dense shadows below the tree, her ears strained through the silence of the night. A low moaning came down from the hills where her flier was hidden. She knew it well—the weird note of the hunting banth. And the great carnivore lay directly in her path. But he was not so close as this other thing, hiding there in the shadows just a little way off. What was it? It was the strain of uncertainty that weighed heaviest upon her. Had she known the nature of the creature lurking there half its menace would have vanished. She cast quickly about her in search of some haven of refuge should the thing prove dangerous.

Again arose the moaning from the hills, but this time closer. Almost immediately it was answered from the opposite side of the valley, behind her, and then from the distance to the right of her, and twice upon her left. Her eyes had found a tree, quite near. Slowly, and without taking her eyes from the shadows of that other tree, she moved toward the overhanging branches that might afford her sanctuary in the event of need, and at her first move a low growl rose from the spot she had been watching and she heard the sudden moving of a big body. Simultaneously the creature shot into the moonlight in full charge upon her, its tail erect, its tiny ears laid flat, its great mouth with its multiple rows of sharp and powerful fangs already yawning for its prey, its ten legs carrying it forward in great leaps, and now from the beast's throat issued the frightful roar with which it seeks to paralyze its prey. It was a banth—the great, maned lion of Barsoom. Tara of Helium saw it coming and leaped for the tree toward which she had been moving, and the banth realized her intention and redoubled his speed. As his hideous roar awakened the echoes in the hills, so too it awakened echoes in the valley; but these echoes came from the living throats of others of his kind, until it seemed to the girl that Fate had thrown her into the midst of a countless multitude of these savage beasts.

Almost incredibly swift is the speed of a charging banth, and fortunate it was that the girl had not been caught farther in the open. As it was, her margin of safety was next to negligible, for as she swung nimbly to the lower branches the creature in pursuit of her crashed among the foliage almost upon her as it sprang upward to seize her. It was only a combination of good fortune and agility that saved her. A stout branch deflected the raking talons of the carnivore, but so close was the call that a giant forearm brushed her flesh in the instant before she scrambled to the higher branches.

Baffled, the banth gave vent to his rage and disappointment in a series of frightful roars that caused the very ground to tremble, and to these were added the roarings and the growlings and the moanings of his fellows as they approached from every direction, in the hope of wresting from him whatever of his kill they could take by craft or prowess. And now he turned snarling upon them as they circled the tree, while the girl, huddled in a crotch above them, looked down upon the gaunt, yellow monsters padding on noiseless feet in a restless circle about her. She wondered now at the strange freak of fate that had permitted her to come down this far into the valley by night unharmed; but even more she wondered how she was to return to the hills. She knew that she would not dare venture it by night and she guessed, too, that by day she might be confronted by even graver perils. To depend upon this valley for sustenance she now saw to be beyond the pale of possibility because of the banths that would keep her from food and water by night, while the dwellers in the towers would doubtless make it equally impossible for her to forage by day. There was but one solution of her difficulty and that was to return to her flier and pray that the wind would waft her to some less terrorful land; but when might she return to the flier? The banths gave little evidence of relinquishing hope of her, and even if they wandered out of sight would she dare risk the attempt? She doubted it.

Hopeless indeed seemed her situation—hopeless it was.

CHAPTER IV

CAPTURED

AS THURIA, SWIFT racer of the night, shot again into the sky the scene changed. As by magic a new aspect fell athwart the face of Nature. It was as though in the instant one had been transported from one planet to another. It was the age-old miracle of the Martian nights that is always new, even to Martians—two moons resplendent in the heavens, where one had been but now; conflicting, fast-changing shadows that altered the very hills themselves; far Cluros, stately, majestic, almost stationary, shedding his steady light upon the world below; Thuria, a great and glorious orb, swinging swift across the vaulted dome of the blue-black night, so low that she seemed to graze the hills, a gorgeous spectacle that held the girl now beneath the spell of its enchantment as it always had and always would.

"Ah, Thuria, mad queen of heaven!" murmured Tara of Helium. "The hills pass in stately procession, their bosoms rising and falling; the trees move in restless circles; the little grasses describe their little arcs; and all is movement, restless, mysterious movement without sound, while Thuria passes." The girl sighed and let her gaze fall again to the stern realities beneath. There was no mystery in the huge banths. He who had discovered her squatted there looking hungrily up at her. Most of the others had wandered away in search of other prey, but a few remained hoping yet to bury their fangs in that soft body.

The night wore on. Again Thuria left the heavens to her lord and master, hurrying on to keep her tryst with the Sun in other skies. But a single banth waited impatiently beneath the tree which harbored Tara of Helium. The others had left, but their roars, and growls, and moans thundered, or rumbled, or floated back to her from near and far. What prey found they in this little valley? There must be something that they were accustomed to find here that they should be drawn in so great numbers. The girl wondered what it could be.

How long the night! Numb, cold, and exhausted, Tara of Helium clung to the tree in growing desperation, for once she had dozed and almost fallen. Hope was low in her brave little heart. How much more could she endure? She asked herself the question and then, with a brave shake of her head, she squared her shoulders. "I still live!" she said aloud.

The banth looked up and growled.

Came Thuria again and after awhile the great Sun—a flaming lover, pursuing his heart's desire. And Cluros, the cold husband, continued his serene way, as placid as before his house had been violated by this hot Lothario. And now the

Sun and both Moons rode together in the sky, lending their far mysteries to make weird the Martian dawn. Tara of Helium looked out across the fair valley that spread upon all sides of her. It was rich and beautiful, but even as she looked upon it she shuddered, for to her mind came a picture of the headless things that the towers and the walls hid. Those by day and the banths by night! Ah, was it any wonder that she shuddered?

With the coming of the Sun the great Barsoomian lion rose to his feet. He turned angry eyes upon the girl above him, voiced a single ominous growl, and slunk away toward the hills. The girl watched him, and she saw that he gave the towers as wide a berth as possible and that he never took his eyes from one of them while he was passing it. Evidently the inmates had taught these savage creatures to respect them. Presently he passed from sight in a narrow defile, nor in any direction that she could see was there another. Momentarily at least the landscape was deserted. The girl wondered if she dared attempt to regain the hills and her flier. She dreaded the coming of the workmen to the fields as she was sure they would come. She shrank from again seeing the headless bodies, and found herself wondering if these things would come out into the fields and work. She looked toward the nearest tower. There was no sign of life there. The valley lay quiet now and deserted. She lowered herself stiffly to the ground. Her muscles were cramped and every move brought a twinge of pain. Pausing a moment to drink again at the stream she felt refreshed and then turned without more delay toward the hills. To cover the distance as quickly as possible seemed the only plan to pursue. The trees no longer offered concealment and so she did not go out of her way to be near them. The hills seemed very far away. She had not thought, the night before, that she had traveled so far. Really it had not been far, but now, with the three towers to pass in broad daylight, the distance seemed great indeed.

The second tower lay almost directly in her path. To make a detour would not lessen the chance of detection, it would only lengthen the period of her danger, and so she laid her course straight for the hill where her flier was, regardless of the tower. As she passed the first enclosure she thought that she heard the sound of movement within, but the gate did not open and she breathed more easily when it lay behind her. She came then to the second enclosure, the outer wall of which she must circle, as it lay across her route. As she passed close along it she distinctly heard not only movement within, but voices. In the world-language of Barsoom she heard a man issuing instructions—so many were to pick usa, so many were to irrigate this field, so many to cultivate that, and so on, as a foreman lays out the day's work for his crew.

Tara of Helium had just reached the gate in the outer wall. Without warning it swung open toward her. She saw that for a moment it would hide her from those within and in that moment she turned and ran, keeping close to the wall, until, passing out of sight beyond the curve of the structure, she came to the opposite side of the enclosure. Here, panting from her exertion and from the excitement of her narrow escape, she threw herself among some tall weeds that grew close to the foot of the wall. There she lay trembling for some time, not even daring to raise her head and look about. Never before had Tara of Helium felt the paralyzing effects of terror. She was shocked and angry at herself, that she, daughter of John Carter, Warlord of Barsoom, should exhibit fear. Not even the fact that there had been none there to witness it lessened her shame and anger, and the worst of it was she knew that under similar circumstances she would again be equally as craven. It was not the fear of death—she knew that. No, it was the thought of those headless bodies and that she might see them and that they might even touch her—lay hands upon her—seize her. She shuddered and trembled at the thought.

After a while she gained sufficient command of herself to raise her head and look about. To her horror she discovered that everywhere she looked she saw people working in the fields or preparing to do so. Workmen were coming from other towers. Little bands were passing to this field and that. There were even some already at work within thirty ads of her—about a hundred yards. There were ten, perhaps, in the party nearest her, both men and women, and all were beautiful of form and grotesque of face. So meager were their trappings that they were practically naked; a fact that was in no way remarkable among the tillers of the fields of Mars. Each wore the peculiar, high leather collar that completely hid the neck, and each wore sufficient other leather to support a single sword and a pocket-pouch. The leather was very old and worn, showing long, hard service, and was absolutely plain with the exception of a single device upon the left shoulder. The heads, however, were covered with ornaments of precious metals and jewels, so that little more than eyes, nose and mouth were discernible. These were hideously inhuman and yet grotesquely human at the same time. The eyes were far apart and protruding, the nose scarce more than two small, parallel slits set vertically above a round hole that was the mouth. The heads were peculiarly repulsive—so much so that it seemed unbelievable to the girl that they formed an integral part of the beautiful bodies below them.

So fascinated was Tara of Helium that she could scarce take her eyes from the strange creatures—a fact that was to prove her undoing, for in order that she might see them she was forced to expose a part of her own head and presently, to her consternation, she saw that one of the creatures had stopped his work and was staring directly at her. She did not dare move, for it was still possible that the thing had not seen her, or at least was only suspicious that some creature lay hid among the weeds. If she could allay this suspicion by remaining motionless the creature might believe that he had been mistaken and return to his work; but, alas, such was not to be the case. She saw the thing call the attention of others to her and almost immediately four or five of them started to move in her direction.

It was impossible now to escape discovery. Her only hope lay in flight. If she could elude them and reach the hills and the flier ahead of them she might escape, and that could be accomplished in but one way—flight, immediate and swift. Leaping to her feet she darted along the base of the wall which she must skirt to the opposite side, beyond which lay the hill that was her goal. Her act was greeted by strange whistling sounds from the things behind her, and casting a glance over her shoulder she saw them all in rapid pursuit. There were also shrill commands that she halt, but to these she paid no attention. Before she had half circled the enclosure she discovered that her chances for successful escape were great, since it was evident to her that her pursuers were not so fleet as she. High indeed then were her hopes as she came in sight of the hill, but they were soon dashed by what lay before her, for there, in the fields that lay between, were fully a hundred creatures similar to those behind her and all were on the alert, evidently warned by the whistling of their fellows. Instructions and commands were shouted to and fro, with the result that those before her spread roughly into a great half circle to intercept her, and when she turned to the right, hoping to elude the net, she saw others coming from fields beyond, and to the left the same was true. But Tara of Helium would not admit defeat. Without once pausing she turned directly toward the center of the advancing semi-circle, beyond which lay her single chance of escape, and as she ran she drew her long, slim dagger. Like her valiant sire, if die she must, she would die fighting. There were gaps in the thin line confronting her and toward the widest of one of these she directed her course. The things on either side of the opening guessed her intent for they closed in to place themselves in her path. This widened the openings on either side of them and as the girl appeared almost to rush into their arms she turned suddenly at right angles, ran swiftly in the new direction for a few yards, and then dashed quickly toward the hill again. Now only a single warrior, with a wide gap on either side of him, barred her clear way to freedom, though all the others were speeding as rapidly as they could to intercept her. If she could pass this one without too much delay she could escape, of that she was certain. Her every hope hinged upon this. The creature before her realized it, too, for he moved cautiously, though swiftly, to intercept her, as a Rugby fullback might maneuver in the realization that he alone stood between the opposing team and a touchdown.

At first Tara of Helium had hoped that she might dodge him, for she could not but guess that she was not only more fleet but infinitely more agile than these strange creatures; but soon there came to her the realization that in the time consumed in an attempt to elude his grasp his nearer fellows would be upon her and escape then impossible, so she chose instead to charge straight for him, and when he guessed her decision he stood, half crouching and with outstretched arms, awaiting her. In one hand was his sword, but a voice arose, crying in tones of authority. "Take her alive! Do not harm her!" Instantly the fellow returned his sword to its scabbard and then Tara of Helium was upon him. Straight for that beautiful body she sprang and in the instant that the arms closed to seize her her sharp blade drove deep into the naked chest. The impact hurled them both to the ground and as Tara of Helium sprang to her feet again she saw, to her horror, that the loathsome head had rolled from the body and was now crawling away from her on six short, spider-like legs. The body struggled spasmodically and lay still. As brief as had been the delay caused by the encounter, it still had been of sufficient duration to undo her, for even as she rose two more of the things fell upon her and instantly thereafter she was surrounded. Her blade sank once more into naked flesh and once more a head rolled free and crawled away. Then they overpowered her and in another moment she was surrounded by fully a hundred of the creatures, all seeking to lay hands upon her. At first she thought that they wished to tear her to pieces in revenge for her having slain two of their fellows, but presently she realized that they were prompted more by curiosity than by any sinister motive.

"Come!" said one of her captors, both of wnom had retained a hold upon her. As he spoke he tried to lead her away with him toward the nearest tower.

"She belongs to me," cried the other. "Did not I capture her? She will come with me to the tower of Moak."

"Never!" insisted the first. "She is Luud's. To Luud I will take her, and whosoever interferes may feel the keenness of my sword—*in the head*!" He almost shouted the last three words.

"Come! Enough of this," cried one who spoke with some show of authority. "She was captured in Luud's fields—she will go to Luud."

"She was discoverd in Moak's fields, at the very foot of the tower of Moak," insisted he who had claimed her for Moak.

"You have heard the Nolach speak," cried the Luud. "It shall be as he says."

"Not while this Moak holds a sword," replied the other. "Rather will I cut her in twain and take my half to Moak than to relinquish her all to Luud," and he drew his sword, or rather he laid his hand upon its hilt in a threatening gesture; but before ever he could draw it the Luud had whipped his out and with a fearful blow cut deep into the head of his adversary. Instantly the big, round head collapsed, almost as a punctured balloon collapses, as a grayish, semi-fluid matter spurted from it. The protruding eyes, apparently lidless, merely stared, the sphincter-like muscle of the mouth opened and closed, and then the head toppled from the body to the ground. The body stood dully for a moment and then slowly started to wander aimlessly about until one of the others seized it by the arm.

One of the two heads crawling about on the ground now approached. "This rykor belongs to Moak," it said. "I am a Moak. I will take it," and without further discussion it commenced to crawl up the front of the headless body, using its six short, spiderlike legs and two stout chelae which grew just in front of its legs and strongly resembled those of an Earthly lobster, except that they were both of the same size. The body in the meantime stood in passive indifference, its arms hanging idly at its sides. The head climbed to the shoulders and settled itself inside the leather collar that now hid its chelae and legs. Almost immediately the body gave evidence of intelligent animation. It raised its hands and adjusted the collar more comfortably, it took the head between its palms and settled it in place and when it moved around it did not wander aimlessly, but instead its steps were firm and to some purpose.

The girl watched all these things in growing wonder, and presently, no other of the Moaks seeming inclined to dispute the right of the Luud to her, she was led off by her captor toward the nearest tower. Several accompanied them, including one who carried the loose head under his arm. The head that was being carried conversed with the head upon the shoulders of the thing that carried it. Tara of Helium shivered. It was horrible! All that she had seen of these frightful creatures was horrible. And to be a prisoner, wholly in their power. Shadow of her first ancestor! What had she done to deserve so cruel a fate?

At the wall enclosing the tower they paused while one opened the gate and then they passed within the enclosure, which, to the girl's horror, she found filled with headless bodies. The creature who carried the bodiless head now set its burden upon the ground and the latter immediately crawled toward one of the bodies that was lying near by. Some wandered stupidly to and fro, but this one lay still. It was a female. The head crawled to it and made its way to the shoulders where it settled itself. At once the body sprang lightly erect. Another of those who had accompanied them from the fields approached with the harness and collar that had been taken from the dead body that the head had formerly topped. The new body now appropriated these and the hands deftly adjusted them. The creature was now as good as before Tara of Helium had struck down its former body with her slim blade. But there was a difference. Before it had been male—now it was female. That, however, seemed to make no difference to the head. In fact, Tara of Helium had noticed during the scramble and the fight about her that sex differences seemed of little moment to her captors. Males and females had taken equal part in her pursuit, both were identically harnessed and both carried swords, and she had seen as many females as males draw their weapons at the moment that a quarrel between the two factions seemed imminent.

The girl was given but brief opportunity for further observation of the pitiful creatures in the enclosure as her captor, after having directed the others to return to the fields, led her toward the tower, which they entered, passing into an apartment about ten feet wide and twenty long, in one end of which was a stairway leading to an upper level and in the other an opening to a similar stairway leading downward. The chamber, though on a level with the ground, was brilliantly lighted by windows in its inner wall, the light coming from a circular court in the center of the tower. The walls of this court appeared to be faced with what resembled glazed, white tile and the whole interior of it was flooded with dazzling light, a fact which immediately explained to the girl the purpose of the glass prisms of which the domes were constructed. The stairways themselves were sufficient to cause remark, since in nearly all Barsoomian architecture inclined runways are utilized for purposes of communication between different levels and especially is this true of the more ancient forms and of those of remote districts where fewer changes have come to alter the customs of antiquity.

Down the stairway her captor led Tara of Helium. Down and down through chambers still lighted from the brilliant well. Occasionally they passed others going in the opposite direction and these always stopped to examine the girl and ask questions of her captor.

"1 know nothing but that she was found in the fields and that I caught her after a fight in which she slew two rykors and in which I slew a Moak, and that I take her to Luud, to whom, of course, she belongs. If Luud wishes to question her that is for Luud to do—not for me." Thus always he answered the curious.

Presently they reached a room from which a circular tunnel led away from the tower, and into this the creature conducted her. The tunnel was some seven feet in diameter and flattened on the bottom to form a walk. For a hundred feet from the tower it was lined with the same tile-like material of the light well and amply illuminated by reflected light from that source. Beyond it was faced with stone of various shapes and sizes, neatly cut and fitted together—a very fine mosaic without a pattern. There were branches, too, and other tunnels which crossed this, and occasionally openings not more than a foot in diameter; these latter being usually close to the floor. Above each of these smaller openings was painted a different device, while upon the walls of the larger tunnels at all intersections and points of convergence hieroglyphics appeared. These the girl could not read though she guessed that they were the names of the tunnels, or notices indicating the points to which they led. She tried to study some of them out, but there was not a character that was familiar to her, which seemed strange, since, while the written languages of the various nations of Barsoom differ, it still is true that they have many characters and words in common.

She had tried to converse with her guard but he had not seemed inclined to talk with her and she had finally desisted. She could not but note that he had offered her no indignities, nor had he been either unnecessarily rough or in any way cruel. The fact that she had slain two of the bodies with her dagger had apparently aroused no animosity or desire for revenge in the minds of the strange heads that surmounted the bodies—even those whose bodies had been killed. She did not try to understand it, since she could not approach the peculiar relationship between the heads and the bodies of these creatures from the basis of any past knowledge or experience of her own. So far their treatment of her seemed to augur naught that might arouse her fears. Perhaps, after all, she had been fortunate to fall into the hands of these strange people, who might not only protect her from harm, but even aid her in returning to Helium. That they were repulsive and uncanny she could not forget, but if they meant her no harm she could, at least, overlook their repulsiveness. Renewed hope aroused within her a spirit of greater cheerfulness, and it was almost blithely now that she moved at the side of her weird companion. She even caught herself humming a gay little tune that was then popular in Helium. The creature at her side turned its expressionless eyes upon her.

"What is that noise that you are making?" it asked.

"I was but humming an air," she replied.

" 'Humming an air,' " he repeated. "I do not know what you mean; but do it again, I like it."

This time she sang the words, while her companion listened intently. His face gave no indication of what was passing in that strange head. It was as devoid of expression as that of a spider. It reminded her of a spider. When she had finished he turned toward her again.

"That was different," he said. "I liked that better, even, than the other. How do you do it?"

"Why," she said, "it is singing. Do you not know what song is?"

"No," he replied. "Tell me how you do it."

"It is difficult to explain," she told him, "since any explanation of it presupposes some knowledge of melody and of music, while your very question indicates that you have no knowledge of either."

"No," he said, "I do not know what you are talking about; but tell me how you do it."

"It is merely the melodious modulations of my voice," she explained. "Listen!" and again she sang.

"I do not understand," he insisted; "but I like it. Could you teach me to do it?"

"I do not know, but I shall be glad to try."

"We will see what Luud does with you," he said. "If he does not want you I will keep you and you shall teach me to make sounds like that."

At his request she sang again as they continued their way along the winding tunnel, which was now lighted by occasional bulbs which appeared to be similar to the radium bulbs with which she was familiar and which were common to all the nations of Barsoom, insofar as she knew, having been perfected at so remote a period that their very origin was lost in antiquity. They consist, usually, of a hemispherical bowl of heavy glass in which is packed a compound containing what, according to John Carter, must be radium. The bowl is then cemented into a metal plate with a heavily insulated back and the whole affair set in the masonry of wall or ceiling as desired, where it gives off light of greater or less intensity, according to the composition of the filling material, for an almost incalculable period of time.

As they proceeded they met a greater number of the inhabitants of this underground world, and the girl noted that among many of these the metal and harness were more ornate than had been those of the workers in the fields above. The heads and bodies, however, were similar, even identical, she thought. No one offered her harm and she was now experiencing a feeling of relief almost akin to happiness, when her guide turned suddenly into an opening on the right side of the tunnel and she found herself in a large, well lighted chamber.

CHAPTER V

THE PERFECT BRAIN

THE SONG THAT had been upon her lips as she entered died there—frozen by the sight of horror that met her eyes. In the center of the chamber a headless body lay upon the floor—a body that had been partially devoured—while over and upon it crawled a half a dozen heads upon their short, spider legs, and they tore at the flesh of the woman with their chelae and carried the bits to their awful mouths. They were eating human flesh—eating it raw!

Tara of Helium gasped in horror and turning away covered her eyes with her palms.

"Come!" said her captor. "What is the matter?"

"They are eating the flesh of the woman," she whispered in tones of horror.

"Why not?" he inquired. "Did you suppose that we kept the rykor for labor alone? Ah, no. They are delicious when kept and fattened. Fortunate, too, are those that are bred for food, since they are never called upon to do aught but eat."

"It is hideous!" she cried.

He looked at her steadily for a moment, but whether in surprise, in anger, or in pity his expressionless face did not reveal. Then he led her on across the room past the frightful thing, from which she turned away her eyes. Lying about the floor near the walls were half a dozen headless bodies in harness. These she guessed had been abandoned temporarily by the feasting heads until they again required their services. In the walls of this room there were many of the small, round openings she had noticed in various parts of the tunnels, the purpose of which she could not guess.

They passed through another corridor and then into a second chamber, larger than the first and more brilliantly illuminated. Within were several of the creatures with heads and bodies assembled, while many headless bodies lay about near the walls. Here her captor halted and spoke to one of the occupants of the chamber.

"I seek Luud," he said. "I bring to Luud a creature that I captured in the fields above."

The others crowded about to examine Tara of Helium. One of them whistled, whereupon the girl learned something of the smaller openings in the walls, for almost immediately there crawled from them, like giant spiders, a score or more of the hideous heads. Each sought one of the recumbent bodies and fastened itself in place. Immediately the bodies reacted to the intelligent direction of the heads. They arose, the hands adjusted the leather collars and put the balance of the harness in order, then the creatures crossed the room to where Tara of Helium stood. She noted that their leather was more highly ornamented than that worn by any of the others she had previously seen, and so she guessed that these must be higher in authority than the others. Nor was she mistaken. The demeanor of her captor indicated it. He addressed them as one who holds intercourse with superiors.

Several of those who examined her felt her flesh, pinching it gently between thumb and forefinger, a familiarity that the girl resented. She struck down their hands. "Do not touch me!" she cried, imperiously, for was she not a princess of Helium? The expressions on those terrible faces did not change. She could not tell whether they were angry or amused, whether her action had filled them with respect for her, or contempt. Only one of them spoke immediately.

"She will have to be fattened more," he said.

The girl's eyes went wide in horror. She turned upon her captor. "Do these frightful creatures intend to devour me?" she cried.

"That is for Luud to say," he replied, and then he leaned closer so that his mouth was near her ear. "That noise you made which you called song pleased me," he whispered, "and I will repay you by warning you not to antagonize these kaldanes. They are very powerful. Luud listens to them. Do not call them frightful. They are very handsome. Look at their wonderful trappings, their gold, their jewels."

"Thank you," she said. "You called them kaldanes—what does that mean?"

"We are all kaldanes," he replied.

"You, too?" and she pointed at him, her slim finger directed toward his chest.

"No, not this," he explained, touching his body; "this is a rykor; but this," and he touched his head, "is a kaldane. It is the brain, the intellect, the power that directs all things. The rykor," he indicated his body, "is nothing. It is not so much even as the jewels upon our harness; no, not so much as the harness itself. It carries us about. It is true that we would find difficulty getting along without it; but it has less value than harness or jewels because it is less difficult to reproduce." He turned again to the other kaldanes. "Will you notify Luud that I am here?" he asked.

"Sept has already gone to Luud. He will tell him," replied one. "Where did you find this rykor with the strange kaldane that cannot detach itself?"

The girl's captor narrated once more the story of her capture. He stated facts just as they had occurred, without embellishment, his voice as expressionless as his face, and his story was received in the same manner that it was delivered. The creatures seemed totally lacking in emotion, or, at least, the capacity to express it. It was impossible to judge what impression the story made upon them, or even if they heard it. Their protruding eyes simply stared and occasionally the muscles of their mouths opened and closed. Familiarity did not lessen the horror the girl felt for them. The more she saw of them the more repulsive they seemed. Often her body was shaken by convulsive shudders as she looked at the kaldanes, but when her eyes wandered to the beautiful bodies and she could for a moment expunge the heads from her consciousness the effect was soothing and refreshing, though when the bodies lay, headless, upon the floor they were quite as shocking as the heads mounted on bodies. But by far the most grewsome and uncanny sight of all was that of the heads crawling about upon their spider legs. If one of these should approach and touch her Tara of Helium was positive that she should scream, while should one attempt to crawl up her person—ugh! the very idea induced a feeling of faintness.

Sept returned to the chamber. "Luud will see you and the captive. Come!" he said, and turned toward a door opposite that through which Tara of Helium had entered the chamber. "What is your name?" His question was directed to the girl's captor.

"I am Ghek, third foreman of the fields of Luud," he answered.

"And hers?"

"I do not know."

"It makes no difference. Come!"

The patrician brows of Tara of Helium went high. It made no difference, indeed! She, a princess of Helium; only daughter of The Warlord of Barsoom!

"Wait!" she cried. "It makes much difference who I am. If you are conducting me into the presence of your jed you may announce The Princess Tara of Helium, daughter of John Carter, The Warlord of Barsoom."

"Hold your peace!" commanded Sept. "Speak when you are spoken to. Come with me!"

The anger of Tara of Helium all but choked her.

"Come," admonished Ghek, and took her by the arm, and Tara of Helium came. She was naught but a prisoner. Her rank and titles meant nothing to these inhuman monsters. They led her through a short, S-shaped passageway into a chamber entirely lined with the white, tile-like material with which the interior of the light wall was faced. Close to the base of the walls were numerous smaller apertures, circular in shape, but larger than those of similar aspect that she had noted elsewhere. The majority of these apertures were sealed. Directly opposite the entrance was one framed in gold, and above it a peculiar device was inlaid in the same precious metal.

Sept and Ghek halted just within the room, the girl between them, and all three stood silently facing the opening in the opposite wall. On the floor beside the aperture lay a headless male body of almost heroic proportions, and on either side of this stood a heavily armed warrior, with drawn sword. For perhaps five minutes the three waited and then something appeared in the opening. It was a pair of large chelae and immediately thereafter there crawled forth a hideous kaldane of enormous proportions. He was half again as large as any that Tara of Helium had yet seen and his whole aspect infinitely more terrible. The skin of the others was a bluish gray—this one was of a little bluer tinge and the eyes were ringed with bands of white and scarlet, as was its mouth. From each nostril a band of white and one of scarlet extended outward horizontally the width of the face.

No one spoke or moved. The creature crawled to the prostrate body and affixed itself to the neck. Then the two rose as one and approached the girl. He looked at her and then he spoke to her captor.

"You are the third foreman of the fields of Luud?" he asked.

"Yes, Luud; I am called Ghek."

"Tell me what you know of this," and he nodded toward Tara of Helium.

Ghek did as he was bid and then Luud addressed the girl.

"What were you doing within the borders of Bantoom?" he asked.

"I was blown hither in a great storm that injured my flier and carried me I knew not where. I came down into the valley at night for food and drink. The banths came and drove me to the safety of a tree, and then your people caught me as I was trying to leave the valley. I do not know why they took me. I was doing no harm. All I ask is that you let me go my way in peace."

"None who enters Bantoom ever leaves," replied Luud.

"But my people are not at war with yours. I am a princess of Helium; my great-grandfather is a jeddak; my grandfather a jed; and my father is Warlord of all Barsoom. You have no right to keep me and I demand that you liberate me at once."

"None who enters Bantoom ever leaves," repeated the creature without expression. "I know nothing of the lesser creatures of Barsoom, of whom you speak. There is but one high race—the race of Bantoomians. All Nature exists to serve them. You shall do your share, but not yet—you are too skinny. We shall have to put some fat upon it, Sept. I tire of rykor. Perhaps this will have a different flavor. The banths are too rank and it is seldom that any other creature enters the valley. And you, Ghek; you shall be rewarded. I shall promote you from the fields to the burrows. Hereafter you shall remain underground as every Bantoomian longs to. No more shall you be forced to endure the hated sun, or look upon the hideous sky, or the hateful growing things that defile the surface. For the present you shall look after this thing that you have brought me, seeing that it sleeps and eats—and does nothing else. You understand me, Ghek; nothing else!!"

"I understand, Luud," replied the other.

"Take it away!" commanded the creature.

Ghek turned and led Tara of Helium from the apartment. The girl was horrified by contemplation of the fate that awaited her—a fate from which it seemed, there was no escape. It was only too evident that these creatures possessed no gentle or chivalric sentiments to which she could appeal, and that she might escape from the labyrinthine mazes of their underground burrows appeared impossible.

Outside the audience chamber Sept overtook them and conversed with Ghek for a brief period, then her keeper led her through a confusing web of winding tunnels until they came to a small apartment.

"We are to remain here for a while. It may be that Luud will send for you again. If he does you will probably not be fattened—he will use you for another purpose." It was fortunate for the girl's peace of mind that she did not realize what he meant. "Sing for me," said Ghek, presently.

Tara of Helium did not feel at all like singing, but she sang, nevertheless, for there was always the hope that she might escape if given the opportunity and if she could win the friendship of one of the creatures, her chances would be increased proportionately. All during the ordeal, for such it was to the overwrought girl, Ghek stood with his eyes fixed upon her.

"It is wonderful," he said, when she had finished; "but I did not tell Luud—you noticed that I did not tell Luud about it. Had he known, he would have had you sing to him and that would have resulted in your being kept with him that he might hear you sing whenever he wished; but now I can have you all the time."

"How do you know he would like my singing?" she asked.

"He would have to," replied Ghek. "If I like a thing he has to like it, for are we not identical—all of us?"

"The people of my race do not all like the same things," said the girl.

"How strange!" commented Ghek. "All kaldanes like the same things and dislike the same things. If I discover something new and like it I know that all kaldanes will like it. That is how I know that Luud would like your singing. You see we are all exactly alike."

"But you do not look like Luud," said the girl.

"Luud is king. He is larger and more gorgeously marked; but otherwise he and I are identical, and why not? Did not Luud produce the egg from which I hatched?"

"What?" queried the girl; "I do not understand you."

"Yes," explained Ghek, "all of us are from Luud's eggs, just as all the swarm of Moak are from Moak's eggs."

"Oh!" exclaimed Tara of Helium understandingly; "you mean that Luud has many wives and that you are the off-spring of one of them."

"No, not that at all," replied Ghek. "Luud has no wife. He lays the eggs himself. You do not understand."

Tara of Helium admitted that she did not.

"I will try to explain then," said Ghek, "if you will prom-ise to sing to me later."

"I promise," she said.

"We are not like the rykors," he began. "They are creatures of a low order, like yourself and the banths and such things.

We have no sex—not one of us except our king, who is bisexual. He produces many eggs from which we, the workers and the warriors, are hatched; and one in every thousand eggs is another king egg, from which a king is hatched. Did you notice the sealed openings in the room where you saw Luud? Sealed in each of those is another king. If one of them escaped he would fall upon Luud and try to kill him and if he succeeded we should have a new king; but there would be no difference. His name would be Luud and all would go on as before, for are we not all alike? Luud has lived a long time and has produced many kings, so he lets only a few live that there may be a successor to him when he dies. The others he kills."

"Why does he keep more than one?" queried the girl.

"Sometimes accidents occur," replied Ghek, "and all the kings that a swarm has saved are killed. When this happens the swarm comes and obtains another king from a neighboring swarm."

"Are all of you the children of Luud?" he asked.

"All but a few, who are from the eggs of the preceding king, as was Luud; but Luud has lived a long time and not many of the others are left."

"You live a long time, or short?" Tara asked.

"A very long time."

"And the rykors, too; they live a long time?"

"No; the rykors live for ten years, perhaps," he said, "if they remain strong and useful. When they can no longer be of service to us, either through age or sickness, we leave them in the fields and the banths come at night and get them."

"How horrible!" she exclaimed.

"Horrible?" he repeated. "I see nothing horrible about that. The rykors are but brainless flesh. They neither see, nor feel, nor hear. They can scarce move but for us. If we did not bring them food they would starve to death. They are less deserving of thought than our leather. All that they can do for themselves is to take food from a trough and put it in their mouths, but with us—look at them!" and he proudly exhibited the noble figure that he surmounted, palpitant with life and energy and feeling.

"How do you do it?" asked Tara of Helium. "I do not understand it at all."

"I will show you," he said, and lay down upon the floor. Then he detached himself from the body, which lay as a thing dead. On his spider legs he walked toward the girl. "Now look," he admonished her. "Do you see this thing?" and he extended what appeared to be a bundle of tentacles from the posterior part of his head. "There is an aperture just back of the rykor's mouth and directly over the upper end of his spinal column. Into this aperture I insert my tentacles and seize the spinal cord. Immediately I control every muscle of the rykor's body—it becomes my own, just as you direct the movement of the muscles of your body. I feel what the rykor would feel if he had a head and brain. If he is hurt, I would suffer if I remained connected with him; but the instant one of them is injured or becomes sick we desert it for another. As we would suffer the pains of their physical injuries, similarly do we enjoy the physical pleasures of the rykors. When your body becomes fatigued you are comparatively useless; if it is sick, you are sick; if it is killed, you die. You are the slave of a mass of stupid flesh and bone and blood. There is nothing more wonderful about your carcass than there is about the carcass of a banth. It is only your brain that makes you super-ior to the banth, but your brain is bound by the limitations of your body. Not so, ours. With us brain is everything. Ninety per centum of our volume is brain. We have only the simplest of vital organs and they are very small for they do not have to assist in the support of a complicated system of nerves, mus-cles, flesh, and bone. We have no lungs, for we do not require air. Far below the levels to which we can take the rykors is a vast network of burrows where the real life of the kaldane is lived. There the airbreathing rykor would perish as you would perish. There we have stored vast quantities of food in hermetically sealed chambers. It will last forever. Far beneath the surface is water that will flow for countless ages after the surface water is exhausted. We are preparing for the time we know must come—the time when the last vestige of the Bar-soomian atmosphere is spent—when the waters and the food are gone. For this purpose were we created, that there might not perish from the planet Nature's divinest creation—the perfect brain."

"But what purpose can you serve when that time comes?" asked the girl.

"You do not understand," he said. "It is too big for you to grasp, but I will try to explain it. Barsoom, the moons, the sun, the stars, were created for a single purpose. From the beginning of time Nature has labored arduously toward the consummation of this purpose. At the very beginning things existed with life, but with no brain. Gradually rudimentary nervous systems and minute brains evolved. Evolution proceeded. The brains became larger and more powerful. In us you see the highest development; but there are those of us who believe that there is yet another step—that some time in the far future our race shall develop into the super-thing —just brain. The incubus of legs and chelae and vital organs will be removed. The future kaldane will be nothing but a great brain. Deaf, dumb, and blind it will lie sealed in its buried vault far beneath the surface of Barsoom—just a great, wonderful, beautiful brain with nothing to distract it from eternal thought."

"You mean it will just lie there and think?" cried Tara of Helium.

"Just that!" he exclaimed. "Could aught be more wonderful?"

"Yes," replied the girl, "I can think of a number of things that would be infinitely more wonderful."

CHAPTER VI

IN THE TOILS OF HORROR

WHAT THE CREATURE had told her gave Tara of Helium food for thought. She had been taught that every created thing fulfilled some useful purpose, and she tried conscientiously to discover just what was the rightful place of the kaldane in the universal scheme of things. She knew that it must have its place but what that place was it was beyond her to conceive. She had to give it up. They recalled to her mind a little group of people in Helium who had forsworn the pleasures of life in the pursuit of knowledge. They were rather patronizing in their relations with those whom they thought not so intellectual. They considered themselves quite superior. She smiled at recollection of a remark her father had once made concerning them, to the effect that if one of them ever dropped his egotism and broke it it would take a week to fumigate Helium. Her father liked normal people—people who knew too little and people who knew too much were equally a bore. Tara of Helium was like her father in this respect and like him, too, she was both sane and normal.

Outside of her personal danger there was much in this strange world that interested her. The rykors aroused her keenest pity, and vast conjecture. How and from what form had they evolved? She asked Ghek.

"Sing to me again and I will tell you," he said. "If Luud would let me have you, you should never die. I should keep you always to sing to me."

The girl marvelled at the effect her voice had upon the creature. Somewhere in that enormous brain there was a chord that was touched by melody. It was the sole link between herself and the brain when detached from the rykor. When it dominated the rykor it might have other human instincts; but these she dreaded even to think of. After she had sung she waited for Ghek to speak. For a long time he was silent, just looking at her through those awful eyes.

"I wonder," he said presently, "if it might not be pleasant to be of your race. Do you sing?"

"Nearly all, a little," she said; "but we do many other interesting and enjoyable things. We dance and play and work and love and sometimes we fight, for we are a race of warriors."

"Love!" said the kaldane. "I think I know what you mean; but we, fortunately, are above sentiment—when we are detached. But when we dominate the rykor—ah, that is different, and when I hear you sing and look at your beautiful body I know what you mean by love. I could love you."

The girl shrank from him. "You promised to tell me the origin of the rykor," she reminded him.

"Ages ago," he commenced, "our bodies were larger and our heads smaller. Our legs were very weak and we could not travel fast or far. There was a stupid creature that went upon four legs. It lived in a hole in the ground, to which it brought its food, so we ran our burrows into this hole and ate the food it brought; but it did not bring enough for all—for itself and all the kaldanes that lived upon it, so we had also to go abroad and get food. This was hard work for our weak legs. Then it was that we commenced to ride upon the backs of these primitive rykors. It took many ages, undoubtedly, but at last came the time when the kaldane had found means to guide the rykor, until presently the latter depended entirely upon the superior brain of his master to guide him to food. The brain of the rykor grew smaller as time went on. His ears went and his eyes, for he no longer had use for them— the kaldane saw and heard for him. By similar steps the rykor came to go upon its hind feet that the kaldane might be able to see farther. As the brain shrank, so did the head. The mouth was the only feature of the head that was used and so the mouth alone remains. Members of the red race fell into the hands of our ancestors from time to time. They saw the beauties and the advantages of the form that nature had given the red race over that which the rykor was developing into. By intelligent crossing the present rykor was achieved. He is really solely the product of the super-intelligence of the kaldane—he is our body, to do with as we see fit, just as you see fit with your body, only we have the advantage of possessing an unlimited supply of bodies. Do you not wish that you were a kaldane?"

For how long they kept her in the subterranean chamber Tara of Helium did not know. It seemed a very long time. She ate and slept and watched the interminable lines of creatures that passed the entrance to her prison. There was a laden line passing from above carrying food, food, food. In the other line they returned empty handed. When she saw them she knew that it was daylight above. When they did not pass she knew it was night, and that the banths were about devouring the rykors that had been abandoned in the fields the previous day. She commenced to grow pale and thin. She did not like the food they gave her—it was not suited to her kind—nor would she have eaten overmuch palatable food, for the fear of becoming fat. The idea of plumpness had a new significance here—a horrible significance.

Ghek noted that she was growing thin and white. He spoke to her about it and she told him that she could not thrive thus beneath the ground—that she must have fresh air and

sunshine, or she would wither and die. Evidently he carried
her words to Luud, since it was not long after that he told her
that the king had ordered that she be confined in the tower
and to the tower she was taken. She had hoped against hope
that this very thing might result from her conversation with
Ghek. Even to see the sun again was something, but now
there sprang to her breast a hope that she had not dared to
nurse before, while she lay in the terrible labyrinth from
which she knew she could never have found her way to the
outer world; but now there was some slight reason to hope.
At least she could see the hills and if she could see them
might there not come also the opportunity to reach them?
If she could have but ten minutes—just ten little minutes!
The flier was still here—she knew that it must be. Just ten
minutes and she would be free—free forever from this frightful place; but the days wore on and she was never alone, not
even for half of ten minutes. Many times she planned her
escape. Had it not been for the banths it had been easy of
accomplishment by night. Ghek always detached his body
then and sank into what seemed a semi-comatose condition.
It could not be said that he slept, or at least it did not appear
like sleep, since his lidless eyes were unchanged; but he lay
quietly in a corner. Tara of Helium enacted a thousand
times in her mind the scene of her escape. She would rush
to the side of the rykor and seize the sword that hung in its
harness. Before Ghek knew what she purposed, she would do
this and then before he could give an alarm she would drive the
blade through his hideous head. It would take but a moment
to reach the enclosure. The rykors could not stop her, for
they had no brains to tell them that she was escaping. She
had watched from her window the opening and closing of
the gate that led from the enclosure out into the fields and
she knew how the great latch operated. She would pass
through and make a quick dash for the hill. It was so near
that they could not overtake her. It was so easy! Or it would
have been but for the banths! The banths at night and the
workers in the fields by day.

Confined to the tower and without proper exercise or food,
the girl failed to show the improvement that her captors
desired. Ghek questioned her in an effort to learn why it was
that she did not grow round and plump; that she did not

even look as well as when they had captured her. His concern was prompted by repeated inquiries on the part of Luud and finally resulted in suggesting to Tara of Helium a plan whereby she might find a new opportunity of escape.

"I am accustomed to walking in the fresh air and the sunlight," she told Ghek. "I cannot become as I was before if I am to be always shut away in this one chamber, breathing poor air and getting no proper exercise. Permit me to go out in the fields every day and walk about while the sun is shining. Then, I am sure, I shall become nice and fat."

"You would run away," he said.

"But how could I if you were always with me?" she asked. "And even if I wished to run away, where could I go? I do not know even the direction of Helium. It must be very far. The very first night the banths would get me, would they not?"

"They would," said Ghek. "'I will ask Luud about it."

The following day he told her that Luud had said that she was to be taken into the fields. He would try that for a time and see if she improved.

"If you do not grow fatter he will send for you anyway," said Ghek; "but he will not use you for food."

Tara of Helium shuddered.

That day and for many days thereafter she was taken from the tower, through the enclosure and out into the fields. Always was she alert for an opportunity to escape; but Ghek was always close by her side. It was not so much his presence that deterred her from making the attempt as the number of workers that were always between her and the hills where the flier lay. She could easily have eluded Ghek, but there were too many of the others. And then, one day, Ghek told her as he accompanied her into the open that this would be the last time.

"Tonight you go to Luud," he said. "I am sorry as I shall not hear you sing again."

"Tonight!" She scarce breathed the word, yet it was vibrant with horror.

She glanced quickly toward the hills. They were so close! Yet between were the inevitable workers—perhaps a score of them.

"Let us walk over there?" she said, indicating them. "I

should like to see what they are doing."

"It is too far," said Ghek. "I hate the sun. It is much pleas-
anter here where I can stand beneath the shade of this tree."

"All right," she agreed; "then you stay here and I will walk
over. It will take me but a minute."

"No," he answered. "I will go with you. You want to escape; but you are not going to."

"I cannot escape," she said.

"I know it," agreed Ghek; "but you might try. I do not
wish you to try. Possibly it will be better if we return to the
tower at once. It would go hard with me should you escape."

Tara of Helium saw her last chance fading into oblivion.
There would never be another after today. She cast about
for some pretext to lure him even a little nearer to the hills.

"It is very little that I ask," she said. "Tonight you will
want me to sing to you. It will be the last time. If you do not
let me go and see what those kaldanes are doing I shall never
sing to you again."

Ghek hesitated. "I will hold you by the arm all the time,
then," he said.

"Why of course, if you wish," she assented. "Come!"

The two moved toward the workers and the hills. The
little party was digging tubers from the ground. She had
noted this and that nearly always they were stooped low over
their work, the hideous eyes bent upon the upturned soil.
She led Ghek quite close to them, pretending that she wished
to see exactly how they did the work, and all the time he held
her tightly by her left wrist.

"It is very interesting," she said, with a sigh, and then,
suddenly: "Look, Ghek!" and pointed quickly back in the
direction of the tower. The kaldane, still holding her turned
half away from her to look in the direction she had indicated
and simultaneously, with the quickness of a banth, she struck
him with her right fist, backed by every ounce of strength she
possessed—struck the back of the pulpy head just above the
collar. The blow was sufficient to accomplish her design, dislodging the kaldane from its rykor and tumbling it to the
ground. Instantly the grasp upon her wrist relaxed as the
body, no longer controlled by the brain of Ghek, stumbled
aimlessly about for an instant before it sank to its knees and
then rolled over on its back; but Tara of Helium waited not

to note the full results of her act. The instant the fingers
loosened upon her wrist she broke away and dashed toward
the hills. Simultaneously a warning whistle broke from
Ghek's lips and in instant response the workers leaped to
their feet, one almost in the girl's path. She dodged the outstretched arms and was away again toward the hills and
freedom, when her foot caught in one of the hoe-like instruments with which the soil had been upturned and which
had been left, half imbedded in the ground. For an instant
she ran on, stumbling, in a mad effort to regain her equilibrium, but the upturned furrows caught at her feet—again
she stumbled and this time went down, and as she scrambled
to rise again a heavy body fell upon her and seized her arms.
A moment later she was surrounded and dragged to her feet
and as she looked around she saw Ghek crawling to his prostrate rykor. A moment later he advanced to her side.

The hideous face, incapable of registering emotion, gave
no clue to what was passing in the enormous brain. Was he
nursing thoughts of anger, of hate, of revenge? Tara of Helium could not guess, nor did she care. The worst had happened. She had tried to escape and she had failed. There
would never be another opportunity.

"Come!" said Ghek. "We will return to the tower." The
deadly monotone of his voice was unbroken. It was worse
than anger, for it revealed nothing of his intentions. It but
increased her horror of these great brains that were beyond
the possibility of human emotions.

And so she was dragged back to her prison in the tower
and Ghek took up his vigil again, squatting by the doorway,
but now he carried a naked sword in his hand and did not
quit his rykor, only to change to another that he had
brought to him when the first gave indications of weariness.
The girl sat looking at him. He had not been unkind to her,
but she felt no sense of gratitude, nor, on the other hand,
any sense of hatred. The brains, incapable themselves of any
of the finer sentiments, awoke none in her. She could not feel
gratitude, or affection, or hatred of them. There was only the
same unceasing sense of horror in their presence. She had
heard great scientists discuss the future of the red race and
she recalled that some had maintained that eventually the
brain would entirely dominate the man. There would be

no more instinctive acts or emotions, nothing would be done on impulse; but on the contrary reason would direct our every act. The propounder of the theory regretted that he might never enjoy the blessings of such a state, which, he argued, would result in the ideal life for mankind. Tara of Helium wished with all her heart that this learned scientist might be here to experience to the full the practical results of the fulfillment of his prophecy. Between the purely physical rykor and the purely mental kaldane there was little choice; but in the happy medium of normal, and imperfect, man, as she knew him, lay the most desirable state of existence. It would have been a splendid object lesson, she thought, to all those idealists who seek mass perfection in any phase of human endeavor, since here they might discover the truth that absolute perfection is as little to be desired as is its antithesis.

Gloomy were the thoughts that filled the mind of Tara of Helium as she awaited the summons from Luud—the summons that could mean for her but one thing: death. She guessed why he had sent for her and she knew that she must find the means for self-destruction before the night was over; but still she clung to hope and to life. She would not give up until there was no other way. She startled Ghek once by exclaiming aloud, almost fiercely: "I still live!"

"What do you mean?" asked the kaldane.

"I mean just what I say," she replied. "I still live and while I live I may still find a way. Dead, there is no hope."

"Find a way to what?" he asked.

"To life and liberty and mine own people," she responded.

"None who enters Bantoom ever leaves," he droned.

She did not reply and after a time he spoke again. "Sing to me," he said.

It was while she was singing that four warriors came to take her to Luud. They told Ghek that he was to remain where he was.

"Why?" asked Ghek.

"You have displeased Luud," replied one of the warriors.

"How?" demanded Ghek.

"You have demonstrated a lack of uncontaminable reasoning power. You have permitted sentiment to influence you, thus demonstrating that you are a defective. You know the fate of defectives."

"I know the fate of defectives, but I am no defective," insisted Ghek.

"You permitted the strange noises which issue from her throat to please and soothe you, knowing well that their origin and purpose had nothing whatever to do with logic or the powers of reason. This in itself constitutes an unimpeachable indictment of weakness. Then, influenced doubtless by an illogical feeling of sentiment, you permitted her to walk abroad in the fields to a place where she was able to make an almost successful attempt to escape. Your own reasoning power, were it not defective, would convince you that you are unfit. The natural, and reasonable, consequence is destruction. Therefore you will be destroyed in such a way that the example will be beneficial to all other kaldanes of the swarm of Luud. In the meantime you will remain where you are."

"You are right," said Ghek. "I will remain here until Luud sees fit to destroy me in the most reasonable manner."

Tara of Helium shot a look of amazement at him as they led her from the chamber. Over her shoulder she called back to him: "Remember, Ghek, you still live!" Then they led her along the interminable tunnels to where Luud awaited her.

When she was conducted into his presence he was squatting in a corner of the chamber upon his six spidery legs. Near the opposite wall lay his rykor, its beautiful form trapped in gorgeous harness—a dead thing without a guiding kaldane. Luud dismissed the warriors who had accompanied the prisoner. Then he sat with his terrible eyes fixed upon her and without speaking for some time. Tara of Helium could but wait. What was to come she could only guess. When it came would be sufficiently the time to meet it. There was no necessity for anticipating the end. Presently Luud spoke.

"You think to escape," he said, in the deadly, expressionless monotone of his kind—the only possible result of orally expressing reason uninfluenced by sentiment. "You will not escape. You are merely the embodiment of two imperfect things—an imperfect brain and an imperfect body. The two cannot exist together in perfection. There you see a perfect body." He pointed toward the rykor. "It has no brain. Here," and he raised one of his chelae to his head, "is the perfect brain. It needs no body to function perfectly and properly as a brain.

You would pit your feeble intellect against mine! Even now
you are planning to slay me. If you are thwarted in that you
expect to slay yourself. You will learn the power of mind over
matter. I am the mind. You are the matter. What brain you
have is too weak and ill-developed to deserve the name of
brain. You have permitted it to be weakened by impulsive
acts dictated by sentiment. It has no value. It has practically
no control over your existence. You will not kill me. You will
not kill yourself. When I am through with you you shall be
killed if it seems the logical thing to do. You have no conception of the possibilities for power which lie in a perfectly developed brain. Look at that rykor. He has no brain. He can
move but slightly of his own volition. An inherent mechanical
instinct that we have permitted to remain in him allows him to
carry food to his mouth; but he could not find food for himself. We have to place it within his reach and always in the
same place. Should we put food at his feet and leave him alone
he would starve to death. But now watch what a real brain
may accomplish."

He turned his eyes upon the rykor and squatted there glaring at the insensate thing. Presently, to the girl's horror,
the headless body moved. It rose slowly to its feet and crossed
the room to Luud; it stooped and took the hideous head in
its hands; it raised the head and set it on its shoulders.

"What chance have you against such power?" asked Luud.
"As I did with the rykor so can I do with you."

Tara of Helium made no reply. Evidently no vocal reply
was necessary.

"You doubt my ability!" stated Luud, which was precisely
the fact, though the girl had only thought it—she had not
said it.

Luud crossed the room and lay down. Then he detached
himself from the body and crawled across the floor until he
stood directly in front of the circular opening through which
she had seen him emerge the day that she had first been
brought to his presence. He stopped there and fastened his
terrible eyes upon her. He did not speak, but his eyes seemed
to be boring straight to the center of her brain. She felt an
almost irresistible force urging her toward the kaldane. She
fought to resist it; she tried to turn away her eyes, but she
could not. They were held as in horrid fascination upon the

glittering, lidless orbs of the great brain that faced her. Slowly, every step a painful struggle of resistance, she moved toward the horrific monster. She tried to cry aloud in an effort to awaken her numbing faculties, but no sound passed her lips. If those eyes would but turn away, just for an instant, she felt that she might regain the power to control her steps; but the eyes never left hers. They seemed but to burn deeper and deeper, gathering up every vestige of control of her entire nervous system.

As she approached the thing it backed slowly away upon its spider legs. She noticed that its chelae waved slowly to and fro before it as it backed, backed, backed, through the round aperture in the wall. Must she follow it there, too? What new and nameless horror lay concealed in that hidden chamber? No! she would not do it. Yet before she reached the wall she found herself down and crawling upon her hands and knees straight toward the hole from which the two eyes still clung to hers. At the very threshold of the opening she made a last, heroic stand, battling against the force that drew her on; but in the end she succumbed. With a gasp that ended in a sob Tara of Helium passed through the aperture into the chamber beyond.

The opening was but barely large enough to admit her. Upon the opposite side she found herself in a small chamber. Before her squatted Luud. Against the opposite wall lay a large and beautiful male rykor. He was without harness or other trappings.

"You see now," said Luud, "the futility of revolt."

The words seemed to release her momentarily from the spell. Quickly she turned away her eyes.

"Look at me!" commanded Luud.

Tara of Helium kept her eyes averted. She felt a new strength, or at least a diminution of the creature's power over her. Had she stumbled upon the secret of its uncanny domination over her will? She dared not hope. With eyes averted she turned toward the aperture through which those baleful eyes had drawn her. Again Luud commanded her to stop, but the voice alone lacked all authority to influence her. It was not like the eyes. She heard the creature whistle and knew that it was summoning assistance; but because she did not dare look toward it she did not see it turn and concentrate its gaze upon the great, headless body lying by the further wall.

The girl was still slightly under the spell of the creature's influence—she had not regained full and independent domination of her powers. She moved as one in the throes of some hideous nightmare—slowly, painfully, as though each limb was hampered by a great weight, or as she were dragging her body through a viscous fluid. The aperture was close, ah, so close, yet, struggle as she would, she seemed to be making no appreciable progress toward it.

Behind her, urged on by the malevolent power of the great brain, the headless body crawled upon all-fours toward her. At last she had reached the aperture. Something seemed to tell her that once beyond it the domination of the kaldane would be broken. She was almost through into the adjoining chamber when she felt a heavy hand close upon her ankle. The rykor had reached forth and seized her, and though she struggled the thing dragged her back into the room with Luud. It held her tight and drew her close, and then, to her horror, it commenced to caress her.

"You see now," she heard Luud's dull voice, "the futility of revolt—and its punishment."

Tara of Helium fought to defend herself, but pitifully weak were her muscles against this brainless incarnation of brute power. Yet she fought, fought on in the face of hopeless odds for the honor of the proud name she bore—fought alone, she whom the fighting men of a mighty empire, the flower of Martian chivalry, would gladly have lain down their lives to save.

CHAPTER VII

A REPELLENT SIGHT

THE CRUISER *VANATOR* careened through the tempest. That she had not been dashed to the ground, or twisted by the force of the elements into tangled wreckage, was due entirely to the caprice of Nature. For all the duration of the storm she rode, a helpless derelict, upon those storm-tossed waves of wind. But for all the dangers and vicissitudes they underwent, she and her crew might have borne charmed lives up to within an hour of the abating of the hurricane. It was then that the catastrophe occurred—a catastrophe indeed to the crew of the *Vanator* and the kingdom of Gathol.

The men had been without food or drink since leaving Helium, and they had been hurled about and buffeted in their lashings until all were worn to exhaustion. There was a brief lull in the storm during which one of the crew attempted to reach his quarters, after releasing the lashings which had held him to the precarious safety of the deck. The act in itself was a direct violation of orders and, in the eyes of the other members of the crew, the effect, which came with startling suddenness, took the form of a swift and terrible retribution. Scarce had the man released the safety snaps ere a swift arm of the storm-monster encircled the ship, rolling it over and over, with the result that the foolhardy warrior went overboard at the first turn.

Unloosed from their lashing by the constant turning and twisting of the ship and the force of the wind, the boarding and landing tackle had been trailing beneath the keel, a tangled mass of cordage and leather. Upon the occasions that the *Vanator* rolled completely over, these things would be wrapped about her until another revolution in the opposite direction, or the wind itself, carried them once again clear of the deck to trail, whipping in the storm, beneath the hurtling ship.

Into this fell the body of the warrior, and as a drowning man clutches at a straw so the fellow clutched at the tangled cordage that caught him and arrested his fall. With the strength of desperation he clung to the cordage, seeking frantically to entangle his legs and body in it. With each jerk of the ship his hand holds were all but torn loose, and though he knew that eventually they would be and that he must be dashed to the ground beneath, yet he fought with the madness that is born of hopelessness for the pitiful seconds which but prolonged his agony.

It was upon this sight then that Gahan of Gathol looked, over the edge of the careening deck of the *Vanator*, as he sought to learn the fate of his warrior. Lashed to the gunwale close at hand a single landing leather that had not fouled the tangled mass beneath whipped free from the ship's side, the hook snapping at its outer end. The Jed of Gathol grasped the situation in a single glance. Below him one of his people looked into the eyes of Death. To the jed's hand lay the means for succor.

There was no instant's hesitation. Casting off his deck lashings, he seized the landing leather and slipped over the ship's side. Swinging like a bob upon a mad pendulum he swung far out and back again, turning and twisting three thousand feet above the surface of Barsoom, and then, at last, the thing he had hoped for occurred. He was carried within reach of the cordage where the warrior still clung, though with rapidly diminishing strength. Catching one leg in a loop of the tangled strands Gahan pulled himself close enough to seize another quite near to the fellow. Clinging precariously to this new hold the jed slowly drew in the landing leather, down which he had clambered until he could grasp the hook at its end. This he fastened to a ring in the warrior's harness, just before the man's weakened fingers slipped from their hold upon the cordage.

Temporarily, at least, he had saved the life of his subject, and now he turned his attention toward insuring his own safety. Inextricably entangled in the mess to which he was clinging were numerous other landing hooks such as he had attached to the warrior's harness, and with one of these he sought to secure himself until the storm should abate sufficiently to permit him to climb to the deck, but even as he reached for one that swung near him the ship was caught in a renewed burst of the storm's fury, the thrashing cordage whipped and snapped to the lunging of the great craft and one of the heavy metal hooks, lashing through the air, struck the Jed of Gathol fair between the eyes.

Momentarily stunned, Gahan's fingers slipped from their hold upon the cordage and the man shot downward through the thin air of dying Mars toward the ground three thousand feet beneath, while upon the deck of the rolling *Vanator* his faithful warriors clung to their lashings all unconscious of the fate of their beloved leader; nor was it until more than an hour later, after the storm had materially subsided, that they realized he was lost, or knew the self-sacrificing

heroism of the act that had sealed his doom. The *Vanator*
now rested upon an even keel as she was carried along by a
strong, though steady, wind. The warriors had cast off their
deck lashings and the officers were taking account of losses
and damage when a weak cry was heard from oversides, attracting their attention to the man hanging in the cordage
beneath the keel. Strong arms hoisted him to the deck and
then it was that the crew of the *Vanator* learned of the heroism of their jed and his end. How far they had traveled since
his loss they could only vaguely guess, nor could they return
in search of him in the disabled condition of the ship. It was
a saddened company that drifted onward through the air
toward whatever destination Fate was to choose for them.

And Gahan, Jed of Gathol—what of him? Plummet-like he
fell for a thousand feet and then the storm seized him in its
giant clutch and bore him far aloft again. As a bit of paper
borne upon a gale he was tossed about in mid-air, the sport
and plaything of the wind. Over and over it turned him and
upward and downward it carried him, but after each new
sally of the element he was brought nearer to the ground.
The freaks of cyclonic storms are the rule of cyclonic storms,
since such storms are in themselves freaks. They uproot and
demolish giant trees, and in the same gust they transport frail
infants for miles and deposit them unharmed in their wake.

And so it was with Gahan of Gathol. Expecting momentarily to be dashed to destruction he presently found himself
deposited gently upon the soft, ochre moss of a dead sea-
bottom, bodily no worse off for his harrowing adventure
than in the possession of a slight swelling upon his forehead
where the metal hook had struck him. Scarcely able to believe that Fate had dealt thus gently with him, the jed arose
slowly, as though more than half convinced that he should
discover crushed and splintered bones that would not support his weight. But he was intact. He looked about him in a
vain effort at orientation. The air was filled with flying dust
and débris. The Sun was obliterated. His vision was confined
to a radius of a few hundred yards of ochre moss and dust-
filled air. Five hundred yards away in any direction there
might have arisen the walls of a great city and he not known
it. It was useless to move from where he was until the air
cleared, since he could not know in what direction he was

moving, and so he stretched himself upon the moss and
waited, pondering the fate of his warriors and his ship, but
giving little thought to his own precarious situation.

Lashed to his harness were his swords, his pistols, and a
dagger, and in his pocket-pouch a small quantity of the con-
centrated rations that form a part of the equipment of the
fighting men of Barsoom. These things together with trained
muscles, high courage, and an undaunted spirit sufficed him
for whatever misadventures might lie between him and Gathol, which lay in what direction he knew not, nor at what
distance.

The wind was falling rapidly and with it the dust that ob-
scured the landscape. That the storm was over he was convinced, but he chafed at the inactivity the low visibility put
upon him, nor did conditions better materially before night
fell, so that he was forced to await the new day at the very
spot at which the tempest had deposited him. Without his
sleeping silks and furs he spent a far from comfortable night,
and it was with feelings of unmixed relief that he saw the
sudden dawn burst upon him. The air was now clear and in
the light of the new day he saw an undulating plain stretching in all directions about him, while to the northwest there
were barely discernible the outlines of low hills. Toward the
southeast of Gathol was such a country, and as Gahan sur-
mised the direction and the velocity of the storm to have
carried him somewhere in the vicinity of the country he
thought he recognized, he assumed that Gathol lay behind
the hills he now saw, whereas, in reality, it lay far to the
northeast.

It was two days before Gahan had crossed the plain and
reached the summit of the hills from which he hoped to see
his own country, only to meet at last with disappointment.
Before him stretched another plain, of even greater proportions than that he had but just crossed, and beyond this
other hills. In one material respect this plain differed from
that behind him in that it was dotted with occasional isolated
hills. Convinced, however, that Gathol lay somewhere in the
direction of his search he descended into the valley and bent
his steps toward the northwest.

For weeks Gahan of Gathol crossed valleys and hills in
search of some familiar landmark that might point his way

toward his native land, but the summit of each succeeding ridge revealed but another unfamiliar view. He saw few animals and no men, until he finally came to the belief that he had fallen upon that fabled area of ancient Barsoom which lay under the curse of her olden gods—the once rich and fertile country whose people in their pride and arrogance had denied the deities, and whose punishment had been extermination.

And then, one day, he scaled low hills and looked into an inhabited valley—a valley of trees and cultivated fields and plots of ground enclosed by stone walls surrounding strange towers. He saw people working in the fields, but he did not rush down to greet them. First he must know more of them and whether they might be assumed to be friends or enemies. Hidden by concealing shrubbery he crawled to a vantage point upon a hill that projected further into the valley, and here he lay upon his belly watching the workers closest to him. They were still quite a distance from him and he could not be quite sure of them, but there was something verging upon the unnatural about them. Their heads seemed out of proportion to their bodies—too large.

For a long time he lay watching them and ever more forcibly it was borne in upon his consciousness that they were not as he, and that it would be rash to trust himself among them. Presently he saw a couple appear from the nearest enclosure and slowly approach those who were working nearest to the hill where he lay in hiding. Immediately he was aware that one of these differed from all the others. Even at the greater distance he noted that the head was smaller and as they approached, he was confident that the harness of one of them was not as the harness of its companion or of that of any of those who tilled the fields.

The two stopped often, apparently in argument, as though one would proceed in the direction that they were going while the other demurred. But each time the smaller won reluctant consent from the other, and so they came closer and closer to the last line of workers toiling between the enclosure from which they had come and the hill where Gahan of Gathol lay watching, and then suddenly the smaller figure struck its companion full in the face. Gahan, horrified, saw the latter's head topple from its body, saw the body stagger and fall to the ground. The man half rose from his concealment the better to view the happenings in the valley below. The creature that had felled its companion was dashing madly in the direction of the hill upon which he was hidden, it dodged one of the workers that sought to seize it. Gahan hoped that it would gain its liberty, why he did not know, other than at closer range it had every appearance of being a creature of his own race. Then he saw it stumble and go down and instantly its pursuers were upon it. Then it was that Gahan's eyes chanced to return to the figure of the creature the fugitive had felled.

What horror was this that he was witnessing? Or were his eyes playing some ghastly joke upon him? No, impossible though it was—it was true—the head was moving slowly to the fallen body. It placed itself upon the shoulders, the body rose, and the creature, seemingly as good as new, ran quickly to where its fellows were dragging the hapless captive to its feet.

The watcher saw the creature take its prisoner by the arm and lead it back to the enclosure, and even across the distance that separated them from him he could note dejection and utter hopelessness in the bearing of the prisoner, and, too, he was half convinced that it was a woman, perhaps a red Martian of his own race. Could he be sure that this was true he must make some effort to rescue her even though the customs of his strange world required it only in case she was of his own country; but he was not sure; she might not be a red Martian at all, or, if she were, it was as possible that she sprang from an enemy people as not. His first duty was to return to his own people with as little personal risk as possible, and though the thought of adventure stirred his blood he put the temptation aside with a sigh and turned away from the peaceful and beautiful valley that he longed to enter, for it was his intention to skirt its eastern edge and continue his search for Gathol beyond.

As Gahan of Gathol turned his steps along the southern slopes of the hills that bound Bantoom upon the south and east, his attention was attracted toward a small cluster of trees a short distance to his right. The low sun was casting long shadows. It would soon be night. The trees were off the path that he had chosen and he had little mind to be diverted from his way; but as he looked again he hesitated. There was something there besides boles of trees, and underbrush. There were suggestions of familiar lines of the handicraft of man. Gahan stopped and strained his eyes in the direction of the thing that had arrested his attention. No, he must be mistaken—the branches of the trees and a low bush had taken on an unnatural semblance in the horizontal rays of the setting sun. He turned and continued upon his way; but as he cast another side glance in the direction of the object of his interest, the sun's rays were shot back into his eyes from a glistening point of radiance among the trees.

Gahan shook his head and walked quickly toward the mystery, determined now to solve it. The shining object still lured him on and when he had come closer to it his eyes went wide in surprise, for the thing they saw was naught else than the jewel-encrusted emblem upon the prow of a small flier. Gahan, his hand upon his short-sword, moved silently forward, but as he neared the craft he saw that he had naught to fear, for it was deserted. Then he turned his attention toward the emblem. As its significance was flashed to his understanding his face paled and his heart went cold—it was the insignia of the house of The Warlord of Barsoom. Instantly he saw the dejected figure of the captive being led back to her prison in the valley just beyond the hills. Tara of Helium! And he had been so near to deserting her to her fate. The cold sweat stood in beads upon his brow.

A hasty examination of the deserted craft unfolded to the young jed the whole tragic story. The same tempest that had proved his undoing had borne Tara of Helium to this distant country. Here, doubtless, she had landed in hope of obtaining food and water since, without a propeller, she could not hope to reach her native city, or any other friendly port, other than by the merest caprice of Fate. The flier seemed intact except for the missing propeller and the fact that it had been carefully moored in the shelter of the clump of trees indicated that the girl had expected to return to it, while the dust and leaves upon its deck spoke of the long days, and even weeks, since she had landed. Mute yet eloquent proofs, these things, that Tara of Helium was a prisoner, and that she was the very prisoner whose bold dash for liberty he had so recently witnessed he now had not the slightest doubt.

The question now revolved solely about her rescue. He knew to which tower she had been taken—that much and no more. Of the number, the kind, or the disposition of her captors he knew nothing; nor did he care—for Tara of Helium he would face a hostile world alone. Rapidly he considered several plans for succoring her; but the one that appealed most strongly to him was that which offered the greatest chance of escape for the girl should he be successful in reaching her. His decision reached he turned his attention quickly toward the flier. Casting off its lashings he dragged it out from beneath the trees, and, mounting to the deck tested out the various controls. The motor started at a touch and purred sweetly, the buoyancy tanks were well stocked, and the ship answered perfectly to the controls which regulated her altitude. There was nothing needed but a propeller to make her fit for the long voyage to Helium. Gahan shrugged impatiently—there might not be a propeller within a thousand haads. But what mattered it? The craft even without a propeller would still answer the purpose his plan required of it—provided the captors of Tara of Helium were a people without ships, and he had seen nothing to suggest that they had ships. The architecture of their towers and enclosures assured him that they had not.

The sudden Barsoomian night had fallen. Cluros rode majestically the high heavens. The rumbling roar of a banth reverberated among the hills. Gahan of Gathol let the ship rise a few feet from the ground, then, seizing a bow rope, he dropped over the side. To tow the little craft was now a thing of ease, and as Gahan moved rapidly toward the brow of the hill above Bantoom the flier floated behind him as lightly as a swan upon a quiet lake. Now down the hill toward the tower dimly visible in the moonlight the Gatholian turned his steps. Closer behind him sounded the roar of the hunting banth. He wondered if the beast sought him or was following some other spoor. He could not be delayed now by any hungry beast of prey, for what might that very instant be befalling Tara of Helium he could not guess; and so he hastened his steps. But closer and closer came the horrid screams of the great carnivore, and now he heard the swift fall of padded feet upon the hillside behind him. He glanced back just in time to see the beast break into a rapid charge. His hand leaped to the hilt of his long-sword, but he did not draw, for in the same instant he saw the futility of armed resistance, since behind the first banth came a herd of at least a dozen others. There was but a single alternative to a futile stand and that he grasped in the instant that he saw the overwhelming number of his antagonists.

Springing lightly from the ground he swarmed up the rope toward the bow of the flier. His weight drew the craft slightly lower and at the very instant that the man drew himself to the deck at the bow of the vessel, the leading banth sprang for the stern. Gahan leaped to his feet and rushed toward the great beast in the hope of dislodging it before it had succeeded in clambering aboard. At the same instant he saw that others of the banths were racing toward them with the quite evident intention of following their leader to the ship's deck. Should they reach it in any numbers he would be lost. There was but a single hope. Leaping for the altitude control Gahan pulled it wide. Simultaneously three banths leaped for the deck. The craft rose swiftly. Gahan felt the impact of a body against the keel, followed by the soft thuds of the great bodies as they struck the ground beneath. His act had not been an instant too soon. And now the leader had gained the deck and stood at the stern with glaring eyes and snarling jaws. Gahan drew his sword. The beast, possibly disconcerted by the novelty of its position, did not charge. Instead it crept slowly toward its intended prey. The craft was rising and Gahan placed a foot upon the control and stopped the ascent. He did not wish to chance rising to some higher air current that would bear him away. Already the craft was moving slowly toward the tower, carried thither by the impetus of the banth's heavy body leaping upon it from astern.

The man watched the slow approach of the monster, the slavering jowls, the malignant expression of the devilish face. The creature, finding the deck stable, appeared to be gaining confidence, and then the man leaped suddenly to one side of the deck and the tiny flier heeled as suddenly in response. The banth slipped and clutched frantically at the deck. Gahan leaped in with his naked sword; the great beast caught itself and reared upon its hind legs to reach forth and seize this presumptuous mortal that dared question its right to the flesh it craved; and then the man sprang to the opposite side of the deck. The banth toppled sideways at the same instant that it attempted to spring; a raking talon passed close to Gahan's head at the moment that his sword lunged through the savage heart, and as the warrior wrenched his blade from the carcass it slipped silently over the side of the ship.

A glance below showed that the vessel was drifting in the direction of the tower to which Gahan had seen the prisoner led. In another moment or two it would be directly over it. The man sprang to the control and let the craft drop quickly toward the ground where followed the banths, still hot for their prey. To land outside the enclosure spelled certain death, while inside he could see many forms huddled upon the ground as in sleep. The ship floated now but a few feet above the wall of the enclosure. There was nothing for it but to risk all on a bold bid for fortune, or drift helplessly past without hope of returning through the banth-infested valley, from many points of which he could now hear the roars and growls of these fierce Barsoomian lions.

Slipping over the side Gahan descended by the trailing anchor-rope until his feet touched the top of the wall, where he had no difficulty in arresting the slow drifting of the ship. Then he drew up the anchor and lowered it inside the enclosure. Still there was no movement upon the part of the sleepers beneath—they lay as dead men. Dull lights shone from openings in the tower; but there was no sign of guard or walking inmate. Clinging to the rope Gahan lowered himself within the enclosure, where he had his first close view of the creatures lying there in what he had thought sleep. With a half smothered exclamation of horror the man drew back from the headless bodies of the rykors. At first he thought them the corpses of decapitated humans like himself, which was quite bad enough; but when he saw them move and realized that they were endowed with life, his horror and disgust became even greater.

Here then was the explanation of the thing he had witnessed that afternoon, when Tara of Helium had struck the head from her captor and Gahan had seen the head crawl back to its body. And to think that the pearl of Helium was in the power of such hideous things as these. Again the man shuddered, but he hastened to make fast the flier, clamber again to its deck and lower it to the floor of the enclosure. Then he strode toward a door in the base of the tower, stepping lightly over the recumbent forms of the unconscious rykors, and crossing the threshold disappeared within.

CHAPTER VIII

CLOSE WORK

GHEK, IN HIS happier days third foreman of the fields of Luud, sat nursing his anger and his humiliation. Recently something had awakened within him the existence of which he had never before even dreamed. Had the influence of the strange captive woman aught to do with this unrest and dissatisfaction? He did not know. He missed the soothing influence of the noise she called singing. Could it be that there were other things more desirable than cold logic and undefiled brain power? Was well balanced imperfection more to be sought after then, than the high development of a single characteristic? He thought of the great, ultimate brain toward which all kaldanes were striving. It would be deaf, and dumb, and blind. A thousand beautiful strangers might sing and dance about it, but it could derive no pleasure from the singing or the dancing since it would possess no perceptive faculties. Already had the kaldanes shut themselves off from most of the gratifications of the senses. Ghek wondered if much was to be gained by denying themselves still further, and with the thought came a question as to the whole fabric of their theory. After all perhaps the girl was right; what purpose could a great brain serve sealed in the bowels of the earth?

And he, Ghek, was to die for this theory. Luud had decreed it. The injustice of it overwhelmed him with rage. But he was helpless. There was no escape. Beyond the enclosure the banths awaited him; within, his own kind, equally as merciless and ferocious. Among them there was no such thing as love, or loyalty, or friendship—they were just brains. He might kill Luud; but what would that profit him? Another

king would be loosed from his sealed chamber and Ghek
would be killed. He did not know it but he would not even
have the poor satisfaction of satisfied revenge, since he was
not capable of feeling so abstruse a sentiment.

Ghek, mounted upon his rykor, paced the floor of the tower
chamber in which he had been ordered to remain. Ordinarily
he would have accepted the sentence of Luud with perfect
equanimity, since it was but the logical result of reason; but
now it seemed different. The stranger woman had bewitched
him. Life appeared a pleasant thing—there were great possibilities in it. The dream of the ultimate brain had receded
into a tenuous haze far in the background of his thoughts.

At that moment there appeared in the doorway of the
chamber a red warrior with naked sword. He was a male
counterpart of the prisoner whose sweet voice had undermined the cold, calculating reason of the kaldane.

"Silence!" admonished the newcomer, his straight brows
gathered in an ominous frown and the point of his long-sword
playing menacingly before the eyes of the kaldane. "I seek the
woman, Tara of Helium. Where is she? If you value your life
speak quickly and speak the truth."

If he valued his life! It was a truth that Ghek had but just
learned. He thought quickly. After all, a great brain is not
without its uses. Perhaps here lay escape from the sentence
of Luud.

"You are of her kind?" he asked. "You come to rescue her?"

"Yes."

"Listen, then, I have befriended her, and because of this
I am to die. If I help you to liberate her, will you take me with
you?"

Gahan of Gathol eyed the weird creature from crown to
foot—the perfect body, the grotesque head, the expressionless face. Among such as these had the beautiful daughter of
Helium been held captive for days and weeks.

"If she lives and is unharmed," he said, "I will take you
with us."

"When they took her from me she was alive and unharmed." replied Ghek. "I cannot say what has befallen her
since. Luud sent for her."

"Who is Luud? Where is he? Lead me to him." Gahan
spoke quickly in tones vibrant with authority.

"Come, then," said Ghek, leading the way from the apartment and down a stairway toward the underground burrows
of the kaldanes. "Luud is my king. I will take you to his
chambers."

"Hasten!" urged Gahan.

"Sheathe your sword," warned Ghek, "so that should we
pass others of my kind I may say to them that you are a new
prisoner with some likelihood of winning their belief."

Gahan did as he was bid, but warning the kaldane that
his hand was ever ready at his dagger's hilt.

"You need have no fear of treachery," said Ghek. "My only
hope of life lies in you."

"And if you fail me," Gahan admonished him, "I can promise you as sure a death as even your king might guarantee
you."

Ghek made no reply, but moved rapidly through the winding subterranean corridors until Gahan began to realize how
truly was he in the hands of this strange monster. If the fellow
should prove false it would profit Gahan nothing to slay him,
since without his guidance the red man might never hope
to retrace his way to the tower and freedom.

Twice they met and were accosted by other kaldanes; but
in both instances Ghek's simple statement that he was taking
a new prisoner to Luud appeared to allay all suspicion, and
then at last they came to the ante-chamber of the king.

"Here, now, red man, thou must fight, if ever," whispered
Ghek. "Enter there!" and he pointed to a doorway before
them.

"And you?" asked Gahan, still fearful of treachery.

"My rykor is powerful," replied the kaldane. "I shall accompany you and fight at your side. As well die thus as in
torture later at the will of Luud. Come!"

But Gahan had already crossed the room and entered the
chamber beyond. Upon the opposite side of the room was a
circular opening guarded by two warriors. Beyond this opening he could see two figures struggling upon the floor, and
the fleeting glimpse he had of one of the faces suddenly endowed him with the strength of ten warriors and the ferocity of a wounded banth. It was Tara of Helium, fighting
for her honor or her life.

The warriors, startled by the unexpected appearance of a

red man, stood for a moment in dumb amazement, and in that moment Gahan of Gathol was upon them, and one was down, a sword-thrust through its heart.

"Strike at the heads," whispered the voice of Ghek in Gahan's ear. The latter saw the head of the fallen warrior crawl quickly within the aperture leading to the chamber where he had seen Tara of Helium in the clutches of a headless body. Then the sword of Ghek struck the kaldane of the remaining warrior from its rykor and Gahan ran his sword through the repulsive head.

Instantly the red warrior leaped for the aperture, while close behind him came Ghek.

"Look not upon the eyes of Luud," warned the kaldane, "or you are lost."

Within the chamber Gahan saw Tara of Helium in the clutches of a mighty body, while close to the wall upon the opposite side of the apartment crouched the hideous, spider-like Luud. Instantly the king realized the menace to himself and sought to fasten his eyes upon the eyes of Gahan, and in doing so he was forced to relax his concentration upon the rykor in whose embraces Tara struggled, so that almost immediately the girl found herself able to tear away from the awful, headless thing.

As she rose quickly to her feet she saw for the first time the cause of the interruption of Luud's plans. A red warrior! Her heart leaped in rejoicing and thanksgiving. What miracle of fate had sent him to her? She did not recognize him, though, this travel-worn warrior in the plain harness which showed no single jewel. How could she have guessed him the same as the scintillant creature of platinum and diamonds that she had seen for a brief hour under such different circumstances at the court of her august sire?

Luud saw Ghek following the strange warrior into the chamber. "Strike him down, Ghek!" commanded the king. "Strike down the stranger and your life shall be yours."

Gahan glanced at the hideous face of the king.

"Seek not his eyes," screamed Tara in warning; but it was too late. Already the horrid hypnotic gaze of the king kaldane had seized upon the eyes of Gahan. The red warrior hesitated in his stride. His sword point dropped slowly toward the floor. Tara glanced toward Ghek. She saw the creature glaring with his expressionless eyes upon the broad back of the stranger. She saw the hand of the creature's rykor creeping stealthily toward the hilt of its dagger.

And then Tara of Helium raised her eyes aloft and poured forth the notes of Mars' most beautiful melody, *The Song of Love*.

Ghek drew his dagger from its sheath. His eyes turned toward the singing girl. Luud's glance wavered from the eyes of the man to the face of Tara, and the instant that the latter's song distracted his attention from his victim, Gahan of Gathols shook himself and as with a supreme effort of will forced his eyes to the wall above Luud's hideous head. Ghek raised his dagger above his right shoulder, took a single quick step forward, and struck. The girl's song ended in a stifled scream as she leaped forward with the evident intention of frustrating the kaldane's purpose; but she was too late, and well it was, for an instant later she realized the purpose of Ghek's act as she saw the dagger fly from his hand, pass Gahan's shoulder, and sink full to the guard in the soft face of Luud.

"Come!" cried the assassin, "we have no time to lose," and started for the aperture through which they had entered the chamber; but in his stride he paused as his glance was arrested by the form of the mighty rykor lying prone upon the floor—a king's rykor; the most beautiful, the most powerful, that the breeders of Bantoom could produce. Ghek realized that in his escape he could take with him but a single rykor, and there was none in Bantoom that could give him better service than this giant lying here. Quickly he transferred himself to the shoulders of the great, inert hulk. Instantly the latter was transformed to a sentient creature, filled with pulsing life and alert energy.

"Now," said the kaldane, "we are ready. Let whoso would revert to nothingness impede me." Even as he spoke he stooped and crawled into the chamber beyond, while Gahan, taking Tara by the arm, motioned her to follow. The girl looked him full in the eyes for the first time. "The Gods of my people have been kind," she said; "you came just in time. To the thanks of Tara of Helium shall be added those of The Warlord of Barsoom and his people. Thy reward shall surpass thy greatest desires."

Gahan of Gathol saw that she did not recognize him, and quickly he checked the warm greeting that had been upon his lips.

"Be thou Tara of Helium or another," he replied, "is immaterial, to serve thus a red woman of Barsoom is in itself sufficient reward."

As they spoke the girl was making her way through the aperture after Ghek, and presently all three had quitted the apartments of Luud and were moving rapidly along the winding corridors toward the tower. Ghek repeatedly urged them to greater speed, but the red men of Barsoom were never keen for retreat, and so the two that followed him moved all too slowly for the kaldane.

"There are none to impede our progress," urged Gahan, "so why tax the strength of the Princess by needless haste?"

"I fear not so much opposition ahead, for there are none there who know the thing that has been done in Luud's chambers this night; but the kaldane of one of the warriors who stood guard before Luud's apartment escaped, and you may count it a truth that he lost no time in seeking aid. That it did not come before we left is due solely to the rapidity with which events transpired in the king's[1] room. Long before we reach the tower they will be upon us from behind, and that they will come in numbers far superior to ours and with great and powerful rykors I well know."

Nor was Ghek's prophecy long in fulfilment. Presently the sounds of pursuit became audible in the distant clanking of accouterments and the whistling *call to arms* of the kaldanes.

"The tower is but a short distance now," cried Ghek. "Make haste while yet you may, and if we can barricade it until the sun rises we may yet escape."

"We shall need no barricades for we shall not linger in the tower," replied Gahan, moving more rapidly as he realized from the volume of sound behind them the great number of their pursuers.

---

[1] I have used the word *king* in describing the rulers or chiefs of the Bantoomian swarms, since the word itself is unpronounceable in English, nor does *jed* or *jeddak* of the red Martian tongue have quite the same meaning as the Bantoomian word, which has practically the same significance as the English word *queen* as applied to the leader of a swarm of bees—J. C.

"But we may not go further than the tower tonight," insisted Ghek. "Beyond the tower await the banths and certain death."

Gahan smiled. "Fear not the banths," he assured them. "Can we but reach the enclosure a little ahead of our pursuers we have naught to fear from any evil power within this accursed valley."

Ghek made no reply, nor did his expressionless face denote either belief or skepticism. The girl looked into the face of the man questioningly. She did not understand.

"Your flier," he said. "It is moored before the tower."

Her face lighted with pleasure and relief. "You found it!" she exclaimed. "What fortune!"

"It was fortune indeed," he replied. "Since it not only told that you were a prisoner here; but it saved me from the banths as I was crossing the valley from the hills to this tower into which I saw them take you this afternoon after your brave attempt at escape."

"How did you know it was I?" she asked, her puzzled brows scanning his face as though she sought to recall from past memories some scene in which he figured.

"Who is there but knows of the loss of the Princess Tara of Helium?" he replied. "And when I saw the device upon your flier I knew at once, though I had not known when I saw you among them in the fields a short time earlier. Too great was the distance for me to make certain whether their captive was man or woman. Had chance not divulged the hiding place of your flier I had gone my way, Tara of Helium. I shudder to think how close was the chance at that. But for the momentary shining of the sun upon the emblazoned device on the prow of your craft, I had passed on unknowing."

The girl shuddered. "The Gods sent you," she whispered reverently.

"The Gods sent me, Tara of Helium," he replied.

"But I do not recognize you," she said. "I have tried to recall you, but I have failed. Your name; what may it be?"

"It is not strange that so great a princess should not recall the face of every roving panthan of Barsoom," he replied with a smile.

"But your name?" insisted the girl.

"Call me Turan," replied the man, for it had come to him

that if Tara of Helium recognized him as the man whose impetuous avowal of love had angered her that day in the gardens of The Warlord, her situation might be rendered infinitely less bearable than were she to believe him a total
stranger. Then, too, as a simple panthan[1] he might win a
greater degree of her confidence by his loyalty and faithful-
ness and a place in her esteem that seemed to have been closed
to the resplendent Jed of Gathol.

They had reached the tower now, and as they entered it
from the subterranean corridor a backward glance revealed
the van of their pursuers—hideous kaldanes mounted upon
swift and powerful rykors. As rapidly as might be the three
ascended the stairways leading to the ground level, but after
them, even more rapidly, came the minions of Luud. Ghek
led the way, grasping one of Tara's hands the more easily to
guide and assist her, while Gahan of Gathol followed a few
paces in their rear, his bared sword ready for the assault that
all realized must come upon them now before ever they
reached the enclosure and the flier.

"Let Ghek drop behind to your side," said Tara, "and fight
with you."

"There is but room for a single blade in these narrow
corridors," replied the Gatholian. "Hasten on with Ghek and
win to the deck of the flier. Have your hand upon the control, and if I come far enough ahead of these to reach the
dangling cable you can rise at my word and I can clamber to
the deck at my leisure; but if one of them emerges first into
the enclosure you will know that I shall never come, and you
will rise quickly and trust to the Gods of our ancestors to
give you a fair breeze in the direction of a more hospitable
people."

Tara of Helium shook her head. "We will not desert you,
panthan," she said.

Gahan, ignoring her reply, spoke above her head to Ghek.
"Take her to the craft moored within the enclosure," he commanded. "It is our only hope. Alone, I may win to its deck;
but have I to wait upon you two at the last moment the
chances are that none of us will escape. Do as I bid." His tone
was haughty and arrogant—the tone of a man who has com-

---

[1] Soldier of Fortune; free-lance warrior.

manded other men from birth, and whose will has been law.
Tara of Helium was both angered and vexed. She was not
accustomed to being either commanded or ignored; but with
all her royal pride she was no fool, and she knew the man was
right; that he was risking his life to save hers, so she hastened
on with Ghek as she was bid, and after the first flush of anger
she smiled, for the realization came to her that this fellow
was but a rough untutored warrior, skilled not in the finer
usages of cultured courts. His heart was right, though; a
brave and loyal heart, and gladly she forgave him the offense
of his tone and manner. But what a tone! Recollection of it
gave her sudden pause. Panthans were rough and ready men.
Often they rose to positions of high command, so it was not
the note of authority in the fellow's voice that seemed remarkable; but something else—a quality that was indefinable,
yet as distinct as it was familiar. She had heard it before when
the voice of her great-grandsire, Tardos Mors, Jeddak of
Helium, had risen in command; and in the voice of her grandfather, Mors Kajak, the jed; and in the ringing tones of her
illustrious sire, John Carter, Warlord of Barsoom, when he
addressed his warriors.

But now she had no time to speculate upon so trivial a
thing, for behind her came the sudden clash of arms and she
knew that Turan, the panthan, had crossed swords with the
first of their pursuers. As she glanced back he was still visible
beyond a turn in the stairway, so that she could see the quick
swordplay that ensued. Daughter of a world's greatest swordsman, she knew well the finest points of the art. She saw the
clumsy attack of the kaldane and the quick, sure return of
the panthan. As she looked down from above upon his
almost naked body, trapped only in the simplest of unadorned
harness, and saw the play of the lithe muscles beneath the
red-bronze skin, and witnessed the quick and delicate play of
his sword point, to her sense of obligation was added a
spontaneous admission of admiration that was but the natural tribute of a woman to skill and bravery and, perchance,
some trifle to manly symmetry and strength.

Three times the panthan's blade changed its position—once
to fend a savage cut; once to feint; and once to thrust. And
as he withdrew it from the last position the kaldane rolled
lifeless from its stumbling rykor and Turan sprang quickly

down the steps to engage the next behind, and then Ghek had drawn Tara upward and a turn in the stairway shut the battling panthan from her view; but still she heard the ring of steel on steel, the clank of accouterments and the shrill whistling of the kaldanes. Her heart moved her to turn back to the side of her brave defender; but her judgment told her that she could serve him best by being ready at the control of the flier at the moment he reached the enclosure.

CHAPTER IX

ADRIFT OVER STRANGE REGIONS

PRESENTLY GHEK PUSHED aside a door that opened from the stairway, and before them Tara saw the moonlight flooding the walled court where the headless rykors lay beside their feeding-troughs. She saw the perfect bodies, muscled as the best of her father's fighting men, and the females whose figures would have been the envy of many of Helium's most beautiful women. Ah, if she could but endow these with the power to act! Then indeed might the safety of the panthan be assured; but they were only poor lumps of clay, nor had she the power to quicken them to life. Ever must they lie thus until dominated by the cold, heartless brain of the kaldane. The girl sighed in pity even as she shuddered in disgust as she picked her way over and among the sprawled creatures toward the flier.

Quickly she and Ghek mounted to the deck after the latter had cast off the moorings. Tara tested the control, raising and lowering the ship a few feet within the walled space. It responded perfectly. Then she lowered it to the ground again and waited. From the open doorway came the sounds of conflict, now nearing them, now receding. The girl, having witnessed her champion's skill, had little fear of the outcome. Only a single antagonist could face him at a time upon the narrow stairway, he had the advantage of position and of the defensive, and he was a master of the sword while they

were clumsy bunglers by comparison. Their sole advantage
was in their numbers, unless they might find a way to come
upon him from behind.

She paled at the thought. Could she have seen him she
might have been further perturbed, for he took no advantage of many opportunities to win nearer the enclosure. He
fought coolly, but with a savage persistence that bore little
semblance to purely defensive action. Often he clambered
over the body of a fallen foe to leap against the next behind,
and once there lay five dead kaldanes behind him, so far had
he pushed back his antagonists. They did not know it, these
kaldanes that he fought, nor did the girl awaiting him upon
the flier, but Gahan of Gathol was engaged in a more alluring
sport than winning to freedom, for he was avenging the indignities that had been put upon the woman he loved; but
presently he realized that he might be jeopardizing her safety
uselessly, and so he struck down another before him and
turning leaped quickly up the stairway, while the leading
kaldanes slipped upon the brain-covered floor and stumbled
in pursuit.

Gahan reached the enclosure twenty paces ahead of them
and raced toward the flier. "Rise!" he shouted to the girl. "I
will ascend the cable."

Slowly the small craft rose from the ground as Gahan
leaped the inert bodies of the rykors lying in his path. The
first of the pursuers sprang from the tower just as Gahan
seized the trailing rope.

"Faster!" he shouted to the girl above, "or they will drag
us down!" But the ship seemed scarcely to move, though in
reality she was rising as rapidly as might have been expected
of a one-man flier carrying a load of three. Gahan swung
free above the top of the wall, but the end of the rope still
dragged the ground as the kaldanes reached it. They were
pouring in a steady stream from the tower into the enclosure.
The leader seized the rope.

"Quick!" he cried. "Lay hold and we will drag them down."

It needed but the weight of a few to accomplish his design.
The ship was stopped in its flight and then, to the horror of
the girl, she felt it being dragged steadily downward. Gahan,
too, realized the danger and the necessity for instant action.
Clinging to the rope with his left hand, he had wound a leg

about it, leaving his right hand free for his long-sword which he had not sheathed. A downward cut clove the soft head of a kaldane, and another severed the taut rope beneath the panthan's feet. The girl heard a sudden renewal of the shrill whistling of her foes, and at the same time she realized that the craft was rising again. Slowly it drifted upward, out of reach of the enemy, and a moment later she saw the figure of Turan clamber over the side. For the first time in many weeks her heart was filled with the joy of thanksgiving; but her first thought was of another.

"You are not wounded?" she asked.

"No, Tara of Helium," he replied. "They were scarce worth the effort of my blade, and never were they a menace to me because of their swords."

"They should have slain you easily," said Ghek. "So great and highly developed is the power of reason among us that they should have known before you struck just where, logically, you must seek to strike, and so they should have been able to parry your every thrust and easily find an opening to your heart."

"But they did not, Ghek," Gahan reminded him. "Their theory of development is wrong, for it does not tend toward a perfectly balanced whole. You have developed the brain and neglected the body and you can never do with the hands of another what you can do with your own hands. Mine are trained to the sword—every muscle responds instantly and accurately, and almost mechanically, to the need of the instant. I am scarcely objectively aware that I think when I fight, so quickly does my point take advantage of every opening, or spring to my defense if I am threatened that it is almost as though the cold steel had eyes and brains. You, with your kaldane brain and your rykor body, never could hope to achieve in the same degree of perfection those things that I can achieve. Development of the brain should not be the sum total of human endeavor. The richest and happiest peoples will be those who attain closest to well-balanced perfection of both mind and body, and even these must always be short of perfection. In absolute and general perfection lies stifling monotony and death. Nature must have contrasts; she must have shadows as well as high lights; sorrow with happiness; both wrong and right; and sin as well as virtue."

"Always have I been taught differently," replied Ghek;
"but since I have known this woman and you, of another
race, I have come to believe that there may be other standards
fully as high and desirable as those of the kaldanes. At least
I have had a glimpse of the thing you call happiness and I
realize that it may be good even though I have no means of
expressing it. I cannot laugh nor smile, and yet within me is
a sense of contentment when this woman sings—a sense
that seems to open before me wondrous vistas of beauty and
unguessed pleasure that far transcend the cold joys of a perfectly functioning brain. I would that I had been born of thy
race."

Caught by a gentle current of air the flier was drifting
slowly toward the northeast across the valley of Bantoom.
Below them lay the cultivated fields, and one after another
they passed over the strange towers of Moak and Nolach and
the other kings of the swarms that inhabited this weird and
terrible land. Within each enclosure surrounding the towers
grovelled the rykors, repellent, headless things, beautiful yet
hideous.

"A lesson, those," remarked Gahan, indicating the rykors
in an enclosure above which they were drifting at the time,
"to that fortunately small minority of our race which worships the flesh and makes a god of appetite. You know them,
Tara of Helium; they can tell you exactly what they had at
the midday meal two weeks ago, and how the loin of the
thoat should be prepared, and what drink should be served
with the rump of the zitidar."

Tara of Helium laughed. "But not one of them could tell
you the name of the man whose painting took the Jeddak's
Award in The Temple of Beauty this year," she said. "Like
the rykors, their development has not been balanced."

"Fortunate indeed are those in which there is combined a
little good and a little bad, a little knowledge of many things
outside their own callings, a capacity for love and a capacity
for hate, for such as these can look with tolerance upon all,
unbiased by the egotism of him whose head is so heavy on one
side that all his brains run to that point."

As Gahan ceased speaking Ghek made a little noise in his
throat as one does who would attract attention. "You speak

as one who has thought upon many subjects. Is it, then, possible that you of the red race have pleasure in thought? Do you know aught of the joys of introspection? Do reason and logic form any part of your lives?"

"Most assuredly," replied Gahan, "but not to the extent of occupying all our time—at least not objectively. You, Ghek, are an example of the egotism of which I spoke. Because you and your kind devote your lives to the worship of mind, you believe that no other created beings think. And possibly we do not in the sense that you do, who think only of yourselves and your great brains. We think of many things that concern the welfare of a world. Had it not been for the red men of Barsoom even the kaldanes had perished from the planet, for while you may live without air the things upon which you depend for existence cannot, and there had been no air in sufficient quantities upon Barsoom these many ages had not a red man planned and built the great atmosphere plant which gave new life to a dying world.

"What have all the brains of all the kaldanes that have ever lived done to compare with that single idea of a single red man?"

Ghek was stumped. Being a kaldane he knew that brains spelled the sum total of universal achievement, but it had never occurred to him that they should be put to use in practical and profitable ways. He turned away and looked down upon the valley of his ancestors across which he was slowly drifting, into what unknown world? He should be a veritable god among the underlings, he knew; but somehow a doubt assailed him. It was evident that these two from that other world were ready to question his preeminence. Even through *his* great egotism was filtering a suspicion that they patronized him; perhaps even pitied him. Then he began to wonder what was to become of him. No longer would he have many rykors to do his bidding. Only this single one and when it died there could not be another. When it tired, Ghek must lie almost helpless while it rested. He wished that he had never seen this red woman. She had brought him only discontent and dishonor and now exile. Presently Tara of Helium commenced to hum a tune and Ghek, the kaldane, was content.

Gently they drifted beneath the hurtling moons above

the mad shadows of a Martian night. The roaring of the banths came in diminishing volume to their ears as their craft passed on beyond the boundaries of Bantoom, leaving behind the terrors of that unhappy land. But to what were they being borne? The girl looked at the man sitting cross-legged upon the deck of the tiny flier, gazing off into the night ahead, apparently absorbed in thought.

"Where are we?" she asked. "Toward what are we drifting?"

Turan shrugged his broad shoulders. "The stars tell me that we are drifting toward the northeast," he replied, "but where we are, or what lies in our path I cannot even guess. A week since I could have sworn that I knew what lay behind each succeeding ridge that I approached; but now I admit in all humility that I have no conception of what lies a mile in any direction. Tara of Helium, I am lost, and that is all that I can tell you."

He was smiling and the girl smiled back at him. There was a slightly puzzled expression on her face—there was something tantalizingly familiar about that smile of his. She had met many a panthan—they came and went, following the fighting of a world—but she could not place this one.

"From what country are you, Turan?" she asked suddenly.

"Know you not, Tara of Helium," he countered, "that a panthan has no country? Today he fights beneath the banner of one master, tomorrow beneath that of another."

"But you must own allegiance to some country when you are not fighting," she insisted. "What banner, then, owns you now?"

He rose and stood before her, then, bowing low. "And I am acceptable," he said, "I serve beneath the banner of the daughter of The Warlord now—and forever."

She reached forth and touched his arm with a slim brown hand. "Your services are accepted," she said; "and if ever we reach Helium I promise that your reward shall be all that your heart could desire."

"I shall serve faithfully, hoping for that reward," he said; but Tara of Helium did not guess what was in his mind, thinking rather that he was mercenary. For how could the proud daughter of The Warlord guess that a simple panthan aspired to her hand and heart?

The dawn found them moving rapidly over an unfamiliar landscape. The wind had increased during the night and had borne them far from Bantoom. The country below them was rough and inhospitable. No water was visible and the surface of the ground was cut by deep gorges, while nowhere was any but the most meager vegetation discernible. They saw no life of any nature, nor was there any indication that the country could support life. For two days they drifted over this horrid wasteland. They were without food or water and suffered accordingly. Ghek had temporarily abandoned his rykor after enlisting Turan's assistance in lashing it safely to the deck. The less he used it the less would its vitality be spent. Already it was showing the effects of privation. Ghek crawled about the vessel like a great spider—over the side, down beneath the keel, and up over the opposite rail. He seemed equally at home one place as another. For his companions, however, the quarters were cramped, for the deck of a one-man flier is not intended for three.

Turan sought always ahead for signs of water. Water they must have, or that water-giving plant which makes life possible upon many of the seemingly arid areas of Mars; but there was neither the one nor the other for these two days and now the third night was upon them. The girl did not complain, but Turan knew that she must be suffering and his heart was heavy within him. Ghek suffered least of all, and he explained to them that his kind could exist for long periods without food or water. Turan almost cursed him as he saw the form of Tara of Helium slowly wasting away before his eyes, while the hideous kaldane seemed as full of vitality as ever.

"There are circumstances," remarked Ghek, "under which a gross and material body is less desirable than a highly developed brain."

Turan looked at him, but said nothing. Tara of Helium smiled faintly. "One cannot blame him," she said, "were we not a bit boastful in the pride of our superiority? When our stomachs were filled," she added.

"Perhaps there is something to be said for their system," Turan admitted. "If we could but lay aside our stomachs when they cried for food and water I have no doubt but that we should do so."

"I should never miss mine now," assented Tara; "It is mighty poor company."

A new day had dawned, revealing a less desolate country and renewing again the hope that had been low within them. Suddenly Turan leaned forward, pointing ahead.

"Look, Tara of Helium!" he cried. "A city! As I am Ga—as I am Turan the panthan, a city."

Far in the distance the domes and walls and slender towers of a city shone in the rising sun. Quickly the man seized the control and the ship dropped rapidly behind a low range of intervening hills, for well Turan knew that they must not be seen until they could discover whether friend or foe inhabited the strange city. Chances were that they were far from the abode of friends and so must the panthan move with the utmost caution; but there was a city and where a city was, was water, even though it were a deserted city, and food if it were inhabited.

To the red man food and water, even in the citadel of an enemy, meant food and drink for Tara of Helium. He would accept it from friends or he would take it from enemies. Just so long as it was there he would have it—and there was shown the egotism of the fighting man, though Turan did not see it, nor Tara who came from a long line of fighting men; but Ghek might have smiled had he known how.

Turan permitted the flier to drift closer behind the screening hills, and then when he could advance no farther without fear of discovery, he dropped the craft gently to ground in a little ravine, and leaping over the side made her fast to a stout tree. For several moments they discussed their plans—whether it would be best to wait where they were until darkness hid their movements and then approach the city in search of food and water, or approach it now, taking advantage of what cover they could, until they could glean something of the nature of its inhabitants.

It was Turan's plan which finally prevailed. They would approach as close as safety dictated in the hope of finding water outside the city; food, too, perhaps. If they did not they could at least reconnoiter the ground by daylight, and then when night came Turan could quickly come close to the city and in comparative safety prosecute his search for food and drink.

Following the ravine upward they finally topped the summit of the ridge, from which they had an excellent view of that part of the city which lay nearest them, though themselves hidden by the brush behind which they crouched. Ghek had resumed his rykor, which had suffered less than either Tara or Turan through their enforced fast.

The first glance at the city, now much closer than when they had first discovered it, revealed the fact that it was inhabited. Banners and pennons broke from many a staff. People were moving about the gate before them. The high white walls were paced by sentinels at far intervals. Upon the roofs of higher buildings the women could be seen airing the sleeping silks and furs. Turan watched it all in silence for some time.

"I do not know them," he said at last. "I cannot guess what city this may be. But it is an ancient city. Its people have no fliers and no firearms. It must be old indeed."

"How do you know they have not these things?" asked the girl.

"There are no landing-stages upon the roofs—not one that can be seen from here; while were we looking similarly at Helium we would see hundreds. And they have no firearms because their defenses are all built to withstand the attack of spear and arrow, with spear and arrow. They are an ancient people."

"If they are ancient perhaps they are friendly," suggested the girl. "Did we not learn as children in the history of our planet that it was once peopled by a friendly, peace-loving race?"

"But I fear they are not as ancient as that," replied Turan, laughing. "It has been long ages since the men of Barsoom loved peace."

"My father loves peace," returned the girl.

"And yet he is always at war," said the man.

She laughed. "But he *says* he likes peace."

"We all like peace," he rejoined; "peace with honor; but our neighbors will not let us have it, and so we must fight."

"And to fight well men must like to fight," she added.

"And to like to fight they must know how to fight," he said, "for no man likes to do the thing that he does not know how to do well."

"Or that some other man can do better than he."

"And so always there will be wars and men will fight," he

concluded, "for always the men with hot blood in their veins will practice the art of war."

"We have settled a great question," said the girl, smiling; "but our stomachs are still empty."

"Your panthan is neglecting his duty," replied Turan; "and how can he with the great reward always before his eyes!"

She did not guess in what literal a sense he spoke.

"I go forthwith," he continued, "to wrest food and drink from the ancients."

"No," she cried, laying a hand upon his arm, "not yet. They would slay you or make you prisoner. You are a brave panthan and a mighty one, but you cannot overcome a city singlehanded."

She smiled up into his face and her hand still lay upon his arm. He felt the thrill of hot blood coursing through his veins. He could have seized her in his arms and crushed her to him. There was only Ghek the kaldane there, but there was something stronger within him that restrained his hand. Who may define it—that inherent chivalry that renders certain men the natural protectors of women?

From their vantage point they saw a body of armed warriors ride forth from the gate, and winding along a well-beaten road pass from sight about the foot of the hill from which they watched. The men were red, like themselves, and they rode the small saddle thoats of the red race. Their trappings were barbaric and magnificent, and in their headdress were many feathers as had been the custom of ancients. They were armed with swords and long spears and they rode almost naked, their bodies being painted in ochre and blue and white. There were, perhaps, a score of them in the party and as they galloped away on their tireless mounts they presented a picture at once savage and beautiful.

"They have the appearance of splendid warriors," said Turan. "I have a great mind to walk boldly into their city and seek service."

Tara shook her head. "Wait," she admonished. "What would I do without you, and if you were captured how could you collect your reward?"

"I should escape," he said. "At any rate I shall try it," and he started to rise.

"You shall not," said the girl, her tone all authority.

The man looked at her quickly—questioningly.

"You have entered my service," she said, a trifle haughtily. "You have entered my service for hire and you shall do as I bid you."

Turan sank down beside her again with a half smile upon his lips. "It is yours to command, Princess," he said.

The day passed. Ghek, tiring of the sunlight, had deserted his rykor and crawled down a hole he had discovered close by. Tara and Turan reclined beneath the scant shade of a small tree. They watched the people coming and going through the gate. The party of horsemen did not return. A small herd of zitidars was driven into the city during the day, and once a caravan of broad-wheeled carts drawn by these huge animals wound out of the distant horizon and came down to the city. It, too, passed from their sight within the gateway. Then darkness came and Tara of Helium bid her panthan search for food and drink; but she cautioned him against attempting to enter the city. Before he left her he bent and kissed her hand as a warrior may kiss the hand of his queen.

<h2 style="text-align:center;">CHAPTER X</h2>

<h1 style="text-align:center;">ENTRAPPED</h1>

TURAN THE PANTHAN approached the strange city under cover of the darkness. He entertained little hope of finding either food or water outside the wall, but he would try and then, if he failed, he would attempt to make his way into the city, for Tara of Helium must have sustenance and have it soon. He saw that the walls were poorly sentineled, but they were sufficiently high to render an attempt to scale them foredoomed to failure. Taking advantage of underbrush and trees, Turan managed to reach the base of the wall without detection. Silently he moved north past the gateway which was closed by a massive gate which effectively barred even the slightest glimpse within the city beyond. It was Turan's hope to find upon the north side of the city away from the hills a level plain where grew the crops of the inhabitants, and here too water from their irrigating system, but though he traveled far along that seemingly interminable wall he found no fields nor any water. He searched also for some means of ingress to the city, yet here, too, failure was his only reward, and now as he went keen eyes watched him from above and a silent stalker kept pace with him for a time upon the summit of the wall; but presently the shadower descended to the pavement within and hurrying swiftly raced ahead of the stranger without.

He came presently to a small gate beside which was a low building and before the doorway of the building a warrior standing guard. He spoke a few quick words to the warrior and then entered the building only to return almost immediately to the street, followed by fully forty warriors. Cautiously opening the gate the fellow peered carefully along the wall upon the outside in the direction from which he had come. Evidently satisfied, he issued a few words of instruction to those behind him, whereupon half the warriors returned to the interior of the building, while the other half followed the man stealthily through the gateway where they crouched low among the shrubbery in a half circle just north of the gateway which they had left open. Here they waited in utter silence, nor had they long to wait before Turan the panthan came cautiously along the base of the wall. To the very gate he came and when he found it and that it was open he paused for a moment, listening; then he approached and looked within. Assured that there was none within sight to apprehend him he stepped through the gateway into the city.

He found himself in a narrow street that paralleled the wall. Upon the opposite side rose buildings of an architecture unknown to him, yet strangely beautiful. While the buildings were packed closely together there seemed to be no two alike and their fronts were of all shapes and heights and of many hues. The skyline was broken by spire and dome and minaret and tall, slender towers, while the walls supported many a balcony and in the soft light of Cluros, the farther moon, now low in the west, he saw, to his surprise and consternation, the figures of people upon the balconies. Directly opposite him were two women and a man. They sat leaning upon the rail of the balcony looking, apparently, directly at him, but if they saw him they gave no sign.

Turan hesitated a moment in the face of almost certain discovery and then, assured that they must take him for one of their own people, he moved boldly into the avenue. Having no idea of the direction in which he might best hope to find what he sought, and not wishing to arouse suspicion by further hesitation, he turned to the left and stepped briskly along the pavement with the intention of placing himself as quickly as possible beyond the observation of those nocturnal watchers. He knew that the night must be far spent; and so he could not but wonder why people should sit upon their balconies when they should have been asleep among their silks and furs. At first he had thought them the late guests of some convivial host; but the windows behind them were shrouded in darkness and utter quiet prevailed, quite upsetting such a theory. And as he proceeded he passed many another group sitting silently upon other balconies. They paid no attention to him, seeming not even to note his passing. Some leaned with a single elbow upon the rail, their chins resting in their palms; others leaned upon both arms across the balcony, looking down into the street, while several that he saw held musical instruments in their hands, but their fingers moved not upon the strings.

And then Turan came to a point where the avenue turned to the right, to skirt a building that jutted from the inside of the city wall, and as he rounded the corner he came full upon two warriors standing upon either side of the entrance to a building upon his right. It was impossible for them not to be aware of his presence, yet neither moved, nor gave other evidence that they had seen him. He stood there waiting, his hand upon the hilt of his long-sword, but they neither challenged nor halted him. Could it be that these also thought him one of their own kind? Indeed upon no other grounds could he explain their inaction.

As Turan had passed through the gateway into the city and taken his unhindered way along the avenue, twenty warriors had entered the city and closed the gate behind them, and then one had taken to the wall and followed along its summit in the rear of Turan, and another had followed him along the avenue, while a third had crossed the street and entered one of the buildings upon the opposite side.

The balance of them, with the exception of a single sentinel beside the gate, had re-entered the building from which they had been summoned. They were well built, strapping, painted fellows, their naked figures covered now by gorgeous robes against the chill of night. As they spoke of the stranger they laughed at the ease with which they had tricked him, and were still laughing as they threw themselves upon their sleeping silks and furs to resume their broken slumber. It was evident that they constituted a guard detailed for the gate beside which they slept, and it was equally evident that the gates were guarded and the city watched much more carefully than Turan had believed. Chagrined indeed had been the Jed of Gathol had he dreamed that he was being so neatly tricked.

As Turan proceeded along the avenue he passed other sentries beside other doors but now he gave them small heed, since they neither challenged nor otherwise outwardly noted his passing; but while at nearly every turn of the erratic avenue he passed one or more of these silent sentinels he could not guess that he had passed one of them many times and that his every move was watched by silent, clever stalkers. Scarce had he passed a certain one of these rigid guardsmen before the fellow awoke to sudden life, bounded across the avenue, entered a narrow opening in the outer wall where he swiftly followed a corridor built within the wall itself until presently he emerged a little distance ahead of Turan, where he assumed the stiff and silent attitude of a soldier upon guard. Nor did Turan know that a second followed in the shadows of the buildings behind him, nor of the third who hastened ahead of him upon some urgent mission.

And so the panthan moved through the silent streets of the strange city in search of food and drink for the woman he loved. Men and women looked down upon him from shadowy balconies, but spoke not; and sentinels saw him pass and did not challenge. Presently from along the avenue before him came the familiar sound of clanking accouterments, the herald of marching warriors, and almost simultaneously he saw upon his right an open doorway dimly lighted from within. It was the only available place where he might seek to hide from the approaching company, and while he had passed several sentries unquestioned he could scarce hope to escape scrutiny and questioning from a patrol, as he naturally assumed this body of men to be.

Inside the doorway he discovered a passage turning abruptly to the right and almost immediately thereafter to the left. There was none in sight within and so he stepped cautiously around the second turn the more effectually to be hidden from the street. Before him stretched a long corridor, dimly lighted like the entrance. Waiting there he heard the party approach the building, he heard someone at the entrance to his hiding place, and then he heard the door past which he had come slam to. He laid his hand upon his sword, expecting momentarily to hear footsteps approaching along the corridor; but none came. He approached the turn and looked around it; the corridor was empty to the closed door. Whoever had closed it had remained upon the outside.

Turan waited, listening. He heard no sound. Then he advanced to the door and placed an ear against it. All was silence in the street beyond. A sudden draft must have closed the door, or perhaps it was the duty of the patrol to see to such things. It was immaterial. They had evidently passed on and now he would return to the street and continue upon his way. Somewhere here would be a public fountain where he could obtain water, and the chance of food lay in the strings of dried vegetables and meat which hung before the doorways of nearly every Barsoomian home of the poorer classes that he had ever seen. It was this district he was seeking, and it was for this reason his search had led him away from the main gate of the city which he knew would not be located in a poor district.

He attempted to open the door only to find that it resisted his every effort—it was locked upon the outside. Here indeed was a sorry contretemps. Turan the panthan scratched his head. "Fortune frowns upon me," he murmured; but beyond the door, Fate, in the form of a painted warrior, stood smiling. Neatly had he tricked the unwary stranger. The lighted doorway, the marching patrol—these had been planned and timed to a nicety by the third warrior who had sped ahead of Turan along another avenue, and the stranger had done precisely what the fellow had thought he would do —no wonder, then, that he smiled.

This exit barred to him Turan turned back into the corridor. He followed it cautiously and silently. Occasionally there was a door on one side or the other. These he tried only to find each securely locked. The corridor wound more erratically the farther he advanced. A locked door barred his way at its end, but a door upon his right opened and he stepped into a dimly-lighted chamber, about the walls of which were three other doors, each of which he tried in turn. Two were locked; the other opened upon a runway leading downward. It was spiral and he could see no farther than the first turn. A door in the corridor he had quitted opened after he had passed, and the third warrior stepped out and followed after him. A faint smile still lingered upon the fellow's grim lips.

Turan drew his short-sword and cautiously descended. At the bottom was a short corridor with a closed door at the end. He approached the single heavy panel and listened. No sound came to him from beyond the mysterious portal. Gently he tried the door, which swung easily toward him at his touch. Before him was a low-ceiled chamber with a dirt floor. Set in its walls were several other doors and all were closed. As Turan stepped cautiously within, the third warrior descended the spiral runway behind him. The panthan crossed the room quickly and tried a door. It was locked. He heard a muffled click behind him and turned about with ready sword. He was alone; but the door through which he had entered was closed—it was the click of its lock that he had heard.

With a bound he crossed the room and attempted to open it; but to no avail. No longer did he seek silence, for he knew now that the thing had gone beyond the sphere of chance. He threw his weight against the wooden panel; but the thick skeel of which it was constructed would have withstood a battering ram. From beyond came a low laugh.

Rapidly Turan examined each of the other doors. They were all locked. A glance about the chamber revealed a wooden table and a bench. Set in the walls were several heavy rings to which rusty chains were attached—all too significant of the purpose to which the room was dedicated. In the dirt floor near the wall were two or three holes resembling the mouths of burrows—doubtless the habitat of the giant Martian rat. He had observed this much when suddenly the dim light was extinguished, leaving him in darkness utter and complete. Turan, groping about, sought the table and the bench. Placing the latter against the wall he drew the table in front of him and sat down upon the bench, his long-sword gripped in readiness before him. At least they should fight before they took him.

For some time he sat there waiting for he knew not what. No sound penetrated to his subterranean dungeon. He slowly revolved in his mind the incidents of the evening—the open, unguarded gate; the lighted doorway—the only one he had seen thus open and lighted along the avenue he had followed; the advance of the warriors at precisely the moment that he could find no other avenue of escape or concealment; the corridors and chambers that led past many locked doors to this underground prison leaving no other path for him to pursue.

"By my first ancestor!" he swore; "but it was simple and I am a simpleton. They tricked me neatly and have taken me without exposing themselves to a scratch; but for what purpose?"

He wished that he might answer that question and then his thoughts turned to the girl waiting there on the hill beyond the city for him—and he would never come. He knew the ways of the more savage peoples of Barsoom. No, he would never come, now. He had disobeyed her. He smiled at the sweet recollection of those words of command that had fallen from her dear lips. He had disobeyed her and now he had lost the reward.

But what of her? What now would be her fate—starving before a hostile city with only an inhuman kaldane for company? Another thought—a horrid thought—obtruded itself upon him. She had told him of the hideous sights she had witnessed in the burrows of the kaldanes and he knew that they ate human flesh. Ghek was starving. Should he eat his rykor he would be helpless; but—there was sustenance there for them both, for the rykor and the kaldane. Turan cursed himself for a fool. Why had he left her? Far better to have remained and died with her, ready always to protect her, than to have left her at the mercy of the hideous Bantoomian.

Now Turan detected a heavy odor in the air. It oppressed him with a feeling of drowsiness. He would have risen to fight off that creeping lethargy, but his legs seemed weak, so that he sank again to the bench. Presently his sword slipped from his fingers and he sprawled forward upon the table, his head resting upon his arms.

Tara of Helium, as the night wore on and Turan did not return, became more and more uneasy, and when dawn broke with no sign of him she guessed that he had failed. Something more than her own unhappy predicament brought a feeling of sorrow to her heart—of sorrow and loneliness. She realized now how she had come to depend upon this panthan not only for protection but for companionship as well. She missed him, and in missing him realized suddenly that he had meant more to her than a mere hired warrior. It was as though a friend had been taken from her—an old and valued friend. She rose from her place of concealment that she might have a better view of the city.

U-Dor, dwar of the 8th Utan of O-Tar, Jeddak of Manator, rode back in the early dawn toward Manator from a brief excursion to a neighboring village. As he was rounding the hills south of the city, his keen eyes were attracted by a slight movement among the shrubbery close to the summit of the nearest hill. He halted his vicious mount and watched more closely. He saw a figure rise facing away from him and peer down toward Manator beyond the hill.

"Come!" he signalled to his followers, and with a word to his thoat turned the beast at a rapid gallop up the hillside. In his wake swept his twenty savage warriors, the padded feet of their mounts soundless upon the soft turf. It was the rattle of sidearms and harness that brought Tara of Helium suddenly about, facing them. She saw a score of warriors with couched lances bearing down upon her.

She glanced at Ghek. What would the spiderman do in this emergency? She saw him crawl to his rykor and attach himself. Then he arose, the beautiful body once again animated and alert. She thought that the creature was preparing for flight. Well, it made little difference to her. Against such as were streaming up the hill toward them a single mediocre swordsman such as Ghek was worse than no defense at all.

"Hurry, Ghek!" she admonished him. "Back into the hills! You may find there a hiding-place;" but the creature only stepped between her and the oncoming riders, drawing his long-sword.

"It is useless, Ghek," she said, when she saw that he intended to defend her. "What can a single sword accomplish against such odds?"

"I can die but once," replied the kaldane. "You and your panthan saved me from Luud and I but do what your panthan would do were he here to protect you."

"It is brave, but it is useless," she replied. "Sheathe your sword. They may not intend us harm."

Ghek let the point of his weapon drop to the ground, but he did not sheathe it, and thus the two stood waiting as U-Dor the dwar stopped his thoat before them while his twenty warriors formed a rough circle about. For a long minute U-Dor sat his mount in silence, looking searchingly first at Tara of Helium and then at her hideous companion.

"What manner of creature are you?" he asked presently. "And what do you before the gates of Manator?"

"We are from far countries," replied the girl, "and we are lost and starving. We ask only food and rest and the privilege to go our way seeking our own homes."

U-Dor smiled a grim smile. "Manator and the hills which guard it alone know the age of Manator," he said; "yet in all the ages that have rolled by since Manator first was, there be no record in the annals of Manator of a stranger departing from Manator."

"But I am a princess," cried the girl haughtily, "and my country is not at war with yours. You must give me and my companions aid and assist us to return to our own land. It is the law of Barsoom."

"Manator knows only the laws of Manator," replied U-Dor; "but come. You shall go with us to the city, where you, being beautiful, need have no fear. I, myself, will protect you if O-Tar so decrees. And as for your companion—but hold! You said 'companions'—there are others of your party then?"

"You see what you see," replied Tara haughtily.

"Be that as it may," said U-Dor. "If there be more they shall not escape Manator; but as I was saying, if your companion fights well he too may live, for O-Tar is just, and just are the laws of Manator. Come!"

Ghek demurred.

"It is useless," said the girl, seeing that he would have stood his ground and fought them. "Let us go with them. Why pit your puny blade against their mighty ones when there should lie in your great brain the means to outwit them?" She spoke in a low whisper, rapidly.

"You are right, Tara of Helium," he replied and sheathed his sword.

And so they moved down the hillside toward the gates of Manator—Tara, Princess of Helium, and Ghek, the kaldane of Bantoom—and surrounding them rode savage, painted warriors of U-Dor, dwar of the 8th Utan of O-Tar, Jeddak of Manator.

CHAPTER XI

THE CHOICE OF TARA

THE DAZZLING SUNLIGHT of Barsoom clothed Manator in an aureole of splendor as the girl and her captors rode into the city through The Gate of Enemies. Here the wall was some fifty feet thick, and the sides of the passageway within the gate were covered with parallel shelves of masonry from bottom to top. Within these shelves, or long, horizontal niches, stood row upon row of small figures, appearing like tiny, grotesque statuettes of men, their long, black hair falling below their feet and sometimes trailing to the shelf beneath. The figures were scarce a foot in height and but for their diminutive proportions might have been the mummified bodies of once living men. The girl noticed that as they passed, the warriors saluted the figures with their spears after the manner of Barsoomian fighting men in extending a military courtesy, and then they rode on into the avenue beyond, which ran, wide and stately, through the city toward the east.

On either side were great buildings wondrously wrought. Paintings of great beauty and antiquity covered many of the walls, their colors softened and blended by the suns of ages. Upon the pavement the life of the newly-awakened city was

already afoot. Women in brilliant trappings, befeathered
warriors, their bodies daubed with paint; artisans, armed but
less gaily caparisoned, took their various ways upon the duties
of the day. A giant zitidar, magnificent in rich harness, rumbled its broad-wheeled cart along the stone pavement toward
The Gate of Enemies. Life and color and beauty wrought together a picture that filled the eyes of Tara of Helium with
wonder and with admiration, for here was a scene out of the
dead past of dying Mars. Such had been the cities of the
founders of her race before Throxeus, mightiest of oceans,
had disappeared from the face of a world. And from balconies
on either side men and women looked down in silence upon
the scene below.

The people in the street looked at the two prisoners, especially at the hideous Ghek, and called out in question or comment to their guard; but the watchers upon the balconies
spoke not, nor did one so much as turn a head to note their
passing. There were many balconies on each building and
not a one that did not hold its silent party of richly trapped
men and women, with here and there a child or two; But
even the children maintained the uniform silence and immobility of their elders. As they approached the center of the
city the girl saw that even the roofs bore companies of these
idle watchers, harnessed and bejeweled as for some gala-day
of laughter and music; but no laughter broke from those
silent lips, nor any music from the strings of the instruments
that many of them held in jeweled fingers.

And now the avenue widened into an immense square, at
the far end of which rose a stately edifice gleaming white in
virgin marble among the gaily painted buildings surrounding it and its scarlet sward and gaily-flowering green-foliaged
shrubbery. Toward this U-Dor led his prisoners and their
guard to the great arched entrance before which a line of
fifty mounted warriors barred the way. When the commander of the guard recognized U-Dor the guardsmen fell
back to either side leaving a broad avenue through which the
party passed. Directly inside the entrance were inclined runways leading upward on either side. U-Dor turned to the
left and led them upward to the second floor and down a long
corridor. Here they passed other mounted men and in chambers upon either side they saw more. Occasionally there was

another runway leading either up or down. A warrior, his steed at full gallop, dashed into sight from one of these and raced swiftly past them upon some errand.

Nowhere as yet had Tara of Helium seen a man afoot in this great building; but when at a turn, U-Dor led them to the third floor she caught glimpses of chambers in which many riderless thoats were penned and others adjoining where dismounted warriors lolled at ease or played games of skill or chance and many there were who played at jetan, and then the party passed into a long, wide hall of state, as magnificent an apartment as even a princess of mighty Helium ever had seen. The length of the room ran an arched ceiling ablaze with countless radium bulbs. The mighty spans extended from wall to wall leaving the vast floor unbroken by a single column. The arches were of white marble, apparently quarried in single, huge blocks from which each arch was cut complete. Between the arches, the ceiling was set solid about the radium bulbs with precious stones whose scintillant fire and color and beauty filled the whole apartment. The stones were carried down the walls in an irregular fringe for a few feet, where they appeared to hang like a beautiful and gorgeous drapery against the white marble of the wall. The marble ended some six or seven feet from the floor, the walls from that point down being wainscoted in solid gold. The floor itself was of marble richly inlaid with gold. In that single room was a vast treasure equal to the wealth of many a large city.

But what riveted the girl's attention even more than the fabulous treasure of decorations were the files of gorgeously harnessed warriors who sat their thoats in grim silence and immobility on either side of the central aisle, rank after rank of them to the farther walls, and as the party passed between them she could not note so much as the flicker of an eyelid, or the twitching of a thoat's ear.

"The Hall of Chiefs," whispered one of her guard, evidently noting her interest. There was a note of pride in the fellow's voice and something of hushed awe. Then they passed through a great doorway into the chamber beyond, a large, square room in which a dozen mounted warriors lolled in their saddles.

As U-Dor and his party entered the room, the warriors came quickly erect in their saddles and formed a line before another door upon the opposite side of the wall. The padwar commanding them saluted U-Dor who, with his party, had halted facing the guard.

"Send one to O-Tar announcing that U-Dor brings two prisoners worthy of the observation of the great jeddak," said U-Dor; "one because of her extreme beauty, the other because of his extreme ugliness."

"O-Tar sits in council with the lesser chiefs," replied the lieutenant; "but the words of U-Dor the dwar shall be carried to him," and he turned and gave instructions to one who sat his thoat behind him.

"What manner of creature is the male?" he asked of U-Dor. "It cannot be that both are of one race."

"They were together in the hills south of the city," explained U-Dor, "and they say that they are lost and starving."

"The woman is beautiful," said the padwar. "She will not long go begging in the city of Manator," and then they spoke of other matters—of the doings of the palace, of the expedition of U-Dor, until the messenger returned to say that O-Tar bade them bring the prisoners to him.

They passed then through a massive doorway, which, when opened, revealed the great council chamber of O-Tar, Jeddak of Manator, beyond. A central aisle led from the doorway the full length of the great hall, terminating at the steps of a marble dais upon which a man sat in a great throne-chair. Upon either side of the aisle were ranged rows of highly carved desks and chairs of skeel, a hard wood of great beauty. Only a few of the desks were occupied—those in the front row, just below the rostrum.

At the entrance U-Dor dismounted with four of his followers who formed a guard about the two prisoners who were then conducted toward the foot of the throne, following a few paces behind U-Dor. As they halted at the foot of the marble steps, the proud gaze of Tara of Helium rested upon the enthroned figure of the man above her. He sat erect without stiffness—a commanding presence trapped in the barbaric splendor that the Barsoomian chieftain loves. He was a large man, the perfection of whose handsome face was marred only by the hauteur of his cold eyes and the suggestion of cruelty imparted by too thin lips. It needed no second glance to assure the least observing that here indeed was a ruler of men—a fighting jeddak whose people might worship but not love, and for whose slightest favor warriors would vie with one another to go forth and die. This was O-Tar, Jeddak of Manator, and as Tara of Helium saw him for the first time she could not but acknowledge a certain admiration for this savage chieftain who so virilely personified the ancient virtues of the God of War.

U-Dor and the jeddak interchanged the simple greetings of Barsoom, and then the former recounted the details of the discovery and capture of the prisoners. O-Tar scrutinized them both intently during U-Dor's narration of events, his expression revealing naught of what passed in the brain behind those inscrutable eyes. When the officer had finished the jeddak fastened his gaze upon Ghek.

"And you," he asked, "what manner of thing are you? From what country? Why are you in Manator?"

"I am a kaldane," replied Ghek; "the highest type of creature upon the face of Barsoom; I am mind, you are matter. I come from Bantoom. I am here because we were lost and starving."

"And you!" O-Tar turned suddenly on Tara. "You, too, are a kaldane?"

"I am a princess of Helium," replied the girl. "I was a prisoner in Bantoom. This kaldane and a warrior of my own race rescued me. The warrior left us to search for food and water. He has doubtless fallen into the hands of your people. I ask you to free him and give us food and drink and let us go upon our way. I am a granddaughter of a jeddak, the daughter of a jeddak of jeddaks, The Warlord of Barsoom. I ask only the treatment that my people would accord you or yours."

"Helium," repeated O-Tar. "I know naught of Helium, nor does the Jeddak of Helium rule Manator. I, O-Tar, am Jeddak of Manator. I alone rule. I protect my own. You have never seen a woman or a warrior of Manator captive in Helium! Why should I protect the people of another jeddak? It is his duty to protect them. If he cannot, he is weak, and his people must fall into the hands of the strong. I, O-Tar, am strong. I will keep you. That—" he pointed at Ghek—"can it fight?"

"It is brave," replied Tara of Helium, "but it has not the skill at arms which my people possess."

"There is none then to fight for you?" asked O-Tar. "We are a just people," he continued without waiting for a reply, "and had you one to fight for you he might win to freedom for himself and you as well."

"But U-Dor assured me that no stranger ever had departed from Manator," she answered.

O-Tar shrugged. "That does not disprove the justice of the laws of Manator," replied O-Tar, "but rather that the warriors of Manator are invincible. Had there come one who could defeat our warriors that one had won to liberty."

"And you fetch my warrior," cried Tara haughtily, "you shall see such swordplay as doubtless the crumbling walls of your decaying city never have witnessed, and if there be no trick in your offer we are already as good as free."

O-Tar smiled more broadly than before and U-Dor smiled, too, and the chiefs and warriors who looked on nudged one another and whispered, laughing. And Tara of Helium knew then that there was trickery in their justice; but though her situation seemed hopeless she did not cease to hope, for was she not the daughter of John Carter, Warlord of Barsoom, whose famous challenge to Fate, "I still live!" remained the one irreducible defense against despair? At thought of her noble sire the patrician chin of Tara of Helium rose a shade higher. Ah! if he but knew where she was there were little to fear then. The hosts of Helium would batter at the gates of Manator, the great green warriors of John Carter's savage allies would swarm up from the dead sea bottoms lusting for pillage and for loot, the stately ships of her beloved navy would soar above the unprotected towers and minarets of the doomed city which only capitulation and heavy tribute could then save.

But John Carter did not know! There was only one other to whom she might hope to look—Turan the panthan; but where was he? She had seen his sword in play and she knew that it had been wielded by a master hand, and who should know swordplay better than Tara of Helium, who had learned it well under the constant tutorage of John Carter himself. Tricks she knew that discounted even far greater physical prowess than her own, and a method of attack that might have been at once the envy and despair of the cleverest of warriors. And so it was that her thoughts turned to Turan the panthan, though not alone because of the protection he might afford her. She had realized, since he had left her in search of food, that there had grown between them a certain comradeship that she now missed. There had been that about him which seemed to have bridged the gulf between their stations in life. With him she had failed to consider that he was a panthan or that she was a princess—they had been comrades. Suddenly she realized that she missed him for himself more than for his sword. She turned toward O-Tar.

"Where is Turan, my warrior?" she demanded.

"You shall not lack for warriors," replied the jeddak. "One of your beauty will find plenty ready to fight for her. Possibly it shall not be necessary to look farther than the jeddak of Manator. You please me, woman. What say you to such an honor?"

Through narrowed lids the Princess of Helium scrutinized the Jeddak of Manator, from feathered headdress to sandaled foot and back to feathered headdress.

" 'Honor'!" she mimicked in tones of scorn. "I please thee, do I? Then know, swine, that thou pleasest me not—that the daughter of John Carter is not for such as thou!"

A sudden, tense silence fell upon the assembled chiefs. Slowly the blood receded from the sinister face of O-Tar, Jeddak of Manator, leaving him a sickly purple in his wrath. His eyes narrowed to two thin slits, his lips were compressed to a bloodless line of malevolence. For a long moment there was no sound in the throne room of the palace at Manator. Then the jeddak turned toward U-Dor.

"Take her away," he said in a level voice that belied his appearance of rage. "Take her away, and at the next games let the prisoners and the common warriors play at jetan for her."

"And this?" asked U-Dor, pointing at Ghek.

"To the pits until the next games," replied O-Tar.

"So this is your vaunted justice!" cried Tara of Helium; "that two strangers who have not wronged you shall be sentenced without trial? And one of them is a woman. The swine of Manator are as just as they are brave."

"Away with her!" shouted O-Tar, and at a sign from U-Dor the guards formed about the two prisoners and conducted them from the chamber.

Outside the palace, Ghek and Tara of Helium were separated. The girl was led through long avenues toward the

center of the city and finally into a low building, topped by
lofty towers of massive construction. Here she was turned
over to a warrior who wore the insignia of a dwar, or captain.

"It is O-Tar's wish," explained U-Dor to this one, "that
she be kept until the next games, when the prisoners and the
common warriors shall play for her. Had she not the tongue
of a thoat she had been a worthy stake for our noblest steel,"
and U-Dor sighed. "Perhaps even yet I may win a pardon for
her. It were too bad to see such beauty fall to the lot of some
common fellow. I would have honored her myself."

"If I am to be imprisoned, imprison me," said the girl. "I
do not recall that I was sentenced to listen to the insults of
every low-born boor who chanced to admire me."

"You see, A-Kor," cried U-Dor, "the tongue that she has.
Even so and worse spoke she to O-Tar the jeddak."

"I see," replied A-Kor, whom Tara saw was with difficulty
restraining a smile. "Come then, with me, woman," he said,
"and we shall find a safe place within The Towers of Jetan
—but stay! what ails thee?"

The girl had staggered and would have fallen had not the
man caught her in his arms. She seemed to gather herself
then and bravely sought to stand erect without support. A-Kor
glanced at U-Dor. "Knew you the woman was ill?" he asked.

"Possibly it is lack of food," replied the other. "She mentioned, I believe, that she and her companions had not eaten
for several days."

"Brave are the warriors of O-Tar," sneered A-Kor; "lavish
their hospitality. U-Dor, whose riches are uncounted, and the
brave O-Tar, whose squealing thoats are stabled within marble halls and fed from troughs of gold, can spare no crust to
feed a starving girl."

The black haired U-Dor scowled. "Thy tongue will yet
pierce thy heart, son of a slave!" he cried. "Once too often
mayst thou try the patience of the just O-Tar. Hereafter
guard thy speech as well as thy towers."

"Think not to taunt me with my mother's state," said A-
Kor. "'Tis the blood of the slave woman that fills my veins
with pride, and my only shame is that I am also the son of thy
jeddak."

"And O-Tar heard this?" queried U-Dor.

"O-Tar has already heard it from my own lips," replied

A-Kor; "this, and more."

He turned upon his heel, a supporting arm still around the waist of Tara of Helium and thus he half led, half carried her into The Towers of Jetan, while U-Dor wheeled his thoat and galloped back in the direction of the palace.

Within the main entrance to The Towers of Jetan lolled a half-dozen warriors. To one of these spoke A-Kor, keeper of the towers. "Fetch Lan-O, the slave girl, and bid her bring food and drink to the upper level of the Thurian tower," then he lifted the half-fainting girl in his arms and bore her along the spiral, inclined runway that led upward within the tower.

Somewhere in the long ascent Tara lost consciousness. When it returned she found herself in a large, circular chamber, the stone walls of which were pierced by windows at regular intervals about the entire circumference of the room. She was lying upon a pile of sleeping silks and furs while there knelt above her a young woman who was forcing drops of some cooling beverage between her parched lips. Tara of Helium half rose upon an elbow and looked about. In the first moments of returning consciousness there were swept from the screen of recollection the happenings of many weeks. She thought that she awoke in the palace of The Warlord at Helium. Her brows knit as she scrutinized the strange face bending over her.

"Who are you?" she asked, and, "Where is Uthia?"

"I am Lan-O the slave girl," replied the other. "I know none by the name of Uthia."

Tara of Helium sat erect and looked about her. This rough stone was not the marble of her father's halls. "Where am I?" she asked.

"In the Thurian Tower," replied the girl, and then seeing that the other still did not understand she guessed the truth. "You are a prisoner in The Towers of Jetan in the city of Manator," she explained. "You were brought to this chamber, weak and fainting, by A-Kor, Dwar of The Towers of Jetan, who sent me to you with food and drink, for kind is the heart of A-Kor."

"I remember, now," said Tara, slowly. "I remember; but where is Turan, my warrior? Did they speak of him?"

"I heard naught of another," replied Lan-O; "you alone were brought to the towers. In that you are fortunate, for there be no nobler man in Manator than A-Kor. It is his mother's blood that makes him so. She was a slave girl from Gathol."

"Gathol!" exclaimed Tara of Helium. "Lies Gathol close by Manator?"

"Not close, yet still the nearest country," replied Lan-O. "About twenty-two degrees[1] east, it lies."

"Gathol!" murmured Tara, "Far Gathol!"

"But you are not from Gathol," said the slave girl; "your harness is not of Gathol."

"I am from Helium," said Tara.

"It is far from Helium to Gathol," said the slave girl, "but in our studies we learned much of the greatness of Helium, we of Gathol, so it seems not so far away."

"You, too, are from Gathol?" asked Tara.

"Many of us are from Gathol who are slaves in Manator," replied the girl. "It is to Gathol, nearest country, that the Manatorians look for slaves most often. They go in great numbers at intervals of three or seven years and haunt the roads that lead to Gathol, and thus they capture whole caravans leaving none to bear warning to Gathol of their fate. Nor do any ever escape from Manator to carry word of us back to Gahan our jed."

Tara of Helium ate slowly and in silence. The girl's words aroused memories of the last hours she had spent in her father's palace and the great midday function at which she had met Gahan of Gathol. Even now she flushed as she recalled his daring words.

Upon her reveries the door opened and a burly warrior appeared in the opening—a hulking fellow, with thick lips and an evil, leering face. The slave girl sprang to her feet, facing him.

"What does this mean, E-Med?" she cried; "was it not the will of A-Kor that this woman be not disturbed?"

"The will of A-Kor, indeed!" and the man sneered. "The will of A-Kor is without power in The Towers of Jetan, or elsewhere, for A-Kor lies now in the pits of O-Tar, and E-Med is dwar of the Towers."

Tara of Helium saw the face of the slave girl pale and the terror in her eyes.

---

[1] Approximately 814 Earth Miles.

CHAPTER XII

GHEK PLAYS PRANKS

WHILE TARA OF HELIUM was being led to The Towers of Jetan, Ghek was escorted to the pits beneath the palace where he was imprisoned in a dimly-lighted chamber. Here he found a bench and a table standing upon the dirt floor near the wall, and set in the wall several rings from which depended short lengths of chain. At the base of the walls were several holes in the dirt floor. These, alone, of the several things he saw, interested him. Ghek sat down upon the bench and waited in silence, listening. Presently the lights were extinguished. If Ghek could have smiled he would have then, for Ghek could see as well in the dark as in the light—better, perhaps. He watched the dark openings of the holes in the floor and waited. Presently he detected a change in the air about him—it grew heavy with a strange odor, and once again might Ghek have smiled, could he have smiled.

Let them replace all the air in the chamber with their most deadly fumes; it would be all the same to Ghek, the kaldane, who, having no lungs, required no air. With the rykor it might be different. Deprived of air it would die; but if only a sufficient amount of the gas was introduced to stupefy an ordinary creature it would have no effect upon the rykor, who had no objective mind to overcome. So long as the excess of carbon dioxide in the blood was not sufficient to prevent heart action, the rykor would suffer only a diminution of vitality; but would still respond to the exciting agency of the kaldane's brain.

Ghek caused the rykor to assume a sitting position with its back against the wall where it might remain without direction from his brain. Then he released his contact with its spinal cord; but remained in position upon its shoulders, waiting and watching, for the kaldane's curiosity was aroused. He had not long to wait before the lights were flashed on and one of the locked doors opened to admit a half-dozen warriors. They approached him rapidly and worked quickly. First they removed all his weapons and then, snapping a fetter about one of the rykor's ankles, secured him to the end of one of the chains hanging from the walls. Next they

dragged the long table to a new position and there bolted it
to the floor so that an end, instead of the middle, was directly
before the prisoner. On the table before him they set food
and water and on the opposite end of the table they laid the
key to the fetter. Then they unlocked and opened all the
doors and departed.

When Turan the panthan regained consciousness it was to
the realization of a sharp pain in one of his forearms. The effects of the gas departed as rapidly as they had overcome him
so that as he opened his eyes he was in full possession of all
his faculties. The lights were on again and in their glow there
was revealed to the man the figure of a giant Martian rat
crouching upon the table and gnawing upon his arm. Snatch-
ing his arm away he reached for his short-sword, while the
rat, growling, sought to seize his arm again. It was then that
Turan discovered that his weapons had been removed—short-
sword, long-sword, dagger, and pistol. The rat charged him
then and striking the creature away with his hand the man
rose and backed off, searching for something with which to
strike a harder blow. Again the rat charged and as Turan
stepped quickly back to avoid the menacing jaws, something
seemed to jerk suddenly upon his right ankle, and as he drew
his left foot back to regain his equilibrium his heel caught
upon a taut chain and he fell heavily backward to the floor
just as the rat leaped upon his breast and sought his throat.

The Martian rat is a fierce and unlovely thing. It is many-
legged and hairless, its hide resembling that of a new-born
mouse in repulsiveness. In size and weight it is comparable to
to a large Airedale terrier. Its eyes are small and close-set, and
almost hidden in deep, fleshy apertures. But its most ferocious and repulsive feature is its jaws, the entire bony structure of which protrudes several inches beyond the flesh,
revealing five sharp, spadelike teeth in the upper jaw and the
same number of similar teeth in the lower, the whole suggesting the appearance of a rotting face from which much of the
flesh has sloughed away.

It was such a thing that leaped upon the breast of the
panthan to tear at his jugular. Twice Turan struck it away
as he sought to regain his feet, but both times it returned
with increased ferocity to renew the attack. Its only weapons
are its jaws since its broad, splay feet are armed with blunt

talons. With its protruding jaws it excavates its winding burrows and with its broad feet it pushes the dirt behind it. To
keep the jaws from his flesh then was Turan's only concern
and this he succeeded in doing until chance gave him a hold
upon the creature's throat. After that the end was but a matter of moments. Rising at last he flung the lifeless thing from
him with a shudder of disgust.

Now he turned his attention to a hurried inventory of
the new conditions which surrounded him since the moment
of his incarceration. He realized vaguely what had happened.
He had been anaesthetized and stripped of his weapons, and
as he rose to his feet he saw that one ankle was fettered to a
chain in the wall. He looked about the room. All the doors
swung wide open! His captors would render his imprison-
ment the more cruel by leaving ever before him tempting
glimpses of open aisles to the freedom he could not attain.
Upon the end of the table and within easy reach was food
and drink. This at least was attainable and at sight of it his
starved stomach seemed almost to cry aloud for sustenance.
It was with difficulty that he ate and drank in moderation.

As he devoured the food his eyes wandered about the confines of his prison until suddenly they seized upon a thing
that lay on the table at the end farthest from him. It was a key.
He raised his fettered ankle and examined the lock. There
could be no doubt of it! The key that lay there on the table
before him was the key to that very lock. A careless warrior
had laid it there and departed, forgetting. Hope surged high
in the breast of Gahan of Gathol, of Turan the panthan. Fur-
tively his eyes sought the open doorways. There was no one
in sight. Ah, if he could but gain his freedom! He would find
some way from this odious city back to *her* side and never
again would he leave her until he had won safety for her or
death for himself.

He rose and moved cautiously toward the opposite end
of the table where lay the coveted key. The fettered ankle
halted his first step, but he stretched at full length along the
table, extending eager fingers toward the prize. They almost
laid hold upon it— a little more and they would touch it. He
strained and stretched, but still the thing lay just beyond
his reach. He hurled himself forward until the iron fetter bit
deep into his flesh, but all futilely. He sat back upon the

bench then and glared at the open doors and the key, realizing now that they were part of a well-laid scheme of re-
fined torture, none the less demoralizing because it inflicted
no physical suffering.

For just a moment the man gave way to useless regret and
foreboding, then he gathered himself together, his brows
cleared, and he returned to his unfinished meal. At least they
should not have the satisfaction of knowing how sorely they
had hit him. As he ate it occurred to him that by dragging
the table along the floor he could bring the key within his
reach, but when he essayed to do so, he found that the table
had been securely bolted to the floor during the period of
his unconsciousness. Again Gahan smiled and shrugged and
resumed his eating.

When the warriors had departed from the prison in which
Ghek was confined, the kaldane crawled from the shoulders
of the rykor to the table. Here he drank a little water and
then directed the hands of the rykor to the balance of it and
to the food, upon which the brainless thing fell with avidity.
While it was thus engaged Ghek took his spider-like way along
the table to the opposite end where lay the key to the fetter.
Seizing it in a chela he leaped to the floor and scurried rapidly toward the mouth of one of the burrows against the wall,
into which he disappeared. For long had the brain been contemplating these burrow entrances. They appealed to his
kaldanean tastes, and further, they pointed a hiding place for
the key and a lair for the only kind of food that the kaldane
relished—flesh and blood.

Ghek had never seen an ulsio, since these great Martian
rats had long ago disappeared from Bantoom, their flesh and
blood having been greatly relished by the kaldanes; but Ghek
had inherited, almost unimpaired, every memory of every
ancestor, and so he knew that ulsio inhabited these lairs and
that ulsio was good to eat, and he knew what ulsio looked
like and what his habits were, though he had never seen
him nor any picture of him. As we breed animals for the transmission of physical attributes, so the kaldanes breed themselves for the transmission of attributes of the mind, including memory and the power of recollection, and thus have they
raised what we term instinct, above the level of the thres-

hold of the objective mind where it may be commanded and utilized by recollection. Doubtless in our own subjective minds lie many of the impressions and experiences of our forebears. These may impinge upon our consciousness in dreams only, or in vague, haunting suggestions that we have before experienced some transient phase of our present existence. Ah, if we had but the power to recall them! Before us would unfold the forgotten story of the lost eons that have preceded us. We might even walk with God in the garden of His stars while man was still but a budding idea within His mind.

Ghek descended into the burrow at a steep incline for some ten feet, when he found himself in an elaborate and delightful network of burrows. The kaldane was elated. This indeed was life! He moved rapidly and fearlessly and he went as straight to his goal as you could to the kitchen of your own home. This goal lay at a low level in a spheroidal cavity about the size of a large barrel. Here, in a nest of torn bits of silk and fur lay six baby ulsios.

When the mother returned there were but five babies and a great spider-like creature, which she immediately sprang to attack only to be met by powerful chelae which seized and held her so that she could not move. Slowly they dragged her throat toward a hideous mouth and in a little moment she was dead.

Ghek might have remained in the nest for a long time, since there was ample food for many days; but he did not do so. Instead he explored the burrows. He followed them into many subterranean chambers of the city of Manator, and upward through walls to rooms above the ground. He found many ingeniously devised traps, and he found poisoned food and other signs of the constant battle that the inhabitants of Manator waged against these repulsive creatures that dwelt beneath their homes and public buildings.

His exploration revealed not only the vast proportions of the net-work of runways that apparently traversed every portion of the city, but the great antiquity of the majority of them. Tons upon tons of dirt must have been removed, and for a long time he wondered where it had been deposited until in following downward a tunnel of great size and length he sensed before him the thunderous rush of subterranean waters, and presently came to the bank of a great, underground river, tumbling onward, no doubt, the length of a world to the buried sea of Omean. Into this torrential sewer had unthinkable generations of ulsios pushed their few handsful of dirt in the excavating of their vast labyrinth.

For only a moment did Ghek tarry by the river, for his seemingly aimless wanderings were in reality prompted by a definite purpose, and this he pursued with vigor and single-ness of design. He followed such runways as appeared to ter-minate in the pits or other chambers of the inhabitants of the city, and these he explored, usually from the safety of a bur-row's mouth, until satisfied that what he sought was not there. He moved swiftly upon his spider legs and covered re-markable distances in short periods of time.

His search not being rewarded with immediate success, he decided to return to the pit where his rykor lay chained and look to its wants. As he approached the end of the burrow that terminated in the pit he slackened his pace, stopping just within the entrance of the runway that he might scan the interior of the chamber before entering it. As he did so he saw the figure of a warrior appear suddenly in a opposite doorway. The rykor sprawled upon the table, his hands grop-ing blindly for more food. Ghek saw the warrior pause and gaze in sudden astonishment at the rykor; he saw the fellow's eyes go wide and an ashen hue replace the copper bronze of his cheek. He stepped back as though someone had struck him in the face. For an instant only he stood thus as in a paral-ysis of fear, then he uttered a smothered shriek and turned and fled. Again was it a catastrophe that Ghek, the kaldane, could not smile.

Quickly entering the room he crawled to the table top and affixed himself to the shoulders of his rykor, and there he waited; and who may say that Ghek, though he could not smile, possessed not a sense of humor? For a half-hour he sat there, and then there came to him the sound of men approach-ing along corridors of stone. He could hear their arms clank against the rocky walls and he knew that they came at a rapid pace; but just before they reached the entrance to his prison they paused and advanced more slowly. In the lead was an officer, and just behind him, wide-eyed and perhaps still a little ashen, the warrior who had so recently departed in haste. At the doorway they halted and the officer turned sternly upon the warrior. With upraised finger he pointed at Ghek.

"There sits the creature! Didst thou dare lie, then, to thy dwar?"

"I swear," cried the warrior, "that I spoke the truth. But a moment since the thing groveled, headless, upon this very table! And may my first ancestor strike me dead upon the spot if I speak other than a true word!"

The officer looked puzzled. The men of Mars seldom if ever lie. He scratched his head. Then he addressed Ghek. "How long have you been here?" he asked.

"Who knows better than those who placed me here and chained me to a wall?" he returned in reply.

"Saw you this warrior enter here a few minutes since?"

"I saw him," replied Ghek.

"And you sat there where you sit now?" continued the officer.

"Look thou to my chain and tell me then where else might I sit!" cried Ghek. "Art the people of thy city all fools?"

Three other warriors pressed behind the two in front, craning their necks to view the prisoner while they grinned at the discomfiture of their fellow. The officer scowled at Ghek.

"Thy tongue is as venomous as that of the she-banth O-Tar sent to The Towers of Jetan," he said.

"You speak of the young woman who was captured with me?" asked Ghek, his expressionless monotone and face revealing naught of the interest he felt.

"I speak of her," replied the dwar, and then turning to the warrior who had summoned him: "Return to thy quarters and remain there until the next games. Perhaps by that time thy eyes may have learned not to deceive thee."

The fellow cast a venomous glance at Ghek and turned away. The officer shook his head. "I do not understand it," he muttered. "Always has U-Van been a true and dependable warrior. Could it be—?" he glanced piercingly at Ghek. "Thou hast a strange head that misfits thy body, fellow," he cried. "Our legends tell us of those ancient creatures that placed hallucinations upon the minds of their fellows. If thou be such then maybe U-Van suffered from thy forbidden powers. If thou be such O-Tar will know well how to deal with thee."

He wheeled about and motioned his warriors to follow him him.

"Wait!" cried Ghek. "Unless I am to be starved, send me food."

"You have had food," replied the warrior.

"Am I to be fed but once a day?" asked Ghek, "I require food oftener than that. Send me food."

"You shall have food," replied the officer. "None may say that the prisoners of Manator are ill-fed. Just are the laws of Manator," and he departed.

No sooner had the sounds of their passing died away in the distance than Ghek clambered from the shoulders of his rykor, and scurried to the burrow where he had hidden the key. Fetching it he unlocked the fetter from about the creature's ankle, locked it empty and carried the key farther down into the burrow. Then he returned to his place upon his brainless servitor. After a while he heard footsteps approaching, whereupon he rose and passed into another corridor from that down which he knew the warrior was coming. Here he waited out of sight, listening. He heard the man enter the chamber and halt. He heard a muttered exclamation, followed by the jangle of metal dishes as a salver was slammed upon a table; then rapidly retreating footsteps, which quickly died away in the distance.

Ghek lost no time in returning to the chamber, recovering the key, relocking the rykor to his chain. Then he replaced the key in the burrow, and squatting on the table beside his headless body, directed its hands toward the food. While the rykor ate Ghek sat listening for the scraping sandals and clattering arms that he knew soon would come. Nor had he long to wait. Ghek scrambled to the shoulders of his rykor as he heard them coming. Again it was the officer who had been summoned by U-Van and with him were three warriors. The one directly behind him was evidently the same who had brought the food, for his eyes went wide when he saw Ghek sitting at the table and he looked very foolish as the dwar turned his stern glance upon him.

"It is even as I said," he cried. "He was not here when I brought his food."

"But he is here now," said the officer grimly, "and his fetter is locked about his ankle. Look! it has not been opened—

but where is the key? It should be upon the table at the end opposite him. Where is the key, creature?" he shouted at Ghek.

"How should I, a prisoner, know better than my jailer the whereabouts of the key to my fetters?" he retorted.

"But it lay here," cried the officer, pointing to the other end of the table.

"Did you see it?" asked Ghek.

The officer hesitated. "No; but it must have been there," he parried.

"Did you see the key lying there?" asked Ghek, pointing to another warrior.

The fellow shook his head negatively. "And you? and you?" continued the kaldane addressing the others.

They both admitted that they never had seen the key. "And if it had been there how could I have reached it?" he continued.

"No, he could not have reached it," admitted the officer; "but there shall be no more of this! I-Zav, you will remain here on guard with this prisoner until you are relieved."

I-Zav looked anything but happy as this intelligence was transmitted to him, and he eyed Ghek suspiciously as the dwar and the other warriors turned and left him to his unhappy lot.

CHAPTER XIII

A DESPERATE DEED

E-MED CROSSED THE tower chamber toward Tara of Helium and the slave girl, Lan-O. He seized the former roughly by a shoulder. "Stand!" he commanded. Tara struck his hand from her and rising, backed away.

"Lay not your hand upon the person of a princess of Helium, beast!" she warned.

E-Med laughed. "Think you that I play at jetan for you without first knowing something of the stake for which I play?" he demanded. "Come here!"

The girl drew herself to her full height, folding her arms across her breast, nor did E-Med note that the slim fingers of her right hand were inserted beneath the broad leather strap of her harness where it passed over her left shoulder.

"And O-Tar learns of this you shall rue it, E-Med," cried the slave girl; "there be no law in Manator that gives you this girl before you shall have won her fairly."

"What cares O-Tar for her fate?" replied E-Med. "Have I not heard? Did she not flout the great jeddak, heaping abuse upon him? By my first ancestor, I think O-Tar might make a jed of the man who subdued her," and again he advanced toward Tara.

"Wait!" said the girl in low, even tone. "Perhaps you know not what you do. Sacred to the people of Helium are the persons of the women of Helium. For the honor of the humblest of them would the great jeddak himself unsheathe his sword. The greatest nations of Barsoom have trembled to the thunders of war in defense of the person of Dejah Thoris, my mother. We are but mortal and so may die; but we may not be defiled. You may play at jetan for a princess of Helium, but though you may win the match, never may you claim the reward. If thou wouldst possess a dead body press me too far, but know, man of Manator, that the blood of The Warlord flows not in the veins of Tara of Helium for naught. I have spoken."

"I know naught of Helium and O-Tar is *our* warlord," replied E-Med; "but I do know that I would examine more closely the prize that I shall play for and win. I would test the lips of her who is to be my slave after the next games; nor is it well, woman, to drive me too far to anger." His eyes narrowed as he spoke, his visage taking on the semblance of that of a snarling beast. "If you doubt the truth of my words ask Lan-O, the slave girl."

"He speaks truly, O woman of Helium," interjected Lan-O. "Try not the temper of E-Med, if you value your life."

But Tara of Helium made no reply. Already had she spoken. She stood in silence now facing the burly warrior who approached her. He came close and then quite suddenly he seized her and, bending, tried to draw her lips to his.

Lan-O saw the woman from Helium half turn, and with a quick movement jerk her right hand from where it had lain upon her breast. She saw the hand shoot from beneath the arm of E-Med and rise behind his shoulder and she saw in the hand a long, slim blade. The lips of the warrior were drawing closer to those of the woman, but they never touched them, for suddenly the man straightened, stiffly, a shriek upon his lips, and then he crumpled like an empty fur and lay, a shrunken heap, upon the floor. Tara of Helium stooped and wiped her blade upon his harness.

Lan-O, wide-eyed, looked with horror upon the corpse. "For this we shall both die," she cried.

"And who would live a slave in Manator?" asked Tara of Helium.

"I am not so brave as thou," said the slave girl, "and life is sweet and there is always hope."

"Life is sweet," agreed Tara of Helium, "but honor is sacred. But do not fear. When they come I shall tell them the truth—that you had no hand in this and no opportunity to prevent it."

For a moment the slave girl seemed to be thinking deeply. Suddenly her eyes lighted. "There is a way, perhaps," she said, "to turn suspicion from us. He has the key to this chamber upon him. Let us open the door and drag him out—maybe we shall find a place to hide him."

"Good!" exclaimed Tara of Helium, and the two immediately set about the matter Lan-O had suggested. Quickly they found the key and unlatched the door and then, between them, they half carried, half dragged, the corpse of E-Med from the room and down the stairway to the next level where Lan-O said there were vacant chambers. The first door they tried was unlatched, and through this the two bore their grisly burden into a small room lighted by a single window. The apartment bore evidence of having been utilized as a living-room rather than as a cell, being furnished with a degree of comfort and even luxury. The walls were paneled to a height of about seven feet from the floor, while the plaster above and the ceiling were decorated with faded paintings of another day.

As Tara's eyes ran quickly over the interior her attention was drawn to a section of paneling that seemed to be separated at one edge from the piece next adjoining it. Quickly she crossed to it, discovering that one vertical edge of an entire panel projected a half-inch beyond the others. There was a possible explanation which piqued her curiosity, and acting upon its suggestion she seized upon the projecting edge and pulled outward. Slowly the panel swung toward her, revealing a dark aperture in the wall behind.

"Look, Lan-O!" she criedl "See what I have found—a hole in which we may hide the thing upon the floor."

Lan-O joined her and together the two investigated the dark aperture, finding a small platform from which a narrow runway led downward into Stygian darkness. Thick dust covered the floor within the doorway, indicating that a great period of time had elapsed since human foot had trod it—a secret way, doubtless, unknown to living Manatorian. Here they dragged the corpse of E-Med, leaving it upon the platform, and as they left the dark and forbidden closet Lan-O would have slammed to the panel had not Tara prevented.

"Wait!" she said, and fell to examining the door frame and the stile.

"Hurry!" whispered the slave girl. "If they come we are lost."

"It may serve us well to know how to open this place again," replied Tara of Helium, and then suddenly she pressed a foot against a section of the carved base at the right of the open panel. "Ah!" she breathed, a note of satisfaction in her tone, and closed the panel until it fitted snugly in its place. "Come!" she said and turned toward the outer doorway of the chamber.

They reached their own cell without detection, and closing the door Tara locked it from the inside and placed the key in a secret pocket in her harness.

"Let them come," she said. "Let them question us! What could two poor prisoners know of the whereabouts of their noble jailer? I ask you, Lan-O, what could they?"

"Nothing," admitted Lan-O, smiling with her companion.

"Tell me of these men of Manator," said Tara presently. "Are they all like E-Med, or are some of them like A-Kor, who seemed a brave and chivalrous character?"

"They are not unlike the peoples of other countries," replied Lan-O. "There be among them both good and bad. They are brave warriors and mighty. Among themselves they are not without chivalry and honor, but in their dealings with strangers they know but one law—the law of might. The weak and unfortunate of other lands fill them with contempt and arouse all that is worst in their natures, which doubtless accounts for their treatment of us, their slaves."

"But why should they feel contempt for those who have suffered the misfortune of falling into their hands?" queried Tara.

"I do not know," said Lan-O; "A-Kor says that he believes that it is because their country has never been invaded by a victorious foe. In their stealthy raids never have they been defeated, because they have never waited to face a powerful force, and so they have come to believe themselves invincible, and the other peoples are held in contempt as inferior in valor and the practice of arms."

"Yet A-Kor is one of them," said Tara.

"He is a son of O-Tar, the jeddak," replied Lan-O; "but his mother was a high born Gatholian, captured and made slave by O-Tar, and A-Kor boasts that in his veins runs only the blood of his mother, and indeed is he different from the others. His chivalry is of a gentler form, though not even his worst enemy has dared question his courage, while his skill with the sword, and the spear, and the thoat is famous throughout the length and breadth of Manator."

"What think you they will do with him?" asked Tara of Helium.

"Sentence him to the games," replied Lan-O. "If O-Tar be not greatly angered he may be sentenced to but a single game, in which case he may come out alive; but if O-Tar wishes really to dispose of him he will be sentenced to the entire series, and no warrior has ever survived the full ten, or rather none who was under a sentence from O-Tar."

"What are the games? I do not understand," said Tara. "I have heard them speak of playing at jetan, but surely no one can be killed at jetan. We play it often at home."

"But not as they play it in the arena at Manator," replied Lan-O. "Come to the window," and together the two approached an aperture facing toward the east.

Below her Tara of Helium saw a great field entirely surrounded by the low building, and the lofty towers of which that in which she was imprisoned was but a unit. About the arena were tiers of seats; but the thing that caught her attention was a gigantic jetan board laid out upon the floor of the arena in great squares of alternate orange and black.

"Here they play at jetan with living pieces. They play for great stakes and usually for a woman—some slave of exceptional beauty. O-Tar himself might have played for you had you not angered him, but now you will be played for in an open game by slaves and criminals, and you will belong to the side that wins—not to a single warrior, but to all who survive the game."

The eyes of Tara of Helium flashed, but she made no comment.

"Those who direct the play do not necessarily take part in it," continued the slave girl, "but sit in those two great thrones which you see at either end of the board and direct their pieces from square to square."

"But where lies the danger?" asked Tara of Helium. "If a piece be taken it is merely removed from the board—this is a rule of jetan as old almost as the civilization of Barsoom."

"But here in Manator, when they play in the great arena with living men, that rule is altered," explained Lan-O. "When a warrior is moved to a square occupied by an opposing piece, the two battle to the death for possession of the square and the one that is successful advantages by the move. Each is caparisoned to simulate the piece he represents and in addition he wears that which indicates whether he be slave, a warrior serving a sentence, or a volunteer. If serving a sentence the number of games he must play is also indicated, and thus the one directing the moves knows which pieces to risk and which to conserve, and further than this, a man's chances are affected by the position that is assigned him for the game. Those whom they wish to die are always Panthans in the game, for the Panthan has the least chance of surviving."

"Do those who direct the play ever actually take part in it?" asked Tara.

"Oh, yes," said Lan-O. "Often when two warriors, even of the highest class, hold a grievance against one another O-Tar compels them to settle it upon the arena. Then it is that they take active part and with drawn swords direct their own players from the position of Chief. The pick their own players, usually the best of their own warriors and slaves, if they be powerful men who possess such, or their friends may volunteer, or they may obtain prisoners from the pits. These are games indeed—the very best that are seen. Often the great chiefs themselves are slain."

"It is within this amphitheater that the justice of Manator is meted, then?" asked Tara.

"Very largely," replied Lan-O.

"How, then, through such justice, could a prisoner win his liberty?" continued the girl from Helium.

"If a man, and he survived ten games his liberty would be his," replied Lan-O.

"But none ever survives?" queried Tara. "And if a woman?"

"No stranger within the gates of Manator ever has survived ten games," replied the slave girl. "They are permitted to offer themselves into perpetual slavery if they prefer that to fighting at jetan. Of course they may be called upon, as any warrior, to take part in a game; but their chances then of surviving are increased, since they may never again have the chance of winning to liberty."

"But a woman," insisted Tara; "how may a woman win her freedom?"

Lan-O laughed. "Very simply," she cried, derisively. "She has but to find a warrior who will fight through ten consecutive games for her and survive."

" 'Just are the laws of Manator,' " quoted Tara, scornfully.

Then it was that they heard footsteps outside their cell and a moment later a key turned in the lock and the door opened. A warrior faced them.

"Hast seen E-Med the dwar?" he asked.

"Yes," replied Tara, "he was here some time ago."

The man glanced quickly about the bare chamber and then searchingly first at Tara of Helium and then at the slave girl, Lan-O. The puzzled expression upon his face increased. He scratched his head. "It is strange," he said. "A score of men saw him ascend into this tower; and though there is but a single exit, and that well guarded, no man has seen him pass out."

Tara of Helium hid a yawn with the back of a shapely hand. "The Princess of Helium is hungry, fellow," she drawled; "tell your master that she would eat."

It was an hour later that food was brought, an officer and several warriors accompanying the bearer. The former examined the room carefully, but there was no sign that aught amiss had occurred there. The wound that had sent E-Med the dwar to his ancestors had not bled, fortunately for Tara of Helium.

"Woman," cried the officer, turning upon Tara, "you were the last to see E-Med the dwar. Answer me now and answer me truthfully. Did you see him leave this room?"

"I did," answered Tara of Helium.

"Where did he go from here?"

"How should I know? Think you that I can pass through a locked door of skeel?" the girl's tone was scornful.

"Of that we do not know," said the officer. "Strange things have happened in the cell of your companion in the pits of Manator. Perhaps you could pass through a locked door of skeel as easily as he performs seemingly more impossible feats."

"Whom do you mean," she cried; "Turan the panthan? He lives, then? Tell me, is he here in Manator unharmed?"

"I speak of that thing which calls itself Ghek the kaldane," replied the officer.

"But Turan! Tell me, padwar, have you heard aught of him?" Tara's tone was insistent and she leaned a little forward toward the officer, her lips slightly parted in expectancy.

Into the eyes of the slave girl, Lan-O, who was watching her, there crept a soft light of understanding; but the officer ignored Tara's question—what was the fate of another slave to him? "Men do not disappear into thin air," he growled, "and if E-Med be not found soon O-Tar himself may take a hand in this. I warn you, woman, if you be one of those horrid Corphals that by commanding the spirits of the wicked dead gains evil mastery over the living, as many now believe the thing called Ghek to be, that lest you return E-Med, O-Tar will have no mercy on you."

"What foolishness is this?" cried the girl. "I am a princess of Helium, as I have told you all a score of times. Even if the fabled Corphals existed, as none but the most ignorant now believes, the lore of the ancients tells us that they entered only into the bodies of wicked criminals of the lowest class. Man of Manator, thou art a fool, and thy jeddak and all his peo-

ple," and she turned her royal back upon the padwar, and
gazed through the window across the Field of Jetan and the
roofs of Manator toward the low hills and the rolling country
and freedom.

"And you know so much of Corphals, then," he cried, "you
know that while no common man dare harm them they may
be slain by the hand of a jeddak with impunity!"

The girl did not reply, nor would she speak again, for all
his threats and rage, for she knew now that none in all Manator dared harm her save O-Tar, the jeddak, and after a
while the padwar left, taking his men with him. And after
they had gone Tara stood for long looking out upon the city
of Manator, and wondering what more of cruel wrongs Fate
held in store for her. She was standing thus in silent meditation when there rose to her the strains of martial music from
the city below—the deep, mellow tones of the long war trumpets of mounted troops, the clear, ringing notes of foot-
soldiers' music. The girl raised her head and looked about,
listening, and Lan-O, standing at an opposite window, looking toward the west, motioned Tara to join her. Now they
could see across roofs and avenues to The Gate of Enemies,
through which troops were marching into the city.

"The Great Jed is coming," said Lan-O; "none other dares
enter thus, with blaring trumpets, the city of Manator. It
is U-Thor, Jed of Manatos, second city of Manator. They call
him The Great Jed the length and breadth of Manator, and
because the people love him, O-Tar hates him. They say, who
know, that it would need but slight provocation to inflame
the two to war. How such a war would end no one could
guess, for the people of Manator worship the great O-Tar,
though they do not love him. U-Thor they love, but he is
not the jeddak," and Tara understood, as only a Martian may,
how much that simple statement encompassed.

The loyalty of a Martian to his jeddak is almost an instinct, and second not even to the instinct of self-preservation
at that. Nor is this strange in a race whose religion includes
ancestor worship, and where families trace their origin back
into remote ages and a jeddak sits upon the same throne
that his direct progenitors have occupied for, perhaps, hundreds of thousands of years, and rules the descendants of the
same people that his forebears ruled. Wicked jeddaks have

been dethroned, but seldom are they replaced by other than members of the imperial house, even though the law gives to the jeds the right to select whom they please.

"U-Thor is a just man and good, then?" asked Tara of Helium.

"There be none nobler," replied Lan-O. "In Manatos none but wicked criminals who deserve death are forced to play at jetan, and even then the play is fair and they have their chance for freedom. Volunteers may play, but the moves are not necessarily to the death—a wound, and even sometimes points in swordplay, deciding the issue. There they look upon jetan as a martial sport—here it is but butchery. And U-Thor is opposed to the ancient slave raids and to the policy that keeps Manator forever isolated from the other nations of Barsoom; but U-Thor is not jeddak and so there is no change."

The two girls watched the column moving up the broad avenue from The Gate of Enemies toward the palace of O-Tar. A gorgeous, barbaric procession of painted warriors in jewel-studded harness and waving feathers; vicious, squealing thoats caparisoned in rich trappings; far above their heads the long lances of their riders bore fluttering pennons; foot-soldiers swinging easily along the stone pavement, their sandals of zitidar hide giving forth no sound; and at the rear of each utan a train of painted chariots, drawn by mammoth zitidars, carrying the equipment of the company to which they were attached. Utan after utan entered through the great gate, and even when the head of the column reached the palace of O-Tar they were not all within the city.

"I have been here many years," said the girl, Lan-O; "but never have I seen even The Great Jed bring so many fighting men into the city of Manator."

Through half-closed eyes Tara of Helium watched the warriors marching up the broad avenue, trying to imagine them the fighting men of her beloved Helium coming to the rescue of their princess. That splendid figure upon the great thoat might be John Carter, himself, Warlord of Barsoom, and behind him utan after utan of the veterans of the empire, and then the girl opened her eyes again and saw the host of painted, befeathered barbarians, and sighed. But yet she watched, fascinated by the martial scene, and now she

noted again the groups of silent figures upon the balconies.
No waving silks; no cries of welcome; no showers of flowers
and jewels such as would have marked the entry of such a
splendid, friendly pageant into the twin cities of her birth.

"The people do not seem friendly to the warriors of Manatos," she remarked to Lan-O; "I have not seen a single wel-
coming sign from the people on the balconies."

The slave girl looked at her in surprise. "It cannot be that
you do not know!" she exclaimed. "Why, they are—" but she
got no further. The door swung open and an officer stood
before them.

"The slave girl, Tara, is summoned to the presence of O-
Tar, the jeddak!" he announced.

CHAPTER XIV

AT GHEK'S COMMAND

TURAN THE PANTHAN chafed in his chains. Time dragged; silence and monotony prolonged minutes into hours. Uncertainty of the fate of the woman he loved turned each hour
into an eternity of hell. He listened impatiently for the sound
of approaching footsteps that he might see and speak to some
living creature and learn, perchance, some word of Tara of
Helium. After torturing hours his ears were rewarded by the
rattle of harness and arms. Men were coming! He waited
breathlessly. Perhaps they were his executioners; but he
would welcome them notwithstanding. He would question
them. But if they knew naught of Tara he would not divulge
the location of the hiding place in which he had left her.

Now they came—a half-dozen warriors and an officer, es-
corting an unarmed man; a prisoner, doubtless. Of this Turan was not left long in doubt, since they brought the newcomer and chained him to an adjoining ring. Immediately
the panthan commenced to question the officer in charge of
the guard.

"Tell me," he demanded, "why I have been made prisoner,
and if other strangers were captured since I entered your city."

"What other prisoners?" asked the officer.

"A woman, and a man with a strange head," replied Turan.

"It is possible," said the officer; "but what were their names?"

"The woman was Tara, Princess of Helium, and the man was Ghek, a kaldane, of Bantoom."

"These were your friends?" asked the officer.

"Yes," replied Turan.

"It is what I would know," said the officer, and with a curt command to his men to follow him he turned and left the cell.

"Tell me of them!" cried Turan after him. "Tell me of Tara of Helium! Is she safe?" but the man did not answer and soon the sound of their departure died in the distance.

"Tara of Helium was safe but a short time since," said the prisoner chained at Turan's side.

The panthan turned toward the speaker, seeing a large man, handsome of face and with a manner both stately and dignified. "You have seen her?" he asked. "They captured her then? She is in danger?"

"She is being held in The Towers of Jetan as a prize for the next games," replied the stranger.

"And who are you?" asked Turan. "And why are you here, a prisoner?"

"I am A-Kor the dwar, keeper of The Towers of Jetan," replied the other. "I am here because I dared speak the truth of O-Tar the jeddak, to one of his officers."

"And your punishment?" asked Turan.

"I do not know. O-Tar has not yet spoken. Doubtless the games—perhaps the full ten, for O-Tar does not love A-Kor, his son."

"You are the jeddak's son," asked Turan.

"I am the son of O-Tar and of a slave, Haja of Gathol, who was a princess in her own land."

Turan looked searchingly at the speaker. A son of Haja of Gathol! A son of his mother's sister, this man, then, was his own cousin. Well did Gahan remember the mysterious disappearance of the Princess Haja and an entire utan of her personal troops. She had been upon a visit far from the city of Gathol and returning home had vanished with her whole escort from the sight of man. So this was the secret of the seeming mystery? Doubtless it explained many other similar disappearances that extended nearly as far back as the history of Gathol. Turan scrutinized his companion, discovering many evidences of resemblance to his mother's people. A-Kor might have been ten years younger than he, but such differences in age are scarce accounted among a people who seldom or never age outwardly after maturity and whose span of life may be a thousand years.

"And where lies Gathol?" asked Turan.

"Almost due east of Manator," replied A-Kor.

"And how far?"

"Some twenty-one degrees it is from the city of Manator to the city of Gathol," replied A-Kor; "but little more than ten degrees between the boundaries of the two countries. Between them, though, there lies a country of torn rocks and yawning chasms."

Well did Gahan know this country that bordered his upon the west—even the ships of the air avoided it because of the treacherous currents that rose from the deep chasms, and the almost total absence of safe landings. He knew now where Manator lay and for the first time in long weeks the way to his own Gathol, and here was a man, a fellow prisoner, in whose veins flowed the blood of his own ancestors—a man who knew Manator; its people, its customs and the country surrounding it—one who could aid him, with advice at least, to find a plan for the rescue of Tara of Helium and for escape. But would A-Kor—could he dare broach the subject? He could do no less than try.

"And O-Tar you think will sentence you to death?" he asked; "and why?"

"He would like to," replied A-Kor, "for the people chafe beneath his iron hand and their loyalty is but the loyalty of a people to the long line of illustrious jeddaks from which he has sprung. He is a jealous man and has found the means of disposing of most of those whose blood might entitle them to a claim upon the throne, and whose place in the affections of the people endowed them with any political significance. The fact that I was the son of a slave relegated me to a position of minor importance in the consideration of O-Tar, yet I am still the son of a jeddak and might sit upon the throne of Manator with as perfect congruity as O-Tar himself. Com-

bined with this is the fact that of recent years the people, and
especially many of the younger warriors, have evinced a
growing affection for me, which I attribute to certain virtues
of character and training derived from my mother, but which
O-Tar assumes to be the result of an ambition upon my part
to occupy the throne of Manator.

"And now, I am firmly convinced, he has seized upon my
criticism of his treatment of the slave girl Tara as a pretext
of ridding himself of me."

"But if you could escape and reach Gathol," suggested
Turan.

"I have thought of that," mused A-Kor; "but how much
better off would I be? In the eyes of the Gatholians I would
be not a Gatholian, but a stranger, and doubtless they would
accord me the same treatment that we of Manator accord
strangers."

"Could you convince them that you are the son of the Princess Haja your welcome would be assured," said Turan;
"while on the other hand you could purchase your freedom
and citizenship with a brief period of labor in the diamond
mines."

"How know you all these things?" asked A-Kor. "I thought
you were from Helium."

"I am a panthan," replied Turan, "and I have served many
countries, among them Gathol."

"It is what the slaves from Gathol have told me," said
A-Kor, thoughtfully, "and my mother, before O-Tar sent her
to live at Manatos. I think he must have feared her power and
influence among the slaves from Gathol and their descendants, who number perhaps a million people throughout the
land of Manator."

"Are these slaves organized?" asked Turan.

A-Kor looked straight into the eyes of the panthan for a
long moment before he replied. "You are a man of honor,"
he said; "I read it in your face, and I am seldom mistaken in
my estimate of a man; but—" and he leaned closer to the other
—"even the walls have ears," he whispered, and Turan's
question was answered.

It was later in the evening that warriors came and unlocked
the fetter from Turan's ankle and led him away to appear
before O-Tar, the jeddak. They conducted him toward the

palace along narrow, winding streets and broad avenues;
but always from the balconies there looked down upon them
in endless ranks the silent people of the city. The palace itself was filled with life and activity. Mounted warriors galloped through the corridors and up and down the runways
connecting adjacent floors. It seemed that no one walked
within the palace other than a few slaves. Squealing, fighting
thoats were stabled in magnificent halls while their riders, if
not upon some duty of the palace, played at jetan with small
figures carved from wood.

Turan noted the magnificence of the interior architecture
of the palace, the lavish expenditure of precious jewels and
metals, the gorgeous mural decorations which depicted almost exclusively martial scenes, and principally duels which
seemed to be fought upon jetan boards of heroic size. The
capitals of many of the columns supporting the ceilings of
the corridors and chambers through which they passed were
wrought into formal likenesses of jetan pieces—everywhere
there seemed a suggestion of the game. Along the same path
that Tara of Helium had been led Turan was conducted
toward the throne room of O-Tar the jeddak, and when he
entered the Hall of Chiefs his interest turned to wonder and
admiration as he viewed the ranks of statuesque thoatmen
decked in their gorgeous, martial panoply. Never, he thought,
had he seen upon Barsoom more soldierly figures or thoats
so perfectly trained to perfection of immobility as these. Not
a muscle quivered, not a tail lashed, and the riders were as
motionless as their mounts—each warlike eye straight to the
front, the great spears inclined at the same angle. It was a
picture to fill the breast of a fighting man with awe and
reverence. Nor did it fail in its effect upon Turan as they
conducted him the length of the chamber, where he waited
before great doors until he should be summoned into the
presence of the ruler of Manator.

When Tara of Helium was ushered into the throne room
of O-Tar she found the great hall filled with the chiefs and
officers of O-Tar and U-Thor, the latter occupying the place
of honor at the foot of the throne, as was his due. The girl
was conducted to the foot of the aisle and halted before the
jeddak, who looked down upon her from his high throne

with scowling brows and fierce, cruel eyes:

"The laws of Manator are just," said O-Tar, addressing her; "thus is it that you have been summoned here again to be judged by the highest authority of Manator. Word has reached me that you are suspected of being a Corphal. What word have you to say in refutation of the charge?"

Tara of Helium could scarce restrain a sneer as she answered the ridiculous accusation of witchcraft. "So ancient is the culture of my people," she said, "that authentic history reveals no defense for that which we know existed only in the ignorant and superstitious minds of the most primitive peoples of the past. To those who are yet so untutored as to believe in the existence of Corphals, there can be no argument that will convince them of their error—only long ages of refinement and culture can accomplish their release from the bondage of ignorance. I have spoken."

"Yet you do not deny the accusation," said O-Tar.

"It is not worthy the dignity of a denial," she responded haughtily.

"And I were you, woman," said a deep voice at her side, "I should, nevertheless, deny it."

Tara of Helium turned to see the eyes of U-Thor, the great jed of Manatos, upon her. Brave eyes they were, but neither cold nor cruel. O-Tar rapped impatiently upon the arm of his throne. "U-Thor forgets," he cried, "that O-Tar is the jeddak."

"U-Thor remembers," replied the jed of Manatos, "that the laws of Manator permit any who may be accused to have advice and counsel before their judge."

Tara of Helium saw that for some reason this man would have assisted her, and so she acted upon his advice.

"I deny the charge," she said, "I am no Corphal."

"Of that we shall learn," snapped O-Tar. "U-Dor, where are those who have knowledge of the powers of this woman?"

And U-Dor brought several who recounted the little that was known of the disappearance of E-Med, and others who told of the capture of Ghek and Tara, suggesting by deduction that having been found together they had sufficient in common to make it reasonably certain that one was as bad as the other, and that, therefore, it remained but to convict one of them of Corphalism to make certain the guilt of both.

And then O-Tar called for Ghek, and immediately the hideous kaldane was dragged before him by warriors who could not conceal the fear in which they held this creature.

"And you!" said O-Tar in cold accusing tones. "Already have I been told enough of you to warrant me in passing through your heart the jeddak's steel—of how you stole the brains from the warrior U-Van so that he thought he saw your headless body still endowed with life; of how you caused another to believe that you had escaped, making him to see naught but an empty bench and a blank wall where you had been."

"Ah, O-Tar, but that is nothing!" cried a young padwar who had come in command of the escort that brought Ghek. "The thing which he did to I-Zav, here, would prove his guilt alone."

"What did he to the warrior I-Zav?" demanded O-Tar. "Let I-Zav speak!"

The warrior I-Zav, a great fellow of bulging muscles and thick neck, advanced to the foot of the throne. He was pale and still trembling visibly as from a nervous shock.

"Let my first ancestor be my witness, O-Tar, that I speak the truth," he began. "I was left to guard this creature, who sat upon a bench, shackled to the wall. I stood by the open doorway at the opposite side of the chamber. He could not reach me, yet, O-Tar, may Iss engulf me if he did not drag me to him helpless as an unhatched egg. He dragged me to him, greatest of jeddaks, *with his eyes!* With his eyes he seized upon my eyes and dragged me to him and he made me lay my swords and dagger upon the table and back off into a corner, and still keeping his eyes upon my eyes his head quitted his body and crawling upon six short legs it decended to the floor and back part way into the hole of an ulsio, but not so far that the eyes were not still upon me and then it returned with the key to its fetter and after resuming its place upon its own shoulders it unlocked the fetter and again dragged me across the room and made me to sit upon the bench where it had been and there it fastened the fetter about my ankle, and I could do naught for the power of its eyes and the fact that it wore my two swords and my dagger. And then the head disappeared down the hole of the ulsio with the key, and when it returned, it resumed its body and

stood guard over me at the doorway until the padwar came
to fetch it hither."

"It is enough!" said O-Tar, sternly. "Both shall receive the
jeddak's steel," and rising from his throne he drew his long
sword and descended the marble steps toward them, while
two brawny warriors seized Tara by either arm and two
seized Ghek, holding them facing the naked blade of the
jeddak.

"Hold, just O-Tar!" cried U-Dor. "There be yet another
to be judged. Let us confront him who calls himself Turan
with these his fellows before they die."

"Good!" exclaimed O-Tar, pausing half way down the
steps. "Fetch Turan, the slave!"

When Turan had been brought into the chamber he was
placed a little to Tara's left and a step nearer the throne. O-
Tar eyed him menacingly.

"You are Turan," he asked, "friend and companion of
these?"

The panthan was about to reply when Tara of Helium
spoke. "I know not this fellow," she said. "Who dares say
that he be a friend and companion of the Princess Tara of
Helium?"

Turan and Ghek looked at her in surprise, but at Turan
she did not look, and to Ghek she passed a quick glance of
warning, as to say: "Hold thy peace!"

The panthan tried not to fathom her purpose for the head
is useless when the heart usurps its functions, and Turan
knew only that the woman he loved had denied him, and
though he tried not even to think it his foolish heart urged
but a single explanation—that she refused to recognize him
lest she be involved in his difficulties.

O-Tar looked first at one and then at another of them; but
none of them spoke.

"Were they not captured together?" he asked of U-Dor.

"No," replied the dwar. "He who is called Turan was
found seeking entrance to the city and was enticed to the
pits. The following morning I discovered the other two upon
the hill beyond The Gate of Enemies."

"But they are friends and companions," said a young padwar, "for this Turan inquired of me concerning these two,
calling them by name and saying that they were his friends."

"It is enough," stated O-Tar, "all three shall die," and he took another step downward from the throne.

"For what shall we die?" asked Ghek. "Your people prate of the just laws of Manator, and yet you would slay three strangers without telling them of what crime they are accused."

"He is right," said a deep voice. It was the voice of U-Thor, the great jed of Manatos. O-Tar looked at him and scowled; but there came voices from other portions of the chamber seconding the demand for justice.

"Then know, though you shall die anyway," cried O-Tar, "that all three are convicted of Corphalism and that as only a jeddak may slay such as you in safety you are about to be honored with the steel of O-Tar."

"Fool!" cried Turan. "Know you not that in the veins of this woman flows the blood of ten thousand jeddaks—that greater than yours is her power in her own land? She is Tara, Princess of Helium, great-granddaughter of Tardos Mors, daughter of John Carter, Warlord of Barsoom. She cannot be a Corphal. Nor is this creature Ghek, nor am I. And you would know more, I can prove my right to be heard and to be believed if I may have word with the Princess Haja of Gathol, whose son is my fellow prisoner in the pits of O-Tar, his father."

At this U-Thor rose to his feet and faced O-Tar. "What means this?" he asked. "Speaks the man the truth? Is the son of Haja a prisoner in thy pits, O-Tar?"

"And what is it to the jed of Manatos who be the prisoners in the pits of his jeddak?" demanded O-Tar, angrily.

"It is this to the jed of Manatos," replied U-Thor in a voice so low as to be scarce more than a whisper and yet that was heard the whole length and breadth of the great throne room of O-Tar, Jeddak of Manator. "You gave me a slave woman, Haja, who had been a princess in Gathol, because you feared her influence among the slaves from Gathol. I have made of her a free woman, and I have married her and made her thus a princess of Manatos. Her son is my son, O-Tar, and though thou be my jeddak, I say to you that for any harm that befalls A-Kor you shall answer to U-Thor of Manatos."

O-Tar looked long at U-Thor, but he made no reply. Then

he turned again to Turan. "If one be a Corphal," he said, "then all of you be Corphals, and we know well from the things that this creature has done," he pointed at Ghek, "that he is a Corphal, for no mortal has such powers as he. And as you are all Corphals you must all die." He took another step downward, when Ghek spoke.

"These two have no such powers as I," he said. "They are but ordinary, brainless things such as yourself. I have done all the things that your poor, ignorant warriors have told you; but this only demonstrates that I am of a higher order than yourselves, as is indeed the fact. I am a kaldane, not a Corphal. There is nothing supernatural or mysterious about me, other than that to the ignorant all things which they cannot understand are mysterious. Easily might I have eluded your warriors and escaped your pits; but I remained in the hope that I might help these two foolish creatures who have not the brains to escape without help. They befriended me and saved my life. I owe them this debt. Do not slay them— they are harmless. Slay me if you will. I offer my life if it will appease your ignorant wrath. I cannot return to Bantoom and so I might as well die, for there is no pleasure in intercourse with the feeble intellects that cumber the face of the world outside the valley of Bantoom."

"Hideous egotist," said O-Tar, "prepare to die and assume not to dictate to O-Tar the jeddak. He has passed sentence and all three of you shall feel the jeddak's naked steel. I have spoken!"

He took another step downward and then a strange thing happened. He paused, his eyes fixed upon the eyes of Ghek. His sword slipped from nerveless fingers, and still he stood here swaying forward and back. A jed rose to rush to his side; but Ghek stopped him with a word.

"Wait!" he cried. "The life of your jeddak is in my hands. You believe me a Corphal and so you believe, too, that only the sword of a jeddak may slay me, therefore your blades are useless against me. Offer harm to any one of us, or seek to approach your jeddak until I have spoken, and he shall sink lifeless to the marble. Release the two prisoners and let them come to my side—I would speak to them, privately. Quick! do I say; I would as lief as not slay O-Tar. I but let him live that I may gain freedom for my friends—obstruct me and he dies."

The guards fell back, releasing Tara and Turan, who came close to Ghek's side.

"Do as I tell you and do it quickly," whispered the kaldane. "I cannot hold this fellow long, nor could I kill him thus. There are many minds working against mine and presently mine will tire and O-Tar will be himself again. You must make the best of your opportunity while you may. Behind the arras that you see hanging in the rear of the throne above you is a secret opening. From it a corridor leads to the pits of the palace, where there are storerooms containing food and drink. Few people go there. From these pits lead others to all parts of the city. Follow one that runs due west and it will bring you to The Gate of Enemies. The rest will then lie with you. I can do no more; hurry before my waning powers fail me—I am not as Luud, who was a king. He could have held this creature forever. Make haste! Go!"

CHAPTER XV

THE OLD MAN OF THE PITS

"I SHALL NOT desert you, Ghek," said Tara of Helium, simply.

"Go! Go!" whispered the kaldane. "You can do me no good. Go, or all I have done is for naught."

Tara shook her head. "I cannot," she said.

"They will slay her," said Ghek to Turan, and the panthan, torn between loyalty to this strange creature who had offered its life for him, and love of the woman, hesitated but a moment, then he swept Tara from her feet and lifting her in his arms leaped up the steps that led to the throne of Manator. Behind the throne he parted the arras and found the secret opening. Into this he bore the girl and down a long, narrow corridor and winding runways that led to lower levels until they came to the pits of the palace of O-Tar. Here was a labyrinth of passages and chambers presenting a thousand hiding-places.

As Turan bore Tara up the steps toward the throne a

score of warriors rose as though to rush forward to intercept them. "Stay!" cried Ghek, "or your jeddak dies," and they halted in their tracks, waiting the will of this strange, uncanny creature.

Presently Ghek took his eyes from the eyes of O-Tar and the jeddak shook himself as one who would be rid of a bad dream and straightened up, half dazed still.

"Look," said Ghek, then, "I have given your jeddak his life, nor have I harmed one of those whom I might easily have slain when they were in my power. No harm have I or my friends done in the city of Manator. Why then should you persecute us? Give us our lives. Give us our liberty."

O-Tar, now in command of his faculties, stooped and regained his sword. In the room was silence as all waited to hear the jeddak's answer.

"Just are the laws of Manator," he said at last. "Perhaps, after all, there is truth in the words of the stranger. Return him then to the pits and pursue the others and capture them. Through the mercy of O-Tar they shall be permitted to win their freedom upon the Field of Jetan, in the coming games."

Still ashen was the face of the jeddak as Ghek was led away and his appearance was that of a man who had been snatched from the brink of eternity into which he has gazed, not with the composure of great courage, but with fear. There were those in the throne room who knew that the execution of the three prisoners had but been delayed and the responsibility placed upon the shoulders of others, and one of those who knew was U-Thor, the great jed of Manatos. His curling lip betokened his scorn of the jeddak who had chosen humiliation rather than death. He knew that O-Tar had lost more of prestige in those few moments than he could regain in a lifetime, for the Martians are jealous of the courage of their chiefs—there can be no evasions of stern duty, no temporizing with honor. That there were others in the room who shared U-Thor's belief was evidenced by the silence and the grim scowls.

O-Tar glanced quickly around. He must have sensed the hostility and guessed its cause, for he went suddenly angry, and as one who seeks by the vehemence of his words to establish the courage of his heart he roared forth what could be considered as naught other than a challenge.

"The will of O-Tar, the jeddak, is the law of Manator,"
he cried, "and the laws of Manator are just—they cannot err.
U-Dor, dispatch those who will search the palace, the pits,
and the city, and return the fugitives to their cells.

"And now for you, U-Thor of Manatos! Think you with
impunity to threaten your jeddak—to question his right to
punish traitors and instigators of treason? What am I to
think of your own loyalty, who takes to wife a woman I
have banished from my court because of her intrigues against
the authority of her jeddak and her master? But O-Tar is
just. Make your explanations and your peace, then, before it
is too late."

"U-Tar has nothing to explain," replied the jed of Manatos; "nor is he at war with his jeddak; but he has the right
that every jed and every warrior enjoys, of demanding justice
at the hands of the jeddak for whomsoever he believes to be
persecuted. With increasing rigor has the jeddak of Manator persecuted the slaves from Gathol since he took to himself the unwilling Princess Haja. If the slaves from Gathol
have harbored thoughts of vengeance and escape 'tis no more
than might be expected from a proud and courageous people. Ever have I counselled greater fairness in our treatment of our slaves, many of whom, in their own lands, are
people of great distinction and power; but always has O-Tar,
the jeddak, flouted with arrogance my every suggestion.
Though it has been through none of my seeking that the
question has arisen now I am glad that it has, for the time
was bound to come when the jeds of Manator would demand from O-Tar the respect and consideration that is their
due from the man who holds his high office at their pleasure.
Know, then, O-Tar, that you must free A-Kor, the dwar,
forthwith or bring him to fair trial before the assembled jeds
of Manator. I have spoken."

"You have spoken well and to the point, U-Thor," cried
O-Tar, "for you have revealed to your jeddak and your fellow
jeds the depth of the disloyalty that I have long suspected.
A-Kor already has been tried and sentenced by the supreme
tribunal of Manator—O-Tar, the jeddak; and you too shall
receive justice from the same unfailing source. In the meantime you are under arrest. To the pits with him! To the pits
with U-Thor the false jed!" He clapped his hands to summon

the surrounding warriors to do his bidding. A score leaped forward to seize U-Thor. They were warriors of the palace, mostly; but two score leaped to defend U-Thor, and with ringing steel they fought at the foot of the steps to the throne of Manator where stood O-Tar, the jeddak, with drawn sword ready to take his part in the mêlée.

At the clash of steel, palace guards rushed to the scene from other parts of the great building until those who would have defended U-Thor were outnumbered two to one, and then the jed of Manatos slowly withdrew with his forces, and fighting his way through the corridors and chambers of the palace came at last to the avenue. Here he was reinforced by the little army that had marched with him into Manator. Slowly they retreated toward The Gate of Enemies between the rows of silent people looking down upon them from the balconies and there, within the city walls, they made their stand.

In a dimly-lighted chamber beneath the palace of O-Tar the jeddak, Turan the panthan lowered Tara of Helium from his arms and faced her. "I am sorry, Princess," he said, "that I was forced to disobey your commands, or to abandon Ghek; but there was no other way. Could he have saved you I would have stayed in his place. Tell me that you forgive me."

"How could I do less?" she replied graciously. "But it seemed cowardly to abandon a friend."

"Had we been three fighting men it had been different," he said. "We could only have remained and died together, fighting; but you know, Tara of Helium, that we may not jeopardize a woman's safety even though we risk the loss of honor."

"I know that, Turan," she said; "but no one may say that you risked honor who knows the honor and bravery that are yours."

He heard her with surprise for these were the first words that she had spoken to him that did not savor of the attitude of a princess to a panthan—though it was more in her tone than the actual words that he apprehended the difference. How at variance were they to her recent repudiation of him! He could not fathom her, and so he blurted out the question that had been in his mind since she had told O-Tar that she did not know him.

"Tara of Helium," he said, "your words are balm to the wound you gave me in the throne room of O-Tar. Tell me, Princess, why you denied me."

She turned her great, deep eyes up to his and in them was a little of reproach.

"You did not guess," she asked, "that it was my lips alone and not my heart that denied you? O-Tar had ordered that I die, more because I was a companion of Ghek than because of any evidence against me, and so I knew that if I acknowledged you as one of us, you would be slain, too."

"It was to save me, then?" he cried, his face suddenly lighting.

"It was to save my brave panthan," she said in a low voice.

"Tara of Helium," said the warrior, dropping to one knee, "your words are as food to my hungry heart," and he took her fingers in his and pressed them to his lips.

Gently she raised him to his feet. "You need not tell me, kneeling," she said, softly.

Her hand was still in his as he rose and they were very close, and the man was still flushed with the contact of her body since he had carried her from the throne room of O-Tar. He felt his heart pounding in his breast and the hot blood surging through his veins as he looked at her beautiful face, with its downcast eyes and the half-parted lips that he would have given a kingdom to possess, and then he swept her to him and as he crushed her against his breast his lips smothered her with kisses.

But only for an instant. Like a tigress the girl turned upon him, striking him, and thrusting him away. She stepped back, her head high and her eyes flashing fire. "You would dare?" she cried. "You would dare thus defile a princess of Helium?"

His eyes met hers squarely and there was no shame and no remorse in them.

"Yes, I would dare," he said. "I would dare love Tara of Helium; but I would not dare defile her or any woman with kisses that were not prompted by love of her alone." He stepped closer to her and laid his hands upon her shoulders. "Look into my eyes, daughter of The Warlord," he said "and tell me that you do not wish the love of Turan, the panthan."

"I do not wish your love," she cried, pulling away. "I hate you!" and then turning away she bent her head into the hollow of her arm, and wept.

The man took a step toward her as though to comfort her when he was arrested by the sound of a cackling laugh behind him. Wheeling about, he discovered a strange figure of a man standing in a doorway. It was one of those rarities occasionally to be seen upon Barsoom—an old man with the signs of age upon him. Bent and wrinkled, he had more the appearance of a mummy than a man.

"Love in the pits of O-Tar!" he cried, and again his thin laughter jarred upon the silence of the subterranean vaults. "A strange place to woo! A strange place to woo, indeed! When I was a young man we roamed in the gardens beneath giant pimalias and stole our kisses in the brief shadows of hurtling Thuria. We came not to the gloomy pits to speak of love; but times have changed and ways have changed, though I had never thought to live to see the time when the way of a man with a maid, or a maid with a man would change. Ah, but we kissed them then! And what if they objected, eh? What if they objected? Why, we kissed them more. Ey, ey, those were the days!" and he cackled again. "Ey, well do I recall the first of them I ever kissed, and I've kissed an army of them since; she was a fine girl, but she tried to slip a dagger into me while I was kissing her. Ey, ey, those were the days! But I kissed her. She's been dead over a thousand years now, but she was never kissed again like that while she lived, I'll swear, nor since she's been dead, either. And then there was that other—" but Turan, seeing a thousand or more years of osculatory memoirs portending, interrupted.

"Tell me, ancient one," he said, "not of thy loves but of thyself. Who are you? What do you here in the pits of O-Tar?"

"I might ask you the same, young man," replied the other. "Few there are who visit the pits other than the dead, except my pupils—ey! That is it—you are new pupils! Good! But never before have they sent a woman to learn the great art from the greatest artist. But times have changed. Now, in my day the women did no work—they were just for kissing and loving. Ey, those were the women. I mind the one we captured in the south—ey! she was a devil, but how she could love. She had breasts of marble and a heart of fire. Why, she ——"

"Yes, yes," interrupted Turan; "We are pupils, and we are

anxious to get to work. Lead on and we will follow."

"Ey, yes! Ey, yes! Come! All is rush and hurry as though there were not another countless myriad of ages ahead. Ey, yes! as many as lie behind. Two thousand years have passed since I broke my shell and always rush, rush, rush, yet I cannot see that aught has been accomplished. Manator is the same today as it was then—except the girls. We had the girls then. There was one that I gained upon The Fields of Jetan. Ey, but you should have seen——"

"Lead on!" cried Turan. "After we are at work you shall tell us of her."

"Ey, yes," said the old fellow and shuffled off down a dimly lighted passage. "Follow me!"

"You are going with him?" asked Tara.

"Why not?" replied Turan. "We know not where we are, or the way from these pits; for I know not east from west; but he doubtless knows and if we are shrewd we may learn from him that which we would know. At least we cannot afford to arouse his suspicions;" and so they followed him—followed along winding corridors and through many chambers, until they came at last to a room in which there were several marble slabs raised upon pedestals some three feet above the floor and upon each slab lay a human corpse.

"Here we are," exclaimed the old man. "These are fresh and we shall have to get to work upon them soon. I am working now on one for The Gate of Enemies. He slew many of our warriors. Truly is he entitled to a place in The Gate. Come, you shall see him."

He led them to an adjoining apartment. Upon the floor were many fresh, human bones and upon a marble slab a mass of shapeless flesh.

"You will learn this later," announced the old man; "but it will not harm you to watch me now, for there are not many thus prepared, and it may be long before you will have the opportunity to see another prepared for The Gate of Enemies. First, you see, I remove all the bones, carefully that the skin may be damaged as little as possible. The skull is the most difficult, but it can be removed by a skillful artist. You see, I have made but a single opening. This I now sew up, and that done, the body is hung so," and he fastened a piece of rope to the hair of the corpse and swung the horrid thing to a ring in the ceiling. Directly below it was a circular manhole in the floor from which he removed the cover revealing a well partially filled with a reddish liquid. "Now we lower it into this, the formula for which you shall learn in due time. We fasten it thus to the bottom of the cover, which we now replace. In a year it will be ready; but it must be examined often in the meantime and the liquid kept above the level of its crown. It will be a very beautiful piece, this one, when it is ready.

"And you are fortunate again, for there is one to come out today." He crossed to the opposite side of the room and raised another cover, reached in and dragged a grotesque looking figure from the hole. It was a human body, shrunk by the action of the chemical in which it had been immersed, to a little figure scarce a foot high.

"Ey! is it not fine?" cried the little old man. "Tomorrow it will take its place in The Gate of Enemies." He dried it off with cloths and packed it away carefully in a basket. "Perhaps you would like to see some of my life work," he suggested, and without waiting for their assent led them to another apartment, a large chamber in which were forty or fifty people. All were sitting or standing quietly about the walls, with the exception of one huge warrior who bestrode a great thoat in the very center of the room, and all were motionless. Instantly there sprang to the minds of Tara and Turan the rows of silent people upon the balconies that lined the avenues of the city, and the noble array of mounted warriors in The Hall of Chiefs, and the same explanation came to both but neither dared voice the question that was in his mind, for fear of revealing by his ignorance the fact that they were strangers in Manator and therefore impostors in the guise of pupils.

"It is very wonderful," said Turan. "It must require great skill and patience and time."

"That it does," replied the old man, "though having done it so long I am quicker than most; but mine are the most natural. Why, I would defy the wife of that warrior to say that insofar as appearances are concerned he does not live," and he pointed at the man upon the thoat. "Many of them, of course, are brought here wasted or badly wounded and these I have to repair. That is where great skill is required, for everyone wants his dead to look as they did at their best in life; but you shall learn—to mount them and paint them and repair them and sometimes to make an ugly one look beautiful. And it will be a great comfort to be able to mount your own. Why, for fifteen hundred years no one has mounted my own dead but myself.

"I have many, my balconies are crowded with them; but I keep a great room for my wives. I have them all, as far back as the first one, and many is the evening I spend with them—quiet evenings and very pleasant. And then the pleasure of preparing them and making them even more beautiful than in life partially recompenses one for their loss. I take my time with them, looking for a new one while I am working on the old. When I am not sure about a new one I bring her to the chamber where my wives are, and compare her charms with theirs, and there is always a great satisfaction at such times in knowing that they will not object. I love harmony."

"Did you prepare all the warriors in The Hall of Chiefs?" asked Turan.

"Yes, I prepare them and repair them," replied the old man. "O-Tar will trust no other. Even now I have two in another room who were damaged in some way and brought down to me. O-Tar does not like to have them gone long, since it leaves two riderless thoats in the Hall; but I shall have them ready presently. He wants them all there in the event any momentous question arises upon which the living jeds cannot agree, or do not agree with O-Tar. Such questions he carried to the jeds in The Hall of Chiefs. There he shuts himself up alone with the great chiefs who have attained wisdom through death. It is an excellent plan and there is never any friction or misunderstandings. O-Tar has said that it is the finest deliberative body upon Barsoom—much more intelligent than that composed of the living jeds. But come, we must get to work; come into the next chamber and I will begin your instruction."

He led the way into the chamber in which lay the several corpses upon their marble slabs, and going to a cabinet he donned a pair of huge spectacles and commenced to select various tools from little compartments. This done he turned again toward his two pupils.

"Now let me have a look at you," he said. "My eyes are not

what they once were, and I need these powerful lenses for my work, or to see distinctly the features of those around me."

He turned his eyes upon the two before him. Turan held his breath for he knew that now the man must discover that they wore not the harness or insignia of Manator. He had wondered before why the old fellow had not noticed it, for he had not known that he was half blind. The other examined their faces, his eyes lingering long upon the beauty of Tara of Helium, and then they drifted to the harness of the two. Turan thought that he noted an appreciable start of surprise on the part of the taxidermist, but if the old man noticed anything his next words did not reveal it.

"Come with I-Gos," he said to Turan, "I have materials in the next room that I would have you fetch hither. Remain here, woman, we shall be gone but a moment."

He led the way to one of the numerous doors opening into the chamber and entered ahead of Turan. Just inside the door he stopped, and pointing to a bundle of silks and furs upon the opposite side of the room directed Turan to fetch them. The latter had crossed the room and was stooping to raise the bundle when he heard the click of a lock behind him. Wheeling instantly he saw that he was alone in the room and that the single door was closed. Running rapidly to it he strove to open it, only to find that he was a prisoner.

I-Gos, stepping out and locking the door behind him, turned toward Tara.

"Your leather betrayed you," he said, laughing his cackling laugh. "You sought to deceive old I-Gos, but you found that though his eyes are weak his brain is not. But it shall not go ill with you. You are beautiful and I-Gos loves beautiful women. I might not have you elsewhere in Manator, but here there is none to deny old I-Gos. Few come to the pits of the dead—only those who bring the dead and they hasten away as fast as they can. No one will know that I-Gos has a beautiful woman locked with his dead. I shall ask you no questions and then I will not have to give you up, for I will not know to whom you belong, eh? And when you die I shall mount you beautifully and place you in the chamber with my other women. Will not that be fine, eh?" He had approached until he stood close beside the horrified girl. "Come!" he cried, seizing her by the wrist. "Come to I-Gos!"

CHAPTER XVI

ANOTHER CHANGE OF NAME

TURAN DASHED HIMSELF against the door of his prison in a vain effort to break through the solid skeel to the side of Tara whom he knew to be in grave danger, but the heavy panels held and he succeeded only in bruising his shoulders and his arms. At last he desisted and set about searching his prison for some other means of escape. He found no other opening in the stone walls, but his search revealed a heterogeneous collection of odds and ends of arms and apparel, of harness and ornaments and insignia, and sleeping silks and furs in great quantities. There were swords and spears and several large, two-bladed battle-axes, the heads of which bore a striking resemblance to the propeller of a small flier. Seizing one of these he attacked the door once more with great fury. He expected to hear something from I-Gos at this ruthless destruction, but no sound came to him from beyond the door, which was, he thought, too thick for the human voice to penetrate; but he would have wagered much that I-Gos heard him. Bits of the hard wood splintered at each impact of the heavy axe, but it was slow work and heavy. Presently he was compelled to rest, and so it went for what seemed hours—working almost to the verge of exhaustion and then resting for a few minutes; but ever the hole grew larger though he could see nothing of the interior of the room beyond because of the hanging that I-Gos had drawn across it after he had locked Turan within.

At last, however, the panthan had hewn an opening through which his body could pass, and seizing a long-sword that he had brought close to the door for the purpose he crawled through into the next room. Flinging aside the arras he stood ready, sword in hand, to fight his way to the side of Tara of Helium—but she was not there. In the center of the room lay I-Gos, dead upon the floor; but Tara of Helium was nowhere to be seen.

Turan was nonplussed. It must have been her hand that had struck down the old man, yet she had made no effort to release Turan from his prison. And then he thought of those last words of hers: "I do not want your love! I hate you," and

the truth dawned upon him—she had seized upon this first
opportunity to escape him. With downcast heart Turan
turned away. What should he do? There could be but one
answer. While he lived and she lived he must still leave no
stone unturned to effect her escape and safe return to the
land of her people. But how? How was he even to find his
way from this labyrinth? How was he to find her again? He
walked to the nearest doorway. It chanced to be that which
led into the room containing the mounted dead, awaiting
transporatation to balcony or grim room or whatever place
was to receive them. His eyes travelled to the great, painted
warrior on the thoat and as they ran over the splendid trappings and the serviceable arms a new light came into the
pain-dulled eyes of the panthan. With a quick step he crossed
to the side of the dead warrior and dragged him from his
mount. With equal celerity he stripped him of his harness
and his arms, and tearing off his own, donned the regalia of
the dead man. Then he hastened back to the room in which
he had been trapped, for there he had seen that which he
needed to make his disguise complete. In a cabinet he found
them—pots of paint that the old taxidermist had used to
place the war-paint in its wide bands across the cold faces of
dead warriors.

A few moments later Gahan of Gathol emerged from the
room a warrior of Manator in every detail of harness, equipment, and ornamentation. He had removed from the leather
of the dead man the insignia of his house and rank so that
he might pass, with the least danger of arousing suspicion,
as a common warrior.

To search for Tara of Helium in the vast, dim labyrinth
of the pits of O-Tar seemed to the Gatholian a hopeless quest,
foredoomed to failure. It would be wiser to seek the streets
of Manator where he might hope to learn first if she had
been recaptured and, if not, then he could return to the pits
and pursue the hunt for her. To find egress from the maze
he must perforce travel a considerable distance through the
winding corridors and chambers, since he had no idea as to
the location or direction of any exit. In fact, he could not
have retraced his steps a hundred yards toward the point at
which he and Tara had entered the gloomy caverns, and
so he set out in the hope that he might find by accident either

Tara of Helium or a way to the street level above.

For a time he passed room after room filled with the cunningly preserved dead of Manator, many of which were piled in tiers after the manner that firewood is corded, and as he moved through corridor and chamber he noticed hieroglyphics painted upon the walls above every opening and at each fork or crossing of corridors, until by observation he reached the conclusion that these indicated the designations of passageways, so that one who understood them might travel quickly and surely through the pits; but Turan did not understand them. Even could he have read the language of Manator they might not materially have aided one unfamiliar with the city; but he could not read them at all since, though there is but one spoken language upon Barsoom, there are as many different written languages as there are nations. One thing, however, soon became apparent to him—the hieroglyphic of a corridor remained the same until the corridor ended.

It was not long before Turan realized from the distance that he had traveled that the pits were part of a vast system undermining, possibly, the entire city. At least he was convinced that he had passed beyond the precincts of the palace. The corridors and chambers varied in appearance and architecture from time to time. All were lighted, though usually quite dimly, with radium bulbs. For a long time he saw no signs of life other than an occasional ulsio, then quite suddenly he came face to face with a warrior at one of the numerous crossings. The fellow looked at him, nodded, and passed on. Turan breathed a sigh of relief as he realized that his disguise was effective, but he was caught in the middle of it by a hail from the warrior who had stopped and turned toward him. The panthan was glad that a sword hung at his side, and glad too that they were buried in the dim recesses of the pits and that there would be but a single antagonist, for time was precious.

"Have you any word of the other?" called the warrior to him.

"No," replied Turan, who had not the faintest idea to whom or what the fellow referred.

"He cannot escape," continued the warrior. "The woman ran directly into our arms, but she swore that she knew not where her companion might be found."

"They took her back to O-Tar?" asked Turan, for now he knew whom the other meant, and he would know more.

"They took her back to The Towers of Jetan," replied the warrior. "Tomorrow the games commence and doubtless she will be played for, though I doubt if any wants her, beautiful as she is. She fears not even O-Tar. By Cluros! but she would make a hard slave to subdue—a regular she-banth she is. Not for me," and he continued on his way shaking his head.

Turan hurried on searching for an avenue that led to the level of the streets above when suddenly he came to the open doorway to a small chamber in which sat a man who was chained to the wall. Turan voiced a low exclamation of surprise and pleasure as he recognized that the man was A-Kor, and that he had stumbled by accident upon the very cell in which he had been imprisoned. A-Kor looked at him questioningly. It was evident that he did not recognize his fellow prisoner. Turan crossed to the table and leaning close to the other whispered to him.

"I am Turan the panthan," he said, "who was chained beside you."

A-Kor looked at him closely. "Your own mother would never know you!" he said; "but tell me, what has transpired since they took you away?"

Turan recounted his experiences in the throne room of O-Tar and in the pits beneath, "and now," he continued, "I must find these Towers of Jetan and see what may be done toward liberating the Princess of Helium."

A-Kor shook his head. "Long was I dwar of the Towers," he said, "and I can say to you, stranger, that you might as well attempt to reduce Manator, single handed, as to rescue a prisoner from The Towers of Jetan."

"But I must," replied Turan.

"Are you better than a good swordsman?" asked A-Kor presently.

"I am accounted so," replied Turan.

"Then there is a way—sst!" he was suddenly silent and pointing toward the base of the wall at the end of the room.

Turan looked in the direction the other's forefinger indicated, to see projecting from the mouth of an ulsio's burrow two large chelae and a pair of protruding eyes.

"Ghek!" he cried and immediately the hideous kaldane

crawled out upon the floor and approached the table. A-Kor drew back with a half-stifled ejaculation of repulsion. "Do not fear," Turan reassured him. "It is my friend—he whom I told you held O-Tar while Tara and I escaped."

Ghek climbed to the table top and squatted between the two warriors. "You are safe in assuming," he said addressing A-Kor, "that Turan the panthan has no master in all Manator where the art of sword-play is concerned. I overheard your conversation—go on."

"You are his friend," continued A-Kor, "and so I may explain safely in your presence the only plan I know whereby he may hope to rescue the Princess of Helium. She is to be the stake of one of the games and it is O-Tar's desire that she be won by slaves and common warriors, since she repulsed him. Thus would he punish her. Not a single man, but all who survive upon the winning side are to possess her. With money, however, one may buy off the others before the game. That you could do, and if your side won and you survived she would become your slave."

"But how may a stranger and a hunted fugitive accomplish this?" asked Turan.

"No one will recognize you. You will go tomorrow to the keeper of the Towers and enlist in that game for which the girl is to be the stake, telling the keeper that you are from Manataj, the farthest city of Manator. If he questions you, you may say that you saw her when she was brought into the city after her capture. If you win her, you will find thoats stabled at my palace and you will carry from me a token that will place all that is mine at your disposal."

"But how can I buy off the others in the game without money?" asked Turan. "I have none—not even of my own country."

A-Kor opened his pocket-pouch and drew forth a packet of Manatorian money.

"Here is sufficient to buy them off twice over," he said, handing a portion of it to Turan.

"But why do you do this for a stranger?" asked the panthan.

"My mother was a captive princess here," replied A-Kor. "I but do for the Princess of Helium what my mother would have me do."

"Under the circumstances, then, Manatorian," replied Turan, "I cannot but accept your generosity on behalf of Tara of Helium and live in hope that some day I may do for you something in return."

"Now you must be gone," advised A-Kor. "At any minute a guard may come and discover you here. Go directly to the Avenue of Gates, which circles the city just within the outer wall. There you will find many places devoted to the lodging of strangers. You will know them by the thoat's head carved above the doors. Say that you are here from Manataj to witness the games. Take the name of U-Kal—it will arouse no suspicion, nor will you if you can avoid conversation. Early in the morning seek the keeper of The Towers of Jetan. May the strength and fortune of all your ancestors be with you!"

Bidding good-bye to Ghek and A-Kor, the panthan, following directions given him by A-Kor, set out to find his way to the Avenue of Gates, nor had he any great difficulty. On the way he met several warriors, but beyond a nod they gave him no heed. With ease he found a lodging place where there were many strangers from other cities of Manator. As he had had no sleep since the previous night he threw himself among the silks and furs of his couch to gain the rest which he must have, was he to give the best possible account of himself in the service of Tara of Helium the following day.

It was already morning when he awoke, and rising he paid for his lodgings, sought a place to eat, and a short time later was on his way toward The Towers of Jetan, which he had no difficulty in finding owing to the great crowds that were winding along the avenues toward the games. The new keeper of The Towers who had succeeded E-Med was too busy to scrutinize entries closely, for in addition to the many volunteer players there were scores of slaves and prisoners being forced into the games by their owners or the government. The name of each must be recorded as well as the position he was to play and the game or games in which he was to be entered, and then there were the substitutes for each that was entered in more than a single game—one for each additional game that an individual was entered for, that no succeeding game might be delayed by the death or disablement of a player.

"Your name?" asked a clerk as Turan presented himself.

"U-Kal," replied the panthan.

"Your city?"

"Manataj."

The keeper, who was standing beside the clerk, looked at Turan. "You have come a great way to play at jetan," he said. "It is seldom that the men of Manataj attend other than the decennial games. Tell me of O-Zar! Will he attend next year? Ah, but he was a noble fighter. If you be half the swordsman, U-Kal, the fame of Manataj will increase this day. But tell me, what of O-Zar?"

"He is well," replied Turan, glibly, "and he sent greetings to his friends in Manator."

"Good!" exclaimed the keeper, "and now in what game would you enter?"

"I would play for the Heliumetic princess, Tara," replied Turan.

"But man, she is to be the stake of a game for slaves and criminals," cried the keeper. "You would not volunteer for such a game!"

"But I would," replied Turan. "I saw her when she was brought into the city and even then I vowed to possess her."

"But you will have to share her with the survivors even if your color wins," objected the other.

"They may be brought to reason," insisted Turan.

"And you will chance incurring the wrath of O-Tar, who has no love for this savage barbarian," explained the keeper.

"And I win her O-Tar will be rid of her," said Turan.

The keeper of The Towers of Jetan shook his head. "You are rash," he said. "I would that I might dissuade the friend of my friend O-Zar from such madness."

"Would you favor the friend of O-Zar?" asked Turan.

"Gladly!" exclaimed the other. "What may I do for him?"

"Make me chief of the Black and give me for my pieces all slaves from Gathol, for I understand that these be excellent warriors," replied the panthan.

"It is a strange request," said the keeper, "but for my friend O-Zar I would do even more, though of course—" he hesitated—"it is customary for one who would be chief to make some slight payment."

"Certainly," Turan hastened to assure him; "I had not forgotten that. I was about to ask you what the customary amount is."

"For the friend of my friend it shall be nominal," replied the keeper, naming a figure that Gahan, accustomed to the high prices of wealthy Gathol, thought ridiculously low.

"Tell me," he said, handing the money to the keeper, "when the game for the Heliumite is to be played."

"It is the second in order of the day's games; and now if you will come with me you may select your pieces."

Turan followed the keeper to a large court which lay between the towers and the jetan field, where hundreds of warriors were assembled. Already chiefs for the games of the day were selecting their pieces and assigning them to positions, though for the principal games these matters had been arranged for weeks before. The keeper led Turan to a part of the courtyard where the majority of the slaves were assembled.

"Take your choice of those not assigned," said the keeper, "and when you have your quota conduct them to the field. Your place will be assigned you by an officer there, and there you will remain with your pieces until the second game is called. I wish you luck, U-Kal, though from what I have heard you will be more lucky to lose than to win the slave from Helium."

After the fellow had departed Turan approached the slaves. "I seek the best swordsmen for the second game," he announced. "Men from Gathol I wish, for I have heard that these be noble fighters."

A slave rose and approached him. "It is all the same in which game we die," he said. "I would fight for you as a panthan in the second game."

Another came. "I am not from Gathol," he said. "I am from Helium, and I would fight for the honor of a princess of Helium."

"Good!" exclaimed Turan. "Art a swordsman of repute in Helium?"

"I was a dwar under the great Warlord, and I have fought at his side in a score of battles from The Golden Cliffs to The Carrion Caves. My name is Val Dor. Who knows Helium, knows my prowess."

The name was well known to Gahan, who had heard the man spoken of on his last visit to Helium, and his mysterious disappearance discussed as well as his renown as a fighter.

"How could I know aught of Helium?" asked Turan; "but

if you be such a fighter as you say no position could suit you better than that of Flier. What say you?"

The man's eyes denoted sudden surprise. He looked keenly at Turan, his eyes running quickly over the other's harness. Then he stepped quite close so that his words might not be overheard.

"Methinks you may know more of Helium than of Manator," he whispered.

"What mean you, fellow?" demanded Turan, seeking to cudgel his brains for the source of this man's knowledge, guess, or inspiration.

"I mean," replied Val Dor, "that you are not of Manator and that if you wish to hide the fact it is well that you speak not to a Manatorian as you did just speak to me of—Fliers! There be no Fliers in Manator and no piece in their game of Jetan bearing that name. Instead they call him who stands next to the Chief or Princess, Odwar. The piece has the same moves and power that the Flier has in the game as played outside Manator. Remember this then and remember, too, that if you have a secret it be safe in the keeping of Val Dor of Helium."

Turan made no reply but turned to the task of selecting the remainder of his pieces. Val Dor, the Heliumite, and Floran, the volunteer from Gathol, were of great assistance to him, since one or the other of them knew most of the slaves from whom his selection was to be made. The pieces all chosen, Turan led them to the place beside the playing field where they were to wait their turn, and here he passed the word around that they were to fight for more than the stake he offered for the princess should they win. This stake they accepted, so that Turan was sure of possessing Tara if his side was victorious, but he knew that these men would fight even more valorously for chivalry than for money, nor was it difficult to enlist the interest even of the Gatholians in the service of the princess. And now he held out the possibility of a still further reward.

"I cannot promise you," he explained, "but I may say I have heard that this day which makes it possible that should we win this game we may even win your freedom!"

They leaped to their feet and crowded around him with many questions.

"It may not be spoken of aloud," he said; "but Floran and Val Dor know and they assure me that you may all be trusted. Listen! What I would tell you places my life in your hands, but you must know that every man will realize that he is fighting today the greatest battle of his life—for the honor and the freedom of Barsoom's most wondrous princess and for his own country and to the woman who awaits him there.

"First, then, is my secret. I am not of Manator. Like yourselves I am a slave, though for the moment disguised as a Manatorian from Manataj. My country and my identity must remain undisclosed for reasons that have no bearing upon our game today. I, then, am one of you. I fight for the same things that you will fight for.

"And now for that which I have but just learned. U-Thor, the great jed of Manatos, quarreled with O-Tar in the palace the day before yesterday and their warriors set upon one another. U-Thor was driven as far as The Gate of Enemies, where he now lies encamped. At any moment the fight may be renewed; but it is thought that U-Thor has sent to Manatos for reinforcements. Now, men of Gathol, here is the thing that interests you. U-Thor has recently taken to wife the Princess Haja of Gathol, who was slave to O-Tar and whose son, A-Kor, was dwar of The Towers of Jetan. Haja's heart is filled with loyalty for Gathol and compassion for her sons who are here enslaved, and this latter sentiment she has to some extent transmitted to U-Thor. Aid me, therefore, in freeing the Princess Tara of Helium and I believe that I can aid you and her and myself to escape the city. Bend close your ears, slaves of O-Tar, that no cruel enemy may hear my words," and Gahan of Gathol whispered in low tones the daring plan he had conceived. "And now," he demanded, when he had finished, "let him who does not dare, speak now." None replied. "Is there none?"

"And it would not betray you should I cast my sword at thy feet, it had been done ere this," said one in low tones pregnant with suppressed feeling.

"And I!" "And I!" "And I!" chorused the others in vibrant whispers.

CHAPTER XVII

A PLAY TO THE DEATH

CLEAR AND SWEET a trumpet spoke across The Fields of Jetan. From The High Tower its cool voice floated across the city of Manator and above the babel of human discords rising from the crowded mass that filled the seats of the stadium below. It called the players for the first game, and simultaneously there fluttered to the peaks of a thousand staffs on tower and battlement and the great wall of the stadium the rich, gay pennons of the fighting chiefs of Manator. Thus was marked the opening of The Jeddak's Games, the most important of the year and second only to the Grand Decennial Games.

Gahan of Gathol watched every play with eagle eye. The match was an unimportant one, being but to settle some petty dispute between two chiefs, and was played with professional jetan players for points only. No one was killed and there was but little blood spilled. It lasted about an hour and was terminated by the chief of the losing side deliberately permitting himself to be out-pointed, that the game might be called a draw.

Again the trumpet sounded, this time announcing the second and last game of the afternoon. While this was not considered an important match, those being reserved for the fourth and fifth days of the games, it promised to afford sufficient excitement since it was a game to the death. The vital difference between the game played with living men and that in which inanimate pieces are used, lies in the fact that while in the latter the mere placing of a piece upon a square occupied by an opponent piece terminates the move, in the former the two pieces thus brought together engage in a duel for possession of the square. Therefore there enters into the former game not only the strategy of jetan but the personal prowess and bravery of each individual piece, so that a knowledge not only of one's own men but of each player upon the opposing side is of vast value to a chief.

In this respect was Gahan handicapped, though the loyalty of his players did much to offset his ignorance of them, since they aided him in arranging the board to the best advantage and told him honestly the faults and virtues of each. One fought best in a losing game; another was too slow; another too impetuous; this one had fire and a heart of steel, but lacked endurance. Of the opponents, though, they knew little or nothing, and now as the two sides took their places upon the black and orange squares of the great jetan board Gahan obtained, for the first time, a close view of those who opposed him. The Orange Chief had not yet entered the field, but his men were all in place. Val Dor turned to Gahan. "They are all criminals from the pits of Manator," he said. "There is no slave among them. We shall not have to fight against a single fellow-countryman and every life we take will be the life of an enemy."

"It is well," replied Gahan; "but where is their Chief, and where the two Princesses?"

"They are coming now, see?" and he pointed across the field to where two women could be seen approaching under guard.

As they came nearer Gahan saw that one was indeed Tara of Helium, but the other he did not recognize, and then they were brought to the center of the field midway between the two sides and there waited until the Orange Chief arrived.

Floran voiced an exclamation of surprise when he recognized him. "By my first ancestor if it is not one of their great chiefs," he said, "and we were told that slaves and criminals were to play for the stake of this game."

His words were interrupted by the keeper of The Towers whose duty it was not only to announce the games and the stakes, but to act as referee as well.

"Of this, the second game of the first day of the Jeddak's Games in the four hundred and thirty-third year of O-Tar, Jeddak of Manator, the Princesses of each side shall be the sole stakes and to the survivors of the winning side shall belong both the Princesses, to do with as they shall see fit. The Orange Princess is the slave woman Lan-O of Gathol; the Black Princess is the slave woman Tara, a princess of Helium. The Black Chief is U-Kal of Manataj, a volunteer player; the Orange Chief is the dwar U-Dor of the 8th Utan of the jeddak of Manator, also a volunteer player. The squares shall be contested to the death. Just are the laws of Manator! I have spoken."

The initial move was won by U-Dor, following which the two Chiefs escorted their respective Princesses to the square each was to occupy. It was the first time Gahan had been alone with Tara since she had been brought upon the field. He saw her scrutinizing him closely as he approached to lead her to her place and wondered if she recognized him; but if she did she gave no sign of it. He could not but remember her last words—"I hate you!" and her desertion of him when he had been locked in the room beneath the palace by I-Gos, the taxidermist, and so he did not seek to enlighten her as to his identity. He meant to fight for her—to die for her, if necessary —and if he did not die to go on fighting to the end for her love. Gahan of Gathol was not easily to be discouraged, but he was compelled to admit that his chances of winning the love of Tara of Helium were remote. Already had she repulsed him twice. Once as jed of Gathol and again as Turan the panthan. Before his love, however, came her safety and the former must be relegated to the background until the latter had been achieved.

Passing among the players already at their stations the two took their places upon their respective squares. At Tara's left was the Black Chief, Gahan of Gathol; directly in front of her the Princess' Panthan, Floran of Gathol; and at her right the Princess' Odwar, Val Dor of Helium. And each of these knew the part that he was to play, win or lose, as did each of the other Black players. As Tara took her place Val Dor bowed low. "My sword is at your feet, Tara of Helium," he said.

She turned and looked at him, an expression of surprise and incredulity upon her face. "Val Dor, the dwar!" she exclaimed. "Val Dor of Helium—one of my father's trusted captains! Can it be possible that my eyes speak the truth?"

"It is Val Dor, Princess," the warrior replied, "and here to die for you if need be, as is every wearer of the Black upon this field of jetan today. Know, Princess," he whispered, "that upon this side is no man of Manator, but each and every is an enemy of Manator."

She cast a quick, meaning glance toward Gahan. "But what of him?" she whispered, and then she caught her breath quickly in surprise. "Shade of the first jeddak!" she exclaimed. "I did but just recognize him through his disguise."

"And you trust him?" asked Val Dor. "I know him not; but he spoke fairly, as an honorable warrior, and we have taken him at his word."

"You have made no mistake," replied Tara of Helium. "I would trust him with my life—with my soul; and you, too, may trust him."

Happy indeed would have been Gahan of Gathol could he have heard those words; but Fate, who is usually unkind to the lover in such matters, ordained it otherwise, and then the game was on.

U-Dor moved his Princess' Odwar three squares diagonally to the right, which placed the piece upon the Black Chief's Odwar's seventh. The move was indicative of the game that U-Dor intended playing—a game of blood, rather than of science—and evidenced his contempt for his opponents.

Gahan followed with his Odwar's Panthan one square straight forward, a more scientific move, which opened up an avenue for himself through his line of Panthans, as well as announcing to the players and spectators that he intended having a hand in the fighting himself even before the exigencies of the game forced it upon him. The move elicited a ripple of applause from those sections of seats reserved for the common warriors and their women, showing perhaps that U-Dor was none too popular with these, and, too, it had its effect upon the morale of Gahan's pieces. A Chief may, and often does, play almost an entire game without leaving his own square, where, mounted upon a thoat, he may overlook the entire field and direct each move, nor may he be reproached for lack of courage should he elect thus to play the game since, by the rules, were he to be slain or so badly wounded as to be compelled to withdraw, a game that might otherwise have been won by the science of his play and the prowess of his men would be drawn. To invite personal combat, therefore, denotes confidence in his own swordsmanship, and great courage, two attributes that were calculated to fill the Black players with hope and valor when evinced by their Chief thus early in the game.

U-Dor's next move placed Lan-O's Odwar upon Tara's Odwar's fourth—within striking distance of the Black Princess. Another move and the game would be lost to Gahan unless the Orange Odwar was overthrown, or Tara moved to a position of safety; but to move his Princess now would be to admit his belief in the superiority of the Orange. In the three squares allowed him he could not place himself upon the square occupied by the Odwar of U-Dor's Princess. There was only one player upon the Black side that might dispute the square with the enemy and that was the Chief's Odwar, who stood upon Gahan's left. Gahan turned upon his thoat and looked at the man. He was a splendid looking fellow, re-splendent in the gorgeous trappings of an Odwar, the five brilliant feathers which denoted his position rising defiantly erect from his thick, black hair. In common with every player upon the field and every spectator in the crowded stands he knew what was passing in his Chief's mind. He dared not speak, the ethics of the game forbade it, but what his lips might not voice his eyes expressed in martial fire, and elo-quently: "The honor of the Black and the safety of our Princess are secure with me!"

Gahan hesitated no longer. "Chief's Odwar to Princess' Odwar's fourth!" he commanded. It was the courageous move of a leader who had taken up the gauntlet thrown down by his opponent.

The warrior sprang forward and leaped into the square occupied by U-Dor's piece. It was the first disputed square of the game. The eyes of the players were fastened upon the contestants, the spectators leaned forward in their seats after the first applause that had greeted the move, and silence fell upon the vast assemblage. If the Black went down to defeat, U-Dor could move his victorious piece on to the square occupied by Tara of Helium and the game would be over—over in four moves and lost to Gahan of Gathol. If the Orange lost U-Dor would have sacrificed one of his most important pieces and more than lost what advantage the first move might have given him.

Physically the two men appeared perfectly matched and each was fighting for his life, but from the first it was appar-ent that the Black Odwar was the better swordsman, and Gahan knew that he had another and perhaps a greater ad-vantage over his antagonist. The latter was fighting for his life only, without the spur of chivalry or loyalty. The Black Odwar had these to strengthen his arm, and besides these the knowledge of the thing that Gahan had whispered into the ears of his players before the game, and so he fought for what is more than life to the man of honor.

It was a duel that held those who witnessed it in spellbound silence. The weaving blades gleamed in the brilliant sunlight, ringing to the parries of cut and thrust. The barbaric harness of the duelists lent splendid color to the savage, martial scene. The Orange Odwar, forced upon the defensive, was fighting madly for his life. The Black, with cool and terrible efficiency, was forcing him steadily, step by step, into a corner of the square—a position from which there could be no escape. To abandon the square was to lose it to his opponent and win for himself ignoble and immediate death before the jeering populace. Spurred on by the seeming hopelessness of his plight, the Orange Odwar burst into a sudden fury of offense that forced the Black back a half dozen steps, and then the sword of U-Dor's piece leaped in and drew the first blood, from the shoulder of his merciless opponent. An illy smothered cry of encouragement went up from U-Dor's men; the Orange Odwar, encouraged by his single success, sought to bear down the Black by the rapidity of his attack. There was a moment in which the swords moved with a rapidity that no man's eye might follow, and then the Black Odwar made a lightning parry of a vicious thrust, leaned quickly forward into the opening he had effected, and drove his sword through the heart of the Orange Odwar—to the hilt he drove it through the body of the Orange Odwar.

A shout arose from the stands, for wherever may have been the favor of the spectators, none there was who could say that it had not been a pretty fight, or that the better man had not won. And from the Black players came a sigh of relief as they relaxed from the tension of the past moments.

I shall not weary you with the details of the game—only the high features of it are necessary to your understanding of the outcome. The fourth move after the victory of the Black Odwar found Gahan upon U-Dor's fourth; an Orange Panthan was on the adjoining square diagonally to his right and the only opposing piece that could engage him other than U-Dor himself.

It had been apparent to both players and spectators for the past two moves, that Gahan was moving straight across the field into the enemy's country to seek personal combat with the Orange Chief—that he was staking all upon his belief in the superiority of his own swordsmanship, since if the two Chiefs engage, the outcome decides the game. U-Dor could move out and engage Gahan, or he could move his Princess' Panthan upon the square occupied by Gahan in the hope that the former would defeat the Black Chief and thus draw the game, which is the outcome if any other than a Chief slays the opposing Chief, or he could move away and escape, temporarily, the necessity for personal combat, or at least that is evidently what he had in mind as was obvious to all who saw him scanning the board about him; and his disappointment was apparent when he finally discovered that Gahan had so placed himself that there was no square to which U-Dor could move that it was not within Gahan's power to reach at his own next move.

U-Dor had placed his own Princess four squares east of Gahan when her position had been threatened, and he had hoped to lure the Black Chief after her and away from U-Dor; but in that he had failed. He now discovered that he might play his own Odwar into personal combat with Gahan; but he had already lost one Odwar and could ill spare the other. His position was a delicate one, since he did not wish to engage Gahan personally, while it appeared that there was little likelihood of his being able to escape. There was just one hope and that lay in his Princess' Panthan, so, without more deliberation he ordered the piece onto the square occupied by the Black Chief.

The sympathies of the spectators were all with Gahan now. If he lost, the game would be declared a draw, nor do they think better of drawn games upon Barsoom than do Earth men. If he won, it would doubtless mean a duel between the two Chiefs, a development for which they all were hoping. The game already bade fair to be a short one and it would be an angry crowd should it be decided a draw with only two men slain. There were great, historic games on record where of the forty pieces on the field when the game opened only three survived—the two Princesses and the victorious Chief.

They blamed U-Dor, though in fact he was well within his rights in directing his play as he saw fit, nor was a refusal on his part to engage the Black Chief necessarily an imputation of cowardice. He was a great chief who had conceived a notion to possess the slave Tara. There was no honor that could accrue to him from engaging in combat with slaves and criminals, or an unknown warrior from Manataj, nor was the stake of sufficient import to warrant the risk.

But now the duel between Gahan and the Orange Panthan was on and the decision of the next move was no longer in other hands than theirs. It was the first time that these Manatorians had seen Gahan of Gathol fight, but Tara of Helium knew that he was master of his sword. Could he have seen the proud light in her eyes as he crossed blades with the wearer of the Orange, he might easily have wondered if they were the same eyes that had flashed fire and hatred at him that time he had covered her lips with mad kisses, in the pits of the palace of O-Tar. As she watched him she could not but compare his swordplay with that of the greatest swordsman of two worlds—her father, John Carter, of Virginia, Prince of Helium, Warlord of Barsoom—and she knew that the skill of the Black Chief suffered little by the comparison.

Short and to the point was the duel that decided posession of the Orange Chief's fourth. The spectators had settled themselves for an interesting engagement of at least average duration when they were brought almost standing by a brilliant flash of rapid swordplay that was over ere one could catch his breath. They saw the Black Chief step quickly back, his point upon the ground, while his opponent, his sword slipping from his fingers, clutched his breast, sank to his knees and then lunged forward upon his face.

And then Gahan of Gathol turned his eyes directly upon U-Dor of Manator, three squares away. Three squares is a Chief's move—three squares in any direction or combination of directions, only provided that he does not cross the same square twice in a given move. The people saw and guessed Gahan's intention. They rose and roared forth their approval as he moved deliberately across the intervening squares toward the Orange Chief.

O-Tar, in the royal enclosure, sat frowning upon the scene. O-Tar was angry. He was angry with U-Dor for having entered this game for possession of a slave, for whom it had been his wish only slaves and criminals should strive. He was angry with the warrior from Manataj for having so far out-

generaled and out-fought the men from Manator. He was
angry with the populace because of their open hostility toward one who had basked in the sunshine of his favor for
long years. O-Tar the jeddak had not enjoyed the afternoon.
Those who surrounded him were equally glum—they, too,
scowled upon the field, the players, and the people. Among
them was a bent and wrinkled old man who gazed through
weak and watery eyes upon the field and the players.

As Gahan entered his square, U-Dor leaped toward him
with drawn sword with such fury as might have overborne
a less skilled and powerful swordsman. For a minute the
fighting was fast and furious and by comparison reducing to
insignificance all that had gone before. Here indeed were two
magnificent swordsmen, and here was to be a battle that bade
fair to make up for whatever the people felt they had been
defrauded of by the shortness of the game. Nor had it continued long before many there were who would have proph-
esied that they were witnessing a duel that was to become
historic in the annals of jetan at Manator. Every trick, every
subterfuge, known to the art of fence these men employed.
Time and again each scored a point and brought blood to his
opponent's copper hide until both were red with gore; but
neither seemed able to administer the *coup de grâce*.

From her position upon the opposite side of the field Tara
of Helium watched the long-drawn battle. Always it seemed
to her that the Black Chief fought upon the defensive, or
when he assumed to push his opponent, he neglected a
thousand openings that her practiced eye beheld. Never did
he seem in real danger, nor never did he appear to exert
himself to quite the pitch needful for victory. The duel already had been long contested and the day was drawing to a
close. Presently the sudden transition from daylight to darkness which, owing to the tenuity of the air upon Barsoom, oc-
curs almost without the warning twilight of Earth, would
occur. Would the fight never end? Would the game be called
a draw after all? What ailed the Black Chief?

Tara wished that she might answer at least the last of
these questions for she was sure that Turan the panthan, as
she knew him, while fighting brilliantly, was not giving of
himself all that he might. She could not believe that fear was
restraining his hand, but that there was something beside

inability to push U-Dor more fiercely she was confident. What it was, however, she could not guess.

Once she saw Gahan glance quickly up toward the sinking sun. In thirty minutes it would be dark. And then she saw and all those others saw a strange transition steal over the swordplay of the Black Chief. It was as though he had been playing with the great dwar, U-Dor, all these hours, and now he still played with him but there was a difference. He played with him terribly as a carnivore plays with its victim in the instant before the kill. The Orange Chief was helpless now in the hands of a swordsman so superior that there could be no comparison, and the people sat in open-mouthed wonder and awe as Gahan of Gathol cut his foe to ribbons and then struck him down with a blow that cleft him to the chin.

In twenty minutes the sun would set! But what of that?

CHAPTER XVIII

A TASK FOR LOYALTY

LONG AND LOUD was the applause that rose above the Field of Jetan at Manator, as The Keeper of the Towers summoned the two Princesses and the victorious Chief to the center of the field and presented to the latter the fruits of his prowess, and then, as custom demanded, the victorious players, headed by Gahan and the two Princesses, formed in procession behind The Keeper of the Towers and were conducted to the place of victory before the royal enclosure that they might receive the commendation of the jeddak. Those who were mounted gave up their thoats to slaves as all must be on foot for this ceremony. Directly beneath the royal enclosure are the gates to one of the tunnels that, passing beneath the seats, give ingress or egress to or from the Field. Before this gate the party halted while O-Tar looked down upon them from above. Val Dor and Floran, passing quietly ahead of the others, went directly to the gates, where they were hidden from those who occupied the enclosure with O-

Tar. The Keeper of the Towers may have noticed them, but so occupied was he with the formality of presenting the victorious Chief to the jeddak that he paid no attention to them.

"I bring you, O-Tar, Jeddak of Manator, U-Kal of Manataj," he cried in a loud voice that might be heard by as many as possible, "victor over the Orange in the second of the Jeddak's Games of the four hundred and thirty-third year of O-Tar, and the slave woman Tara and the slave woman Lan-O that you may bestow these, the stakes, upon U-Kal."

As he spoke, a little, wrinkled, old man peered over the rail of the enclosure down upon the three who stood directly behind The Keeper, and strained his weak and watery eyes in an effort to satisfy the curiosity of old age in a matter of no particular import, for what were two slaves and a common warrior from Manataj to any who sat with O-Tar the jeddak?

"U-Kal of Manataj," said O-Tar, "you have deserved the stakes. Seldom have we looked upon more noble swordplay. And you tire of Manataj there be always here in the city of Manator a place for you in The Jeddak's Guard."

While the jeddak was speaking the little, old man, failing clearly to discern the features of the Black Chief, reached into his pocket-pouch and drew forth a pair of thick-lensed spectacles, which he placed upon his nose. For a moment he scrutinized Gahan closely, then he leaped to his feet and addressing O-Tar pointed a shaking finger at Gahan. As he rose Tara of Helium clutched the Black Chief's arm.

"Turan!" she whispered. "It is I-Gos, whom I thought to have slain in the pits of O-Tar. It is I-Gos and he recognizes you and will——"

But what I-Gos would do was already transpiring. In his falsetto voice he fairly screamed: "It is the slave Turan who stole the woman Tara from your throne room, O-Tar. He desecrated the dead chief I-Mal and wears his harness now!"

Instantly all was pandemonium. Warriors drew their swords and leaped to their feet. Gahan's victorious players rushed forward in a body, sweeping The Keeper of the Towers from his feet. Val Dor and Floran threw open the gates beneath the royal enclosure, opening the tunnel that led to the avenue in the city beyond the Towers. Gahan, surrounded by his men, drew Tara and Lan-O into the passageway, and at a rapid pace the party sought to reach the

opposite end of the tunnel before their escape could be cut
off. They were successful and when they emerged into the
city the sun had set and darkness had come, relieved only by
an antiquated and ineffective lighting system, which cast but
a pale glow over the shadowy streets.

Now it was that Tara of Helium guessed why the Black
Chief had drawn out his duel with U-Dor and realized that
he might have slain his man at almost any moment he had
elected. The whole plan that Gahan had whispered to his
players before the game was thoroughly understood. They
were to make their way to The Gate of Enemies and there
offer their services to U-Thor, the great Jed of Manatos. The
fact that most of them were Gatholians and that Gahan could
lead rescuers to the pit where A-Kor, the son of U-Thor's
wife, was confined, convinced the Jed of Gathol that they
would meet with no rebuff at the hands of U-Thor. But
even should he refuse them, still were they bound together
to go on toward freedom, if necessary cutting their way
through the forces of U-Thor at The Gate of Enemies—
twenty men against a small army; but of such stuff are the
warriors of Barsoom.

They had covered a considerable distance along the almost deserted avenue before signs of pursuit developed and
then there came upon them suddenly from behind a dozen
warriors mounted on thoats—a detachment, evidently, from
The Jeddak's Guard. Instantly the avenue was a pandemonium of clashing blades, cursing warriors, and squealing
thoats. In the first onslaught life blood was spilled upon both
sides. Two of Gahan's men went down, and upon the enemies'
side three riderless thoats attested at least a portion of their
casualties.

Gahan was engaged with a fellow who appeared to have
been selected to account for him only, since he rode straight
for him and sought to cut him down without giving the
slightest heed to several who slashed at him as he passed
them. The Gatholian, practiced in the art of combating a
mounted warrior from the ground, sought to reach the left
side of the fellow's thoat a little to the rider's rear, the only
position in which he would have any advantage over his
antagonist, or rather the position that would most greatly
reduce the advantage of the mounted man, and, similarly,

the Manatorian strove to thwart his design. And so the guardsman wheeled and turned his vicious, angry mount while Gahan leaped in and out in an effort to reach the coveted vantage point, but always seeking some other opening in his foe's defense.

And while they jockeyed for position a rider swept swiftly past them. As he passed behind Gahan the latter heard a cry of alarm.

"Turan, they have me!" came to his ears in the voice of Tara of Helium.

A quick glance across his shoulder showed him the galloping thoatman in the act of dragging Tara to the withers of the beast, and then, with the fury of a demon, Gahan of Gathol leaped for his own man, dragged him from his mount and as he fell smote his head from his shoulders with a single cut of his keen sword. Scarce had the body touched the pavement when the Gatholian was upon the back of the dead warrior's mount, and galloping swiftly down the avenue after the diminishing figures of Tara and her abductor, the sounds of the fight waning in the distance as he pursued his quarry along the avenue that passes the palace of O-Tar and leads to The Gate of Enemies.

Gahan's mount, carrying but a single rider, gained upon that of the Manatorian, so that as they neared the palace Gahan was scarce a hundred yards behind, and now, to his consternation, he saw the fellow turn into the great entrance-way. For a moment only was he halted by the guards and then he disappeared within. Gahan was almost upon him then, but evidently he had warned the guards, for they leaped out to intercept the Gatholian. But no! the fellow could not have known that he was pursued, since he had not seen Gahan seize a mount, nor would he have thought that pursuit would come so soon. If he had passed then, so could Gahan pass, for did he not wear the trappings of a Manatorian? The Gatholian thought quickly, and stopping his thoat called to the guardsmen to let him pass, "In the name of O-Tar!" They hesitated a moment.

"Aside!" cried Gahan. "Must the jeddak's messenger parley for the right to deliver his message?"

"To whom would you deliver it?" asked the padwar of the guard.

"Saw you not him who just entered?" cried Gahan, and without waiting for a reply urged his thoat straight past them into the palace, and while they were deliberating what was best to be done, it was too late to do anything—which is not unusual.

Along the marble corridors Gahan guided his thoat, and because he had gone that way before, rather than because he knew which way Tara had been taken, he followed the runways and passed through the chambers that led to the throne room of O-Tar. On the second level he met a slave.

"Which way went he who carried the woman before him?" he asked.

The slave pointed toward a nearby runway that led to the third level and Gahan dashed rapidly on in pursuit. At the same moment a thoatman, riding at a furious pace, approached the palace and halted his mount at the gate.

"Saw you aught of a warrior pursuing one who carried a woman before him on his thoat?" he shouted to the guard.

"He but just passed in," replied the padwar, "saying that he was O-Tar's messenger."

"He lied," cried the newcomer. "He was Turan, the slave, who stole the woman from the throne room two days since. Arouse the palace! He must be seized, and alive if possible. It is O-Tar's command."

Instantly warriors were dispatched to search for the Gatholian and warn the inmates of the palace to do likewise. Owing to the games there were comparatively few retainers in the great building, but those whom they found were immediately enlisted in the search, so that presently at least fifty warriors were seeking through the countless chambers and corridors of the palace of O-Tar.

As Gahan's thoat bore him to the third level the man glimpsed the hind quarters of another thoat disappearing at the turn of a corridor far ahead. Urging his own animal forward he raced swiftly in pursuit and making the turn discovered only an empty corridor ahead. Along this he hurried to discover near its farther end a runway to the fourth level, which he followed upward. Here he saw that he had gained upon his quarry who was just turning through a doorway fifty yards ahead. As Gahan reached the opening he saw that the warrior had dismounted and was dragging Tara

toward a small door on the opposite side of the chamber.
At the same instant the clank of harness to his rear caused
him to cast a glance behind where, along the corridor he had
just traversed, he saw three warriors approaching on foot at
a run. Leaping from his thoat Gahan sprang into the chamber where Tara was struggling to free herself from the grasp
of her captor, slammed the door behind him, shot the great
bolt into its seat, and drawing his sword crossed the room
at a run to engage the Manatorian. The fellow, thus menaced,
called aloud to Gahan to halt, at the same time thrusting
Tara at arm's length and threatening her heart with the
point of his short-sword. "Stay!!" he cried, "or the woman
dies, for such is the command of O-Tar, rather than that
she again fall into your hands."

Gahan stopped. But a few feet separated him from Tara
and her captor, yet he was helpless to aid her. Slowly the warrior backed toward the open doorway behind him, dragging
Tara with him. The girl struggled and fought, but the warrior was a powerful man and having seized her by the harness
from behind was able to hold her in a position of helplessness.

"Save me, Turan!" she cried. "Let them not drag me to a
fate worse than death. Better that I die now while my eyes
behold a brave friend than later, fighting alone among enemies in defense of my honor."

He took a step nearer. The warrior made a threatening
gesture with his sword close to the soft, smooth skin of
the princess, and Gahan halted.

"I cannot, Tara of Helium," he cried. "Think not ill of me
that I am weak—that I cannot see you die. Too great is my
love for you, daughter of Helium."

The Manatorian warrior, a derisive grin upon his lips,
backed steadily away. He had almost reached the doorway
when Gahan saw another warrior in the chamber toward
which Tara was being borne—a fellow who moved silently,
almost stealthily, across the marble floor as he approached
Tara's captor from behind. In his right hand he grasped a
long-sword.

"Two to one," thought Gahan, and a grim smile touched
his lips, for he had no doubt that once they had Tara safely in
the adjoining chamber the two would set upon him. If he
could not save her, he could at least die for her.

And then, suddenly, Gahan's eyes fastened with amazement upon the figure of the warrior behind the grinning fellow who held Tara and was forcing her to the doorway. He saw the newcomer step almost within arm's reach of the other. He saw him stop, an expression of malevolent hatred upon his features. He saw the great sword swing through the arc of a great circle, gathering swift and terrific momentum from its own weight backed by the brawn of the steel thews that guided it; he saw it pass through the feathered skull of the Manatorian, splitting his sardonic grin in twain, and open him to the middle of his breast bone.

As the dead hand relaxed its grasp upon Tara's wrist the girl leaped forward, without a backward glance, to Gahan's side. His left arm encircled her, nor did she draw away, as with ready sword the Gatholian awaited Fate's next decree. Before them Tara's deliverer was wiping the blood from his sword upon the hair of his victim. He was evidently a Manatorian, his trappings those of the Jeddak's Guard, and so his act was inexplicable to Gahan and to Tara. Presently he sheathed his sword and approached them.

"When a man chooses to hide his identity behind an assumed name," he said, looking straight into Gahan's eyes, "whatever friend pierces the deception were no friend if he divulged the other's secret."

He paused as though awaiting a reply.

"Your integrity has perceived and your lips voiced an unalterable truth," replied Gahan, whose mind was filled with wonder if the implication could by any possibility be true—that this Manatorian had guessed his identity.

"We are thus agreed," continued the other, "and I may tell you that though I am here known as A-Sor, my real name is Tasor." He paused and watched Gahan's face intently for any sign of the effect of this knowledge and was rewarded with a quick, though guarded expression of recognition.

Tasor! Friend of his youth. The son of that great Gatholian noble who had given his life so gloriously, however futilely, in an attempt to defend Gahan's sire from the daggers of the assassins. Tasor an under-padwar in the guard of O-Tar, Jeddak of Manator! It was inconceivable—and yet it was he; there could be no doubt of it.

"Tasor," Gahan repeated aloud. "But it is no Manatorian

name." The statement was half interrogatory, for Gahan's curiosity was aroused. He would know how his friend and loyal subject had become a Manatorian. Long years had passed since Tasor had disappeared as mysteriously as the Princess Haja and many other of Gahan's subjects. The Jed of Gathol had long supposed him dead.

"No," replied Tasor, "nor is it a Manatorian name. Come, while I search for a hiding place for you in some forgotten chamber in one of the untenanted portions of the palace, and as we go I will tell you briefly how Tasor the Gatholian became A-Sor the Manatorian.

"It befell that as I rode with a dozen of my warriors along the western border of Gathol searching for zitidars that had strayed from my herds, we were set upon and surrounded by a great company of Manatorians. They overpowered us, though not before half our number was slain and the balance helpless from wounds. And so I was brought a prisoner to Manataj, a distant city of Manator, and there sold into slavery. A woman bought me—a princess of Manataj whose wealth and position were unequaled in the city of her birth. She loved me and when her husband discovered her infatuation she beseeched me to slay him, and when I refused she hired another to do it. Then she married me; but none would have aught to do with her in Manataj, for they suspected her guilty knowledge of her husband's murder. And so we set out from Manataj for Manatos accompanied by a great caravan bearing all her worldly goods and jewels and precious metals, and on the way she caused the rumor to be spread that she and I had died. Then we came to Manator instead, she taking a new name and I the name A-Sor, that we might not be traced through our names. With her great wealth she bought me a post in The Jeddak's Guard and none knows that I am not a Manatorian, for she is dead. She was beautiful, but she was a devil."

"And you never sought to return to your native city?" asked Gahan.

"Never has the hope been absent from my heart, or my mind empty of a plan," replied Tasor. "I dream of it by day and by night, but always must I return to the same conclusion—that there can be but a single means for escape. I must wait until Fortune favors me with a place in a raiding party to Gathol. Then, once within the boundaries of my own country, they shall see me no more."

"Perhaps your opportunity lies already within your grasp," said Gahan, "has not your fealty to your own Jed been undermined by years of association with the men of Manator." The statement was half challenge.

"And my Jed stood before me now," cried Tasor, "and my avowal could be made without violating his confidence, I should cast my sword at his feet and beg the high privilege of dying for him as my sire died for his sire."

There could be no doubt of his sincerity nor any that he was cognizant of Gahan's identity. The Jed of Gathol smiled. "And if your Jed were here there is little doubt but that he would command you to devote your talents and your prowess to the rescue of the Princess Tara of Helium," he said, meaningly. "And he possessed the knowledge I have gained during my captivity he would say to you, 'Go, Tasor, to the pit where A-Kor, son of Haja of Gathol, is confined and set him free and with him arouse the slaves from Gathol and march to The Gate of Enemies and offer your services to U-Thor of Manataj, who is wed to Haja of Gathol, and ask of him in return that he attack the palace of O-Tar and rescue Tara of Helium and when that thing is accomplished that he free the slaves of Gathol and furnish them with the arms and the means to return to their own country.' That, Tasor of Gathol, is what Gahan your Jed would demand of you."

"And that, Turan the slave, is what I shall bend my every effort to accomplish after I have found a safe refuge for Tara of Helium and her panthan," replied Tasor.

Gahan's glance carried to Tasor an intimation of his Jed's gratification and filled him with a chivalrous determination to do the thing required of him, or die, for he considered that he had received from the lips of his beloved ruler a commission that placed upon his shoulders a responsibility that encompassed not alone the life of Gahan and Tara but the welfare, perhaps the whole future, of Gathol. And so he hastened them onward through the musty corridors of the old palace where the dust of ages lay undisturbed upon the marble tiles. Now and again he tried a door until he found one that was unlocked. Opening it he ushered them into a chamber, heavy with dust. Crumbling silks and furs adorned the walls, with ancient weapons, and great paintings whose colors were toned by age to wondrous softness.

"This be as good as any place," he said. "No one comes here. Never have I been here before, so I know no more of the other chambers than you; but this one, at least, can I find again when I bring you food and drink. O-Mai the Cruel occupied this portion of the palace during his reign, five thousand years before O-Tar. In one of these apartments he was found dead, his face contorted in an expression of fear so horrible that it drove to madness those who looked upon it; yet there was no mark of violence upon him. Since then the quarters of O-Mai have been shunned for the legends have it that the ghosts of Corphals pursue the spirit of the wicked Jeddak nightly through these chambers, shrieking and moaning as they go. But," he added, as though to reassure himself as well as his companions, "such things may not be countenanced by the culture of Gathol or Helium."

Gahan laughed. "And if all who looked upon him were driven mad, who then was there to perform the last rites or prepare the body of the Jeddak for them?"

"There was none," replied Tasor. "Where they found him they left him and there to this very day his mouldering bones lie hid in some forgotten chamber of this forbidden suite."

Tasor left them then assuring them that he would seek the first opportunity to speak with A-Kor, and upon the following day he would bring them food and drink.[1]

After Tasor had gone Tara turned to Gahan and approaching laid a hand upon his arm. "So swiftly have events transpired since I recognized you beneath your disguise," she said, "that I have had no opportunity to assure you of my gratitude and the high esteem that your valor has won for you in my consideration. Let me now acknowledge my indebtedness; and if promises be not vain from one whose life and liberty are in grave jeopardy, accept my assurance of the great reward that awaits you at the hand of my father in

---

[1] Those who have read John Carter's description of the Green Martians in *A Princess of Mars* will recall that these strange people could exist for considerable periods of time without food or water, and to a lesser degree is the same true of all Martians.

Helium."

"I desire no reward," he replied, "other than the happiness of knowing that the woman I love is happy."

For an instant the eyes of Tara of Helium blazed as she
drew herself haughtily to her full height, and then they
softened and her attitude relaxed as she shook her head
sadly.

"I have it not in my heart to reprimand you, Turan," she
said, "however great your fault, for you have been an honorable and a loyal friend to Tara of Helium; but you must not
say what my ears must not hear."

"You mean," he asked, "that the ears of a Princess must
not listen to words of love from a panthan?"

"It is not that, Turan," she replied; "but rather that I may
not in honor listen to words of love from another than him
to whom I am betrothed—a fellow countryman, Djor Kantos."

"You mean, Tara of Helium," he cried, "that were it not
for that you would——"

"Stop!" she commanded. "You have no right to assume
aught else than my lips testify."

"The eyes are ofttimes more eloquent than the lips, Tara,"
he replied; "and in yours I have read that which is neither
hatred nor contempt for Turan the panthan, and my heart
tells me that your lips bore false witness when they cried in
anger: 'I hate you!' "

"I do not hate you, Turan, nor yet may I love you," said
the girl, simply.

"When I broke my way out from the chamber of I-Gos I
was indeed upon the verge of believing that you did hate
me," he said, "for only hatred, it seemed to me, could account
for the fact that you had gone without making an effort to
liberate me; but presently both my heart and my judgment
told me that Tara of Helium could not have deserted a
companion in distress, and though I still am in ignorance of
the facts I know that it was beyond your power to aid me."

"It was indeed," said the girl. "Scarce had I-Gos fallen at
the bite of my dagger than I heard the approach of warriors.
I ran then to hide until they had passed, thinking to return
and liberate you; but in seeking to elude the party I had
heard I ran full into the arms of another. They questioned
me as to your whereabouts, and I told them that you had

gone ahead and that I was following you and thus I led them
from you."

"I knew," was Gahan's only comment, but his heart was
glad with elation, as a lover's must be who has heard from
the lips of his divinity an avowal of interest and loyalty,
however little tinged by a suggestion of warmer regard it may
be. To be abused, even, by the mistress of one's heart is better
than to be ignored.

As the two conversed in the ill-lit chamber, the dim bulbs
of which were encrusted with the accumulated dust of centuries, a bent and withered figure traversed slowly the gloomy
corridors without, his weak and watery eyes peering through
thick lenses at the signs of passage written upon the dusty
floor.

CHAPTER XIX

THE MENACE OF THE DEAD

THE NIGHT WAS STILL young when there came one to
the entrance of the banquet hall where O-Tar of Manator
dined with his chiefs, and brushing past the guards entered
the great room with the insolence of a privileged character,
as in truth he was. As he approached the head of the long
board O-Tar took notice of him.

"Well, hoary one!" he cried. "What brings you out of your
beloved and stinking burrow again this day? We thought
that the sight of the multitude of living men at the games
would drive you back to your corpses as quickly as you could
go."

The cackling laugh of I-Gos acknowledged the royal sally.
"Ey, ey, O-Tar," squeaked the ancient one, "I-Gos goes out
not upon pleasure bound; but when one does ruthlessly dese-
crate the dead of I-Gos, vengeance must be had!"

"You refer to the act of the slave Turan?" demanded O-Tar.

"Turan, yes, and the slave Tara, who slipped beneath my
hide a murderous blade. Another fraction of an inch, O-Tar,
and I-Gos' ancient and wrinkled covering were even now in
some apprentice tanner's hands, ey, ey!"

"But they have again eluded us," cried O-Tar. "Even in the palace of the great jeddak twice have they escaped the stupid knaves I call The Jeddak's Guard." O-Tar had risen and was angrily emphasizing his words with heavy blows upon the table, dealt with a golden goblet.

"Ey, O-Tar, they elude thy guard but not the wise old calot, I-Gos."

"What mean you? Speak!" commanded O-Tar.

"I know where they are hid," said the ancient taxidermist. "In the dust of unused corridors their feet have betrayed them."

"You followed them? You have seen them?" demanded the jeddak.

"I followed them and I heard them speaking beyond a closed door," replied I-Gos; "but I did not see them."

"Where is that door?" cried O-Tar. "We will send at once and fetch them," he looked about the table as though to decide to whom he would entrust this duty. A dozen warrior chiefs arose and laid their hands upon their swords.

"To the chambers of O-Mai the Cruel I traced them," squeaked I-Gos. "There you will find them where the moaning Corphals pursue the shrieking ghost of O-Mai; ey!" and he turned his eyes from O-Tar toward the warriors who had arisen, only to discover that, to a man, they were hurriedly resuming their seats.

The cackling laughter of I-Gos broke derisively the hush that had fallen on the room. The warriors looked sheepishly at the food upon their plates of gold. O-Tar snapped his fingers impatiently.

"Be there only cravens among the chiefs of Manator?" he cried. "Repeatedly have these presumptuous slaves flouted the majesty of your jeddak. Must I command one to go and fetch them?"

Slowly a chief arose and two others followed his example, though with ill concealed reluctance. "All, then, are not cowards," commented O-Tar. "The duty is distasteful. Therefore all three of you shall go, taking as many warriors as you wish."

"But do not ask for volunteers," interrupted I-Gos, "or you will go alone."

The three chiefs turned and left the banquet hall, walking slowly like doomed men to their fate.

Gahan and Tara remained in the chamber to which Tasor
had led them, the man brushing away the dust from a deep
and comfortable bench where they might rest in comparative
comfort. He had found the ancient sleeping silks and fur too
far gone to be of any service, crumbling to powder at a touch,
thus removing any chance of making a comfortable bed for
the girl, and so the two sat together, talking in low tones, of
the adventures through which they already had passed and
speculating upon the future; planning means of escape and
hoping Tasor would not be long gone. They spoke of many
things—of Hastor, and Helium, and Ptarth, and finally the
conversation reminded Tara of Gathol.

"You have served there?" she asked.

"Yes," replied Turan.

"I met Gahan the Jed of Gathol at my father's palace,"
she said "the very day before the storm snatched me from
Helium—he was a presumptuous fellow, magnificently trapped in platinum and diamonds. Never in my life saw I so gorgeous a harness as his, and you must well know, Turan, that
the splendor of all Barsoom passes through the court at
Helium; but in my mind I could not see so resplendent a
creature drawing that jeweled sword in mortal combat. I fear
me that the Jed of Gathol, though a pretty picture of a man,
is little else."

In the dim light Tara did not perceive the wry expression
upon the half-averted face of her companion.

"You thought little then of the Jed of Gathol?" he asked.

"Then or now," she replied, and with a little laugh; "how
it would pique his vanity to know, if he might, that a poor
panthan had won a higher place in the regard of Tara of
Helium," and she laid her fingers gently upon his knee.

He seized the fingers in his and carried them to his lips.
"O, Tara of Helium," he cried. "Think you that I am a man
of stone?" One arm slipped about her shoulders and drew
the yielding body toward him.

"May my first ancestor forgive me my weakness," she cried,
as her arms stole about his neck and she raised her panting
lips to his. For long they clung there in love's first kiss and
then she pushed him away, gently. "I love you, Turan," she
half sobbed; "I love you so! It is my only poor excuse for having done this wrong to Djor Kantos, whom now I know I

never loved, who knew not the meaning of love. And if you love me as you say, Turan, your love must protect me from greater dishonor, for I am but as clay in your hands."

Again he crushed her to him and then as suddenly released her, and rising, strode rapidly to and fro across the chamber as though he endeavored by violent exercise to master and subdue some evil spirit that had laid hold upon him. Ringing through his brain and heart and soul like some joyous paean were those words that had so altered the world for Gahan of Gathol: "I love you, Turan; I love you so!" And it had come so suddenly. He had thought that she felt for him only gratitude for his loyalty and then, in an instant, her barriers were all down, she was no longer a princess; but instead a— his reflections were interrupted by a sound from beyond the closed door. His sandals of zitidar hide had given forth no sound upon the marble floor he strode, and as his rapid pacing carried him past the entrance to the chamber there came faintly from the distance of the long corridor the sound of metal on metal—the unmistakable herald of the approach of armed men.

For a moment Gahan listened intently, close to the door, until there could be no doubt but that a party of warriors was approaching. From what Tasor had told him he guessed correctly that they would be coming to this portion of the palace but for a single purpose—to search for Tara and him-self—and it behooved him therefore to seek immediate means for eluding them. The chamber in which they were had other doorways beside that at which they had entered, and to one of these he must look for some safer hiding place. Crossing to Tara he acquainted her with his suspicion, lead-ing her to one of the doors which they found unsecured. Beyond it lay a dimly-lighted chamber at the threshold of which they halted in consternation, drawing back quickly into the chamber they had just quitted, for their first glance revealed four warriors seated around a jetan board.

That their entrance had not been noted was attributed by Gahan to the absorption of the two players and their friends in the game. Quietly closing the door the fugitives moved silently to the next, which they found locked. There was now but another door which they had not tried, and this they approached quickly as they knew that the searching party must be close to the chamber. To their chagrin they found this avenue of escape barred.

Now indeed were they in a sorry plight, for should the searchers have information leading them to this room they were lost. Again leading Tara to the door behind which were the jetan players Gahan drew his sword and waited, listening. The sound of the party in the corridor came distinctly to their ears—they must be quite close, and doubtless they were coming in force. Beyond the door were but four warriors who might be readily surprised. There could, then, be but one choice and acting upon it Gahan quietly opened the door again, stepped through into the adjoining chamber, Tara's hand in his, and closed the door behind them. The four at the jetan board evidently failed to hear them. One player had either just made or was contemplating a move, for his fingers grasped a piece that still rested upon the board. The other three were watching his move. For an instant Gahan looked at them, playing jetan there in the dim light of this forgotten and forbidden chamber, and then a slow smile of understanding lighted his face.

"Come!" he said to Tara. "We have nothing to fear from these. For more than five thousand years they have sat thus, a monument to the handiwork of some ancient taxidermist."

As they approached more closely they saw that the lifelike figures were coated with dust, but that otherwise the skin was in as fine a state of preservation as the most recent of I-Gos' groups, and then they heard the door of the chamber they had quitted open and knew that the searchers were close upon them. Across the room they saw the opening of what appeared to be a corridor and which investigation proved to be a short passageway, terminating in a chamber in the center of which was an ornate sleeping dais. This room, like the others, was but poorly lighted, time having dimmed the radiance of its bulbs and coated them with dust. A glance showed that it was hung with heavy goods and contained considerable massive furniture in addition to the sleeping platform, a second glance at which revealed what appeared to be the form of a man lying partially on the floor and partially on the dais. No doorways were visible other than that at which they had entered, though both knew that others might be concealed by the hangings.

Gahan, his curiosity aroused by the legends surrounding
this portion of the palace, crossed to the dais to examine the
figure that apparently had fallen from it, to find the dried
and shrivelled corpse of a man lying upon his back on the
floor with arms outstretched and fingers stiffly outspread. One
of his feet was doubled partially beneath him, while the other
was still entangled in the sleeping silks and furs upon the dais.
After five thousand years the expression of the withered face
and the eyeless sockets retained the aspect of horrid fear to
such an extent, that Gahan knew that he was looking upon
the body of O-Mai the Cruel.

Suddenly Tara, who stood close beside him, clutched his
arm and pointed toward a far corner of the room. Gahan
looked and looking felt the hairs upon his neck rising. He
threw his left arm about the girl and with bared sword
stood between her and the hangings that they watched, and
then slowly Gahan of Gathol backed away, for in this grim
and somber chamber, which no human foot had trod for
five thousand years and to which no breath of wind might
enter, the heavy hangings in the far corner had moved. Not
gently had they moved as a draught might have moved them
had there been a draught, but suddenly they had bulged
out as though pushed against from behind. To the opposite
corner backed Gahan until they stood with their backs a-
gainst the hangings there, and then hearing the approach
of their pursuers across the chamber beyond Gahan pushed
Tara through the hangings and, following her, kept open
with his left hand, which he had disengaged from the girl's
grasp, a tiny opening through which he could view the apartment and the doorway upon the opposite side through which
the pursuers would enter, if they came this far.

Behind the hangings there was a space of about three feet
in width between them and the wall, making a passageway
entirely around the room, broken only by the single entrance
opposite them; this being a common arrangement especially
in the sleeping apartments of the rich and powerful upon
Barsoom. The purposes of this arrangement were several.
The passageway afforded a station for guards in the same
room with their master without intruding entirely upon his
privacy; it concealed secret exits from the chamber; it permitted the occupant of the room to hide eavesdroppers and

assassins for use against enemies that he might lure to his chamber.

The three chiefs with a dozen warriors had had no difficulty in following the tracks of the fugitives through the dust of the corridors and chambers they had traversed. To enter this portion of the palace at all had required all the courage they possessed, and now that they were within the very chambers of O-Mai their nerves were pitched to the highest key—another turn and they would snap; for the people of Manator are filled with weird superstitions. As they entered the outer chamber they moved slowly, with drawn swords, no one seeming anxious to take the lead, and the twelve warriors hanging back in unconcealed and shameless terror, while the three chiefs, spurred on by fear of O-Tar and by pride, pressed together for mutual encouragement as they slowly crossed the dimly-lighted room.

Following the tracks of Gahan and Tara they found that though each doorway had been approached only one threshold had been crossed and this door they gingerly opened, revealing to their astonished gaze the four warriors at the jetan table. For a moment they were on the verge of flight, for though they knew what they were, coming as they did upon them in this mysterious and haunted suite, they were as startled as though they had beheld the very ghosts of the departed. But they presently regained their courage sufficiently to cross this chamber too and enter the short passageway that led to the ancient sleeping apartment of O-Mai the Cruel. They did not know that this awful chamber lay just before them, or it were doubtful that they would have proceeded farther; but they saw that those they sought had come this way and so they followed, but within the gloomy interior of the chamber they halted, the three chiefs urging their followers, in low whispers, to close in behind them, and there just within the entrance they stood until, their eyes becoming accustomed to the dim light, one of them pointed suddenly to the thing lying upon the floor with one foot tangled in the coverings of the dais.

"Look!" he gasped. "It is the corpse of O-Mai! Ancestor of ancestors! we are in the forbidden chamber." Simultaneously there came from behind the hangings beyond the grewsome dead a hollow moan followed by a piercing scream, and the hangings shook and bellied before their eyes.

With one accord, chieftains and warriors, they turned and bolted for the doorway; a narrow doorway, where they jammed, fighting and screaming in an effort to escape. They threw away their swords and clawed at one another to make a passage for escape; those behind climbed upon the shoulders of those in front; and some fell and were trampled upon; but at last they all got through, and, the swiftest first, they bolted across the two intervening chambers to the outer corridor beyond, nor did they halt their mad retreat before they stumbled, weak and trembling, into the banquet hall of O-Tar. At sight of them the warriors who had remained with the jeddak leaped to their feet with drawn swords, thinking that their fellows were pursued by many enemies; but no one followed them into the room, and the three chieftains came and stood before O-Tar with bowed heads and trembling knees.

"Well?" demanded the jeddak. "What ails you? Speak!"

"O-Tar," cried one of them when at last he could master his voice. "When have we three failed you in battle or combat? Have our swords been not always among the foremost in defense of your safety and your honor?"

"Have I denied this?" demanded O-Tar.

"Listen then, O Jeddak, and judge us with leniency. We followed the two slaves to the apartment of O-Mai the Cruel. We entered the accursed chambers and still we did not falter. We came at last to that horrid chamber no human eye had scanned before in fifty centuries and we looked upon the dead face of O-Mai, lying as he has lain for all this time. To the very death chamber of O-Mai the Cruel we came and yet we were ready to go farther; when suddenly there broke upon our horrified ears the moans and the shrieking that mark these haunted chambers and the hangings moved and rustled in the dead air. O-Tar, it was more than human nerves could endure. We turned and fled. We threw away our swords and fought with one another to escape. With sorrow, but without shame, I tell it, for there be no man in all Manator that would not have done the same. If these slaves be Corphals they are safe among their fellow ghosts. If they be not Corphals, then already are they dead in the chambers of O-Mai, and there may they rot for all of me, for

I would not return to that accursed spot for the harness of a jeddak and the half of Barsoom for an empire. I have spoken."

O-Tar knitted his scowling brows. "Are all my chieftains cowards and cravens?" he demanded presently in sneering tones.

From among those who had not been of the searching party a chieftain arose and turned a scowling face upon O-Tar.

"The jeddak knows," he said, "that in the annals of Manator her jeddaks have ever been accounted the bravest of her warriors. Where my jeddak leads I will follow, nor may any jeddak call me a coward or a craven unless I refuse to go where he dares go. I have spoken."

After he had resumed his seat there was a painful silence, for all knew that the speaker had challenged the courage of O-Tar the Jeddak of Manator and all awaited the reply of their ruler. In every mind was the same thought—O-Tar must lead them at once to the chamber of O-Mai the Cruel, or accept forever the stigma of cowardice, and there could be no coward upon the throne of Manator. That they all knew and that O-Tar knew, as well.

But O-Tar hesitated. He looked about upon the faces of those around him at the banquet board; but he saw only the grim visages of relentless warriors. There was no trace of leniency in the face of any. And then his eye wandered to a small entrance at one side of the great chamber. An expression of relief expunged the scowl of anxiety from his features.

"Look!" he exclaimed. "See who has come!"

CHAPTER XX

THE CHARGE OF COWARDICE

GAHAN, WATCHING THROUGH the aperture between the hangings, saw the frantic flight of their pursuers. A grim smile rested upon his lips as he viewed the mad scramble for safety and saw them throw away their swords and fight with one another to be first from the chamber of fear, and when they were all gone he turned back toward Tara, the smile still upon his lips; but the smile died the instant that he turned, for he saw that Tara had disappeared.

"Tara!" he called in a loud voice, for he knew that there was no danger that their pursuers would return; but there was no response, unless it was a faint sound as of cackling laughter from afar. Hurriedly he searched the passageway behind the hangings finding several doors, one of which was ajar. Through this he entered the adjoining chamber which was lighted more brilliantly for the moment by the soft rays of hurtling Thuria taking her mad way through the heavens. Here he found the dust upon the floor disturbed, and the imprint of sandals. They had come this way—Tara and whatever the creature was that had stolen her.

But what could it have been? Gahan, a man of culture and high intelligence, held few if any superstitions. In common with nearly all races of Barsoom he clung, more or less inherently, to a certain exalted form of ancestor worship, though it was rather the memory or legends of the virtues and heroic deeds of his forebears that he deified rather than themselves. He never expected any tangible evidence of their existence after death; he did not believe that they had the power either for good or for evil other than the effect that their example while living might have had upon following generations; he did not believe therefore in the materialization of dead spirits. If there was a life hereafter he knew nothing of it, for he knew that science had demonstrated the existence of some material cause for every seemingly supernatural pheonomenon of ancient religions and superstitions. Yet he was at a loss to know what power might have removed Tara so suddenly and mysteriously from his side in a chamber that had not known the presence of man for five thousand years.

In the darkness he could not see whether there were the imprints of other sandals than Tara's—only that the dust was disturbed—and when it led him into gloomy corridors he lost the trail altogether. A perfect labyrinth of passages and apartments was now revealed to him as he hurried on through the deserted quarter of O-Mai. Here was an ancient bath—doubtless that of the jeddak himself, and again he passed through a room in which a meal had been laid upon a table five thousand years before—the untasted breakfast of O-Mai, perhaps. There passed before his eyes in the brief moments that he traversed the chambers, a wealth of ornaments and jewels and precious metals that surprised even the Jed of Gathol whose harness was of diamonds and platinum and whose riches were the envy of a world. But at last his search of O-Mai's chambers ended in a small closet in the floor of which was the opening to a spiral runway leading straight down into Stygian darkness. The dust at the entrance of the closet had been freshly disturbed, and as this was the only possible indication that Gahan had of the direction taken by the abductor of Tara it seemed as well to follow on as to search elsewhere. So, without hesitation, he descended into the utter darkness below. Feeling with a foot before taking a forward step his descent was necessarily slow, but Gahan was a Barsoomian and so knew the pitfalls that might await the unwary in such dark, forbidden portions of a jeddak's palace.

He had descended for what he judged might be three full levels and was pausing, as he occasionally did, to listen, when he distinctly heard a peculiar shuffling, scraping sound approaching him from below. Whatever the thing was it was ascending the runway at a steady pace and would soon be near him. Gahan laid his hand upon the hilt of his sword and drew it slowly from its scabbard that he might make no noise that would apprise the creature of his presence. He wished that there might be even the slightest lessening of the darkness. If he could see but the outline of the thing that approached him he would feel that he had a fairer chance in the meeting; but he could see nothing, and then because he could see nothing the end of his scabbard struck the stone side of the runway, giving off a sound that the stillness and the narrow confines of the passage and the darkness seemed to magnify to a terrific clatter.

Instantly the shuffling sound of approach ceased. For a moment Gahan stood in silent waiting, then casting aside discretion he moved on again down the spiral. The thing, whatever it might be, gave forth no sound now by which Gahan might locate it. At any moment it might be upon him and so he kept his sword in readiness. Down, ever downward the steep spiral led. The darkness and the silence of the tomb surrounded him, yet somewhere ahead was something. He was not alone in that horrid place—another presence that he could not hear or see hovered before him—of that he was positive. Perhaps it was the thing that had stolen Tara. Perhaps Tara herself, still in the clutches of some nameless horror, was just ahead of him. He quickened his pace—it became almost a run at the thought of the danger that threatened the woman he loved, and then he collided with a wooden door that swung open to the impact. Before him was a lighted corridor. On either side were chambers. He had advanced but a short distance from the bottom of the spiral when he recognized that he was in the pits below the palace. A moment later he heard behind him the shuffling sound that had attracted his attention in the spiral runway. Wheeling about he saw the author of the sound emerging from a doorway he had just passed. It was Ghek the kaldane.

"Ghek!" exclaimed Gahan. "It was you in the runway? Have you seen Tara of Helium?"

"It was I in the spiral," replied the kaldane; "but I have not seen Tara of Helium. I have been searching for her. Where is she?"

"I do not know," replied the Gatholian; "but we must find her and take her from this place."

"We may find her," said Ghek; "but I doubt our ability to take her away. It is not so easy to leave Manator as it is to enter it. I may come and go at will, through the ancient burrows of the ulsios; but you are too large for that and your lungs need more air than may be found in some of the deeper runways."

"But U-Thor!" exclaimed Gahan. "Have you heard aught of him or his intentions?"

"I have heard much," replied Ghek. "He camps at The Gate of Enemies. That spot he holds and his warriors lie just beyond The Gate; but he has not sufficient force to enter the city and take the palace. An hour since and you might have made your way to him; but now every avenue is strongly guarded since O-Tar learned that A-Kor had escaped to U-Thor."

"A-Kor has escaped and joined U-Thor!" exclaimed Gahan.

"But little more than an hour since. I was with him when a warrior came—a man whose name is Tasor—who brought a message from you. It was decided that Tasor should accompany A-Kor in an attempt to reach the camp of U-Thor, the great jed of Manatos, and exact from him the assurances you required. Then U-Thor was to return and take food to you and the Princess of Helium. I accompanied them. We won through easily and found U-Thor more than willing to respect your every wish, but when Tasor would have returned to you the way was blocked by the warriors of O-Tar. Then it was that I volunteered to come to you and report and find food and drink and then go forth among the Gatholian slaves of Manator and prepare them for their part in the plan that U-Thor and Tasor conceived."

"And what was this plan?"

"U-Thor has sent for reinforcements. To Manatos he has sent and to all the outlying districts that are his. It will take a month to collect and bring them hither and in the meantime the slaves within the city are to organize secretly, stealing and hiding arms against the day that the reinforcements arrive. When that day comes the forces of U-Thor will enter The Gate of Enemies and as the warriors of O-Tar rush to repulse them the slaves from Gathol will fall upon them from the rear with the majority of their numbers, while the balance will assault the palace. They hope thus to divert so many from The Gate that U-Thor will have little difficulty in forcing an entrance to the city."

"Perhaps they will succeed," commented Gahan; "but the warriors of O-Tar are many, and those who fight in defense of their homes and their jeddak have always an advantage. Ah, Ghek, would that we had the great warships of Gathol or of Helium to pour their merciless fire into the streets of Manator while U-Thor marched to the palace over the corpses of the slain." He paused, deep in thought, and then turned his gaze again upon the kaldane. "Heard you aught of the party that escaped with me from The Field of Jetan—of Floran, Val Dor, and the others? What of them?"

"Ten of these won through to U-Thor at The Gate of Enemies and were well received by him. Eight fell in the fighting upon the way. Val Dor and Floran live, I believe, for I am sure that I heard U-Thor address two warriors by these names."

"Good!" exclaimed Gahan. "Go then, through the burrows

of the ulsios, to The Gate of Enemies and carry to Floran the
message that I shall write in his own language. Come, while I
write the message."

In a nearby room they found a bench and table and there
Gahan sat and wrote in the strange, stenographic characters
of Martian script a message to Floran of Gathol. "Why," he
asked, when he had finished it, "did you search for Tara
through the spiral runway where we nearly met?"

"Tasor told me where you were to be found, and as I have
explored the greater part of the palace by means of the ulsio
runways and the darker and less frequented passages I knew
precisely where you were and how to reach you. This secret
spiral ascends from the pits to the roof of the loftiest of the
palace towers. It has secret openings at every level; but there
is no living Manatorian, I believe, who knows of its existence.
At least never have I met one within it and I have used it
many times. Thrice have I been in the chamber where O-Mai
lies, though I knew nothing of his identity or the story of his
death until Tasor told it to us in the camp of U-Thor."

"You know the palace thoroughly then?" Gahan interrupted.

"Better than O-Tar himself or any of his servants."

"Good! And you would serve the Princess Tara, Ghek, you
may serve her best by accompanying Floran and following his
instructions. I will write them here at the close of my message
to him, for the walls have ears, Ghek, while none but a Gatholian may read what I have writ to Floran. He will transmit it
to you. Can I trust you?"

"I may never return to Bantoom," replied Ghek. "Therefore I have but two friends in all Barsoom. What better may I
do than serve them faithfully? You may trust me, Gatholian,
who with a woman of your kind has taught me that there be
finer and nobler things than perfect mentality uninfluenced
by the unreasoning tuitions of the heart. I go."

As O-Tar pointed to the little doorway all eyes turned in
the direction he indicated and surprise was writ large upon
the faces of the warriors when they recognized the two who
had entered the banquet hall. There was I-Gos, and he dragged behind him one who was gagged and whose hands were
fastened behind with a ribbon of tough silk. It was Tara the

slave girl. I-Gos' cackling laughter rose above the silence of
the room.

"Ey, ey," he shrilled. "What the young warriors of O-Tar
cannot do, old I-Gos does alone."

"Only a Corphal may capture a Corphal," growled one
of the chiefs who had fled from the chambers of O-Mai.

I-Gos laughed. "Terror turned your heart to water," he
replied; "and shame your tongue to libel. This be no Corphal, but only a woman of Helium; her companion a warrior who can match blades with the best of you and cut out
your putrid hearts. Not so in the days of I-Gos' youth. Ah,
then were there men in Manator. Well do I recall that day
that I——"

"Peace, doddering fool!" commanded O-Tar. "Where is
the man?"

"Where I found the woman—in the death chamber of O-
Mai. Let your wise and brave chieftains go thither and
fetch him. I am an old man, and could bring but one."

"You have done well, I-Gos," O-Tar hastened to assure
him, for when he learned that Gahan might still be in the
haunted chambers he wished to appease the wrath of I-Gos,
knowing well the vitriolic tongue and temper of the ancient
one. "You think she is no Corphal, then, I-Gos?" he asked,
wishing to carry the subject from the man who was still at
large.

"No more than you," replied the ancient taxidermist.

O-Tar looked long and searchingly at Tara of Helium.
All the beauty that was hers seemed suddenly to be carried to
every fibre of his consciousness. She was still garbed in the
rich harness of a Black Princess of Jetan, and as O-Tar the
Jeddak gazed upon her he realized that never before had his
eyes rested upon a more perfect figure—a more beautiful
face.

"She is no Corphal," he murmured to himself. "She is no
Corphal and she is a princess—a princess of Helium, and, by
the golden hair of the Holy Hekkador, she is beautiful. Take
the gag from her mouth and release her hands," he commanded aloud. "Make room for the Princess Tara of Helium
at the side of O-Tar of Manator. She shall dine as becomes
a princess."

Slaves did as O-Tar bid and Tara of Helium stood with

flashing eyes behind the chair that was offered her. "Sit,"
commanded O-Tar.

The girl sank into the chair. "I sit as a prisoner," she said;
"not as a guest at the board of my enemy, O-Tar of Manator."

O-Tar motioned his followers from the room. "I would
speak alone with the Princess of Helium," he said. The company and the slaves withdrew and once more the Jeddak of
Manator turned toward the girl. "O-Tar of Manator would
be your friend," he said.

Tara of Helium sat with arms folded upon her small, firm
breasts, her eyes flashing from behind narrowed lids, nor did
she deign to answer his overture. O-Tar leaned closer to her.
He noted the hostility of her bearing and he recalled his first
encounter with her. She was a she-banth, but she was beautiful. She was by far the most desirable woman that O-Tar
had ever looked upon and he was determined to possess her.
He told her so.

"I could take you as my slave," he said to her; "but it
pleases me to make you my wife. You shall be Jeddara of
Manator. You shall have seven days in which to prepare for
the great honor that O-Tar is conferring upon you, and at
this hour of the seventh day you shall become an empress
and the wife of O-Tar in the throne room of the jeddaks of
Manator." He struck a gong that stood beside him upon the
table and when a slave appeared he bade him recall the company. Slowly the chiefs filed in and took their places at the
table. Their faces were grim and scowling, for there was still
unanswered the question of their jeddak's courage. If O-Tar
had.hoped they would forget he had been mistaken in his
men.

O-Tar arose. "In seven days," he announced, "there will
be a great feast in honor of the new Jeddara of Manator,"
and he waved his hand toward Tara of Helium. "The ceremony will occur at the beginning of the seventh zode[1] in the
throne room. In the meantime the Princess of Helium will
be cared for in the tower of the women's quarters of the
palace. Conduct her thither, E-Thas, with a suitable guard
of honor and see to it that slaves and eunuchs be placed at

---

[1] About 8:30 P.M. Earth Time.

her disposal, who shall attend upon all her wants and guard her carefully from harm."

Now E-Thas knew that the real meaning concealed in these fine words was that he should conduct the prisoner under a strong guard to the women's quarters and confine her there in the tower for seven days, placing about her trustworthy guards who would prevent her escape or frustrate any attempted rescue.

As Tara was departing from the chamber with E-Thas and the guard, O-Tar leaned close to her ear and whispered: "Consider well during these seven days the high honor I have offered you, and—its sole alternative." As though she had not heard him the girl passed out of the banquet hall, her head high and her eyes straight to the front.

After Ghek had left him Gahan roamed the pits and the ancient corridors of the deserted portions of the palace seeking some clue to the whereabouts or the fate of Tara of Helium. He utilized the spiral runway in passing from level to level until he knew every foot of it from the pits to the summit of the high tower, and into what apartments it opened at the various levels as well as the ingenious and hidden mechanism that operated the locks of the cleverly concealed doors leading to it. For food he drew upon the stores he found in the pits and when he slept he lay upon the royal couch of O-Mai in the forbidden chamber, sharing the dais with the dead foot of the ancient jeddak.

In the palace about him seethed, all unknown to Gahan, a vast unrest. Warriors and chieftains pursued the duties of their vocations with dour faces, and little knots of them were collecting here and there and with frowns of anger discussing some subject that was uppermost in the minds of all. It was upon the fourth day following Tara's incarceration in the tower that E-Thas, the major-domo of the palace and one of O-Tar's creatures, came to his master upon some trivial errand. O-Tar was alone in one of the smaller chambers of his personal suite when the major-domo was announced, and after the matter upon which E-Thas had come was disposed of the jeddak signed him to remain.

"From the position of an obscure warrior I have elevated you, E-Thas, to the honors of a chief. Within the confines of the palace your word is second only to mine. You are not loved for this, E-Thas, and should another jeddak ascend the throne of Manator what would become of you, whose enemies are among the most powerful of Manator?"

"Speak not of it, O-Tar," begged E-Thas. "These last few days I have thought upon it much and I would forget it; but I have sought to appease the wrath of my worst enemies. I have been very kind and indulgent with them."

"You, too, read the voiceless message in the air?" demanded the jeddak.

E-Thas was palpably uneasy and he did not reply.

"Why did you not come to me with your apprehensions?" demanded O-Tar. "Be this loyalty?"

"I feared, O mighty jeddak!" replied E-Thas. "I feared that you would not understand and that you would be angry."

"What know you? Speak the whole truth!" commanded O-Tar.

"There is much unrest among the chieftains and the warriors," replied E-Thas. "Even those who were your friends fear the power of those who speak against you."

"What say they?" growled the jeddak.

"They say that you are afraid to enter the apartments of O-Mai in search of the slave Turan—oh, do not be angry with me, Jeddak; it is but what they say that I repeat. I, your loyal E-Thas, believe no such foul slander."

"No, no; why should I fear?" demanded O-Tar. "We do not know that he is there. Did not my chiefs go thither and see nothing of him?"

"But they say that *you* did not go," pursued E-Thas, "and that they will have none of a coward upon the throne of Manator."

"They said that treason?" O-Tar almost shouted.

"They said that and more, great jeddak," answered the major-domo. "They said that not only did you fear to enter the chambers of O-Mai, but that you feared the slave Turan, and they blame you for your treatment of A-Kor, whom they all believe to have been murdered at your command. They were fond of A-Kor and there are many now who say aloud that A-Kor would have made a wondrous jeddak."

"They dare?" screamed O-Tar. "They dare suggest the name of a slave's bastard for the throne of O-Tar!"

"He is your son, O-Tar," E-Thas reminded him, "nor is there a more beloved man in Manator—I but speak to you of facts which may not be ignored, and I dare do so because only when you realize the truth may you seek a cure for the ills that draw about your throne."

O-Tar had slumped down upon his bench—suddenly he looked shrunken and tired and old. "Cursed be the day," he cried, "that saw those three strangers enter the city of Manator. Would that U-Dor had been spared to me. He was strong —my enemies feared him; but he is gone—dead at the hands of that hateful slave, Turan; may the curse of Issus be upon him!"

"My jeddak, what shall we do?" begged E-Thas. "Cursing the slave will not solve your problems."

"But the great feast and the marriage is but three days off," plead O-Tar. "It shall be a great gala occasion. The warriors and the chiefs all know that—it is the custom. Upon that day gifts and honors shall be bestowed. Tell me, who are most bitter against me? I will send you among them and let it be known that I am planning rewards for their past services to the throne. We will make jeds of chiefs and chiefs of warriors, and grant them palaces and slaves. Eh, E-Thas?"

The other shook his head. "It will not do, O-Tar. They will have nothing of your gifts or honors. I have heard them say as much."

"What do they want?" demanded O-Tar.

"They want a jeddak as brave as the bravest," replied E-Thas, though his knees shook as he said it.

"They think I am a coward?" cried the jeddak.

"They say you are afraid to go to the apartments of O-Mai the Cruel."

For a long time O-Tar sat, his head sunk upon his breast, staring blankly at the floor.

"Tell them," he said at last in a hollow voice that sounded not at all like the voice of a great jeddak; "tell them that I will go to the chambers of O-Mai and search for Turan the slave."

CHAPTER XXI

A RISK FOR LOVE

"EY, EY, HE IS A CRAVEN and he called me 'doddering fool'!" The speaker was I-Gos and he addressed a knot of chieftains in one of the chambers of the palace of O-Tar, Jeddak of Manator: "If A-Kor was alive there were a jeddak for us!"

"Who says that A-Kor is dead?" demanded one of the chiefs.

"Where is he then?" asked I-Gos. "Have not others disappeared whom O-Tar thought too well beloved for men so near the throne as they?"

The chief shook his head. "And I thought that, or knew it, rather, I'd join U-Thor at The Gate of Enemies."

"S-s-st," cautioned one; "here comes the licker of feet," and all eyes were turned upon the approaching E-Thas.

"Kaor, friends!" he exclaimed as he stopped among them, but his friendly greeting elicited naught but a few surly nods. "Have you heard the news?" he continued, unabashed by treatment to which he was becoming accustomed.

"What—has O-Tar seen an ulsio and fainted?" demanded I-Gos with broad sarcasm.

"Men have died for less than that, ancient one," E-Thas reminded him.

"I am safe," retorted I-Gos, "for I am not a brave and popular son of the jeddak of Manator."

This was indeed open treason, but E-Thas feigned not to hear it. He ignored I-Gos and turned to the others. "O-Tar goes to the chamber of O-Mai this night in search of Turan the slave," he said. "He sorrows that his warriors have not the courage for so mean a duty and that their jeddak is thus compelled to arrest a common slave," with which taunt E-Thas passed on to spread the word in other parts of the palace. As a matter of fact the latter part of his message was purely original with himself, and he took great delight in delivering it to the discomfiture of his enemies. As he was leaving the little group of men I-Gos called after him. "At what hour does O-Tar intend visiting the chambers of O-Mai?" he asked.

"Toward the end of the eighth zode[1]," replied the major-domo, and went his way.

"We shall see," stated I-Gos.

"What shall we see?" asked a warrior.

"We shall see whether O-Tar visits the chamber of O-Mai."

"I shall be there myself and if I see him I will know that he has been there. If I don't see him I will know that he has not," explained the old taxidermist.

"Is there anything there to fill an honest man with fear?" asked a chieftain. "What have you seen?"

"It was not so much what I saw, though that was bad enough, as what I heard," said I-Gos.

"Tell us! What heard and saw you?"

"I saw the dead O-Mai," said I-Gos. The others shuddered.

"And you went not mad?" they asked.

"Am I mad?" retorted I-Gos.

"And you will go again?"

"Yes."

"Then indeed you are mad," cried one.

"You saw the dead O-Mai; but what heard you that was worse?" whispered another.

"I saw the dead O-Mai lying upon the floor of his sleeping chamber with one foot tangled in the sleeping silks and furs upon his couch. I heard horrid moans and frightful screams."

"And you are not afraid to go there again?" demanded several.

"The dead cannot harm me," said I-Gos. "He has lain thus for five thousand years. Nor can a sound harm me. I heard it once and live—I can hear it again. It came from almost at my side where I hid behind the hangings and watched the slave Turan before I snatched the woman away from him."

"I-Gos, you are a very brave man," said a chieftain.

"O-Tar called me 'doddering fool' and I would face worse dangers than lie in the forbidden chambers of O-Mai to know it if he does not visit the chamber of O-Mai. Then indeed shall O-Tar fall!"

The night came and the zodes dragged and the time approached when O-Tar, Jeddak of Manator, was to visit the chamber of O-Mai in search of the slave Turan. To us, who

---

[1] About 1:00 A.M. Earth Time.

may doubt the existence of malignant spirits, his fear may seem unbelievable, for he was a strong man, an excellent swordsman, and a warrior of great repute; but the fact remained that O-Tar of Manator was nervous with apprehension as he strode the corridors of his palace toward the deserted halls of O-Mai and when he stood at last with his hand upon the door that opened from the dusty corridor to the very apartments themselves he was almost paralyzed with terror. He had come alone for two very excellent reasons, the first of which was that thus none might note his terror-stricken state nor his defection should he fail at the last moment, and the other was that should he accomplish the thing alone or be able to make his chiefs believe that he had, the credit would be far greater than were he to be accompanied by warriors.

But though he had started alone he had become aware that he was being followed, and he knew that it was because his people had no faith in either his courage or his veracity. He did not believe that he would find the slave Turan. He did not very much want to find him, for though O-Tar was an excellent swordsman and a brave warrior in physical combat, he had seen how Turan had played with U-Dor and he had no stomach for a passage at arms with one whom he knew outclassed him.

And so O-Tar stood with his hand upon the door—afraid to enter; afraid not to. But at last his fear of his own warriors, watching behind him, grew greater than the fear of the unknown behind the ancient door and he pushed the heavy skeel aside and entered.

Silence and gloom and the dust of centuries lay heavy upon the chamber. From his warriors he knew the route that he must take to the horrid chamber of O-Mai and so he forced his unwilling feet across the room before him, across the room where the jetan players sat at their eternal game, and came to the short corridor that led into the room of O-Mai. His naked sword trembled in his grasp. He paused after each forward step to listen and when he was almost at the door of the ghost-haunted chamber, his heart stood still within his breast and the cold sweat broke from the clammy skin of his forehead, for from within there came to his affrighted ears the sound of muffled breathing. Then it was that O-Tar of

Manator came near to fleeing from the nameless horror
that he could not see, but that he knew lay waiting for him
in that chamber just ahead. But again came the fear of the
wrath and contempt of his warriors and his chiefs. They
would degrade him and they would slay him into the bar-
gain. There was no doubt of what his fate would be should
he flee the apartments of O-Mai in terror. His only hope,
therefore, lay in daring the unknown in preference to the
known.

He moved forward. A few steps took him to the doorway.
The chamber before him was darker than the corridor, so
that he could but indistinctly make out the objects in the
room. He saw a sleeping dais near the center, with a darker
blotch of something lying on the marble floor beside it. He
moved a step farther into the doorway, and the scabbard of
his sword scraped against the stone frame. To his horror he
saw the sleeping silks and furs upon the central dais move.
He saw a figure slowly arising to a sitting posture from the
death bed of O-Mai the Cruel. His knees shook, but he gathered all his moral forces, and gripping his sword more tightly
in his trembling fingers prepared to leap across the chamber
upon the horrid apparition. He hesitated just a moment. He
felt eyes upon him—ghoulish eyes that bored through the
darkness into his withering heart—eyes that he could not see.
He gathered himself for the rush—and then there broke from
the thing upon the couch an awful shriek, and O-Tar sank
senseless to the floor.

Gahan rose from the couch of O-Mai, smiling, only to
swing quickly about with drawn sword as the shadow of a
noise impinged upon his keen ears from the shadows behind
him. Between the parted hangings he saw a bent and wrinkled figure. It was I-Gos.

"Sheathe your sword, Turan," said the old man. "You
have naught to fear from I-Gos."

"What do you here?" demanded Gahan.

"I came to make sure that the great coward did not cheat us.
Ey, and he called me 'doddering fool'; but look at him now!
Stricken insensible by terror, but, ey, one might forgive him
that who had heard your uncanny scream. It all but blasted
my own courage. And it was you, then, who moaned and
screamed when the chiefs came the day that I stole Tara from

you?"

"It was you, then, old scoundrel?" demanded Gahan, moving threateningly toward I-Gos.

"Come, come!" expostulated the old man; "it was I, but then I was your enemy. I would not do it now. Conditions have changed."

"How have they changed? What has changed them?" asked Gahan.

"Then I did not fully realize the cowardice of my jeddak, or the bravery of you and the girl. I am an old man from another age and I love courage. At first I resented the girl's attack upon me, but later I came to see the bravery of it and it won my admiration, as have all her acts. She feared not O-Tar, she feared not me, she feared not all the warriors of Manator. And you! Blood of a million sires! but how you fight! I am sorry that I exposed you at The Fields of Jetan. I am sorry that I dragged the girl Tara back to O-Tar. I would make amends. I would be your friend. Here is my sword at your feet," and drawing his weapon I-Gos cast it to the floor in front of Gahan.

The Gatholian knew that scarce the most abandoned of knaves would repudiate this solemn pledge, and so he stooped, and picking up the old man's sword returned it to him, hilt first, in acceptance of his friendship.

"Where is the Princess Tara of Helium?" asked Gahan. "Is she safe?"

"She is confined in the tower of the women's quarters awaiting the ceremony that is to make her Jeddara of Manator," replied I-Gos.

"This thing dared think that Tara of Helium would mate with him?" growled Gahan. "I will make short work of him if he is not already dead from fright," and he stepped toward the fallen O-Tar to run his sword through the jeddak's heart.

"No!" cried I-Gos. "Slay him not and pray that he be not dead if you would save your princess."

"How is that?" asked Gahan.

"If word of O-Tar's death reached the quarters of the women the Princess Tara would be lost. They know O-Tar's intention of taking her to wife and making her Jeddara of Manator, so you may rest assured that they all hate her with the hate of jealous women. Only O-Tar's power protects her now from harm. Should O-Tar die they would turn her over to the warriors and the male slaves, for there would be none to avenge her."

Gahan sheathed his sword. "Your point is well taken; but what shall we do with him?"

"Leave him where he lies," counseled I-Gos. "He is not dead. When he revives he will return to his quarters with a fine tale of his bravery and there will be none to impugn his boasts—none but I-Gos. Come! he may revive at any moment and he must not find us here."

I-Gos crossed to the body of his jeddak, knelt beside it for an instant, and then returned past the couch to Gahan. The two quit the chamber of O-Mai and took their way toward the spiral runway. Here I-Gos led Gahan to a higher level and out upon the roof of that portion of the palace from where he pointed to a high tower quite close by. "There," he said, "lies the Princess of Helium, and quite safe she will be until the time of the ceremony."

"Safe, possibly, from other hands, but not from her own," said Gahan. "She will never become Jeddara of Manator—first will she destroy herself."

"She would do that?" asked I-Gos.

"She will, unless you can get word to her that I still live and that there is yet hope," replied Gahan.

"I cannot get word to her," said I-Gos. "The quarters of his women O-Tar guards with jealous hand. Here are his most trusted slaves and warriors, yet even so, thick among them are countless spies, so that no man knows which be which. No shadow falls within those chambers that is not marked by a hundred eyes."

Gahan stood gazing at the lighted windows of the high tower in the upper chambers of which Tara of Helium was confined. "I will find a way, I-Gos," he said.

"There is no way," replied the old man.

For some time they stood upon the roof beneath the brilliant stars and hurtling moons of dying Mars, laying their plans against the time that Tara of Telium should be brought from the high tower to the throne room of O-Tar. It was then, and then alone, argued I-Gos, that any hope of rescuing her might be entertained. Just how far he might trust the other Gahan did not know, and so he kept to him-

self the knowledge of the plan that he had forwarded to Floran and Val Dor by Ghek, but he assured the ancient taxidermist that if he were sincere in his oft-repeated declaration
that O-Tar should be denounced and superseded he would
have his opportunity on the night that the jeddak sought to
wed the Heliumetic princess.

"Your time shall come then, I-Gos," Gahan assured the
other, "and if you have any party that thinks as you do, prepare them for the eventuality that will succeed O-Tar's
presumptuous attempt to wed the daughter of The Warlord.
Where shall I see you again, and when? I go now to speak
with Tara, Princess of Helium."

"I like your boldness," said I-Gos; "but it will avail you
naught. You will not speak with Tara, Princess of Helium,
though doubtless the blood of many Manatorians will drench
the floors of the women's quarters before you are slain."

Gahan smiled. "I shall not be slain. Where and when shall
we meet? But you may find me in O-Mai's chamber at night.
That seems the safest retreat in all Manator for an enemy of
the jeddak in whose palace it lies. I go!"

"And may the spirits of your ancestors surround you,"
said I-Gos.

After the old man had left him Gahan made his way across
the roof to the high tower, which appeared to have been
constructed of concrete and afterward elaborately carved, its
entire surface being covered with intricate designs cut deep
into the stone-like material of which it was composed.
Though wrought ages since, it was but little weather-worn
owing to the aridity of the Martian atmosphere, the infre-
quency of rains, and the rarity of dust storms. To scale it,
though, presented difficulties and danger that might have
deterred the bravest of men—that would, doubtless, have
deterred Gahan, had he not felt that the life of the woman he
loved depended upon his accomplishing the hazardous feat.

Removing his sandals and laying aside all of his harness
and weapons other than a single belt supporting a dagger,
the Gatholian essayed the dangerous ascent. Clinging to the
carvings with hands and feet he worked himself slowly aloft,
avoiding the windows and keeping upon the shadowy side
of the tower, away from the light of Thuria and Cluros. The
tower rose some fifty feet above the roof of the adjacent part

of the palace, comprising five levels or floors with windows looking in every direction. A few of the windows were balconied, and these more than the others he sought to avoid, although, it being now near the close of the ninth zode, there was little likelihood that many were awake within the tower.

His progress was noiseless and he came at last, undetected, to the windows of the upper level. These, like several of the others he had passed at lower levels, were heavily barred, so that there was no possibility of his gaining ingress to the apartment where Tara was confined. Darkness hid the interior behind the first window that he approached. The second opened upon a lighted chamber where he could see a guard sleeping at his post outside a door. Here also was the top of the runway leading to the next level below. Passing still farther around the tower Gahan approached another window, but now he clung to that side of the tower which ended in a courtyard a hundred feet below and in a short time the light of Thuria would reach him. He realized that he must hasten and he prayed that behind the window he now approached he would find Tara of Helium.

Coming to the opening he looked in upon a small chamber dimly lighted. In the center was a sleeping dais upon which a human form lay beneath silks and furs. A bare arm, protruding from the coverings, lay exposed against a black and yellow striped orluk skin—an arm of wondrous beauty about which was clasped an armlet that Gahan knew. No other creature was visible within the chamber, all of which was exposed to Gahan's view. Pressing his face to the bars the Gatholian whispered her dear name. The girl stirred, but did not awaken. Again he called, but this time louder. Tara sat up and looked about and at the same instant a huge eunuch leaped to his feet from where he had been lying on the floor close by that side of the dais farthest from Gahan. Simultaneously the brilliant light of Thuria flashed full upon the window where Gahan clung silhouetting him plainly to the two within.

Both sprang to their feet. The eunuch drew his sword and leaped for the window where the helpless Gahan would have fallen an easy victim to a single thrust of the murderous weapon the fellow bore, had not Tara of Helium leaped upon her guard dragging him back. At the same time she drew the slim dagger from its hiding place in her harness and even as the eunuch sought to hurl her aside its keen point found his heart. Without a sound he died and lunged forward to the floor. Then Tara ran to the window.

"Turan, my chief!" she cried. "What awful risk is this you take to seek me here, where even your brave heart is powerless to aid me."

"Be not so sure of that, heart of my heart," he replied. "While I bring but words to my love, they be the forerunner of deeds, I hope, that will give her back to me forever. I feared that you might destroy yourself, Tara of Helium, to escape the dishonor that O-Tar would do you, and so I came to give you new hope and beg that you live for me through whatever may transpire, in the knowledge that there is yet a way and that if all goes well we shall be freed at last. Look for me in the throne room of O-Tar the night that he would wed you. And now, how may we dispose of this fellow?" He pointed to the dead eunuch upon the floor.

"We need not concern ourselves about that," she replied. "None dares harm me for fear of the wrath of O-Tar—otherwise I should have been dead so soon as ever I entered this portion of the palace, for the women hate me. O-Tar alone may punish me, and what cares O-Tar for the life of a eunuch? No, fear not upon this score."

Their hands were clasped between the bars and now Gahan drew her nearer to him.

"One kiss," he said, "before I go, my princess," and the proud daughter of Dejah Thoris, Princess of Helium, and The Warlord of Barsoom whispered: "My chieftain!" and pressed her lips to the lips of Turan, the common panthan.

CHAPTER XXII

AT THE MOMENT OF MARRIAGE

THE SILENCE OF THE TOMB lay heavy about him as O-Tar, Jeddak of Manator, opened his eyes in the chamber of O-Mai. Recollection of the frightful apparition that had confronted him swept to his consciousness. He listened, but heard naught. Within the range of his vision there was nothing apparent that might cause alarm. Slowly he lifted his head and looked about. Upon the floor beside the couch lay the thing that had first attracted his attention and his eyes closed in terror as he recognized it for what it was; but it moved not, nor spoke. O-Tar opened his eyes again and rose to his feet. He was trembling in every limb. There was nothing on the dais from which he had seen the thing arise.

O-Tar backed slowly from the room. At last he gained the outer corridor. It was empty. He did not know that it had emptied rapidly as the loud scream with which his own had mingled had broken upon the startled ears of the warriors who had been sent to spy upon him. He looked at the timepiece set in a massive bracelet upon his left forearm. The ninth zode was nearly half gone. O-Tar had lain for an hour unconscious. He had spent an hour in the chamber of O-Mai and he was not dead! He had looked upon the face of his predecessor and was still sane! He shook himself and smiled. Rapidly he subdued his rebelliously shaking nerves, so that by the time he reached the tenanted portion of the palace he had gained control of himself. He walked with chin high and something of a swagger. To the banquet hall he went, knowing that his chiefs awaited him there and as he entered they arose and upon the faces of many were incredulity and amaze, for they had not thought to see O-Tar the jeddak again after what the spies had told them of the horrid sounds issuing from the chambers of O-Mai. Thankful was O-Tar that he had gone alone to that chamber of fright, for now no one could deny the tale that he should tell.

E-Thas rushed forward to greet him, for E-Thas had seen black looks directed toward him as the *tals* slipped by and his benefactor failed to return.

"O brave and glorious jeddak!" cried the major-domo. "We rejoice at your safe return and beg of you the story of your adventure."

"It was naught," exclaimed O-Tar. "I searched the chambers carefully and waited in hiding for the return of the slave, Turan, if he were temporarily away; but he came not. He is not there and I doubt if he ever goes there. Few men would choose to remain long in such a dismal place."

"You were not attacked?" asked E-Thas. "You heard no screams, nor moans?"

"I heard hideous noises and saw phantom figures; but they fled before me so that never could I lay hold of one, and I looked upon the face of O-Mai and I am not mad. I even rested in the chamber beside his corpse."

In a far corner of the room a bent and wrinkled old man hid a smile behind a golden goblet of strong brew.

"Come! Let us drink!" cried O-Tar and reached for the dagger, the pommel of which he was accustomed to use to strike the gong which summoned slaves, but the dagger was not in its scabbard. O-Tar was puzzled. He knew that it had been there just before he entered the chamber of O-Mai, for he had carefully felt of all his weapons to make sure that none was missing. He seized instead a table utensil and struck the gong, and when the slaves came bade them bring the strongest brew for O-Tar and his chiefs. Before the dawn broke many were the expressions of admiration bellowed from drunken lips—admiration for the courage of their jeddak; but some there were who still looked glum.

Came at last the day that O-Tar would take the Princess Tara of Helium to wife. For hours slaves prepared the unwilling bride. Seven perfumed baths occupied three long and weary hours, then her whole body was anointed with the oil of pimalia blossoms and massaged by the deft fingers of a slave from distant Dusar. Her harness, all new and wrought for the occasion, was of the white hide of the great white apes of Barsoom, hung heavily with platinum and diamonds—fairly encrusted with them. The glossy mass of her jet hair had been built into a coiffure of stately and becoming grandeur, into which diamond-headed pins were stuck until the whole scintillated as the stars in heaven upon a moonless night.

But it was a sullen and defiant bride that they led from the high tower toward the throne room of O-Tar. The corridors were filled with slaves and warriors, and the women of the palace and the city who had been commanded to attend the ceremony. All the power and pride, wealth and beauty of Manator were there.

Slowly Tara, surrounded by a heavy guard of honor,

moved along the marble corridors filled with people. At the entrance to The Hall of Chiefs E-Thas, the major-domo, received her. The Hall was empty except for its ranks of dead chieftains upon their dead mounts. Through this long chamber E-Thas escorted her to the throne room which also was empty, the marriage ceremony in Manator differing from that of other countries of Barsoom. Here the bride would await the groom at the foot of the steps leading to the throne. The guests followed her in and took their places, leaving the central aisle from The Hall of Chiefs to the throne clear, for up this O-Tar would approach his bride alone after a short solitary communion with the dead behind closed doors in The Hall of Chiefs. It was the custom.

The guests had all filed through The Hall of Chiefs; the doors at both ends had been closed. Presently those at the lower end of the hall opened and O-Tar entered. His black harness was ornamented with rubies and gold; his face was covered by a grotesque mask of the precious metal in which two enormous rubies were set for eyes, though below them were narrow slits through which the wearer could see. His crown was a fillet supporting carved feathers of the same metal as the mask. To the least detail his regalia was that demanded of a royal bridegroom by the customs of Manator, and now in accordance with that same custom he came alone to The Hall of Chiefs to receive the blessings and the council of the great ones of Manator who had preceded him.

As the doors at the lower end of the Hall closed behind him O-Tar the Jeddak stood alone with the great dead. By the dictates of ages no mortal eye might look upon the scene enacted within that sacred chamber. As the mighty of Manator respected the traditions of Manator, let us, too, respect those traditions of a proud and sensitive people. Of what concern to us the happenings in that solemn chamber of the dead?

Five minutes passed. The bride stood silently at the foot of the throne. The guests spoke together in low whispers until the room was filled with the hum of many voices. At length the doors leading into The Hall of Chiefs swung open, and the resplendent bridegroom stood framed for a moment in the massive opening. A hush fell upon the wedding guests. With measured and impressive step the groom approached the bride. Tara felt the muscles of her heart contract with the apprehension that had been growing upon her as the coils of Fate settled more closely about her and no sign came from Turan. Where was he? What, indeed, could he accomplish now to save her? Surrounded by the power of O-Tar with never a friend among them, her position seemed at last without vestige of hope.

"I still live!" she whispered inwardly in a last brave attempt to combat the terrible hopelessness that was overwhelming her, but her fingers stole for reassurance to the slim blade that she had managed to transfer, undetected, from her old harness to the new. And now the groom was at her side and taking her hand was leading her up the steps to the throne, before which they halted and stood facing the gathering below. Came then, from the back of the room a procession headed by the high dignitary whose office it was to make these two man and wife, and directly behind him a richly-clad youth bearing a silken pillow on which lay the golden handcuffs connected by a short length of chain-of-gold with which the ceremony would be concluded when the dignitary clasped a handcuff about the wrist of each symbolizing their indissoluble union in the holy bonds of wedlock.

Would Turan's promised succor come too late? Tara listened to the long, monotonous intonation of the wedding service. She heard the virtues of O-Tar extolled and the beauties of the bride. The moment was approaching and still no sign of Turan. But what could he accomplish should he succeed in reaching the throne room, other than to die with her? There could be no hope of rescue.

The dignitary lifted the golden handcuffs from the pillow upon which they reposed. He blessed them and reached for Tara's wrist. The time had come! The thing could go no further, for alive or dead, by all the laws of Barsoom she would be the wife of O-Tar of Manator the instant the two were locked together. Even should rescue come then or later she could never dissolve those bonds and Turan would be lost to her as surely as though death separated them.

Her hand stole toward the hidden blade, but instantly the hand of the groom shot out and seized her wrist. He had guessed her intention. Through the slits in the grotesque mask she could see his eyes upon her and she guessed the sardonic smile that the mask hid. For a tense moment the two stood thus. The people below them kept breathless silence for the play before the throne had not passed unnoticed.

Dramatic as was the moment it was suddenly rendered trebly so by the noisy opening of the doors leading to The Hall of Chiefs. All eyes turned in the direction of the interruption to see another figure framed in the massive opening —a half-clad figure buckling the half-adjusted harness hurriedly in place—the figure of O-Tar, Jeddak of Manator.

"Stop!" he screamed, springing forward along the aisle toward the throne. "Seize the impostor!"

All eyes shot to the figure of the groom before the throne. They saw him raise his hand and snatch off the golden mask, and Tara of Helium in wide-eyed incredulity looked up into the face of Turan the panthan.

"Turan, the slave," they cried then. "Death to him! Death to him!"

"Wait!" shouted Turan, drawing his sword, as a dozen warriors leaped forward.

"Wait!" screamed another voice, old and cracked, as I-Gos, the ancient taxidermist, sprang from among the guests and reached the throne steps ahead of the foremost warriors.

At sight of the old man the warriors paused, for age is held in great veneration among the peoples of Barsoom, as is true, perhaps, of all peoples whose religion is based to any extent upon ancestor worship. But O-Tar gave no heed to him, leaping instead swiftly toward the throne. "Stop, coward!" cried I-Gos.

The people looked at the little old man in amazement. "Men of Manator," he cackled in his thin, shrill voice, "wouldst be ruled by a coward and a liar?"

"Down with him!" shouted O-Tar.

"Not until I have spoken," retorted I-Gos. "It is my right. If I fail my life is forfeit—that you all know and I know. I demand therefore to be heard. It is my right!"

"It is his right," echoed the voices of a score of warriors in various parts of the chamber.

"That O-Tar is a coward and a liar I can prove," continued I-Gos. "He said that he faced bravely the horrors of the chamber of O-Mai and saw nothing of the slave Turan. I was there, hiding behind the hangings, and I saw all that transpired. Turan had been hiding in the chamber and was even then lying upon the couch of O-Mai when O-Tar, trembling with fear, entered the room. Turan, disturbed, arose to a sitting position at the same time voicing a piercing shriek. O-Tar screamed and swooned."

"It is a lie!" cried O-Tar.

"It is *not* a lie and I can prove it," retorted I-Gos. "Didst notice the night that he returned from the chambers of O-Mai and was boasting of his exploit, that when he would summon slaves to bring wine he reached for his dagger to strike the gong with its pommel as is always his custom? Didst note that, any of you? And that he had no dagger? O-Tar, where is the dagger that you carried into the chamber of O-Mai? You do not know; but I know. While you lay in the swoon of terror I took it from your harness and hid it among the sleeping silks upon the couch of O-Mai. There it is even now, and if any doubt it let them go thither and there they will find it and know the cowardice of their jeddak."

"But what of this impostor?" demanded one. "Shall he stand with impunity upon the throne of Manator whilst we squabble about our ruler?"

"It is through his bravery that you have learned the cowardice of O-Tar," replied I-Gos, "and through him you will be given a greater jeddak."

"We will choose our own jeddak. Seize and slay the slave!" There were cries of approval from all parts of the room. Gahan was listening intently, as though for some hoped-for sound. He saw the warriors approaching the dais, where he now stood with drawn sword and with one arm about Tara of Helium. He wondered if his plans had miscarried after all. If they had it would mean death for him, and he knew that Tara would take her life if he fell. Had he, then, served her so futilely after all his efforts?

Several warriors were urging the necessity for sending at once to the chamber of O-Mai to search for the dagger that would prove, if found, the cowardice of O-Tar. At last three consented to go. "You need not fear," I-Gos assured them. "There is naught there to harm you. I have been there often of late and Turan the slave has slept there for these many nights. The screams and moans that frightened you and O-Tar were voiced by Turan to drive you away from his hiding place." Shamefacedly the three left the apartment to search for O-Tar's dagger.

And now the others turned their attention once more to Gahan. They approached the throne with bared swords, but they came slowly for they had seen this slave upon the Field of Jetan and they knew the prowess of his arm. They had reached the foot of the steps when from far above there sounded a deep boom, and another, and another, and Turan smiled and breathed a sigh of relief. Perhaps, after all, it had not come too late. The warriors stopped and listened as did the others in the chamber. Now there broke upon their ears a loud rattle of musketry and it all came from above as though men were fighting upon the roofs of the palace.

"What is it?" they demanded, one of the other.

"A great storm has broken over Manator," said one.

"Mind not the storm until you have slain the creature who dares stand upon the throne of your jeddak," demanded O-Tar. "Seize him!"

Even as he ceased speaking the arras behind the throne parted and a warrior stepped forth upon the dais. An exclamation of surprise and dismay broke from the lips of the warriors of O-Tar. "U-Thor!" they cried. "What treason is this?"

"It is no treason," said U-Thor in his deep voice. "I bring you a new jeddak for all of Manator. No lying poltroon, but a courageous man whom you all love."

He stepped aside then and another emerged from the corridor hidden by the arras. It was A-Kor, and at sight of him there rose exclamations of surprise, of pleasure, and of anger, as the various factions recognized the *coup d'état* that had been arranged so cunningly. Behind A-Kor came other warriors until the dais was crowded with them—all men of Manator from the city of Manatos.

O-Tar was exhorting his warriors to attack, when a bloody and disheveled padwar burst into the chamber through a side entrance. "The city has fallen!" he cried aloud. "The hordes of Manatos pour through The Gate of Enemies. The slaves from Gathol have arisen and destroyed the palace guards. Great ships are landing warriors upon the palace roof and in the Fields of Jetan. The men of Helium and Gathol are marching through Manator. They cry aloud for the Princess of Helium and swear to leave Manator a blazing funeral pyre consuming the bodies of all our people. The skies are black with ships. They come in great processions from the east and from the south."

And then once more the doors from The Hall of Chiefs swung wide and the men of Manator turned to see another figure standing upon the threshold—a mighty figure of a man with white skin, and black hair, and gray eyes that glittered now like points of steel and behind him The Hall of Chiefs was filled with fighting men wearing the harness of far countries. Tara of Helium saw him and her heart leaped in exultation, for it was John Carter, Warlord of Barsoom, come at the head of a victorious host to the rescue of his daughter, and at his side was Djor Kantos to whom she had been betrothed.

The Warlord eyed the assemblage for a moment before he spoke. "Lay down your arms, men of Manator," he said. "I see my daughter and that she lives, and if no harm has befallen her no blood need be shed. Your city is filled with the fighting men of U-Thor, and those from Gathol and from Helium. The palace is in the hands of the slaves from Gathol, beside a thousand of my own warriors who fill the halls and chambers surrounding this room. The fate of your jeddak lies in your own hands. I have no wish to interfere. I come only for my daughter and to free the slaves from Gathol. I have spoken!" and without waiting for a reply and as though the room had been filled with his own people rather than a hostile band he strode up the broad main aisle toward Tara of Helium.

The chiefs of Manator were stunned. They looked to O-Tar; but he could only gaze helplessly about him as the enemy entered from The Hall of Chiefs and circled the throne room until they had surrounded the entire company. And then a dwar of the army of Helium entered.

"We have captured three chiefs," he reported to The Warlord, "who beg that they be permitted to enter the throne room and report to their fellows some matter which they say will decide the fate of Manator."

"Fetch them," ordered The Warlord.

They came, heavily guarded, to the foot of the steps leading to the throne and there they stopped and the leader turned toward the others of Manator and raising high his right hand displayed a jeweled dagger. "We found it," he said, "even where I-Gos said that we would find it," and he looked menacingly upon O-Tar.

"A-Kor, Jeddak of Manator!" cried a voice, and the cry was taken up by a hundred hoarse-throated warriors.

"There can be but one jeddak in Manator," said the chief who held the dagger; his eyes still fixed upon the hapless O-Tar he crossed to where the latter stood and holding the dagger upon an outstretched palm proffered it to the discredited ruler. "There can be but one jeddak in Manator," he repeated meaningly.

O-Tar took the proffered blade and drawing himself to his full height plunged it to the guard into his breast, in that single act redeeming himself in the esteem of his people and winning an eternal place in The Hall of Chiefs.

As he fell all was silence in the great room, to be broken presently by the voice of U-Thor. "O-Tar is dead!" he cried. "Let A-Kor rule until the chiefs of all Manator may be summoned to choose a new jeddak. What is your answer?"

"Let A-Kor rule! A-Kor, Jeddak of Manator!" The cries filled the room and there was no dissenting voice.

A-Kor raised his sword for silence. "It is the will of A-Kor," he said, "and that of the Great Jed of Manatos, and the commander of the fleet from Gathol, and of the illustrious John Carter, Warlord of Barsoom, that peace lie upon the city of Manator and so I decree that the men of Manator 'go forth and welcome the fighting men of these our allies as guests and friends and show them the wonders of our ancient city and the hospitality of Manator. I have spoken."

And U-Thor and John Carter dismissed their warriors and bade them accept the hospitality of Manator. As the room emptied Djor Kantos reached the side of Tara of Helium. The girl's happiness at rescue had been blighted by sight of this man whom her virtuous heart told her she had wronged. She dreaded the ordeal that lay before her and the dishonor that she must admit before she could hope to be freed from the understanding that had for long existed between them. And now Djor Kantos approached and kneeling raised her fingers to his lips.

"Beautiful daughter of Helium," he said, "how may I tell

you the thing that I must tell you—of the dishonor that I have all unwittingly done you? I can but throw myself upon your generosity for forgiveness; but if you demand it I can receive the dagger as honorably as did O-Tar."

"What do you mean?" asked Tara of Helium. "What are you talking about—why speak thus in riddles to one whose heart is already breaking?"

Her heart already breaking! The outlook was anything but promising, and the young padwar wished that he had died before ever he had had to speak the words he now must speak.

"Tara of Helium," he continued, "we all thought you dead. For a long year have you been gone from Helium. I mourned you truly and then, less than a moon since, I wed with Olvia Marthis." He stopped and looked at her with eyes that might have said: "Now, strike me dead!"

"Oh, foolish man!" cried Tara. "Nothing you could have done could have pleased me more. Djor Kantos, I could kiss you!"

"I do not think that Olvia Marthis would mind," he said, his face now wreathed with smiles. As they spoke a body of men had entered the throne room and approached the dais. They were tall men trapped in plain harness, absolutely without ornamentation. Just as their leader reached the dais Tara had turned to Gahan, motioning him to join them.

"Djor Kantos," she said, "I bring you Turan the panthan, whose loyalty and bravery have won my love."

John Carter and the leader of the new come warriors, who were standing near, looked quickly at the little group. The former smiled an inscrutable smile, the latter addressed the Princess of Helium. " 'Turan the panthan!' " he cried. "Know you not, fair daughter of Helium, that this man you call panthan is Gahan, Jed of Gathol?"

For just a moment Tara of Helium looked her surprise; and then she shrugged her beautiful shoulders as she turned her head to cast her eyes over one of them at Gahan of Gathol.

"Jed or panthan," she said; "what difference does it make what one's slave has been?" and she laughed roguishly into the smiling face of her lover.

His story finished, John Carter rose from the chair opposite me, stretching his giant frame like some great forest-bred lion.

"You must go?" I cried, for I hated to see him leave and it seemed that he had been with me but a moment.

"The sky is already red beyond those beautiful hills of yours," he replied, "and it will soon be day."

"Just one question before you go," I begged.

"Well?" he assented, good-naturedly.

"How was Gahan able to enter the throne room garbed in O-Tar's trappings?" I asked.

"It was simple—for Gahan of Gathol," replied The War-Lord. "With the assistance of I-Gos he crept into The Hall of Chiefs before the ceremony, while the throne room and Hall of Chiefs were vacated to receive the bride. He came from the pits through the corridor that opened behind the arras at the rear of the throne, and passing into The Hall of Chiefs took his place upon the back of a riderless thoat, whose warrior was in I-Gos' repair room. When O-Tar entered and came near him Gahan fell upon him and struck him with the butt of a heavy spear. He thought that he had killed him and was surprised when O-Tar appeared to denounce him."

"And Ghek? What became of Ghek?" I insisted.

"After leading Val Dor and Floran to Tara's disabled flier, which they repaired, he accompanied them to Gathol, from where a message was sent to me in Helium. He then led a large party including A-Kor and U-Thor from the roof, where our ships landed them, down a spiral runway into the palace and guided them to the throne room. We took him back to Helium with us, where he still lives, with his single rykor which we found all but starved to death in the pits of Manator. But come! No more questions now."

I accompanied him to the east arcade where the red dawn was glowing beyond the arches.

"Good-bye!" he said.

"I can scarce believe that it is really you," I exclaimed. "Tomorrow I will be sure that I have dreamed all this."

He laughed and drawing his sword scratched a rude cross upon the concrete of one of the arches.

"If you are in doubt tomorrow," he said, "come and see if you dreamed this."

A moment later he was gone.

JETAN, OR MARTIAN CHESS

FOR THOSE WHO care for such things, and would like to try the game, I give the rules of Jetan as they were given me by John Carter. By writing the names and moves of the various pieces on bits of paper and pasting them on ordinary checker-men the game may be played quite as well as with the ornate pieces used upon Mars.

THE BOARD: Square board consisting of one hundred alternate black and orange squares.

THE PIECES: In order, as they stand upon the board in the first row, from left to right of each player.

Warrior: 2 feathers; 2 spaces straight in any direction or combination.

Padwar: 2 feathers; 2 spaces diagonal in any direction or combination.

Dwar: 3 feathers; 3 spaces straight in any direction or combination.

Flier: 3 bladed propeller; 3 spaces diagonal in any direction or combination; and may jump intervening pieces.

Chief: Diadem with ten jewels; 3 spaces in any direction; straight or diagonal or combination.

Princess: Diadem with one jewel; same as Chief, except may jump intervening pieces.

Flier: See above.

Dwar: See above.

Padwar: See above.

Warrior: See above.

And in the second row from left to right:

Thoat: Mounted warrior 2 feathers; 2 spaces, one straight and one diagonal in any direction.

Panthans (8 of them) : 1 feather; 1 space, forward, side or diagonal, but not backward.

Thoat: See above.

The game is played with twenty black pieces by one player and twenty orange by his opponent, and is presumed to have originally represented a battle between the Black race of the south and the Yellow race of the north. On Mars the board is usually arranged so that the Black pieces are played from the south and the Orange from the north.

The game is won when any piece is placed on same square with opponent's Princess, or a Chief takes a Chief.

The game is drawn when either Chief is taken by a piece other than the opposing Chief, or when both sides are reduced to three pieces, or less, of equal value and the game is not won in the ensuing ten moves, five apiece.

The Princess may not move onto a threatened square, nor may she take an opposing piece. She is entitled to one ten-space move at any time during the game. This move is called *the escape*.

Two pieces may not occupy the same square except in the final move of a game where the Princess is taken.

When a player, moving properly and in order, places one of his pieces upon a square occupied by an opponent piece, the opponent piece is considered to have been killed and is removed from the game.

The moves explained. Straight moves mean due north, south, east, or west; diagonal moves mean northeast, southeast, southwest, or northwest. A Dwar might move straight north three spaces, or north one space and east two spaces, or any similar combination of straight moves, so long as he did not cross the same square twice in a single move. This example explains combination moves.

The first move may be decided in any way that is agreeable to both players; after the first game the winner of the preceding game moves first if he chooses, or may instruct his opponent to make the first move.

Gambling: The Martians gamble at Jetan in several ways. Of course the outcome of the game indicates to whom the main stake belongs; but they also put a price upon the head of each piece, according to its value, and for each piece that a player loses he pays its value to his opponent.

The Master Mind of Mars

By

EDGAR RICE BURROUGHS

*An attendant appeared bearing the body of the
beautiful girl*

CONTENTS

"The transplanted portions of the brain are more active — that is why the ape behaves in a more human manner."

A LETTER

Helium, June 8th, 1925

My Dear Mr. Burroughs:

It was in the Fall of nineteen seventeen at an officers' training camp that I first became acquainted with John Carter,
War Lord of Barsoom, through the pages of your novel "A
Princess of Mars." The story made a profound impression
upon me and while my better judgment assured me that it
was but a highly imaginative piece of fiction, a suggestion of
the verity of it pervaded my inner consciousness to such an
extent that I found myself dreaming of Mars and John Carter,
of Dejah Thoris, of Tars Tarkas and of Woola as they had
been entities of my own experience rather than the figments
of your imagination.

It is true that in those days of strenuous preparation there
was little time for dreaming, yet there were brief moments
before sleep claimed me at night and there were my dreams.
Such dreams! Always of Mars, and during my waking hours
at night my eyes always sought out the Red Planet when he
was above the horizon and clung there seeking a solution of
the seemingly unfathomable riddle he has presented to the
Earthman for ages.

Perhaps the thing became an obsession. I know it clung to
me all during my training camp days and at night, on the
deck of the transport, I would lie on my back gazing up into
the red eye of the god of battle—my god—and wishing that,
like John Carter, I might be drawn across the great void to
the haven of my desire.

And then came the hideous days and nights in the trenches
—the rats, the vermin, the mud—with an occasional glorious
break in the monotony when we were ordered over the top. I
loved it then and I loved the bursting shells, the mad, wild
chaos of the thundering guns, but the rats and the vermin
and the mud—God! how I hated them. It sounds like boasting
I know, and I am sorry; but I wanted to write you just the

359

truth about myself. I think you will understand. And it may account for much that happened afterward.

There came at last to me what had come to so many others upon those bloody fields. It came within the week that I had received my first promotion and my captaincy, of which I was greatly proud, though humbly so; realizing as I did my youth, the great responsibility that it placed upon me as well as the opportunities it offered, not only in service to my country but, in a personal way, to the men of my command. We had advanced a matter of two kilometers and with a small detachment I was holding a very advanced position when I received orders to fall back to the new line. That is the last I remember until I regained consciousness after dark. A shell must have burst among us. What became of my men I never knew. It was cold and very dark when I awoke and at first, for an instant, I was quite comfortable—before I was fully conscious, I imagine—and then I commenced to feel pain. It grew until it seemed unbearable. It was in my legs. I reached down to feel of them, but my hand recoiled from what it found, and when I tried to move my legs I discovered that I was dead from the waist down. Then the moon came out from behind a cloud and I saw that I lay within a shell hole and that I was not alone—the dead were all about me.

It was a long time before I found the moral courage and the physical strength to draw myself up on one elbow that I might view the havoc that had been done me. One look was enough, I sank back in an agony of mental and physical anguish—my legs had been blown away from midway between the hips and knees. For some reason I was not bleeding excessively, yet I know that I had lost a great deal of blood and that I was gradually losing enough to put me out of my misery in a short time if I were not soon found; and as I lay there on my back, tortured with pain, I prayed that they would not come in time, for I shrank more from the thought of going maimed through life than I shrank from the thought of death. Then my eyes suddenly focused upon the bright red eye of Mars and there surged through me a sudden wave of hope. I stretched out my arms toward Mars, I did not seem to question or to doubt for an instant as I prayed to the god of my vocation to reach forth and succor me. I knew that he would do it, my faith was complete, and yet so great was the mental ef-

fort that I made to throw off the hideous bonds of my mutilated flesh that I felt a momentary qualm of nausea and then a
sharp click as of the snapping of a steel wire, and suddenly I
stood naked upon two good legs looking down upon the bloody
distorted thing that had been I. Just for an instant did I stand
thus before I turned my eyes aloft again to my star of destiny
and with outstretched arms stand there in the cold of that
French night—waiting.

Suddenly I felt myself drawn with the speed of thought
through the trackless wastes of interplanetary space. There
was an instant of extreme cold and utter darkness, then—

But the rest is in the manuscript that, with the aid of one
greater than either of us, I have found the means to transmit
to you with this letter. You and a few others of the chosen
will believe in it—for the rest it matters not as yet. The time
will come—but why tell you what you already know?

My salutations and my congratulations—the latter on your
good fortune in having been chosen as the medium through
which Earthmen shall become better acquainted with the
manners and customs of Barsoom, against the time that they
shall pass through space as easily as John Carter and visit the
scenes that he has described to them through you, as have I.

Your sincere friend,
ULYSSES PAXTON,
Late Captain,—th Inf.,
US. Army.

It was my first experience with a Martian watch dog.

CHAPTER I

THE HOUSE OF THE DEAD

I MUST HAVE closed my eyes involuntarily during the transition for when I opened them I was lying flat on my back gazing up into a brilliant, sun-lit sky, while standing a few feet from me and looking down upon me with the most mystified expression was as strange a looking individual as my eyes ever had rested upon. He appeared to be quite an old man, for he was wrinkled and withered beyond description. His limbs were emaciated; his ribs showed distinctly beneath his shrunken hide; his cranium was large and well developed, which, in conjunction with his wasted limbs and torso, lent him the appearance of top heaviness, as though he had a head beyond all proportion to his body, which was, I am sure, really not the case.

As he stared down upon me through enormous, many lensed spectacles I found the opportunity to examine him as minutely in return. He was, perhaps, five feet five in height, though doubtless he had been taller in youth, since he was somewhat bent; he was naked except for some rather plain and well worn leather harness which supported his weapons and pocket pouches, and one great ornament, a collar, jewel studded, that he wore around his scraggy neck—such a collar as a dowager empress of pork or real estate might barter her soul for, if she had one. His skin was red, his scant locks gray. As he looked at me his puzzled expression increased in intensity, he grasped his chin between the thumb and fingers of his left hand and slowly raising his right hand he scratched his head most deliberately. Then he spoke to me, but in a language I did not understand.

At his first words I sat up and shook my head. Then I looked about me. I was seated upon a crimson sward within a high walled enclosure, at least two, and possibly three, sides of which were formed by the outer walls of a structure that in some respects resembled more closely a feudal castle of Europe than any familiar form of architecture that comes to my mind. The façade presented to my view was ornately carved and of most irregular design, the roof line being so broken as to almost suggest a ruin, and yet the whole seemed harmonious and not without beauty. Within the enclosure grew a number of trees and shrubs, all weirdly strange and all, or almost all, profusely flowering. About them wound walks of colored pebbles among which scintillated what appeared to be rare and beautiful gems, so lovely were the strange, unearthly rays that leaped and played in the sunshine.

The old man spoke again, peremptorily this time, as though repeating a command that had been ignored, but again I shook my head. Then he lay a hand upon one of his two swords, but as he drew the weapon I leaped to my feet, with such remarkable results that I cannot even now say which of us was the more surprised. I must have sailed ten feet into the air and back about twenty feet from where I had been sitting; then I was sure that I was upon Mars (not that I had for one instant doubted it), for the effects of the lesser gravity, the color of the sward and the skin-hue of the red Martians I had seen described in the manuscripts of John Carter, those marvellous and as yet unappreciated contributions to the scientific literature of a world. There could be no doubt of it, I stood upon the soil of the Red Planet, I had come to the world of my dreams—to Barsoom.

So startled was the old man by my agility that he jumped a bit himself, though doubtless involuntarily, but, however, with certain results. His spectacles tumbled from his nose to the sward, and then it was that I discovered that the pitiful old wretch was practically blind when deprived of these artificial aids to vision, for he got to his knees and commenced to grope frantically for the lost glasses, as though his very life depended upon finding them in the instant. Possibly he thought that I might take advantage of his helplessness and slay him. Though the spectacles were enormous and lay within a couple of feet of him he could not find them, his hands, seemingly afflicted by that strange perversity that sometimes confounds our simplest acts, passing all about the lost object of their search, yet never once coming in contact with it.

As I stood watching his futile efforts and considering the advisability of restoring to him the means that would enable him more readily to find my heart with his sword point, I became aware that another had entered the enclosure.

Looking toward the building I saw a large red-man running rapidly toward the little old man of the spectacles. The newcomer was quite naked, he carried a club in one hand, and there was upon his face such an expression as unquestionably boded ill for the helpless husk of humanity grovelling, mole-like, for its lost spectacles.

My first impulse was to remain neutral in an affair that it seemed could not possibly concern me and of which I had no slightest knowledge upon which to base a predilection toward either of the parties involved; but a second glance at the face of the club-bearer aroused a question as to whether it might not concern me after all. There was that in the expression upon the man's face that betokened either an inherent savageness of disposition or a maniacal cast of mind which might turn his evidently murderous attentions upon me after he had dispatched his elderly victim, while, in outward appearance at least, the latter was a sane and relatively harmless individual. It is true that his move to draw his sword against me was not indicative of a friendly disposition toward me, but at least, if there were any choice, he seemed the lesser of two evils.

He was still groping for his spectacles and the naked man was almost upon him as I reached the decision to cast my lot upon the side of the old man. I was twenty feet away, naked and unarmed, but to cover the distance with my Earthly muscles required but an instant, and a naked sword lay by the old man's side where he had discarded it the better to search for his spectacles. So it was that I faced the attacker at the instant that he came within striking distance of his victim, and the blow which had been intended for another was aimed at me. I side-stepped it and then I learned that the greater agility of my Earthly muscles had its disadvantages as well as its advantages, for, indeed, I had to learn to walk at the very instant that I had to learn to fight with a new weapon against a maniac armed with a bludgeon, or at least, so I assumed him to be and I think that it is not strange that I should have done so, what with his frightful show of rage and the terrible expression upon his face.

As I stumbled about endeavoring to accustom myself to the new conditions, I found that instead of offering any serious opposition to my antagonist I was hard put to it to escape death at his hands, so often did I stumble and fall sprawling upon the scarlet sward; so that the duel from its inception became but a series of efforts, upon his part to reach and crush me with his great club, and upon mine to dodge and elude him. It was mortifying, but it is the truth. However, this did not last indefinitely, for soon I learned, and quickly too under the exigencies of the situation, to command my muscles, and then I stood my ground and when he aimed a blow at me, and I had dodged it, I touched him with my point and brought blood along with a savage roar of pain. He went more cautiously then, and taking advantage of the change I pressed him so that he fell back. The effect upon me was magical, giving me new confidence, so that I set upon him in good earnest, thrusting and cutting until I had him bleeding in a half dozen places, yet taking good care to avoid his mighty swings, any one of which would have felled an ox.

In my attempts to elude him in the beginning of the duel we had crossed the enclosure and were now fighting at a considerable distance from the point of our first meeting. It now happened that I stood facing toward that point at the moment that the old man regained his spectacles which he quickly adjusted to his eyes. Immediately he looked about until he discovered us, whereupon he commenced to yell excitedly at us at the same time running in our direction and drawing his short-sword as he ran. The red-man was pressing me hard, but I had gained almost complete control of myself, and fearing that I was soon to have two antagonists instead of one I set upon him with redoubled intensity. He missed me by the fraction of an inch, the wind in the wake of his bludgeon fanning my scalp, but he left an opening into which I stepped, running my sword fairly through his heart. At least I thought that I had pierced his heart, but I had forgotten what I had once read in one of John Carter's manuscripts to the effect that all the Martian internal organs are not disposed identically with those of Earthmen. However, the immediate results were quite as satisfactory as though I had found his heart, for the wound was sufficiently grievous to place him *hors de combat*, and at that instant the old gentleman arrived. He found me ready, but I had mistaken his intentions. He made no unfriendly gestures with his weapon, but seemed to be trying to convince me that he had no intention of harming me. He was very excited and apparently tremendously annoyed that I could not understand him, and perplexed, too. He hopped about screaming strange sentences at me that bore the tones of peremptory commands, rabid invective and impotent rage. But the fact that he had returned his sword to its scabbard had greater significance than all his jabbering, and when he ceased to yell at me and commenced to talk in a sort of pantomime I realized that he was making overtures of peace if not of friendship, so I lowered my point and bowed. It was all that I could think of to assure him that I had no immediate intention of spitting him.

He seemed satisfied and at once turned his attention to the fallen man. He examined his pulse and listened to his heart, then nodding his head, he arose and taking a whistle from one of his pocket pouches sounded a single loud blast. There emerged immediately from one of the surrounding buildings a score of naked red-men who came running toward us. None was armed. To these he issued a few curt orders, whereupon they gathered the fallen one in their arms and bore him off. Then the old man started toward the building, motioning me to accompany him. There seemed nothing else for me to do but obey. Wherever I might be upon Mars, the chances were a million to one that I would be among enemies; and so I was as well off here as elsewhere and must depend upon my own resourcefulness, skill and agility to make my way upon the Red Planet.

The old man led me into a small chamber from which opened numerous doors, through one of which they were just bearing my late antagonist. We followed into a large, brilliantly lighted chamber wherein there burst upon my astounded vision the most gruesome scene that I ever had beheld. Rows upon rows of tables arranged in parallel lines filled the room and with few exceptions each table bore a similar grisly burden, a partially dismembered or otherwise mutilated human corpse. Above each table was a shelf bearing containers of various sizes and shapes, while from the bottom of the shelf depended numerous surgical instruments, suggesting that my entrance upon Barsoom was to be through a gigantic medical college.

At a word from the old man, those who bore the Barsoomian I had wounded laid him upon an empty table and left the apartment. Whereupon my host, if so I may call him, for certainly he was not as yet my captor, motioned me forward. While he conversed in ordinary tones, he made two incisions in the body of my late antagonist; one, I imagine, in a large vein and one in an artery, to which he deftly attached the ends of two tubes, one of which was connected with an empty glass receptacle and the other with a similar receptacle filled with a colorless, transparent liquid resembling clear water. The connections made, the old gentleman pressed a button controlling a small motor, whereupon the victim's blood was pumped into the empty jar while the contents of the other was forced into the emptying veins and arteries.

The tones and gestures of the old man as he addressed me during this operation convinced me that he was explaining in detail the method and purpose of what was transpiring, but as I understood no word of all he said I was as much in the dark when he had completed his discourse as I was before he started it, though what I had seen made it appear reasonable to believe that I was witnessing an ordinary Barsoomian embalming. Having removed the tubes the old man closed the openings he had made by covering them with bits of what appeared to be heavy adhesive tape and then motioned me to follow him. We went from room to room, in each of which were the same gruesome exhibits. At many of the bodies the old man paused to make a brief examination or to refer to what appeared to be a record of the case, that hung upon a hook at the head of each of the tables.

From the last of the chambers we visited upon the first floor my host led me up an inclined runway to the second floor where there were rooms similar to those below, but here the tables bore whole rather than mutilated bodies, all of which were patched in various places with adhesive tape. As we were passing among the bodies in one of these rooms a Barsoomian girl, whom I took to be a servant or slave, entered and addressed the old man, whereupon he signed me to follow him and together we descended another runway to the first floor of another building.

Here, in a large, gorgeously decorated and sumptuously furnished apartment an elderly red-woman awaited us. She appeared to be quite old and her face was terribly disfigured as by some injury. Her trappings were magnificent and she was attended by a score of women and armed warriors, suggesting that she was a person of some consequence, but the little old man treated her quite brusquely, as I could see, quite to the horror of her attendants.

Their conversation was lengthy and at the conclusion of it, at the direction of the woman, one of her male escort advanced and opening a pocket pouch at his side withdrew a handful of what appeared to me to be Martian coins. A quantity of these he counted out and handed to the little old man, who then beckoned the woman to follow him, a gesture which included me. Several of her women and guard started to accompany us, but these the old man waved back peremptorily; whereupon there ensued a heated discussion between the woman and one of her warriors on one side and the old man on the other, which terminated in his proffering the return of the woman's money with a disgusted air. This seemed to settle the argument, for she refused the coins, spoke briefly to her people and accompanied the old man and myself alone.

He led the way to the second floor and to a chamber which I had not previously visited. It closely resembled the others except that all the bodies therein were of young women, many of them of great beauty. Following closely at the heels of the old man the woman inspected the gruesome exhibit with painstaking care. Thrice she passed slowly among the tables examining their ghastly burdens. Each time she paused longest before a certain one which bore the figure of the most beautiful creature I had ever looked upon; then she returned the fourth time to it and stood looking long and earnestly into the dead face. For awhile she stood there talking with the old man, apparently asking innumerable questions, to which he returned quick, brusque replies, then she indicated the body with a gesture and nodded assent to the withered keeper of this ghastly exhibit.

Immediately the old fellow sounded a blast upon his whistle, summoning a number of servants to whom he issued brief instructions, after which he led us to another chamber, a smaller one in which were several empty tables similar to those upon which the corpses lay in adjoining rooms. Two female slaves or attendants were in this room and at a word from their master they removed the trappings from the old woman, unloosed her hair and helped her to one of the tables. Here she was thoroughly sprayed with what I presume was an anti-septic solution of some nature, carefully dried and removed to another table, at a distance of about twenty inches from which stood a second parallel table.

Now the door of the chamber swung open and two attendants appeared bearing the body of the beautiful girl we had seen in the adjoining room. This they deposited upon the table the old woman had just quitted and as she had been sprayed so was the corpse, after which it was transferred to the table beside that on which she lay. The little old man now made two incisions in the body of the old woman, just as he had in the body of the red-man who had fallen to my sword; her blood was drawn from her veins and the clear liquid pumped into them, life left her and she lay upon the polished ersite slab that formed the table top, as much a corpse as the poor, beautiful, dead creature at her side.

The little, old man, who had removed the harness down to his waist and been thoroughly sprayed, now selected a sharp knife from among the instruments above the table and re-moved the old woman's scalp, following the hair line entirely around her head. In a similar manner he then removed the scalp from the corpse of the young woman, after which, by means of a tiny circular saw attached to the end of a flexible, revolving shaft he sawed through the skull of each, follow-ing the line exposed by the removal of the scalps. This and the balance of the marvellous operation was so skillfully per-formed as to baffle description. Suffice to say that at the end of four hours he had transferred the brain of each woman to the brain pan of the other, deftly connected the severed nerves and ganglia, replaced the skulls and scalps and bound both heads securely with his peculiar adhesive tape, which was not only antiseptic and healing but anaesthetic, locally, as well.

He now reheated the blood that he had withdrawn from the body of the old woman, adding a few drops of some clear chemical solution, withdrew the liquid from the veins of the beautiful corpse, replacing it with the blood of the old woman and simultaneously administering a hypodermic injection.

During the entire operation he had not spoken a word. Now he issued a few instructions in his curt manner to his

assistants, motioned me to follow him, and left the room. He
led me to a distant part of the building or series of buildings
that composed the whole, ushered me into a luxurious apartment, opened the door to a Barsoomian bath and left me in the
hands of trained servants. Refreshed and rested I left the bath
after an hour of relaxation to find harness and trappings awaiting me in the adjoining chamber. Though plain, they were of
good material, but there were no weapons with them.

Naturally I had been thinking much upon the strange
things I had witnessed since my advent upon Mars, but what
puzzled me most lay in the seemingly inexplicable act of the
old woman in paying my host what was evidently a considerable sum to murder her and transfer to the inside of her skull
the brain of a corpse. Was it the outcome of some horrible religious fanaticism, or was there an explanation that my Earthly
mind could not grasp?

I had reached no decision in the matter when I was summoned to follow a slave to another and near-by apartment
where I found my host awaiting me before a table loaded with
delicious foods, to which, it is needless to say, I did ample
justice after my long fast and longer weeks of rough army fare.

During the meal my host attempted to converse with me,
but, naturally, the effort was fruitless of results. He waxed
quite excited at times and upon three distinct occasions laid
his hand upon one of his swords when I failed to comprehend
what he was saying to me, an action which resulted in a growing conviction upon my part that he was partially demented;
but he evinced sufficient self-control in each instance to avert
a catastrophe for one of us.

The meal over he sat for a long time in deep meditation,
then a sudden resolution seemed to possess him. He turned
suddenly upon me with a faint suggestion of a smile and
dove headlong into what was to prove an intensive course of
instruction in the Barsoomian language. It was long after
dark before he permitted me to retire for the night, conducting me himself to a large apartment, the same in which I
had found my new harness, where he pointed out a pile of
rich sleeping silks and furs, bid me a Barsoomian good-night
and left me, locking the door after him upon the outside,
and leaving me to guess whether I were more guest or prisoner.

CHAPTER II

PREFERMENT

THREE WEEKS PASSED rapidly. I had mastered enough of the Barsoomian tongue to enable me to converse with my host in a reasonably satisfactory manner, and I was also progressing slowly in the mastery of the written language of his nation, which is different, of course, from the written language of all other Barsoomian nations, though the spoken language of all is identical. In these three weeks I had learned much of the strange place in which I was half guest and half prisoner and of my remarkable host-jailer, Ras Thavas, the old surgeon of Toonol, whom I had accompanied almost constantly day after day until gradually there had unfolded before my astounded faculties an understanding of the purposes of the institution over which he ruled and in which he labored practically alone; for the slaves and attendants that served him were but hewers of wood and carriers of water. It was his brain alone and his skill that directed the sometimes beneficent, the sometimes malevolent, but always marvellous activities of his life's work.

Ras Thavas himself was as remarkable as the things he accomplished. He was never intentionally cruel; he was not, I am sure, intentionally wicked. He was guilty of the most diabolical cruelties and the basest of crimes; yet in the next moment he might perform a deed that if duplicated upon Earth would have raised him to the highest pinnacle of man's esteem. Though I know that I am safe in saying that he was never prompted to a cruel or criminal act by base motives, neither was he ever urged to a humanitarian one by high motives. He had a purely scientific mind entirely devoid of the cloying influences of sentiment, of which he possessed none. His was a practical mind, as evidenced by the enormous fees he demanded for his professional services; yet I know that he would not operate for money alone and I have seen him devote days to the study of a scientific problem the solution of which could add nothing to his wealth, while the quarters that he furnished his waiting clients were overflowing with wealthy patrons waiting to pour money into his coffers.

His treatment of me was based entirely upon scientific requirements. I offered a problem. I was either, quite evidently, not a Barsoomian at all, or I was of a species of which he had no knowledge. It therefore best suited the purposes of science that I be preserved and studied. I knew much about my own planet. It pleased Ras Thavas' scientific mind to milk me of all I knew in the hope that he might derive some suggestion that would solve one of the Barsoomian scientific riddles that still baffle their savants; but he was compelled to admit that in this respect I was a total loss, not alone because I was densely ignorant upon practically all scientific subjects, but because the learned sciences on Earth have not advanced even to the swaddling-clothes stage as compared with the remarkable progress of corresponding activities on Mars. Yet he kept me by him, training me in many of the minor duties of his vast laboratory. I was entrusted with the formula of the "embalming fluid" and taught how to withdraw a subject's blood and replace it with this marvellous preservative that arrests decay without altering in the minutest detail the nerve or tissue structure of the body. I learned also the secret of the few drops of solution which, added to the rewarmed blood before it is returned to the veins of the subject, revitalizes the latter and restores to normal and healthy activity each and every organ of the body.

He told me once why he had permitted me to learn these things that he had kept a secret from all others and why he kept me with him at all times in preference to any of the numerous individuals of his own race that served him and me in lesser capacities both day and night.

"Vad Varo," he said, using the Barsoomian name that he had given me because he insisted that my own name was meaningless and impractical, "for many years I have needed an assistant, but heretofore I have never felt that I had discovered one who might work here for me wholeheartedly and disinterestedly without ever having reason to go elsewhere or to divulge my secrets to others. You, in all Barsoom, are unique—you have no other friend or acquaintance than myself. Were you to leave me you would find yourself in a world of enemies, for all are suspicious of a stranger. You would not survive a dozen dawns and you would be cold and hungry and miserable—a wretched outcast in a hostile world. Here you have every luxury that the mind of man can devise or the hand of man produce, and you are occupied with work of such engrossing interest that your every hour must be fruitful of unparalleled satisfaction. There is no selfish reason, therefore, why you should leave me and there is every reason why you should remain. I expect no loyalty other than that which may be prompted by egoism. You make an ideal assistant, not only for the reasons I have just given you, but because you are intelligent and quick witted, and now I have decided, after observing you carefully for a sufficient time, that you can serve me in yet another capacity—that of personal body-guard.

"You may have noticed that I alone of all those connected with my laboratory am armed. This is unusual upon Barsoom, where people of all classes, and all ages and both sexes habitually go armed. But many of these people I could not trust armed as they would slay me; and were I to give arms to those whom I might trust, who knows but that the others would obtain possession of them and slay me, or even those whom I had trusted turn against me, for there is not one who might not wish to go forth from this place back among his own people—only you, Vad Varo, for there is no other place for you to go. So I have decided to give you weapons.

"You saved my life once. A similar opportunity might again present itself. I know that, being a reasoning and reasonable creature, you will not slay me, for you have nothing to gain and everything to lose by my death, which would leave you friendless and unprotected in a world of strangers where assassination is the order of society and natural death one of the rarest of phenomena. Here are your arms." He stepped to a cabinet which he unlocked, displaying an assortment of weapons, and selected for me a long-sword, a short-sword, a pistol and a dagger.

"You seem sure of my loyalty, Ras Thavas," I said.

He shrugged his shoulders. "I am only sure that I know perfectly where your interests lie—sentimentalists have words: love, loyalty, friendship, enmity, jealousy, hate, a thousand others; a waste of words—one word defines them all: self-interest. All men of intelligence realize this. They analyse an individual and by his predilections and his needs they classify him as a friend or foe, leaving to the weak minded idiots who like to be deceived the drooling drivel of sentiment."

I smiled as I buckled my weapons to my harness, but I held my peace. Nothing could be gained by arguing with the man and, too, I felt quite sure that in any purely academic controversy I should get the worst of it; but many of the matters of which he had spoken had aroused my curiosity and one had reawakened in my mind a matter to which I had given considerable thought. While partially explained by some of his remarks I still wondered why the red-man from whom I had rescued him had seemed so venomously bent upon slaying him the day of my advent upon Barsoom, and so, as we sat chatting after our evening meal, I asked him.

"A sentimentalist," he said. "A sentimentalist of the most pronounced type. Why that fellow hated me with a venom absolutely unbelievable by any of the reactions of a trained, analytical mind such as mine; but having witnessed his reactions I become cognizant of a state of mind that I cannot of myself even imagine. Consider the facts. He was the victim of assassination—a young warrior in the prime of life, possessing a handsome face and a splendid physique. One of my agents paid his relatives a satisfactory sum for the corpse and brought it to me. It is thus that I obtain practically all of my material. I treated it in the manner with which you are familiar. For a year the body lay in the laboratory, there being no occasion during that time that I had use for it; but eventually a rich client came, a not overly prepossessing man of considerable years. He had fallen desperately in love with a young woman who was attended by many handsome suitors. My client had more money than any of them, more brains, more experience, but he lacked the one thing that each of the others had that always weighs heavily with the undeveloped, unreasoning, sentiment-ridden minds of young females —good looks.

"Now 378-J-493811-P had what my client lacked and could afford to purchase. Quickly we reached an agreement as to price and I transferred the brain of my rich client to the head of 378-J-493811-P and my client went away and for all I know won the hand of the beautiful moron; and 378-J-493811-P might have rested on indefinitely upon his ersite slab until I needed him or a part of him in my work, had I not, merely by chance, selected him for resurgence because of an existing need for another male slave.

"Mind you now, the man had been murdered. He was dead. I bought and paid for the corpse and all there was in it. He might have lain dead forever upon one of my ersite slabs had I not breathed new life into his dead veins. Did he have the brains to view the transaction in a wise and dispassionate manner? He did not. His sentimental reactions caused him to reproach me because I had given him another body, though it seemed to me that, looking at the matter from a standpoint of sentiment, if one must, he should have considered me as a benefactor for having given him life again in a perfectly healthy, if somewhat used, body.

"He had spoken to me upon the subject several times, begging me to restore his body to him, a thing which, of course, as I explained to him, was utterly out of the question unless chance happened to bring to my laboratory the corpse of the client who had purchased his carcass—a contingency quite beyond the pale of possibility for one as wealthy as my client. The fellow even suggested that I permit him to go forth and assassinate my client, bringing the body back that I might reverse the operation and restore his body to his brain. When I refused to divulge the name of the present possessor of his body he grew sulky, but until the very hour of your arrival, when he attacked me, I did not suspect the depth of his hate complex.

"Sentiment is indeed a bar to all progress. We of Toonol are probably less subject to its vagaries than most other nations upon Barsoom, but yet most of my fellow countrymen are victims of it in varying degrees. It has its rewards and compensations, however. Without it we could preserve no stable form of government and the Phundahlians, or some other people, would overrun and conquer us; but enough of our lower classes have sentiment to a sufficient degree to give them loyalty to the Jeddak of Toonol and the upper classes are brainy enough to know that it is to their own best interests to keep him upon his throne.

"The Phundahlians, upon the other hand, are egregious sentimentalists, filled with crass stupidities and superstitions, slaves to every variety of brain withering conceit. Why the very fact that they keep the old termagant, Xaxa, on the throne brands them with their stupid idiocy. She is an igno-

rant, arrogant, selfish, stupid, cruel virago, yet the Phundahlians would fight and die for her because her father was Jeddak of Phundahl. She taxes them until they can scarce
stagger beneath their burden, she misrules them, exploits
them, betrays them, and they fall down and worship at her
feet. Why? Because her father was Jeddak of Phundahl and
his father before him and so on back into antiquity; because
they are ruled by sentiment rather than reason; because their
wicked rulers play upon this sentiment.

"She had nothing to recommend her to a sane person—
not even beauty. You know, you saw her."

"I saw her?" I demanded.

"You assisted me the day that we gave her old brain a new
casket—the day you arrived from what you call your Earth."

"She! That old woman was Jeddara of Phundahl?"

"That was Xaxa," he assured me.

"Why, you did not accord her the treatment that one of
the Earth would suppose would be accorded a ruler, and
so I had no idea that she was more than a rich old woman."

"I am Ras Thavas," said the old man. "Why should I incline
my head to any other? In my world nothing counts but
brain and in that respect, and without egotism, I may say
that I acknowledge no superior."

"Then you are not without sentiment," I said, smiling. "You
acknowledge pride in your intellect!"

"It is not pride," he said, patiently, for him, "it is merely a
fact that I state. A fact that I should have no difficulty in proving. In all probability I have the most highly developed and
perfectly functioning mind among all the learned men of my
acquaintance, and reason indicates that this fact also sug-
gests that I possess the most highly developed and perfectly
functioning mind upon Barsoom. From what I know of Earth
and from what I have seen of you, I am convinced that there
is no mind upon your planet that may even faintly approxi-
mate in power that which I have developed during a thous-
and years of active study and research. Rasoom (Mercury) or
Cosoom (Venus) may possibly support intelligences equal to
or even greater than mine. While we have made some study
of their thought waves, our instruments are not yet sufficiently
developed to more than suggest that they are of extreme refinement, power and flexibility."

"And what of the girl whose body you gave to the Jeddara?" I asked, irrelevantly, for my mind could not efface the memory of that sweet body that must, indeed, have possessed an equally sweet and fine brain.

"Merely a subject! Merely a subject!" he replied with a wave of his hand.

"What will become of her?" I insisted.

"What difference does it make?" he demanded. "I bought her with a batch of prisoners of war. I do not even recall from what country my agent obtained them, or from whence they originated. Such matters are of no import."

"She was alive when you bought her?" I demanded.

"Yes. Why?"

"You—er—ah—killed her, then?"

"Killed her! No; I preserved her. That was some ten years ago. Why should I permit her to grow old and wrinkled? She would no longer have the same value then, would she? No, I preserved her. When Xaxa bought her she was just as fresh and young as the day she arrived. I kept her a long time. Many women looked at her and wanted her face and figure, but it took a Jeddara to afford her. She brought the highest price that I have ever been paid.

"Yes, I kept her a long time, but I knew that some day she would bring my price. She was indeed beautiful and so sentiment has its uses—were it not for sentiment there would be no fools to support this work that I am doing, thus permitting me to carry on investigations of far greater merit. You would be surprised, I know, were I to tell you that I feel that I am almost upon the point of being able to reproduce rational human beings through the action upon certain chemical combinations of a group of rays probably entirely undiscovered by your scientists, if I am to judge by the paucity of your knowledge concerning such things."

"I would not be surprised," I assured him. "I would not be surprised by anything that you might accomplish."

CHAPTER III

VALLA DIA

I LAY AWAKE a long time that night thinking of 4296-E-2631-H, the beautiful girl whose perfect body had been stolen to furnish a gorgeous setting for the cruel brain of a tyrant. It seemed such a horrid crime that I could not rid my mind of it and I think that contemplation of it sowed the first seed of my hatred and loathing for Ras Thavas. I could not conjure a creature so utterly devoid of bowels of compassion as to even consider for a moment the frightful ravishing of that sweet and lovely body for even the holiest of purposes, much less one that could have been induced to do so for filthy pelf.

So much did I think upon the girl that night that her image was the first to impinge upon my returning consciousness at dawn, and after I had eaten, Ras Thavas not having appeared, I went directly to the storage room where the poor thing was. Here she lay, identified only by a small panel, bearing a number: 4296-E-2631-H. The body of an old woman with a disfigured face lay before me in the rigid immobility of death; yet that was not the figure that I saw, but instead, a vision of radiant loveliness whose imprisoned soul lay dormant beneath those graying locks.

The creature here with the face and form of Xaxa was not Xaxa at all, for all that made the other what she was had been transferred to this cold corpse. How frightful would be the awakening, should awakening ever come! I shuddered to think of the horror that must overwhelm the girl when first she realized the horrid crime that had been perpetrated upon her. Who was she? What story lay locked in that dead and silent brain? What loves must have been hers whose beauty was so great and upon whose fair face had lain the indelible imprint of graciousness! Would Ras Thavas ever arouse her from this happy semblance of death?—far happier than any quickening ever could be for her. I shrank from the thought of her awakening and yet I longed to hear her speak, to know that the brain lived again, to learn her name, to listen to the story of this gentle life that had been so rudely snatched from its proper environment and so cruelly bandied by the hand of Fate. And suppose she were awakened!

Suppose she were awakened and that I—A hand was laid upon my shoulder and I turned to look into the face of Ras Thavas.

"You seem interested in this subject," he said.

"I was wondering," I replied, "what the reaction of this girl's brain would be were she to awaken to the discovery that she had become an old, disfigured woman."

He stroked his chin and eyed me narrowly. "An interesting experiment," he mused. "I am gratified to discover that you are taking a scientific interest in the labors that I am carrying on. The psychological phases of my work I have, I must confess, rather neglected during the past hundred years or so, though I formerly gave them a great deal of attention. It would be interesting to observe and study several of these cases. This one, especially, might prove of value to you as an initial study, it being simple and regular. Later we will let you examine into a case where a man's brain has been transferred to a woman's skull, and a woman's brain to a man's. There are also the interesting cases where a portion of diseased or injured brain has been replaced by a portion of the brain from another subject; and, for experimental purposes alone, those human brains that have been transplanted to the craniums of beasts, and *vice versa*, offer tremendous opportunities for observation. I have in mind one case in which I transferred half the brain of an ape to the skull of a man, after having removed half of his brain, which I grafted upon the remaining part of the brain in the ape's skull. That was a matter of several years ago and I have often thought that I should like to recall these two subjects and note the results. I shall have to have a look at them—as I recall it they are in vault L-42-X, beneath building 4-J-21. We shall have to look at them some day soon—it has been years since I have been below. There must be some very interesting specimens there that have escaped my mind. But come! let us recall 4296-E-2631-H."

"No!" I exclaimed, laying a hand upon his arm. "It would be horrible."

He turned a surprised look upon me and then a nasty, sneering smile curled his lips. "Maudlin, sentimental fool!" he cried. "Who dare say no to me?"

I laid a hand upon the hilt of my long-sword and looked him steadily in the eye. "Ras Thavas," I said, "you are mas-

ter in your own house; but while I am your guest treat me
with courtesy."

He returned my look for a moment but his eyes wavered.
"I was hasty," he said. "Let it pass." That, I let answer for an
apology—really it was more than I had expected—but the
event was not unfortunate. I think he treated me with far
greater respect thereafter; but now he turned immediately
to the slab bearing the mortal remains of 4296-E-2631-H.

"Prepare the subject for revivification," he said, "and
make what study you can of·all its reactions." With that he
left the room.

I was now fairly adept at this work which I set about with
some misgivings but with the assurance that I was doing right
in obeying Ras Thavas while I remained a member of his
entourage. The blood that had once flowed through the veins
of the beautiful body that Ras Thavas had sold to Xaxa reposed in an hermetically sealed vessel upon the shelf above
the corpse. As I had before done in other cases beneath the
watchful eyes of the old surgeon I now did for the first time
alone. The blood heated, the incisions made, the tubes attached and the few drops of life-giving solution added to the
blood, I was now ready to restore life to that delicate brain
that had lain dead for ten years. As my finger rested upon
the little button that actuated the motor that was to send
the revivifying liquid into those dormant veins, I experienced
such a sensation as I imagine no mortal man has ever felt.

I had become master of life and death, and yet at this moment that I stood there upon the point of resurrecting the
dead I felt more like a murderer than a savior. I tried to view
the procedure dispassionately through the cold eye of science,
but I failed miserably. I could only see a stricken girl grieving
for her lost beauties. With a muffled oath I turned away. I
could not do it! And then, as though an outside force had
seized upon me, my finger moved unerringly to the button
and pressed it. I cannot explain it, unless upon the theory of
dual mentality, which may explain many things. Perhaps
my subjective mind directed that act. I do not know. Only I
know that I did it, the motor started, the level of the blood
in the container commenced gradually to lower.

Spell-bound, I stood watching. Presently the vessel was
empty. I shut off the motor, removed the tubes, sealed the

openings with tape. The red glow of life tinged the body, replacing the sallow, purplish hue of death. The breasts rose and fell regularly, the head turned slightly and the eyelids moved. A faint sigh issued from between the parting lips. For a long time there was no other sign of life, then, suddenly, the eyes opened. They were dull at first, but presently they commenced to fill with questioning wonderment. They rested on me and then passed on about that portion of the room that was visible from the position of the body. Then they came back to me and remained steadily fixed upon my countenance after having once surveyed me up and down. There was still the questioning in them, but there was no fear.

"Where am I?" she asked. The voice was that of an old woman—high and harsh. A startled expression filled her eyes. "What is the matter with me? What is wrong with my voice? What has happened?"

I laid a hand upon her forehead. "Don't bother about it now," I said, soothingly. "Wait until sometime when you are stronger. Then I will tell you."

She sat up. "I am strong," she said, and then her eyes swept her lower body and limbs and a look of utter horror crossed her face. "What has happened to me? In the name of my first ancestor, what has happened to me?"

The shrill, harsh voice grated upon me. It was the voice of Xaxa and Xaxa now must possess the sweet musical tones that alone would have harmonized with the beautiful face she had stolen. I tried to forget those strident notes and think only of the pulchritude of the envelope that had once graced the soul within this old and withered carcass.

She extended a hand and laid it gently upon mine. The act was beautiful, the movements graceful. The brain of the girl directed the muscles, but the old, rough vocal chords of Xaxa could give forth no sweeter notes. "Tell me, please!" she begged. There were tears in the old eyes, I'll venture for the first time in many years. "Tell me! You do not seem unkind."

And so I told her. She listened intently and when I was through she sighed. "After all," she said, "it is not so dreadful, now that I really know. It is better than being dead." That made me glad that I had pressed the button. She was glad to be alive, even draped in the hideous carcass of Xaxa.

I told her as much.

"You were so beautiful," I told her.

"And now I am so ugly?" I made no answer.

"After all, what difference does it make?" she inquired presently. "This old body cannot change me, or make me different from what I have always been. The good in me remains and whatever of sweetness and kindness, and I can be happy to be alive and perhaps to do some good. I was terrified at first, because I did not know what had happened to me. I thought that maybe I had contracted some terrible disease that had so altered me—that horrified me; but now that I know—pouf! what of it?"

"You are wonderful," I said. "Most women would have gone mad with the horror and grief of it—to lose such wondrous beauty as was yours—and you do not care."

"Oh, yes, I care, my friend," she corrected me, "but I do not care enough to ruin my life in all other respects because of it, or to cast a shadow upon the lives of those around me. I have had my beauty and enjoyed it. It is not an unalloyed happiness I can assure you. Men killed one another because of it; two great nations went to war because of it; and perhaps my father lost his throne or his life—I do not know, for I was captured by the enemy while the war still raged. It may be raging yet and men dying because I was too beautiful. No one will fight for me now, though," she added, with a rueful smile.

"Do you know how long you have been here?" I asked.

"Yes," she replied. "It was day before yesterday that they brought me hither."

"It was ten years ago," I told her.

"Ten years! Impossible."

I pointed to the corpses around us. "You have lain like this for ten years," I explained. "There are subjects here who have lain thus for fifty, Ras Thavas tells me."

"Ten years! Ten years! What may not have happened in ten years! It is better thus. I should fear to go back now. I should not want to know that my father, my mother too, perhaps, were gone. It is better thus. Perhaps you will let me sleep again? May I not?"

"That remains with Ras Thavas," I replied; "but for a while I am to observe you."

"Observe me?"

"Study you—your reactions."

"Ah! and what good will that do?"

"It may do some good in the world."

"It may give this horrid Ras Thavas some new ideas for his torture chamber—some new scheme for coining money from the suffering of his victims," she said, her harsh voice saddened.

"Some of his works are good," I told her. "The money he makes permits him to maintain this wonderful establishment where he constantly carries on countless experiments. Many of his operations are beneficent. Yesterday a warrior was brought in whose arm was crushed beyond repair. Ras Thavas gave him a new arm. A demented child was brought. Ras Thavas gave her a new brain. The arm and the brain were taken from two who had met violent deaths. Through Ras Thavas they were permitted, after death, to give life and happiness to others."

She thought for a moment. "I am content," she said. "I only hope that you will always be the observer."

Presently Ras Thavas came and examined her. "A good subject," he said. He looked at the chart where I had made a very brief record following the other entries relative to the history of Case No. 4296-E-2631-H. Of course this is, naturally, a rather free translation of this particular identification number. The Barsoomians have no alphabet such as ours and their numbering system is quite different. The thirteen characters above were represented by four Toonolian characters, yet the meaning was quite the same—they represented, in contracted form, the case number, the room, the table and the building.

"The subject will be quartered near you where you may regularly observe it," continued Ras Thavas. "There is a chamber adjoining yours. I will see that it is unlocked. Take the subject there. When not under your observation, lock it in." *It* was only another *case* to him.

I took the girl, if I may so call her, to her quarters. On the way I asked her her name, for it seemed to me an unnecessary discourtesy always to address her and refer to her as 4296-E-2631-H, and this I explained to her.

"It is considerate of you to think of that," she said, "but

really that is all that I am here—just another subject for vivisection."

"You are more than that to me," I told her. "You are friendless and helpless. I want to be of service to you—to make your lot easier if I can."

"Thank you again," she said. "My name is Valla Dia, and yours?"

"Ras Thavas calls me Vad Varo," I told her.

"But that is not your name?"

"My name is Ulysses Paxton."

"It is a strange name, unlike any that I have ever heard, but you are unlike any man I have ever seen—you do not seem Barsoomian. Your color in unlike that of any race."

"I am not of Barsoom, but from Earth, the planet you sometimes call Jasoom. That is why I differ in appearance from any you have known before."

"Jasoom! There is another Jasoomian here whose fame has reached to the remotest corners of Barsoom, but I never have seen him."

"John Carter?" I asked.

"Yes, the Warlord. He was of Helium and my people were not friendly with those of Helium. I never could understand how he came here. And now there is another from Jasoom—how can it be? How did you cross the great void?"

I shook my head. "I cannot even guess," I told her.

"Jasoom must be peopled with wonderful men," she said. It was a pretty compliment.

"As Barsoom is with beautiful women," I replied.

She glanced down ruefully at her old and wrinkled body.

"I have seen the real you," I said gently.

"I hate to think of my face," she said. "I know it is a frightful thing."

"It is not you, remember that when you see it and do not feel too badly."

"Is it as bad as that?" she asked.

I did not reply. "Never mind," she said presently. "If I had not beauty of the soul, I was not beautiful, no matter how perfect my features may have been; but if I possessed beauty of the soul then I have it now. So I can think beautiful thoughts and perform beautiful deeds and that, I think, is the real test of beauty, after all."

"And there is hope," I added, almost in a whisper.

"Hope? No, there is no hope, if what you mean to suggest is that I may some time regain my lost self. You have told me enough to convince me that that can never be."

"We will not speak of it," I said; 'but we may think of it and sometimes thinking a great deal of a thing helps us to find a way to get it, if we want it badly enough."

"I do not want to hope," she said, "for it will but mean disappointment for me. I shall be happy as I am. Hoping, I should always be unhappy."

I had ordered food for her and after it was brought Ras Thavas sent for me and I left her, locking the door of her chamber as the old surgeon had instructed. I found Ras Thavas in his office, a small room which adjoined a very large one in which were a score of clerks arranging and classifying reports from various departments of the great laboratory. He arose as I entered.

"Come with me, Vad Varo," he directed. "We will have a look at the two cases in L-42-X, the two of which I spoke."

"The man with half a simian brain and the ape with a half human brain?" I asked.

He nodded and preceded me toward the runway that led to the vaults beneath the building. As we descended, the corridors and passageways indicated long disuse. The floors were covered with an impalpable dust, long undisturbed; the tiny radium bulbs that faintly illuminated the sub-barsoomian depths were likewise coated. As we proceeded, we passed many doorways on either side, each marked with its descriptive hieroglyphic. Several of the openings had been tightly sealed with masonry. What gruesome secrets were hid within? At last we came to L-42-X. Here the bodies were arranged on shelves, several rows of which almost completely filled the room from floor to ceiling, except for a rectangular space in the center of the chamber, which accommodated an ersite topped operating table with its array of surgical instruments, its motor and other laboratory equipment.

Ras Thavas searched out the subjects of his strange experiment and together we carried the human body to the table. While Ras Thavas attached the tubes I returned for the vessel of blood which reposed upon the same shelf with the corpse. The now familiar method of revivification was soon accomplished and presently we were watching the return of consciousness to the subject.

The man sat up and looked at us, then he cast a quick glance about the chamber; there was a savage light in his eyes as they returned to us. Slowly he backed from the table to the floor, keeping the former between us.

"We will not harm you," said Ras Thavas.

The man attempted to reply, but his words were unintelligible gibberish, then he shook his head and growled. Ras Thavas took a step toward him and the man dropped to all fours, his knuckles resting on the floor, and backed away, growling.

"Come!" cried Ras Thavas. "We will not harm you." Again he attempted to approach the subject, but the man only backed quickly away, growling more fiercely; and then suddenly he wheeled and climbed quickly to the top of the highest shelf, where he squatted upon a corpse and gibbered at us.

"We shall have to have help," said Ras Thavas and, going to the doorway, he blew a signal upon his whistle.

"What are you blowing that for?" demanded the man suddenly. "Who are you? What am I doing here? What has happened to me?"

"Come down," said Ras Thavas, "We are friends."

Slowly the man descended to the floor and came toward us, but he still moved with his knuckles to the pavement. He looked about at the corpses and a new light entered his eyes.

"I am hungry!" he cried." I will eat!" and with that he seized the nearest corpse and dragged it to the floor.

"Stop! Stop!" cried Ras Thavas, leaping forward. "You will ruin the subject," but the man only backed away, dragging the corpse along the floor after him. It was then that the attendants came and with their help we subdued and bound the poor creature. Then Ras Thavas had the attendants bring the body of the ape and he told them to remain, as we might need them.

The subject was a large specimen of the Barsoomian white ape, one of the most savage and fearsome denizens of the Red Planet, and because of the creature's great strength and ferocity Ras Thavas took the precaution to see that it was securely bound before resurgence.

It was a colossal creature about ten or fifteen feet tall,

standing erect, and had an intermediary set of arms or legs midway between its upper and lower limbs. The eyes were close together and non-protruding; the ears were high set, while its snout and teeth were strikingly like those of our African gorilla.

With returning consciousness the creature eyed us questioningly. Several times it seemed to essay to speak, but only inarticulate sounds issued from its throat. Then it lay still for a period.

Ras Thavas spoke to it. "If you understand my words, nod your head." The creature nodded.

"Would you like to be freed of your bonds?" asked the surgeon.

Again the creature nodded an affirmative.

"I fear that you will attempt to injure us, or escape," said Ras Thavas.

The ape was apparently trying very hard to articulate and and at last there issued from its lips a sound that could not be misunderstood. It was the single word no.

"You will not harm us or try to escape?" Ras Thavas repeated his question.

"No," said the ape, and this time the word was clearly enunciated.

"We shall see," said Ras Thavas. "But remember that with our weapons we may dispatch you quickly if you attack us."

The ape nodded, and then, very laboriously: "I will not harm you."

At a sign from Ras Thavas the attendants removed the bonds and the creature sat up. It stretched its limbs and slid easily to the floor, where it stood erect upon two feet, which was not surprising, since the white ape goes more often upon two feet than six; a fact of which I was not cognizant at the time, but which Ras Thavas explained to me later in commenting upon the fact that the human subject had gone upon all fours, which, to Ras Thavas, indicated a reversion to type in the fractional ape-brain transplanted to the human skull.

Ras Thavas examined the subject at considerable length and then resumed his examination of the human subject which continued to evince more simian characteristics than human, though it spoke more easily than the ape, because, undoubtedly, of its more perfect vocal organs. It was only by exerting the closest attention that the diction of the ape became understandable at all.

"There is nothing remarkable about these subjects," said Ras Thavas, after devoting half a day to them. "They bear out what I had already determined years ago in the transplanting of entire brains; that the act of transplanting stimulates growth and activity of brain cells. You will note that in each subject the transplanted portions of the brains are more active—they, in a considerable measure, control. That is why we have the human subject displaying distinctly simian characteristics, while the ape behaves in a more human manner; though if longer and closer observation were desirable you would doubtless find that each reverted at times to his own nature—that is the ape would be more wholly an ape and the human more manlike—but it is not worth the time, of which I have already given too much to a rather unprofitable forenoon. I shall leave you now to restore the subjects to anesthesia while I return to the laboratories above. The attendants will remain here to assist you, if required."

The ape, who had been an interested listener, now stepped forward. "Oh, please, I pray you," it mumbled, "do not again condemn me to these horrid shelves. I recall the day that I was brought here securely bound, and though I have no recollection of what has transpired since I can but guess from the appearance of my own skin and that of these dusty corpses that I have lain here long. I beg that you will permit me to live and either restore me to my fellows or allow me to serve in some capacity in this establishment, of which I saw something between the time of my capture and the day that I was carried into this laboratory, bound and helpless, to one of your cold, ersite slabs."

Ras Thavas made a gesture of impatience. "Nonsense!" he cried. "You are better off here, where you can be preserved in the interests of science."

"Accede to his request," I begged, "and I will myself take over all responsibility for him while I profit by the study that he will afford me."

"Do as you are directed," snapped Ras Thavas as he quit the room.

I shrugged my shoulders. "There is nothing for it, then,"

I said.

"I might dispatch you all and escape," mused the ape, aloud, "but you would have helped me. I could not kill one who would have befriended me—yet I shrink from the thought of another death. How long have I lain here?"

I referred to the history of his case that had been brought and suspended at the head of the table. "Twelve years," I told him.

"And yet, why not?" he demanded of himself. "This man would slay me—why should I not slay him first."

"It would do you no good," I assured him, "for you could never escape. Instead you would be really killed, dying a death from which Ras Thavas would probably think it not worth while ever to recall you, while I, who might find the opportunity at some later date and who have the inclination, would be dead at your hands and thus incapable of saving you."

I had been speaking in a low voice, close to his ear, that the attendants might not overhear me. The ape listened intently.

"You will do as you suggest?" he asked.

"At the first opportunity that presents itself," I assured him.

"Very well," he said, "I will submit, trusting to you."

A half hour later both subjects had been returned to their shelves.

CHAPTER IV

THE COMPACT

DAYS RAN INTO WEEKS, weeks into months, as day by day I labored at the side of Ras Thavas, and more and more the old surgeon took me into his confidence, more and more he imparted to me the secrets of his skill and his profession. Gradually he permitted me to perform more and more important functions in the actual practice of his vast laboratory. I started transferring limbs from one subject to another, then internal organs of the digestive tract. Then he intrusted to me a complete operation upon a paying client. I removed the kidneys from a rich old man, replacing them with healthy ones from a young subject. The following day I gave a stunted child new thyroid glands. A week later I transferred two hearts and then, at last, came the great day for me—unassisted, with Ras Thavas standing silently beside me, I took the brain of an old man and transplanted it within the cranium of a youth.

When I had done Ras Thavas laid a hand upon my shoulder. "I could not have done better myself," he said. He seemed much elated and I could not but wonder at this unusual demonstration of emotion upon his part, he who so prided himself upon his lack of emotionalism. I had often pondered the purpose which influenced Ras Thavas to devote so much time to my training, but never had I hit upon any more satisfactory explanation than that he had need of assistance in his growing practice. Yet when I consulted the records, that were now open to me, I discovered that his practice was no greater than it had been for many years; and even had it been there was really no reason why he should have trained me in preference to one of his red-Martian assistants, his belief in my loyalty not being sufficient warrant, in my mind, for this preferment when he could, as well as not, have kept me for a bodyguard and trained one of his own kind to aid him in his surgical work.

But I was presently to learn that he had an excellent reason for what he was doing—Ras Thavas always had an excellent reason for whatever he did. One night after we had finished our evening meal he sat looking at me intently as he so often did, as though he would read my mind, which, by the way, he was totally unable to do, much to his surprise and chagrin; for unless a Martian is constantly upon the alert any other Martian can read clearly his every thought; but Ras Thavas was unable to read mine. He said that it was due to the fact that I was not a Barsoomian. Yet I could often read the minds of his assistants, when they were off their guard, though never had I read aught of Ras Thavas' thoughts, nor, I am sure, had any other read them. He kept his brain sealed like one of his own blood jars, nor was he ever for a moment found with his barriers down.

He sat looking at me this evening for a long time, nor did it in the least embarrass me, so accustomed was I to his peculiarities. "Perhaps," he said presently, "one of the reasons that I trust you is due to the fact that I cannot ever, at any time, fathom your mind; so, if you harbor traitorous thoughts concerning me I do not know it, while the others, every one of them, reveal their inmost souls to my searching mind and in each one there is envy, jealousy or hatred of me. Them, I know, I cannot trust. Therefore I must accept the risk and place all my dependence upon you, and my reason tells me that my choice is a wise one—I have told you upon what grounds it based my selection of you as my bodyguard. The same holds true in my selection of you for the thing I have in mind. You cannot harm me without harming yourself and no man will intentionally do that; nor is there any reason why you should feel any deep antagonism toward me.

"You are, of course, a sentimentalist and doubtless you look with horror upon many of the acts of a sane, rational, scientific mind; but you are also highly intelligent and can, therefore, appreciate better than another, even though you may not approve them, the motives that prompt me to do many of those things of which your sentimentality disapproves. I may have offended you, but I have never wronged you, nor have I wronged any creature for which you might have felt some of your so-called friendship or love. Are my premises incorrect, or my reasoning faulty?"

I assured him to the contrary.

"Very well! Now let me explain why I have gone to such pains to train you as no other human being, aside from myself, has ever been trained. I am not ready to use you yet, or rather you are not ready; but if you know my purpose you will realize the necessity for bending your every energy to the consummation of my purpose, and to that end you will strive even more diligently than you have to perfect yourself in the high scientific art I am imparting to you.

"I am a very old man," he continued after a brief pause, "even as age goes upon Barsoom. I have lived more than a thousand years. I have passed the allotted natural span of life, but I am not through with my life's work—I have but barely started it. I must not die. Barsoom must not be robbed of this wondrous brain and skill of mine. I have long had in mind a plan to thwart death, but it required another with skill equal to mine—two such might live forever. I have selected you to be that other, for reasons that I already have explained—they are undefiled by sentimentalism. I did not choose you because I love you, or because I feel friendship for you, or because I think that you love me, or feel friendship toward me. I chose you because I knew that of all the inhabitants of a world you were the one least likely to fail me. For a time you will have my life in your hands. You will understand now why I have not been able to choose carelessly.

"This plan that I have chosen is simplicity itself provided that I can count upon just two essential factors—skill and self-interested loyalty in an assistant. My body is about worn out. I must have a new one. My laboratory is filled with wonderful bodies, young and complete with potential strength and health. I have but to select one of these and have my skilled assistant transfer my brain from this old carcass to the new one." He paused.

"I understand now, why you have trained me," I said. "It has puzzled me greatly."

"Thus and thus only may I continue my labors," he went on, "and thus may Barsoom be assured a continuance, practically indefinitely, of the benefits that my brain may bestow upon her children. I may live forever, provided I always have a skilled assistant, and I may assure myself of such by seeing to it that he never dies; when he wears out one organ, or his whole body, I can replace either from my great storehouse of perfect parts, and for me he can perform the same service. Thus may we continue to live indefinitely; for the brain, I believe, is almost deathless, unless injured or attacked by disease.

"You are not ready as yet to be intrusted with this important task. You must transfer many more brains and meet with and overcome the various irregularities and idiosyncrasies that constitute the never failing differences that render no two operations identical. When you gain sufficient proficiency I shall lose no time in making Barsoom safe for posterity."

The old man was far from achieving hatred of himself.

However, his plan was an excellent one, both for himself and for me. It assured us immortality—we might live forever and always with strong, healthy, young bodies. The outlook was alluring—and what a wonderful position it placed me in. If the old man could be assured of my loyalty because of self-interest, similarly might I depend upon his loyalty; for he could not afford to antagonize the one creature in the world who could assure him immortality, or withhold it from him. For the first time since I had entered his establishment I felt safe.

As soon as I had left him I went directly to Valla Dia's apartment, for I wanted to tell her this wonderful news. In the weeks that had passed since her resurrection I had seen much of her and in our daily intercourse there had been revealed to me little by little the wondrous beauties of her soul, until at last I no longer saw the hideous, disfigured face of Xaxa when I looked upon her, but the eyes of my heart penetrated deeper to the loveliness that lay within that sweet mind. She had become my confidant, as I was hers, and this association constituted the one great pleasure of my existence upon Barsoom.

Her congratulations, when I told her of what had come to me, were very sincere and lovely. She said that she hoped I would use this great power of mine to do good in the world. I assured her that I would and that among the first things that I should demand of Ras Thavas was that he should give Valla Dia a beautiful body; but she shook her head.

"No, my friend," she said, "if I may not have my own body this old one of Xaxa's is quite as good for me as another. Without my own body I should not care to return to my native country; while were Ras Thavas to give me the beautiful body of another, I should always be in danger of the covetousness of his clients, any one of whom might see and desire to purchase it, leaving to me her old husk, conceivably one quite terribly diseased or maimed. No, my friend, I am satisfied with the body of Xaxa, unless I may again possess my own, for Xaxa at least bequeathed me a tough and healthy envelope, however ugly it may be; and for what do looks count here? You, alone, are my friend—that I have your friendship is enough. You admire me for what I am, not for what I look like, so let us leave well enough alone."

"If you could regain your own body and return to your native country, you would like that?" I demanded.

"Oh, do not say it!" she cried. "The simple thought of it drives me mad with longing. I must not harbor so hopeless a dream that at best may only tantalize me into greater abhorrence of my lot."

"Do not say that it is hopeless," I urged. "Death, only, renders hope futile."

"You mean to be kind," she said, "but you are only hurting me. There can be no hope."

"May I hope for you, then?" I asked. "For I surely see a way; however slight a possibility for success it may have, still, it is a way."

She shook her head. "There is no way," she said, with finality. "No more will Duhor know me."

"Duhor?" I repeated. "Your—some one you care for very much?"

"I care for Duhor very much," she answered with a smile, "but Duhor is not someone—Duhor is my home, the country of my ancestors."

"How came you to leave Duhor?" I asked. "You have never told me, Valla Dia."

"It was because of the ruthlessness of Jal Had, Prince of Amhor," she replied. "Hereditary enemies were Duhor and Amhor; but Jal Had came disguised into the city of Duhor, having heard, they say, of the great beauty attributed to the only daughter of Kor San, Jeddak of Duhor; and when he had seen her he determined to possess her. Returning to Amhor he sent ambassadors to the court of Kor San to sue for the hand of the Princess of Duhor; but Kor San, who had no son, had determined to wed his daughter to one of his own Jeds, that the son of this union, with the blood of Kor San in his veins, might rule over the people of Duhor; and so the offer of Jal Had was declined.

"This so incensed the Amhorian that he equipped a great fleet and set forth to conquer Duhor and take by force that which he could not win by honorable methods. Duhor was, at that time, at war with Helium and all her forces were far afield in the south, with the exception of a small army that had been left behind to guard the city. Jal Had, therefore, could not have selected a more propitious time for an attack.

Duhor fell, and while his troops were looting the fair city Jal Had, with a picked force, sacked the palace of the jeddak and searched for the princess; but the princess had no mind to go back with him as Princess of Amhor. From the moment that the vanguard of the Amhorian fleet was seen in the sky she had known, with the others of the city, the purpose for which they came and so she used her head to defeat that purpose.

"There was in her retinue a cosmetologist whose duty it was to preserve the lustrous beauty of the princess' hair and skin and prepare her for public audiences, for fetes and for the daily intercourse of the court. He was a master of his art; he could render the ugly pleasant to look upon, he could make the plain lovely, and he could make the lovely radiant. She called him quickly to her and commanded him to make the radiant ugly; and when he had done with her none might guess that she was the Princess of Duhor, so deftly had he wrought with his pigments and his tiny brushes.

When Jal Had could not find the princess within the palace, and no amount of threat or torture could force a statement of her whereabouts from the loyal lips of her people, the Amhorian ordered that every woman within the palace be seized and taken to Amhor; there to be held as hostages until the princess of Duhor should be delivered to him in marriage. We were, therefore, all seized and placed upon an Amhorian war ship which was sent back to Amhor ahead of the balance of the fleet, which remained to complete the sacking of Duhor.

"When the ship, with its small convoy, had covered some four thousand of the five thousand haads that separate Duhor from Amhor, it was sighted by a fleet from Phundahl which immediately attacked. The convoying ships were destroyed or driven off and that which carried us was captured. We were taken to Phundahl where we were put upon the auction block and I fell to the bid of one of Ras Thavas' agents. The rest you know."

"And what became of the princess?" I asked.

"Perhaps she died—her party was separated in Phundahl —but death could not more definitely prevent her return to Duhor. The Princess of Duhor will never again see her native country."

"But you may!" I cried, for I had suddenly hit upon a plan.

"Where is Duhor?"

"You are going there?" she asked, laughingly.

"Yes!"

"You are mad, my friend," she said. "Duhor lies a full seven thousand, eight hundred haads from Toonol, upon the opposite side of the snow clad Artolian Hills. You, a stranger and alone, could never reach it; for between lie the Toonolian Marshes, wild hordes, savage beasts and warlike cities. You would but die uselessly within the first dozen haads, even could you escape from the island upon which stands the laboratory of Ras Thavas; and what motive is there to prompt you to such a useless sacrifice?"

I could not tell her. I could not look upon that withered figure and into that hideous and disfigured face and say: "It is because I love you, Valla Dia." But that, alas, was my only reason. Gradually, as I had come to know her through the slow revealment of the wondrous beauty of her mind and soul, there had crept into my heart a knowledge of my love; and yet, explain it I cannot, I could not speak the words to that frightful old hag. I had seen the gorgeous mundane tabernacle that had housed the equally gorgeous spirit of the real Valla Dia—*that* I could love; her heart and soul and mind I could love; but I could not love the body of Xaxa. I was torn, too, by other emotions, induced by a great doubt—could Valla Dia return my love. Habilitated in the corpse of Xaxa, with no other suitor, nay, with no other friend, she might, out of gratitude or through sheer loneliness, be attracted to me; but once again were she Valla Dia the beautiful and returned to the palace of her king, surrounded by the great nobles of Duhor, would she have either eyes or heart for a lone and friendless exile from another world? I doubted it—and yet that doubt did not deter me from my determination to carry out, as far as Fate would permit, the mad scheme that was revolving in my brain.

"You have not answered my question, Vad Varo," she interrupted my surging thoughts. "Why would you do this thing?"

"To right the wrong that has been done you, Valla Dia," I said.

She sighed. "Do not attempt it, please," she begged. "You would but rob me of my one friend, whose association is the only source of happiness remaining to me. I appreciate your generosity and your loyalty, even though I may not understand them; your unselfish desire to serve me at such suicidal risk touches me more deeply than I can reveal, adding still further to the debt I owe you; but you must not attempt it—you must not."

"If it troubles you, Valla Dia," I replied, "we will not speak of it again; but know always that it is never from my thoughts. Some day I shall find a way, even though the plan I now have fails me."

The days moved on and on, the gorgeous Martian nights, filled with her hurtling moons, followed one upon another. Ras Thavas spent more and more time in directing my work of brain transference. I had long since become an adept; and I realized that the time was rapidly approaching when Ras Thavas would feel that he could safely intrust to my hands and skill his life and future. He would be wholly within my power and he knew that I knew it. I could slay him; I could permit him to remain forever in the preserving grip of his own anesthetic; or I could play any trick upon him that I chose, even to giving him the body of a calot or a part of the brain of an ape; but he must take the chance and that I knew, for he was failing rapidly. Already almost stone blind, it was only the wonderful spectacles that he had himself invented that permitted him to see at all; long deaf, he used artificial means for hearing; and now his heart was showing symptoms of fatigue that he could not longer ignore.

One morning I was summoned to his sleeping apartment by a slave. I found the old surgeon lying, a shrunken, pitiful heap of withered skin and bones.

"We must hasten, Vad Varo," he said in a weak whisper. "My heart was like to have stopped a few tals ago. It was then that I sent for you." He pointed to a door leading from his chamber. "There," he said, "you will find the body I have chosen. There, in the private laboratory I long ago built for this very purpose, you will perform the greatest surgical operation that the universe has ever known, transferring its most perfect brain to the most beautiful and perfect body that ever has passed beneath these ancient eyes. You will find the head already prepared to receive my brain; the brain of the subject having been removed and destroyed—totally de-

stroyed by fire. I could not possibly chance the existence of a
brain desiring and scheming to regain its wondrous body.
No, I destroyed it. Call slaves and have them bear my body
to the ersite slab."

"That will not be necessary," I told him; and lifting his
shrunken form in my arms as he had been an earthly babe,
I carried him into the adjoining room where I found a perfectly lighted and appointed laboratory containing two operating tables, one of which was occupied by the body of a
red-man. Upon the surface of the other, which was vacant,
I laid Ras Thavas, then I turned to look at the new envelope
he had chosen. Never, I believe, had I beheld so perfect a
form, so handsome a face—Ras Thavas had indeed chosen
well for himself. Then I turned back to the old surgeon.
Deftly, as he had taught me, I made the two incisions and
attached the tubes. My finger rested upon the button that
would start the motor pumping his blood from his veins and
his marvellous preservative-anesthetic into them. Then I
spoke.

"Ras Thavas," I said, "you have long been training me to
this end. I have labored assiduously to prepare myself that
there might be no slightest cause for apprehension as to the
outcome. You have, coincidentally, taught me that one's every
act should be prompted by self-interest only. You are satisfied, therefore, that I am not doing this for you because I
love you, or because I feel any friendship for you; but you
think that you have offered me enough in placing before me
a similar opportunity for immortality.

"Regardless of your teaching I am afraid that I am still
somewhat of a sentimentalist. I crave the redressing of wrongs.
I crave friendship and love. The price you offer is not enough.
Are you willing to pay more that this operation may be successfully concluded?"

He looked at me steadily for a long minute. "What do you
want?" he asked. I could see that he was trembling with
anger, but he did not raise his voice.

"Do you recall 4296-E-2631-H?" I inquired.

"The subject with the body of Xaxa? Yes, I recall the case.
What of it?"

"I wish her body returned to her. That is the price you
must pay for this operation."

He glared at me. "It is impossible. Xaxa has the body. Even if I cared to do so, I could never recover it. Proceed with the operation!"

"When you have promised me," I insisted.

"I cannot promise the impossible—I cannot obtain Xaxa. Ask me something else. I am not unwilling to grant any reasonable request."

"That is all I wish—just that; but I do not insist that you obtain the body. If I bring Xaxa here will you make the transfer?"

"It would mean war between Toonol and Phundahl," he fumed.

"That does not interest me," I said. "Quick! Reach a decision. In five tals I shall press this button. If you promise what I ask, you shall be restored with a new and beautiful body; if you refuse you shall lie here in the semblance of death forever."

"I promise," he said slowly, "that when you bring the body of Xaxa to me I will transfer to that body any brain that you select from among my subjects."

"Good!" I exclaimed, and pressed the button.

CHAPTER V

DANGER

RAS THAVAS awakened from the anesthetic a new and gorgeous creature—a youth of such wondrous beauty that he seemed of heavenly rather than worldly origin; but in that beautiful head was the hard, cold, thousand-year-old brain of the master surgeon. As he opened his eyes he looked upon me coldly.

"You have done well," he said.

"What I have done, I have done for friendship—perhaps for love," I said, "so you can thank the sentimentalism you decry for the success of the transfer."

He made no reply.

"And now," I continued, "I shall look to you for the fulfillment of the promise you have made me."

"When you bring Xaxa's body I shall transfer to it the brain of any of my subjects you may select," he said, "but were I you, I would not risk my life in such an impossible venture—you cannot succeed. Select another body—there are many beautiful ones—and I will give it the brain of 4296-E-2631-H."

"None other than the body now owned by the Jeddara Xaxa will fulfill your promise to me," I said.

He shrugged and there was a cold smile upon his handsome lips. "Very well," he said, "fetch Xaxa. When do you start?"

"I am not yet ready. I will let you know when I am."

"Good and now begone—but wait! First go to the office and see what cases await us and if there be any that do not require my personal attention, and they fall within your skill and knowledge, attend to them yourself."

As I left him I noticed a crafty smile of satisfaction upon his lips. What had aroused that? I did not like it and as I walked away I tried to conjure what could possibly have passed through that wondrous brain to call forth at that particular instant so unpleasant a smile. As I passed through the doorway and into the corridor beyond I heard him summon his personal slave and body servant, Yamdor, a huge fellow whose loyalty he kept through the bestowal of lavish gifts and countless favors. So great was the fellow's power that all feared him, as a word to the master from the lips of Yamdor might easily send any of the numerous slaves or attendants to an ersite slab for eternity. It was rumored that he was the result of an unnatural experiment which had combined the brain of a woman with the body of a man, and there was much in his actions and mannerisms to justify this general belief. His touch, when he worked about his master, was soft and light, his movements graceful, his ways gentle, but his mind was jealous, vindictive and unforgiving.

I believed that he did not like me, through jealousy of the authority I had attained in the establishment of Ras Thavas; for there was no questioning the fact that I was a lieutenant, while he was but a slave; yet he always accorded me the utmost respect. He was, however, merely a minor cog in the machinery of the great institution presided over by the sovereign mind of Ras Thavas, and as such I had given him little consideration; nor did I now as I bent my steps toward the office.

I had gone but a short distance when I recalled a matter of importance upon which it was necessary for me to obtain instructions from Ras Thavas immediately; and so I wheeled about and retraced my way toward his apartments, through the open doorway of which, as I approached, I heard the new voice of the master surgeon. Ras Thavas had always spoken in rather loud tones, whether as a vocal reflection of his naturally domineering and authoritative character, or because of his deafness, I do not know; and now, with the fresh young vocal chords of his new body, his words rang out clearly and distinctly in the corridor leading to his room.

"You will, therefore, Yamdor," he was saying, "go at once and, selecting two slaves in whose silence and discretion you may trust, take the subject from the apartments of Vad Varo and destroy it—let no vestige of body or brain remain. Immediately after, you will bring the two slaves to the laboratory F-30-L, permitting them to speak to no one, and I will consign them to silence and forgetfulness for eternity.

"Vad Varo will discover the absence of the subject and report the matter to me. During my investigation you will confess that you aided 4296-E-2631-H to escape, but that you have no idea where it intended going. I will sentence you to death as punishment, but at last, explaining how urgently I need your services and upon your solemn promise never to transgress again, I will defer punishment for the term of your continued good behavior. Do you thoroughly understand the entire plan?"

"Yes, master," replied Yamdor.

"Then depart at once and select the slaves who are to assist you."

Quickly and silently I sped along the corridor until the first intersection permitted me to place myself out of sight of anyone coming from Ras Thavas' apartment; then I went directly to the chamber occupied by Valla Dia. Unlocking the door I threw it open and beckoned her to come out. "Quick! Valla Dia!" I cried. "No time is to be lost. In attempting to save you I have but brought destruction upon you. First we must find a hiding place for you, and that at once—afterward we can plan for the future."

The place that first occurred to me as affording adequate concealment was the half forgotten vaults in the pits beneath the laboratories, and toward these I hastened Valla Dia. As we proceeded I narrated all that had transpired, nor did she once reproach me; but, instead, expressed naught but gratitude for what she was pleased to designate as my unselfish friendship. That it had miscarried, she assured me, was no reflection upon me and she insisted that she would rather die in the knowledge that she possessed one such friend than to live on indefinitely, friendless.

We came at last to the chamber I sought—vault L-42-X, in building 4-J-21, where reposed the bodies of the ape and the man, each of which possessed half the brain of the other. Here I was forced to leave Valla Dia for the time, that I might hasten to the office and perform the duties imposed upon me by Ras Thavas, lest his suspicions be aroused when Yamdor reported that he had found her apartment vacant.

I reached the office without it being discovered by anyone who might report the fact to Ras Thavas that I had been a long time coming from his apartment. To my relief, I found there were no cases. Without appearing in any undue haste, I nevertheless soon found an excuse to depart and at once made my way toward my own quarters, moving in a leisurely and unconcerned manner and humming, as was my wont (a habit which greatly irritated Ras Thavas), snatches from some song that had been popular at the time that I quit Earth. In this instance it was "Oh, Frenchy."

I was thus engaged when I met Yamdor moving hurriedly along the corridor leading from my apartment, in company with two male slaves. I greeted him pleasantly, as was my custom, and he returned my greeting; but there was an expression of fear and suspicion in his eyes. I went at once to my quarters, opened the door leading to the chamber formerly occupied by Valla Dia and then hastened immediately to the apartment of Ras Thavas, where I found him conversing with Yamdor. I rushed in apparently breathless and simulating great excitement.

"Ras Thavas," I demanded, "what have you done with 4296-E-2631-H? She has disappeared; her apartment is empty; and as I was approaching it I met Yamdor and two other slaves coming from that direction." I turned then upon Yamdor and pointed an accusing finger at him. "Yamdor!" I cried. "What have you done with this woman?"

Both Ras Thavas and Yamdor seemed genuinely puzzled and I congratulated myself that I had thus readily thrown them off the track. The master surgeon declared that he would make an immediate investigation; and he at once ordered a thorough search of the grounds and of the island outside the enclosure. Yamdor denied any knowledge of the woman and I, at least, was aware of the sincerity of his protestations, but not so Ras Thavas. I could see a hint of suspicion in his eyes as he questioned his body servant; but evidently he could conjure no motive for any such treasonable action on the part of Yamdor as would have been represented by the abduction of the woman and the consequent gross disobedience of orders.

Ras Thavas' investigation revealed nothing. I think as it progressed that he became gradually more and more imbued with a growing suspicion that I might know more about the disappearance of Valla Dia than my attitude indicated, for I presently became aware of a delicately concealed espionage. Up to this time I had been able to smuggle food to Valla Dia every night, after Ras Thavas had retired to his quarters. Then, on one occasion, I suddenly became subsconsciously aware that I was being followed, and instead of going to the vaults I went to the office, where I added some observations to my report upon a case I had handled that day. Returning to my room I hummed a few bars from "Over There," that the suggestion of my unconcern might be accentuated. From the moment that I quit my quarters until I returned to them I was sure that eyes had been watching my every move. What was I to do? Valla Dia must have food, without it she would die; and were I to be followed to her hiding place while taking it to her, she would die; Ras Thavas would see to that.

Half the night I lay awake, racking my brains for some solution to the problem. There seemed only one way—I must elude the spies. If I could do this but one single time I could carry out the balance of a plan that had occurred to me, and which was, I thought, the only one feasible that might eventually lead to the resurrection of Valla Dia in her own body. The way was long, the risks great; but I was young, in love and utterly reckless of consequences in-so-far as they concerned me; it was Valla Dia's happiness alone that I could not risk too greatly, other than under dire stress. Well, the stress existed and I must risk that, even as I risked my life.

My plan was formulated and I lay awake upon my sleeping silks and furs in the darkness of my room, awaiting the time when I might put it into execution. My window, which was upon the third floor, overlooked the walled enclosure, upon the scarlet sward of which I had made my first bow to Barsoom. Across the open casement I had watched Cluros, the farther moon, take his slow deliberate way. He had already set. Behind him, Thuria, his elusive mistress, fled through the heavens. In five xats (about 15 minutes) she would set; and then for about three and three quarters Earth hours the heavens would be dark, except for the stars.

In the corridor, perhaps, lurked those watchful eyes. I prayed God that they might not be elsewhere as Thuria sank at last beneath the horizon and I swung to my window ledge, in my hand a long rope fabricated from braided strips torn from my sleeping silks while I had awaited the setting of the moons. One end I had fastened to a heavy sorapus bench which I had drawn close to the window. I dropped the free end of the rope and started my descent. My Earthly muscles, untried in such endeavors, I had not trusted to the task of carrying me to my window ledge in a single leap, when I should be returning. I felt that they would, but I did not know; and too much depended upon the success of my venture to risk any unnecessary chance of failure. And so I had prepared the rope.

Whether I was being observed I did not know. I must go on as though none were spying upon me. In less than four hours Thuria would return (just before the sudden Barsoomian dawn) and in the interval I must reach Valla Dia, persuade her of the necessity of my plan and carry out its details, returning to my chamber before Thuria could disclose me to any accidental observer. I carried my weapons with me and in my heart was unbending determination to slay whoever might cross my path and recognize me during the course of my errand, however innocent of evil intent against me he might be.

The night was quiet except for the usual distant sounds

that I had heard ever since I had been here—sounds that I had interpreted as the cries of savage beasts. Once I had asked Ras Thavas about them, but he had been in ill humor and had ignored my question. I reached the ground quickly and without hesitation moved directly to the nearest entrance of the building, having previously searched out and determined upon the route I would follow to the vault. No one was visible and I was confident, when at last I reached the doorway, that I had come through undetected. Valla Dia was so happy to see me again that it almost brought the tears to my eyes.

"I thought that something had happened to you," she cried, "for I knew that you would not remain away so long of your own volition."

I told her of my conviction that I was being watched and that it would not be possible for me longer to bring food to her without incurring almost certain detection, which would spell immediate death for her.

"There is a single alternative," I said, "and that I dread even to suggest and would not were there any other way. You must be securely hidden for a long time, until Ras Thavas' suspicions have been allayed; for as long as he has me watched I cannot possibly carry out the plans I have formulated for your eventual release, the restoration of your own body and your return to Duhor."

"Your will shall be my law, Vad Varo."

I shook my head. "It will be harder for you than you imagine."

"What is the way?" she asked.

I pointed to the ersite topped table. "You must pass again through that ordeal that I may hide you away in this vault until the time is ripe for the carrying out of my plans. Can you endure it?"

She smiled. "Why not?" she asked. "It is only sleep—if it lasts forever I shall be no wiser."

I was surprised that she did not shrink from the idea, but I was very glad since I knew that it was the only way that we had a chance for success. Without my help she disposed herself upon the ersite slab.

"I am ready, Vad Varo," she said bravely; "but first promise me that you will take no risks in this mad venture. You cannot succeed. When I close my eyes I know that it will be for the last time if my resurrection depends upon the successful outcome of the maddest venture that ever man conceived; yet I am happy, because I know that it is inspired by the greatest friendship with which any mortal woman has ever been blessed."

As she talked I had been adjusting the tubes and now I stood beside her with my finger upon the starting button of the motor.

"Good-bye, Vad Varo," she whispered.

"Not good-bye, Valla Dia, but only a sweet sleep for what to you will be the briefest instant. You will seem but to close your eyes and open them again. As you see me now, I shall be standing here beside you as though I never had departed from you. As I am the last that you look upon tonight before you close your eyes, so shall I be the first that you shall look upon as you open them on that new and beautiful morning; but you shall not again look forth through the eyes of Xaxa, but from the limpid depths of your own beautiful orbs."

She smiled and shook her head. Two tears formed beneath her lids. I pressed her hand in mine and touched the button.

CHAPTER VI

SUSPICIONS

IN-SO-FAR as I could know I reached my apartment without detection. Hiding my rope where I was sure it would not be discovered, I sought my sleeping silks and furs and was soon asleep.

The following morning as I emerged from my quarters I caught a fleeting glimpse of a figure in a nearby corridor and from then on for a long time I had further evidence that Ras Thavas suspicioned me. I went at once to his quarters, as had been my habit. He seemed restless, but he gave me no hint that he held any assurance that I had been responsible for the disappearance of Valla Dia, and I think that he was far from positive of it. It was simply that his judgment pointed to

the fact that I was the only person who might have any reason for interfering in any way with this particular subject,
and he was having me watched to either prove or disprove
the truth of his reasonable suspicions. His restlessness he explained to me himself.

"I have often studied the reaction of others who have un-
dergone brain transference," he said, "and so I am not wholly
surprised at my own. Not only has my brain energy been stim-
ulated, resulting in an increased production of nervous
energy, but I also feel the effects of the young tissue and
youthful blood of my new body. They are affecting my consciousness in a way that my experiments had vaguely indicated, but which I now see must be actually experienced to
be fully understood. My thoughts, my inclinations, even my
ambitions have been changed, or at least colored, by the
transfer. It will take some time for me to find myself."

Though uninterested, I listened politely until he was
through and then I changed the subject. "Have you located
the missing woman?" I asked.

He shook his head, negatively.

"You must appreciate, Ras Thavas," I said, "that I fully
realize that you must have known that the removal or destruction of that woman would entirely frustrate my entire
plan. You are master here. Nothing that passes is without
your knowledge."

"You mean that I am responsible for the disappearance
of the woman?" he demanded.

"Certainly. It is obvious. I demand that she be restored."

He lost his temper. "Who are you to demand?" he shouted.
"You are naught but a slave. Cease your impudence or I shall
erase you—erase you. It will be as though you never had existed."

I laughed in his face. "Anger is the most futile attribute
of the sentimentalist," I reminded him. "You will not erase
me, for I alone stand between you and mortality."

"I can train another," he parried.

"But you could not trust him," I pointed out.

"But you bargained with me for my life when you had me
in your power," he cried.

"For nothing that it would have harmed you to have
granted willingly. I did not ask anything for myself. Be that

as it may, you will trust me again. You will trust, for no other reason than that you will be forced to trust me. So why not win my gratitude and my loyalty by returning the woman to me and carrying out in spirit as well as in fact the terms of our agreement?"

He turned and looked steadily at me. "Vad Varo," he said, "I give you the word of honor of a Barsoomian noble that I know absolutely nothing concerning the whereabouts of 4296-E-2631-H."

"Perhaps Yamdor does," I persisted.

"Nor Yamdor. Of my knowledge no person in any way connected with me knows what became of it. I have spoken the truth."

Well, the conversation was not as profitless as it might appear, for I was sure that it had almost convinced Ras Thavas that I was equally as ignorant of the fate of Valla Dia as was he. That it had not wholly convinced him was evidenced by the fact that the espionage continued for a long time, a fact which determined me to use Ras Thavas' own methods in my own defense. I had had allotted to me a number of slaves and these I had won over by kindness and understanding until I knew that I had the full measure of their loyalty. They had no reason to love Ras Thavas and every reason to hate him; on the other hand they had no reason to hate me, and I saw to it that they had every reason to love me.

The result was that I had no difficulty in enlisting the services of a couple of them to spy upon Ras Thavas' spies, with the result that I was soon apprised that my suspicions were well founded—I was being constantly watched every minute that I was out of my apartments, but the spying did not come beyond my outer chamber walls. That was why I had been successful in reaching the vault in the manner that I had; the spies having assumed that I would leave my chamber only by its natural exit, had been content to guard that and permit my windows to go unwatched.

I think it was about two of our months that the spying continued and then my men reported that it seemed to have ceased entirely. All that time I was fretting at the delay, for I wanted to be about my plans which would have been absolutely impossible for me to carry out if I were being watched. I had spent the interval in studying the geography of the northeastern Barsoomian hemisphere where my activities were to be carried on, and also in scanning a great number of case histories and inspecting the subjects to which they referred; but at last, with the removal of the spies, it began to look as though I might soon commence to put my plans in active operation.

Ras Thavas had for some time permitted me considerable freedom in independent investigation and experiment, and this I determined to take advantage of in every possible way that might forward my plans for the resurrection of Valla Dia. My study of the histories of many of the cases had been with the possibility in mind of discovering subjects that might be of assistance to me in my venture. Among those that had occupied my careful attention were, quite naturally, the cases with which I had been most familiar, namely: 378-J-493811-P, the red-man from whose vicious attack I had saved Ras Thavas upon the day of my advent upon Mars; and he whose brain had been divided with an ape.

The former, 378-J-493811-P, had been a native of Phundahl—a young warrior attached to the court of Xaxa, Jeddara of Phundhal—and a victim of assassination. His body had been purchased by a Phundahlian noble for the purpose, as Ras Thavas had narrated, of winning the favor of a young beauty. I felt that I might possibly enlist his services, but that would depend upon the extent of his loyalty toward Xaxa, which I could only determine by reviving and questioning him.

He whose brain had been divided with an ape had originated in Ptarth, which lay at a considerable distance to the west of Phundahl and a little south and about an equal distance from Duhor, which lay north and a little west of it. An inhabitant of Ptarth, I reasoned, would know much of the entire country included in the triangle formed by Phundahl, Ptarth and Duhor; the strength and ferocity of the great ape would prove of value in crossing beast infested wastes; and I felt that I could hold forth sufficient promise to the human half of the great beast's brain, which really now dominated the creature, to win its support and loyalty. The third subject that I had tentatively selected had been a notorious Toonolian assassin, whose audacity, fearlessness

and swordsmanship had won for him a reputation that had
spread far beyond the boundaries of his country.

Ras Thavas, himself a Toonolian, had given me something
of the history of this man whose grim calling is not without
honor upon Barsoom, and which Gor Hajus had raised still
higher in the esteem of his countrymen through the fact
that he never struck down a woman or a good man and that
he never struck from behind. His killings were always the
results of fair fights in which the victim had every opportunity to defend himself and slay his attacker; and he was famous for his loyalty to his friends. In fact this very loyalty
had been a contributing factor in his downfall which had
brought him to one of Ras Thavas' ersite slabs some years
since, for he had earned the enmity of Vobis Kan, Jeddak
of Toonol, through his refusal to assassinate a man who once
had befriended Gor Hajus in some slight degree; following
which Vobis Kan conceived the suspicion that Gor Hajus had
him marked for slaying. The result was inevitable: Gor Hajus
was arrested and condemned to death; immediately following the execution of the sentence an agent of Ras Thavas had
purchased the body.

These three, then, I had chosen to be my partners in my
great adventure. It is true that I had not discussed the matter
with any one of them, but my judgment assured me that I
would have no difficulty in enlisting their services and loyalty
in return for their total resurrection.

My first task lay in renewing the organs of 378-J-493811-P
and of Gor Hajus which had been injured by the wounds
that had layed them low; the former requiring a new lung
and the latter a new heart, his executioner having run him
through with a short-sword. I hesitated to ask Ras Thavas'
permission to experiment on these subjects for fear of the
possibility of arousing his suspicions, in which event he would
probably have them destroyed; and so I was forced to accomplish my designs by subterfuge and stealth. To this end I
made it a practice for weeks to carry my regular laboratory
work far into the night, often requiring the service of various
assistants that all might become accustomed to the sight of
me at work at unusual hours. In my selection of these assistants I made it a point to choose two of the very spies that
Ras Thavas had set to watching me. While it was true that

they were no longer employed in this particular service, I had hopes that they would carry word of my activities to their master; and I was careful to see that they received from me the proper suggestions that would mold their report in language far from harmful to me. By the merest suggestion I carried to them the idea that I worked thus late purely for the love of the work itself and the tremendous interest in it that Ras Thavas had awakened within my mind. Some nights I worked with assistants and as often I did not, but always I was careful to assure myself that the following morning those in the office were made aware that I had labored far into the preceding night.

This groundwork carefully prepared, I had comparatively little fear of the results of actual discovery when I set to work upon the warrior of Phundahl and the assassin of Toonol. I chose the former first. His lung was badly injured where my blade had passed through it, but from the laboratory where were kept fractional bodies I brought a perfect lung, with which I replaced the one that I had ruined. The work occupied but half the night. So anxious was I to complete my task that I immediately opened up the breast of Gor Hajus, for whom I had selected an unusually strong and powerful heart, and by working rapidly I succeeded in completing the transference before dawn. Having known the nature of the wounds that had dispatched these two men, I had spent weeks in performing similar operations that I might perfect myself especially in this work; and having encountered no unusual pathological conditions in either subject, the work had progressed smoothly and with great rapidity. I had completed what I had feared would be the most difficult part of my task and now, having removed as far as possible all signs of the operation except the therapeutic tape which closed the incisions, I returned to my quarters for a few minutes of much needed rest, praying that Ras Thavas would not by any chance examine either of the subjects upon which I had been working; although I had fortified myself against such a contingency by entering full details of the operation upon the history card of each subject that, in the event of discovery, any suspicion of ulterior motives upon my part might be allayed by my play of open frankness.

I arose at the usual time and went at once to Ras Thavas'

apartment, where I was met with a bomb shell that nearly wrecked my composure. He eyed me closely for a long minute before he spoke.

"You worked late last night, Vad Varo," he said.

"I often do," I replied, lightly; but my heart was heavy as a stone.

"And what might it have been that so occupied your interest?" he inquired.

I felt as a mouse with which the cat is playing. "I have been doing quite a little lung and heart transference of late," I replied, "and I became so engrossed with my work that I did not note the passage of time."

"I have known that you worked late at night. Do you think it wise?"

At that moment I felt that it had been very unwise, yet I assured him to the contrary.

"I was restless," he said. "I could not sleep and so I went to your quarters after midnight, but you were not there. I wanted someone with whom to talk, but your slaves knew only that you were not there—where you were they did not know—so I set out to search for you." My heart went into my sandals. "I guessed that you were in one of the laboratories, but though I visited several I did not find you." My heart arose with the lightness of a feather. "Since my own transference I have been cursed with restlessness and sleeplessness, so that I could almost wish for the return of my old corse—the youth of my body harmonizes not with the antiquity of my brain. It is filled with latent urges and desires that comport illy with the serious subject matter of my mind."

"What your body needs," I said, "is exercise. It is young, strong, virile. Work it hard and it will let your brain rest at night."

"I know that you are right," he replied. "I have reached that same conclusion myself. In fact, not finding you, I walked in the gardens for an hour or more before returning to my quarters, and then I slept soundly. I shall walk every night when I cannot sleep, or I shall go into the laboratories and work as do you."

This news was most disquieting. Now I could never be sure but that Ras Thavas was wandering about at night and I had one more very important night's work to do, perhaps two. The only way that I could be sure of him was to be with him.

"Send for me when you are restless," I said, "and I will walk and work with you. You should not go about thus at night alone."

"Very well," he said, "I may do that occasionally."

I hoped that he would do it always, for then I would know that when he failed to send for me he was safe in his own quarters. Yet I saw that I must henceforth face the menace of detection; and knowing this I determined to hasten the completion of my plans and to risk everything on a single bold stroke.

That night I had no opportunity to put it into action as Ras Thavas sent for me early and informed me that we would walk in the gardens until he was tired. Now, as I needed a full night for what I had in mind and as Ras Thavas walked until midnight, I was compelled to forego everything for that evening, but the following morning I persuaded him to walk early on the pretext that I should like to go beyond the enclosure and see something of Barsoom beside the inside of his laboratories and his gardens. I had little confidence that he would grant my request, yet he did so. I am sure he never would have done it had he possessed his old body; but thus greatly had young blood changed Ras Thavas.

I had never been beyond the buildings, nor had I seen beyond, since there were no windows in the outside walls of any of the structures and upon the garden side the trees had grown to such a height that they obstructed all view beyond them. For a time we walked in another garden just inside the outer wall, and then I asked Ras Thavas if I might go even beyond this.

"No," he said. "It would not be safe."

"And why not?" I asked.

"I will show you and at the same time give you a much broader view of the outside world than you could obtain by merely passing through the gate. Come, follow me!"

He led me immediately to a lofty tower that rose at the corner of the largest building of the group that comprised his vast establishment. Within was a circular runway which led not only upward, but down as well. This we ascended, passing openings at each floor, until we came at last out upon its lofty summit. About me spread the first Barsoomian landscape of any extent upon which my eyes had yet rested during the long months that I had spent upon the Red Planet. For almost an Earthly year I had been immured within the grim walls of Ras Thavas' bloody laboratory, until, such creatures of habit are we, the weird life there had grown to seem quite natural and ordinary; but with this first glimpse of open country there surged up within me an urge for freedom, for space, for room to move about, such as I knew would not be long denied.

Directly beneath lay an irregular patch of rocky land elevated perhaps a dozen feet or more above the general level of the immediately surrounding country. Its extent was, at a rough guess, a hundred acres. Upon this stood the buildings and grounds, which were enclosed in a high wall. The tower upon which we stood was situated at about the center of the total area enclosed. Beyond the outer wall was a strip of rocky ground on which grew a sparse forest of fair sized trees interspersed with patches of a jungle growth, and beyond all, what appeared to be oozy marsh through which were narrow water courses connecting occasional open water—little lakes, the largest of which could have comprised scarce two acres. This landscape extended as far as the eye could reach, broken by occasional islands similar to that upon which we were, and at a short distance by the skyline of a large city, whose towers and domes and minarets glistened and sparkled in the sun as though plated with shining metals and picked out with precious gems.

This, I knew, must be Toonol and all about us the Great Toonolian Marshes which extend nearly eighteen hundred earth miles east and west and in some places have a width of three hundred miles. Little is known about them in other portions of Barsoom as they are frequented by fierce beasts, afford no landing places for fliers and are commanded by Phundahl at their western end and Toonol at the east; inhospitable kingdoms that invite no intercourse with the outside world and maintain their independence alone by their inaccessibility and savage aloofness.

As my eyes returned to the island at our feet I saw a huge form emerge from one of the nearby patches of jungle a short distance beyond the outer wall. It was followed by a second and a third. Ras Thavas saw that the creatures had attracted my notice.

"There," he said, pointing to them, "are three of a number of similar reasons why it would not have been safe for us to venture outside the enclosure."

They were great white apes of Barsoom, creatures so savage that even that fierce Barsoomian lion, the banth, hesitates to cross their path.

"They serve two purposes," explained Ras Thavas. "They discourage those who might otherwise creep upon me by night from the city of Toonol, where I am not without many good enemies, and they prevent desertion upon the part of my slaves and assistants."

"But how do your clients reach you?" I asked "How are your supplies brought in?"

He turned and pointed down toward the highest portion of the irregular roof of the building below us. Built upon it was a large, shed-like structure. "There," he said, "I keep three small ships. One of them goes every day to Toonol."

I was overcome with eagerness to know more about these ships, in which I thought I saw a much needed means of escape from the island; but I dared not question him for fear of arousing his suspicions.

As we turned to descend the tower runway I expressed interest in the structure which gave evidence of being far older than any of the surrounding buildings.

"This tower," said Ras Thavas, "was built some twenty-three thousand years ago by an ancestor of mine who was driven from Toonol by the reigning jeddak of the time. Here, and upon other islands, he gathered a considerable following, dominated the surrounding marshes and defended himself successfully for hundreds of years. While my family has been permitted to return to Toonol since, this has been their home; to which, one by one, have been added the various buildings which you see about the tower, each floor of which connects with the adjacent building from the roof to the lowest pits beneath the ground."

This information also interested me greatly since I thought that I saw where it too might have considerable bearing upon my plan of escape, and so, as we descended the runway, I encouraged Ras Thavas to discourse upon the construction of the tower, its relation to the other buildings and especially its accessibility from the pits. We walked again in the outer garden and by the time we returned to Ras Thavas' quarters it was almost dark and the master surgeon was considerably fatigued.

"I feel that I shall sleep well tonight," he said as I left him.

"I hope so, Ras Thavas," I replied.

CHAPTER VII
ESCAPE

IT WAS USUALLY about three hours after the evening meal, which was served immediately after dark, that the establishment quieted down definitely for the night. While I should have preferred waiting longer before undertaking that which I had in mind, I could not safely do so, since there was much to be accomplished before dawn. So it was that with the first indications that the occupants of the building in which my work was to be performed had retired for the night, I left my quarters and went directly to the laboratory, where, fortunately for my plans, the bodies of Gor Hajus, the assassin of Toonol, and 378-J-493811-P both reposed. It was the work of a few minutes to carry them to adjoining tables, where I quickly strapped them securely against the possibility that one or both of them might not be willing to agree to the proposition I was about to make them, and thus force me to anesthetize them again. At last the incisions were made, the tubes attached and the motors started. 378-J-493811-P, whom I shall hereafter call by his own name, Dar Tarus, was the first to open his eyes; but he had not regained full consciousness when Gor Hajus showed signs of life.

I waited until both appeared quite restored. Dar Tarus was eyeing me with growing recognition that brought a most venomous expression of hatred to his countenance. Gor Hajus was frankly puzzled. The last he remembered was the scene in the death chamber at the instant that his executioner had run a sword through his heart. It was I who broke the silence.

"In the first place," I said, "let me tell you where you are, if you do not already know."

"I know well enough where I am," growled Dar Tarus.

"Ah!" exclaimed Gor Hajus, whose eyes had been roaming about the chamber. "I can guess where I am. What Toonolian has not heard of Ras Thavas? So they sold my corpse to the old butcher, did they? And what now? Did I just arrive?"

"You have been here six years," I told him, "and you may stay here forever unless we three can reach an agreement within the next few minutes, and that goes for you too, Dar Tarus."

"Six years!" mused Gor Hajus. "Well, out with it, man. What do you want? If it is to slay Ras Thavas, no! He has saved me from utter destruction; but name me some other, preferably Vobis Kan, Jeddak of Toonol. Find me a blade and I will slay a hundred to regain life."

"I seek the life of none unless he stands in the way of the fulfilment of my desire in this matter that I have in mind. Listen! Ras Thavas had here a beautiful Duhorian girl. He sold her body to Xaxa, Jeddara of Phundahl, transplanting the girl's brain to the wrinkled and hideous body of the jeddara. It is my intention to regain the body, restore it to its own brain and return the girl to Duhor."

Gor Hajus grinned. "You have a large contract on your hands," he said, "but I can see that you are a man after my own heart and I am with you. It will give freedom and fighting, and all that I ask is a chance for one thrust at Vobis Kan."

"I promise you life," I replied; "but with the understanding that you serve me faithfully and none other, undertaking no business of your own, until mine has been carried to a successful conclusion."

"That means that I shall have to serve you for life," he replied, "for the thing you have undertaken you can never accomplish; but that is better than lying here on a cold ersite slab waiting for old Ras Thavas to come along and carve out my gizzard. I am yours! Let me up, that I may feel a good pair of legs under me again."

"And you?" I asked, turning to Dar Tarus as I released the

bonds that held Gor Hajus. For the first time I now noticed that the ugly expression that I had first noted upon the face of Dar Tarus had given place to one of eagerness.

"Strike off my bonds!" he cried. "I will follow you to the ends of Barsoom and the way leads thus far to the fulfilment of your design; but it will not. It will lead to Phundahl and to the chamber of the wicked Xaxa, where, by the generosity of my ancestors, I may be given the opportunity to avenge the hideous wrong the creature did me. You could not have chosen one better fitted for your mission than Dar Tarus, one time soldier of the Jeddara's Guard, whom she had slain that in my former body one of her rotten nobles might woo the girl I loved."

A moment later the two men stood at my side, and without more delay I led them toward the runway that descended to the pits beneath the building. As we went, I described to them the creature I had chosen to be the fourth member of our strange party. Gor Hajus questioned the wisdom of my choice, saying that the ape would attract too much attention to us. Dar Tarus, however, believed that it might be helpful in many respects, since it was possible that we might be compelled to spend some time among the islands of the marshes which were often infested with these creatures; while, once in Phundahl, the ape might readily be used in the furtherance of our plans and would cause no considerable comment in a city where many of these beasts are held in captivity and often are seen performing for the edification of street crowds.

We went at once to the vault where the ape lay and where I had concealed the anesthetized body of Valla Dia. Here I revived the great anthropoid and to my great relief found that the human half of its brain still was dominant. Briefly I explained my plan as I had to the other two and won the hearty promise of his support upon my engaging to restore his brain to its rightful place upon the completion of our venture.

First we must get off the island, and I outlined two plans I had in mind. One was to steal one of Ras Thavas' three fliers and set out directly for Phundahl, and the other, in the event that the first did not seem feasible, was to secret ourselves aboard one of them on the chance that we might either overpower the crew and take over the ship after we had left the island, or escape undetected upon its arrival in Toonol. Dar Tarus liked the first plan; the ape, whom we now called by the name belonging to the human half of his brain, Hovan Du, preferred the first alternative of the second plan; and Gor Hajus the second alternative.

Dar Tarus explained that as our principal objective was Phundahl, the quicker we got there the better. Hovan Du argued that by seizing the ship after it had left the island we would have longer time in which to make our escape before the ship was missed and pursuit instituted, than by seizing it now in the full knowledge that its absence would be discovered within a few hours. Gor Hajus thought that it would be better if we could come into Toonol secretly and there, through one of his friends, secure arms and a flier of our own. It would never do, he insisted, to attempt to go far without arms for himself and Dar Tarus, nor could we hope to reach Phundahl without being overhauled by pursuers; for we must plan on the hypothesis that Ras Thavas would immediately discover my absence; that he would at once investigate; that he would find Dar Tarus and Gor Hajus missing and thereupon lose no time in advising Vobis Kan, Jeddak of Toonol, that Gor Hajus the assassin was at large, whereupon the Jeddak's best ships would be sent in pursuit.

Gor Hajus' reasoning was sound and coupled with my recollection that Ras Thavas had told me that his three ships were slow, I could readily foresee that our liberty would be of short duration were we to steal one of the old surgeon's fliers.

As we discussed the matter we had made our way through the pits and I had found the exit to the tower. Silently we passed upward along the runway and out upon the roof. Both moons were winging low through the heavens and the scene was almost as light as day. If anyone was about discovery was certain. We hastened toward the hangar and were soon within it, where, for a moment at least, I breathed far more easily than I had beneath those two brilliant moons upon the exposed roof.

The fliers were peculiar looking contrivances, low, squat, with rounded bows and sterns and covered decks, their every line proclaiming them as cargo carriers built for anything but speed. One was much smaller than the other two and a second was evidently undergoing repairs. The third I entered and examined carefully. Gor Hajus was with me and pointed out several places where we might hide with little likelihood of discovery unless it were suspected that we might be aboard, and that of course constituted a very real danger; so much so that I had about decided to risk all aboard the small flier, which Gor Hajus assured me would be the fastest of the three, when Dar Tarus stuck his head into the ship and motioned me to come quickly.

"There is someone about," he said when I reached his side.

"Where?" I demanded.

"Come," he said, and led me to the rear of the hangar, which was flush with the wall of the building upon which it stood, and pointed through one of the windows into the inner garden where, to my consternation, I saw Ras Thavas walking slowly to and fro. For an instant I was sick with despair, for I knew that no ship could leave that roof unseen while anyone was abroad in the garden beneath, and Ras Thavas least of all people in the world; but suddenly a great light dawned upon me. I called the three close to me and explained my plan.

Instantly they grasped the possibilities in it and a moment later we had run the small flier out upon the roof and turned her nose toward the east, away from Toonol. Then Gor Hajus entered her, set the various controls as we had decided, opened the throttle, slipped back to the roof. The four of us hastened into the hangar and ran to the rear window where we saw the ship moving slowly and gracefully out over the garden and the head of Ras Thavas, whose ears must instantly have caught the faint purring of the motor, for he was looking up by the time we reached the window.

Instantly he hailed the ship and stepping back from the window that he might not see me I answered: "Good-bye, Ras Thavas! It is I, Vad Varo, going out into a strange world to see what it is like. I shall return. The spirits of your ancestors be with you until then." That was a phrase I had picked up from reading in Ras Thavas' library and I was quite proud of it.

"Come back at once," he shouted up in reply, "or you will be with the spirits of your own ancestors before another day is done."

I made no reply. The ship was now at such a distance that

I feared my voice might no longer seem to come from it and that we should be discovered. Without more delay we concealed ourselves aboard one of the remaining fliers, that upon which no work was being done, and there commenced as long and tiresome a period of waiting as I can recall ever having passed through.

I had at last given up any hope of the ship's being flown that day when I heard voices in the hangar, and presently the sound of footsteps aboard the flier. A moment later a few commands were given and almost immediately the ship moved slowly out into the open.

The four of us were crowded into a small compartment built into a tiny space between the forward and aft starboard buoyancy tanks. It was very dark and poorly ventilated, having evidently been designed as a storage closet to utilize otherwise waste space. We dared not converse for fear of attracting attention to our presence, and for the same reason we moved about as little as possible, since we had no means of knowing but that some member of the crew might be just beyond the thin door that separated us from the main cabin of the ship. Altogether we were most uncomfortable; but the distance to Toonol is not so great but that we might hope that our situation would soon be changed—at least if Toonol was to be the destination of the ship. Of this we soon had cheering hope. We had been out but a short time when, faintly, we heard a hail and then the motors were immediately shut down and the ship stopped.

"What ship?" we heard a voice demand, and from aboard our own came the reply:

"The Vosar, Tower of Thavas for Toonol." We heard a scraping as the other ship touched ours.

"We are coming aboard to search you in the name of Vobis Kan, Jeddak of Toonol. Make way!" shouted one from the other ship. Our cheer had been of short duration. We heard the shuffling of many feet and Gor Hajus whispered in my ear.

"What shall we do?" he asked.

I slipped my short-sword into his hand. "Fight!" I replied.

"Good, Vad Varo," he replied, and then I handed him my pistol and told him to pass it on to Dar Tarus. We heard the voices again, but nearer now.

"What ho!" cried one. "It is Bal Zak himself, my old friend Bal Zak!"

"None other," replied a deep voice. "And whom did you expect to find in command of the Vosar other than Bal Zak?"

"Who could know but that it might have been this Vad Varo himself, or even Gor Hajus," said the other, "and our orders are to search all ships."

"I would that they were here," replied Bal Zak, "for the reward is high. But how could they, when Ras Thavas himself with his own eyes saw them fly off in the Pinsar before dawn this day and disappear in the east?"

"Right you are, Bal Zak," agreed the other, "and it were a waste of time to search your ship. Come men! to our own!"

I could feel the muscles about my heart relax with the receding footfalls of Vobis Kan's warriors as they quitted the deck of the Vosar for their own ship, and my spirits rose with the renewed purring of our own motor as Ras Thavas' flier again got under way. Gor Hajus bent his lips close to my ear.

"The spirits of our ancestors smile upon us," he whispered. "It is night and the darkness will aid in covering our escape from the ship and the landing stage."

"What makes you think it is night?" I asked.

"Vobis Kan's ship was close by when it hailed and asked our name. By daylight it could have seen what ship we were."

He was right. We had been locked in that stuffy hole since before dawn, and while I had thought that it had been for a considerable time, I also had realized that the darkness and the inaction and the nervous strain would tend to make it seem much longer than it really had been; so that I would not have been greatly surprised had we made Toonol by daylight.

The distance from the Tower of Thavas to Toonol is inconsiderable, so that shortly after Vobis Kan's ship had spoken us we came to rest upon the landing stage at our destination. For a long time we waited, listening to the sounds of movement aboard the ship and wondering, upon my part at least, as to what the intentions of the captain might be. It is quite possible that Bal Zak might return to Thavas this same night, especially if he had come to Toonol to fetch a rich or powerful patient to the laboratories; but if he had come only for supplies he might well lie here until the morrow. This much I had learned from Gor Hajus, my own knowledge of the movements of the fliers of Ras Thavas being considerably less than nothing; for, though I had been months a lieutenant of the master surgeon, I had learned only the day before of the existence of his small fleet, it being according to the policy of Ras Thavas to tell me nothing unless the telling of it coincided with and furthered his own plans.

Questions which I asked he always answered, if he reasoned that the effects would not be harmful to his own interests, but he volunteered nothing that he did not particularly wish me to know; and the fact that there were no windows in the outside walls of the buildings facing toward Toonol, that I had never before the previous day been upon the roof and that I never had seen a ship sail over the inner court toward the east all tended to explain my ignorance of the fleet and its customary operations.

We waited quietly until silence fell upon the ship, betokening either that the crew had retired for the night or that they had gone down into the city. Then, after a whispered consultation with Gor Hajus, we decided to make an attempt to leave the flier. It was our purpose to seek a hiding place within the tower of the landing stage from which we might investigate possible avenues of escape into the city, either at once or upon the morrow when we might more easily mix with the crowd that Gor Hajus said would certainly be in evidence from a few hours after sunrise.

Cautiously I opened the door of our closet and looked into the main cabin beyond. It lay in darkness. Silently we filed out. The silence of the tomb lay upon the flier, but from far below arose the subdued noises of the city. So far, so good! Then, without sound, without warning, a burst of brilliant light illuminated the interior of the cabin. I felt my fingers tighten upon my sword hilt as I glanced quickly about.

Directly opposite us, in the narrow doorway of a small cabin, stood a tall man whose handsome harness betokened the fact that he was no common warrior. In either hand he held a heavy Barsoomian pistol, into the muzzles of which we found ourselves staring.

CHAPTER VIII
HANDS UP!

IN QUIET TONES he spoke the words of the Barsoomian equivalent of our earthly *hands up!* The shadow of a grim smile touched his lips, and as he saw us hesitate to obey his commands he spoke again.

"Do as I tell you and you will be well off. Keep perfect silence. A raised voice may spell your doom; a pistol shot most assuredly."

Gor Hajus raised his hands above his head and we others followed his example.

"I am Bal Zak," announced the stranger. My heart slumped.

"Then you had better commence firing," said Gor Hajus, "for you will not take us alive and we are four to one."

"Not so fast, Gor Hajus," admonished the captain of the Vosar, "until you learn what is in my mind."

"That, we already know for we heard you speak of the large reward that awaited the captor of Vad Varo and Gor Hajus," snapped the assassin of Toonol.

"Had I craved that reward so much I could have turned you over to the dwar of Vobis Kan's ship when he boarded us," said Bal Zak.

"You did not know we were aboard the Vosar," I reminded him.

"Ah, but I did."

Gor Hajus snorted his disbelief.

"How then," Bal Zak reminded us, "was I able to be ready upon this very spot when you emerged from your hiding place? Yes, I knew that you were aboard."

"But how?" demanded Dar Tarus.

"It is immaterial," replied Bal Zak, "but to satisfy your natural curiosity I will tell you that I have quarters in a small room in the Tower of Thavas, my windows overlook the roof and the hangar. My long life spent aboard fliers has made me very sensitive to every sound of a ship—motors changing their speed will awaken me in the dead of night, as quickly as will their starting or their stopping. I was awakened by the starting of the motors of the Pinsar; I saw three of you upon the roof and the fourth drop from the deck of the flier as

she started and my judgment told me that the ship was being sent out unmanned for some reason of which I had no
knowledge. It was too late for me to prevent the act and so I
waited in silence to learn what would follow. I saw you hasten
into the hangar and I heard Ras Thavas' hail and your reply,
and then I saw you board the Vosar. Immediately I descended
to the roof and ran noiselessly to the hangar, apprehending
that you intended making away with this ship; but there
was no one about the controls; and from a tiny port in the
control room, through which one has a view of the main
cabin, I saw you enter that closet. I was at once convinced that
your only purpose was to stow away for Toonol and conse-
quently, aside from keeping an eye upon your hiding place,
I went about my business as usual."

"And you did not advise Ras Thavas?" I asked.

"I advised no one," he replied. "Years ago I learned to mind
my own business, to see all, to hear all and to tell nothing unless it profited me to do so."

"But you said that the reward is high for our apprehension,"
Gor Hajus reminded him. "Would it not be profitable to collect it?"

"There are in the breasts of honorable men," replied Bal
Zak, "forces that rise superior to the lust for gold, and while
Toonolians are supposedly a people free from the withering influences of sentiment yet I for one am not totally unconscious of the demand of gratitude. Six years ago, Gor
Hajus, you refused to assassinate my father, holding that he
was a good man, worthy to live and one that had once befriended you slightly. Today, through his son, you reap your
reward and in some measure are repaid for the punishment
that was meted out to you by Vobis Kan because of your refusal to slay the sire of Bal Zak. I have sent my crew away that
none aboard the Vosar but myself might have knowledge of
your presence. Tell me your plans and command me in what
way I may be of further service to you."

"We wish to reach the streets, unobserved," replied Gor
Hajus. "Can you but help us in that we shall not put upon
your shoulders further responsibility for our escape. You have
our gratitude and in Toonol, I need not remind you, the gratitude of Gor Hajus is a possession that even the Jeddak has
craved."

"Your problem is complicated," said Bal Zak, after a moment of thought, "by the personnel of your party. The ape would immediately attract attention and arouse suspicion. Knowing much of Ras Thavas' experiments I realized at once this morning, after watching him with you, that he had the brain of a man; but this very fact would attract to him and to you the closer attention of the masses."

"I do not need acquaint them with the fact," growled Hovan Du. "To them I need be but a captive ape. Are such unknown in Toonol?"

"Not entirely, though they are rare," replied Bal Zak. "But there is also the white skin of Vad Varo! Ras Thavas appears to have known nothing of the presence of the ape with you; but he full well knew of Vad Varo, and your description has been spread by every means at his command. You would be recognized immediately by the first Toonolian that lays eyes upon you, and then there is Gor Hajus. He has been as dead for six years, yet I venture there is scarce a Toonolian that broke the shell prior to ten years ago who does not know the face of Gor Hajus as well as he knows that of his own mother. The jeddak himself was not better known to the people of Toonol than Gor Hajus. That leaves but one who might possibly escape suspicion and detection in the streets of Toonol."

"If we could but obtain weapons for these others," I suggested, "we might even yet reach the house of Gor Hajus' friend."

"Fight your way through the city of Toonol?" demanded Bal Zak.

"I admire the will," commented the commander of the Vosar, "but fear that the flesh is without sufficient strength. Wait! there is a way—perhaps. On the stage just below this there is a public depot where equilibrimotors are kept and rented. Could we find the means to obtain four of these there would be a chance, at least, for you to elude the air patrols and reach the house of Gor Hajus' friend; and I think I see a way to the accomplishment of that. The landing tower is closed for the night but there are several watchmen distributed through it at different levels. There is one at the equilibrimotor depot and, as I happen to know, he is a devotee of jetan. He would rather play jetan than attend to his duties as watchman. I often remain aboard the Vosar at night and occasionally he and I indulge in a game. I will ask him up tonight and while he is thus engaged you may go to the depot, help yourselves to equilibrimotors and pray to your ancestors that no air patrol suspicions you as you cross the city toward your destination. What think you of this plan, Gor Hajus?"

"It is splendid," replied the assassin. "And you, Vad Varo?"

"If I knew what an equilibrimotor is I might be in a better position to judge the merits of the plan," I replied. "However, I am satisfied to abide by the judgment of Gor Hajus. I can assure you, Bal Zak, of our great appreciation, and as Gor Hajus has put the stamp of his approval upon your plan I can only urge you to arrange that we may put it into effect with as little delay as possible."

"Good!" exclaimed Bal Zak. "Come with me and I will conceal you until I have lured the watchman to the jetan game within my cabin. After that your fate will be in your own hands."

We followed him from the ship onto the deck of the landing stage and close under the side of the Vosar opposite that from which the watchman must approach the ship and enter it. Then, bidding us good luck, Bal Zak departed.

From the summit of the landing tower I had my first view of a Martian city. Several hundred feet below me lay spread the broad, well lighted avenues of Toonol, many of which were crowded with people. Here and there, in this central district, a building was raised high upon its supporting, cylindrical metal shaft; while further out, where the residences predominated, the city took on the appearance of a colossal and grotesque forest. Among the larger palaces only an occasional suite of rooms was thus raised high above the level of the others, these being the sleeping apartments of the owners, their servants or their guests; but the smaller homes were raised in their entirety, a precaution necessitated by the constant activities of the followers of Gor Hajus' ancient profession that permitted no man to be free from the constant menace of assassination. Throughout the central district the sky was pierced by the lofty towers of several other landing stages; but, as I was later to learn, these were comparatively few in number. Toonol is in no sense a flying nation, supporting no such enormous fleets of merchant ships and vessels of war as, for example, the twin cities of Helium or the great capitol of Ptarth.

A peculiar feature of the street lighting of Toonol, and in fact the same condition applies to the lighting of other Barsoomian cities I have visited, I noted for the first time that night as I waited upon the landing stage for the return of Bal Zak with the watchman. The luminosity below me seemed confined directly to the area to be lighted; there was no diffusion of light upward or beyond the limits the lamps were designed to light. This was effected, I was told, by lamps designed upon principles resulting from ages of investigation of the properties of light waves and the laws governing them which permit Barsoomian scientists to confine and control light as we confine and control matter. The light waves leave the lamp, pass along a prescribed circuit and return to the lamp. There is no waste nor, strange this seemed to me, are there any dense shadows when lights are properly installed and adjusted; for the waves in passing around objects to return to the lamp, illuminate all sides of them.

The effect of this lighting from the great height of the tower was rather remarkable. The night was dark, there being no moons at that hour upon this night, and the effect was that obtained when sitting in a darkened auditorium and looking upon a brilliantly lighted stage. I was still intent upon watching the life and color beneath when we heard Bal Zak returning. That he had been successful in his mission was apparent from the fact that he was conversing with another.

Five minutes later we crept quietly from our hiding place and descended to the stage below where lay the equilibrimotor depot. As theft is practically unknown upon Barsoom, except for purposes entirely disassociated from a desire to obtain pecuniary profit through the thing stolen, no precautions are taken against theft. We therefore found the doors of the depot open and Gor Hajus and Dar Tarus quickly selected four equilibrimotors and adjusted them upon us. They consist of a broad belt, not unlike the life belt used aboard trans-oceanic liners upon Earth; these belts are filled with the eighth Barsoomian ray, or ray of propulsion, to a sufficient degree to just about equalize the pull of gravity and thus to maintain a person in equilibrium between that force and the opposite force exerted by the eighth ray. Permanently attached to the back of the belt is a small radium motor, the controls for which are upon the front of the belt. Rigidly attached to and projecting from each side of the upper rim of the belt is a strong, light wing with small hand levers for quickly altering its position.

Gor Hajus quickly explained the method of control, but I could apprehend that there might be embarrassment and trouble awaiting me before I mastered the art of flying in an equilibrimotor. He showed me how to tilt the wings downward in walking so that I would not leave the ground at every step, and thus he led me to the edge of the landing stage.

"We will rise here," he said, "and keeping in the darkness of the upper levels seek to reach the house of my friend without being detected. If we are pursued by air patrol we must separate; and later those who escape may gather just west of the city wall where you will find a small lake with a deserted tower upon its northern rim—this tower will be our rendezvous in event of trouble. Follow me!" He started his motor and rose gracefully into the air.

Hovan Du followed him and then it was my turn. I rose beautifully for about twenty feet, floating out over the city which lay hundreds of feet below, and then, quite suddenly, I turned upside down. I had done something wrong—I was quite positive of it. It was a most startling sensation, I can assure you, floating there with my head down, quite helpless; while below me lay the streets of a great city and no softer, I was sure, than the streets of Los Angeles or Paris. My motor was still going, and as I manipulated the controls which operated the wings I commenced to describe all sorts of strange loops and spirals and spins; and then Dar Tarus came to my rescue. First he told me to lie quietly and then directed the manipulation of each wing until I had gained an upright position. After that I did fairly well and was soon rising in the wake of Gor Hajus and Hovan Du.

I need not describe in detail the hour of flying, or rather floating, that ensued. Gor Hajus led us to a considerable altitude and there, through the darkness above the city, our slow motors drove us toward a district of magnificent homes surrounded by spacious grounds; and here, as we hovered over a large palace, we were suddenly startled by a sharp challenge coming from directly above us.

"Who flies by night?" a voice demanded.

"Friends of Mu Tel, Prince of the House of Kan," replied Gor Hajus quickly.

"Let me see your night flying permit and your flier's license," ordered the one above us, at the same time swooping suddenly to our level and giving me my first sight of a Martian policeman. He was equipped with a much swifter and handier equilibrimotor than ours. I think that was the first fact to impress us deeply, and it demonstrated the futility of flight; for he could have given us ten minutes start and overhauled each of us within another ten minutes, even though we had elected to fly in different directions. The fellow was a warrior rather than a policeman, though detailed to duty such as our earthly police officers perform; the city being patroled both day and night by the warriors of Vobis Kan's army.

He dropped now close to the assassin of Toonol, again demanding permit and license and at the same time flashing a light in the face of my comrade.

"By the sword of the jeddak!" he cried. "Fortune heaps her favors upon me. Who would have thought an hour since that it would be I who would collect the reward for the capture of Gor Hajus?"

"Any other fool might have thought it," returned Gor Hajus, "but he would have been as wrong as you," and as he spoke he struck with the short-sword I had loaned him.

The blow was broken by the wing of the warrior's equilibrimotor, which it demolished, yet it inflicted a severe wound in the fellow's shoulder. He tried to back off, but the damaged wing caused him to only wheel around erratically; and then he seized upon his whistle and attempted to blow a mighty blast that was cut short by another blow from Gor Hajus' sword that split the man's head open to the bridge of his nose.

"Quick!" cried the assassin. "We must drop into the gardens of Mu Tel, for that signal will bring a swarm of air patrols about our heads."

The others I saw falling rapidly toward the ground, but again I had trouble. Depress my wings as I would I moved only slightly downward and upon a path that, if continued, would have landed me at a considerable distance from the gardens of Mu Tel. I was approaching one of the elevated portions of the palace, what appeared to be a small suite that was raised upon its shining metal shaft far above the ground. From all directions I could hear the screaming whistles of the air patrols answering the last call of their comrade whose corpse floated just above me, a guide even in death to point the way for his fellows to search us out. They were sure to discover him and then I would be in plain view of them and my fate sealed.

Perhaps I could find ingress to the apartments looming darkly near! There I might hide until the danger had passed, provided I could enter, undetected. I directed my course toward the structure; an open window took form through the darkness and then I collided with a fine wire netting—I had run into a protecting curtain that fends off assassins of the air from these high flung sleeping apartments. I felt that I was lost. If I could but reach the ground I might find concealment among the trees and shrubbery that I had seen vaguely outlined beneath me in the gardens of this Barsoomian prince; but I could not drop at a sufficient angle to bring me to ground within the garden, and when I tried to spiral down I turned over and started up again. I thought of ripping open my belt and letting the eighth ray escape; but in my unfamiliarity with this strange force I feared that such an act might precipitate me to the ground with too great violence, though I was determined to have recourse to it as a last alternative if nothing less drastic presented itself.

In my last attempt to spiral downward I rose rapidly feet foremost to a sudden and surprising collision with some object above me. As I frantically righted myself, fully expecting to be immediately seized by a member of the air patrol, I found myself face to face with the corpse of the warrior Gor Hajus had slain. The whistling of the air patrols sounded ever nearer—it could be only a question of seconds now before I was discovered—and with the stern necessity that confronted me, with death looking me in the face, there burst upon me a possible avenue of escape from my dilemma.

Seizing tightly with my left hand the harness of the dead Toonolian, I whipped out my dagger and slashed his buoyancy belt a dozen times. Instantly, as the rays escaped, his body started to drag me downward. Our descent was rapid, but not precipitate, and it was but a matter of seconds before we landed gently upon the scarlet sward of the gardens of Mu

Tel, Prince of the House of Kan, close beside a clump of heavy shrubbery. Above me sounded the whistles of the circling patrols as I dragged the corpse of the warrior into the concealing depth of the foliage. Nor was I an instant too soon for safety, as almost immediately the brilliant rays of a searchlight shot downward from the deck of a small patrol ship, illuminating the open spaces of the garden all about me. A hurried glance through the branches and the leaves of my sanctuary revealed nothing of my companions and I breathed a sigh of relief in the thought that they, too, had found concealment.

The light played for a short time about the gardens and then passed on, as did the sound of the patrol's whistles, as the search proceeded elsewhere; thus giving me the assurance that no suspicion was directed upon our hiding place.

Left in darkness I appropriated such of the weapons of the dead warrior as I coveted, after having removed my equilibrimotor, which I was first minded to destroy, but which I finally decided to moor to one of the larger shrubs against the possibility that I might again have need for it; and now, secure in the conviction that the danger of discovery by the air patrol had passed, I left my concealment and started in search of my companions.

Keeping well in the shadows of the trees and shrubs I moved in the direction of the main building, which loomed darkly near at hand; for in this direction I believed Gor Hajus would lead the others as I knew that the palace of Mu Tel was to have been our destination. As I crept along, moving with utmost stealth, Thuria, the nearer moon, shot suddenly above the horizon, illuminating the night with her brilliant rays. I was close to the building's ornately carved wall at the moment; beside me was a narrow niche, its interior cast in deepest shadow by Thuria's brilliant rays; to my left was an open bit of lawn upon which, revealed in every detail of its terrifying presence, stood as fearsome a creature as my earthly eyes ever had rested upon. It was a beast about the size of a Shetland pony, with ten short legs and a terrifying head that bore some slight resemblance to that of a frog, except that the jaws were equipped with three rows of long, sharp tusks.

The thing had its nose in the air and was sniffing about, while its great pop eyes moved swiftly here and there, assuring me, beyond the shadow of a doubt, that it was searching for someone. I am not inclined to be egotistical, yet I could not avoid the conviction that it was searching for me. It was my first experience of a Martian watch dog; and as I sought concealment within the dark shadows of the niche behind me, at the very instant that the creature's eyes alighted upon me, and heard his growl and saw him charge straight toward me, I had a premonition that it might prove my last experience with one.

I drew back my long-sword as I backed into the niche, but with a sense of the utter inadequacy of the unaccustomed weapon in the face of this three or four hundred pounds of ferocity incarnate. Slowly I backed away into the shadows as the creature bore down upon me and then, as it entered the niche, my back collided with a solid obstacle that put an end to further retreat.

CHAPTER IX

THE PALACE OF MU TEL

AS THE CALOT entered the niche I experienced, I believe, all of the reactions of the cornered rat, and I certainly know that I set myself to fight in that proverbial manner. The beast was almost upon me and I was metaphorically kicking myself for not having remained in the open where there were many tall trees when the support at my back suddenly gave way, a hand reached out of the darkness behind me and seized my harness and I was drawn swiftly into inky blackness. A door slammed and the silhouette of the calot against the moonlit entrance to the niche was blotted out.

A gruff voice spoke in my ear. "Come with me!" it said. A hand found mine and thus I was led along through the darkness of what I soon discovered was a narrow corridor from the constantly recurring collisions I had first with one side of it and then with the other.

Ascending gradually, the corridor turned abruptly at right angles and I saw beyond my guide a dim luminosity that grad-

ually increased until another turn brought us to the threshold of a brilliantly lighted chamber—a magnificent apartment,
the gorgeous furnishings and decorations of which beggar the
meager descriptive powers of my native tongue. Gold, ivory,
precious stones, marvellous woods, resplendent fabrics, gorgeous furs and startling architecture combined to impress
upon my earthly vision such a picture as I had never even
dreamed of dreaming; and in the center of this room, surrounded by a little group of Martians, were my three companions.

My guide conducted me toward the party, the members of
which had turned toward us as we entered the chamber,
and stopped before a tall Barsoomian, resplendent in jewel
encrusted harness.

"Prince," he said, "I was scarce a tal too soon. In fact, as
I opened the door to step out into the garden in search of
him, as you directed, there he was upon the opposite side
with one of the calots of the garden almost upon him."

"Good!" exclaimed he who had been addressed as prince,
and then he turned to Gor Hajus. "This is he, my friend, of
whom you told me?"

"This is Vad Varo, who claims to be from the planet Jasoom," replied Gor Hajus; "and this, Vad Varo, is Mu Tel,
Prince of the House of Kan."

I bowed and the prince advanced and placed his right hand
upon my left shoulder in true Barsoomian acknowledgment
of an introduction; when I had done similarly, the ceremony
was over. There was no silly pleased-to-meet-you, how-do-
you-do? or it's-a-pleasure-I-assure-you.

At Mu Tel's request I narrated briefly what had befallen
me between the time I had become separated from my companions and the moment that one of his officers had snatched
me from impending disaster. Mu Tel gave instructions that
all traces of the dead patrol be removed before dawn lest
their discovery bring upon him the further suspicion of his
uncle, Vobis Kan, Jeddak of Toonol, whom it seemed had
long been jealous of his nephew's growing popularity and
fearful that he harbored aspirations for the throne.

It was later in the evening, during one of those elaborate
meals for which the princes of Barsoom are justly famous,
when mellowed slightly by the rare vintages with which he

delighted his guests, that Mu Tel discoursed with less restraint upon his imperial uncle.

"The nobles have long been tired of Vobis Kan," he said, "and the people are tiring of him—he is a conscienceless tyrant—but he is our hereditary ruler, and so they hesitate to change. We are a practical people, little influenced by sentiment; yet there is enough to keep the masses loyal to their jeddak even after he has ceased to deserve their loyalty, while the fear of the wrath of the masses keeps the nobles loyal. There is also the natural suspicion that I, the next in line for succession, would make them no less tyrannical a jeddak than has Vobis Kan, while, having youth, I might be much more active in cruel and nefarious practices.

"For myself, I would not hesitate to destroy my uncle and seize his throne were I sure of the support of the army, for with the warriors of Vobis Kan at my back I might defy the balance of Toonol. It is because of this that I long since offered my friendship to Gor Hajus; not that he might slay my uncle, but that when I had slain him in fair fight Gor Hajus might win to me the loyalty of the jeddak's warriors, for great is the popularity of Gor Hajus among the soldiers, who ever look up to such a great fighter with reverence and devotion. I have offered Gor Hajus a high place in the affairs of Toonol should he cast his lot with me; but he tells me that he has first to fulfill his obligations to you, Vad Varo, and for the furtherance of your adventure he has asked me to give you what assistance I may. This I offer gladly, from purely practical motives, since your early success will hasten mine. Therefore I propose to place at your disposal a staunch flier that will carry you and your companions to Phundahl."

This offer I naturally accepted, after which we fell to discussing plans for our departure which we finally decided to attempt early the following night, at a time when neither of the moons would be in the heavens. After a brief discussion of equipment we were, at my request, permitted to retire since I had not slept for more than thirty-six hours and my companions for twenty-four.

Slaves conducted us to our sleeping apartments, which were luxuriously furnished, and arranged magnificent sleeping silks and furs for our comfort. After they had left us Gor Hajus touched a button and the room rose swiftly upon its metal shaft to a height of forty or fifty feet; the wire netting automatically dropped about us, and we were safe for the night.

The following morning, after our apartment had been lowered to its daylight level and before I was permitted to leave it, a slave was sent to me by Mu Tel with instructions to stain my entire body the beautiful copper-red of my Barsoomian friends; furnishing me with a disguise which I well knew to be highly essential to the success of my venture, since my white skin would have drawn unpleasant notice upon me in any city of Barsoom. Another slave brought harness and weapons for Gor Hajus, Dar Tarus and myself, and a collar and chain for Hovan Du, the ape-man. Our harness, while of heavy material and splendid workmanship, was quite plain, being free of all insignia either of rank or service—such harness as is customarily worn by the Barsoomian panthan, or soldier of fortune, at such times as he is not definitely in the service of any nations or individual. These panthans are virtually men without a country, being roving mercenaries ready to sell their swords to the highest bidder. Although they have no organization they are ruled by a severe code of ethics and while in the employ of a master are, almost without exception, loyal to him. They are generally supposed to be men who have flown from the wrath of their own jeddaks or the justice of their own courts,but there is among them a sprinkling of adventurous souls who have adopted their calling because of the thrills and excitement it offers. While they are well paid, they are also great gamblers and notorious spenders, with the result that they are almost always without funds and often reduced to strange expedients for the gaining of their livelihoods between engagements; a fact which gave great plausibility to our possession of a trained ape, which upon Mars would appear no more remarkable than would to us the possession of a monkey or parrot by an old salt just returned, from a long cruise, to one of our Earthly ports.

This day that I stayed in the palace of Mu Tel I spent much in the company of the prince, who found pleasure in questioning me concerning the customs, the politics, the civilization and the geography of Earth, with much of which, I was surprised to note, he seemed quite familiar; a fact which he explained was due to the marvellous development of Barsoomian astronomical instruments, wireless photography and wireless telephony; the last of which has been brought to such a state of perfection that many Barsoomian savants have succeeded in learning several Earthly languages, notably Urdu, English and Russian, and, a few, Chinese also. These have doubtless been the first languages to attract their attention because of the fact that they are spoken by great numbers of people over large areas of the world.

Mu Tel took me to a small auditorium in his palace that reminded me somewhat of private projection rooms on Earth. It had, I should say, a capacity of some two hundred persons and was built like a large camera obscura; the audience sitting within the instrument, their backs toward the lens and in front of them, filling one entire end of the room, a large ground glass upon which is thrown the image to be observed.

Mu Tel seated himself at a table upon which was a chart of the heavens. Just above the chart was a movable arm carrying a pointer. This pointer Mu Tel moved until it rested upon the planet Earth, then he switched off the light in the room and immediately there appeared upon the ground glass plate a view such as one might obtain from an aeroplane riding at an elevation of a thousand feet. There was something strangely familiar about the scene before me. It was of a desolate, wasted country. I saw shattered stumps whose orderly arrangement proclaimed that here once an orchard had blossomed and borne fruit. There were great, unsightly holes in the earth and over and across all a tangle of barbed wire. I asked Mu Tel how we might change the picture to another locality. He lighted a small radio bulb between us and I saw a globe there, a globe of Earth, and a small pointer fixed over it.

"The side of this globe now presented to you represents the face of the Earth turned toward us," explained Mu Tel. "You will note that the globe is slowly revolving. Place this pointer where you will upon the globe and that portion of Jasoom will be revealed for you."

I moved the pointer very slowly and the picture changed. A ruined village came into view. I saw some people moving among its ruins. They were not soldiers. A little further on I came upon trenches and dug-outs—there were no soldiers here, either. I moved the pointer rapidly north and south along a vast line of trenches. Here and there in villages there were soldiers, but they were all French soldiers and never were they in the trenches. There were no German soldiers and no fighting. The war was over, then! I moved the pointer to the Rhine and across. There were soldiers in Germany —French soldiers, English soldiers, American soldiers. We had won the war! I was glad, but it seemed very far away and quite unreal—as though no such world existed and no such peoples had ever fought—it was as though I were recalling through its illustrations a novel that I had read a long time since.

"You seem much interested in that war torn country," remarked Mu Tel.

"Yes," I explained, "I fought in that war. Perhaps I was killed. I do not know."

"And you won?" he asked.

"Yes, my people won," I replied. "We fought for a great principle and for the peace and happiness of a world. I hope that we did not fight in vain."

"If you mean that you hope that your principle will triumph because you fought and won, or that peace will come, your hopes are futile. War never brought peace—it but brings more and greater wars. War is Nature's natural state—it is folly to combat it. Peace should be considered only as a time for preparation for the principal business of man's existence. Were it not for constant warring of one form of life upon another, and even upon itself, the planets would be so overrun with life that it would smother itself out. We found upon Barsoom that long periods of peace brought plagues and terrible diseases that killed more than the wars killed and in a much more hideous and painful way. There is neither pleasure nor thrill nor reward of any sort to be gained by dying in bed of a loathesome disease. We must all die—let us therefore go out and die in a great and exciting game, and make room for the millions who are to follow us. We have tried it out upon Barsoom and we would not be without war."

Mu Tel told me much that day about the peculiar philosophy of Toonolians. They believe that no good deed was ever performed except for a selfish motive; they have no god and no religion; they believe, as do all educated Barsoomians, that man came originally from the Tree of Life, but unlike most of their fellows they do not believe that an omnipotent being created the Tree of Life. They hold that the only sin is failure—success, however achieved, is meritorious; and yet, paradoxical as it may seem, they never break their given word. Mu Tel explained that they overcame the baneful results of this degrading weakness—this sentimental bosh—by seldom, if ever, binding themselves to loyalty to another, and then only for a definitely prescribed period.

As I came to know them better, and especially Gor Hajus, I began to realize that much of their flaunted contempt of the finer sensibilities was specious. It is true that generations of inhibition had to some extent atrophied those characterstcs of heart and soul which the noblest among us so highly esteem; that friendship's ties were lax and that blood kinship awakened no high sense of responsibility or love even between parents and children; yet Gor Hajus was essentially a man of sentiment, though he would doubtless have run through the heart any who had dared accuse him of it, thus perfectly proving the truth of the other's accusation. His pride in his reputation for integrity and loyalty proved him a man of heart as truly as did his jealousy of his reputation for heartlessness prove him a man of sentiment; and in all this he was but typical of the people of Toonol. They denied deity, and in the same breath worshipped the fetish of science that they had permitted to obsess them quite as harmfully as do religious fanatics accept the unreasoning rule of their imaginary gods; and so, with all their vaunted knowledge, they were unintelligent because unbalanced.

As the day drew to a close I became the more anxious to be away. Far to the west across desolate leagues of marsh lay Phundahl, and in Phundahl the beauteous body of the girl I loved and that I was sworn to restore to its rightful owner. The evening meal was over and Mu Tel himself had conducted us to a secret hangar in one of the towers of his palace. Here artisans had prepared a flier for us, having removed during the day all signs of its real ownership, even to slightly altering its lines; so that in the event of capture Mu Tel's name might in no way be connected with the expedition. Provisions were stored, including plenty of raw meat for Hovan Du, and, as the farther moon sank below the horizon and darkness fell, a panel of the tower wall, directly in front of the flier's nose, slid aside, Mu Tel wished us luck and the ship slipped silently out into the night. The flier, like many of her type, was without cockpit or cabin; a low, metal hand-rail surmounted her gunwale; heavy rings were set substantially in her deck and to these her crew was supposed to cling or attach themselves by means of their harness hooks provided for this and similar purposes; a low wind shield, with a rakish slant, afforded some protection from the wind; the motor and controls were all exposed, as all the space below decks was taken up by the buoyancy tanks. In this type everything is sacrificed to speed; there is no comfort aboard. When moving at high speed each member of the crew lies extended at full length upon the deck, each in his allotted place to give the necessary trim, and hangs on for dear life. These Toonolian crafts, however, are not overly fast, so I was told, being far outstripped in speed by the fliers of such nations as Helium and Ptarth who have for ages devoted themselves to the perfection of their navies; but this one was quite fast enough for our purposes, to the consummation of which it would be pitted against fliers of no higher rating, and it was certainly fast enough for me. In comparison with the slow moving Vosar, it seemed to shoot through the air like an arrow.

We wasted no time in strategy or stealth, but opened her wide as soon as we were in the clear, and directed her straight toward the west and Phundahl. Scarcely had we passed over the gardens of Mu Tel when we met with our first adventure. We shot by a solitary figure floating in the air and almost simultaneously there shrilled forth the warning whistle of an air patrol. A shot whistled above us harmlessly and we were gone; but within a few seconds I saw the rays of a searchlight shining down from above and moving searchingly to and fro through the air.

"A patrol boat!" shouted Gor Hajus in my ear. Hovan Du growled savagely and shook the chain upon his collar. We raced on, trusting to the big gods and the little gods and all our ancestors that that relentless eye of light would not find us out; but it did. Within a few seconds it fell full upon our deck from above and in front of us and there it clung as the patrol boat dropped rapidly toward us while it maintained a high rate of speed upon a course otherwise identical with ours. Then, to our consternation, the ship opened fire on us with explosive bullets. These projectiles contain a high explosive that is detonated by light rays when the opaque covering of the projectile is broken by impact with the target. It is therefore not at all necessary to make a direct hit for a shot to be effective. If the projectile strikes the ground or the deck of a vessel or any solid substance near its target, it does considerably more damage when fired at a group of men than as though it struck but one of them, since it will then explode if its outer shell is broken and kill or wound several; while if it enters the body of an individual the light rays cannot reach it and it accomplishes no more than a non-explosive bullet. Moonlight is not powerful enough to detonate this explosive and so projectiles fired at night, unless touched by the powerful rays of searchlights, detonate at sunrise the following morning, making a battle field a most unsafe place at that time even though the contending forces are no longer there. Similarly they make the removal of unexploded projectiles from the bodies of the wounded a most ticklish operation which may well result in the instant death of both the patient and the surgeon.

Dar Tarus, at the controls, turned the nose of our flier upward directly toward the patrol boat and at the same time shouted to us to concentrate our fire upon her propellers. For myself, I could see little but the blinding eye of the searchlight, and at that I fired with the strange weapon to which I had received my first introduction but a few hours since when it was presented to me by Mu Tel. To me that all searching eye represented the greatest menace that confronted us, and could we blind it the patrol boat would have no great advantage over us. So I kept my rifle straight upon it, my finger on the button that controlled the fire, and prayed for a hit. Gor Hajus knelt at my side, his weapon spitting bullets at the patrol boat. Dar Tarus' hands were busy with the controls and Hovan Du squatted in the bow and growled.

Suddenly Dar Tarus voiced an exclamation of alarm. "The controls are hit!" he shouted. "We can't alter our course—the ship is useless." Almost the same instant the searchlight was extinguished—one of my bullets evidently having found it. We were quite close to the enemy now and heard their shout of anger. Our own craft, out of control, was running swiftly toward the other. It seemed that if there was not a collision we would pass directly beneath the keel of the air patrol. I asked Dar Tarus if our ship was beyond repair.

"We could repair it if we had time," he replied, "but it would take hours and while we were thus delayed the whole air patrol force of Toonol would be upon us."

"Then we must have another ship," I said.

Dar Tarus laughed. "You are right, Vad Varo," he replied, "but where shall we find it?"

I pointed to the patrol boat. "We shall not have to look far."

Dar Tarus shrugged his shoulders. "Why not!" he exclaimed. "It would be a glorious fight and a worthy death."

Gor Hajus slapped me on the shoulder. "To the death, my captain!" he cried.

Hovan Du shook his chain and roared.

The two ships were rapidly approaching one another. We had stopped firing now for fear that we might disable the craft we hoped to use for our escape; and for some reason the crew of the patrol ship had ceased firing at us—I never learned why. We were moving in a line that would bring us directly beneath the other ship. I determined to board her at all costs. I could see her keel boarding tackle slung beneath her, ready to be lowered to the deck of a quarry when once her grappling hooks had seized the prey. Doubtless they were already manning the latter, and as soon as we were beneath her the steel tentacles would reach down and seize us as her crew swarmed down the boarding tackle to our deck.

I called Hovan Du and he crept back to my side where I whispered my instructions in his ear. When I was done he nodded his head with a low growl. I cast off the harness hook that held me to the deck, and the ape and I moved to our bow after I had issued brief, whispered instructions to Gor Hajus and Dar Tarus. We were now almost directly beneath the enemy craft; I could see the grappling hooks being prepared for lowering. Our bow ran beneath the stern of the other ship and the moment was at hand for which I had been waiting. Now those upon the deck of the patrol boat could not see Hovan Du or me. The boarding tackle of the other ship swung fifteen feet above our heads; I whispered a word of command to the ape and simultaneously we crouched and sprang for the tackle. It may sound like a mad chance—failure meant almost certain death—but I felt that if two of us could reach the deck of the patrol boat while her crew was busy with the grappling gear it would be well worth the risk.

Gor Hajus had assured me that there would not be more than six men aboard the patrol ship; that one would be at the controls and the others manning the grappling hooks. It would be a most propitious time to gain a footing on the enemy's deck.

Hovan Du and I made our leaps and Fortune smiled upon us, though the huge ape but barely reached the tackle with one outstretched hand, while my Earthly muscles carried me easily to my goal. Together we made our way rapidly toward the bow of the patrol craft and without hesitation, and as previously arranged, he clambered quickly up the starboard side and I the port. If I were the more agile jumper Hovan Du far outclassed me in climbing, with the result that he reached the rail and was clambering over while my eyes were still below the level of the deck, which was, perhaps, a fortunate thing for me since, by chance, I had elected to gain the deck directly at a point where, unknown to me, one of the crew of the ship was engaged with the grappling hooks. Had his eyes not been attracted elsewhere by the shout of one of his fellows who was first to see Hovan Du's savage face rise above the gunwale, he could have dispatched me with a single blow before ever I could have set foot upon the deck.

The ape had also come up directly in front of a Toonolian warrior and this fellow had let out a yell of surprise and sought to draw his sword, but the ape, for all his great bulk, was too quick for him; and as my eyes topped the rail I saw the mighty anthropoid seize the unfortunate man by the harness, drag him to the side and hurl him to destruction far below. Instantly we were both over the rail and squarely on deck while the remaining members of the craft's crew, abandoning their stations, ran forward to overpower us. I think that the sight of the great, savage beast must have had a demoralizing effect upon them, for they hesitated, each seeming to be willing to accord his fellow the honor of first engaging us; but they did come on, though slowly. This hesitation I was delighted to see, for it accorded perfectly with the plan that I had worked out, which depended largely upon the success which might attend the efforts of Gor Hajus and Dar Tarus to reach the deck of the patrol when our craft had risen sufficiently close beneath the other to permit them to reach the boarding tackle, which we were utilizing with reverse English, as one might say.

Gor Hajus had cautioned me to dispatch the man at the controls as quickly as possible, since his very first act would be to injure them the instant that there appeared any possibility that we might be successful in our attempt to take his ship, and so I ran quickly toward him and before he could draw I cut him down. There were now four against us and we waited for them to advance that we might gain time for our fellows to reach the deck.

The four moved slowly forward and were almost within striking distance when I saw Gor Hajus' head appear above the stern rail, quickly followed by that of Dar Tarus.

"Look!" I cried to the enemy, "and surrender," and I pointed astern.

One of them turned to look and what he saw brought an exclamation of surprise to his lips. "It is Gor Hajus," he cried, and then, to me: "What is your purpose with us if we surrender?"

"We have no quarrel with you," I replied. "We but wish to leave Toonol and go our way in peace—we shall not harm you."

He turned to his fellows while, at a sign from me, my three companions stopped their advance and waited. For a few minutes the four warriors conversed in low tones, then he who had first spoken addressed me.

"There are few Toonolians," he said, "who would not be glad to serve Gor Hajus, whom we had thought long dead, but to surrender our ship to you would mean certain death for us when we reported our defeat at our headquarters. On the other hand were we to continue our defense most of us here upon the deck of this flier would be killed. If you can assure us that your plans are not aimed at the safety of Toonol I can make a suggestion that will afford an avenue of escape and safety for us all."

"We only wish to leave Toonol," I replied. "No harm can come to Toonol because of what I seek to accomplish."

"Good! and where do you wish to go?"

"That I may not tell you."

"You may trust us, if you accept my proposal," he assured

me, "which is that we convey you to your destination, after which we can return to Toonol and report that we engaged you and that after a long running fight, in which two of our number were killed, you eluded us in the darkness and escaped."

"Can we trust these men?" I asked, addressing Gor Hajus, who assured me that we could, and thus the compact was entered into which saw us speeding rapidly toward Phundahl aboard one of Vobis Kan's own fliers.

CHAPTER X

PHUNDAHL

THE FOLLOWING NIGHT the Toonolian crew set us down just inside the wall of the city of Phundahl, following the directions of Dar Tarus who was a native of the city, had been a warrior of the Jeddara's Guard and, prior to that, seen service in Phundahl's tiny navy. That he was familiar with every detail of Phundahl's defenses and her systems of patrols was evidenced by the fact that we landed without detection and that the Toonolian ship rose and departed apparently unnoticed.

Our landing place had been the roof of a low building built within and against the city wall. From this roof Dar Tarus led us down an inclined runway to the street, which, at this point, was quite deserted. The street was narrow and dark, being flanked upon one side by the low buildings built against the city wall and upon the other by higher buildings, some of which were windowless and none showing any light. Dar Tarus explained that he had chosen this point for our entrance because it was a district of storage houses, and while a hive of industry during the day, was always deserted at night, not even a watchman being required owing to the almost total absence of thievery upon Barsoom.

By devious and roundabout ways he led us finally to a section of second rate shops, eating places and hotels such as are frequented by the common soldiers, artisans and slaves,

where the only attention we attracted was due to the curios-
ity aroused by Hovan Du. As we had not eaten since leaving
Mu Tel's palace, our first consideration was food. Mu Tel had
furnished Gor Hajus with money, so that we had the means
to gratify our wants. Our first stop was at a small shop where
Gor Hajus purchased four or five pounds of thoat steak for
Hovan Du, and then we repaired to an eating place of which
Dar Tarus knew. At first the proprietor would not let us bring
Hovan Du inside, but finally, after much argument, he per-
mitted us to lock the great ape in an inner room where Hovan
Du was forced to remain with his thoat meat while we sat at
a table in the outer room.

I will say for Hovan Du that he played his role well, nor
was there once when the proprietor of the place, or any of his
patrons, or the considerable crowd that gathered to listen to
the altercation, could have guessed that the body of the great,
savage beast was animated by a human brain. It was really
only when feeding or fighting that the simian half of Hovan
Du's brain appeared to exercise any considerable influence
upon him; yet there seemed little doubt that it always colored all his thoughts and actions to some extent, accounting for
his habitual taciturnity and the quickness with which he
was aroused to anger, as well as to the fact that he never
smiled, nor appeared to appreciate in any degree the humor
of a situation. He assured me, however, that the human half
of his brain not only appreciated but greatly enjoyed the
lighter episodes and occurences of our adventure and the
witty stories and anecdotes related by Gor Hajus, the Assassin,
but that his simian anatomy had developed no muscles wherewith to evidence physical expression of his mental reactions.

We dined heartily, though upon rough and simple fare,
but were glad to escape the prying curiosity of the garrulous
and gossipy proprietor, who plied us with so many questions
as to our past performances and future plans that Dar Tarus,
who was our spokesman here, was hard put to it to quickly
fabricate replies that would be always consistent. However,
escape we did at last, and once again in the street, Dar Tarus
set out to lead us to a public lodging house of which he knew.
As we went we approached a great building of wondrous
beauty in and out of which constant streams of people were
pouring, and when we were before it Dar Tarus asked us to

wait without as he must enter. When I asked him why, he told me that this was a temple of Tur, the god worshipped by the people of Phundahl.

"I have been away for a long time," he said, "and have had no opportunity to do honor to my god. I shall not keep you waiting long. Gor Hajus, will you loan me a few pieces of gold?"

In silence the Toonolian took a few pieces of money from one of his pocket pouches and handed them to Dar Tarus, but I could see that it was only with difficulty that he hid an expression of contempt, since the Toonolians are atheists.

I asked Dar Tarus if I might accompany him into the temple, which seemed to please him very much; and so we fell in with the stream approaching the broad entrance. Dar Tarus gave me two of the gold pieces that he had borrowed from Gor Hajus and told me to follow directly behind him and do whatever I saw him doing. Directly inside the main entrance, and spread entirely across it at intervals that permitted space for the worshippers to pass between them, was a line of priests, their entire bodies, including their heads and faces, covered by a mantle of white cloth. In front of each was a substantial stand upon which rested a cash drawer. As we approached one of these we handed him a piece of gold which he immediately changed into many pieces of lesser value, one of which we dropped into a box at his side; whereupon he made several passes with his hands above our heads, dipped one of his fingers into a bowl of dirty water which he rubbed upon the ends of our noses, mumbled a few words which I could not understand and turned to the next in line as we passed on into the interior of the great temple. Never have I seen such a gorgeous display of wealth and lavish ornamentation as confronted my eyes in this, the first of the temples of Tur that it was my fortune to behold.

The enormous floor was unbroken by a single pillar and arranged upon it at regular intervals were carven images resting upon gorgeous pedestals. Some of these images were of men and some of women and many of them were beautiful; and there were others of beasts and of strange, grotesque creatures and many of these were hideous indeed. The first we approached was that of a beautiful female figure; and about the pedestal of this lay a number of men and women prone upon the floor against which they bumped their heads seven times and then arose and dropped a piece of money into a receptacle provided for that purpose, moving on then to another figure. The next that Dar Tarus and I visited was that of a man with the body of a *silian,* about the pedestal of which was arranged a series of horizontal wooden bars in concentric circles. The bars were about five feet from the floor and hanging from them by their knees were a number of men and women repeating monotonously, over and over again, something that sounded to me like, *bibble-babble-blup.*

Dar Tarus and I swung to the bars like the others and mumbled the meanless phrase for a minute or two, then we swung down, dropped a coin into the box, and moved on. I asked Dar Tarus what the words were that we had repeated and what they meant, but he said he did not know. I asked him if anyone knew, but he appeared shocked and said that such a question was sacrilegious and revealed a marked lack of faith. At the next figure we visited the people were all upon their hands and knees crawling madly in a circle about the pedestal. Seven times around they crawled and then they arose and put some money in a dish and went their ways. At another the people rolled about, saying, "Tur is Tur; Tur is Tur; Tur is Tur," and dropping money in a golden bowl when they were done.

"What god was that?" I whispered to Dar Tarus when we had quit this last figure, which had no head, but eyes, nose and mouth in the center of its belly.

"There is but one god," replied Dar Tarus, solemnly, "and he is Tur!"

"Was that Tur?" I inquired.

"Silence, man," whispered Dar Tarus. "They would tear you to pieces were they to hear such heresy."

"Oh, I beg your pardon," I exclaimed. "I did not mean to offend. I see now that that is merely one of your idols."

Dar Tarus clapped a hand over my mouth. "S-s-s-t!" he cautioned to silence. "We do not worship idols—there is but one god and he is Tur!"

"Well, what are these?" I insisted, with a sweep of a hand that embraced the several score images about which were gathered the thousands of worshippers.

"We must not ask," he assured me. "It is enough that we

have faith that all the works of Tur are just and righteous. Come! I shall soon be through and we may join our companions."

He led me next to the figure of a monstrosity with a mouth that ran entirely around its head. It had a long tail and the breasts of a woman. About this image were a great many people, each standing upon his head. They also were repeating, over and over, "Tur is Tur; Tur is Tur; Tur is Tur." When we had done this for a minute or two, during which I had a devil of a time maintaining my equilibrium, we arose, dropped a coin into the box by the pedestal and moved on.

"We may go now," said Dar Tarus. "I have done well in the sight of Tur."

"I notice," I remarked, "that the people repeated the same phase before this figure that they did at the last—Tur is Tur."

"Oh, no," exclaimed Dar Tarus. "On the contrary they said just exactly the opposite from what they said at the other. At that they said, Tur is Tur; while at this they absolutely reversed it and said, Tur is Tur. Do you not see? They turned it right around backwards, which makes a very great difference."

"It sounded the same to me," I insisted.

"That is because you lack faith," he said sadly, and we passed out of the temple after depositing the rest of our money in a huge chest, of which there were many standing about almost filled with coins.

We found Gor Hajus and Hovan Du awaiting us impatiently, the center of a large and curious throng among which were many warriors in the metal of Xaxa, the Jeddara of Phundahl. They wanted to see Hovan Du perform, but Dar Tarus told them that he was tired and in an ugly mood.

"Tomorrow," he said, "when he is rested I shall bring him out upon the avenues to amuse you.'

With difficulty we extricated ourselves, and passing into a quieter avenue, took a roundabout way to the lodging place, where Hovan Du was confined in a small chamber while Gor Hajus, Dar Tarus and I were conducted by slaves to a large sleeping apartment where sleeping silks and furs were arranged for us upon a low platform that encircled the room and was broken only at the single entrance to the chamber. Here were already sleeping a considerable number of men, while two armed slaves patrolled the aisle to guard the guests from assassins.

It was still early and some of the other lodgers were conversing in low whispers so I sought to engage Dar Tarus in conversation relative to his religion, about which I was curious.

"The mysteries of religions always fascinate me, Dar Tarus," I told him.

"Ah, but that is the beauty of the religion of Tur," he exclaimed, "it has no mysteries. It is simple, natural, scientific and every word and work of it is susceptible of proof through the pages of Turgan, the great book written by Tur himself.

"Tur's home is upon the sun. There, one hundred thousand years ago, he made Barsoom and tossed it out into space. Then he amused himself by creating man in various forms and two sexes; and later he fashioned animals to be food for man and each other, and caused vegetation and water to appear that man and the animals might live. Do you not see how simple and scientific it all is?"

But it was Gor Hajus who told me most about the religion of Tur one day when Dar Tarus was not about. He said that the Phundahlians maintained that Tur still created every living thing with his own hands. They denied vigorously that man possessed the power to reproduce his kind and taught their young that all such belief was vile; and always they hid every evidence of natural procreation, insisting to the death that even those things which they witnessed with their own eyes and experienced with their own bodies in the bringing forth of their young never transpired.

Turgan taught them that Barsoom is flat and they shut their minds to every proof to the contrary. They would not leave Phundahl far for fear of falling off the edge of the world; they would not permit the development of aeronautics because should one of their ships circumnavigate Barsoom it would be a wicked sacrilege in the eyes of Tur who made Barsoom flat.

They would not permit the use of telescopes, for Tur taught them that there was no other world than Barsoom and to look at another would be heresy; nor would they permit the teaching in their schools of any history of Barsoom that antedated the creation of Barsoom by Tur, though Barsoom has a well authenticated written history that reaches back more than one hundred thousand years; nor would they permit any geography of Barsoom except that which appears in Turgan, nor any scientific researches along biological lines. Turgan is their only text book—if it is not in Turgan it is a wicked lie.

Much of all this and a great deal more I gathered from one source or another during my brief stay in Phundahl, whose people are, I believe, the least advanced in civilization of any of the red nations upon Barsoom. Giving, as they do, all their best thought to religious matters, they have become ig- norant, bigoted and narrow, going as far to one extreme as the Toonolians do to the other.

However, I had not come to Phundahl to investigate her culture but to steal her queen, and that thought was upper- most in my mind when I awoke to a new day—my first in Phundahl. Following the morning meal we set out in the direction of the palace to reconnoiter, Dar Tarus leading us to a point from which he might easily direct us the balance of the way, as he did not dare accompany us to the immediate vicinity of the royal grounds for fear of recognition, the body he now possessed having formerly belonged to a well known noble.

It was arranged that Gor Hajus should act as spokesman and I as keeper of the ape. This arranged, we bade farewell to Dar Tarus and set forth, the three of us, along a broad and beautiful avenue that led directly to the palace gates. We had been planning and rehearsing the parts that we were to play and which we hoped would prove so successful that they would open the gates to us and win us to the presence of the Jeddara.

As we strolled with seeming unconcern along the avenue, I had ample opportunity to enjoy the novel and beautiful sights of this rich boulevard of palaces. The sun shone down upon vivid scarlet lawns, gorgeous flowered pimalia and a score of other rarely beautiful Barsoomian shrubs and trees, while the avenue itself was shaded by almost perfect speci- mens of the magnificent sorapus. The sleeping apartments of the buildings had all been lowered to their daytime level, and from a hundred balconies gorgeous silks and furs were airing in the sun. Slaves were briskly engaged with their duties about the grounds, while upon many a balcony wo- men and children sat at their morning meal. Among the children we aroused considerable enthusiasm, or at least Ho-van Du did, nor was he without interest to the adults. Some of them would have detained us for an exhibition, but we moved steadily on toward the palace, for no where else had we business or concern within the walls of Phundahl.

Around the palace gates was the usual crowd of loitering curiosity seekers; for after all human nature is much the same every where, whether skins be black or white, red or yellow or brown, upon Earth or upon Mars. The crowd before Xaxa's gates was largely made up of visitors from the islands of that part of the Great Toonolian Marshes which owes allegiance to Phundahl's queen, and like all provincials eager for a glimpse of royalty; though none the less to be interested by the antics of a simian, wherefore we had a ready made audience awaiting our arrival. Their natural fear of the great brute caused them to fall back a little at our approach so that we had a clear avenue to the very gates themselves, and here we halted while the crowds closed in behind, forming a half circle about us. Gor Hajus addressed them in a loud tone of voice that might be overheard by the warriors and their officers beyond the gates, for it was really them we had come to entertain, not the crowds in which we had not the slightest interest.

"Men and women of Phundahl," cried Gor Hajus, "behold two poor panthans, who, risking their lives, have captured and trained one of the most savage and ferocious and at the same time most intelligent specimens of the great white ape of Barsoom ever before seen in captivity and at great expense have brought it to Phundahl for your entertainment and edification. My friends, this wonderful ape is endowed with human intelligence; he understands every word that is spoken to him. With your kind attention, my friends, I will endeavor to demonstrate the remarkable intelligence of this ferocious, man-eating beast—an intelligence that has entertained the crowned heads of Barsoom and mystified the minds of her most learned savants."

I thought Gor Hajus did pretty well as a bally-hoo artist. I had to smile as I listened, here upon Mars, to the familiar lines that I had taught him out of my Earthly experience of county fairs and amusement parks, so highly ludicrous they sounded falling from the lips of the Assassin of Toonol; but they evidently interested his auditors and impressed them, too, for they craned their necks and stood in earnest eyed silence awaiting the performance of Hovan Du. Even better, several members of the Jeddara's Guard pricked up their ears and sauntered toward the gates; and among them was an officer.

Gor Hajus caused Hovan Du to lie down at word of command, to get up, to stand upon one foot, and to indicate the number of fingers that Gor Hajus held up by growling once for each finger, thus satisfying the audience that he could count; but these simple things were only by way of leading up to the more remarkable achievements which we hoped would win an audience before the Jeddara. Gor Hajus borrowed a set of harness and weapons from a man in the crowd and had Hovan Du don it and fence with him, and then indeed did we hear exclamations of amazement.

The warriors and the officer of Xaxa had drawn near the gates and were interested spectators, which was precisely what we wished, and now Gor Hajus was ready for the final astounding revelation of Hovan Du's intelligence.

"These things that you have witnessed are as nothing," he cried. "Why this wonderful beast can even read and write. He was captured in a deserted city near Ptarth and can read and write the language of that country. Is there among you one who, by chance, comes from that distant country?"

A slave spoke up. "I am from Ptarth."

"Good!" said Gor Hajus. "Write some simple instructions and hand them to the ape. I will turn my back that you may know that I cannot assist him in any way."

The slave drew forth a tablet from a pocket pouch and wrote briefly. What he wrote he handed to Hovan Du. The ape read the message and without hesitation moved quickly to the gate and handed it to the officer standing upon the other side, the gate being constructed of wrought metal in fanciful designs that offered no obstruction to the view or to the passage of small articles. The officer took the message and examined it.

"What does it say?" he demanded of the slave that had penned it.

"It says," replied the latter: "Take this message to the officer who stands just within the gates."

There were exclamations of surprise from all parts of the crowd and Hovan Du was compelled to repeat his performance several times with different messages which directed him to do various things, the officer always taking a great interest in the proceedings.

"It is marvellous," said he at last. "The Jeddara would be amused by the performance of this beast. Wait here, therefore, until I have sent word to her that she may, if she so desires, command your presence."

Nothing could have better suited us and so we waited with what patience we might for the messenger to return; and while we waited Hovan Du continued to mystify his audience with new proofs of his great intelligence.

CHAPTER XI

XAXA

THE OFFICER RETURNED, the gates swung out and we were commanded to enter the courtyard of the palace of Xaxa, Jeddara of Phundahl. After that events transpired with great rapidity—surprising and totally unexpected events. We were led through an intricate maze of corridors and chambers until I became suspicious that we were purposely being confused, and convinced that whether such was the intention or not the fact remained that I could no more have retraced my steps to the outer courtyard than I could have flown without wings. We had planned that, in the event of gaining admission to the palace, we would carefully note whatever might be essential to a speedy escape; but when, in a whisper, I asked Gor Hajus if he could find his way out again he assured me that he was as confused as I.

The palace was in no sense remarkable nor particularly interesting, the work of the Phundahlian artists being heavy and oppressing and without indication of high imaginative genius. The scenes depicted were mostly of a religious nature illustrating passages from Turgan, the Phundahlian bible, and, for the most part, were a series of monotonous repetitions.

There was one, which appeared again and again, depicting Turgan creating a round, flat Mars and hurling it into Space, that always reminded me of a culinary artist turning a flap jack in Childs' window.

There were also numerous paintings of what appeared to be court scenes delineating members of the Phundahlian royal line in various activities; it was noticeable that the more recent ones in which Xaxa appeared had had the principal figure repainted so that there confronted me from time to time portraits, none too well done, of the beautiful face and figure of Valla Dia in the royal trappings of a jeddara. The effect of these upon me is not easy of description. They brought home to me the fact that I was approaching, and should presently be face to face with, the person of the woman to whom I had consecrated my love and my life, and yet in that same person I should be confronting one whom I loathed and would destroy.

We were halted at last before a great door and from the number of warriors and nobles congregated before it I was confident that we were soon to be ushered into the presence of the Jeddara. As we waited those assembled about us eyed us with, it seemed to me, more of hostility than curiosity and when the door swung open they accompanied us, with the exception of a few warriors, into the chamber beyond. The room was of medium size and at the farther side, behind a massive table, sat Xaxa. About her were grouped a number of heavily armed nobles. As I looked them over I wondered if among them was he for whom the body of Dar Tarus had been filched; for we had promised him that if conditions were favorable we would attempt to recover it.

Xaxa eyed us coldy as we were halted before her. "Let us see the beast perform," she commanded, and then suddenly: "What mean you by permitting strangers to enter my presence bearing arms?" she cried. "Sag Or, see that their weapons are removed!" and she turned to a handsome young warrior standing near her.

Sag Or! That was the name. Before me stood the noble for whom Dar Tarus had suffered the loss of his liberty, his body and his love. Gor Hajus had also recognized the name and Hovan Du, too; I could tell by the way they eyed the man as he advanced. Curtly he instructed us to hand our

weapons to two warriors who advanced to receive them. Gor
Hajus hesitated. I admit that I did not know what course to
pursue.

Everyone seemed hostile and yet that might be, and doubtless was, but a reflection of their attitude toward all strangers.
If we refused to disarm we were but three against a room full,
if they chose to resort to force; or if they turned us out of
the palace because of it we would be robbed of this seemingly
god given opportunity to win to the very heart of Xaxa's
palace and to their very presence, where we must eventually
win before we could strike. Would such an opportunity ever
be freely offered us again? I doubted it and felt that we had
better assume a vague risk now than by refusing their demand, definitely arm their suspicions. So I quietly removed
my weapons and handed them to the warrior waiting to receive them; and following my example, Gor Hajus did likewise, though I can imagine with what poor grace.

Once again Xaxa signified that she would see Hovan Du
perform. As Gor Hajus put him through his antics she
watched listlessly; nor did anything that the ape did arouse
the slightest flicker of interest among the entire group assembled about the Jeddara. As the thing dragged on I became obsessed with apprehensions that all was not right. It
seemed to me that an effort was being made to detain us for
some purpose—to gain time. I could not understand, for
instance, why Xaxa required that we repeat several times the
least interesting of the ape's performances. And all the time
Xaxa sat playing with a long, slim dagger, and I saw that she
watched me quite as much as she watched Hovan Du, while
I found it difficult to keep my eyes averted from that perfect
face, even though I knew that it was but a stolen mask behind which lurked the cruel mind of a tyrant and a murderess.

At last came an interruption to the performance. The
door opened and a noble entered, who went directly to the
Jeddara whom he addressed briefly and in a low tone. I saw
that she asked him several questions and that she seemed
vexed by his replies. Then she dismissed him with a curt
gesture and turned toward us.

"Enough of this!" she cried. Her eyes rested upon mine
and she pointed her slim dagger at me. "Where is the other?"
she demanded.

"What other?" I inquired.

"There were three of you, beside the ape. I know nothing about the ape, nor where, nor how you acquired it; but I do know all about you, Vad Varo, and Gor Hajus, the Assassin of Toonol, and Dar Tarus. Where is Dar Tarus?" her voice was low and musical and entirely beautiful—the voice of Valla Dia—but behind it I knew was the terrible personality of Xaxa, and I knew too that it would be hard to deceive her, for she must have received what information she had directly from Ras Thavas. It had been stupid of me not to foresee that Ras Thavas would immediately guess the purpose of my mission and warn Xaxa. I perceived instantly that it would be worse than useless to deny our identity, rather I must explain our presence—if I could.

"Where is Dar Tarus?" she repeated.

"How should I know?" I countered. "Dar Tarus has reasons to believe that he would not be safe in Phundahl and I imagine that he is not anxious that any one should know his whereabouts—myself included. He helped me to escape from the Island of Thavas, for which his liberty was to be his reward. He has not chosen to accompany me further upon my adventures."

Xaxa seemed momentarily disarmed that I did not deny my identity—evidently she had supposed that I would do so.

"You admit then," she said, "that you are Vad Varo, the assistant of Ras Thavas?"

"Have I ever sought to deny it?"

"You have disguised yourself as a red-man of Barsoom."

"How could I travel in Barsoom otherwise, where every man's hand is against a stranger?"

"And why would you travel in Barsoom?" Her eyes narrowed as she waited for my reply.

"As Ras Thavas has doubtless sent you word, I am from another world and I would see more of this one," I told her. "Is that strange?"

"And you come to Phundahl and seek to gain entrance to my presence and bring with you the notorious Assassin of Toonol that you may see more of Barsoom?"

"Gor Hajus may not return to Toonol," I explained, "and so he must seek service for his sword at some other court than that of Vobis Kan—in Phundahl perhaps, or if not

here he must move on. I hope that he will decide to accompany me as I am a stranger in Barsoom, unaccustomed
to the manners and ways of her people. I would fare ill without a guide and mentor."

"You shall fare ill," she cried. "You have seen all of Barsoom that you are destined to see—you have reached the end
of your adventure. You think to deceive me, eh? You do not
know, perhaps, that I have heard of your infatuation for
Valla Dia or that I am fully conversant with the purpose of
your visit to Phundahl." Her eyes left me and swept her
warriors. "To the pits with them!" she cried. "Later we
shall choose the manner of their passing."

Instantly we were surrounded by a score of naked blades.
There was no escape for Gor Hajus or me, but I thought
that I saw an opportunity for Hovan Du to get away. I had
had the possibility of such a contingency in mind from the
first and always I had been on the lookout for an avenue of
escape for one of us, and so the open windows at the right
of the Jeddara had not gone unnoticed, nor the great trees
growing in the courtyard beneath. Hovan Du was close beside me as Xaxa spoke.

"Go!" I whispered. "The windows are open. Go, and tell
Dar Tarus what has happened to us," and then I fell back
away from him and dragged Gor Hajus with me as though
we would attempt to resist arrest; and while I thus distracted
their attention from him Hovan Du turned toward an open
window. He had taken but a few steps when a warrior attempted to halt him; with that the ferocious brain of the
anthropoid seemed to seize dominion over the great creature.
With a hideous growl he leaped with the agility of a cat
upon the unfortunate Phundahlian, swung him high in giant
hands and using his body as a flail tumbled his fellows to
right and left as he cut a swath toward the open window nearest him.

Instantly pandemonium reigned in the apartment. The
attention of all seemed centered upon the great ape and
even those who had been confronting us turned to attack
Hovan Du. And in the midst of the confusion I saw Xaxa step
to some heavy hangings directly behind her desk, part them
and disappear.

"Come!" I whispered to Gor Hajus. Apparently intent only

upon watching the conflict between the ape and the warriors I moved forward with the fighters but always to the
left toward the desk that Xaxa had just quitted. Hovan Du
was giving a good account of himself. He had discarded his
first victim and one by one had seized others as they came
within range of his long arms and powerful hands, sometimes
four at a time as he stood well braced upon two of his hand-
like feet and fought with the other four. His shock of bristling hair stood erect upon his skull and his fierce eyes blazed
with rage as, towering high above his antagonists, he fought
for his life—the most feared of all the savage creatures of
Barsoom. Perhaps his greatest advantage lay in the inherent
fear of him that was a part of every man in that room who
faced him, and it forwarded my quickly conceived plan, too,
for it kept every eye turned upon Hovan Du, so that Gor
Hajus and I were able to work our way to the rear of the
desk. I think Hovan Du must have sensed my intention then,
for he did the one thing best suited to attract every eye from
us to him and, too, he gave me notice that the human half
of his brain was still alert and watchful of our welfare.

Heretofore the Phundahlians must have looked upon him
as a remarkable specimen of great ape, marvellously trained,
but now, of a sudden, he paralyzed them with awe, for his
roars and growls took the form of words and he spoke with
the tongue of a human. He was near the window now. Several
of the nobles were pushing bravely forward. Among them
was Sag Or. Hovan Du reached forth and seized him, wrench-
ing his weapons from him. "I go," he cried, "but let harm befall my friends and I shall return and tear the heart from
Xaxa. Tell her that, from the Great Ape of Ptarth."

For an instant the warriors and the nobles stood trans-
fixed with awe. Every eye was upon Hovan Du as he stood
there with the struggling figure of Sag Or in his mighty
grasp. Gor Hajus and I were forgotten. And then Hovan Du
turned and leaped to the sill of the window and from there
lightly to the branches of the nearest tree; and with him
went Sag Or, the favorite of Xaxa, the Jeddara. At the same
instant I drew Gor Hajus with me between the hangings in
the rear of Xaxa's desk, and as they fell behind us we found
ourselves in the narrow mouth of a dark corridor.

Without knowledge of where the passage led we could

only follow it blindly, urged on by the necessity for discovering a hiding place or an avenue of escape from the palace before the pursuit, which we knew would be immediately instituted, overtook us. As our eyes became accustomed to the gloom, which was partially dispelled by a faint luminosity, we moved more rapidly and presently came to a narrow spiral runway which descended into a dark hole below the level of the corridor and also arose into equal darkness above.

"Which way?" I asked Gor Hajus.

"They will expect us to descend," he replied, "for in that direction lies the nearest avenue of escape."

"Then we will go up."

"Good!" he exclaimed. "All we seek now is a place to hide until night has fallen, for we may not escape by day."

We had scarcely started to ascend before we heard the first sound of pursuit—the clank of accouterments in the corridor beneath. Yet, even with this urge from behind, we were forced to move with great caution, for we knew not what lay before. At the next level there was a doorway, the door closed and locked, but there was no corridor, nor anywhere to hide, and so we continued on upward. The second level was identical with that just beneath, but at the third a single corridor ran straight off into darkness and at our right was a door, ajar. The sounds of pursuit were appreciably nearer now and the necessity for concealment seemed increasing as the square of their growing proportions until every other consideration was overwhelmed by it. Nor is this so strange when the purpose of my adventure is considered and that discovery now must assuredly spell defeat and blast forever the slender ray of hope that remained for the resurrection of Valla Dia in her own flesh.

There was scarce a moment for consideration. The corridor before us was shrouded in darkness—it might be naught but a blind alley. The door was close and ajar. I pushed it gently inward. An odor of heavy incense greeted our nostrils and through the small aperture we saw a portion of a large chamber garishly decorated. Directly before us, and almost wholly obstructing our view of the entire chamber, stood a colossal statue of a squatting man-like figure. Behind us we heard voices—our pursuers already were ascending the spiral—they would be upon us in a few seconds. I examined the door and discovered that it fastened with a spring lock. I looked again into the chamber and saw no one within the range of our vision, and then I motioned Gor Hajus to follow me and stepping into the room closed the door behind us. We had burned our bridges. As the door closed the lock engaged with a sharp, metallic click.

"What was that?" demanded a voice, originating, seemingly, at the far end of the chamber.

Gor Hajus looked at me and shrugged his shoulders in resignation (he must have been thinking what I was thinking—that with two avenues we had chosen the wrong one) but he smiled and there was no reproach in his eyes.

"It sounded from the direction of the Great Tur," replied a second voice.

"Perhaps someone is at the door," suggested the first speaker.

Gor Hajus and I were flattened against the back of the statue that we might postpone as long as possible our inevitable discovery should the speakers decide to investigate the origin of the noise that had attracted their suspicions. I was facing against the polished stone of the figure's back, my hands outspread upon it. Beneath my fingers were the carven bits of its ornamental harness—jutting protuberances that were costly gems set in these trappings of stone, and there were gorgeous inlays of gold filigree; but these things I had no eyes for now. We could hear the two conversing as they came nearer. Perhaps I was nervous. I do not know, I am sure I never shrank from an encounter when either duty or expediency called; but in this instance both demanded that we avoid conflict and remain undiscovered. However that may be, my fingers must have been moving nervously over the jeweled harness of the figure when I became vaguely, perhaps subconsciously, aware that one of the gems was loose in its setting. I do not recall that this made any impression upon my conscious mind, but I do know that it seemed to catch the attention of my wandering fingers and they must have paused to play with the loosened stone.

The voices seemed quite close now—it could be but a matter of seconds before we should be confronted by their owners. My muscles seemed to tense for the anticipated encounter and unconsciously I pressed heavily upon the loosened setting —whereat a portion of the figure's back gave noiselessly inward revealing to us the dimly lighted interior of the statue. We needed no further invitation; simultaneously we stepped across the threshold and in almost the same movement I turned and closed the panel gently behind us. I think that there was absolutely no sound connected with the entire transaction; and following it we remained in utter silence, motionless—scarce breathing. Our eyes became quickly accustomed to the dim interior which we discovered was lighted through numerous small orifices in the shell of the statue, which was entirely hollow, and through these same orifices every outside sound came clearly to our ears.

We had scarcely closed the opening when we heard the voices directly outside it and simultaneously there came a hammering on the door by which we had entered the apartment from the corridor. "Who seeks entrance to Xaxa's Temple?" demanded one of the voices within the room.

" 'Tis I, dwar of the Jeddara's Guard," boomed a voice from without. "We are seeking two who came to assassinate Xaxa."

"Came they this way?"

"Think you, priest, that I should be seeking them here had they not?"

"How long since?"

"Scarce twenty tals since," replied the dwar.

"Then they are not here," the priest assured him, "for we have been here for a full zode* and no other has entered the temple during that time. Look quickly to Xaxa's apartments above and to the roof and the hangars, for if you followed them up the spiral there is no other where they might flee."

"Watch then the temple carefully until I return," shouted the warrior and we heard him and his men moving on up the spiral.

Now we heard the priests conversing as they moved slowly past the statue.

"What could have caused the noise that first attracted our attention?" asked one.

---

* A tal is about one second, and a zode approximately two and one-half hours, Earth time.

"Perhaps the fugitives tried the door," suggested the other.

"It must have been that, but they did not enter or we should have seen them when they emerged from behind the Great Tur, for we were facing him at the time, nor have we once turned our eyes from this end of the temple."

"Then at least they are not within the temple."

"And where else they may be is no concern of ours."

"No, nor if they reached Xaxa's apartment, if they did not pass through the temple."

"Perhaps they did reach it."

"And they were assassins!"

"Worse things might befall Phundahl."

"Hush! the gods have ears."

"Of stone."

"But the ears of Xaxa are not of stone and they hear many things that are not intended for them."

"The old she-banth!"

"She is Jeddara and High Priestess."

"Yes, but——" the voices passed beyond the range of our ears at the far end of the temple, yet they had told me much —that Xaxa was feared and hated by the priesthood and that the priests themselves had none too much reverence for their deity, as evidenced by the remark of one that the gods have ears of stone. And they had told us other things, important things, when they conversed with the dwar of the Jeddara's Guard.

Gor Hajus and I now felt that we had fallen by chance upon a most ideal place of concealment, for the very guardians of the temple would swear that we were not, could not be, where we were. Already had they thrown the pursuers off our track.

Now, for the first time, we had an opportunity to examine our hiding place. The interior of the statue was hollow and far above us, perhaps forty feet, we could see the outside light shining through the mouth, ears and nostrils, just below which a circular platform could be discerned running around the inside of the neck. A ladder with flat rungs led upward from the base to the platform. Thick dust covered the floor on which we stood, and the extremity of our position suggested a careful examination of this dust, with the result that I was at once impressed by the evidence that it revealed; which indicated that we were the first to enter the statue for a long time, possibly for years, as the fine coating of almost impalpable dust that covered the floor was undistrubed. As I searched for this evidence my eyes fell upon something lying huddled close to the base of the ladder and approaching nearer I saw that it was a human skeleton, while a closer examination revealed that the skull was crushed and one arm and several ribs broken. About it lay, dust covered, the most gorgeous trappings I had ever seen. Its position at the foot of the ladder, as well as the crushed skull and broken bones, appeared quite conclusive evidence of the manner in which death had come—the man had fallen head foremost from the circular platform forty feet above, carrying with him to eternity, doubtless, the secret of the entrance of the interior of the Great Tur.

I suggested this to Gor Hajus who was examining the dead man's trappings and he agreed with me that such must have been the manner of his death.

"He was a high priest of Tur," whispered Gor Hajus, "and probably a member of the royal house—possibly a jeddak. He has been dead a long time."

"I am going up above," I said. "I will test the ladder. If it is safe, follow me up. I think we shall be able to see the interior of the temple through the mouth of Tur."

"Go carefully," Gor Hajus admonished. "The ladder is very old."

I went carefully, testing each rung before I trusted my weight to it, but I found the old sorapus wood of which it was constructed sound and as stanch as steel. How the high priest came to his death must always remain a mystery, for the ladder or the circular platform would have carried the weight of a hundred red-men.

From the platform I could see through the mouth of Tur. Below me was a large chamber along the sides of which were ranged other, though lesser, idols. They were even more grotesque than those I had seen in the temple in the city and their trappings were rich beyond the conception of man—Earthman—for the gems of Barsoom scintillate with rays unknown to us and of such gorgeous and blinding beauty as to transcend description. Directly in front of the Great Tur was an altar of palthon, a rare and beautiful stone, blood red, in which are traced in purest white Nature's most fanciful designs; the whole vastly enhanced by the wondrous polish which the stone takes beneath the hand of the craftsman.

Gor Hajus joined me and together we examined the interior of the temple. Tall windows lined two sides, letting in a flood of light. At the far end, opposite the Great Tur, were two enormous doors, closing the main entrance to the chamber, and here stood the two priests whom we had heard conversing. Otherwise the temple was deserted. Incense burned upon tiny altars before each of the minor idols, but whether any burned before the Great Tur we could not see.

Having satisfied our curiosity relative to the temple, we returned our attention to a further examination of the interior of Tur's huge head and were rewarded by the discovery of another ladder leading upward against the rear wall to a higher and smaller platform that evidently led to the eyes. It did not take me long to investigate and here I found a most comfortable chair set before a control that operated the eyes, so that they could be made to turn from side to side, or up or down, according to the whim of the operator; and here too was a speaking tube leading to the mouth. This again I must needs investigate and so I returned to the lower platform and there I discovered a device beneath the tongue of the idol, and this device, which was in the nature of an amplifier, was connected with the speaking tube from above. I could not repress a smile as I considered these silent witnesses to the perfidy of man and thought of the broken thing lying at the foot of the ladder. Tur, I could have sworn, had been silent for many years.

Together Gor Hajus and I returned to the higher platform and again I made a discovery—the eyes of Tur were veritable periscopes. By turning them we could see any portion of the temple and what we saw through the eyes was magnified. Nothing could escape the eyes of Tur and presently, when the priests began to talk again, we discovered that nothing could escape Tur's ears, for every slightest sound in the temple came clearly to us. What a valuable adjunct to high priesthood this Great Tur must have been in the days when that broken skeleton lying below us was a thing of blood and life!

CHAPTER XII

THE GREAT TUR

THE DAY DRAGGED wearily for Gor Hajus and me. We watched the various priests who came in pairs at intervals to relieve those who had preceded them, and we listened to their prattle, mostly idle gossip of court scandals. At times they spoke of us and we learned that Hovan Du had escaped with Sag Or, nor had they been located as yet, nor had Dar Tarus. The whole court was mystified by our seemingly miraculous disappearance. Three thousand people, the inmates and attaches of the palace, were constantly upon the lookout for us. Every part of the palace and the palace grounds had been searched and searched again. The pits had been explored more thoroughly than they had been explored within the memory of the oldest retainer, and it seemed that queer things had been unearthed there—things of which not even Xaxa dreamed; and the priests whispered that at least one great and powerful house would fall because of what a dwar of the Jeddara's Guard had discovered in a remote precinct of the pits.

As the sun dropped below the horizon and darkness came, the interior of the temple was illuminated by a soft white light, brilliantly but without the glare of Earthly artificial illumination. More priests came and many young girls, priestesses. They performed before the idols, chanting meaningless gibberish. Gradually the chamber filled with worshippers, nobles of the Jeddara's court with their women and their retainers, forming in two lines along either side of the temple before the lesser idols, leaving a wide aisle from the great entrance to the foot of the Great Tur and toward this aisle they all faced, waiting. For what were they waiting? Their eyes were turned expectantly toward the closed doors of the great entrance and Gor Hajus and I felt our eyes held there too, fascinated by the suggestion that they were about to open and reveal some stupendous spectacle.

And presently the doors did swing slowly open and all we saw was what appeared to be a great roll of carpet lying upon its side across the opening. Twenty slaves, naked but for their scant leather harness, stood behind the huge roll;

and as the doors swung fully open they rolled the carpet inward to the very feet of the altar before the Great Tur, covering the wide aisle from the entranceway almost to the idol with a thick, soft rug of gold and white and blue. It was the most beautiful thing in the temple where all else was blatant, loud and garish, or hideous, or grotesque. And then the doors closed and again we waited; but not for long. Bugles sounded from without, the sound increasing as they neared the entrance. Once more the doors swung in. Across the entrance stood a double rank of gorgeously trapped nobles. Slowly they entered the temple and behind them came a splendid chariot drawn by two banths, the fierce Barsoomian lion, held in leash by slaves on either side. Upon the chariot was a litter and in the litter, reclining at ease, lay Xaxa. As she entered the temple the people commenced to chant her praises in a monotonous sing-song. Chained to the chariot and following on foot was a red warrior and behind him a procession composed of fifty young men and an equal number of young girls.

Gor Hajus touched my arm. "The prisoner," he whispered, "do you recognize him?"

"Dar Tarus!" I exclaimed.

It was Dar Tarus—they had discovered his hiding place and arrested him, but what of Hovan Du? Had they taken him, also? If they had it must have been only after slaying him, for they never would have sought to capture the fierce beast, nor would he have brooked capture. I looked for Sag Or, but he was no where to be seen within the temple and this fact gave me hope that Hovan Du might be still at liberty.

The chariot was halted before the altar and Xaxa alighted; the lock that held Dar Tarus' chain to the vehicle was opened and the banths were led away by their attendants to one side of the temple behind the lesser idols. Then Dar Tarus was dragged roughly to the altar and thrown upon it and Xaxa, mounting the steps at its base, came close to his side and with hands outstretched above him looked up at the Great Tur towering above her. How beautiful she was! How richly trapped! Ah, Valla Dia! that your sweet form should be debased to the cruel purposes of the wicked mind that now animates you!

Xaxa's eyes now rested upon the face of the Great Tur. "O,

I saw the mighty anthropoid hurl him to destruction far below.

"Speak, Great Tur, ere I strike."

Tur, Father of Barsoom," she cried, "behold the offering we place before you, All-seeing, All-knowing, All-powerful One, and frown no more upon us in silence. For a hundred years you have not deigned to speak aloud to your faithful slaves; never since Hora San, the high priest, was taken away by you on that long gone night of mystery have you unsealed your lips to your people. Speak, Great Tur! Give us some sign, ere we plunge this dagger into the heart of our offering, that our works are pleasing in thine eyes. Tell us whither went the two who came here today to assassinate your high priestess; reveal to us the fate of Sag Or. Speak, Great Tur, ere I strike," and she raised her slim blade above the heart of Dar Tarus and looked straight upward into the eyes of Tur.

And then, as a bolt from the blue, I was struck by the great inspiration. My hand sought the lever controlling the eyes of Tur and I turned them until they completed a full circuit of the room and rested again upon Xaxa. The effect was magical. Never before had I seen a whole room full of people so absolutely stunned and awe struck as were these. As the eyes returned to Xaxa she seemed turned to stone and her copper skin to have taken on an ashen purple hue. Her dagger remained stiffly poised above the heart of Dar Tarus. Not for a hundred years had they seen the eyes of the Great Tur move. Then I placed the speaking tube to my lips and the voice of Tur rumbled through the chamber. As from one great throat a gasp arose from the crowded temple floor and the people fell upon their knees and buried their faces in their hands.

"Judgment is mine!" I cried. "Strike not lest ye be struck! To Tur is the sacrifice!"

I was silent then, attempting to plan how best to utilize the advantage I had gained. Fearfully, one by one, the bowed heads were raised and frightened eyes sought the face of Tur. I gave them another thrill by letting the god's eyes wander slowly over the upturned faces, and while I was doing this I had another inspiration, which I imparted to Gor Hajus in a low whisper. I could hear him chuckle as he started down the ladder to carry my new plan into effect. Again I had recourse to the speaking tube.

"The sacrifice is Tur's." I rumbled. "Tur will strike with his own hand. Extinguish the lights and let no one move

under pain of instant death until Tur gives the word. Prostrate yourselves and bury your eyes in your palms, for whosoever sees shall be blinded when the spirit of Tur walks
among his people."

Down they went again and one of the priests hurriedly extinguished the lights, leaving the temple in total darkness;
and while Gor Hajus was engaged with his part of the performance I tried to cover any accidental noise he might make
by keeping up a running fire of celestial revelation.

"Xaxa, the high priestess, asks what has become of the two
whom she believed came to assassinate her. I, Tur, took them
to myself. Vengeance is Tur's! And Sag Or I took, also. In
the guise of a great ape I came and took Sag Or and none
knew me; though even a fool might have guessed, for who
is there ever heard a great ape speak with tongue of man
unless he was animated by the spirit of Tur?"

I guess that convinced them, it being just the sort of logic
suited to their religion, or it would have convinced them
if they had not already been convinced. I wondered what
might be passing in the mind of the doubting priest who
had remarked that the gods had ears of stone.

Presently I heard a noise upon the ladder beneath me
and a moment later someone climbed upon the circular landing.

"All's well," whispered the voice of Gor Hajus. "Dar Tarus is with me."

"Light the temple!" I commanded through the speaking
tube. "Rise and look upon your altar."

The lights flashed on and the people rose, trembling, to
their feet. Every eye was bent upon the altar and what they
saw there seemed to crush them with terror. Some of the
women screamed and fainted. It all impressed me with the
belief that none of them had taken this god of theirs with
any great amount of seriousness, and now when they were
confronted with absolute proof of his miraculous powers
they were swept completely off their feet. Where, a few moments before, they had seen a live sacrifice awaiting the knife
of the high priestess they saw now only a dust covered human
skull. I grant you that without an explanation it might have
seemed a miracle to almost anyone so quickly had Gor Hajus
run from the base of the idol with the skull of the dead

high priest and returned again leading Dar Tarus with him. I had been a bit concerned as to what the attitude of Dar Tarus might be, who was no more conversant with the hoax than were the Phundahlians, but Gor Hajus had whispered "For Valla Dia" in his ear and he had understood and come quickly.

"The Great Tur," I now announced, "is angry with his people. For a long time they have denied him in their hearts even while they made open worship of him. The Great Tur is angry with Xaxa. Only through Xaxa may the people of Phundahl be saved from destruction, for the Great Tur is angry. Go then from the temple and the palace leaving no human being here other than Xaxa, the high priestess of Tur. Leave her here in solitude beside the altar. Tur would speak with her alone."

I could see Xaxa fairly shrivel in fright.

"Is the Jeddara Xaxa, High Priestess of the Great God Tur, afraid to meet her master?" I demanded. The woman's jaw trembled so that she could not reply. "Obey! or Xaxa and all her people shall be struck dead!" I fairly screamed at them.

Like cattle they turned and fled toward the entrance and Xaxa, her knees shaking so that she could scarce stand erect, staggered after them. A noble saw her and pushed her roughly back, but she shrieked and ran after him when he had left her. Then others dragged her to the foot of the altar and threw her roughly down and one menaced her with his sword, but at that I called aloud that no harm must befall the Jeddara if they did not wish the wrath of Tur to fall upon them all. They left her lying there and so weak from fright was she that she could not rise, and a moment later the temple was empty, but not until I had shouted after them to clear the whole palace within a quarter zode, for my plan required a free and unobstructed as well as unobserved field of action.

The last of them was scarce out of sight ere we three descended from the head of Tur and stepped out upon the temple floor behind the idol. Quickly I ran toward the altar, upon the other side of which Xaxa had dropped to the floor in a swoon. She still lay there and I gathered her into my arms and ran quickly back to the door in the wall behind the idol—the doorway through which Gor Hajus and I had entered the temple earlier in the day.

Preceded by Gor Hajus and followed by Dar Tarus, I ascended the runway toward the roof where the conversation of the priests had informed us were located the royal hangars. Had Hovan Du and Sag Or been with us my cup of happiness would have been full, for within half a day what had seemed utter failure and defeat had been turned almost to assured success. At the landing where lay Xaxa's apartments we halted and looked within, for the long night voyage I contemplated would be cold and the body of Valla Dia must be kept warm with suitable robes even though it was inhabited by the spirit of Xaxa. Seeing no one we entered and soon found what we required. As I was adjusting a heavy robe of orluk about the Jeddara she regained consciousness. Instantly she recognized me and then Gor Hajus and finally Dar Tarus. Mechanically she felt for her dagger, but it was not there, and when she saw my smile she paled with anger. At first she must have jumped to the conclusion that she had been the victim of a hoax, but presently a doubt seemed to enter her mind—she must have been recalling some of the things that had transpired within the temple of the Great Tur, and these, neither she nor any other mortal might explain.

"Who are you?" she demanded.

"I am Tur," I replied, brazenly.

"What is your purpose with me?"

"I am going to take you away from Phundahl," I replied.

"But I do not wish to go. You are not Tur. You are Vad Varo. I shall call for help and my guards will come and slay you."

"There is no one in the palace," I reminded her. "Did I, Tur, not send them away?"

"I shall not go with you," she announced firmly. "Rather would I die."

"You shall go with me, Xaxa," I replied, and though she fought and struggled we carried her from her apartment and up the spiral runway to the roof where, I prayed, I should find the hangars and the royal fliers; and as we stepped out into the fresh night air of Mars we did see the hangars before us, but we saw something else—a group of Phundahlian warriors of the Jeddara's Guard whom they had evidently failed to notify of the commands of Tur. At sight of them Xaxa cried aloud in relief.

"To me! To the Jeddara!" she cried. "Strike down these assassins and save me!"

There were three of them and there were three of us, but they were armed and between us we had but Xaxa's slender dagger. Gor Hajus carried that. Victory seemed turned to defeat as they rushed toward us; but it was Gor Hajus who gave them pause. He seized Xaxa and raised the blade, its point above her heart. "Halt!" he cried, "or I strike."

The warriors hesitated; Xaxa was silent, stricken with fear. Thus we stood in stalemate when, just beyond the three Phundahlian warriors, I saw a movement at the roof's edge. What was it? In the dim light I saw something that seemed a human head, and yet unhuman, rise slowly above the edge of the roof, and then, silently, a great form followed, and then I recognized it—Hovan Du, the great white ape.

"Tell them," I cried to Xaxa in a loud voice that Hovan Du might hear, "that I am Tur, for see, I come again in the semblance of a white ape!" and I pointed to Hovan Du. "I would not destroy these poor warriors. Let them lay down their weapons and go in peace."

The men turned, and seeing the great ape standing there behind them, materialized, it might have been, out of thin air, were shaken.

"Who is he, Jeddara?" demanded one of the men.

"It is Tur," replied Xaxa in a weak voice; "but save me from him! Save me from him!"

"Throw down your weapons and your harness and fly!" I commanded, "or Tur will strike you dead. Heard you not the people rushing from the palace at Tur's command? How think you we brought Xaxa hither with a lesser power than Tur's when all her palace was filled with her fighting men? Go, while yet you may in safety."

One of them unbuckled his harness and threw it with his weapons upon the roof, and as he started at a run for the spiral his companions followed his example. Then Hovan Du approached us.

"Well done, Vad Varo," he growled, "though I know not what it is all about."

"That you shall know later," I told him, "but now we must find a swift flier and be upon our way. Where is Sag Or?

Does he still live?"

"I have him securely bound and safely hidden in one of the high towers of the palace," replied the ape. "It will be easy to get him when we have launched a flier."

Xaxa was eyeing us ragefully. "You are not Tur!" she cried. "The ape has exposed you."

"But too late to profit you in any way, Jeddara," I assured her. "Nor could you convince one of your people who stood in the temple this night that I am not Tur. Nor do you, yourself, know that I am not. The ways of Tur, the all-powerful, all-knowing, are beyond the conception of mortal man. To you, then Jeddara, I am Tur, and you will find me all-powerful enough for my purposes."

I think she was still perplexed as we found and dragged forth a flier, aboard which we placed her, and turned the craft's nose toward a lofty tower where Hovan Du told us lay Sag Or.

"I shall be glad to see myself again," said Dar Tarus, with a laugh.

"And you shall be yourself again, Dar Tarus," I told him, "as soon as ever we can come again to the pits of Ras Thavas."

"Would that I might be reunited with my sweet Kara Vasa," he sighed. "Then, Vad Varo, the last full measure of my gratitude would be yours."

"Where may we find her?"

"Alas, I do not know. It was while I was searching for her that I was apprehended by the agents of Xaxa. I had been to her father's palace only to learn that he had been assassinated and his property confiscated. The whereabouts of Kara Vasa they either did not know or would not divulge; but they held me there upon one pretext or another until a detachment of the Jeddara's Guard could come and arrest me."

"We shall have to make inquiries of Sag Or," I said.

We were now coming to a stop alongside a window of the tower Hovan Du had indicated, and he and Dar Tarus leaped to the sill and disappeared within. We were all armed now, having taken the weapons discarded by the three warriors at the hangars, and with a good flier beneath our feet and all our little company reunited, with Xaxa and Sag Or, whom they were now conducting aboard, we were indeed in high spirits.

As we got under way again, setting our nose toward the east, I asked Sag Or if he knew what had become of Kara Vasa, but he assured me, in surly tones, that he did not.

"Think again, Sag Or," I admonished him, "and think hard, for perhaps upon your answer your life depends."

"What chance have I for life?" he sneered, casting an ugly look toward Dar Tarus.

"You have every chance," I replied. "Your life lies in the hollow of my hand; and you serve me well it shall be yours, though in your own body and not in that belonging to Dar Tarus."

"You do not intend destroying me?"

"Neither you nor Xaxa," I answered. "Xaxa shall live on in her own body and you in yours."

"I do not wish to live in my own body," snapped the Jeddara.

Dar Tarus stood looking at Sag Or—looking at his own body like some disembodied soul—as weird a situation as I have ever encountered.

"Tell me, Sag Or," he said, "what has become of Kara Vasa. When my body has been restored to me and yours to you I shall hold no enmity against you if you have not harmed Kara Vasa and will tell me where she be."

"I cannot tell you, for I do not know. She was not harmed, but the day after you were assassinated she disappeared from Phundahl. We were positive that she was spirited away by her father, but from him we could learn nothing. Then he was assassinated," the man glanced at Xaxa, "and since, we have learned nothing. A slave told us that Kara Vasa, with some of her father's warriors, had embarked upon a flier and set out for Helium, where she purposed placing herself under the protection of the great War Lord of Barsoom; of the truth of that we know nothing. This is the truth. I, Sag Or, have spoken!"

It was futile then to search Phundahl for Kara Vasa and so we held our course toward the east and the Tower of Thavas.

CHAPTER XIII

BACK TO THAVAS

ALL THAT NIGHT we sped beneath the hurtling moons of Mars, as strange a company as was ever foregathered upon any planet, I will swear. Two men, each possessing the body of the other, an old and wicked empress whose fair body belonged to a youthful damsel beloved by another of this company, a great white ape dominated by half the brain of a human being, and I, a creature of a distant planet, with Gor Hajus, the Assassin of Toonol, completed the mad roster.

I could scarce keep my eyes from the fair form and face of Xaxa, and it is well that I was thus fascinated for I caught her in the act of attempting to hurl herself overboard, so repugnant to her was the prospect of living again in her own old and hideous corpse. After that I kept her securely bound and fastened to the deck, though it hurt me to see the bonds upon those fair limbs.

Dar Tarus was almost equally fascinated by the contemplation of his own body, which he had not seen for many years.

"By my first ancestor," he ejaculated. "It must be that I was the least vain of fellows, for I give you my word I had no idea that I was so fair to look upon. I can say this now without seeming egotism, since I am speaking of Sag Or," and he laughed aloud at his little joke.

But the fact remained that the body and face of Dar Tarus were beautiful indeed, though there was a hint of steel in the eyes and the set of the jaw that betokened fighting blood. Little wonder, then, that Sag Or had coveted the body of his young warrior; for his own, which Dar Tarus now possessed, was marked by dissipation and age; nor that Dar Tarus yearned to come again into his own.

Just before dawn we dropped to one of the numerous small islands that dot the Great Toonolian Marshes and nosing the ship between the boles of great trees we came to rest upon the surface of the ground, half buried in the lush and gorgeous jungle grasses, well hidden from the sight of possible pursuers. Here Hovan Du found fruits and nuts for us which the simian section of his brain pronounced safe for human consumption, and instinct led him to a nearby spring from which there bubbled delicious water. We four were half famished and much fatigued, so that the food and water were most welcome to us; nor did Xaxa and Sag Or refuse them. Having eaten, three of us lay down upon the ship's deck to sleep, after securely chaining our prisoners, while the fourth stood watch. In this way, taking turns, we slept away most of the day and when night fell, rested and refreshed, we were ready to resume our flight.

Making a wide detour to the south we avoided Toonol and about two hours before dawn we sighted the high Tower of Thavas. I think we were all keyed up to the highest pitch of excitement, for there was not one aboard that flier but whose whole life would be seriously affected by the success or failure of our venture. As a first precaution we secured the hands of Xaxa and Sag Or behind their backs and placed gags in their mouths, lest they succeed in giving warning of our approach.

Cluros had long since set and Thuria was streaming toward the horizon as we stopped our motor and drifted without lights a mile or two south of the tower while we waited impatiently for Thuria to leave the heavens to darkness and the world to us. To the northwest the lights of Toonol shone plainly against the dark background of the sky, and there were lights too in some of the windows of the great laboratory of Ras Thavas, but the tower itself was dark from plinth to pinnacle.

And now the nearer moon dropped plummet-like beneath the horizon and left the scene to darkness and to us. Dar Tarus started the motor, the wonderful, silent motor of Barsoom, and we moved slowly, close to the ground, toward Ras Thavas' island, with no sound other than the gentle whirring of our propeller; nor could that have been heard scarce a hundred feet so slowly was it turning. Close off the island we came to a stop behind a cluster of giant trees and Hovan Du, going into the bow, uttered a few low growls. Then we stood waiting in silence, listening. There was a rustling in the dense undergrowth upon the shore. Again Hovan Du voiced his low, grim call and this time there came an answer from the black shadows. Hovan Du spoke in the language of the great apes and the invisible creature replied.

For five minutes, during which time we were aware from

the different voices that others had joined in the conversation from the shore, the apes conversed, and then Hovan Du turned to me.

"It is arranged," he said. "They will permit us to hide our ship beneath these trees and they will permit us to pass out again when we are ready and board her, nor will they harm us in any way. All they ask is that when we are through we shall leave the gate open that leads to the inner court."

"Do they understand that while an ape goes in with us none will return with us?" I asked.

"Yes; but they will not harm us."

"Why do they wish the gate left open?"

"Do not inquire too closely, Vad Varo," replied Hovan Du. "It should be enough that the great apes make it possible for you to restore Valla Dia's body to her brain and escape with her from this terrible place."

"It is enough," I replied. "When may we land?"

"At once. They will help us drag the ship beneath the trees and make her fast."

"But first we must top the wall to the inner court," I reminded him.

"Yes, true—I had forgotten that we cannot open the gate from this side."

He spoke again, then, to the apes, whom we had not yet seen; and then he told me that all was arranged and that he and Dar Tarus would return with the ship after landing us inside the wall.

Again we got under way and rising slowly above the outer wall dropped silently to the courtyard beyond. The night was unusually dark, clouds having followed Thuria and blotted out the stars after the moon had set. No one could have seen the ship at a distance of fifty feet, and we moved almost without noise. Quietly we lowered our prisoners over the side and Gor Hajus and I remained with them while Dar Tarus and Hovan Du rose again and piloted the ship back to its hiding place.

I moved at once to the gate and, unlatching it, waited. I heard nothing. Never, I think, have I endured such utter silence. There came no sound from the great pile rising behind me, nor any from the dark jungle beyond the wall. Dimly I could see the huddled forms of Gor Hajus, Xaxa and Sag Or beside me—otherwise I might have been alone in the darkness and immensity of space.

It seemed an eternity that I waited there before I heard a soft scratching on the panels of the heavy gate. I pushed it open and Dar Tarus and Hovan Du stepped silently within as I closed and relatched it. No one spoke. All had been carefully planned so that there was no need of speech. Dar Tarus and I led the way, Gor Hajus and Hovan Du brought up the rear with the prisoners. We moved directly to the entrance to the tower, found the runway and descended to the pits. Every fortune seemed with us. We met no one, we had no difficulty in finding the vault we sought, and once within we secured the door so that we had no fear of interruption—that was our first concern—and then I hastened to the spot where I had hidden Valla Dia behind the body of a large warrior, tucked far back against the wall in a dark corner. My heart stood still as I dragged aside the body of the warrior, for always had I feared that Ras Thavas, knowing my interest in her and guessing the purpose of my venture, would cause every chamber and pit to be searched and every body to be examined until he found her for whom he sought; but my fears had been baseless, for there lay the body of Xaxa, the old and wrinkled casket of the lovely brain of my beloved, where I had hidden it against this very night. Gently I lifted it out and bore it to one of the two ersite topped tables. Xaxa, standing there bound and gagged, looked on with eyes that shot hate and loathing at me and at that hideous body to which her brain was so soon to be restored.

As I lifted her to the adjoining slab she tried to wriggle from my grasp and hurl herself to the floor, but I held her and soon had strapped her securely in place. A moment later she was unconscious and the re-transference was well under way. Gor Hajus, Sag Or and Hovan Du were interested spectators, but to Dar Tarus, who stood ready to assist me, it was an old story, for he had worked in the laboratory and seen more than enough of similar operations. I will not bore you with a description of it—it was but a repetition of what I had done many times in preparation for this very event.

At last it was completed and my heart fairly stood still as I replaced the embalming fluid with Valla Dia's own life blood and saw the color mount to her cheeks and her rounded bosoms rise and fall to her gentle breathing. Then she opened her eyes and looked up into mine.

"What has happened, Vad Varo?" she asked. "Has something gone amiss that you have recalled me so soon, or did I not respond to the fluid?"

Her eyes wandered past me to the faces of the others standing about. "What does it mean?" she asked. "Who are these?"

I raised her gently in my arms and pointed at the body of Xaxa lying deathlike on the ersite slab beside her. Valla Dia's eyes went wide. "It is done?" she cried, and clapped her hands to her face and felt of all her features and of the soft, delicate contours of her smooth neck; and yet she could scarce believe it and asked for a glass and I took one from Xaxa's pocket pouch and handed it to her. She looked long into it and the tears commenced to roll down her cheeks, and then she looked up at me through the mist of them and put her dear arms about my neck and drew my face down to hers. "My chieftain," she whispered—that was all. But it was enough. For those two words I had risked my life and faced unknown dangers, and gladly would I risk my life again for that same reward and always, forever.

Another night had fallen before I had completed the restoration of Dar Tarus and Hovan Du. Xaxa, and Sag Or and the great ape I left sleeping the death-like sleep of Ras Thavas's marvellous anesthetic. The great ape I had no intention of restoring, but the others I felt bound to return to Phundahl, though Dar Tarus, now resplendent in his own flesh and the gorgeous trappings of Sag Or, urged me not to inflict them again upon the long suffering Phundhlians.

"But I have given my word," I told him.

"Then they must be returned," he said.

"Though what I may do afterward is another matter," I added, for there had suddenly occurred to me a bold scheme.

I did not tell Dar Tarus what it was nor would I have had time, for at that very instant we heard someone without trying the door and then we heard voices and presently the door was tried again, this time with force. We made no noise, but just waited. I hoped that whoever it was would go away. The door was very strong and when they tried to force it they must soon have realized the futility of it because they quickly desisted and we heard their voices for only a short time thereafter and then they seemed to have gone away.

"We must leave," I said, "before they return."

Strapping the hands of Xaxa and Sag Or behind them and placing gags in their mouths I quickly restored them to life, nor ever did I see two less grateful. The looks they cast upon me might well have killed could looks do that, and with what disgust they viewed one another was writ plain in their eyes.

Cautiously unbolting the door I opened it very quietly, a naked sword in my right hand and Dar Tarus, Gor Hajus and Hovan Du ready with theirs at my shoulder, and as it swung back it revealed two standing in the corridor watching—two of Ras Thavas' slaves; and one of them was Yamdor, his body servant. At sight of us the fellow gave a loud cry of recognition and before I could leap through the doorway and prevent they had both turned and were flying up the corridor as fast as their feet would carry them.

Now there was no time to be lost—everything must be sacrificed to speed. Without thought of caution or silence we hastened through the pits toward the runway in the tower; and when we stepped into the inner court it was night again, but the farther moon was in the heavens and there were no clouds. The result was that we were instantly discovered by a sentry who gave the alarm as he ran forward to intercept us.

What was a sentry doing in the courtyard of Ras Thavas? I could not understand. And what were these? A dozen armed warriors were hurrying across the court on the heels of the sentry.

"Toonolians!" shouted Gor Hajus. "The warriors of Vobis Kan, Jeddak of Toonol!"

Breathlessly we raced for the gate. If we could but reach it first! But we were handicapped by our prisoners who held back the moment they discovered how they might embarrass us, and so it was that we all met in front of the gate. Dar Tarus and Gor Hajus and Hovan Du and I put Valla Dia and our prisoners behind us and fought the twenty warriors of Toonol with the odds five to one against us; but we had more heart in the fight than they and perhaps that gave us an advantage, though I am sure that Gor Hajus was as ten men himself so terrible was the effect of his name alone upon the men of Toonol.

"Gor Hajus!" cried one, the first to recognize him.

"Yes, it is Gor Hajus," replied the assassin. "Prepare to meet your ancestors!" and he drove into them like a racing propeller, and I was upon his right and Hovan Du and Dar Tarus upon his left.

It was a pretty fight, but it must eventually have gone against us, so greatly were we outnumbered, had I not thought of the apes and the gate beside us. Working my way to it I threw it open and there upon the outside, attracted by the noise of the conflict, stood a full dozen of the great beasts. I called to Gor Hajus and the others to fall back beside the gate, and as the apes rushed in I pointed to the Toonolian warriors.

I think the apes were at a loss to know which were friends and which were foes, but the Toonolians apprised them by attacking them, while we stood aside with our points upon the ground. Just a moment we stood thus waiting. Then as the apes rushed among the Toonolian warriors, we slipped into the darkness of the jungle beyond the outer wall and sought our flier. Behind us we could hear the growls and the roars of the beasts mingled with the shouts and the curses of the men; and the sound still rose from the courtyard as we clambered aboard the flier and pushed off into the night.

As soon as we felt that we were safely escaped from the Island of Thavas I removed the gags from the mouths of Xaxa and Sag Or and I can tell you that I immediately regretted it, for never in my life had I been subjected to such horrid abuse as poured from the wrinkled old lips of the Jeddara; and it was only when I started to gag her again that she promised to desist.

My plans were now well laid and they included a return to Phundahl since I could not start for Duhor with Valla Dia without provisions and fuel; nor could I obtain these elsewhere than in Phundahl since I felt that I held the key that would unlock the resources of that city to me; whereas all Toonol was in arms against us owing to Vobis Kan's fear of Gor Hajus.

So we retraced our way toward Phundahl as secretly as we had come, for I had no mind to be apprehended before we had gained entrance to the palace of Xaxa.

Again we rested over daylight upon the same island that had given us sanctuary two days before, and at dark we set out upon the last leg of our journey to Phundahl. If there had been pursuit we had seen naught of it; and that might easily be explained by the great extent of the uninhabited marshes across which we flew and the far southerly course that we followed close above the ground.

As we neared Phundahl I caused Xaxa and Sag Or to be again gagged, and further, I had their heads bandaged so that none might recongize them; and then we sailed straight over the city toward the palace, hoping that we would not be discovered and yet ready in the event that we should be.

But we came to the hangars on the roof apparently unseen and constantly I coached each upon the part he was to play. As we were settling slowly to the roof Dar Tarus, Hovan Du and Valla Dia quickly bound Gor Hajus and me and wrapped our heads in bandages, for we had seen below the figures of the hangar guard. Had we found the roof unguarded the binding of Gor Hajus and me had been unnecessary.

As we dropped nearer one of the guard hailed us. "What ship?" he cried.

"The royal flier of the Jeddara of Phundahl," replied Dar Tarus, "returning with Xaxa and Sag Or."

The warriors whispered among themselves as we dropped nearer and I must confess that I felt a bit nervous as to the outcome of our ruse; but they permitted us to land without a word and when they saw Valla Dia they saluted her after the manner of Barsoom, as, with the regal carriage of an empress, she descended from the deck of the flier.

"Carry the prisoners to my apartments!" she commanded, addressing the guard, and with the help of Hovan Du and Dar Tarus the four bound and muffled figures were carried from the flier down the spiral runway to the apartments of Xaxa, Jeddara of Phundahl. Here excited slaves hastened to do the bidding of the Jeddara. Word must have flown through the palace with the speed of light that Xaxa had returned, for almost immediately court functionaries began to arrive and be announced; but Valla Dia sent word that she would see no one for a while. Then she dismissed her slaves, and at my suggestion Dar Tarus investigated the apartments with a view to finding a safe hiding place for Gor Hajus, me, and the prisoners. This he soon found in a small antechamber directly off the main apartment of the royal suite; the bonds were removed from the assassin and myself and together we carried Xaxa and Sag Or into the room.

The entrance here was furnished with a heavy door over which there were hangings that completely hid it. I bade Hovan Du, who, like the rest of us, wore Phundahlian harness, stand guard before the hangings and let no one enter but members of our own party. Gor Hajus and I took up our positions just within the hangings through which we cut small holes that permitted us to see all that went on within the main chamber, for I was greatly concerned for Valla Dia's safety while she posed as Xaxa, whom I knew to be both feared and hated by her people and therefore always liable to assassination.

Valla Dia summoned the slaves and bade them admit the officials of the court, and as the doors opened fully a score of nobles entered. They appeared ill at ease and I could guess that they were recalling the episode in the temple when they had deserted their jeddara and even hurled her roughly at the feet of the Great Tur, but Valla Dia soon put them at their ease.

"I have summoned you," she said, "to hear the word of Tur. Tur would speak again to his people. Three days and three nights have I spent with Tur. His anger against Phundahl is great. He bids me summon all the higher nobles to the temple after the evening meal tonight, and all the priests, and the commanders and dwars of the Guard, and as many of the lesser nobles as be in the palace; and then shall the people of Phundahl hear the word and the law of Tur and all those who shall obey shall live and all those who shall not obey shall die; and woe be to him who, having been summoned, shall not be in the temple this night. I, Xaxa, Jeddara of Phundahl, have spoken! Go!"

They went and they seemed glad to go. Then Valla Dia summoned the odwar of the Guard, who would be in our world a general, and she told him to clear the palace of every living being from the temple level to the roof an hour before the evening meal, nor to permit any one to enter the temple or the levels above it until the hour appointed for the assembling in the temple to hear the word of Tur, excepting however those who might be in her own apartments, which were not to be entered upon pain of death. She made it all very clear and plain and the odwar understood and I think he trembled a trifle, for all were in great fear of the Jeddara Xaxa; and then he went away and the slaves were dismissed and we were alone.

CHAPTER XIV

JOHN CARTER

HALF AN HOUR before the evening meal we carried Xaxa and Sag Or down the spiral runway and placed them in the base of the Great Tur and Gor Hajus and I took our places on the upper platform behind the eyes and voice of the idol. Valla Dia, Dar Tarus and Hovan Du remained in the royal apartment. Our plans were well formulated. There was no one between the door at the rear of the Great Tur and the flier that lay ready on the roof in the event that we were forced to flee through any miscarriage of our mad scheme.

The minutes dragged slowly by and darkness fell. The time was approaching. We heard the doors of the temple open and beyond we saw the great corridor brilliantly lighted. It was empty except for two priests who stood hesitating nervously in the doorway. Finally one of them mustered up sufficient courage to enter and switch on the lights. More bravely now they advanced and prostrated themselves before the altar of the Great Tur. When they arose and looked up into the face of the idol I could not resist the temptation to turn those huge eyes until they had rolled completely about the interior of the chamber and rested again upon the priests; but I did not speak and I think the effect of the awful silence in the presence of the living god was more impressive than would words have been. The two priests simply collapsed. They slid to the floor and lay there trembling, moaning and supplicating Tur to have mercy on them, nor did they rise before the first of the worshippers arrived.

Thereafter the temple filled rapidly and I could see that the word of Tur had been well and thoroughly disseminated. They came as they had before; but there were more this time, and they ranged upon either side of the central aisle and there they waited, their eyes divided between the doorway and the god. About the time that I thought the next scene was about to be enacted I let Tur's eyes travel over the assemblage that they might be keyed to the proper pitch for what was to follow. They reacted precisely as had the priests, falling upon the floor and moaning and supplicating; and there they remained until the sounds of bugles announced the coming of the Jeddara. Then they rose unsteadily to their feet. The great doors swung open and there was the carpet and the slaves behind it. As they rolled it down toward the altar the bugles sounded louder and the head of the royal procession came into view. I had ordered it thus to permit of greater pageantry than was possible when the doors opened immediately upon the head of the procession. My plan permitted the audience to see the royal retinue advancing down the long corridor and the effect was splendid. First came the double rank of nobles and behind these the chariot drawn by the two banths, bearing the litter upon which reclined Valla Dia. Behind her walked Dar Tarus, but all within that room thought they were looking upon the Jeddara Xaxa and her favorite, Sag Or. Hovan Du walked behind Sag Or and following came the fifty young men and the fifty maidens.

The chariot halted before the altar and Valla Dia descended and knelt and the voices that had been chanting the praises of Xaxa were stilled as the beautiful creature extended her hands toward the Great Tur and looked up into his face. "We are ready, Master!" she cried. "Speak! We await the word of Tur!"

A gasp arose from the kneeling assemblage, a gasp that ended in a sob. I felt that they were pretty well worked up and that everything ought to go off without a hitch. I placed the speaking tube to my lips.

"I am Tur!" I thundered and the people trembled. "I come to pass judgment on the men of Phundahl. As you receive my word so shall you prosper or so shall you perish. The sins of the people may be atoned by two who have sinned most in my sight." I let the eyes of Tur rove about over the audience and then brought them to rest upon Valla Dia. "Xaxa, are you ready to atone for your sins and for the sins of your people?"

Valla Dia bowed her beautiful head. "Thy will is law, Master!" she replied.

"And Sag Or," I continued, "you have sinned. Are you prepared to pay?"

"As Tur shall require," said Dar Tarus.

"Then it is my will," I boomed, "that Xaxa and Sag Or shall give back to those from whom they stole them, the beautiful bodies they now wear; that he from whom Sag Or took this body shall become Jeddak of Phundahl and High Priest of Tur; and that she from whom Xaxa stole her body shall be returned in pomp to her native country. I have spoken. Let any who would revolt against my word speak now or forever hold his peace."

There was no objection voiced. I had felt pretty certain that there would not be. I doubt if any god ever looked down upon a more subdued and chastened flock. As I had talked, Gor Hajus had descended to the base of the idol and removed the bonds from the feet and legs of Xaxa and Sag Or.

"Extinguish the lights!" I commanded. A trembling priest did my bidding.

Valla Dia and Dar Tarus were standing side by side before the altar when the lights went out. In the next minute they and Gor Hajus must have worked fast, for when I heard a low whistle from the interior of the idol's base, the pre-arranged signal that Gor Hajus had finished his work, and ordered the lights on again, there stood Xaxa and Sag Or where Valla Dia and Dar Tarus had been, and the latter were no where in sight. I think the dramatic effect of that transformation upon the people there was the most stupend-ous thing I have ever seen. There was no cord or gag upon either Xaxa or Sag Or, nothing to indicate they they had been brought hither by force—no one about who might have so brought them. The illusion was perfect—it was a gesture of omnipotence that simply staggered the intellect. But I wasn't through.

"You have heard Xaxa renounce her throne," I said, "and Sag Or submit to the judgment of Tur."

"I have not renounced my throne!" cried Xaxa. "It is all a——"

"Silence!" I thundered. "Prepare to greet the new jeddak, Dar Tarus of Phundahl!" I turned my eyes toward the great doors and the eyes of the assemblage followed mine. They swung open and there stood Dar Tarus, resplendent in the trappings of Hora San, the long dead jeddak and high priest, whose bones we had robbed in the base of the idol an hour earlier. How Dar Tarus had managed to make the change so quickly is beyond me, but he had done it and the effect was colossal. He looked every inch a jeddak as he moved with slow dignity up the wide aisle along the blue and gold and white carpet. Xaxa turned purple with rage. "Impostor!" she shrieked. "Seize him! Kill him!" and she ran forward to meet him as though she would slay him with her bare hands.

"Take her away," said Dar Tarus in a quiet voice, and at that Xaxa fell foaming to the floor. She shrieked and gasped and then lay still—a wicked old woman dead of apoplexy. And when Sag Or saw her lying there he must have been the first to realize that she was dead and that there was now no one to protect him from the hatreds that are levelled always at the person of a ruler's favorite. He looked wildly about for an instant and then threw himself at the feet of Dar Tarus.

"You promised to protect me!" he cried.

"None shall harm you," replied Dar Tarus. "Go your way and live in peace." Then he turned his eyes upward toward the face of the Great Tur. "What is thy will, Master?" he cried. "Dar Tarus, thy servant, awaits thy commands!"

I permitted an impressive silence before I replied.

"Let the priests of Tur, the lesser nobles and a certain number of the Jeddak's Guard go forth into the city and spread the word of Tur among the people that they may know that Tur smiles again upon Phundahl and that they have a new jeddak who stands high in the favor of Tur. Let the higher nobles attend presently in the chambers that were Xaxa's and do honor to Valla Dia in whose perfect body their Jeddara once ruled them, and effect the necessary arrangements for her proper return to Duhor, her native city. There also will they find two who have served Tur well and these shall be accorded the hospitality and friendship of every Phundahlian—Gor Hajus of Toonol and Vad Varo of Jasoom. Go! and when the last has gone let the temple be darkened. I, Tur, have spoken!"

Valla Dia had gone directly to the apartments of the former jeddara and the moment that the lights were extinguished

Gor Hajus and I joined her. She could not wait to hear the outcome of our ruse, and when I assured her that there had been no hitch the tears came to her eyes for very joy.

"You have accomplished the impossible, my chieftain," she murmured, "and already can I see the hills of Duhor and the towers of my native city. Ah, Vad Varo, I had not dreamed that life might again hold for me such happy prospects. I owe you life and more than life."

We were interrupted by the coming of Dar Tarus, and with him were Hovan Du and a number of the higher nobles. The latter received us pleasantly, though I think they were mystified as to just how we were linked with the service of their god; nor, I am sure, did one of them ever learn. They were frankly delighted to be rid of Xaxa; and while they could not understand Tur's purpose in elevating a former warrior of the Guard to the throne, yet they were content if it served to relieve them from the wrath of their god, now a very real and terrible god, since the miracles that had been performed in the temple. That Dar Tarus had been of a noble family relieved them of embarrassment, and I noted that they treated him with great respect. I was positive that they would continue to treat him so, for he was also high priest and for the first time in a hundred years he would bring to the Great Tur in the Royal Temple the voice of god, for Hovan Du had agreed to take service with Dar Tarus, and Gor Hajus as well, so that there would never be lacking a tongue wherewith Tur might speak. I foresaw great possibilities for the reign of Dar Tarus, Jeddak of Phundahl.

At the meeting held in the apartments of Xaxa it was decided that Valla Dia should rest two days in Phundahl while a small fleet was preparing to transport her to Duhor. Dar Tarus assigned Xaxa's apartments for her use and gave her slaves from different cities to attend upon her, all of whom were to be freed and returned with Valla Dia to her native land.

It was almost dawn before we sought our sleeping silks and furs and the sun was high before we awoke. Gor Hajus and I breakfasted with Valla Dia, outside of whose door we had spread our beds that we might not leave her unprotected for a moment that it was not necessary. We had scarce finished our meal when a messenger came from Dar Tarus summoning us to the audience chamber, where we found some of the higher officers of the court gathered about the throne upon which Dar Tarus sat, looking every inch an emperor. He greeted us kindly, rising and descending from his dais to receive Valla Dia and escort her to one of the benches he had had placed beside the throne for her and for me.

"There is one," he said to me, "who has come to Phundahl over night and now begs audience of the jeddak—one whom I thought you might like to meet again," and he signed to one of his attendants to admit the petitioner; and when the doors at the opposite end of the room opened I saw Ras Thavas standing there. He did not recognize me or Valla Dia or Gor Hajus until he was almost at the foot of the throne, and when he did he looked puzzled and glanced again quickly at Dar Tarus.

"Ras Thavas of the Tower of Thavas, Toonol," announced an officer.

"What would Ras Thavas of the Jeddak of Phundahl?" asked Dar Tarus.

"I came seeking audience of Xaxa," replied Ras Thavas, "not knowing of her death or your accession until this very morning; but I see Sag Or upon Xaxa's throne and beside him one whom I thought was Xaxa, though they tell me Xaxa is dead, and another who was my assistant at Thavas and one who is the Assassin of Toonol, and I am confused, Jeddak, and do not know whether I be among friends or foes."

"Speak as though Xaxa still sat upon the throne of Phundahl," Dar Tarus told him, "for though I am Dar Tarus, whom you wronged, and not Sag Or, yet need you have no fear in the court of Phundahl."

"Then let me tell you that Vobis Kan, Jeddak of Toonol, learning that Gor Hajus had escaped me, swore that I had set him free to assassinate him, and he sent warriors who took my island and would have imprisoned me had I not been warned in time to escape; and I came hither to Xaxa to beg her to send warriors to drive the men of Toonol from my island and restore it to me that I may carry on my scientific labors."

Dar Tarus turned to me. "Vad Varo, of all others you are most familiar with the work of Ras Thavas. Would you see him again restored to his island and his laboratory?"

"Only on condition that he devote his great skill to the amelioration of human suffering." I replied, "and no longer prostitute it to the foul purposes of greed and sin." This led to a discussion which lasted for hours, the results of which were of far reaching significance. Ras Thavas agreed to all that I required and Dar Tarus commissioned Gor Hajus to head an army against Toonol.

But these matters, while of vast interest to those most directly concerned, have no direct bearing upon the story of my adventures upon Barsoom, as I had no part in them, since upon the second day I boarded a flier with Valla Dia and, escorted by a Phundahlian fleet, set out toward Duhor. Dar Tarus accompanied us for a short distance. When the fleet was stopped at the shore of the great marsh he bade us farewell and was about to step to the deck of his own ship and return to Phundahl when a shout arose from the deck of one of the other ships and word was soon passed that a lookout had sighted what appeared to be a great fleet far to the southwest. Nor was it long before it became plainly visible to us all and equally plain that it was headed for Phundahl.

Dar Tarus told me then that as much as he regretted it, there seemed nothing to do but return at once to his capital with the entire fleet, since he could not spare a single ship or man if this proved an enemy fleet, nor could Valla Dia or I interpose any objection; and so we turned about and sped as rapidly as the slow ships of Phundahl permitted back toward the city.

The stranger fleet had sighted us at about the same time that we had sighted it, and we saw it change its course and bear down upon us; and as it came nearer it fell into single file and prepared to encircle us. I was standing at Dar Tarus' side when the colors of the approaching fleet became distinguishable and we first learned that it was from Helium.

"Signal and ask if they come in peace," directed Dar Tarus.

"We seek word with Xaxa, Jeddara of Phundahl," came the reply. "The question of peace or war will be hers to decide."

"Tell them that Xaxa is dead and that I, Dar Tarus, Jeddak of Phundahl, will receive the commander of Helium's fleet in peace upon the deck of this ship, or that I will receive him in war with all my guns. I, Dar Tarus, have spoken!"

From the bow of a great ship of Helium there broke the flag

of truce and when Dar Tarus' ship answered it in kind the other drew near and presently we could see the men of Helium upon her decks. Slowly the great flier came alongside our smaller ship and when the two had been made fast a party of officers boarded us. They were fine looking men, and at their head was one whom I recognized immediately though I had never before laid eyes upon him. I think he was the most impressive figure I have ever seen as he advanced slowly across the deck toward us—John Carter, Prince of Helium, Warlord of Barsoom.

"Dar Tarus," he said, "John Carter greets you in peace, though it had been different, I think, had Xaxa still reigned."

"You came to war upon Xaxa?" asked Dar Tarus.

"We came to right a wrong," replied the Warlord. "But from what we know of Xaxa that could have been done only by force."

"What wrong has Phundahl done Helium?" demanded Dar Tarus.

"The wrong was against one of your own people—even against you in person."

"I do not understand," said Dar Tarus.

"There is one aboard my ship who may be able to explain to you, Dar Tarus," replied John Carter, with a smile. He turned and spoke to one of his aides in a whisper, and the man saluted and returned to the deck of his own ship. "You shall see with your own eyes, Dar Tarus." Suddenly his eyes narrowed. "This is indeed Dar Tarus who was a warrior of the Jeddara's Guard and supposedly assassinated by her command?"

"It is," replied Dar Tarus.

"I must be certain," said the Warlord.

"There is no question about it, John Carter," I spoke up in English.

His eyes went wide, and when they fell upon me and he noted my lighter skin, from which the dye was wearing away, he stepped forward and held out his hand.

"A countryman?" he asked.

"Yes, an American," I replied.

"I was almost surprised," he said. "Yet why should I be? I have crossed—there is no reason why others should not. And you have accomplished it! You must come to Helium with me and tell me all about it."

Further conversation was interrupted by the return of the
aide, who brought a young woman with him. At sight of her
Dar Tarus uttered a cry of joy and sprang forward, and I did
not need to be told that this was Kara Vasa.

There is little more to tell that might not bore you in the
telling—of how John Carter himself took Valla Dia and me
to Duhor after attending the nuptials of Dar Tarus and Kara
Vasa; and of the great surprise that awaited me in Duhor,
where I learned for the first time that Kor San, Jeddak of
Duhor, was the father of Valla Dia; and of the honors and the
great riches that he heaped upon me when Valla Dia and I
were wed.

John Carter was present at the wedding and we initiated
upon Barsoom a good old American custom, for the Warlord
acted as best man; and then he insisted that we follow that
up with a honeymoon and bore us off to Helium, where I am
writing this.

Even now it seems like a dream that I can look out of my
window and see the scarlet and the yellow towers of the twin
cities of Helium; that I have met, and see daily, Carthoris,
Thuvia of Ptarth, Tara of Helium, Gahan of Gathol and that
peerless creature, Dejah Thoris, Princess of Mars. Though to
me, beautiful as she is, there is another even more beautiful
—Valla Dia, Princess of Duhor—Mrs. Ulysses Paxton.

A GLOSSARY OF NAMES AND TERMS USED IN THE MARTIAN BOOKS*

Aaanthor. A dead city of ancient Mars.

Aisle of Hope. An aisle leading to the courtroom in Helium.

Apt. An Arctic monster. A huge, white-furred creature with six limbs, four of which, short and heavy, carry it over the snow and ice; the other two, which grow forward from its shoulders on either side of its long, powerful neck, terminate in white, hairless hands with which it seizes and holds it prey. Its head and mouth are similar in appearance to those of a hippopotamus except that from the sides of the lower jawbone two mighty horns curve slightly downward toward the front. Its two huge eyes extend in two vast oval patches from the center of the top of the cranium down either side of the head to below the roots of the horns, so that these weapons really grow out from the lower part of the eyes, which are composed of several thousand ocelli each. Each ocellus is furnished with its own lid, and the apt can, at will, close as many of the facets of his huge eyes as he chooses. (See THE WARLORD OF MARS.)

Astok. Prince of Dusar.

Avenue of Ancestors. A street in Helium.

Banth. Barsoomian lion. A fierce beast of prey that roams the low hills surrounding the dead seas of ancient Mars. It is almost hairless, having only a great, bristly mane about its thick neck. Its long, lithe body is supported by ten powerful legs, its enormous jaws are equipped with several rows of long needle-like fangs, and its mouth reaches to a point far back of its tiny ears. It has enormous protruding eyes of green. (See THE GODS OF MARS.)

Bar Comas. Jeddak of Warhoon. (See A PRINCESS OF MARS.)

Barsoom. Mars.

Black pirates of Barsoom. Men six feet and over in height. Have clear-cut and handsome features; their eyes are well

---

*This Glossary originally appeared as an appendix to *Thuvia, Maid of Mars.*

set and large, though a slight narrowness lends them a
crafty appearance. The iris is extremely black while the
eyeball itself is quite white and clear. Their skin has the
appearance of polished ebony. (See THE GODS OF MARS.)

Calot. A dog. About the size of a Shetland pony and has ten
short legs. The head bears a slight resemblance to that of
a frog, except that the jaws are equipped with three rows
of long, sharp tusks. (See A PRINCESS OF MARS.)

Carter, John. Warlord of Mars.

Carthoris of Helium. Son of John Carter and Dejah Thoris.

Dak Kova. Jed among the Warhoons (later jeddak).

Darseen. Chameleon-like reptile.

Dator. Chief or prince among the First Born.

Dejah Thoris. Princess of Helium.

Djor Kantos. Son of Kantos Kan; padwar of the Fifth Utan.

Dor. Valley of Heaven.

Dotar Sojat. John Carter's Martian name, from the surnames
of the first two warrior chieftains he killed.

Dusar. A Martian kingdom.

Dwar. Captain.

Ersite. A kind of stone.

Father of Therns. High Priest of religious cult.

First Born. Black race; black pirates.

Kar Komak. Odwar of Lotharian bowmen.

Gate of Jeddaks. A gate in Helium.

Gozava. Tars Tarkas' dead wife.

Gur Tus. Dwar of the Tenth Utan.

Haad. Martian mile.

Hal Vas. Son of Vas Kor, the Dusarian noble.

Hastor. A city of Helium.

Hekkador. Title of Father of Therns.

Helium. The empire of the grandfather of Dejah Thoris.

Holy Therns. A Martian religious cult.

Hortan Gur. Jeddak of Torquas.

Hor Vastus. Padwar in the navy of Helium.

Horz. Deserted city; Barsoomian Greenwich.

Ilall. A city of Okar.

Iss. River of Death. (See A PRINCESS OF MARS.)

Issus. Goddess of Death, whose abode is upon the banks of
the Lost Sea of Korus. (See THE GODS OF MARS.)

Jav. A Lotharian.

Jed. King.

Jeddak. Emperor.

Kab Kadja. Jeddak of the Warhoons of the south.

Kadabra. Capital of Okar.

Kadar. Guard.

Kalksus. Cruiser-transport under Vas Kor.

Kantos Kan. Padwar in the Helium navy.

Kaol. A Martian kingdom in the eastern hemisphere.

Kaor. Greeting.

Karad. Martian degree.

Komal. The Lotharian god; a huge banth.

Korad. A dead city of ancient Mars. (SEE A PRINCESS OF MARS.)

Korus. The Lost Sea of Dor.

Kulan Tith. Jeddak of Kaol. (SEE THE WARLORD OF MARS.)

Lakor. A thern.

Larok. A Dusarian warrior; artificer.

Lorquas Ptomel. Jed among the Tharks. (SEE A PRINCESS OF MARS.)

Lothar. The forgotten city.

Marentina. A principality of Okar.

Matai Shang. Father of Therns. (SEE THE GODS OF MARS.)

Mors Kajak. A jed of lesser Helium.

Notan. Royal psychologist of Zodanga.

Nutus. Jeddak of Dusar.

Od. Martian foot.

Odwar. A commander, or general.

Okar. Land of the yellow men.

Old Ben (or *Uncle Ben*). The writer's body-servant (colored).

Omad. Man with one name.

Omean. The buried sea.

Orluk. A black and yellow striped Arctic monster.

Otz Mountains. Surrounding the Valley Dor and the Lost Sea of Korus.

Padwar. Lieutenant.

Panthan. A soldier of fortune.

Parthak. The Zodangan who brought food to John Carter in the pits of Zat Arras. (SEE THE GODS OF MARS.)

Pedestal of Truth. Within the courtroom of Helium.

Phaidor. Daughter of Matai Shang. (SEE THE GODS OF MARS.)

Pimalia. Gorgeous flowering plant.

Plant men of Barsoom. A race inhabiting the Valley Dor. They are ten or twelve feet in height when standing erect; their arms are very short and fashioned after the manner of an elephant's trunk, being sinuous; the body is hairless and ghoulish blue except for a broad band of white which encircles the protruding, single eye, the pupil, iris, and ball of which are dead white. The nose is a ragged, inflamed, circular hole in the center of the blank face, resembling a fresh bullet wound which has not yet commenced to bleed. There is no mouth in the head. With the exception of the face, the head is covered by a tangled mass of jet-black hair some eight or ten inches in length. Each hair is about the thickness of a large angleworm. The body, legs and feet are of human shape but of monstrous proportions, the feet being fully three feet long and very flat and broad. The method of feeding consists in running their odd hands over the surface of the turf, cropping off the tender vegetation with razor-like talons and sucking it up from two mouths, which lie one in the palm of each hand. They are equipped with a massive tail about six feet long, quite round where it joins the body, but tapering to a flat, thin blade toward the end, which trails at right angles to the ground. (See THE GODS OF MARS.)

Prince Soran. Overlord of the navy of Ptarth.

Ptarth. A Martian kingdom.

Ptor. Family name of three Zodangan brothers.

Sab Than. Prince of Zodanga. (See A PRINCESS OF MARS.)

Safad. A Martian inch.

Sak. Jump.

Salensus Oll. Jeddak of Okar. (SEE THE WARLORD OF MARS.)

Saran Tal. Carthoris' major-domo.

Sarkoja. A green Martian woman. (See A PRINCESS OF MARS.)

Sator Throg. A Holy Thern of the Tenth Cycle.

Shador. Island in Omean used as a prison.

Silian. Slimy reptiles inhabiting the Sea of Korus.

Sith. Hornet-like monster. Bald-faced and about the size of a Hereford bull. Has frightful jaws in front and mighty poisoned sting behind. The eyes, of myriad facets, cover three-fourths of the head, permitting the creature to see in all directions at one and the same time. (See THE WARLORD OF MARS.)

Skeel. A Martian hardwood.

Sola. A young green Martian woman.

Solan. An official of the palace.

Sompus. A kind of tree.

Sorak. A little pet animal among the red Martian women, about the size of a cat.

Sorapus. A Martian hardwood.

Sorav. An officer of Salensus Oll.

Tal. A Martian second.

Tal Hajus. Jeddak of Thark.

Talu. Rebel Prince of Marentina.

Tan Gama. Warhoon warrior.

Tardos Mors. Grandfather of Dejah Thoris and jeddak of Helium.

Tario. Jeddak of Lothar.

Tars Tarkas. A green man, chieftain of the Tharks.

Temple of Reward. In Helium.

Tenth Cycle. A sphere, or plane of eminence, among the Holy Therns.

Thabis. Issus' chief.

Than Kosis. Jeddak of Zodanga. (See A PRINCESS OF MARS.)

Thar Ban. Jed among the green men of Tarquas.

Thark. City and name of a green Martian horde.

Thoat. A green Martian horse. Ten feet high at the shoulder, with four legs on either side; a broad, flat tail, larger at the tip than at the root which it holds straight out behind while running; a mouth splitting its head from snout to the long, massive neck. It is entirely devoid of hair and is of a dark slate color and exceedingly smooth and glossy. It has a white belly and the legs are shaded from slate at the shoulders and hips to a vivid yellow at the feet. The feet are heavily padded and nailless. (See A PRINCESS OF MARS.)

Thorian. Chief of the lesser Therns.

Throne of Righteousness. In the courtroom of Helium.

Throxus. Mightiest of the five oceans.

Thurds. A green horde inimical to Torquas.

Thuria. The nearer moon. (Also airship under Astok.)

Thurid. A black dator.

Thuvan Dihn. Jeddak of Ptarth.

Thuvia. Princess of Ptarth.

Torith. Officer of the guards at submarine pool.

Torkar Bar. Kaolian noble; dwar of the Kolian Road.

Torquas. A green horde.

Turjun. Carthoris' alias.

Utan. A company of one hundred men (military).

Vas Kor. A Dusarian noble.

Warhoon. A community of green men; enemy of Thark.

Woola. A Barsoomian calot.

Xat. A Martian minute.

Xavarian. A Helium warship.

Xodar. Dator among the First Born.

Yersted. Commander of the submarine.

Zad. Tharkian warrior.

Zat Arrras. Jed of Zodanga.

Zithad. Dator of the guards of Issus. (See THE GODS OF MARS.)

Zitidars. Mastodonian draught animals.

Zodanga. Martian city of red men at war with Helium.

Zode. A Martian hour.

A CATALOGUE OF SELECTED DOVER BOOKS
IN ALL FIELDS OF INTEREST

A CATALOGUE OF SELECTED DOVER BOOKS
IN ALL FIELDS OF INTEREST

THE DEVIL'S DICTIONARY, Ambrose Bierce. Barbed, bitter, brilliant witticisms in the form of a dictionary. Best, most ferocious satire America has produced. 145pp. 20487-1 Pa. $1.75

ABSOLUTELY MAD INVENTIONS, A.E. Brown, H.A. Jeffcott. Hilarious, useless, or merely absurd inventions all granted patents by the U.S. Patent Office. Edible tie pin, mechanical hat tipper, etc. 57 illustrations. 125pp. 22596-8 Pa. $1.50

AMERICAN WILD FLOWERS COLORING BOOK, Paul Kennedy. Planned coverage of 48 most important wildflowers, from Rickett's collection; instructive as well as entertaining. Color versions on covers. 48pp. 8¼ x 11. 20095-7 Pa. $1.50

BIRDS OF AMERICA COLORING BOOK, John James Audubon. Rendered for coloring by Paul Kennedy. 46 of Audubon's noted illustrations: red-winged blackbird, cardinal, purple finch, towhee, etc. Original plates reproduced in full color on the covers. 48pp. 8¼ x 11. 23049-X Pa. $1.50

NORTH AMERICAN INDIAN DESIGN COLORING BOOK, Paul Kennedy. The finest examples from Indian masks, beadwork, pottery, etc. — selected and redrawn for coloring (with identifications) by well-known illustrator Paul Kennedy. 48pp. 8¼ x 11. 21125-8 Pa. $1.50

UNIFORMS OF THE AMERICAN REVOLUTION COLORING BOOK, Peter Copeland. 31 lively drawings reproduce whole panorama of military attire; each uniform has complete instructions for accurate coloring. (Not in the Pictorial Archives Series). 64pp. 8¼ x 11. 21850-3 Pa. $1.50

THE WONDERFUL WIZARD OF OZ COLORING BOOK, L. Frank Baum. Color the Yellow Brick Road and much more in 61 drawings adapted from W.W. Denslow's originals, accompanied by abridged version of text. Dorothy, Toto, Oz and the Emerald City. 61 illustrations. 64pp. 8¼ x 11. 20452-9 Pa. $1.50

CUT AND COLOR PAPER MASKS, Michael Grater. Clowns, animals, funny faces ... simply color them in, cut them out, and put them together, and you have 9 paper masks to play with and enjoy. Complete instructions. Assembled masks shown in full color on the covers. 32pp. 8¼ x 11. 23171-2 Pa. $1.50

STAINED GLASS CHRISTMAS ORNAMENT COLORING BOOK, Carol Belanger Grafton. Brighten your Christmas season with over 100 Christmas ornaments done in a stained glass effect on translucent paper. Color them in and then hang at windows, from lights, anywhere. 32pp. 8¼ x 11. 20707-2 Pa. $1.75

CREATIVE LITHOGRAPHY AND HOW TO DO IT, Grant Arnold. Lithography as art form: working directly on stone, transfer of drawings, lithotint, mezzotint, color printing; also metal plates. Detailed, thorough. 27 illustrations. 214pp.
21208-4 Pa. $3.00

DESIGN MOTIFS OF ANCIENT MEXICO, Jorge Enciso. Vigorous, powerful ceramic stamp impressions — Maya, Aztec, Toltec, Olmec. Serpents, gods, priests, dancers, etc. 153pp. 6¹/8 x 9¼. 20084-1 Pa. $2.50

AMERICAN INDIAN DESIGN AND DECORATION, Leroy Appleton. Full text, plus more than 700 precise drawings of Inca, Maya, Aztec, Pueblo, Plains, NW Coast basketry, sculpture, painting, pottery, sand paintings, metal, etc. 4 plates in color. 279pp. 8³/8 x 11¼. 22704-9 Pa. $4.50

CHINESE LATTICE DESIGNS, Daniel S. Dye. Incredibly beautiful geometric designs: circles, voluted, simple dissections, etc. Inexhaustible source of ideas, motifs. 1239 illustrations. 469pp. 6¹/8 x 9¼. 23096-1 Pa. $5.00

JAPANESE DESIGN MOTIFS, Matsuya Co. Mon, or heraldic designs. Over 4000 typical, beautiful designs: birds, animals, flowers, swords, fans, geometric; all beautifully stylized. 213pp. 11³/8 x 8¼. 22874-6 Pa. $5.00

PERSPECTIVE, Jan Vredeman de Vries. 73 perspective plates from 1604 edition; buildings, townscapes, stairways, fantastic scenes. Remarkable for beauty, surrealistic atmosphere; real eye-catchers. Introduction by Adolf Placzek. 74pp. 11³/8 x 8¼. 20186-4 Pa. $2.75

EARLY AMERICAN DESIGN MOTIFS, Suzanne E. Chapman. 497 motifs, designs, from painting on wood, ceramics, appliqué, glassware, samplers, metal work, etc. Florals, landscapes, birds and animals, geometrics, letters, etc. Inexhaustible. Enlarged edition. 138pp. 8³/8 x 11¼. 22985-8 Pa. $3.50
23084-8 Clothbd. $7.95

VICTORIAN STENCILS FOR DESIGN AND DECORATION, edited by E.V. Gillon, Jr. 113 wonderful ornate Victorian pieces from German sources; florals, geometrics; borders, corner pieces; bird motifs, etc. 64pp. 9³/8 x 12¼. 21995-X Pa. $2.75

ART NOUVEAU: AN ANTHOLOGY OF DESIGN AND ILLUSTRATION FROM THE STUDIO, edited by E.V. Gillon, Jr. Graphic arts: book jackets, posters, engravings, illustrations, decorations; Crane, Beardsley, Bradley and many others. Inexhaustible. 92pp. 8¹/8 x 11. 22388-4 Pa. $2.50

ORIGINAL ART DECO DESIGNS, William Rowe. First-rate, highly imaginative modern Art Deco frames, borders, compositions, alphabets, florals, insectals, Wurlitzer-types, etc. Much finest modern Art Deco. 80 plates, 8 in color. 8³/8 x 11¼. 22567-4 Pa. $3.50

HANDBOOK OF DESIGNS AND DEVICES, Clarence P. Hornung. Over 1800 basic geometric designs based on circle, triangle, square, scroll, cross, etc. Largest such collection in existence. 261pp. 20125-2 Pa. $2.75

VICTORIAN HOUSES: A TREASURY OF LESSER-KNOWN EXAMPLES, Edmund Gillon and Clay Lancaster. 116 photographs, excellent commentary illustrate distinct characteristics, many borrowings of local Victorian architecture. Octagonal houses, Americanized chalets, grand country estates, small cottages, etc. Rich heritage often overlooked. 116 plates. 11⅜ x 10.   22966-1 Pa. $4.00

STICKS AND STONES, Lewis Mumford. Great classic of American cultural history; architecture from medieval-inspired earliest forms to 20th century; evolution of structure and style, influence of environment. 21 illustrations. 113pp.
20202-X Pa. $2.50

ON THE LAWS OF JAPANESE PAINTING, Henry P. Bowie. Best substitute for training with genius Oriental master, based on years of study in Kano school. Philosophy, brushes, inks, style, etc. 66 illustrations. 117pp. 6⅛ x 9¼.   20030-2 Pa. $4.50

A HANDBOOK OF ANATOMY FOR ART STUDENTS, Arthur Thomson. Virtually exhaustive. Skeletal structure, muscles, heads, special features. Full text, anatomical figures, undraped photos. Male and female. 337 illustrations. 459pp.
21163-0 Pa. $5.00

AN ATLAS OF ANATOMY FOR ARTISTS, Fritz Schider. Finest text, working book. Full text, plus anatomical illustrations; plates by great artists showing anatomy. 593 illustrations. 192pp. 7⅞ x 10¾.   20241-0 Clothbd. $6.95

THE HUMAN FIGURE IN MOTION, Eadweard Muybridge. More than 4500 stopped-action photos, in action series, showing undraped men, women, children jumping, lying down, throwing, sitting, wrestling, carrying, etc. "Unparalleled dictionary for artists," American Artist. Taken by great 19th century photographer. 390pp. 7⅞ x 10⅝.   20204-6 Clothbd. $12.50

AN ATLAS OF ANIMAL ANATOMY FOR ARTISTS, W. Ellenberger et al. Horses, dogs, cats, lions, cattle, deer, etc. Muscles, skeleton, surface features. The basic work. Enlarged edition. 288 illustrations. 151pp. 9⅜ x 12¼.   20082-5 Pa. $4.50

LETTER FORMS: 110 COMPLETE ALPHABETS, Frederick Lambert. 110 sets of capital letters; 16 lower case alphabets; 70 sets of numbers and other symbols. Edited and expanded by Theodore Menten. 110pp. 8⅛ x 11.   22872-X Pa. $3.00

THE METHODS OF CONSTRUCTION OF CELTIC ART, George Bain. Simple geometric techniques for making wonderful Celtic interlacements, spirals, Kells-type initials, animals, humans, etc. Unique for artists, craftsmen. Over 500 illustrations. 160pp. 9 x 12.   USO 22923-8 Pa. $4.00

SCULPTURE, PRINCIPLES AND PRACTICE, Louis Slobodkin. Step by step approach to clay, plaster, metals, stone; classical and modern. 253 drawings, photos. 255pp. 8⅛ x 11.   22960-2 Pa. $5.00

THE ART OF ETCHING, E.S. Lumsden. Clear, detailed instructions for etching, drypoint, softground, aquatint; from 1st sketch to print. Very detailed, thorough. 200 illustrations. 376pp.   20049-3 Pa. $3.75

CATALOGUE OF DOVER BOOKS

CONSTRUCTION OF AMERICAN FURNITURE TREASURES, Lester Margon. 344 detail drawings, complete text on constructing exact reproductions of 38 early American masterpieces: Hepplewhite sideboard, Duncan Phyfe drop-leaf table, mantel clock, gate-leg dining table, Pa. German cupboard, more. 38 plates. 54 photographs. 168pp. 8⅜ x 11¼.   23056-2 Pa. $4.00

JEWELRY MAKING AND DESIGN, Augustus F. Rose, Antonio Cirino. Professional secrets revealed in thorough, practical guide: tools, materials, processes; rings, brooches, chains, cast pieces, enamelling, setting stones, etc. Do not confuse with skimpy introductions: beginner can use, professional can learn from it. Over 200 illustrations. 306pp.   21750-7 Pa. $3.00

METALWORK AND ENAMELLING, Herbert Maryon. Generally conceded best all-around book. Countless trade secrets: materials, tools, soldering, filigree, setting, inlay, niello, repoussé, casting, polishing, etc. For beginner or expert. Author was foremost British expert. 330 illustrations. 335pp.   22702-2 Pa. $3.50

WEAVING WITH FOOT-POWER LOOMS, Edward F. Worst. Setting up a loom, beginning to weave, constructing equipment, using dyes, more, plus over 285 drafts of traditional patterns including Colonial and Swedish weaves. More than 200 other figures. For beginning and advanced. 275pp. 8¾ x 6⅜ .   23064-3 Pa. $4.50

WEAVING A NAVAJO BLANKET, Gladys A. Reichard. Foremost anthropologist studied under Navajo women, reveals every step in process from wool, dyeing, spinning, setting up loom, designing, weaving. Much history, symbolism. With this book you could make one yourself. 97 illustrations. 222pp.   22992-0 Pa. $3.00

NATURAL DYES AND HOME DYEING, Rita J. Adrosko. Use natural ingredients: bark, flowers, leaves, lichens, insects etc. Over 135 specific recipes from historical sources for cotton, wool, other fabrics. Genuine premodern handicrafts. 12 illustrations. 160pp.   22688-3 Pa. $2.00

THE HAND DECORATION OF FABRICS, Francis J. Kafka. Outstanding, profusely illustrated guide to stenciling, batik, block printing, tie dyeing, freehand painting, silk screen printing, and novelty decoration. 356 illustrations. 198pp. 6 x 9.
                                    21401-X Pa. $3.00

THOMAS NAST: CARTOONS AND ILLUSTRATIONS, with text by Thomas Nast St. Hill. Father of American political cartooning. Cartoons that destroyed Tweed Ring; inflation, free love, church and state; original Republican elephant and Democratic donkey; Santa Claus; more. 117 illustrations. 146pp. 9 x 12.
                                    22983-1 Pa. $4.00
                                    23067-8 Clothbd. $8.50

FREDERIC REMINGTON: 173 DRAWINGS AND ILLUSTRATIONS. Most famous of the Western artists, most responsible for our myths about the American West in its untamed days. Complete reprinting of *Drawings of Frederic Remington* (1897), plus other selections. 4 additional drawings in color on covers. 140pp. 9 x 12.
                                    20714-5 Pa. $3.95

EARLY NEW ENGLAND GRAVESTONE RUBBINGS, Edmund V. Gillon, Jr. 43 photographs, 226 rubbings show heavily symbolic, macabre, sometimes humorous primitive American art. Up to early 19th century. 207pp. 8⅜ x 11¼.
21380-3 Pa. $4.00

L.J.M. DAGUERRE: THE HISTORY OF THE DIORAMA AND THE DAGUERREOTYPE, Helmut and Alison Gernsheim. Definitive account. Early history, life and work of Daguerre; discovery of daguerreotype process; diffusion abroad; other early photography. 124 illustrations. 226pp. 6⅙ x 9¼.
22290-X Pa. $4.00

PHOTOGRAPHY AND THE AMERICAN SCENE, Robert Taft. The basic book on American photography as art, recording form, 1839-1889. Development, influence on society, great photographers, types (portraits, war, frontier, etc.), whatever else needed. Inexhaustible. Illustrated with 322 early photos, daguerreotypes, tintypes, stereo slides, etc. 546pp. 6⅛ x 9¼.
21201-7 Pa. $5.95

PHOTOGRAPHIC SKETCHBOOK OF THE CIVIL WAR, Alexander Gardner. Reproduction of 1866 volume with 100 on-the-field photographs: Manassas, Lincoln on battlefield, slave pens, etc. Introduction by E.F. Bleiler. 224pp. 10¾ x 9.
22731-6 Pa. $5.00

THE MOVIES: A PICTURE QUIZ BOOK, Stanley Appelbaum & Hayward Cirker. Match stars with their movies, name actors and actresses, test your movie skill with 241 stills from 236 great movies, 1902-1959. Indexes of performers and films. 128pp. 8⅜ x 9¼.
20222-4 Pa. $2.50

THE TALKIES, Richard Griffith. Anthology of features, articles from Photoplay, 1928-1940, reproduced complete. Stars, famous movies, technical features, fabulous ads, etc.; Garbo, Chaplin, King Kong, Lubitsch, etc. 4 color plates, scores of illustrations. 327pp. 8⅜ x 11¼.
22762-6 Pa. $6.95

THE MOVIE MUSICAL FROM VITAPHONE TO "42ND STREET," edited by Miles Kreuger. Relive the rise of the movie musical as reported in the pages of Photoplay magazine (1926-1933): every movie review, cast list, ad, and record review; every significant feature article, production still, biography, forecast, and gossip story. Profusely illustrated. 367pp. 8⅜ x 11¼.
23154-2 Pa. $7.95

JOHANN SEBASTIAN BACH, Philipp Spitta. Great classic of biography, musical commentary, with hundreds of pieces analyzed. Also good for Bach's contemporaries. 450 musical examples. Total of 1799pp.
EUK 22278-0, 22279-9 Clothbd., Two vol. set $25.00

BEETHOVEN AND HIS NINE SYMPHONIES, Sir George Grove. Thorough history, analysis, commentary on symphonies and some related pieces. For either beginner or advanced student. 436 musical passages. 407pp.
20334-4 Pa. $4.00

MOZART AND HIS PIANO CONCERTOS, Cuthbert Girdlestone. The only full-length study. Detailed analyses of all 21 concertos, sources; 417 musical examples. 509pp.
21271-8 Pa. $6.00

THE FITZWILLIAM VIRGINAL BOOK, edited by J. Fuller Maitland, W.B. Squire. Famous early 17th century collection of keyboard music, 300 works by Morley, Byrd, Bull, Gibbons, etc. Modern notation. Total of 938pp. 8⅜ x 11.
ECE 21068-5, 21069-3 Pa., Two vol. set $15.00

COMPLETE STRING QUARTETS, Wolfgang A. Mozart. Breitkopf and Härtel edition. All 23 string quartets plus alternate slow movement to K156. Study score. 277pp. 9⅜ x 12¼. 22372-8 Pa. $6.00

COMPLETE SONG CYCLES, Franz Schubert. Complete piano, vocal music of Die Schöne Müllerin, Die Winterreise, Schwanengesang. Also Drinker English singing translations. Breitkopf and Härtel edition. 217pp. 9⅜ x 12¼.
22649-2 Pa. $4.50

THE COMPLETE PRELUDES AND ETUDES FOR PIANOFORTE SOLO, Alexander Scriabin. All the preludes and etudes including many perfectly spun miniatures. Edited by K.N. Igumnov and Y.I. Mil'shteyn. 250pp. 9 x 12. 22919-X Pa. $5.00

TRISTAN UND ISOLDE, Richard Wagner. Full orchestral score with complete instrumentation. Do not confuse with piano reduction. Commentary by Felix Mottl, great Wagnerian conductor and scholar. Study score. 655pp. 8⅛ x 11.
22915-7 Pa. $11.95

FAVORITE SONGS OF THE NINETIES, ed. Robert Fremont. Full reproduction, including covers, of 88 favorites: Ta-Ra-Ra-Boom-De-Aye, The Band Played On, Bird in a Gilded Cage, Under the Bamboo Tree, After the Ball, etc. 401pp. 9 x 12.
EBE 21536-9 Pa. $6.95

SOUSA'S GREAT MARCHES IN PIANO TRANSCRIPTION: ORIGINAL SHEET MUSIC OF 23 WORKS, John Philip Sousa. Selected by Lester S. Levy. Playing edition includes: The Stars and Stripes Forever, The Thunderer, The Gladiator, King Cotton, Washington Post, much more. 24 illustrations. 111pp. 9 x 12.
USO 23132-1 Pa. $3.50

CLASSIC PIANO RAGS, selected with an introduction by Rudi Blesh. Best ragtime music (1897-1922) by Scott Joplin, James Scott, Joseph F. Lamb, Tom Turpin, 9 others. Printed from best original sheet music, plus covers. 364pp. 9 x 12.
EBE 20469-3 Pa. $6.95

ANALYSIS OF CHINESE CHARACTERS, C.D. Wilder, J.H. Ingram. 1000 most important characters analyzed according to primitives, phonetics, historical development. Traditional method offers mnemonic aid to beginner, intermediate student of Chinese, Japanese. 365pp. 23045-7 Pa. $4.00

MODERN CHINESE: A BASIC COURSE, Faculty of Peking University. Self study, classroom course in modern Mandarin. Records contain phonetics, vocabulary, sentences, lessons. 249 page book contains all recorded text, translations, grammar, vocabulary, exercises. Best course on market. 3 12" 33⅓ monaural records, book, album. 98832-5 Set $12.50

THE BEST DR. THORNDYKE DETECTIVE STORIES, R. Austin Freeman. The Case of Oscar Brodski, The Moabite Cipher, and 5 other favorites featuring the great scientific detective, plus his long-believed-lost first adventure — 31 New Inn — reprinted here for the first time. Edited by E.F. Bleiler. USO 20388-3 Pa. $3.00

BEST "THINKING MACHINE" DETECTIVE STORIES, Jacques Futrelle. The Problem of Cell 13 and 11 other stories about Prof. Augustus S.F.X. Van Dusen, including two "lost" stories. First reprinting of several. Edited by E.F. Bleiler. 241pp.
20537-1 Pa. $3.00

UNCLE SILAS, J. Sheridan LeFanu. Victorian Gothic mystery novel, considered by many best of period, even better than Collins or Dickens. Wonderful psychological terror. Introduction by Frederick Shroyer. 436pp.   21715-9 Pa. $4.00

BEST DR. POGGIOLI DETECTIVE STORIES, T.S. Stribling. 15 best stories from EQMM and The Saint offer new adventures in Mexico, Florida, Tennessee hills as Poggioli unravels mysteries and combats Count Jalacki. 217pp.   23227-1 Pa. $3.00

EIGHT DIME NOVELS, selected with an introduction by E.F. Bleiler. Adventures of Old King Brady, Frank James, Nick Carter, Deadwood Dick, Buffalo Bill, The Steam Man, Frank Merriwell, and Horatio Alger — 1877 to 1905. Important, entertaining popular literature in facsimile reprint, with original covers. 190pp. 9 x 12.   22975-0 Pa. $3.50

ALICE'S ADVENTURES UNDER GROUND, Lewis Carroll. Facsimile of ms. Carroll gave Alice Liddell in 1864. Different in many ways from final Alice. Handlettered, illustrated by Carroll. Introduction by Martin Gardner. 128pp. 21482-6 Pa. $1.50

ALICE IN WONDERLAND COLORING BOOK, Lewis Carroll. Pictures by John Tenniel. Large-size versions of the famous illustrations of Alice, Cheshire Cat, Mad Hatter and all the others, waiting for your crayons. Abridged text. 36 illustrations. 64pp. 8¼ x 11.   22853-3 Pa. $1.50

AVENTURES D'ALICE AU PAYS DES MERVEILLES, Lewis Carroll. Bué's translation of "Alice" into French, supervised by Carroll himself. Novel way to learn language. (No English text.) 42 Tenniel illustrations. 196pp.   22836-3 Pa. $2.50

MYTHS AND FOLK TALES OF IRELAND, Jeremiah Curtin. 11 stories that are Irish versions of European fairy tales and 9 stories from the Fenian cycle — 20 tales of legend and magic that comprise an essential work in the history of folklore. 256pp.   22430-9 Pa. $3.00

EAST O' THE SUN AND WEST O' THE MOON, George W. Dasent. Only full edition of favorite, wonderful Norwegian fairytales — Why the Sea is Salt, Boots and the Troll, etc. — with 77 illustrations by Kittelsen & Werenskiöld. 418pp.
22521-6 Pa. $4.00

PERRAULT'S FAIRY TALES, Charles Perrault and Gustave Doré. Original versions of Cinderella, Sleeping Beauty, Little Red Riding Hood, etc. in best translation, with 34 wonderful illustrations by Gustave Doré. 117pp. 8⅛ x 11. 22311-6 Pa. $2.50

MOTHER GOOSE'S MELODIES. Facsimile of fabulously rare Munroe and Francis "copyright 1833" Boston edition. Familiar and unusual rhymes, wonderful old woodcut illustrations. Edited by E.F. Bleiler. 128pp. 4½ x 6⅜. 22577-1 Pa. $1.50

MOTHER GOOSE IN HIEROGLYPHICS. Favorite nursery rhymes presented in rebus form for children. Fascinating 1849 edition reproduced in toto, with key. Introduction by E.F. Bleiler. About 400 woodcuts. 64pp. 6⅞ x 5¼. 20745-5 Pa. $1.00

PETER PIPER'S PRACTICAL PRINCIPLES OF PLAIN & PERFECT PRONUNCIATION. Alliterative jingles and tongue-twisters. Reproduction in full of 1830 first American edition. 25 spirited woodcuts. 32pp. 4½ x 6⅜. 22560-7 Pa. $1.00

MARMADUKE MULTIPLY'S MERRY METHOD OF MAKING MINOR MATHEMATICIANS. Fellow to Peter Piper, it teaches multiplication table by catchy rhymes and woodcuts. 1841 Munroe & Francis edition. Edited by E.F. Bleiler. 103pp. 4⅝ x 6.
22773-1 Pa. $1.25
20171-6 Clothbd. $3.00

THE NIGHT BEFORE CHRISTMAS, Clement Moore. Full text, and woodcuts from original 1848 book. Also critical, historical material. 19 illustrations. 40pp. 4⅝ x 6. 22797-9 Pa. $1.25

THE KING OF THE GOLDEN RIVER, John Ruskin. Victorian children's classic of three brothers, their attempts to reach the Golden River, what becomes of them. Facsimile of original 1889 edition. 22 illustrations. 56pp. 4⅝ x 6⅜.
20066-3 Pa. $1.50

DREAMS OF THE RAREBIT FIEND, Winsor McCay. Pioneer cartoon strip, unexcelled for beauty, imagination, in 60 full sequences. Incredible technical virtuosity, wonderful visual wit. Historical introduction. 62pp. 8⅜ x 11¼. 21347-1 Pa. $2.50

THE KATZENJAMMER KIDS, Rudolf Dirks. In full color, 14 strips from 1906-7; full of imagination, characteristic humor. Classic of great historical importance. Introduction by August Derleth. 32pp. 9¼ x 12¼. 23005-8 Pa. $2.00

LITTLE ORPHAN ANNIE AND LITTLE ORPHAN ANNIE IN COSMIC CITY, Harold Gray. Two great sequences from the early strips: our curly-haired heroine defends the Warbucks' financial empire and, then, takes on meanie Phineas P. Pinchpenny. Leapin' lizards! 178pp. 6⅛ x 8⅜. 23107-0 Pa. $2.00

THE BEST OF GLUYAS WILLIAMS. 100 drawings by one of America's finest cartoonists: The Day a Cake of Ivory Soap Sank at Proctor & Gamble's, At the Life Insurance Agents' Banquet, and many other gems from the 20's and 30's. 118pp. 8⅜ x 11¼. 22737-5 Pa. $2.50

THE MAGIC MOVING PICTURE BOOK, Bliss, Sands & Co. The pictures in this book move! Volcanoes erupt, a house burns, a serpentine dancer wiggles her way through a number. By using a specially ruled acetate screen provided, you can obtain these and 15 other startling effects. Originally "The Motograph Moving Picture Book." 32pp. 8¼ x 11.   23224-7 Pa. $1.75

STRING FIGURES AND HOW TO MAKE THEM, Caroline F. Jayne. Fullest, clearest instructions on string figures from around world: Eskimo, Navajo, Lapp, Europe, more. Cats cradle, moving spear, lightning, stars. Introduction by A.C. Haddon. 950 illustrations. 407pp.   20152-X Pa. $3.50

PAPER FOLDING FOR BEGINNERS, William D. Murray and Francis J. Rigney. Clearest book on market for making origami sail boats, roosters, frogs that move legs, cups, bonbon boxes. 40 projects. More than 275 illustrations. Photographs. 94pp.
20713-7 Pa. $1.25

INDIAN SIGN LANGUAGE, William Tomkins. Over 525 signs developed by Sioux, Blackfoot, Cheyenne, Arapahoe and other tribes. Written instructions and diagrams: how to make words, construct sentences. Also 290 pictographs of Sioux and Ojibway tribes. 111pp. 6⅛ x 9¼.   22029-X Pa. $1.50

BOOMERANGS: HOW TO MAKE AND THROW THEM, Bernard S. Mason. Easy to make and throw, dozens of designs: cross-stick, pinwheel, boomabird, tumblestick, Australian curved stick boomerang. Complete throwing instructions. All safe. 99pp.   23028-7 Pa. $1.75

25 KITES THAT FLY, Leslie Hunt. Full, easy to follow instructions for kites made from inexpensive materials. Many novelties. Reeling, raising, designing your own. 70 illustrations. 110pp.   22550-X Pa. $1.25

TRICKS AND GAMES ON THE POOL TABLE, Fred Herrmann. 79 tricks and games, some solitaires, some for 2 or more players, some competitive; mystifying shots and throws, unusual carom, tricks involving cork, coins, a hat, more. 77 figures. 95pp.   21814-7 Pa. $1.25

WOODCRAFT AND CAMPING, Bernard S. Mason. How to make a quick emergency shelter, select woods that will burn immediately, make do with limited supplies, etc. Also making many things out of wood, rawhide, bark, at camp. Formerly titled Woodcraft. 295 illustrations. 580pp.   21951-8 Pa. $4.00

AN INTRODUCTION TO CHESS MOVES AND TACTICS SIMPLY EXPLAINED, Leonard Barden. Informal intermediate introduction: reasons for moves, tactics, openings, traps, positional play, endgame. Isolates patterns. 102pp. USO 21210-6 Pa. $1.35

LASKER'S MANUAL OF CHESS, Dr. Emanuel Lasker. Great world champion offers very thorough coverage of all aspects of chess. Combinations, position play, openings, endgame, aesthetics of chess, philosophy of struggle, much more. Filled with analyzed games. 390pp.   20640-8 Pa. $4.00

DRIED FLOWERS, Sarah Whitlock and Martha Rankin. Concise, clear, practical guide to dehydration, glycerinizing, pressing plant material, and more. Covers use of silica gel. 12 drawings. Originally titled "New Techniques with Dried Flowers." 32pp. 21802-3 Pa. $1.00

ABC OF POULTRY RAISING, J.H. Florea. Poultry expert, editor tells how to raise chickens on home or small business basis. Breeds, feeding, housing, laying, etc. Very concrete, practical. 50 illustrations. 256pp. 23201-8 Pa. $3.00

HOW INDIANS USE WILD PLANTS FOR FOOD, MEDICINE & CRAFTS, Frances Densmore. Smithsonian, Bureau of American Ethnology report presents wealth of material on nearly 200 plants used by Chippewas of Minnesota and Wisconsin. 33 plates plus 122pp. of text. 6⅛ x 9¼. 23019-8 Pa. $2.50

THE HERBAL OR GENERAL HISTORY OF PLANTS, John Gerard. The 1633 edition revised and enlarged by Thomas Johnson. Containing almost 2850 plant descriptions and 2705 superb illustrations, Gerard's Herbal is a monumental work, the book all modern English herbals are derived from, and the one herbal every serious enthusiast should have in its entirety. Original editions are worth perhaps $750. 1678pp. 8½ x 12¼. 23147-X Clothbd. $50.00

A MODERN HERBAL, Margaret Grieve. Much the fullest, most exact, most useful compilation of herbal material. Gigantic alphabetical encyclopedia, from aconite to zedoary, gives botanical information, medical properties, folklore, economic uses, and much else. Indispensable to serious reader. 161 illustrations. 888pp. 6½ x 9¼. USO 22798-7, 22799-5 Pa., Two vol. set $10.00

HOW TO KNOW THE FERNS, Frances T. Parsons. Delightful classic. Identification, fern lore, for Eastern and Central U.S.A. Has introduced thousands to interesting life form. 99 illustrations. 215pp. 20740-4 Pa. $2.75

THE MUSHROOM HANDBOOK, Louis C.C. Krieger. Still the best popular handbook. Full descriptions of 259 species, extremely thorough text, habitats, luminescence, poisons, folklore, etc. 32 color plates; 126 other illustrations. 560pp. 21861-9 Pa. $4.50

HOW TO KNOW THE WILD FRUITS, Maude G. Peterson. Classic guide covers nearly 200 trees, shrubs, smaller plants of the U.S. arranged by color of fruit and then by family. Full text provides names, descriptions, edibility, uses. 80 illustrations. 400pp. 22943-2 Pa. $4.00

COMMON WEEDS OF THE UNITED STATES, U.S. Department of Agriculture. Covers 220 important weeds with illustration, maps, botanical information, plant lore for each. Over 225 illustrations. 463pp. 6⅛ x 9¼. 20504-5 Pa. $4.50

HOW TO KNOW THE WILD FLOWERS, Mrs. William S. Dana. Still best popular book for East and Central USA. Over 500 plants easily identified, with plant lore; arranged according to color and flowering time. 174 plates. 459pp. 20332-8 Pa. $3.50

DRIED FLOWERS, Sarah Whitlock and Martha Rankin. Concise, clear, practical guide to dehydration, glycerinizing, pressing plant material, and more. Covers use of silica gel. 12 drawings. Originally titled "New Techniques with Dried Flowers." 32pp. 21802-3 Pa. $1.00

ABC OF POULTRY RAISING, J.H. Florea. Poultry expert, editor tells how to raise chickens on home or small business basis. Breeds, feeding, housing, laying, etc. Very concrete, practical. 50 illustrations. 256pp. 23201-8 Pa. $3.00

HOW INDIANS USE WILD PLANTS FOR FOOD, MEDICINE & CRAFTS, Frances Densmore. Smithsonian, Bureau of American Ethnology report presents wealth of material on nearly 200 plants used by Chippewas of Minnesota and Wisconsin. 33 plates plus 122pp. of text. 6⅛ x 9¼. 23019-8 Pa. $2.50

THE HERBAL OR GENERAL HISTORY OF PLANTS, John Gerard. The 1633 edition revised and enlarged by Thomas Johnson. Containing almost 2850 plant descriptions and 2705 superb illustrations, Gerard's Herbal is a monumental work, the book all modern English herbals are derived from, and the one herbal every serious enthusiast should have in its entirety. Original editions are worth perhaps $750. 1678pp. 8½ x 12¼. 23147-X Clothbd. $50.00

A MODERN HERBAL, Margaret Grieve. Much the fullest, most exact, most useful compilation of herbal material. Gigantic alphabetical encyclopedia, from aconite to zedoary, gives botanical information, medical properties, folklore, economic uses, and much else. Indispensable to serious reader. 161 illustrations. 888pp. 6½ x 9¼. USO 22798-7, 22799-5 Pa., Two vol. set $10.00

HOW TO KNOW THE FERNS, Frances T. Parsons. Delightful classic. Identification, fern lore, for Eastern and Central U.S.A. Has introduced thousands to interesting life form. 99 illustrations. 215pp. 20740-4 Pa. $2.75

THE MUSHROOM HANDBOOK, Louis C.C. Krieger. Still the best popular handbook. Full descriptions of 259 species, extremely thorough text, habitats, luminescence, poisons, folklore, etc. 32 color plates; 126 other illustrations. 560pp. 21861-9 Pa. $4.50

HOW TO KNOW THE WILD FRUITS, Maude G. Peterson. Classic guide covers nearly 200 trees, shrubs, smaller plants of the U.S. arranged by color of fruit and then by family. Full text provides names, descriptions, edibility, uses. 80 illustrations. 400pp. 22943-2 Pa. $4.00

COMMON WEEDS OF THE UNITED STATES, U.S. Department of Agriculture. Covers 220 important weeds with illustration, maps, botanical information, plant lore for each. Over 225 illustrations. 463pp. 6⅛ x 9¼. 20504-5 Pa. $4.50

HOW TO KNOW THE WILD FLOWERS, Mrs. William S. Dana. Still best popular book for East and Central USA. Over 500 plants easily identified, with plant lore; arranged according to color and flowering time. 174 plates. 459pp. 20332-8 Pa. $3.50

THE STYLE OF PALESTRINA AND THE DISSONANCE, Knud Jeppesen. Standard analysis of rhythm, line, harmony, accented and unaccented dissonances. Also pre-Palestrina dissonances. 306pp. 22386-8 Pa. $4.50

DOVER OPERA GUIDE AND LIBRETTO SERIES prepared by Ellen H. Bleiler. Each volume contains everything needed for background, complete enjoyment: complete libretto, new English translation with all repeats, biography of composer and librettist, early performance history, musical lore, much else. All volumes lavishly illustrated with performance photos, portraits, similar material. Do not confuse with skimpy performance booklets.

CARMEN, Georges Bizet. 66 illustrations. 222pp. 22111-3 Pa. $3.00
DON GIOVANNI, Wolfgang A. Mozart. 92 illustrations. 209pp. 21134-7 Pa. $2.50
LA BOHÈME, Giacomo Puccini. 73 illustrations. 124pp. USO 20404-9 Pa. $1.75
AÏDA, Giuseppe Verdi. 76 illustrations. 181pp. 20405-7 Pa. $2.25
LUCIA DI LAMMERMOOR, Gaetano Donizetti. 44 illustrations. 186pp.
22110-5 Pa. $2.00

ANTONIO STRADIVARI: HIS LIFE AND WORK, W. H. Hill, et al. Great work of musicology. Construction methods, woods, varnishes, known instruments, types of instruments, life, special features. Introduction by Sydney Beck. 98 illustrations, plus 4 color plates. 315pp. 20425-1 Pa. $4.00

MUSIC FOR THE PIANO, James Friskin, Irwin Freundlich. Both famous, little-known compositions; 1500 to 1950's. Listing, description, classification, technical aspects for student, teacher, performer. Indispensable for enlarging repertory. 448pp. 22918-1 Pa. $4.00

PIANOS AND THEIR MAKERS, Alfred Dolge. Leading inventor offers full history of piano technology, earliest models to 1910. Types, makers, components, mechanisms, musical aspects. Very strong on offtrail models, inventions; also player pianos. 300 illustrations. 581pp. 22856-8 Pa. $5.00

KEYBOARD MUSIC, J.S. Bach. Bach-Gesellschaft edition. For harpsichord, piano, other keyboard instruments. English Suites, French Suites, Six Partitas, Goldberg Variations, Two-Part Inventions, Three-Part Sinfonias. 312pp. 8⅛ x 11.
22360-4 Pa. $5.00

COMPLETE STRING QUARTETS, Ludwig van Beethoven. Breitkopf and Härtel edition. 6 quartets of Opus 18; 3 quartets of Opus 59; Opera 74, 95, 127, 130, 131, 132, 135 and Grosse Fuge. Study score. 434pp. 9⅜ x 12¼. 22361-2 Pa. $7.95

COMPLETE PIANO SONATAS AND VARIATIONS FOR SOLO PIANO, Johannes Brahms. All sonatas, five variations on themes from Schumann, Paganini, Handel, etc. Vienna Gesellschaft der Musikfreunde edition. 178pp. 9 x 12. 22650-6 Pa. $4.50

PIANO MUSIC 1888-1905, Claude Debussy. Deux Arabesques, Suite Bergamesque, Masques, 1st series of Images, etc. 9 others, in corrected editions. 175pp. 9⅜ x 12¼. 22771-5 Pa. $4.00

INCIDENTS OF TRAVEL IN YUCATAN, John L. Stephens. Classic (1843) exploration of jungles of Yucatan, looking for evidences of Maya civilization. Travel adventures, Mexican and Indian culture, etc. Total of 669pp.
20926-1, 20927-X Pa., Two vol. set $6.00

LIVING MY LIFE, Emma Goldman. Candid, no holds barred account by foremost American anarchist: her own life, anarchist movement, famous contemporaries, ideas and their impact. Struggles and confrontations in America, plus deportation to U.S.S.R. Shocking inside account of persecution of anarchists under Lenin. 13 plates. Total of 944pp.
22543-7, 22544-5 Pa., Two vol. set $9.00

AMERICAN INDIANS, George Catlin. Classic account of life among Plains Indians: ceremonies, hunt, warfare, etc. Dover edition reproduces for first time all original paintings. 312 plates. 572pp. of text. 6⅛ x 9¼.
22118-0, 22119-9 Pa., Two vol. set $8.00
22140-7, 22144-X Clothbd., Two vol. set $16.00.

THE INDIANS' BOOK, Natalie Curtis. Lore, music, narratives, drawings by Indians, collected from cultures of U.S.A. 149 songs in full notation. 45 illustrations. 583pp. 6⅝ x 9⅜.
21939-9 Pa. $6.95

INDIAN BLANKETS AND THEIR MAKERS, George Wharton James. History, old style wool blankets, changes brought about by traders, symbolism of design and color, a Navajo weaver at work, outline blanket, Kachina blankets, more. Emphasis on Navajo. 130 illustrations, 32 in color. 230pp. 6⅛ x 9¼.
22996-3 Pa. $5.00
23068-6 Clothbd. $10.00

AN INTRODUCTION TO THE STUDY OF THE MAYA HIEROGLYPHS, Sylvanus Griswold Morley. Classic study by one of the truly great figures in hieroglyph research. Still the best introduction for the student for reading Maya hieroglyphs. New introduction by J. Eric S. Thompson. 117 illustrations. 284pp.
23108-9 Pa. $4.00

THE ANALECTS OF CONFUCIUS, THE GREAT LEARNING, DOCTRINE OF THE MEAN, Confucius. Edited by James Legge. Full Chinese text, standard English translation on same page, Chinese commentators, editor's annotations; dictionary of characters at rear, plus grammatical comment. Finest edition anywhere of one of world's greatest thinkers. 503pp.
22746-4 Pa. $5.00

THE I CHING (THE BOOK OF CHANGES), translated by James Legge. Complete translation of basic text plus appendices by Confucius, and Chinese commentary of most penetrating divination manual ever prepared. Indispensable to study of early Oriental civilizations, to modern inquiring reader. 448pp.
21062-6 Pa. $3.50

THE EGYPTIAN BOOK OF THE DEAD, E.A. Wallis Budge. Complete reproduction of Ani's papyrus, finest ever found. Full hieroglyphic text, interlinear transliteration, word for word translation, smooth translation. Basic work, for Egyptology, for modern study of psychic matters. Total of 533pp. 6½ x 9¼.
EBE 21866-X Pa. $4.95

BUILD YOUR OWN LOW-COST HOME, L.O. Anderson, H.F. Zornig. U.S. Dept. of Agriculture sets of plans, full, detailed, for 11 houses: A-Frame, circular, conventional. Also construction manual. Save hundreds of dollars. 204pp. 11 x 16.
21525-3 Pa. $6.00

HOW TO BUILD A WOOD-FRAME HOUSE, L.O. Anderson. Comprehensive, easy to follow U.S. Government manual: placement, foundations, framing, sheathing, roof, insulation, plaster, finishing — almost everything else. 179 illustrations. 223pp. 7⅞ x 10¾.
22954-8 Pa. $3.50

CONCRETE, MASONRY AND BRICKWORK, U.S. Department of the Army. Practical handbook for the home owner and small builder manual contains basic principles, techniques, and important background information on construction with concrete, concrete blocks, and brick. 177 figures, 37 tables. 200pp. 6½ x 9¼.
23203-4 Pa. $4.00

THE STANDARD BOOK OF QUILT MAKING AND COLLECTING, Marguerite Ickis. Full information, full-sized patterns for making 46 traditional quilts, also 150 other patterns. Quilted cloths, lamé, satin quilts, etc. 483 illustrations. 273pp. 6⅞ x 9⅝.
20582-7 Pa. $3.50

101 PATCHWORK PATTERNS, Ruby S. McKim. 101 beautiful, immediately useable patterns, full-size, modern and traditional. Also general information, estimating, quilt lore. 124pp. 7⅞ x 10¾.
20773-0 Pa. $2.50

KNIT YOUR OWN NORWEGIAN SWEATERS, Dale Yarn Company. Complete instructions for 50 authentic sweaters, hats, mittens, gloves, caps, etc. Thoroughly modern designs that command high prices in stores. 24 patterns, 24 color photographs. Nearly 100 charts and other illustrations. 58pp. 8⅜ x 11¼.
23031-7 Pa. $2.50

IRON-ON TRANSFER PATTERNS FOR CREWEL AND EMBROIDERY FROM EARLY AMERICAN SOURCES, edited by Rita Weiss. 75 designs, borders, alphabets, from traditional American sources printed on translucent paper in transfer ink. Reuseable. Instructions. Test patterns. 24pp. 8¼ x 11.
23162-3 Pa. $1.50

AMERICAN INDIAN NEEDLEPOINT DESIGNS FOR PILLOWS, BELTS, HANDBAGS AND OTHER PROJECTS, Roslyn Epstein. 37 authentic American Indian designs adapted for modern needlepoint projects. Grid backing makes designs easily transferable to canvas. 48pp. 8¼ x 11.
22973-4 Pa. $1.50

CHARTED FOLK DESIGNS FOR CROSS-STITCH EMBROIDERY, Maria Foris & Andreas Foris. 278 charted folk designs, most in 2 colors, from Danube region: florals, fantastic beasts, geometrics, traditional symbols, more. Border and central patterns. 77pp. 8¼ x 11.
USO 23191-7 Pa. $2.00

Prices subject to change without notice.
Available at your book dealer or write for free catalogue to Dept. GI, Dover Publications, Inc., 180 Varick St., N.Y., N.Y. 10014. Dover publishes more than 150 books each year on science, elementary and advanced mathematics, biology, music, art, literary history, social sciences and other areas.